Tara Flynn

Tara Flynn

Geraldine O'Neill

ORION

First published in Great Britain in 2003 by Orion Books
an imprint of The Orion Publishing Group
Orion House, 5 Upper St Martin's Lane, London WC2H 9EA

A CIP catalogue record for this book is
available from the British Library

ISBN (hardback) 0 75286 010 0
ISBN (trade paperback) 0 75286 011 9

Typeset at The Spartan Press Ltd,
Lymington, Hants.

Printed and bound in Great Britain by
Clays Ltd, St Ives plc

Acknowledgements

I would like to thank Kate Mills and her colleagues at Orion for the extremely warm welcome I was given, and for their enthusiasm and support of *Tara Flynn*.

Thanks to my agent, Sugra Zaman from Watson, Little Ltd., London, for her total belief in *Tara Flynn* and in my writing.

Thanks to the Offaly Writers' Group for their long-term support, especially Malcolm Ross-McDonald for his guidance and expertise. A warm thanks to Peter Brady for his advice and suggestions, and to Pauline Walshe for her encouragement.

Thanks to my mother, Be-be O'Neill for information about Offaly during Tara Flynn's time and to my mother-in law, Mary Hynes for details about Stockport.

Thanks to my own family; my father Teddy O'Neill, sisters Teresa, Kate and Berni, my brother Eamonn and brother-in-law, Eddie McManus, for their support in a difficult year.

Loving thanks to my children, Christopher and Clare, who have always praised and encouraged me in my writing.

And a final thanks to my old college boyfriend, Michael Brosnahan, for his endless support and constant encouragement.

PART ONE

If you have built castles in the air,
your work need not be lost:
That is where they should be.
Now put the foundations under them.

HENRY DAVID THOREAU

County Offaly, Ireland

ෙ෨෩

1956

Ballygrace House stood in several acres of neglected gardens, about a mile outside Ballygrace village, and three miles west of Tullamore. The house was large, rambling and run-down, but still had the imposing charm that had long led the local children to refer to it as 'Ballygrace Castle'.

According to the auctioneers' brochure, it had been built first in the late eighteenth century, then badly damaged during the Troubles, and later rebuilt in the 1920s. It waited patiently for its new owner. Someone fortunate enough to have the asking price, and another small fortune to pay for the running costs. The house was waiting to soak up money – like the miles of bog surrounding it would soak up water.

The auctioneer observed the tall elegant woman as she paced up and down the large marble hallway with its sweeping staircase. Meticulously wrapped in her brown velvet coat and extravagant matching hat, she had examined every inch of the house, making notes in a leather-bound notebook.

John Costelloe followed her Italian crocodile shoes as they tapped up and down stairs, in and out of rooms, and then out into the overgrown gardens. She obviously had no need or wish for him to show her around the house. She had started off at a confident pace the moment she had stepped inside Ballygrace House, as though she knew exactly where she was going.

Strangely, she had returned several times to one particular bedroom door on the upstairs landing – but had hovered outside the room, as

3

though afraid to cross the threshold. Instinctively, John Costelloe retreated back downstairs, not wishing her to feel that her movements were being observed. He made no comments whatsoever, knowing that she was perfectly capable of asking for his help when it was required.

She had asked him none of the usual questions that a female viewer might ask, and paid scant attention to the existing furniture or decor – apart from the grand piano. The first time she had stepped into the drawing-room, she had made straight for the carefully covered instrument. She had thrown the dusty sheets aside, and then placed her graceful hands on the cool, ebony wood.

It was on her second visit to the drawing-room that she had lifted the lid of the piano, and ran her fingers over the black and ivory keys. While John Costelloe had loitered in the hallway, she pulled out the velvet-covered stool and started to play the most beautiful, haunting music.

When the piece was finished, she had remained silent in the room for several minutes, then she came out into the hallway for one last look around the rest of the house. As she passed by the auctioneer, her head bowed, he was convinced he saw her wipe away a stray tear. But John Costelloe's thoughts were quickly diverted by the subtle tones of her perfume and her graceful carriage as she made her way back upstairs.

The odd comment she had made about the house had surprised the auctioneer. He was taken aback by her knowledge about the structure of the property, her observations of the stonework and the pointing, and the general condition of the building. These were all the areas he would have scrutinised if he were buying such a house, but that was his business. It was an *auctioneer's* business to know such things – hardly the business of a wealthy, elegant young woman.

John Costelloe felt very little would escape this particular lady's notice. The longer they spent together, the more curious he became. 'You seem familiar with the house,' he dared to venture.

The well-manicured hands snapped the notebook shut. She lifted her green, penetrating eyes, and studied him for a few moments. 'I used to know it very well,' she said in a measured tone. 'But that was a long time ago.'

'You haven't been back in recent years?'

She walked across the hallway and looked out through the stained-glass window at the late autumn sky. 'I haven't been in Ballygrace House since I was eighteen years old.'

John detected an Irish accent beneath the polished, English veneer – and his interest was whetted even more. Everything about the woman spoke of breeding and money – from the expensive clothes to the exquisite pearls in her ears and around her elegant throat. If anyone could be described as the perfect owner for Ballygrace House – she was that person.

'It feels all right,' she suddenly said, her face breaking into a smile. 'The house feels much better than I thought it would.'

John Costelloe smiled back, then wondered how old she was. Her polished, confident bearing had made him estimate her as approaching thirty. But now, her face relaxed and smiling, she looked much younger. She looked younger than his own age of twenty-eight. She must come from a very well-heeled family, he thought, to contemplate viewing a house like this. He suddenly wondered how she would look without the hat. He watched her now ascend the staircase again and fancied he could see wisps of flame-coloured hair trying to escape from under it.

She reached the upstairs landing and hesitated outside the same room once again. Then he felt his own body tense as she finally threw open the bedroom door and walked in. After a few minutes of pacing around the bedroom, she came back downstairs. Her face revealed nothing. 'I need time to think about it,' she told him now – her manner brusque and businesslike again. 'To move over to Ireland would be a considerable upheaval.'

'Of course,' John Costelloe replied. 'I imagine a property like this will be on the market for some time yet . . . it's not everyone who could afford the asking price. You have our phone number.'

The auctioneer carefully locked up Ballygrace House and together they descended the mossy stone steps. 'Would you like a lift to the end of the driveway?' he asked, knowing she had arranged to be picked up from that spot.

She checked her watch. 'Yes, thank you,' she replied. 'We're a little earlier than I thought.'

He held the passenger door open for her as she climbed gracefully into the car. She loosened her coat and then a hand came up to sweep the hat from her head.

John Costelloe had been right about her hair. He held his breath as a cascade of russet curls tumbled down around her shoulders. He was not the first man who had felt the desire to run his fingers through that beautiful, unruly mane of hair.

Chapter One

ॐ

1937

The draught from the open door scattered a flurry of snow-flakes across the stone floor of the thatched cottage.

'You've left it till the last minute, as usual.' The old Irishman's voice was low and full of reproach. He straightened his spine against the wooden rocking chair, prepared for the usual conflict. 'For God's sake close the door behind you or we'll lose the bit of heat we have.'

Shay Flynn carefully negotiated the step down into his father's cottage. Too many times lately – due to the drink – he had missed it, and gone sprawling his full length across the floor. He closed the door and, with great concentration, made for a three-legged stool on the opposite side of the turf fire from his father.

'I've come straight from Midnight Mass,' Shay said in a pious whisper. 'I never wasted a minute.'

Old Noel gave a grunt of disbelief and closed the book he was reading. 'Well,' he said, thumbing towards the small settle bed in the corner, 'did you bring her anything?'

Shay stood up and fumbled deep in his overcoat pocket. 'I got her a few apples and oranges . . . that's all I could find.' He placed them on the mantelpiece, beside the stocking that was pinned down by a heavy candlestick. 'The shops were closing by the time I got into town . . .'

Noel Flynn cleared his throat and spat in the fire. 'Pity about the shop selling porter and whiskey. By the cut of you, you'd no trouble finding that.'

Shay bent his knees to sit back down on the stool; then he

remembered. He straightened up again and dug into his other pocket. 'Oh . . . an' Mrs Kelly gave me a few nuts and sugar sticks for her, too.'

The old man looked over at the little bed again, checking the child was still asleep, then he got up and went into his bedroom. A few moments later he came back with a small package wrapped in brown paper. It was a child's story book. 'Here,' he said gruffly, 'put that in the stocking for her. If that and the other things don't fill it, you may dig deep in your pocket for any coppers the pub didn't get.' He lifted his pipe from the mantelpiece. 'I don't suppose it will make any difference what you put in . . . nothing but the doll will please her.'

Shay's shoulders slumped. He pulled off his damp cap and twisted it between his hands. 'Christ Almighty . . . how could I afford ten bob for a china doll? Where the hell does she think the money comes from?'

'It's not where the money comes from that matters,' Noel replied, 'but where it goes.'

Shay shook his curly dark head. 'I have her brother to think of, too,' he whispered heatedly. 'By the time I give the ould aunties somethin' for *him* every week, and pay for the bite to eat here and everythin' . . . sure I'm left with nothing.'

'Your priorities are all wrong,' his father stated. 'The child's doll would have been paid for long ago if you'd left the porter alone.'

'Oh, feck off about the doll, will you?' Shay grabbed viciously at the stocking, wishing it was his father's scrawny old neck. 'She'll get what I can afford to give her and it'll have to do – whether it pleases her or not. This oul' Christmas *craic* is nothin' but a heap of shite!'

Shay had come home tonight with more on his mind than Christmas. He'd come home with news that would benefit them all, but his father had spoiled things as usual – with his oul' moanin' and groanin'. Well, his father could feck off. He would keep his good news until he was sure it would be properly received.

'You have Tara spoiled,' Shay said bitterly. 'She's nothin' but a little oul' brat . . . lookin' for china dolls, when we've hardly a bit to ate in the house at times.' He sighed, suddenly weighed down by all the demands made on him. 'An' I'm going to have to go into Tullamore tomorrow, to give Joe a few coppers, as well.' He shook his head. 'I can't make meat of one and bones of the other.' It suited Shay to visit Tullamore for another, more important reason, but they could all wait until tomorrow to be told about that.

The slur in his voice and his coarse language made the old man cluck his tongue in annoyance. 'Put the stuff in the stocking, will you – and get yourself off to bed. I don't want the child disturbed at this hour of the night.'

There was a hostile silence between father and son. Shay fumbled about, dropping apples and oranges on the floor, while Noel struggled to hold his tongue and smoke his pipe at the same time. It was only the sleeping child that stopped him from venting his temper on his drunken, widowed son.

But neither of the warring men knew that Tara Flynn was not asleep.

She was lying on her little hay mattress, pretending. Pretending as usual, that she did not hear the adult conversations that went on in the room around her. Pretending that there was a Santy, when now she knew there was none. At five years of age – and as bright as a button – the flame-haired Tara Flynn was an expert at pretending.

The following morning, dressed in a second-hand night-gown, which had come all the way from America, Tara wiped away a tear and sucked thoughtfully on Mrs Kelly's sugar stick. She was thinking of her friend, and how poor Biddy Hart wouldn't have got anything at all for Christmas. Not even a bit of fruit. Her little friend didn't even have a daddy – never mind a mammy. Biddy only had oul' Lizzie Lawless to look after her and the other girl, and she was horrible to them. She was always in bad humour and they didn't get very much to eat.

Sometimes Tara had to share her bit of cakebread at dinner time in school. Poor Biddy hardly ever had bread with her, and she would eat anything, she was so hungry. Tara decided to keep one of her oranges and give it to Biddy at ten o'clock Mass.

'Are you going to eat your stirabout, now?' Noel asked, lifting a small pot of oatmeal out of the fire.

'Don't want it!' Tara said with a pout, still thinking of the china doll she never got.

'You'll eat it,' her grandfather said slowly and firmly, 'or you'll have no dinner after Mass.'

'Don't want it,' she repeated, but her tone was less certain now.

'Suit yourself, but don't complain when we're all eating the goose and you're going hungry.' There was a pause. 'And your Uncle Mick's made a currant cake, too.'

Tara sucked on the sugar stick a bit longer and worked things out in her mind. When she had cried earlier this morning over the doll, her father had mentioned something about it not being long until her birthday. Her sixth birthday was in January and that wasn't long after Christmas. January was the first month of the year.

Maybe the china doll would still be in Dolan's window until then.

'I'll eat me stirabout,', she announced, 'when I've put on me good skirt and jumper.'

'You'll eat it now,' Noel stated, spooning it into her small dish, '*before* you put on your skirt and jumper, or you'll be a lovely-looking sight going to Mass with stains all down them.'

The smell of the hot oatmeal made Noel's stomach clench with hunger, but years of practice at going without ensured he ignored it. The Catholic Church's rule of fasting from twelve o'clock the previous night before receiving Holy Communion was firmly ingrained in him. In just over a year's time, the child would make her First Holy Communion, and she would also follow the age-old tradition like the rest of the family.

Tara folded her little arms, the sugar cane sticking out of her mouth, and shook her red ringlets. 'D'you know, Granda? It'll be me birthday in a few weeks. I learnt all about the months and dates in school from Miss Molloy I can even say them in the Irish, too. Miss Molloy says I'm very good at working things out in me head. She says I'm very clever.'

'You are,' Noel Flynn replied, 'too clever by half.'

An hour later, Noel stood in his dark, sober suit, carefully attaching his silver watch and chain. This was a ritual he performed every Sunday morning and every Holy Day. Every time he slid the cold smooth timepiece into his little pocket, he thought of his wife, because Hannah had bought the watch for him. She had paid it off – at so much a week – in a jeweller's shop in Tullamore. In their forty-odd years of marriage, it was the one and only gift she had been able to afford to give him. The watch had counted off all the minutes, and the weeks, and the months – of the two years since Hannah had died.

Then, just under a year after Hannah's death, Shay's wife went down with scarlet fever and died within a short time. Shay, who had been living with his in-laws, asked if he and Tara could come back to live at the cottage until he had got back on his feet again.

Noel's first thoughts were not favourable. He had not been keen on the idea of having a child around the place. A year later, he could not imagine life without her, and he now realised that if it hadn't been for the child he would have sunk into depression and lethargy. With the motherless Tara depending on him, he couldn't allow himself that luxury.

Biddy was delighted with the orange. 'I got a lovely prayer book off a neighbour,' she told Tara as they stood outside the church gates after Mass. She looked down at her hobnailed boots. 'It's too hard for me to read but it has nice pictures of Our Lady an' the angels an' everythin'. She says I've not to tell Lizzie. Lizzie says that Christmas is a load of nonsense and, apart from going to Mass, that it's the same as any other day.'

'We're havin' a goose for our dinner,' Tara said proudly. 'And me Uncle Mick has made a currant cake with cherries in it. He says he made it especially for Christmas.'

'Maybe we'll have a chicken,' Biddy said hopefully. Then she added, 'But I think we're only havin' soup.'

Suddenly, a hush descended on the groups of churchgoers, and everyone turned to look as a particularly well-clad family made their way out through the crowds.

'It's the Fitzgeralds,' Tara informed her friend. '*And* they've got a new car. It's up the road a bit.' She pointed now. 'I saw it when me granda brought me in on the ass and cart. Will we go and look at it?'

The youngsters in the churchyard, and some of the more curious adults, followed the Fitzgeralds out of the gates and along the road. Tara and Biddy moved first at a quick trot, and then they broke into an excited run as the car engine started up with a loud roar.

Suddenly Tara felt a firm hand grab her by the arm. 'Back to the cart!' her granda said sternly.

Tara tried to wriggle out of his grip. 'I'll only be a minute,' she argued. 'We're goin' to have a look at the Fitzgerald's new car.'

Noel swept her up into his arms, his face dark with annoyance. 'You're gawping at no new car – or anything else belonging to the Fitzgeralds,' he told her firmly. He looked down at Biddy. 'You'd better go home. Lizzie Lawless was callin' for you at the church gate – and she didn't look one bit happy.'

Head bent, Biddy scuttled off as fast as her hobnailed boots would allow.

'Could Biddy have a bit of our goose, Granda?' Tara said, stroking her grandfather's closely shaved chin. 'She says she's only havin' soup for her Christmas dinner.'

'Lizzie Lawless is paid to feed those girls,' Noel replied, putting the child back down on the ground. 'She wouldn't thank us for bringin' them into the house, and anyway, we have enough mouths of our own.' He led her by the hand towards the ass and cart, where Shay and Mick, dressed in their good suits, stood chatting with a group of men. Tara fished the end of a sugar stick out of her pocket and stuck it in her mouth. She wished her granda and her Uncle Mick had a new car like the Fitzgeralds, instead of an oul' ass and cart. She wished Biddy could have her dinner at their house, every day. She wished she could have that china doll, with the red satin dress and hat, for her birthday. And she wished – most of all – that she could have a mammy.

Chapter Two

'All the women in Tullamore,' Noel Flynn gasped, 'and you have to take up with a widow with three children!'

When they all sat down at the fire – stomachs full with roast potatoes, carrots and the goose – Shay announced the news about his forthcoming second marriage. He had sent Tara over to Mrs Kelly's cottage to show the old woman her new book, and to get her out of earshot. 'Sure it's the best thing all round for me to get married again,' he said with a beaming smile, trying not to think of Tessie Devine's bosom. 'As far as I'm concerned, the quicker the better.'

'You're taking on a quare handful there, with five young ones between ye,' his brother warned him. 'I would weigh things up carefully, if I was in yer shoes.'

'And *what*,' Shay said, getting to his feet, 'would an oul' bachelor like you know about marriage and childer?'

Mick shrugged his shoulders, not a man for arguing. 'True . . . true,' he muttered. He said no more, leaving his father to carry the cudgel further if he so wished.

Noel reached for his pipe and tobacco. There was an uneasy silence for a while, as he packed the pipe, and then lit it. After a few puffs to get it going, he glanced in Shay's direction. 'Your mind is set on it?'

'Me mind is fixed,' Shay replied. 'She's agreed to marry me, and it can't be undone now.'

'*Five* childer,' Noel repeated, with a shake of his head. 'I hope to God you know what you're about.'

'Oh, I do. I've given it a good deal of thought. Make no mistake about that.'

'The mistake may be on your part,' his father told him. 'And once you're married, there's no changing it.'

'Haven't I been married before?' Shay's voice took on a higher note. 'And wouldn't it be better for poor Tara and Joe if they had a mother?'

Noel felt a cold hand clutch his heart. 'You're not thinking of taking the child?'

'I would, of course,' Shay stated. 'Where would I be goin' without her? How could I look after three of Tessie's, and neglect me own?'

'Where,' the old man said wearily, 'are you going to find the means of looking after five children? You find it tight enough looking after the two you have – and that's with meself and the aunties helping you out.'

'You won't have to help me out much longer,' Shay said proudly. 'The priest in Tullamore told Tessie that he's going to put a word in for me in the new factory.' He raised his eyebrows. 'They pay big money in the factory – far better than I'm gettin' in the mill in Ballygrace.'

'No doubt you'll live in Tullamore?' Mick said. 'You'd find it hard cycling to the factory every morning in the winter.'

Shay nodded. 'Tessie has the house well set up . . . and with the bits of furniture the aunties have kept for me, we should be fine.'

Mick rubbed his hands. 'By the sounds of everything, you'll be on the pig's back, so!'

'We will,' Shay agreed. 'Please God we will.'

Nelly Kelly was delighted with her little visitor, and gave her a drink of milk and a piece of apple tart. A day of rest, such as Christmas Day, was not something she relished. She usually filled her long, empty days scrubbing floors, cleaning windows, washing already-gleaming delph from the dresser, and tidying her turf shed. Sunday was a long enough day to abstain from her tasks, without having this extra Holy Day as well. She was a lonely old lady since her husband had died several years ago, and her family grown up and scattered to the wind. Occasionally, she had a visit from a son or a daughter, but they never seemed to have the money or the time to travel from Dublin or England too often. Originally from Galway, Nelly had always had a notion to return there, but the opportunity had never come. Some time back, she had recognised that her roots were now in Offaly, and she might as well be content to finish her days there.

'Do you like me new book, Mrs Kelly?' Tara asked. 'It's a fairy-tale book, and it's got lots of pictures in it. Me granda has got loads of books, but his big books are awful hard to read. This one is easier for me.'

Nelly examined the book. 'Your granda's a very educated man and you're a clever girleen to be reading a book like this.'

'It hasn't got many words, and they're only for little children. Can you read, Mrs Kelly?'

The old woman drew her shawl across her shoulders – it was her best one and worn only on special occasions like today. 'Very little. I can just about write me name, and a few other words. I wasn't as lucky as you. I never went to school.'

Tara's face was a picture. 'You never went to school?' she said in a shocked voice. Then recovering quickly, she added, 'I could teach you to read, if you like.'

'I think,' Nelly said, trying not to laugh, 'that I'm a bit old for that now. But you could read me a bit of your new book. I'd like to hear you reading.'

Tara needed no prompting. She sat up dead straight in her chair, as if she was in school. 'It's all about fairies . . . and everything.'

Just as she opened her mouth to read the first word, a loud knock sounded on the door. Nelly clucked her tongue and rushed to answer it.

'I'm sorry for disturbing you, Mrs Kelly,' Shay said in a respectful tone, dragging his cap from his head, 'but I've to go to Tullamore on a bit of business and Tara has to come with me.'

'Sure you're not disturbing me,' Nelly told him in her soft Galway lilt. 'I'll get her for you now.' When she saw the disappointed look on Tara's face, she said, 'You can bring your book over tonight, if it's not too late.'

Tara climbed down off the chair, and wiping a crumb from the corner of her mouth, said in a solemn voice, 'Thanks for the apple tart, Mrs Kelly – it was lovely.'

*

Tara's face dropped as Shay appeared wheeling his rickety old bicycle. 'Can we not take the ass and cart?'

He gave a sigh. 'Don't start yer complainin' already. We're goin' on the bike, and that's the end of it.' He threw his leg over the bike, and reached his arms out to lift Tara up onto the crossbar.

The child's lip quivered and she took a step back, shaking her head. 'Don't want to go on yer oul' bike.'

Shay's arm shot out and caught her. 'You're going on the feckin' bike,' he told her, 'whether you like it or not.'

A mile or so along the road, Shay attempted to mollify his young daughter. 'The oul' ass is in bad form,' he explained. 'The last time I took her to Tullamore, she took nearly two hours. Sure we can be there in half an hour on the bike, and I have a few sweets here in my pocket for you.'

'Are we goin' to see Joe, Daddy?' she asked, brightening up.

'We are, my girleen. We are,' he said jovially. 'And then we're going to visit a grand, nice woman and her three children.'

'What ages are they?' Tara asked curiously, her burnished hair flying in the breeze.

'All ages,' Shay replied, his mind wandering back to Tessie. 'And don't be asking me any more questions – you'll find out when we get there.'

The old aunties were all over Tara and her father when they arrived. Their pristine little house in Tullamore had such an air of excitement that Shay immediately wondered what was going on. The house usually had an atmosphere more suited to a church, with holy pictures adorning the walls, and the rosary and prayers being said at every opportune moment.

Joe was a rather solemn, sensitive child. He was very different from Tara, both in demeanour and appearance, he being dark-haired and dark-eyed like his father, while Tara took after her reddish-haired mother. Joe was quiet and respectful towards his father, regarding him in the way that a polite stranger might. To Tara, he was patient and kind, but in the time they had been separated, he had become as remote towards her as he was to his father and the rest of the family.

Noel's spinster sisters were like two young schoolgirls, giggling over a secret. They gave Tara a bag of sweets and a sixpence, then they told her to be a good girl and sit and listen to the music on the radio with her brother. Molly poured a large glass of whiskey for Shay, and then they ushered him into the privacy of their bedroom.

'We have great news for you, Shay,' Maggie the eldest said breathlessly, her hands joined as though in prayer. 'Great news altogether! We got a letter from the seminary yesterday, and they say there's a place for Joe after the summer.'

'Begod!' Shay said, nearly choking on his whiskey. 'As soon as that? Isn't he a bit young to be goin' away?'

'He'll be eleven on March the nineteenth – his patron saint's day,' Molly reminded him. 'Just the right age to start. If you leave him any longer, he could lose his vocation. His mind is dead set on being a priest, and has been since his poor mother died.' She took a deep breath. 'We spoke to Father Higgins at Midnight Mass, and he said he would call round to talk to us in the New Year.'

Shay's mind rattled along, trying to make sense of this new development. He had geared himself up to explain about his forthcoming marriage to his son. He had been going to suggest that Joe might like to come and live with him and Tessie after the wedding. Exactly where he might fit in the two-bedroomed cottage, Shay had not yet worked out.

This business about Joe going away to a seminary was a bolt out of the blue. He knew Molly and Maggie had been going on about him being a priest this long time, but he hadn't given it much attention, thinking it was wishful thinking on their parts.

No doubt about it, this news had taken the wind out of his sails. Really, it would have suited everyone fine for Joe to stay with his great-aunties. The boy was not a good mixer and inclined to be on the timid side. Maybe, Shay thought, the seminary was the answer to everybody's prayers. It would solve the problem of trying to mix the two families together in little or no space. At eleven, it would be harder for Joe than it would be for Tara. She was only an infant yet, and could come to look upon Tessie as her mother.

On the other hand, Tara could be a spoiled little brat at times.

Hopefully, she wouldn't kick up any trouble about the wedding. She had been going on about that feckin' china doll since first thing this morning. Maybe he could find the money for it by her birthday and when she was all delighted and in great humour, he could tell her about the wedding, and about moving to Tullamore. Shay drained his glass, suddenly thinking that things might be working out for him, at long last.

'So,' Maggie said, interrupting her nephew's thoughts, 'we'll see what the priest has to say about Joe, when he comes round in the New Year.'

'We'll be guided by the priest's advice,' Shay said carefully. 'If the boy has a vocation, then it wouldn't be for me to stand between himself and God.'

'Indeed not!' Maggie agreed. 'And we'll all help him out in any way we can, with the bits of things he needs for the seminary. Sure, wouldn't it be a privilege?' She sighed with delight and patted Shay on the back. 'He'll be first priest in the Flynn family. Isn't that something for a father to be proud of?'

After a cup of tea and a slice of fruit cake, followed by another celebratory glass of whiskey, Shay and Tara set off for Tessie's little terraced house in the middle of the town. He decided against introducing Joe to them at this stage. What was the point now? Sure, he might not be involved in the set-up at all, if he was going to the seminary.

Tessie had the kettle boiling and the delph on the table, waiting for her visitors. She opened the door to them smiling and blushing at the same time. 'Welcome to ye both,' she said, ushering them into the neat little house.

Tara, initially shy and clinging to her father, soon changed her tune, when she saw the colouring book and crayons that were waiting for her on the table, and the other little hands all too willing to help her to colour in the pictures. Sean, Mary and Assumpta were five, four and three respectively – the youngest born the month after her father died. Tara was unaware of the scrimping and scraping Tessie Devine had gone through to provide the few bits extra for Christmas for her own crowd, without having to stretch it to buy for Shay's daughter, too. The young widow looked on it as an investment, for if things worked out, they would be a lot better off in the near future.

Hopefully, she would soon be married – and to a man with a good job in the new spinning factory in Tullamore.

Tessie's previous husband had been a hard worker, and had provided well for her and the children. But a year of struggling on a widow's pension had taught her that her only chance of survival now was to find another man. Although Shay had a bit of a reputation as a drinker, she was confident she could knock him into shape. A good dinner every day, and a warm bed every night would keep him a satisfied and happy man.

'You'll have some cakebread and a bit of ham?' Tessie asked Shay, handing him a mug of steaming tea.

Shay had to think for a moment, as his stomach was unusually full with all the festive food. 'Go on,' he said, giving her a wink, 'you've twisted me arm.'

She ruffled his boyish dark curls. 'A growing man like you needs to be kept well-fed.'

'And no better woman to do it!' he said, gripping her hand playfully. He then proceeded to demolish the plate of bread and meat she put in front of him.

'How soon d'you think the wedding will be?' Tessie asked when Tara took the younger children to play outside.

'As soon as things are fixed up at the factory, then we can chat the priest about the arrangements,' Shay said, stretching his feet out in front of the fire. 'A month or so should see everything fixed up.'

'Won't it be great for you, to be able to walk up the road to work? Sure, you can fall out of bed and straight into the factory.'

The mention of bed brought Shay up on his feet and over to the table, where Tessie was sitting. His hands came to rest on her shoulders, and he bent down to kiss her cheek. She gave a little moan, which encouraged him more, and his hands slid further down her arms, and then moved to cup her voluptuous breasts. When her face turned up towards him, Shay crushed his mouth down hand on hers.

God, it was ages since he'd been with a woman – over three years! Although they hadn't had much time on their own, from the response he had from Tessie, hopefully, it would be well worth the wait. After a promising start, Tara's pale, delicate mother had not been great in that department. She was either pregnant, or recovering from the birth or the loss of a child. Out of six pregnancies, she had only managed to give birth to Joe and Tara, and then she had gone down with scarlet fever.

Shay felt Tessie was promising in more ways than one. She was only twenty-six, and her full, firm figure had hardly been changed by childbirth. By the looks of the house and the children, she was also a good housekeeper. And by the way she was pushing her breasts against him and opening the buttons on his shirt, she was likely to be good sport in bed.

As the sound of children's voices came nearer the house, Shay suddenly reckoned that the answer to all his problems was to get married.

To get married – and as quickly as he possibly could.

Chapter Three

There had never been such activity and excitement in the Flynn spinsters' house, except perhaps when it was their turn to host a Station Mass. But even so, this particular occasion outshone any other, for it singled the family out from the common herd in Tullamore. To have a priest in the making was the highest honour any Irish Catholic family could wish for. And no price was too high to pay for someone who forgave sins.

For months, Molly and Maggie had been gathering up the things for the trunk which Joe had to take to the seminary in Dublin. They had dragged the whole procedure out much longer than was necessary, substituting the trunk for the bottom drawer they had never had as brides. They picked sheets and blankets and pillowslips for Joe's bed, sets of stripy towels and soaps, and pyjamas, vests, underpants and socks. And every assistant, in every shop they patronised, was told in great detail about the contents and the quality of the stuff in Joe's trunk, and how his great-aunts had spared no expense.

'He has the loveliest uniform of a dark green blazer,' Molly elaborated to Mrs Finlay in the drapery shop, 'and a matching cap with a badge.'

'And a gabardine overcoat,' Maggie added. 'Everything has to be the best of quality.'

'And aren't they entitled to it?' Mrs Finlay said with a grim look on her pinched face. 'The poor little *gossuns!* Away from their homes and families from eleven years of age, to have their lessons beat into them by those cruel priests.' Mrs Finlay had a son who had attended a seminary some years ago, and had been devastated when he was sent home with ill-health.

He had since left Tullamore for England, and rumour had it he was now married to a Protestant girl and that the wedding ceremony had taken place in a registry office.

The Flynn spinsters were both aware of this fact, and Mrs Finlay was painfully aware that they knew it, too. Nothing was said for a moment while Molly re-positioned her pearl-encrusted hatpin and Maggie examined the quality of a boy's grey schoolshirt.

'Father Higgins was very careful when he picked the seminary in Dublin for us,' Molly gushed in the high-pitched girlish tone she used when talking about the clergy, 'and we were delighted with it when he took us up on a visit in the spring.'

'We were assured that Joe would be more than looked after,' Maggie added, 'and if there were any problems they would inform us immediately.'

Mrs Finlay reached across the shop counter and almost pulled the shirt out of Maggie's hands. 'Do you want the shirt or not?' she said in an uppity tone. 'It makes no odds to me. I have plenty of customers who know good quality when they see it, without having to study it for half an hour.'

'We'll take *one*, thank you,' Molly said primly. 'We'll see how it washes. Then we'll decide about buying another one.'

'Sure, won't it give you more time to save for it,' Mrs Finlay said, wrapping the shirt in a piece of brown paper. 'It makes it easier on you, buying the odd item every now and then.' Her voice took on a nasal tone. 'It's all right for the well-to-do families buying these expensive uniforms and the rest of the stuff for the seminary – but it's not easy on the *likes of you*.'

Then, the wrapped shirt was clapped down on the counter in front of the two sisters.

Molly took her purse out of her bag and put a ten-shilling note down on the counter. 'Isn't it amazing the short memory some people have?' she said to no one in particular. 'And how they can forget the ordinary families they came from, themselves?'

'It is,' Maggie agreed, starting towards the door. 'At least any money we have is our own, and we were never tempted into marrying for it. Nor do we have to rely on the good humour of a man to give it to us, instead of giving it to other women.'

A dreadful silence descended on the shop while Mrs Finlay fiddled around at the till with her back to the two sisters. Then, she turned and came back to the counter, her face like thunder and her mind full of dire thoughts. She heartily wished she had never made the biting comments about the seminary which had started this diatribe off. But it was too late now. After all these years, she had never got over the disappointment of *nearly* having a priest in her family. It was a wound she would carry to the grave.

But, the gloves were off now and she had to defend her corner.

She banged the change down loudly in front of Molly. 'Those who have never had a man shouldn't comment. Marriage is an area two oul' spinsters like yourselves know nothing about.'

Molly scooped the coins into her neat little purse and put the brown paper parcel into her shopping bag. 'True,' she agreed, 'and from what we've heard of your husband at the weekends with other women – *younger* women – it's just as well we know nothing about it!'

Having had the last word – and before Mrs Finlay could catch her breath – the victorious spinsters made a quick but dainty exit from the drapery shop.

The Sunday evening in September that Joe left his great-aunts' house in Tullamore for the junior seminary in Dublin was the climax of months of preparation. Noel and Mick Flynn, plus Tara in a new straw hat, had made their way out on the ass and cart from Ballygrace after their dinner. Shay and Tessie, his wife this six months, and noticeably pregnant with their first child, were also there. They had walked the half-mile from their own house, leaving Tessie's three children in the care of a neighbour, to wish the boy farewell.

'Doesn't he look lovely in his uniform and cap?' Molly gushed, as she handed tea round in the parlour that was only used for special occasions. There was a great smell of spicy furniture polish and floor wax that helped to cover up the usual musty smell.

'He certainly does, begod!' Shay said, loosening the tie which Tessie had forced him to wear. He was unusually dapper, clad in the suit he had worn to both his weddings and his first wife's funeral.

As he looked across the room at Joe now, he felt slightly in awe of this smartly dressed young stranger who was his son. 'And how does it feel,' he asked, 'to be goin' to an important place like Dublin . . . and to be amongst the likes of all those clever priests?'

Joe looked down at his black shiny school shoes and shrugged. 'I . . . I don't really know.'

'I don't think I've been in Dublin more than half a dozen times in me life,' his father elaborated, 'and that was enough. Cars and people everywhere, and the price of everythin' in the shops! Sure, ye couldn't *look* at anythin', far less buy it.'

'Sure Joe won't be anywhere *near* the shops and cars,' Molly cut in hastily, lest the boy should have fears setting in at the last minute. 'It's the grandest seminary in Dublin. Father Higgins said it himself. Isn't that right, Maggie?'

'Indeed it is,' Maggie called from the kitchen, where she was carefully cutting up a newly baked currant cake, which would be handed round when the priest arrived. She came into the parlour, where some of the adults were seated on straight-backed chairs, and others on a highly polished, folded-up settle bed. Tara sat, unusually quiet, on her grandfather's knee, with her thumb in her mouth. On this unheard-of occasion, Joe was allowed to sit on the wine, velvet-upholstered rocking chair, which had belonged to the aunty who had left the house to the two sisters.

'Joe's a lucky boy to have the chance of such a good education.' Maggie said to the group, then she nodded over to Noel. 'Your granda had high hopes of going to a seminary when he was a boy, but there was no one in the family who could afford to send him there. That's the truth – isn't it, Noel?'

'That was a long time ago,' Noel said quietly, shifting Tara onto his other knee. 'And it wasn't meant to be.'

'Well for it!' Shay laughed out loud. 'Where would me and Mick and the rest of us be, if you'd gone in for the priesthood? What d'you say, Mick?'

Mick grinned and rubbed his hands together in embarrassment – but he said nothing as usual.

Molly shook her head, her mouth laughing but her eyes serious. 'There was never any fear of *you* having any vocation, Shay. And if you had, God help the parish that would have been landed with you!'

'What's this I'm missing about parishes and priests?' a voice beloved by Molly and Maggie said from the half-opened front door. It was Father Higgins.

The atmosphere in the house became distinctly tense. Shay straightened his tie, and Joe moved out of the chair to offer it to the Parish Priest.

'Good man yourself!' the priest said, giving the young boy a pat on the head. 'You'll do fine in the seminary if you keep up your manners.' He sank down into the rocking chair. 'Sure, isn't this the happiest day there ever was for the Flynn family?'

'Indeed it is!' the two elderly sisters chorused, while Noel nodded his head slowly and Shay and Tessie grinned ingratiatingly at the priest, as they did with anyone they considered to be their 'better'.

Father Higgins graciously accepted the china cup of tea that was thrust into his hands, and the plate of buttered soda bread and currant cake that was placed on a little table by his left elbow. 'Currant cake!' he exclaimed in mock delight. 'You ladies have certainly risen to the occasion today.'

Molly's heart soared and her cheeks flamed at the priest's compliment, while Maggie scurried about refilling empty cups and offering the celebratory cake to everyone else, now that the priest had been attended to.

'Do you know something, Joe?' Father Higgins said, wiping a stray crumb from his black jacket. 'I have a feeling – a very strong feeling – that your mother is watching down on you from heaven today.'

A gasp went around the room. For the first time during the proceedings, Tara Flynn's ears pricked up, and her eyes travelled to the ceiling, as though expecting to see her dead mother's face smiling down.

'I have a feeling,' the priest elaborated in the same tone he used for his sermon at Sunday mass, 'that she is celebrating with the family today. Celebrating the fact that her son – Joseph Flynn – has been chosen to join the priesthood.'

All eyes descended on Joe, who shifted uncomfortably in his new uniform. The shirt was rubbing against his neck, and the elastic garters that his Auntie Maggie had made to hold his socks up were pinching him because they were too tight.

For the hundredth time that afternoon, he ran a finger under his collar to ease the chafed skin, and said another silent prayer that he would like the seminary, and not get teased by the other pupils, as he had been at National School in Tullamore.

Joe had always been different from the other children his own age. When the other boys were out kicking football and going to the cinema, he had been at home quietly reading his books and playing the piano in the musty, damp parlour.

He hoped and prayed with all his eleven-year-old heart that things would be better in the seminary, and that the other boys who were training to be priests would be nicer than the ones in his school.

Several cups of tea and half an hour of awakward chat later, Father Higgins and Joe waved goodbye to the Flynn family and an assembly of neighbours, and set off in the priest's car for the seminary in Dublin. The two spinsters' feelings swung from elation because of Joe's great public send-off, and abject misery every time they thought of the big void he would leave in their daily life.

'D'you think Joe will settle in all right in the seminary?' Tessie asked, as she and Shay walked back to their house.

Shay shrugged, loosening his tie and opening the top button on his shirt. 'You wouldn't know what's in that fella's mind,' he said. 'You'd never really get to know him. He was a bit of a mammy's boy, and he did nothing but cry for weeks when she died. That's why Molly and Maggie took him. They said he needed a woman to mind him more than Tara did.'

Tessie pulled her cardigan across her ample chest. 'You wouldn't believe Tara and Joe were brother and sister. They don't look a bit alike, Tara with the red curly hair and him with the black straighter hair. And they have different ways altogether.' She stopped when they reached the corner of their road. 'You know, Shay,' Tessie said quietly, 'I sometimes feel a bit guilty when I think about Joe and Tara. Maybe if we hadn't got married, you might have had more time with them. It's sad for them both to be livin' with elderly people, and not having a mother or a father to see to them.'

Shay shrugged again. 'I've done my best by them both – how many fathers can say that their son has gone to be a priest? Molly and Maggie are good to Joe. Did you see the way they had him dressed up? And everythin' in the finest of material too.'

'What about Tara?' Tessie said. 'I felt pity for the poor child, sitting up on her grandfather's knee. It's sad to think of her with no womankind in that cottage. How will she manage when she gets older, and she has no woman to talk to?'

'Tara's grand,' Shay said, feeling uncomfortable with the conversation. For all he had an ever-increasing houseful of children and was on to his second wife, he felt lost when presented with any kind of a problem. 'It's her own choice to be living with me father – we gave her a fair crack at our house, and the little divil wouldn't stay.' He paused for a moment. 'But if you like, we could always encourage her to come back to our house again.'

'You could go across next weekend and see yer father about it,' Tessie said. 'They can't blame you then for not asking. Even if she doesn't want to come, our consciences would be clear.'

'Grand,' Shay agreed, for the sake of peace. Tara was fine where she was. Sure, didn't she have her own room and half-decent furniture and everything? She wouldn't take kindly to being put into a room with Tessie's children again. She hadn't taken to it the first time, and she was unlikely to take to it now. She was that determined she wouldn't sleep with the others, that they had ended up making up a bed on the floor for her. Sure, Tara had everything she needed out in Ballygrace. At his father's cottage they had plenty of milk and eggs, and butter and spuds, without having to buy them at the shops in Tullamore like he had to do. Many's the night Shay wished he could just go out to the cow and bring in a pitcher of milk, instead of having to find the money to pay for it. And he was often glad to bring a bit of butter or a bag of spuds or carrots back from his father's place, when he visited Tara at the weekends. Every little helped to make the wages go that bit further.

Tara was far better off living in the cottage in Ballygrace, Shay decided. He found it hard going feeding all the little mouths that he had in Tullamore, without adding her healthy appetite to them. If the truth be told, if he had to make the choice again, he would have stayed in the cottage himself and forgotten the idea of a second marriage.

He had been well off then, with his father and Mick – and he didn't know it.

It was a terrible pity, that in order to get a bit of sport with a woman, you had to be shackled with all the other responsibilities that went with marriage. Shay shook his head. Men were the greatest eedjits going – led by their mickeys instead of their heads.

'What are you muttering and shakin' yer head about now?' Tessie suddenly demanded.

'Nothin',' Shay replied. 'Sure, I was only trying to remember the words of an ould song.'

'Well for you!' Tessie told him. 'Well for you to have so little thoughts in your head, that you can be worryin' about the words of a song.' She held her hands up to the evening sky. 'Oh, the Lord be good to them! Don't men have it nice and easy?'

The drive up to Dublin in Father Higgins's car should have been a treat for Joe. It would have been a treat for any other boy. But Joe was not like any other boy. He had always been different, and in his eleven-year-old mind, he knew that he would always be that way. When they went on the visit to the seminary in the spring, he had enjoyed the day out then. He had loved sitting in the back of the shiny black Ford car with its leather seats and beautiful walnut dashboard. But as he drove along now through Daingean and Edenderry and beyond to the main road for Dublin, Joe could not summon up the same enthusiasm.

All sorts of thoughts were going through his mind about the seminary and about leaving his aunties behind in their neat little house in Tullamore. Although he often felt sad in the house – for reasons his childish mind could not make any sense of – he was aware of being very safe and secure with the two sisters. Apart from leaving them behind, Joe had also left his beloved piano, and it would be Christmas before he would get the chance to play it again.

Hot tears welled up in his eyes as he thought about all the things he would miss about his old life. Then, it suddenly struck him as being odd that he wouldn't miss his father or Tara. They were like strangers to him and he could hardly remember having ever lived with them. His life seemed to have been always with Molly and Maggie.

His thoughts flitted from one thing to another, then came to rest on Father Higgins's words about his mother. He liked the bit about her being up in heaven, because that was exactly where an angel like his mother should be. He just wished she had been alive until he had grown up. He might have got to know his father better then, instead of having to sit quietly every other Sunday when he came to visit him at his aunties' house.

He hoped Father Higgins was right about his mother looking down on him, and he hoped he was right about the seminary. A cold feeling stole over Joe's heart. He knew that if Father Higgins was wrong – there would be no one up in Dublin to save him.

Chapter Four

❧❧❧

Spring, 1943

'I've got another little sister, Mrs Kelly,' Tara proudly told her neighbour. 'Tessie had her early this morning – so that makes her a Saturday child. Do you know that poem, Mrs Kelly? It starts – "Monday's child is fair of face.". I was born on a Sunday, so that makes me – "bonny and blithe, and good and gay!" '

'Is that right?' The old woman said, not understanding a word of what Tara was going on about. 'So that's another little Flynn born today. Begod, that's how many ye have now?' Nelly was busy boiling flour bags in a large cauldron on the blazing turf fire, and was glad of the excuse to sit down at the table for a few minutes. It was four o'clock in the afternoon, and she'd been on the go since six that morning.

Tara tilted her head to the side. 'I have one stepbrother and two stepsisters, and two half-sisters, and me big brother Joe, that's away to be a priest. That makes seven of us all together.'

'Would you not think of moving to Tullamore, to try living with your father again?'

Tara's red curls flew wildly as she shook her head. 'Sure, me granda and me Uncle Mick need me more here,' she said, in a manner more suited to an old woman than an eleven-year-old girl.

The very mention of going to live in Tullamore sent a shiver through Tara's bones. She had lasted only a week out there, When Shay and Tessie had first got married. Night after night of crying, making herself sick, and ultimately wetting the bed, had ensured that she was returned to Ballygrace and her granda. Not under any circumstances would she go back to live in Tullamore, to have to share a bed with Mary and Assumpta, and to have Sean in the same room. Worst of all – Tara could hardly bear to think of it – had been the noises coming from her father's and Tessie's room nearly every night. The smothered laughter, the creaking of the marital bed, and the groans and grunts were the final straw.

She would stay put in her granda's cottage, where she now had her own bedroom. Her Uncle Mick had moved in with her granda to let her have more privacy because she was growing up. He'd bought a new bed for her – one with a proper mattress – although Tara thought that the old straw mattress on the settle bed had been more comfortable.

'Have you finished knitting the baby's jacket yet?' Nelly asked, pouring two mugs of strong tea.

Tara nodded. 'I took it into school to show to Miss O'Hanlon, our knitting teacher, and she said I'd made a lovely job of it. She says we'll be learning how to knit socks soon.'

Nelly lifted a quarter of a soda-bread loaf out of her small cupboard, and cut it into slices. She spread butter thickly on it, then some raspberry jam, and set it on the table between them. 'I spent ages this morning sieving that damned black flour – you have to put plenty of butter and jam on the bread to cover up the taste.'

'Mick won't let me bake anything till the Emergency is over,' Tara confided in an irritable tone. 'He says that I'd only waste the flour, and we can't afford it. He thinks I'm just a child, but I'm not. I can bake every bit as well as him.' She took a bite of her bread and jam. 'I'm sick of this oul' war, and the rationing and everything.'

'Sure there's a lot worse off than us, me darlin',' Nelly said quietly. 'At least we can bake our own bread – such as it is – and we have our own butter and cheese, and jam and milk. We have potatoes and vegetables from the garden, and the bit of meat we're allowed.' She shook her head. 'The ones in England are havin' a terrible time, altogether. We're well off, and we don't know it.'

Tara drank her tea and ate her bread, pondering over Mrs Kelly's words. She didn't feel at all well off. Compared to someone like her friend Biddy, she was well off – but compared to some of the girls in her class, she was definitely poor. She thought of Madeleine

Fitzgerald, and her lovely coats and dresses, and her father's car. Her granda said the Emergency had put a spoke in the wheel of Fitzgerald's car, for they were allowed hardly any petrol to run it. He had nearly laughed out loud the first Sunday they had all turned up for Mass in the old pony and trap.

Tara didn't think it was funny; the Fitzgeralds were too fancy to use a pony and trap. They had a big house, and nice clothes – the sort of clothes Tara would have when she was grown up and married.

Then Tara thought of Gabriel Fitzgerald – Madeleine's older brother – and she blushed. He was in the class above her in school. He was quiet and nice. Nice clothes, nice hair and nice manners. When their car arrived at Mass every Sunday, it was always Gabriel that she looked out for. She'd never *really* spoken to him – just the odd word here and there in school – but there was something about him that made him stand out from all the other boys.

Mrs Kelly heaved herself up from the table, and lifted a pile of old newspapers from the top of a cupboard. She spread a thick layer on the corner of the table. 'Would you ever be a good girl, Tara, and give me a hand to lift the pot out of the fire?'

Tara got to her feet immediately. They went over to the fireplace, and, taking the damp cloth the old woman gave her, Tara wrapped it round one of the pot handles. Mrs Kelly did the same with the other handle, and then they lifted the pot out of the dying embers of the turf fire and set it on top of the newspapers.

'I'll leave it there to cool for a bit,' she told Tara, panting from the exertion, 'and then I'll drain the water off.'

'What are you going to make with the flour bags, Mrs Kelly?' the young girl asked. 'Is it more sheets?'

'Pillowcases, darlin',' the old Galway woman replied. 'I'm going to boil them a few more times, to get the flour-maker's name off them. When I've finished bleachin' them and they're lovely and soft, I'll do a bit of lacework on them. I'm going to give them as a wedding present to the young girl that works in the bakery. She's very good to me, giving me a few extra ounces of flour now and again.'

'Would you teach me how to do lacework, Mrs Kelly?' Tara asked.

Nelly took a deep breath. She had taught the child how to knit, how to sew, even how to do basic embroidery – but lacework was a different matter altogether. It was much more intricate and required a great deal of concentration. 'Maybe in the winter,' she hedged. 'We'll be glad of something to occupy us during the long, dark nights.'

Tara smiled with delight. She wanted to learn how to do all the fancy things – she liked the things that the better-class families had. She wanted to learn them, because they were the sort of things she would have when she got married.

They sat chatting a bit longer, and then Tara said she would have to go home to get the potatoes on for her granda and Mick. 'Mick'll be in from the bakery soon, and me granda's been out in the field all afternoon, fixing one of the fences,' she said, 'so they'll be fit to eat a horse when they come in.'

'Aren't you a grand little girleen, able to cook and do all the household things for the men?' Mrs Kelly said. 'Sure, you'll make someone a grand wife in a few years.'

'Mrs Kelly,' Tara said suddenly, 'do you have any pictures of my mammy? Only . . . I don't like to ask daddy any more . . . now he's married again . . . and with the new babbies and everything. I don't think he likes me remindin' him about it.'

Nelly paused for a moment, her heart going out to the child. 'I haven't any meself,' she said slowly, 'but I think I know a woman who could have some. Leave it with me, darlin', and I'll see what I can do.'

'Thanks, Mrs Kelly,' Tara said, and closed the door quietly behind her.

Biddy was sitting on the doorstep waiting on her friend. 'Where were you?' she snapped in an accusing voice. 'I've been lookin' for you for ages.'

Tara took a deep breath, surprised at her friend's sharp manner. It wasn't Biddy's usual way at all. 'I was havin' my tea at Mrs Kelly's.'

'I've had nothin' to eat all day,' Biddy said with a sob in her voice. 'Lizzie blamed me for the cow kicking over the bucket of milk this morning, and she gave me no dinner because of it.' She halted, giving a great sniff. 'An' I had had no breakfast either.' She pulled her shrunken, threadbare cardigan across her chest, trying to keep warm. Even in the height of summer, Biddy often looked cold. 'She sent me out to look for sticks for the fire, so I took me chance to come and see you.'

Tara opened the front door of the whitewashed cottage. 'Come on in,' she said kindly. 'There's some cake-bread left from yesterday. We'll get the fire goin' and we can make some toast.'

'What if yer granda comes in?' Biddy said fearfully. 'He might run me.'

'I'll tell him you're helping me to make the butter,' Tara told her. 'He always says it's good luck if a neighbour gives a hand to churn it, so he won't mind you.' She pointed to the turf basket by the side of the dying fire. 'You throw a few sods on the fire, and I'll go and get the churn.'

Tara poured milk from the crockery pan into the churn, then carried it into the kitchen. She set it down by the table, then she went and got the churn lid and the dash. 'There you are,' she said to Biddy. 'You can stand there and be doin' the butter, and I'll toast you a bit of bread at the fire. Do you want a drink of milk?'

Biddy nodded her head. 'I'm not feeling too grand today,' she said. 'I've got a pain in me head and a pain in me belly.'

Tara poured a cup of fresh milk from the jug and handed it to Biddy. She studied her sad, scrawny friend for a moment. Biddy was often not well. She was always complaining, and a few times at school recently she had fainted. When she had come round, they had taken her home to Lizzie Lawless, although Biddy had protested, saying she wanted to stay at school. Tara would never have told anybody, but really she felt a bit jealous. She'd never fainted, and she always wondered what it was like. A few times she'd felt funny on a Sunday morning at Mass, a kind of dizzy feeling, but it never came to anything. Her granda had said it was fasting from the night before that made some people weak. Tara would love to have fainted – for a bit of excitement at Mass – instead of just feeling weak.

She held the toasting fork over the flickering flames, while Biddy pulled the dash – a long wooden paddle – up and down through the hole in the churn lid.

'I'll just sit down for a minute,' Biddy said after a few minutes. 'Me arms are a bit sore.'

'Here y'are,' Tara said, handing her the toasted bread. She lifted a saucer from the cupboard that held a small pat of butter and a knife, and placed it in front of her friend. 'You'll feel better after that, Biddy. I'll make you another slice while you're eating it.'

'Thanks, Tara,' the little orphan said gratefully, spreading the butter thickly. 'I wish I could bring you into Lizzie's house, but she'd kill me if she found out.' She wolfed the piece of toast down in a matter of seconds. 'Nora brought a friend into the house one evenin' when Lizzie was out, and when she heard the next day, she hit her over the head with the brush.'

'That Lizzie Lawless is nothin' but an ould witch!' Tara stated. 'Me granda says she shouldn't be allowed to look after children – that she only does it for the money.'

Biddy shrugged and bit the ragged sleeve of her cardigan. 'She never gives us the clothes that are handed in for us either.' She looked down at her battered old boots. 'She got a lovely pair of shoes in a parcel and when I asked her if I could have them, she gave me a slap. She said, "Those shoes are not for the likes of you!" Then she put them away in a box and I never saw them again.'

'Never mind,' Tara consoled her. 'When you leave school and get a job, you can buy your own shoes.' She put another piece of slightly burned toast down in front of her friend.

Biddy shrugged and bit into the bread. 'I don't think I'll ever get a job – sure I can hardly read an' write.'

'You're getting better,' Tara said encouragingly. 'I heard the teacher telling you when you read out in the class yesterday.'

Biddy sighed. 'She wasn't so nice when I told her Lizzie wasn't sending in any turf for the class fire. She told me that I was stupid, and it wasn't worth me while coming to school any more.'

The two friends chatted about school while Biddy did her best at churning the butter, and Tara scrubbed the potatoes and cut up a cabbage, and put them on the blazing fire to boil. She then took a piece of cold, boiled bacon from the cupboard, and cut it into thick slices, to have it ready for her granda and Mick when they came in.

'Here y'are, Biddy,' Tara said, handing her friend a piece of the fatty ham rind. 'That'll fill you up.'

The skinny orphan devoured the meat in two bites, then she plunged the dash up and down in the churn a few more times. 'I'll have to go, Tara,' she said apologetically. 'If I don't gather up the sticks, Lizzie will beat me when I get home.'

Tara stood, eyes blazing and her hands on her hips. 'It's a good beating Lizzie Lawless needs, to see how she likes it.' She moved towards the back door. 'Me granda has a pile of kindling he chopped up this morning. He won't notice if you take a handful, an' if he does, I'll tell him I had to use it to get the fire going.'

'Thanks, Tara,' Biddy said again. She always seemed to be saying thanks to her friend.

'Oh, Biddy –' Tara suddenly remembered, 'have you finished with me American comic yet?'

The little orphan's face flushed. 'Oh . . . I forgot about it. I'll bring it up to you tomorrow.'

Biddy walked the half-mile back to the house, hugging the firewood to her chest, and saying a prayer to God, for giving her such a nice friend. Tara had plenty of friends in school, but she was always kind to Biddy, and never left her out of games at playtime. She stuck up for her, too, when other boys and girls laughed at her big boots and the old-fashioned clothes that Lizzie made her wear.

If it wasn't for Tara and Dinny the lodger, Biddy didn't know what she'd do.

Nora – the other orphan who lived at Lizzie's – had warned Biddy about Dinny. She'd told her not to go into the hayshed on her own with him. Nora had said to be careful when Lizzie wasn't about, because he was worse then.

Biddy didn't care. She liked Dinny. Even though he was quite old – thirty-six – he was always nice to her. He saved her bits of his breakfast, and gave her toffees and sugar sticks that he brought back from Dublin. He was a lorry driver. He drove up to Dublin some days, and went to Galway on others. He picked things up on his travels, although it was usually oul' bottles of *poitín*. Dinny hid these in a case under his bed, and sold them to men who he met up with in the pub. Even with the Emergency, and things being short everywhere, Dinny still managed to pick up odds and ends.

And sometimes – if Biddy did what he asked – he would give her things. He would give her a drop of his *poitín* with lemonade in it first, or maybe a glass of his beer, and then he would tell her stories and jokes. When she was in a heap giggling, Dinny would start to tickle her – and then he would ask her for a kiss.

At first Biddy hated him kissing her, because his teeth were all crooked and his bristly cheeks rubbed her skin raw – but she'd got used to it. She liked Dinny carrying on with her, for no one else had ever tickled and teased or played with her.

Biddy sighed, and hugged the sticks closer to her. She stopped every now and then, and picked up a few other bits from the ditch. She even found two sods of turf, which must have fallen off somebody's cart on the way back from the bog. Biddy hoped that it might put Lizzie in a better mood, for she got very little turf in. She said she wasn't wasting money on big fires. She went about the house wearin' a coat all the time – even in the height of the summer. And she told Nora and Biddy to do the same, she said it was their own fault if they were cold. She expected them to wear thick woollen stockings and hobnailed boots into the spring, and then they went barefoot until the cooler autumn days drew in. Any day now, Biddy thought, she would be able to throw off the boots and go in her bare feet. And nobody would laugh at her, because in the good weather all the children ran about in their bare feet.

Nora was a bit better off now she'd left school. She was turned fourteen years old, and was helping out at Father Daly's house during the week. The priest's housekeeper gave her dinner there, and gave her bits to bring home to Biddy. Biddy reckoned that some of the people in Ballygrace must know what an old miser Lizzie was, because they always said – '*Don't tell Lizzie*' when they gave you anything. Biddy couldn't wait until she was old enough to get away from Lizzie's house. She was past twelve now, and in a few years she was going to get a job and eventually get a nice house of her own.

There was nobody in the cottage when Biddy got back. She brushed the floor and tidied around a bit, then she settled back, relieved and glad to have the place to herself. There was a small pot by the side of the fire, with some leftover cooked potatoes and onions in it. Biddy reckoned it must be for colcannon for Dinny's tea. If Lizzie didn't come in before the lodger, then Biddy would have to add milk to the mixture and mash it up on the fire. She scooped a few pieces of the cold potato out with her fingers and ate them. Then she put the sticks and turf on the dying fire to revive it, and when it was going, she put the kettle on to boil. She would make some tea for herself before Lizzie got back, and she would sit and read Tara's American comic in front of the fire.

Ten minutes later Biddy heard the sound of whistling and a bike coming up the path. She looked out of the window that she had spent ages cleaning the day before. A smile came over her face. It was Dinny. Every evening, he dropped the lorry off at the depot in Tullamore, collected his bike and cycled back out to Ballygrace.

The lodger came in the front door of the cottage. He immediately knew by the casual, relaxed manner of Biddy that the woman of the house was not around.

'Where's Herself?' Dinny asked, taking off his cap and running his hands through his greasy brown hair.

'Out,' said Biddy in a light-hearted tone. She could talk to Dinny any way she liked and she knew he wouldn't give out to her. 'There was nobody here when I came back from gatherin' sticks.'

'Where's Nora?'

Biddy shrugged. 'She must still be at the priest's house.'

Dinny rubbed his hands together. 'Just yerself and meself.'

Biddy giggled. 'That's all.' She went over and poked the fire a bit. 'Will I put yer dinner on now? Lizzie's left some spuds for you . . . and I could fry you some bacon and eggs to go with it.'

'Could you now?' Dinny said, in a low, throaty voice. 'Aren't you the great little housekeeper?' He moved towards her, rolling up the sleeves of his stained working shirt.

Biddy giggled again, and threw back her lank, shoulder-length hair. 'Sure, won't I make a fine wife for somebody one day?'

'You will . . . you'll make some man a grand wife,' Dinny said, searching for the stick of liquorice in his waistcoat pocket. He held it out to her between finger and thumb. 'Well, now,' he said in a wheedling voice, 'what would a man get for this?'

Biddy stretched an eager hand out. 'Where did you get that, Dinny? Have you any more?'

He held the liquorice high above his head. 'Hold yer horses,' he said laughing. 'I don't give these away for nothing . . . sweeties are priceless at the minute.'

Biddy jumped up and down, trying to reach his hand.

'C'mon now,' he said, stretching higher and angling his body away from her. 'Surely, you can think of *something* to give me . . . something that could make a man feel happy?'

Biddy stopped jumping, and put a grubby finger under her chin in a coy manner. 'I wonder,' said she, 'what kind of a thing that would be?'

Biddy knew full well what he was looking for. Since he had come to live in the cottage, he had played around with her like this – when Lizzie wasn't around. He had started carrying on with her shortly after he arrived, teasing and tickling her . . . and touching her in places that she had never imagined a man would want to touch her. And funnily enough, she had liked it. She had liked the attention that Dinny paid her. She didn't always like the things he wanted her to do – but she had got used to it. And after a bit, she didn't mind. Dinny always gave her sweeties for doing it, and that made everything all right.

Dinny lowered his arm. 'Maybe a kiss?' he said in a thick voice.

The little orphan rolled her eyes to the ceiling as though considering the bargain. Then, a wide grin spread over her face. 'Okay!' she agreed, throwing her arms around him. As his rough lips came crushing down on her childish mouth, Biddy felt a wave of delight. It was grand, just grand, that someone liked her enough to hug and kiss her.

Never, at any point in her young life, could she remember being held and kissed. Nobody, except Dinny the Lodger, had been kind and nice to her. Her mother – whom she never knew – must have held her once. But not for long. Within days of her birth she was taken away. The nuns in the orphanage certainly never held and kissed her. Oh, they were kind enough to her, but in a strict, religious way. Once, when she was four years old, she was out playing in the orphanage garden and she fell over and cut her knee badly. One of the younger nuns had lifted her up in her arms, and then taken her to the doctor to have it stitched. Biddy had almost cried with joy at being held in someone's arms, and had held on so tightly when she came back to the orphanage that it had taken two other nuns to wrestle her out of the younger nun's arms.

And then Biddy had come to live at Lizzie Lawless's in Ballygrace. Instinctively – even as a young child – she had known not to expect any kisses and cuddles from that quarter. Lizzie was a pinched little spinster, who had a grudge against the world, and she took great delight in venting her spleen on Nora and Biddy.

From the moment Biddy had arrived in Ballygrace, their foster-mother had made her carry heavy buckets of water from the pump at the bottom of the road. She then had to heat the water in a pan over the fire, and then she had to wash the delph and pots. As she got older she had learned how to cook and wash and sew – and how to do them well – because Lizzie was very pernickety about how things were done. If they weren't done right first time, then Lizzie reckoned a good slap was all that was needed, to ensure it was done right the second time. Nora and Biddy had been quick learners due to the slaps.

Everything had changed when Dinny arrived at the cottage last year. Everything had become brighter and lighter in Lizzie's house, with his jocular manner and easy-going ways. He was distantly connected to the Lawless family, and when he was offered his new job in the area, the elderly spinster had suggested that he move in as a lodger. It meant that the girls had to give up their bedroom for him, and move their double bed into Lizzie's smaller room, while she moved her settle bed into the kitchen.

'I can see all that's going on from me bed, now,' she had warned, 'and there's no one can come in or out without me knowin'. Nobody knows what young ones would get up to these days.'

The arrangement had initially been temporary, but since both parties were happy with things, no mention had been made of Dinny looking elsewhere. Lizzie had been particularly happy with the dig money that the lodger tipped up every Friday night. It was another source of income to add to the money she was paid for rearing the girls. Another bit to add to the growing nest-egg that Lizzie had locked in a small wooden chest in her wardrobe drawer.

One of Dinny's hands slowly moved Biddy's hand to the hard ridge in the front of his rough working trousers, and the other moved to the garter at the top of her woollen stocking.

Biddy gave a loud, snorting giggle, pulled her hand away from him and shook her thin, lanky brown hair. 'The liquorice,' she said in a teasing voice, which she knew he liked. 'No sport until I get the stick of liquorice!'

Dinny lowered his dark head and pulled her hand back to caress him. 'Give my mickey a bit of a rub,' he murmured, 'and then you'll get the sweetie . . . I've got more than the one sweetie for you, if you do it the way I showed you last time.'

Biddy giggled again, delighted with his pleading manner. She couldn't believe how stupid a grown man could be. What could he possibly like about her touching him there? Up until a few weeks ago, he'd been content with just tickling and kissing her, but then this 'rubbing his mickey' business had started. It just seemed stupid and silly to Biddy, she couldn't see what Dinny liked about it at all. She couldn't understand why he would close his eyes, and make all those groaning noises as if she was hurting him.

Last time, in the turf shed, he had tried to make her put her hand down the front of his trousers. Biddy had laughed and wriggled away from him. She'd told him that she'd only do it if she got a fancy china doll like the one that Tara had. Dinny had sighed and said that when she was grown up, he would buy her lots of nice things, but at the minute he couldn't, because Lizzie would wonder where it came from.

As her hand moved up and down the bulge in his trousers, a thought suddenly came into Biddy's mind. 'What if Lizzie or Nora come in?' The laughter drained from her voice. 'We'd be in a lot of trouble then.'

'They won't come in,' Dinny said, in the funny, husky voice he always used when she touched him. 'And we can stop if they do.' He looked anxiously towards the door. 'We could go out into the turf shed . . . we would hear anybody before they came in on top of us.' He pressed her little hand harder against his body and closed his eyes again.

Then, a crunching of footsteps sounded on the path outside, heralding the arrival of Lizzie and Nora.

'Aw . . . feck it!' the lodger muttered, giving a deep, noisy sigh. He quickly moved away from Biddy, and readjusted the front of his trousers.

'What about me liquorice?' Biddy whispered urgently.

'I'll give it to you later – out in the turf shed,' Dinny said. Then, leaving a disappointed Biddy to greet the other two, he disappeared into his bedroom.

Chapter Five

William Fitzgerald lived a lie. He was regarded as the most prosperous and respectable member of Ballygrace parish. And indeed, this was exactly how he intended to present himself, when he moved from Blackrock – a small town on the south-east coast of Dublin – to County Offaly in the Midlands.

Exactly why he had moved with his family to Ballygrace House – a large rambling residence outside the village – none of the locals really knew. And it certainly wasn't for the want of enquiring. Not that they would have dared ask William Fitzgerald *directly*, for they could tell he was not a man to be approached with personal questions. Nor would they approach his stand-offish, pale-skinned, uppity wife.

There were ways and means of acquiring information in Ballygrace, some subtle and some not so subtle. The teachers in school made it their business to enquire, in a roundabout way, through the children. Others approached the two local women and the gardener who worked at the house, hoping for some nugget of information with which they could entertain their neighbours over the fence, or at night around the fire.

They were all given the same answer. The Fitzgeralds had moved to Ballygrace because Elisha Fitzgerald's delicate health was more suited to the country than the city, and because of William Fitzgerald's business interests. No other explanations were forthcoming.

Had the good people of Ballygrace known that William Fitzgerald had left Blackrock under a cloud, their tongues would have had something to wag about. And had they known that he had owned several residences in Blackrock equal in size to Ballygrace House – and

43

lost it all through drink and gambling – their tongues would have wagged all the harder.

But they didn't know, and William Fitzgerald would do his damnedest to make sure that they never found out. His good reputation meant everything to him. It meant his wife – who had put almost every penny of her family inheritance into financing the move to Offaly – would remain as his wife. It meant that his son, Gabriel, and his daughter, Madeleine – who knew nothing of their father's misdemeanours – could go about Tullamore with heads held high, as would befit a family living in Ballygrace House. Living in such a rural environment – far away from Blackrock – meant there was no likelihood of them being informed of the family's fallen fortunes.

The ambiguity of his children's schooling, however, was not lost on William Fitzgerald. It was the sorest point between him and Elisha, that they had to attend the Ballygrace National School. There were two reasons for this – finance and location.

To send the children to the nearest, suitable school would have been a huge drain on their rather depleted finances. It would also have taken too long to travel to Tullamore in a pony and trap, especially in the winter.

Elisha had put her daintily clad foot down firmly on the matter. She would not have the children travelling three miles in the dark to school in the morning and then three miles back home again in the dark. The children would attend Ballygrace National School, which – depending on their father's future fortunes – they could walk to, if the need arose.

'We have already learned one hard lesson,' Elisha Fitzgerald pointed out, 'and I have no wish to go through that uncertainty again. From now on, until your new business ventures start showing a reasonable profit, we shall cut our coats according to our cloth. Ballygrace School will serve our purposes quite well, without incurring any unnecessary expense.' She gave a little smile, which she knew would infuriate her husband. 'I'm sure we can quite comfortably afford the load of turf that the school requires each pupil to bring every term.'

The mention of the word 'turf' was enough to bring a curl to

William Fitzgerald's moustache-covered lip. The fact that Ballygrace village was largely built on a bog had escaped his notice in the family's hurry to buy and move into the house.

'There is no point in comparing things down here with Dublin standards,' Elisha had scolded her husband. 'Our life in Dublin society is finished. We have to start afresh here, mixing with the people around us, and living according to those standards. Ballygrace may not be the sophisticated place we have been used to, but we have a fine Georgian house and several acres of grounds. We can bring them both back to their former beauty with a bit of hard work. Surely,' she said, 'it should be a balm to your wounded pride that the local people here hold us in the high esteem we were held in Blackrock?'

'What about the children Gabriel and Madeleine will have to mix with in this local school?' William had snorted. 'They may pick up the habits and manners of the local peasants.'

'They will maintain the same standards at home, and that is the most important place for them. Besides, there are children whose fathers have substantial farms in the area attending the school, and several shopkeepers. The head teacher informed me when I enrolled them.'

'He probably only said that to impress you,' William argued. 'As far as I can see, there are few wealthy farmers or shopkeepers in this area. If there is any money, then it doesn't show in their outward appearance. If you ask me, all their money must be in trunks under the bed, because they don't appear to spend it on clothing or transport.'

'Outward trappings do not always tell the truth,' Elisha had answered pointedly. 'And thank God for it – or we might find *ourselves* the subject of considerable gossip!'

Odd whispers about William's misdemeanours had reached Tullamore over the years since the Fitzgeralds had arrived, but nothing had actually been verified. The children had settled in and flourished in their country environment, as had Elisha's health.

After a shaky start, William had thrown himself into his auctioneer's business and the adjoining undertaker's business which he had also purchased. He also bought up several old buildings in Tullamore and the surrounding district. He hired local workers at much lower rates than he would have paid in the city to renovate and restore them, and then sell them to businesses for a decent profit.

The property business was much smaller and slower in Offaly, and William found that he was dealing more with buying and selling of land around the Midlands and Kildare, rather than buildings. There was only the odd house for sale when people decided to up sticks and move to England or America.

But things were not all bad, and William was surprised to learn that a good profit came from the undertaker's office, where business was always brisk. He took nothing to do with the actual running of it himself, as he found that side of things rather distasteful. He carefully averted his eyes from the coffins any time he entered the room behind the office. He had two men working for him who managed all the undertaking work from the start to the finish of the funerals. And according to the local people and the accounts books – a good job they made of it, too.

As a result of his hard work and employing local people, William found that his reputation had gradually built up in his adopted County Offaly, and before long, he was being asked to join the various clubs and committees in Tullamore. It may not have been anywhere near the same exciting standards as Dublin, but where had that got the Fitzgerald family?

This all went some way to restoring Elisha's faith in her husband, but deep down they both knew that she would never fully trust him again. As far as she was concerned, William had kept his promise about never gambling, and he now drank only on social occasions, mostly accompanied by his wife.

Having arrived in Ballygrace at such a young age, the golden-haired Madeleine and Gabriel had settled down to country life as though born into it. When William's business ventures started to pay off, he invested more and more money into Ballygrace House to restore it to its former glory, and the children benefited from this when the decrepit stables were rebuilt.

Bessie and Tessie – two dumpy little ponies – became the focus of home life in Ballygrace House for the children. Gabriel, a quiet, sensitive boy, found confidence in his physical capabilities through learning to ride, even if both ponies were somewhat over the hill. Madeleine, slightly more adventurous than her brother, took to the saddle like a duck to water. Within a few years a larger horse, Daisy, was added to the stable, ostensibly between both children, but the younger sister was the one to use it most.

The horses and the brightly painted 'jumps' scattered over the fields drew great attention from the younger generation in Ballygrace. On warm spring days, when the idea of rambling further afield came into the minds of the children, groups of them made for 'Ballygrace Castle' and the excitement of watching as the Fitzgeralds put their ponies through their paces.

On one particularly warm afternoon in May, Tara Flynn checked her appearance in the old pine wardrobe mirror in her bedroom. She turned this way and that, making sure that the hem on her suit skirt was even. Her Aunty Mona in America – actually a younger cousin of Noel's – had sent her a box of clothes, and for a change some of the things had fitted her without alterations.

Mona's daughters had always seemed much older and taller than Tara, but she knew she must be catching up on them, as some of the clothes the thirteen- and fourteen-year olds had grown out of now fitted her.

Tara thought her new suit was lovely, though it was a pity it hadn't come in time for wearing to church on Easter Sunday, a few weeks ago. Church was the best place to wear new clothes. It was like being on a stage, where everyone could get a good look at you when you walked up the aisle to receive Holy Communion.

The suit was intended for the American summer weather, made from a light silky material, with tiny flowers in blue and yellow on a pale green background. The blouse had a Peter Pan collar and gathered sleeves down to the elbows. It had the loveliest little pearl buttons all the way down the front, and a button on each of the sleeve bands. The skirt swirled down to mid-calf length, now that Tara had carefully lifted and hand-stitched the original hem. Her best cotton ankle socks showed up sparkling white against her cream, open-toed sandals.

She stepped away from the wardrobe to get a better look at herself, and then she smiled. None of the other girls in the class had a suit like this – apart from Madeleine Fitzgerald. And that made Tara Flynn feel very happy.

She wanted to look like the Fitzgeralds – or at least like a guest of the Fitzgeralds. It was very important to her, because she was going to visit their house. It was the first time that Madeleine Fitzgerald had *officially* asked any of her classmates to come to Ballygrace House, and Tara felt very privileged. Really, she was only going to help her friend with some mathematics homework. The blonde-haired Madeleine had ended up crying in class last week because she couldn't under-stand how to multiply and divide fractions.

Being humiliated by the teacher in front of the whole class had been bad enough, but having to go home and tell her father that she was having problems at school was worse. Tara and Biddy had comforted Madeleine during their dinner-break, although Biddy had got even more sums wrong than the upset girl.

'My father will stop my riding lessons if I don't pass the test next week!' Madeleine had wailed. 'He went mad at my last test marks . . . he said I wasn't concentrating enough in school because my mind was full of horses.'

'I'll help you,' Tara had offered. 'You could come to my house after school and I'll go over the fractions with you.'

Madeleine shook her head frantically. 'No . . . no. I'm not allowed to visit any houses in Ballygrace.' She had paused, not wishing to reveal anything about her father's attitude which might offend her schoolfriend. 'Anyway, Mr Molloy will be there with the pony and trap when school comes out, and I can't keep him back from his gardening, or Daddy will go mad.'

And so, Tara had invited herself up to Ballygrace House, to tutor her friend in fractions, because she was top of the class in both maths and English. Tara was lucky. She seemed to understand everything easily.

The girls had decided upon Saturday afternoon, because Madelei-ne's parents and Gabriel would be out of the house then. They were taking her brother for an interview at a boarding school for boys near the Slieve Bloom mountains. After September, Gabriel would leave Ballygrace National School, and would become a student there.

'If you come on Saturday afternoon,' Madeleine said, 'we can have some cakes and lemonade while you show me how to do the sums.'

Tara brushed her red curly hair, which had now grown well past her shoulders. When she was younger, her granda had made her keep it on the short side because it was easier to manage. 'You can grow it whatever way you like when you're old enough to look after it yourself,' he had told her.

Tara had learned how to wash and brush her hair until it shone like burnished gold, and how to plait it and tie it up in a bun for school. It was simple, she thought, how you could learn new things when you put your mind to it. Tara put her brush back on the dressingtable beside its matching comb and mirror.

She checked that her bed was tidy, and then straightened the few things on her rickety old dressingtable. She wondered what Madeleine's bedroom would look like. It would be a lot bigger and a lot grander than her little room. In fact, the whole of her granda's cottage would probably fit into Madeleine's bedroom.

She came back into the kitchen, and threw a few more sods of turf on the fire. She would be in trouble with her granda if she let the fire go out. It was the one thing he went mad about – especially on a Saturday. Mick baked the soda bread in the evening, to have it fresh for breakfast on the Sunday morning after Mass.

Everything was prepared for making the dinner when she came back in. There was a pot of stew already cooked this morning, and the potatoes and carrots were scrubbed, ready for boiling when she came back from Ballygrace House. She had got up early and cleaned the cottage from top to bottom in preparation for her afternoon out – and so that her granda couldn't complain that she'd neglected the housework.

Tara gave a little sigh as she closed the door of the cottage behind her. Madeleine Fitzgerald wouldn't have done any housework this morning. She had probably lain in bed for hours, reading books and comics, and then had her breakfast brought upstairs on a silver tray.

Tara would absolutely love a house with stairs in it. Apart from Doyle's shop in Ballygrace, she'd never been upstairs in a house before. If you came in looking for something like thread, Mrs Doyle often said, 'Run upstairs, and you'll find a box of coloured thread in the front room.'

It was only yesterday that Tara had gone into the shop looking for green thread, and had been sent upstairs to look for it. The rooms in Doyle's house were really just an extension of the shop, because they were full of boxes and tea chests. Even their kitchen and bedrooms – which were disappointingly furnished like her granda's rooms – were full of the boring boxes.

After closing the cottage door, Tara went round the back of the house to check on her chickens, and the three baby goslings that her granda had bought her at the market earlier in the spring. He had told her that she could sell any eggs they didn't use, and keep the money for herself. The goslings would be reared until Christmas, when they would have a goose for themselves, and give one to the aunties in Tullamore and the other to Shay and Tessie. Tara was determined to save any money she made from the eggs. When she had a bit saved, she planned to dip into it, and buy some nice clothes from a new shop that had opened in Tullamore.

As Tara started on the mile and a half walk to her friend's house, she wondered what Ballygrace House would look like inside. She imagined that it would have a big staircase and lots of fancy rooms with real carpets on the floor. It would be exactly the sort of house that Tara was going to have when she was older. She planned to study hard at school, and then get a good job in Tullamore or maybe even Dublin.

Her heart suddenly sank. What would her granda and Mick do if she went to live in Dublin? They were used to her doing all the woman's work in the house now. How would they manage without her? Her granda was getting older . . . he was over seventy now. He could drop dead any day!

The frightening thought made Tara walk all the quicker. What would she do if her granda died? Who would want her then? Not her father, that's for sure. He had enough to do, looking after the children living with him and Tessie. And anyway, Tara wouldn't want to live with them. Sometimes her father and his wife argued and she couldn't stand it.

Life with her granda and Mick was more peaceful, and she could come and go with her friends as long as she did her work about the house first. She hadn't mentioned anything about going to the Fitzgeralds' house, because she knew her granda would stop her. She couldn't work out why he didn't like them, but for some reason he seemed to have a grudge against them. He was always making comments about Madeleine's father thinking he was 'God Almighty, himself'.

As she side-stepped a muddy bit of the path, Tara thought how lucky Madeleine was living in a big house with servants, as well as having a mother and a father. She wondered if she would see Gabriel at the house, or maybe out riding his horse. Madeleine had said something about them taking him to see his new school. Tara quickened her steps – he might not have left the house yet.

The road out to Fitzgeralds' was very quiet today. She had hardly met anyone, just the odd ass and cart and a few people on bicycles. Tara was hoping to get a bicycle herself for her next Christmas and birthday present together.

Her father had laughed out loud when she told him that she wanted one the other week. 'In yer dreams, Tara!' he'd said, folding up his newspaper. 'Sure I can't afford to get me own bike fixed for work, never mind buyin' one for the likes of you. You can start savin' for one out of yer first week's wages.' He'd pointed at Tara's two half-sisters. 'Have you any idea how much milk and bread we go through in this house? I've all this crowd to feed, plus helpin' out with you and Joe. New bikes are the last thing I'll be buyin'.'

Tara had flounced out of the house, feeling badly done by.

When she had gone, Tessie had rounded on Shay. 'Maybe you could afford a bike for the girl if you didn't spend so much on beer!' She pointed to her swollen stomach. 'And maybe I could have afforded a new winter coat this year if there wasn't another little Flynn on the way! Between your drinking and your carry-on in bed every other night – we'll never be the penny better off.'

Shay had flushed at his wife's coarse talk, and stuck his head back in the newspaper. It was no good arguing with Tessie when she was like this. Every feckin' time there was a child on the way, there was no living with her. It seemed as though she was only gettin' back to normal, givin' him a bit of wifely affection, when she was down the same road again, expectin' another one. He wondered again, as he did often, why he hadn't stayed with his father and brother, and lived the lucky life of a bachelor.

Thoughts of a bicycle were forgotten as Tara enjoyed her walk to Fitzgeralds' house on this sunny spring day. The thrushes were singing and the swallows were making dizzy circles in the sky, and then suddenly swooping down low. She walked along, looking at the fields of yellow gorse and the splashes of wild yellow primroses.

Tara loved flowers. When she grew up and had a fine big house, she was going to have flowers everywhere. She had nagged her granda last year, and he had put a few rose bushes and some nice shrubs round the front of the cottage. Some of the rose bushes had grown up the wall and trailed lots of lovely pink scented roses round her bedroom window. This year, he had planted some pansies and petunias, and had bought Tara a watering can when he was at the Tullamore fair a few weeks ago. They were going to have the nicest garden in Ballygrace if Tara had her way.

Tara suddenly noticed a cyclist coming towards her, and the nearer the rickety old bike came, the quicker her heart started to pound. She looked to the field on her left, and then the wood on her right. Then she looked back again as the figure started gesturing towards her, and a voice called out '*Tara!*' very loudly. There was nowhere for her to escape. She had to carry straight on. To the grilling that her father would give her, for being so far away from home, on her own.

'Where the hell d'you think you're goin'?' he called, swinging one leg off his bike and coming to a halt beside her.

'Nowhere . . .' Tara heard herself say defensively.

'Nowhere?' Shay jeered. 'She says she's goin' nowhere and her dressed up to the knockers!'

Tara looked at her father from under lowered eyelids. Who was *he* to question her? He didn't live with her or look after her. He had no business asking her anything.

'What d'you think yer granda will have to say if he catches you round here?' Shay asked, as if reading her thoughts.

She took a deep breath, and then said in a haughty tone: 'I'm only goin' to visit my friend. Granda lets me visit my friends any time.'

'Does he now, begod? And does he happen to know who the friend is, that yer visiting today?'

'He was up the bog with Mick when I left . . . so I hadn't time to tell him.'

'Indeed!' Shay said, holding his head to the side 'So he doesn't know that you're visitin' the Fitzgeralds?'

Tara flushed with annoyance at being caught out. 'How do you know where I'm goin'?' she said cheekily.

'It doesn't take much of a brain to work that out. Where else would you be goin' around here?'

She tilted her chin defiantly. 'I've been asked to visit Madeleine Fitzgerald, to help her with her homework.'

'And who asked you to help her?'

There was a little pause. '*She* did. Madeleine's havin' a lot of trouble with her homework, and she's gettin' into bother at home about it.'

'Is she now?' said Shay. 'And what business would that be of yours?'

Tara gave a great big sigh and hugged the schoolbooks tight to her chest. 'Sure I'm her best friend.'

'And does her father and mother know all about this? Did they ask ye to come up to the big house and help her?'

Tara shrugged. 'I don't know if she's told them.'

Shay clapped his cap back on his head. 'Up here,' he said, rapping his knuckle on the crossbar of his bike. 'Get up here, and I'll take you back home before yer granda knows you're even missing. We'll be home in a quarter of an hour, and there'll be no more said about it.'

Tara backed away, holding the books behind her back. 'I'll not go home!' she said in a rising tone. 'I've come this far and I'm not goin' home 'til I've visited my friend!'

Shay reached towards her, trying to keep his bike steady at the same time. 'Come on now, Tara, and don't be givin' me any trouble. I've no time to waste. I'm supposed to be up the bog wi'yer granda and yer uncle Mick. You can come up and help us foot the turf. All the other girls and lads your age will be up there.' He gave a conspiratorial wink. 'Trickacting and messin' about on the bog would be better *craic* than goin' up to Ballygrace House.'

Tara backed off further, her face determined. 'Madeleine's waiting on me. I won't be long . . . only an hour or little more. I'll have the meat and potatoes ready for ye all when you're finished for the evening.' She turned in the drive of Ballygrace House. 'I've some eggs and butter put by for you and Tessie an' I'll give ye them later.'

Shay shook his head and gave a deep sigh. 'Fine feathers don't make fine birds, Tara,' he called, repeating one of his father's proverbs. 'Yer fancy clothes won't make the Fitzgeralds think any more of ye.' He pointed upwards. 'The Fitzgeralds are up there with the Quality.' Then he pointed to the ground. 'And we're down there with the ordinary people. They're only interested in you, if you're off the right connections. If you have big money and plenty of land. We have neither, so yer only wastin' yer time. Ould Fitzgerald will run you, the very minute he claps eyes on you.'

Tara started to walk up the rhododendron-lined drive. 'I'm just helpin' Madeleine with her homework,' she called back over her shoulder. 'I'll see you later.'

'You will,' said Shay, pushing off on his bike, 'and yer granda will be seeing you, too.' He gave a salute of farewell. 'Good luck to you!'

Anger and a determination to distance herself from her interfering father put a spring in Tara's step. Before she realised it, she was halfway up the Fitzgerald's drive. She suddenly stopped dead, an uneasy feeling creeping over her. What would she do when she got to the house? Supposing Madeleine's mother and father hadn't gone out? What would they say if they saw her?

All the thoughts and fears she had pushed to the back of her mind now stared her in the face. Her determination to see inside this huge elegant house, and to see with her own eyes the lives that the Quality led, now drained away. Just looking up the rhododendron-lined path made Tara feel nervous.

She stood debating whether to carry on, or go back as her father had advised. Then, a loud roaring noise coming from the direction of the big house suddenly startled her. Instinctively, Tara moved backwards into the rhododendrons.

The sound got louder and louder, and then a few moments later, a large shiny motor car came noisily down the drive towards her. Suddenly realising that it was Gabriel and his parents in the car, Tara pressed further back into the greenery. The bushes scraped against her bare arms and legs, and then a particularly thick branch made her drop the schoolbooks. The nearer the car came, the harder her heart thumped.

Although Madeleine hadn't *actually* said it, Tara knew that her parents would not be pleased if they saw her anywhere near the house. Tara also knew that everything her own father had said was true about them – and true about her. But, as the car hurtled past her, Tara knew that she would continue up the drive and walk to the front door of Ballygrace House. She felt almost compelled to go, as though the house were beckoning her inside. Beckoning her to come and look at all the nice things she was missing, living the life of a poor child from a poor family.

Madeleine was standing by some flower-beds in the garden, staring out into the distance. She didn't notice her schoolmate until Tara called her name. Then she came running down the drive to meet her, her long blonde hair blowing in the breeze.

'Did anyone in the car see you?' she asked anxiously.

'No,' Tara replied. 'I was standing out of the way, in the bushes.'

Madeleine's face and shoulders relaxed with relief. 'It's not because it's you . . .' she explained weakly. 'They don't like me having any friends at the house. Mother says that I'll make lots of new friends at boarding school next year, and that I won't have time to see any from around here.'

Tara looked down at the ground. 'Maybe I should just go back home,' she said in a hurt, stained voice. 'I met my father out on the road, and he gave out to me for coming up to see you. He'll tell my granda, and when I go back home . . . I'll be in trouble, too.'

Madeleine bit her lip. 'I'm sorry, Tara. It's all my fault for telling you to come up here. I don't want to get you in trouble, but I'm really happy you came. You look very different . . . you look very nice in your new suit.' In truth, Madeleine felt the suit was much too fancy for an ordinary Saturday afternoon in May, but she didn't want to hurt Tara's feelings. 'Come into the house, and I'll get you a drink of lemonade. You must be thirsty after walking all that way from Ballygrace.'

Tara – mollified by her friend's compliment about her outfit –

followed her across the gravel path and up the huge white steps of the Georgian house. 'Are you really glad I came?' she checked.

'Oh, yes!' Madeleine said, coming to a halt on the top step. 'I'm delighted you came . . . I like you much better than all the other girls in the class.'

'Do you?' Tara said, pleased and curious at the same time. 'What do you like about me?'

Madeleine suddenly giggled. 'I don't know – everything, I suppose. I like your lovely curly hair and your nice long fingers. I could play the piano much better if I had fingers like yours.'

Tara held her own hands up in front of her face, as though seeing them for the first time. 'My hands?' she said incredulously. 'Everybody always likes my hair – even though I wish it was straight like yours – but nobody ever said I had nice hands before!' And she started to giggle, too. It was funny, she thought, how she found it easy to believe anything that Madeleine said. Tara felt she always told the truth, whether you liked it or not – whereas Biddy always said the things that she knew would please you.

Madeleine pushed the heavy, polished wooden door open and Tara Flynn walked into Ballygrace House for the very first time. She did not know where to look first, as huge mirrors, fancy rugs, vases of flowers and paintings overwhelmed her. She followed Madeleine through the magnificent hallway, trying to drink in every detail as she passed.

Never, ever, had she imagined being in a house so grand. And never would she have pushed for an invitation had she known just how intimidated it would make her feel. After following her friend through several narrower corridors, Tara found herself in the biggest kitchen she had ever seen. Her eyes roamed round it, taking in the huge dressers full of fancy-patterned delph and the magnificent cooker, from which emanated a mouth-watering smell of meat cooking in the oven.

'Here you are,' Madeleine said, setting a glass of pale-coloured lemonade and a plate of home-made shortbread down on the pine kitchen table. 'When you've finished, we'll go upstairs to my bedroom to do the fractions.'

'That'll be grand,' Tara said taking a dainty bite from a piece of shortbread. It was made from white flour she noticed, and wondered how Mrs Fitzgerald had managed to get pure flour, when everyone else had to make do with the horrible dark stuff with the bits in it.

Madeleine stood out in the hallway, obviously eager for Tara to finish her snack, and go upstairs to do the fractions. But Tara was in no hurry to be out of the warm, spicy-smelling kitchen. She was enjoying herself and was going to take her time.

She wanted to remember every single detail, so that she could describe it to Biddy and Mrs Kelly when she got back home. With the glass in her hand, Tara walked casually over to examine the ornaments in one of the dressers. She took a sip of the lemonade and nearly choked with shock. It tasted awful! It didn't taste a bit like the minerals she was used to.

'What's wrong?' Madeleine asked, noticing her friend's puckered face.

'The lemonade . . .' Tara said, sniffing the glass suspiciously. 'It tastes a bit funny.'

'It's *real* lemonade. Mrs Scully makes it using lemons and sugar.' She gave Tara a funny look. 'Don't you have it at home?'

Tara felt her face flush, realising she had said something stupid. 'Yes,' she said quickly, 'but this just tasted a bit different.' She took another sip of the strange drink. 'It's fine when ye get used to it.'

'Well,' Madeleine said, glancing anxiously out into the hallway again, 'hurry up and finish it, and then we can go upstairs.'

Madeleine's bedroom was even fancier than Tara had imagined. It was like something out of the American magazines her Aunty Mona sent over last year, with lovely wallpaper and curtains and blinds and rugs. She also had a collection of teddy bears, a big rocking horse and a doll's house with tiny wooden furniture. When Tara commented on her toys, Madeleine shrugged and said that most of her and Gabriel's things were in the nursery. Tara wanted to say: 'Can I have a look in the nursery?' because she had read about a nursery in one of her books – but she felt it wasn't the right thing to say.

While Madeleine rummaged in a big wooden desk looking for her maths book, Tara's eyes scanned the room. There was a huge mirrored wardrobe which almost took up a full wall, and a matching dressing table and bedside cabinet. Even the bed was fancy, with wooden cherubs carved into the headboard and bottom of it, and a lace cover over the quilt and snow-white pillowcases.

Real pillowcases, Tara thought enviously, not ones made from old flour bags.

'You're really lucky having a bedroom like this,' Tara said quietly. 'When I grow up, I'm going to live in a big house and have nice things like this. I'm going to work hard at school and get a good job with lots of money.'

Madeleine's gaze moved from her maths book to Tara's determined face. 'There's a much easier way to have nice things than working for them . . .'

'What d'you mean?' Tara asked.

'You just have to marry a rich man. Mother always tells me that. She says I've to make sure that I don't get lumbered with someone like my father.' She looked out of the window now, a strange look on her face. 'My mother's family were very rich, you know. They weren't happy with her marrying my father . . . his family were quite poor, really. He went to American when he was young and made his fortune out there. Then he came back to Dublin and married my mother. After a few years, he lost every bit of the money he had made and he nearly lost my mother's money, too.' She turned back to Tara, who was all ears at the amazing story. 'My mother says if she had her time over again, that she would pick a wealthy, older man to marry. She says life is much easier if the man has the money. She says all you have to do is look nice and agree with everything they say.' She gave Tara a sidelong glance. 'You'd do very well, Tara, with your lovely red hair and pretty face. I bet you could marry a rich man if you really tried.'

Tara looked appalled. 'Oh, I could never marry a man I didn't love! You'd be tied to him for the rest of your life.'

'Not if he was older,' Madeleine said lightly. 'He would probably die before you, and then you could marry someone else.' She laughed. 'My mother says she wishes she'd done that. A friend of my grandfather's wanted to marry her when she was eighteen – he was an American millionaire – but she turned him down.' She spread the maths book, opened at the section on multiplying fractions, on top of the desk. 'My mother says turning him down was the biggest mistake of her life. Apart,' she gave a high-pitched giggle, 'apart from marrying my father!'

For once, Tara couldn't think of a thing to say. She had never heard of such a thing in her life as ordinary people marrying for money. But then, Madeleine wasn't ordinary – and neither were her family.

After an hour, and having mastered the basics of multiplying fractions, Madeleine suggested that they could have a little break. 'Have you ever ridden a pony, Tara?' she asked, as they bounded down the stairs.

'Well . . .' Tara said cagily, 'I've sat on the ass's back loads of times . . . and I was on Fox's pony last summer.'

Madeleine giggled again. 'No . . . no – I meant on a pony with a saddle.'

Tara swallowed hard on her pride. 'I haven't actually ridden a pony with a saddle,' she reluctantly admitted. Then she quickly added, 'Not that I can remember anyway.'

They went out into the afternoon sunshine. Tara followed Madeleine through the carefully manicured lawn, and down the path flanked on either side by rose beds. She walked past the two large greenhouses filled with plants and tomatoes, through the gate and into the field where the ponies were grazing.

'My saddle is in the shed,' Madeleine said, leading Tara to the far end of the field. 'I'll put it on Daisy and then you can have a go at riding her.'

A rush of excitement ran through Tara's veins. This was even better than she had dared hope for. She had seen all round the big fancy house, had sat in the kitchen drinking posh lemonade and eating shortbread. And now she was going to ride a pony wearing a real saddle! She had often watched Madeleine and Gabriel riding round the field with their boots and riding hats on – but she had only watched from a distance, and as part of a group.

'That's it!' Madeleine called. She led the pony down the field with Tara perched on its back, wearing her friend's riding boots and hat. 'She's going into a trot now.'

'Am I doing it right?' Tara replied, anxious to learn the rudiments of riding with a saddle quickly, and trying not to think of how silly she looked with the boots and hat and her fancy suit.

'You're doing fine,' Madeleine assured her. 'Just keep your back straight and your eyes looking ahead. It helps to keep your balance.'

And as they had walked and trotted the pony round and round the field – Tara felt as though she were floating on a cloud rather than sitting on the pony's back. She felt more elated than she had ever felt in her life.

This, she thought passionately, *is the way I want to live. Ballygrace House is the sort of house I want to live in.*

As she bobbed along, the fact that she was dressed all wrong in her floral American suit suddenly hit Tara like a bolt out of the blue. She didn't know exactly *what* was wrong with it, but she suddenly knew that it was wrong for the occasion. She thought now about the funny look that Madeleine had given her when she had first arrived, and now she knew why. Madeleine's plain skirt and checked blouse, and her hair now tied back in a ribbon – was the sort of thing she should have worn.

'Shall we go back in?' Madeleine said a while later. 'I suppose I'd better learn a few more horrible fractions before you have to go home.' She led the pony back to the shed where she kept the tackle, and helped Tara to dismount. 'Are you all right?' she said anxiously, noticing that her friend had gone all quiet.

Tara nodded, but to her horror she felt tears start to form in her eyes. Then – before she could stop herself – she suddenly blurted out, 'You think my new suit's awful, don't you? You would never wear a suit like this.'

Madeleine's mouth opened in shock, and she seemed stuck for words. Then, she put her arm round her friend's shoulder and said: 'Your new suit is lovely, Tara. It looks really nice on you.'

'But you wouldn't wear it, would you?' Tara persisted. 'Your skirt and blouse are not like this . . .'

Madeleine took a deep breath. 'I would love to have a suit like yours, Tara, but my mother would only let me wear it if I were going to church . . . or to a wedding. I would have to keep it for a *very special* occasion.' She patted Tara's shoulder. 'She says I have to wear my sensible, hard-wearing clothes at school and at the weekends. I wouldn't be allowed to wear something expensive like your suit on an *ordinary* day . . . although I would love to.'

Tara wiped the back of her hand over her eyes. 'Would you? You're not just codding me to make me feel better?'

Madeleine made the sign of the cross on her chest with her thumb. 'Hate God if I tell a lie.'

Tara's brows furrowed in thought. 'My school-clothes are real dull, and I have to wear my old skirts and jumpers for working about the cottage. I don't have any *nice* ordinary clothes like yours . . . I have only old things and my best clothes.'

Madeleine shrugged. 'I think it's because our families are a little bit different. My mother's very strict about my clothes . . . some of the things she buys me are very old-fashioned.'

'You're lucky to have a mammy to buy you clothes,' Tara said sadly. 'Me granda doesn't know anything about girls' clothes, and me father's always promisin' to buy me things . . . but he never does. He wouldn't even get me a bike.'

At a loss at how to comfort her friend, Madeleine said, 'Shall we go back into the house? We haven't much time left for doing the fractions . . .'

Tara cheered up. Things weren't that bad. Madeleine really liked her new suit, so she would wear again it to Mass tomorrow. She had learned how to ride a pony with a saddle, and she was going back into Ballygrace House for another little while.

Walking along the upstairs corridor to the bedroom, Madeleine suggested that they should wash their hands in the bathroom. It was there, when her friend flung the door open, that Tara noticed the true difference in their domestic conditions. The bathroom, which was much bigger than Tara's bedroom, was like nothing she had ever seen before. Her eyes were large with amazement, as she looked at the huge enamel bath with its claw feet and gold taps, and the sink that had blue flowers painted all over it. But the sight that completely took her breath away was the lavatory. The porcelain toilet bowl was lavishly decorated on the inside and the outside, with the same blue flowers.

After a whispered word with Madeleine, she was soon ensconced in the room, and sitting up on the floral throne with the highly polished seat.

What a difference from the makeshift toilet in her granda's garden shed! That was only a plank of wood with a hole in it, balanced precariously on some big nails, above a tin bucket. The wooden shed also let in big drops of rain and rattled with the slightest gust of wind. On one occasion, Tara had to endure the peeping eyes of a neighbour's son, when she was trying to do her business in privacy. Her granda had given him a good kick up the backside when he'd caught him, which had made her feel only slightly better.

Having used a proper lavatory now, Tara knew she would never be happy with the tin bucket again.

Two hours and six pages of multiplying and dividing fractions later, Madeleine suddenly jumped up and closed her books. 'You'll have to go home now,' she said regretfully to Tara. 'My mother and father will be back soon . . . and I'll be in trouble if they find you here.'

Tara slowly got to her feet. 'I'll have to go home anyway, me granda and me uncle Mick will be back from . . . will be back in soon.' She had nearly said *from the bog*, but something had stopped her. Madeleine wouldn't know about things like cutting turf up the bog. Not like her and Biddy, who had to stack the sods into big piles, and go home with a sore back every night for a week. The Fitzgeralds would probably pay people to cut and rear the turf, and then have it drawn home. They did everything different from ordinary people.

Tara stopped at the bottom of the staircase, reluctant to leave the fairytale house so quickly. 'Could I have another little drink of that lemonade before I go home?' she asked. 'It's a fair walk back home and it's hot outside.'

'I don't know . . .' Madeleine said weakly. 'It's just that Mother and Father could come back any time . . .'

Tara was determined not to go before she was ready. 'Sure they wouldn't give out to you, when you tell them all the help I gave you with yer fractions, would they?'

Madeleine's eyes darted anxiously to the front door, and then back down the hallway towards the kitchen. 'Wait here,' she said, and then moved quickly towards the kitchen door.

Tara sighed with delight at having another few minutes to scrutinise her impressive surroundings. She looked down at the pale blue, white and salmon-pink tiles on the hall floor and then she looked up at the huge coatstand with the mirror surrounded by stained glass.

She recognised the navy woollen overcoat that Gabriel wore to school every day.

She felt a little twinge of regret that he hadn't seen her all dressed up in her new American suit. He wouldn't have said anything about it – he was too shy. And she was sure he wouldn't notice that it was a bit fancy for a Saturday.

The sound of a piano key being struck brought Tara's attention to one of the closed doors in the hallway. She checked if there was any sign of Madeleine coming, and when there wasn't she turned back to the door she had heard the noise coming from.

She bent down and closed her left eye, then stuck her right eye to the keyhole. She could see a few chairs and a great big sofa and a huge, black, grand piano. Madeleine had moaned to her about having to practise, and Tara had imagined that she had an ordinary brown upright piano like the one Joe played. How could Madeleine complain about playing on a beautiful piano like that?

Tara moved about, then changed to her other eye, to see if she could see better. She pressed hard against the door, then without any warning, the door suddenly flew open. Tara found herself looking up at a small, blocky, elderly woman, dressed in a maid's pinafore and cap.

The look on the woman's face went from one of shock to raging anger, when she saw Tara. 'What the hell d'you think you're doing in here?' she roared. 'Who let the likes of you in this house?'

Tara straightened up quickly, her face chalk-white. She knew once the woman had a good look at her fancy suit she would realise that she was a friend of Madeleine.

'Well?' the woman demanded. 'Are you going to answer me? Who let *you* in? You've no business being in this house.'

'I did, Mrs Scully,' Madeleine called in a breathless voice, as she came rushing down the hallway. 'It's my friend from school.' She came towards Tara, her arm outstretched with the glass of lemonade. She had moved so quickly that the liquid spilled out over the top of the glass as she handed it to Tara, and several splashes landed on the patterned tiles.

'Oh, no – you feckin' well don't!' the purple-faced woman said, grabbing the glass out of Tara's hand. 'I just mopped that floor this morning – an' I didn't mop it for the likes of you to be trampin' in and out of here, as if you owned the place!' She turned to Madeleine, her stubby finger wagging. 'You're for it, me girl, when yer mammy and daddy gets home.' She whirled back to Tara. 'What name have they for you?'

Tara put her hands behind her back, the way she did with the teachers in school. 'Tara . . . Tara Flynn.'

'Flynn? Flynn . . . and what Flynns would that be?' Rosie Scully stared closely at Tara, as though she were examining an insect under a microscope. 'Where are you from? Yer not one of the Flynns that owns the pub in Tullamore – that's for sure. There's no foxy-haired ones in that family.'

'I'm one of the Flynns from Ballygrace,' Tara said in a shaky voice.

'And who's yer mammy and daddy? What's their names? What's yer mammy's own name . . . and where are they from?' She fired one question after another, like shots out of a gun.

'My daddy's Shay Flynn . . . and my mammy's dead. I think she came from Edenderry.'

Mrs Scully stopped for a moment, the wind taken out of her sails. She gave a little cough, and then gathered her composure to start again. 'So . . . would that make you ould Noel Flynn's granddaughter?'

Tara nodded, afraid to say a word. There were plenty of women like this one in Ballygrace, and there was no point arguing with them. Her granda had warned her about them. They had a long memory, and made sure they got back at you every chance they got – even if it was years later.

The housekeeper turned on Madeleine again. 'You're a bold girl – bringing people in here, when yer parents are out. You'll be in trouble when they get back and they hear all about this.' She pointed to the stairs. 'Get up to yer bedroom until they come back in.'

'Goodbye, Tara,' Madeleine whispered, and then she ran up the stairs, two at a time.

The elderly maid marched forward to the front door, and opened it. She held the door wide and motioned to Tara to get out. 'I'm sure yer a grand little girl,' she said in a strained tone, 'but *this* house is not for the likes of you. We all have to know our stations in life.'

Tara passed out by the housekeeper silently, her eyes downcast.

'As I said,' the woman called after her as she descended the outside stairs, 'I'm sure ye are a good enough little girl, but Madeleine's father would ate you without salt if he caught you anywhere near the house. He could send the *Gardaí* out to yer family, if he took it into his head . . . he's not the kind of man you could cross.'

When she reached the bottom step, Tara whirled round to face the elderly maid, a feeling of rage rising up inside her. How dare this cross ould cratur threaten her granda with the *Gardaí*! How dare she! Her granda was one of the finest and well-thought of men in Ballygrace. Even the parish priest had been known to come to him for advice. *The parish priest* . . . Tara suddenly remembered.

'In Ballygrace church, a few weeks ago,' she said in a loud, clear voice, 'the priest gave a grand sermon.'

Mrs Scully's face crumpled in confusion. '*What?*' she said, her voice on a rising note. 'What nonsense are you talkin' now?'

'The priest was explainin' about what makes people good . . . and what makes them bad,' Tara went on. 'He was sayin' that just because some people have more money, that it doesn't make them any better.'

Mrs Scully's eyes bulged with rage, and for a few moments was rendered speechless. She stepped forward, planting both hands firmly on her hefty hips. 'You . . . bold . . . girl!' she finally said, enunciating every word.

'It says in the Bible,' Tara continued in a high voice, ' "*As a man thinketh in his heart – so he is.*" It means we're all as good as each other, an' that we should judge people by their actions – not by their money.'

'And there's a say in' that springs to *my* mind,' Rosie Scully spat out. ' "Put a beggar on horseback, and she'll ride to hell!" ' Her eyes narrowed dangerously. 'Now,' she said through clenched teeth, 'go home, you foxy-haired, little oul' brat – before I bring me sweeping brush down on the broad of yer back!'

'I'm going home this minute,' Tara said, turning on her heel, 'and I'll be lettin' me granda know what you called me – and what you said about sending the *Gardaí* out to the house!'

Rage and indignation lent speed to Tara's feet, and she was back home in half the time it had taken her to walk to Ballygrace House.

She passed no one she knew, and was releived that she had made it to the cottage before the men came home from the bog.

She quickly raked the fire out and got it flaming again in minutes, and then she rushed into her bedroom to take off the fancy suit and change back into her old clothes. As she pulled on her dark grey skirt and a green jumper that Mrs Kelly had knitted for her, she remembered Madeleine's nice blouse and skirt.

Then, all the angry feelings about the housekeeper came flooding back.

'I'm as good as Madeleine Fitzgerald!' she said out loud, as she tied up her long red hair with a green checked ribbon. 'One day I'll live in a big house like hers, and I'll have servants to look after me.' She paused for a moment. 'And I'll *never* treat anybody as terrible as I was treated today.'

Chapter Six

'You are *not*,' Noel Flynn stated for the third time, 'going for piano lessons.'

'But I've already organised my first lesson,' Tara said calmly, taking a cake of soda bread out of the hot pot-oven. 'I've to be at Mrs Foley's house for seven o'clock tomorrow evenin'.'

Noel took off his reading glasses, and put his book down by the side of his rocking-chair. 'Where's the money to come from?' he asked quietly.

'I've saved up me egg money . . . I've enough put by to pay for lessons until September, and I walked out as far as the bike shop in Daingean to see about a cheap second-hand bike. He says I can pay it off at so much a week.'

Noel shook his head in exasperation. 'When yer father suggested a second-hand bike before, you nearly took the nose off him!'

Tara sighed. 'I know . . . but that was *before* I thought of the piano lessons. I don't mind what sort of a bike it is, if it takes me as far as Daingean or Tullamore.'

'But, sure, you have no piano to play at home.'

'I was hopin',' Tara explained, 'that you might ask Aunty Molly and Aunty Maggie if I can use their piano to practise on. I thought we could go into Tullamore tomorrow after the dinner, and you could have a word with them then.' She smiled engagingly. 'Once I have the bike, I'll be able to go everywhere by myself. Sure, I'll be no bother to you at all.'

Noel gave a deep sigh. 'You have it all worked out, don't you? Molly and Maggie could just as easily say "no" about ye using their piano. They're a fussy little pair – they mightn't be in agreement with

67

the idea at all. Where will you be with yer lessons if ye have no piano to practise on?'

Tara busied herself wrapping the soda bread up in a piece of clean flour bag, hoping that her granda wouldn't notice the delighted grin on her face. 'Sure, the oul' piano's only goin' damp and fusty from lack of use. It only gets used when Joe's home from the seminary. They should be glad of someone to play it now and again.'

'I wouldn't count yer chickens, mavourneen,' the old man said. 'Those two women are not easily got round.' He reached for his pipe from the mantelpiece now, tapped the spent tobacco out of it into the fire and then proceeded to clean it. First with a little penknife, and then with a pipe-cleaner. 'Explain to me, Tara,' he said seriously, 'exactly why ye want to start piano lessons at this stage. You're never shown any interest in it before.'

Tara set the covered soda bread down to cool by the open window. 'I don't really know,' she hedged. 'I've just taken a notion to learn it.'

'Would it be anything to do with that young one you went visiting last weekend?' Noel said innocently. 'Yer father told me he met you outside Fitzgeralds', all dressed up like the Quality in yer fine clothes.'

Tara blushed. She thought her granda knew nothing at all about last Saturday. When they all came back from the bog, there had been no mention of it. She thought her father had taken her side for once, that he had decided to keep her secret, to save her granda giving out to her. But if her granda knew, why had he waited so long to mention it?

'Well?' he said now, patiently waiting for her answer.

Tara took a deep breath. 'I want to learn the piano, Granda, because I have a notion to do it . . . that's all.'

There was another pause. 'Have you now? And what other notions would you have in that young head of yours?'

'I want to better myself,' she said quietly. 'I want to have nice things when I grow up . . . a big house . . . a car . . . nice clothes.'

'We'd all like those things, Tara, but it's not easy,' the old man said. 'If you are born into money, like the Fitzgeralds, then there's no problem. But the likes of our family would find it very hard. There's not much work round here, and what work there is, is very poorly paid.'

Tara came over to the fire to sit on the three-legged stool. She waited while her grandfather carried out the ritual of paring thin slivers from a hard piece of black tobacco, and then packing his clean pipe.

'The only way a young girl like you can get on,' the old man told her, 'is to work hard at school, and get a good job. Have you ever thought that you could be a schoolteacher if ye worked hard enough?'

'Most of the teachers I know aren't married . . . they're oul' maids.'

'What's that got to do with it?'

'Nothin' . . . I was just saying.'

Noel took a deep puff of his pipe. 'Sometimes you have the quarest thoughts in yer head, Tara. Where do you get them from, I'm wonderin'?'

Tara shook her red curls. 'So . . . ' she said, with a wheedling little smile, 'will ye bring me into Tullamore tomorrow to ask Aunty Molly and Aunty Maggie?'

Noel looked at his granddaughter, and wondered once again where all these ambitious ideas of hers came from. Certainly not from her father. To Shay, work was only a means to an end. As long as his wages put food on the table and gave him a few glasses of beer at the weekend, he was happy enough. It wasn't her mother – God rest her soul – she was a quiet enough woman and wouldn't have got in with the likes of Shay if she had wanted more out of life.

'We'll see,' Noel finally replied, 'but only if you promise me never to set foot on Fitzgeralds' land again.' He pointed the end of his pipe warningly at his granddaughter. 'You're worth a hundred of their kind, and I'm not havin' you belittling yerself by hanging around their coat-tails.'

'Oh thanks, Granda!' Tara said delightedly, giving the old man a hug.

'I only said "*we'd see*" – nothing more.'

'I promise I won't go near Ballygrace House again . . . and I promise that I'll practise the piano every chance I get!'

Agreeing with her granda now was easy, for Tara had *no* intentions of returning to Ballygrace House. Never again would she hide from Madeleine's parents, or do battle with the cantankerous Mrs Scully. Madeleine would be leaving the local school shortly and going to a private girls' boarding school. Sadly, their friendship would soon be coming to an end, in any case.

Later that evening, Tara skipped excitedly along the road to Lizzie Lawless's house, to tell Biddy all about her piano lessons and the new bike she was getting. She decided she would not mention what had happened at Ballygrace House earlier in the week.

Tara Flynn had learned already that it was better to look forward with hope, than look back holding a grudge.

Chapter Seven

❦

September, 1947

'I'm nearly fifteen years old,' Biddy said in an even tone to Lizzie Lawless, 'and I'm entitled to go to the pictures if I want. Sure, I've done everythin' for you . . . the meat's cooked and the spuds are scrubbed, and the cabbage is washed and in its pot.' She shook her head and tutted. 'And that's after spendin' the whole mornin' working up in the priest's house.'

Lizzie lifted her wizened old head up from the settle bed, her movement disturbing one of the three cats on top of it. 'But I'm not well . . . I might need you to help me outside to the toilet.'

Biddy pointed to the chamber pot on the floor by the side of the bed. 'You can do the same as you do at night, and anyway, you're just back from doin' it – you can't have anything left inside you.'

Lizzie moaned and lay back down on the lumpy pillow. 'I could be dyin' and nobody cares,' she whined. 'All that I've done for you and that ungrateful bitch, Nora, and look at the thanks I get. Running away and causin' me all that trouble wi' the parish priest. You'd think I'd murdered her and buried her body up the bog, the way he was carrying on!'

Biddy rolled her eyes to the ceiling and placed her hands on her hips. If Lizzie started on about Nora again she'd scream. She'd gone on about it for the last three months, since the older girl had mysteriously disappeared one night, taking all her bits of belongings. 'You'll be all right,' she said. 'Didn't the doctor say he could find nothin' wrong with you?'

There was a silence for a few moments, then Lizzie said in a tearful voice, 'I've no faith in doctors. They told ould Annie Rooney the very same thing, and she was dead within the week. She started off with the diarrhoea too.'

There's no fear of this ould bugger dyin' and giving us all peace, Biddy thought to herself. 'If you like,' she said now, 'I could call in at Mrs Galvin's and get a cure off her for you. When she heard you weren't well the last time, she offered to give me something' for you.'

'Father Daly says he doesn't hold wi' these cures.' Lizzie's voice had reduced to a self-pitying tremble. 'But it's not him that's weak wi' the diarrhoea . . . an' he has an inside toilet as well. He doesn't have to go outside in the pouring rain and the freezin' cold, and bare his arse to an oul' bucket.' She sighed deeply. 'Ask Mrs Galvin for a cure for me . . . I'm at the stage I'll try anythin'.'

'Ye have the pot there if yer caught short,' Biddy said, lifting her cardigan from the table, 'and I brought back more newspapers from the priest's house. I've torn them up into little squares for you. I'll only be gone a couple of hours anyway.'

'I only hope I'm still here when you come back from yer pictures,' Lizzie called weakly as the door closed behind Biddy. Then, she said forlornly to herself, 'With the way I'm feelin' . . . I could be meeting my Maker at any time.'

Biddy closed the outside door quietly behind her and then, once out in the open air on her own, she punched her fist in the air triumphantly. By running away – and consequently bringing the priest to Lizzie's door – Nora had done her the biggest favour imaginable.

Father Daly had quizzed Lizzie endlessly, about what went on in the house, and how she treated the girls. He had asked Biddy questions too, but had got very little out of her. She knew if she told the truth that she'd be moved from the only home she'd known, and more importantly, her best friend, Tara.

There was a long queue outside the Town Hall in Daingean when Tara arrived carrying Biddy on the back of her bicycle. They were beckoned excitedly to join a group of giggling girls who had kept a place for them in the queue.

'Does my hair look all right? And my dress and cardigan?' Biddy asked anxiously, as they dismounted the bicycle.

'Your hair is lovely now – it looks real natural,' Tara told her. 'You should wash it more often. You've no excuse, now that Lizzie's a bit more easy-going with you.'

'I'm brushing it a hundred times every night, like you advised me,' Biddy confided. She didn't mention the compliments that Dinny the lodger had given her about the change in her appearance, and how he had promised to marry her as soon as she was old enough. She felt that Tara would be shocked at the difference in their ages, and even more shocked if she found out about all the things they did together when Lizzie wasn't around.

'And what about the dress and cardigan?' Biddy prompted her friend. 'Do they look all right?'

'They're lovely, too,' Tara replied in a patient but distracted tone, as she scanned the crowds to see who was there. Then, seeing the anxiety on the orphan's face, she elaborated further. 'The white cardigan goes lovely with the navy and white polka-dot dress, and with your navy sandals.'

Biddy checked that the narrow belt was in the middle of her waist once again, and then she stepped out after her long-legged friend to join the crowds. It never struck her as odd that Tara rarely asked for reassurance on her own appearance.

According to Biddy, Tara seemed to get everything just right. At fifteen years old, she outwardly had the confidence and poise of a girl several years older. Her long auburn curls were restrained with a russet bow, but still managed to bob along with a life of their own as she walked with a ram rod straight back, and her head held high. On this warm Sunday afternoon in September, Tara wore a sparkling white blouse with half sleeves and a lace collar, and a mid-calf-length skirt the same colour as the bow in her hair. Brown open-toed sandals matched the neat little leather bag strung over her shoulder.

Tara knew that the other girls in the queue were scrutinising her outfit as she crossed the courtyard to join them – but it did not concern her one iota. She knew she was different from them in many ways, and her clothing was only the outward sign. Most of the others in her class had left school and were working in the factories in Tullamore or in the local hotels or shops, but Tara was one of the few who had moved on to a convent school in Tullamore to do her Leaving Certificate.

Thankfully, her granda had not argued about her staying on in school. This was partly due to the fact that he was proud of her doing so well, and partly because she was earning reasonable money doing the books for two of the local shops in Ballygrace. She was also making a little more money since she had expanded her egg business.

With the help of her granda and her Uncle Mick, Tara had extended into their field at the back of the garden, and had widened her range of poultry to include turkeys and a few ducks. So much so, that the previous Christmas she had made enough money from selling turkeys and geese to buy a brand-new ladies' bike – cash instead of paying it up – and was slowly, but steadily, adding to her collection of good-quality clothes.

Most of the time, her granda and Mick had no idea of the origins of her clothes. She could appear in clothes which had come in an American parcel, skirts she had learned to make on a treadle sewing-machine at school, or a dress she had paid up weekly in the exclusive ladies' wear shop in Tullamore. The men were none the wiser about where they came from, or of the balance in the little wooden box which was kept under Tara's bed.

This afternoon's outfit was American. The previous month her Aunty Mona had come on a visit to the aunties in Tullamore, and had brought a full suitcase of clothes for Tara. With the skilful use of a needle, she had adapted any which were too long or too wide, until they fitted her tall but curvaceous figure perfectly. She had passed on any others which were too small to the shorter and thinner – and everlastingly grateful – Biddy.

'You can have them on one condition,' Tara had warned her friend. 'That you keep them spotlessly clean, and that you must be spotlessly clean, too – before you put them on.'

'I promise you that I will be clean, Tara,' Biddy had assured her. 'Oh, indeed I will . . . no doubts about that.'

'I'll take them straight off you, if I catch you lookin' like a tinker!' Tara had threatened. She had heard Biddy's promises before, only to find her wearing good clothes that were all messed up from doing dirty jobs.

Biddy made the sign of the cross on her chest. 'I promise I'll look after them. Cross my heart and hope to die.'

'You will,' Tara grinned, 'if I catch you with those good clothes all messed up.'

The two girls joined the others in the queue for the Sunday afternoon matinee, Tara standing a good head above the rest. She first cast a casual glance to the front of the queue, and then to the back. Two equally tall figures – with the autumn sun glinting on their whitish-blonde hair – caught her eye. Then, when one of them waved and a familiar voice called out 'Tara!' her heart skipped a beat. It was Madeleine Fitzgerald and, standing beside her, was her brother Gabriel. For a few seconds Tara froze, then, mustering all her composure, she gathered herself together and slowly moved towards the back of the queue.

'How are you, Tara?' Madeleine asked with a big smile on her face. 'I haven't seen you for ages.'

'Grand,' Tara replied in a breathless voice. 'Have you been away for the summer?' She was surprised to notice that Madeleine's face was sort of pasty-looking, and that she had put on quite a bit of weight. However, her well-cut, shiny blonde hair and her expensive clothes ensured that she still stood out from the rest of the crowd.

Madeleine nodded and looked at Gabriel. 'Yes, we were over in London. Mother has a sister there . . . and we spent a month in Scotland, too. What about you?'

Tara shielded her eyes against the sun. 'We've had visitors over from America . . . my Aunty Mona and her oldest daughter. Joe's been back in Tullamore for the summer too. We all had a day out in Galway, and another day up in Dublin. The shops are brilliant up in Dublin . . . we got some new music books.' Tara paused for a moment, trying to think of something to make her summer sound more interesting. 'I haven't really had much time for holidays . . . I've been kept busy doing bookkeeping for some of the local shops.' She deliberately didn't mention all the work she had done up the bog, footing and heaping the turf with her father and her Uncle Mick. Neither did she mention the unglamorous hours she had put in with looking after the poultry. She knew instinctively that those sort of details would not impress the Fitzgeralds.

'Bookkeeping?' Gabriel asked, with a curious note in his voice.

Tara's face flushed. 'Yes,' she replied, avoiding his eyes. 'I've been doing it this past few months.'

'Do you deal with stock and wages . . . that sort of thing?'

Tara nodded, amazed at his interest. Without thinking, she lifted her head, and suddenly met Gabriel's piercing blue eyes staring straight into hers. For a moment, their gaze held, then she quickly turned away and tried desperately to ignore the tight sensation which had gripped her chest.

Tara couldn't believe how handsome and mature he seemed since she last had seen him at Sunday Mass. Exactly three months and one week ago. It was very rare to see the Fitzgeralds at Mass in Ballygrace these days, as their parents now favoured the larger parish of Tullamore.

'The shops are only small,' Tara explained, in a voice which sounded funny to her own ears. 'They don't carry a lot of stock, or have many staff. It's only the baker's shop in Ballygrace and the hardware shop. I check their order sheets every week, and balance the books.'

'Didn't I tell you how clever Tara was in school?' Madeleine said to her brother in a high-pitched, excited tone. 'She was always the top of the class. She's also a wonderful pianist. She's been playing the organ in Ballygrace church this year, and from the pieces I've heard, she's *miles* ahead of us. Her brother Joe's a gifted pianist, too. It obviously runs in the family.'

Tara blushed at her friend's exaggerated praise. 'I'm not really that good,' she argued. 'Half the time I only play by ear.'

'Don't be so modest,' Madeleine told her. 'Mother always says that women should be more positive about themselves and have confidence in their talents.' She gave a little laugh. 'She would be delighted if she had a daughter like you, Tara. If I had half the talent that you have, she'd be ecstatic. Have you decided what you're going to do when you leave school? Do you think you'll go to somewhere like England or America?'

'I'm not sure,' Tara said. 'It all depends on my granda . . .'

Madeleine's hand flew to her mouth. 'Oh, I'm sorry, Tara! I forgot all about your grandfather . . . I heard he was ill over the summer. Mrs Scully mentioned it to me. How is he now?'

A picture of the cross old maid who had thrown her out of Ballygrace House flashed through Tara's mind. How dare that old witch even mention her granda's name! Then, seeing the concern on her friend's face, she swallowed her anger and said: 'He's much better now, thanks. The doctor gave him some tablets and told him that he has to take it a lot easier.'

Because of that advice, Tara had found herself volunteering to spend the summer evenings up on the bog with her Uncle Mick and her father – doing the work which her granda had loved to do in the fine weather. The work which Tara knew he would never do again.

'I'm glad to hear he's better,' Madeleine said, and then added in a surprisingly light-hearted manner, 'It would be awful for you if anything happened to him, wouldn't it? You'd almost be an orphan . . . just like poor Biddy.'

There was a shocked silence for a moment, during which Gabriel glared into his sister's face, trying to alert her to the terrible blunder she had just made.

Tara found herself rooted to the spot by Madeleine's words. *How could she?* How could she have said such a thing about her granda? And then – adding insult to injury – how could she have compared her situation to poor Biddy's?

Never, since the day Mrs Scully had thrown her out of Ballygrace House, had Tara felt so hurt and belittled. She looked around now to see if anyone else had been close enough to hear Madeleine Fitzgerald's comments. Thankfully, the rest of the youngsters were too taken up with the impending entertainment. As she turned back to Madeleine, the crowd suddenly cheered as the film projectionist came round the corner, jangling the keys to the Town Hall.

'*Nothing* is going to happen to my granda,' Tara said in a low voice. She narrowed her eyes. 'What else did that Mrs Scully say about him?'

'She said something about him having a *heart attack*,' Madeleine said airily, oblivious to the ill feelings she had aroused in her friend.

'It wasn't a heart attack!' Tara said furiously. 'The doctors said they weren't sure what it was – but nobody mentioned the words *heart attack*.'

'Oh, well,' Madeleine said, giving a little shrug, 'Mrs Scully often gets things wrong . . . doesn't she, Gabriel?'

Gabriel looked at his sister, in dread of what she might say next. It was because of this recent change in her behaviour – her tendency to say the first thing that came into her head – that he had been asked to accompany Madeleine to the film show. Only last week she had ruined a dinner party at home, by rushing downstairs and accusing one of the guests of having entered her bedroom and taken one of her books.

'Gabriel?' Madeleine prompted, as though he were the one behaving strangely.

'Yes . . . yes,' he said quickly. 'Mrs Scully gets things very wrong at times.' Then, he turned to Tara, praying that Madeleine would not say anything else which would make the situation worse. 'In the future . . . Father reckons that there are likely to be more businesses opening in the Midlands . . . and I'm sure that they will all need bookkeepers. It would be quite well paid, too. I'm sure you could negotiate a position when you leave school. There are classes at night school, where you could sit some sort of certificate in accounts.'

Tara took a deep breath, then smoothed the top of her hair back with both hands. 'Do you think so?' she said quietly.

'Yes.' He coughed to clear his throat. 'From what Madeleine has told me about your mathematical abilities . . . I'm quite sure *you* would find it a doddle.' He ran a finger around the neck of his white collar. 'If you like, I could find out about the training and qualifications necessary.' He cleared his throat again, smiled, and when he looked at Tara he was alarmed to see that her green eyes were brimming with tears.

Gently, he gripped her by the elbow and guided her to a quiet spot away from Madeleine and the rest of the moving queue. 'I'm so sorry, Tara,' Gabriel said in a low voice. 'Madeleine didn't mean to upset you . . . she's not been herself lately . . . she says things without thinking, and doesn't realise the hurt she's causing.' He dug both hands deep into his jacket pocket, deeply embarrassed. 'My father took her to a specialist in Mullingar, who deals with this sort of thing . . . apparently, she'll grow out of it. Please don't mind what she said – only someone who is ill could find a similarity between you and poor Biddy.' His face suddenly flushed red. 'In my opinion . . . you're likely to grow into a more refined and beautiful lady than Madeleine could ever hope to be.'

Several little sparks ignited in Tara's heart at his kind words. A spark of delight that he had commented on her good looks, and a spark of hope about her aspirations to become a real lady. But the brightest spark of all told Tara Flynn that she had fallen in love – for the first time in her young life.

It was seven o'clock by the time Biddy hopped off Tara's bike, at the top of her lane. As she walked along, Biddy giggled to herself recalling the antics of Laurel and Hardy in the film they'd seen that afternoon. She also giggled every time she thought of the lads who had sat in the row behind her and Tara and Madeleine. They had messed about, pulling at the girls' hair and putting their feet up on the backs of their chairs.

Sick of their messing, Tara had turned round and really given out to them, telling them they should either act their age or move seats down to the front beside the younger children.

They had quietened down after that, but one of the lads had kept leaning forward every now and then, touching Biddy's hair or pressing the toe of his shoe into the back of her chair, whispering. 'How's it goin'? The film is great oul' *craic*, isn't it?'

Biddy had giggled out loud but had stopped abruptly when Tara told her off, saying she was only encouraging them.

Madeleine had leaned across Tara, who was in between her and Biddy, and whispered: 'I think that one with the fair hair fancies you, Biddy! That's what happens when girls get all dressed up in their finery. Men can only judge a book by its cover.' And then she had gone into peals of laughter, as although someone had just told her a hilarious joke.

Tara had seemed a bit annoyed with Madeleine, Biddy thought. In fact, Tara had seemed annoyed at *everything*. First, she had moaned about the number of younger children who had been let in, and the noise they were making. Then she had criticised the mess people were making of the hall, throwing sweetie wrappers on the floor.

Later, Tara had given out again to Biddy for whispering and

smiling back at the boy with the fair hair. He had just told her his name was PJ Murphy, and then asked Biddy what her name was.

'Surely you don't want to get landed with the likes of them?' Tara had hissed in Biddy's ear. 'They're no-users. If you give them the slightest encouragement, they'll be after you every time you come into Daingean.'

'Sure, they're only messin,' Biddy had said. 'They don't mean any harm.' Then, as Tara stood up to straighten her skirt, Biddy noticed the lingering glance she gave the back corner of the hall where Gabriel Fitgerald was sitting, and she realised the real reason for Tara's bad humour. It was obvious to Biddy that the only boy Tara wanted to sit beside was Gabriel, but unfortunately for her he was too shy to sit with three girls on his own.

During a quiet part of the film, one of the lads behind them cleared his throat loudly, and then spat on the wooden hall floor. When Tara turned round and gave him a look of contempt, the whole group started to jeer and laugh at him.

'Isn't that a fine fella for you?' Tara said loudly. 'The oul' pig we have at home would have better manners!'

Once again, Madeleine went into her irritating shrieks of uncontrolled laughter.

Biddy's face had burned with embarrassment at Madeleine's silly behaviour and Tara's uppity manner. She decided that next time she escaped to the pictures, she would go with some of the more ordinary crowd from Ballygrace or Daingean. At least they wouldn't show her up. There was no point in fighting with Lizzie, getting her hair washed, and getting all dressed up in her good clothes, if she couldn't even have a laugh with a few of the lads.

Still, the afternoon hadn't been completely spoiled. Biddy suddenly smiled to herself. Unknown to both Madeleine and Tara, she had managed to make a date with PJ Murphy. When they had gone to buy minerals and sweets at the interval, he had leaned forward and asked her to go to the cinema in Tullamore the following weekend. 'We'll have great *craic* in Tullamore,' he told her, '*without* yer miserable friends. Howsabout it?'

Biddy had not been slow to agree. He might not have asked the second time.

As she walked past the kitchen window, Biddy could see Lizzie lying fast asleep in the bed. She smiled to herself, wondering how long the diarrhoea would last. Hopefully, for another day or two, because an incapacitated Lizzie was much easier to handle than Lizzie in the whole of her health.

Dinny obviously thought the same, and was passing the time chopping up some firewood, as he waited for Biddy coming back from the pictures. As soon as he heard the bike's brakes screeching to a halt in the lane, he put the axe down and came to the side of the house, waiting for her to come in the path to the cottage.

'Biddy!' he softly called, motioning her to come round to the turf shed. 'Come here, quick – I've got something to show you.'

Biddy walked towards him, trying not to make too much noise in case Lizzie heard her.

'It's all right,' Dinny reassured her in a low voice. 'She's been asleep this ten minutes. I gave her a good sup of brandy in hot milk and a couple of tablets. It should knock her out for a while.'

'What is it?' Biddy said with a frown, thinking how old and wrinkled the lodger looked compared to the lads in the hall. 'What'd you want to show me?'

Dinny winked meaningfully and reached for the buckle of his belt.

'Ah, no –' Biddy stepped back, shaking her head. 'Not if you haven't anythin' for me.' She turned away from him, as though making towards the cottage. Dinny knew the score by now, she thought. Nothing for nothing. If he wanted to have his way with her, he had to pay the price. And the more he wanted, the higher the price.

'Wait now, won't you?' Dinny said quickly. 'I have a real surprise for you . . . something you've been hopin' for, this long time.'

'Well?' Biddy demanded in an impatient tone, knowing she held all the cards. 'I'm waitin'.'

He pointed to the back of the turf shed. 'I have it round there . . . go on and see for yerself.'

Biddy folded her arms defensively and made round the back of the shed. There, leaning up against it, was a well-used but serviceable ladies' bicycle. 'Dinny!' she screeched in childish excitement, all pretence at being casual and aloof gone. Apart from Tara, Dinny was the only person who had ever given her anything in her life. She ran her hands over the worn leather seat, and along the back wheel. 'Where did you get it?'

'Never mind where I got it.' He gave a suggestive leer and sidled up next to her. 'I'm more interested in what you're goin to give me now.'

Biddy turned towards him, her eyelashes fluttering and her hands on her hips. 'It'll have to be quick,' she said with a playful smile. 'Lizzie could come out any minute and catch us.'

'It'll only be as long as it takes,' Dinny told her, delighted to be in charge of the situation again. He gave a quick glance round the side of the cottage, to make sure there was nobody about, then he motioned Biddy to go round to their usual spot at the back of the turf shed.

In the time that it took Dinny to unbutton his trousers and release his straining erection, Biddy had quickly stepped out of the new knickers she had bought in Tullamore with Tara last weekend, and was unbuttoning the front of her polka-dot dress. She held the dress up around her thighs and then leaned up against the trunk of the massive hawthorn tree for support.

'You'll pull out before anything happens, won't ye?' Biddy checked. 'The last time ye nearly left it too late.'

'I promise I'll pull out in plenty of time,' he said thickly, his eyes roaming over the exposed parts of her ripe teenage body. As they moved together, one of Dinny's hands found its way down the front of her brassiere, while the other worked between her legs.

'Your hair smells lovely,' he grunted, then he lifted her left foot to rest on a log, placed there for the purpose so that she could accommodate him more easily. Then, he pushed upwards and thrust himself deep inside her young body.

'I washed my hair for goin' to the pictures,' Biddy replied, and then – as he started moving in and out of her – Biddy closed her eyes. She imagined that it was PJ Murphy who was holding and touching her, and she found the whole procedure surprisingly easy to endure.

Chapter Eight

❧

October, 1949

'I can't imagine why you should want to ask a girl like that to your birthday party,' said Elisha Fitzgerald in an exasperated tone. 'She'll feel completely out of her depth with all your friends from boarding school.' She paused for a moment to stifle the huge sigh which she knew would only antagonise her daughter further. They had been at loggerheads since the summer holidays and it was late October. Every weekend that Madeleine came home from school brought fresh conflicts between the two women. It had now reached the point where Elisha dreaded her daughter's arrival on a Friday evening.

'Tara's not typical of the girls from Ballygrace,' Madeleine answered evenly, leaning forward to take another blank invitation card, from the pile on the dining-room table. 'And anyway, you've never even spoken to her, Mother. You can't judge a person if you haven't given them a chance.' She started to write Tara's name on the envelope.

'Mrs Scully says she's from a *very* ordinary family, and that the girl has had to practically bring herself up.'

'I should think that's to Tara's credit.' Madeleine's voice was taking on an edge now, and she was starting to rub her right hand over her left forearm – a sign that she was getting agitated. A sign that her mother should not push the issue any further.

'But she won't know anyone at the party,' Elisha persisted. 'The poor girl will be like a fish out of water! Her clothes – everything – will be different from the other girls.'

'Mother!' Madeleine's eyes were wide and starting to fill up with

83

tears. 'I will be eighteen years old in two weeks' time. You've got to let me make my own decisions. I've been friends with Tara since we moved to Ballygrace, and I want her to come to my birthday party! I like her better than any of the other girls I know from school.' She halted for a moment to catch her breath. 'I've agreed that it's not suitable to ask Biddy Hart to the party. I can understand that Biddy would feel out of her depth with the other girls – but you have to have faith in my judgement over *Tara*. You know nothing whatsoever about her . . . she speaks very well, and there are times when she wears better clothes than I do.'

Disbelief was stamped all over Elisha Fitzgeralds's face.

'I can assure you,' Madeleine reiterated, 'she is *very* different to the other girls from Ballygrace.'

Elisha took a deep breath. 'All right!' she snapped. 'Invite her if you must.'

Madeleine stopped rubbing her arm and calmly laid her hands on the table. 'Thank you,' she said quietly. Then, looking her mother straight in the eye, she added, 'I intend to ask her to stay overnight, because it will be much too late, and too cold, to have her cycle home in the dark. As you well know, her family don't have a car like the other girls.' Then, ignoring the indignant look which had spread on her mother's face, she reached for a pen to continue writing Tara's invitation.

As she mounted the stairs to her bedroom, Elisha Fitzgerald wondered what she had done to deserve this latest thorn in her side. Things had only recently settled down to a more civilised basis between herself and William, now that their financial situation had improved.

The move from Dublin to Offaly, he had decided, was a blessing in disguise. Just last month, William had come rushing home excitedly one afternoon, and asked Elisha if they could talk privately. 'I have something to ask you – and I want you to think carefully before answering.'

'What is it?' she had replied warily, her hands smoothing her severely coiffuired hair as she led the way to her husband's study.

William had walked over to the window and looked out at the berry-laden bushes and the late autumn roses, as though gathering inspiration. Then, he had strode across the room and taken both her hands in his and kissed them. The first gesture of affection he had shown her in a long time.

He said beseechingly: 'I want you to have faith in me, and back me in a new business venture.' He placed a finger on her lips, to silence any protest. 'Hear me out before saying anything – and remember – I vow that I will never let you down again.'

The outcome of the conversation was Elisha's agreeing to fund William's buying into another auctioneer's office in Naas in Country Kildare. A profitable business was due to go up for sale with a solid, dependable manager already at the helm. William reckoned that it was just the stepping-stone he needed to regain the business acumen he had lost in Dublin.

He pointed out that Kildare was more lucrative land-wise due to the Curragh racing course and the growing number of stud farms. Another factor worth considering, was that the auctioneering busi- nesses would provide careers for Gabriel and Madeleine, should they show any interest.

After some thought, Elisha conceded that her husband had, after all, settled into rural life in the Midlands much better than she had hoped at the beginning. He had worked harder than she had ever seen him work at building up this new business. She did not admit to her husband that the idea of a position for Madeleine in his business had swayed her decision considerably. Gabriel was not a worry. He was a quiet, academic boy who would clearly do well in his chosen career. His sister was a different kettle of fish altogether.

On a Wednesday, two days later, Tara's hands shook with excitement as she read the invitation that she had just received in the post. She had not seen Madeleine for months, although she had looked out for her – and Gabriel – at Mass in Ballygrace Church every Sunday. She presumed that since the family's business concerns were firmly rooted in Tullamore, they had decided to patronise the town's church on a more regular basis.

'I can't believe it!' she said to herself, turning the thick, gilt-edged card over and over in her hands. As she read the PS on the back, inviting her to stay overnight, an anxious little frown creased her forehead. It was just over seven years ago since the day she was shown the door in Ballygrace House by that horrible Mrs Scully. And a lot had changed in seven years.

Tara herself would be eighteen in January, and had been working full-time in the offices of a Tullamore whiskey distillery since May the previous year. She had kept up her piano classes and had passed every exam with honours so far. She had taken Gabriel Fitzgerald's advice and was now in her second year attending bookkeeping and typing classes in Tullamore. Two evenings a week – on Tuesdays and Thursdays – she went straight from work to Molly and Maggie's for her dinner, had a couple of hours' practice on the piano, and then went on to her evening classes. Around ten o'clock she cycled back to Ballygrace with another local girl who was taking evening classes, too.

Tara had kept up her little egg and poultry business over the years, and a few hours over the weekend doing the books for some of the little shops in Ballygrace and Daingean. As a result, her bank account had grown larger and larger – and she had grown more and more secretive about the money, knowing that her father would only be too delighted to get his hands on anything he thought she could spare.

Shay never looked further than the few days – or at most, the week – ahead. Tessie, having seen the youngest child start school, had got herself a part-time job cleaning in a hotel in Tullamore. This was supposed to have given the family a bit extra, but Shay had seen it as an opportunity to allow himself a few extra jars of stout after his hard week's work. He gave no thought to the work involved bringing up the houseful of children, and indeed after a few jars at the weekend, he often bemoaned his lot to his elderly father and bachelor brother.

'If I had been anyway wise,' Tara had heard him rambling on to her granda and Uncle Mick the previous Friday evening, from the refuge of her bedroom, 'I would have stayed here at home, where I was well off. If I had known what I know now . . . I would have contented meself with bein' a bachelor again.' He'd gestured towards the glowing turf fire. 'I could be happy sittin' here nights with Tara to make me a cup of tea, and to bring me my bit to eat after work. I could have gone up the road for a few pints in the evenin' without havin' to explain meself. There's never a penny I can call me own.' He had shook his head in sorrow. 'Women are the ruination of men.'

'Away with you! You're nothing short of a fool, man.' Noel Flynn's voice was now thin and frail, as was his body. He had struggled up from his old armchair, made his painful way to the door and unbolted it. 'Go home, ya *amadán* – will you? Go home to your wife and childer! The wife and childer ye were well warned about. The road ye were determined to go down.'

When Shay got up unsteadily to his feet, Mick laid a firm hand on his shoulder and guided him towards the open cottage door. 'You made yer bed, Shay,' he said quietly, 'now you may lie in it.'

'Jaysus!' Shay had said, staggering out into the night air. 'It's great sympathy I'm gettin' from ye all.' He gave a drunken, strangled sob. 'I thought me own kind at least would have had a sympathetic word for me.'

'Mind yourself and go easy on the bike,' Mick had called into the darkness. Then, with a sigh of relief, he closed the door.

Tara had also heaved a sigh of relief when she heard her father departing. The older she grew, the more grateful she grew that her father had had little or nothing to do with her upbringing. Though she often felt the lack of a mother, she knew that she was better off with her granda and her Uncle Mick than her father. Since she had reached womanhood, they had let her come and go as she pleased, and left any major decisions in her life up to herself. Her granda was always there to offer advice if she asked for it, but he never interfered with her business.

Lately, Tara had been out very little, apart from her evening classes and her piano lessons, and the odd Saturday afternoon at the pictures. Since her granda had not been so great, she felt happier staying at home. In fairness to him and her Uncle Mick, they both encouraged her to go out in Tullamore or to the dances in the town hall in Daingean, but recently she always refused. The local boys from Ballygrace and the surrounding villages held no great interest for her, although she got on well with them. Apart from the ones who came into the dances with a drink on them. She had seen enough of that in her father, and couldn't bring herself to be pleasant to anybody who remotely resembled him after a few pints.

If somebody like Gabriel Fitzgerald had gone to the dances – then that would have been different. But it wasn't the type of place he would go. He had left school this year, too, and was now in his first year at UCD. Tara supposed it made no difference where he was, whether it was boarding school or university in Dublin, because she never saw much of him anyway.

She derived some comfort from the fact that his name had never been mentioned with any local girls. The talk amongst Biddy and the others she met at Mass revolved around who was at the pictures last night or the local dances – and Gabriel never seemed to be there.

Tara always stood just on the fringe of the circle of giggling girls, waiting for Biddy to have a chat on their own. It didn't matter that she and Biddy never went out together very often; they were still good friends, and always kept each other up to date on what they were doing.

Meanwhile, Tara was busy at her night classes, her music, reading up on the latest fashions – and improving herself generally. Since leaving school, Tara realised that there was no point in dressing like a lady, if she didn't sound like one. Working on the telephone in the office had sorted out her problem, and forced her into adopting a more 'refined' accent.

When she first started in the office, many of the people who rang the distillery from Dublin and England had expressed difficulty in understanding her Ballygrace brogue. Initially, Tara was mortified and very self-conscious, and on one particular occasion went home and cried on her granda's shoulder.

'You sound fine to me, mavourneen,' he comforted her, 'but if you're going to travel any distance, you'll have to lose some of the ould Ballygrace brogue if you want to be understood. Rightly or wrongly, you're judged by the way you look and by what comes out of your mouth. You need to make sure you sound right if you want to get on in the world.' The old man leaned over and patted her hand. 'You're not going to be one of the ones that stay around Ballygrace, Tara, and you need to know how to adjust to the big world outside. My own sisters and brothers had to adjust when they went to America and England. Who knows,' he said softly, 'you might end up in one of them places yerself.'

'I'm quite content where I am,' Tara had quickly replied. 'I wouldn't like to live anywhere else other than here – with you and my Uncle Mick.'

'That's grand for *now*, girleen,' Noel said with a smile, 'but time changes many a thing. It's like the tide coming in with the sea. It comes in whether we like it or not.'

Tara meant what she said. Her life had changed enough recently – leaving school and going to night classes and all the cycling to and from Tullamore every day. For the time being, she wanted everything else to continue as it was. She wanted to come home from work in the evenings, make supper for the three of them, then tidy up. She spent the rest of the evening studying or maybe visiting Mrs Kelly, who – like her granda – was now housebound. During October, Tara had gone to Devotions in church with Biddy on the evenings she didn't have night school, but the rest of the night was spent with her granda and Mick.

Recently, when Tara studied the old man, a cold hand clutched at her heart, for she could see a big change in him. Over the last two years he had undoubtedly lost weight, and his normally ruddy cheeks had a sickly grey pallor to them. Tara had tried to tempt his failing appetite by giving him larger portions of his favourite plain, but nourishing, meals. But Noel Flynn was no longer fit to digest the slices of harm and beef which Tara and Mick made sure they had in plenty for him.

Tara looked down at the card once again and wondered why she had received the invitation to Ballygrace House. It most certainly would have been discussed with Madeleine's parents, because she would not dare to invite her without their permission.

As she pondered over it, a little knot of doubt tightened in her stomach. The last time she had been in Ballygrace House, she had been a naive eleven-year-old girl, too curious for her own good. But Tara was no longer that naive child. In those intervening years she had studied carefully from magazines and books, and had more insight into how the other half lived. She had studied the clothes and habits of people like the Fitzgeralds, until she knew by heart the cutlery that they used and the sorts of dishes that they ate. She had read up on table settings and napkins, and had tried out new recipes from cookery magazines whenever she could find the ingredients.

Never again would Tara Flynn be told by the likes of Mrs Scully that she wasn't good enough. She owed it to herself and her granda to prove that she could hold her head up in any kind of company. She knew that she was the smartest dressed girl in Ballygrace Church every Sunday, and was constantly being asked where she had bought this hat or that pair of shoes from. The look of amazement on some of the girls' faces, when she told them that she had bought them in Dublin, said it all. Since she was sixteen years of age, Tara had found her way up to the city. She had cycled into Tullamore, then caught the train up to Dublin, and had made her way to the glamorous shops that she saw advertised in the national newspaper and in the ladies' magazines. After she had found the big department stores in Grafton Street and O'Connell Street, Tara knew she would never be satisfied with the smaller shops in Tullamore, ever again.

She put the invitation down on the old pine table and decided that she *would* go. Even if Madeleine's parents were not very welcoming, she would still go to the party and stay the night. She would not put a foot wrong, because she would keep silent rather than risk saying the wrong thing.

She would attend the party because she wanted to keep friends with Madeleine . . . and because she wanted to see Gabriel Fitzgerald again. But the real reason she would attend had nothing to do with other people. It was because she was determined to test herself out. To put into practice all the things she had learned over the last few years. To show how much she had changed, to anyone who might doubt her suitability as a friend of Madeleine Fitzgerald's and as a guest at her home. More than anything, she was determined to pass herself with these people and to fit in with their surroundings.

The following Monday, Tara took a day's holiday from work. She took a carefully counted six pounds from her savings, and cycled to Tullamore to catch the early morning train to Dublin. She had looked in on her granda, and given him a cup of tea and a slice of soda bread and butter before leaving. He didn't look too bad this morning, and he gave her his usual parting of 'Mind yourself,' as she quietly left the house.

The train went just after seven, necessitating that Tara leave Ballygrace around twenty past six to give herself plenty of time to cycle into Tullamore. As she stepped out into the cold, dark November morning, she paused for a few moments to tie her hair under a

floral scarf. She then debated with herself as to whether she should go
back into the cottage and get her warmer camel-haired coat, as
opposed to the light grey one she was wearing. Two reasons made
her decide to brave the cold autumn morning in the lighter coat. First,
she had all too often had favourite skirts and dresses ruined by smears
of oil from the bike – and the camel coat had cost too much to let that
happen. Secondly, it was likely to be warmer later on in Dublin, and
she didn't want to be laden down with a heavy coat all day.

On the open road to Tullamore, as the icy wind bit at her cheeks,
and nipped at her hands and legs, Tara wondered about her choice of
coat, and hoped and prayed that the weather would improve as the
day progressed. At this time of the morning, there was little life about
apart from the shadowy cows and sheep standing motionless in the
fields, their warm breath forming white clouds around their heads.

As she pedalled along through Cappincur, a townland just outside
Tullamore, some signs of human life began to stir in the form of an
elderly man with a pony and cart, and several cyclists, huddled over
the bike handlebars against the morning chill. By the time she reached
the station, Tara had warmed up considerably. She left the bike
against the side of the station building. Then, after smoothing her
clothes and removing her headscarf, she took her black leather clutch
bag from the carrier basket and made her way to the ticket office.

The train was only a couple of minutes late – good by the usual
lackadaisical standards. Tara boarded it with mounting excitement at
the thought of the whole day which lay ahead of her in Dublin. She
found a quiet carriage and, after removing her coat, she sat back in the
seat, enjoying the journey as they passed through the expansive, misty
fields of Offaly then out through the less familiar territory of Kildare.

When she wasn't occupied looking out of the little space she had
rubbed in the steamed-up window, Tara stole discreet glances at the
other passengers, most of them heading off for their day's work in the
big city, intermingled with the odd shopper or nun.

She compared the outfits the other girls were wearing with her own
emerald-green dress with the buttoned-down collar and nipped-in
waist, and the matching velvet band she wore in her loose red hair.

After eyeing up a number of girls she eventually decided that she
was very satisfied with her own outfit. While her mind fluttered from

the shops she intended to visit, to the sort of birthday present she should take to the party – she sat completely oblivious to the admiring glances the men in the carriage were giving her.

The green fields and hedges and grazing cattle gave way to buildings that got taller and closer together – and heralding the train's arrival in Dublin. Tara felt her heartbeat quicken at the thought of the exciting day in front of her. She made her way purposefully out through the city station and, saving the coppers she could have spent on a tram, she headed down along the Quays. She walked along in her neat low-heeled shoes, past the busy Guinness Brewery on one side and the Collins Barracks on the other, enjoying the hustle and bustle of the city traffic. It would have been nice to have company with her for the day, but Tara knew that there was no point in asking Biddy or any of the other girls from Ballygrace to come up to Dublin. For a start, Biddy would not have been allowed. Lizzie Lawless reckoned that Dublin embodied all that was wrong in the world, with loose women and fast cars – little knowing the carnal deeds that were taking place under her own pinched nose.

Besides, Biddy would not have had the money or the confidence to enter the big shops that Tara intended to patronise. An example of her backwardness had been her reaction to Tara's party invitation. 'You're hardly going to go?' she had said with wide eyes, after scanning the printed card.

'I am,' Tara had replied.

'I would die!' Biddy said, clutching her throat at the thought. 'Imagine having to walk into that place, and you only knowing Madeleine.' Her eyes rolled in horror. 'All the ones from that posh school in their fancy cars and their fancy clothes . . .' And then she had hesitated, pondering something over in her mind. 'Sure, it will be no bother to the likes of you, Tara. The way you dress yerself and the way you go on is nearly the same as them.'

Tara's eyebrows had shot up defensively. 'What d'you mean? The way I go on?'

Biddy had looked flustered, not wishing to incur her friend's wrath. 'What I mean is,' she said, deliberating each word carefully, 'that you can nearly pass yerself off as Quality . . . ye have a fancier – a nicer – way of talkin' and goin' on than the likes of me.'

Eventually, Tara decided to accept her friend's remarks as a compliment – for Biddy was adamant that she was indeed praising her.

Later on that same evening, when her Uncle Mick was out the back fixing a fence, she had told her granda about the invitation, and asked him if he minded her going to the party. Noel had put the book he was reading down on his lap, and looked into the glowing turf fire for a good minute before replying. 'Tara,' he said, turning to look at her, 'you're growing up, and you're going to have to learn to make a lot of decisions from now on.' He'd paused and pursed his blue-tinged lips together. 'You'll just have to learn – like the rest of us – to make up yer own mind about people. I'm not going to argue with you any more, about who you should be chattin' to, and who ye should be keepin' away from. You're a clever girl . . . all the teachers at school and the parish priest have told me and yer father that. From here on in – it's up to yourself. If you have a mind to go to the party – or anywhere else for that matter – then please yerself and go.'

Half of Tara had felt pleased at her granda's reply and half of her had felt confused. It was good that he thought she was growing up and mature enough to make up her own mind – but there was something worrying about her granda not giving his usual advice. 'D'you still not like the Fitzgeralds, Granda?' she asked quietly.

Noel Flynn reached down for his pipe and tobacco to the little table he now kept beside his rocking chair. This was to save him having to get to his feet to reach the mantelpiece – an action which now left him dizzy. He took his penknife out of his waistcoat pocket, and after opening the wrapping of the small hard block of tobacco, started to peel fine slices off it. 'It makes no difference in the world,' he said, 'whether I like them or not. If the truth be told, I don't know the people. I only know their sort – and their sort wouldn't normally give the likes of us the time of day. This friend of yours – the young Madeleine one – she seems different to the others. She obviously looks for more in people than just money.' Then, slowly, he lifted his gaze back to meet Tara's eyes. 'It's up to you, and whether you feel you can take it. Whether you can keep yer tongue between yer teeth, and have yer own thoughts, or whether you think you can match them. You have the looks and the brains, and you have a determination in you to be as good as anybody else. That might be what makes the difference. You're entitled to better yerself, and you're entitled to have all the things that comes from doing well. If you have the guts – and the determination – then all I can say is good luck to you.'

'So,' Tara said hesitantly, 'do you think it's all right for me to go to the party?'

Noel struck a match and then lit his pipe with a shaky hand. 'If that's what you want to do, then don't let anybody stop you. Life's too short to waste on trying to please other people. It was different when you were small and we had to show you the right road to do everything. You're nearly a woman now and you'll have to find yer own road.' He reached out his frail, work-worn hand and took hers. 'Whatever you do, my little darlin' – be careful. You're a grand-looking girl, Tara, and there's many a man will set his cap at ye. Just make sure they're good to you, and don't be like yer father – always thinkin' that the grass is greener on the other side. Once you have your bed made, you'll have no option but to lie in it.'

When she reached the 'Ha'penny Bridge' – the little iron bridge which spans the Liffey – Tara decided to head straight for Grafton Street. There was a Bewley's cafe around there where she knew she could get a good cooked breakfast for a reasonable price. It was one of the places that the parish priest had recommended, when she and the old aunties were on a day's visit to see Joe in the seminary. She had been in Bewley's several times, and felt more comfortable going there than into one she didn't know.

Dublin city – although busy to country folk – was still in its sleepy, early morning state. It was only half-past eight and the shops were not open until nine or after. Many of the stores were lifeless with blinds pulled and brown paper or newspaper covering any goods which might fade in the early morning sun.

Tara walked along at a leisurely pace, occasionally halting to look into some of the shop windows which caught her eye. Several times she paused outside a cheaper restaurant or cafe, tempted by the smell of bacon and sausages frying, but she pressed on. Instinctively, and no matter how uncomfortable it initially felt, Tara would from now on push herself into the situations and places that she knew the Quality would frequent. Like her foray into Bewley's – she knew that the more she went into these places, the more familiar and relaxed she would become. And the more she studied the people who patronised the premises – the more like them *she* would become.

As on her last visit to the restaurant, Tara ordered a small glass of orange juice with her breakfast, and then a pot of coffee for afterwards. The hot drink did not taste as bitter or strange as the first time she had tried it, and she confidently spooned in some *brown* sugar – and chose cream instead of milk.

Tara was also pleased with the attention she had received from the young waitress, in her long white frilled pinafore and little frilled cap, who had called her *Madam*. After paying at the till, she stepped confidently out into Grafton Street to enjoy the rest of her adventure in Dublin.

In the hour she had spent having her breakfast, the city had both livened up and warmed up. Tara left the buttons open on her coat, glad that she had opted for the lightweight garment after all. She made her way up the street, stopping every so often to look in at the ladies' wear shops, and if the prices looked within her range, she went inside and had a look at the clothes on display.

Choosing just the right outfit for the party was not an easy task. Early November was cool enough to venture into winter colours and heavier weight materials, but not near enough to Christmas to warrant the really fancy clothes she could have chosen for the festive season.

Tara carefully inspected the racks of dresses and suits and studied the outfits on the shop dummies, trying to gauge the sort of accessories that would complete the right look for the party. She saw one or two promising dresses early on in her shopping, but decided to carry on checking out the rest of the shops in case she saw something better.

Towards the top of Grafton Street, a jewellery display in the window of a large department store caught Tara's eye and as she scanned the items on one of the black velvet pads she saw the perfect gift for Madeleine's birthday. It was a beautiful little brooch with a white profile of a lady's face set on a brown background. The card at the top of the display said 'Cameo Collection', and as Tara stared at it, she knew it was exactly the type of present her friend would love.

'The setting and the clip at the back of the brooch are nine-carat gold, madam,' the elderly sales assistant told Tara. Then she asked: 'Is it for yourself?'

Tara shook her head. 'No, it's a present for a friend.'

'Well, you'll be delighted to know that it comes with a special gift box.'

The brooch was slightly more than Tara had budgeted for, but she felt sure that it was just right. It was worth the extra few shillings, both to please Madeleine and to feel confident that she wasn't letting herself down.

Spurred on by her purchase, Tara came out of the shop delighted with herself, and looking forward to completing the rest of her shopping. She paused outside the shop, first looking towards the top of Grafton Street and St Stephen's Green, and then back down towards O'Connell Street – debating which would be the best direction to take. She had almost exhausted all the ladies' wear shops in Grafton Street, and was wondering whether it was worth checking out the few that she had not been in yet.

She decided to try the last few shops in the immediate area, as she knew she might regret it later, when she had trudged all the way over O'Connell Bridge to the shops on the other side. She looked at the little watch her granda and Uncle Mick had bought her last Christmas. It was nearly two o'clock. A wave of panic washed over her, as she realised she had only a few more hours to pick her outfit for the party.

She turned quickly now, in the direction of the next ladies' wear shop, and bumped straight into a young man who had been looking into the shop window next to her.

'Tara?' a very surprised voice said. 'It is you, isn't it?'

When she lifted her head to look at the young man in the dark overcoat and university scarf, she got the shock of her life. 'Gabriel!' she gasped, her legs suddenly weak. 'What are you doing here?'

He pushed his blond hair back off his forehead in an embarrassed manner. 'I was just about to ask you the same question,' he laughed. 'I've got the afternoon off lectures. I had a dentist appointment – I'm having trouble with a wisdom tooth and I had to have an X-ray.'

'Was it painful?' she asked sympathetically.

'It wasn't too bad.' He gave a grin that made Tara's heart lurch.

'Having it out is going to be a different matter, I'm definitely *not* looking forward to that.'

As Tara looked at Gabriel, she suddenly felt all awkward and shy. Then, she realised she would have to think of something to say to keep the conversation going, or he would go about his business. 'D'you often get time off from your classes?' she asked, nervously moving her brown bag from one hand to the other.

'It depends if you can talk your way out of it . . . anyway, I'm off the hook for a couple of hours, thanks be to God!' He paused. 'What about yourself? What plans have you?'

'Nothing really,' she said. 'I'm just shopping.'

'Have you had lunch yet?'

Tara hesitated, not sure what to say. 'I had breakfast in Bewley's when I arrived.'

'That's exactly where I'm heading for,' he said. 'I don't suppose you feel ready to eat again, do you?'

Tara held her breath, and gripped the handles of the brown-paper bag tightly. She didn't know how to reply to his question, because she didn't really know what he was asking. Did he want her to join him for lunch – or was he just chatting for the sake of it? A sudden breeze lifted the back of her hair. Grateful for the excuse, she turned her head away to smooth her hair down.

'I will, of course, pay for lunch,' Gabriel said quickly. 'I'd love the company . . . I hate going into restaurants on my own.'

'No – no – you will not!' Tara protested. 'I have my own money.'

His eyes lit up, and he bent his head towards her. 'I've invited you, so I'm paying. No arguments.' Then he put his hand under her elbow and guided her down Grafton Street.

Tara felt very proud, but nervous, as she walked into the restaurant with Gabriel Fitzgerald. The palms of her hands were damp, and her throat was tight and strange. She also felt as if she had just eaten a huge meal, even though it had been several hours before. If it had been any other person, she knew she would have made her excuses and left. She would not have dreamt of wasting the precious time she had left in Dublin. But Gabriel was not *any other* person – and there was nothing else in the world she wanted to do but sit across a table from him for the rest of the afternoon.

As Tara's head was bent over the menu, Gabriel found his gaze drawn to the abundant flaming hair, held in submission by the velvet band, and the long slim fingers curving round the hard-backed menu. Tara Flynn had always caught his eye. When they were younger, he had been acutely aware of her presence. Even when she was silent, she always looked lively and interested in everything. She looked so bright – so *vital*.

Madeleine had brought a number of friends home from boarding school, on special weekends or at the holidays, but none of them were like the young woman sitting opposite him now. They always seemed boring and childish to him, or silly and giggly.

He hadn't given Tara any thought recently. Why should he, when she hardly ever crossed his path? University had taken up all his attention, what with moving up to Dublin, and studying – and getting used to having girls around him everywhere. Getting used to girls – that was the strangest part, after spending years in a boys' boarding school.

His eyes were now drawn from Tara's hair to her shoulders, and then – like magnets he had no control over – to her generous breasts. He was amazed that he had missed this particular asset of hers and, as he stared, he deduced that she had either kept them well wrapped up, or they had developed since the last time they had met.

As his eyes lingered longingly, Gabriel wondered if Tara had a boyfriend. He suddenly wondered if she had a rich boyfriend, who had bought her nice clothes and gifts. Surely, there must be someone for her to dress up like this? Someone who worked with her in the distillery perhaps? Or maybe someone she had met in Dublin.

'Have you decided yet?' she suddenly asked, looking up at him.

Gabriel snapped the menu shut, feeling guilty, as though she had read his thoughts. 'I'll have the steak and roast potatoes,' he answered, then he laughed lightly. 'It's still early in the term, so I can afford to eat reasonably. It's a different matter when my allowance is nearly gone.'

'I'll just have a sandwich and a coffee,' Tara said decisively. 'I had a big breakfast not too long ago.'

A frown crossed his lightly tanned face. 'You're not just saying that, because I made the joke about my allowance, are you?'

'No . . . no!' Tara insisted. 'Honestly, I'm not a bit hungry. A sandwich will do me fine until I get home this evening.'

When the waitress came to take their order, Tara turned her attention to asking about the sandwich fillings, Gabriel's eyes were drawn to scrutinise her strong-featured but beautiful face. As she looked up at the waitress, he noticed the smooth texture of her skin, and the little tilt at the end of her nose. Then he noticed that when she smiled, her eyes – a startling green, framed with thick lashes – lit up her whole face.

He could not help but notice her easy confidence in the surroundings, her excellent vocabulary and her clear diction. It all added up to a confusion in Gabriel's head. How could a girl from such an ordinary – even lowly – background, know all these things? How could she afford the expensive clothes she was wearing? Who had encouraged the confidence which allowed her to move about the city as she moved about the small towns in Offaly? Once again – it all pointed to a rich boyfriend.

To Gabriel, Tara seemed no different to the girls he had come across at university. She spoke as well, and she certainly dressed better than a lot of them. How he mused – and perhaps more importantly why, had she come to be like this?

As they sat back in their high wooden chairs, Gabriel Fitzgerald decided that he would make it his business to find out the answers to some of his questions, if the opportunity arose. He would ask Tara herself, if it came up in the conversation. If not – he would carefully ask around in Tullamore.

It would satisfy not only his own curiosity but his mother's, who had been on the phone ranting and raving, about Madeleine having asked such a person to her birthday party. Madeleine, it seemed, was the only person prepared to take Tara at face value. And given her disturbed frame of mind at the minute, she was perhaps not the best person to trust in these judgements.

Later that evening, on the train going back to Tullamore, Tara stared out into the dim light, going over every little detail of the time she and Gabriel had spent together. She could still picture him in his dark overcoat, and the pale blue v-neck sweater he had worn underneath.

She could feel his hands on her shoulders, when he had helped her to slip off her coat.

She hugged the coat tightly to her now, imagining she could feel his arms folding around her, and she shivered in the same delicious way as when he had actually touched her. Tara thought back in amazement that she had been able to eat anything at all, because the minute she had bumped into him in Grafton Street she felt she would never need food again. She had somehow managed to drink two cups of coffee and pick at a ham sandwich, while Gabriel had eaten his meal. And the biggest miracle of all – she had talked to him – quite naturally, about everything under the sun.

Gabriel had asked her all about her music and her nightclasses, and then about her brother Joe. She had even talked to him about her granda's failing health, and how she did her best to look after him. It was strange how comfortable she had felt talking to Gabriel. She even felt confident enough to tell him all about her ambitions at work, and how determined she was to improve her skills in bookkeeping and shorthand. She was surprised at how interested he seemed in every-thing about her. He had asked her lots of questions about her work and about the other little bits and pieces she did at weekends. Later, she showed him the cameo brooch she had bought Madeleine and he had liked it so much that he said he might look in the same shop for a gift for Madeleine himself.

Gabriel had talked a little bit about himself, but he seemed more curious about her. He had even asked if she had any special boyfriend, and when she had told him that she didn't have the time, he looked surprised. He said he was pleased that she was coming to Madeleine's party, and wasn't it strange – after not seeing each other for ages – that they should be meeting twice in as many weeks.

After her second cup of coffee, Tara checked the time and then, very unwillingly, said she had to go. It was the last thing she wanted, but she knew she had little over an hour to complete her shopping, before making her way back for the train home. She resisted Gabriel's offer of another drink, because she did not want to give the impression that she was desperate for his company.

Instinctively, she did not want him to be the first to leave, and so she had parted with him outside the restaurant in a friendly and polite manner, and gone about her business.

Tara found great difficulty concentrating for the rest of the afternoon – and was sure that she wouldn't be able to find anything suitable for the party in the short time she had left. Then, as she walked towards the last ladies store in Grafton Street, a dummy stood in the doorway wearing the perfect outfit. A fine crepe wool dress and jacket in a deep burgundy, which she knew would pick up the darker tones of her hair. On closer examination, the dress had a low but modest neckline, short sleeves and a toning satin band on the bustline which twisted into a neat little bow.

When she tried the outfit on, it looked as if it had been designed with her and the special party in mind. The dress, which came just below her knee, looked perfect either on its own or with the matching short jacket with the 'Peter Pan' collar and satin burgundy buttons. If the house was warm or there was any dancing, the dress on its own would be cool enough for comfort. And for when she first arrived, or if they were all sitting around listening to music, then the jacket would be sophisticated but warm. All in all, it was an attractive outfit, which would let her blend in with the other guests and hopefully catch Gabriel Fitzgerald's eye.

The lady who served her brought the other two girls out from the back to see how well the costume looked on Tara. 'Of course, she has the height and the posture to carry it off,' the saleslady had commented to her colleagues. She then produced a satin clutch bag in the same colour, and told her that a shoe shop just off O'Connell Street had satin shoes in all colours at a reasonable price.

Tara had taken a deep breath when the lady had rung up the suit and bag on the till. She fleetingly thought of her father's reaction, if he had known the money she was about to hand over. Enough to keep him in beer for months. Then she remembered his drunken antics of late and quickly put him out of her mind as she rushed all the way down Grafton Street and across O'Connell Bridge to get her shoes.

When the train pulled in at the station in Tullamore, Tara stepped out on to the platform and then headed for her bicycle at the end of the building. She carefully tied her costume on to the carrier at the back of her bike, and then she put Madeleine's gift, her shoes and bag, and sweets for her granda, in the basket at the front. Then, almost bursting with happiness, she set off to cycle home to Ballygrace.

Chapter Nine

On Friday – the night before Madeleine's party – Shay Flynn
made his weekly drunken visit to Ballygrace. The original
reason for the regular visit was to give a few shillings to help
towards Tara's keep, but since Tara was now working, she insisted on
paying for her own keep.

This ostensibly left Shay with the extra money for the rest of his
family, but more often than not – the local publican was the main
beneficiary. After receiving his wages, Shay would visit one or two
pubs in Tullamore, then cycle out to the cottage to look in on his
father and daughter. Later, he would accompany Mick to the pub in
Ballygrace for a last few drinks. At the end of the night – usually the
worse for wear – he would call back at the cottage and have some
supper. On his way out, he would collect a bag of spuds, eggs and
milk, and then take them home with the remains of his wages, as a
softener to his long-suffering wife.

Around eleven o'clock, just after her granda had gone to bed, the
latch on the front door lifted. Mick came in first, his face red and
beaming after the few pints, with Shay trailing behind in a badly
inebriated fashion. Without saying a word, Mick made straight for
the back door to answer the call of nature, brought on by the cold
porter. Shay made his unsteady way across the stone floor to his
father's vacant rocking chair by the fireplace.

Tara, keeping to the opposite side from him, lifted the kettle from
the fire and poured the boiling water into the teapot. She had earlier
put two spoons of tea leaves in it, so that she didn't waste a second in
making her father's drink, to let him get off on his road home.
Depending on his mood, he could make a cup of tea last an hour but

tonight Tara was in no humour to listen to the nonsense he came out with when inebriated.

'I hear there's a right posh "do" going on at yer oul' pals, the Fitzgeralds, tomorrow night. No doubt it's for all the big nobs,' Shay said scathingly. He shifted forward in the rocking chair to warm his hands at the flames. 'One of the cooks in the hotel was tellin' Tessie all about it. Some friend of hers that takes to do with catering has been taken on to make up the buffet. There's to be bottles of champagne, along with wine and various minerals. An' seemingly the food list is as long as yer arm. And,' he elaborated, his arms waving in the air, 'you wouldn't know where to start pronouncin' the names of half the dishes! Foreign stuff and everythin'! You wouldn't mind . . . but that young Madeleine one . . .' He laughed heartily. 'She's not the full shillin'! I heard that she started giving out to everybody in the cemetery last week – talkin' a load of rubbish. Made a holy show of herself – and had to be led out of the place like a lamb.'

Tara banged the teapot down on the hearth. She turned to her father – cheeks flushed red with anger. 'I don't think it's very holy of you,' she said, 'to be jeering at someone who's not in the whole of her health.'

Shay raised one dark eyebrow, with the careless disinterest of one who was used to being corrected. 'Oh, d'you not think so?' he replied slowly. 'Sure, I'm only speakin' the truth . . . repeatin' what the whole town is sayin'.'

'There are some things that don't need saying, whether it's the truth or not.' Tara was not letting him off the hook. Her father was far too smart at the jeering. 'And in any case, that was last year. She's been seeing a doctor up in Dublin and she's fine now.'

'It's to be hoped that she's fine,' Shay said, lifting his cap off, and scratching at the black curls underneath. 'It'll be a fine state of affairs if she throws one of her mad turns at the posh party!' He went into gales of laughter at the thought of it. 'All the Quality there . . . stuffin' their faces and drinkin' the champagne . . . an' yer wan comin' floatin' down the stairs like a banshee let loose!'

'Aren't you the fine one to be talking about anybody!' Tara was on her feet, hands on hips, facing him. 'You come here every week after drinking your fill in the pub, spending money you should be giving to your wife and children – and then you have the nerve to talk about a girl who's never done you any harm.' A defiant smile spread over her face. 'For your information, I happen to be invited to Madeleine Fitzgerald's birthday party! And furthermore, I'm going to stay the night in her house!'

Shay's mouth opened but nothing came out. His silence did not matter, for his expression said it all. Then, just as he gathered himself together, another voice sounded.

'Go home this minute, Shay Flynn!' Old Noel called in a thin, faraway voice from inside his bedroom. 'You're nothing but a disturber of the peace! Go home – you drunken *amadán!*'

Mick came in the back door and on hearing the commotion asked: 'What's goin' on? I could hear youse all bawlin' and shoutin' out the back. It's loud enough to waken the dead.'

Shay ignored his brother and his father. 'You – are – a spoilt – little – oul' – brat – Tara – Flynn!' His head nodding to emphasise each word. He thumbed in the direction of his father's bedroom. 'An' that oul' eedjit in there is to blame for lettin' you away with it. By rights, I should have kept you in Tullamore to help Tessie mind yer young brothers and sisters. I would soon have put manners on you! You would have none of these uppity ideas if I'd reared you.'

'Let it be, Shay, for God's sake!' implored the good-natured Mick. He lifted the sack of spuds and stuff from the kitchen table. 'You'd better head off home. Tessie will be wondering where you've got to.'

Shay wheeled round in the chair to face his brother. 'Don't *you* be startin' now! I've enough listening to me own daughter cheekin' me back. Me own flesh and blood – and d'you hear the way she's talking to me? Isn't that the fine daughter for any man – turning on her father like that?'

'And aren't you the good example, to be talking?' Tara retorted. 'Why d'you think I wouldn't live with you when I was a child? By the time I was five I'd heard enough of your drunken ramblings to know where I was better off.' She pointed to the door. 'Your father and your brother have both shown you the door – and now I'm showing it to you! Go home and leave us all in peace.'

Shay got to his feet and put his cap back on his head. 'I'll not stay where I'm not welcome. I wouldn't take a cup of tea off ye now, if ye feckin' well paid me!' He shambled across the floor to take the sack from Mick. 'It's a sorry day when yer own flesh and blood thinks it's too damn good for you . . . when they prefer black strangers just because they've got money.' He gave a snort of derision in his daughter's direction. 'The Fitzgeralds won't want the likes of *you* there . . . they're only tolerating you because of the mad daughter. You'd be better off stayin' at home – or going to the dance in the town hall in Daingean, and mixin' with yer own kind. But no doubt an ordinary fella like meself wouldn't be good enough for you!'

Tara straightened up to her full height. 'That's the truest words you've spoken tonight,' she said venomously. 'The way you behave when you have drink taken makes you good for nobody! Sure, everybody thinks Tessie's a saint to put up with you.'

The mention of his wife's name was like a thorn suddenly searing into Shay's flesh. The last thing he needed reminding of was Tessie. Tessie, who had warned him not to come home tonight if he went on to the pub in Ballygrace. Tessie, who told him she was throwing him out if he didn't pull himself together soon.

Shay felt behind him for the latch on the door, then – determined determined to have the last word – he turned back to the poker-faced Tara. 'D'you know what they call people like you?' he said in a low vicious voice.

'I'm not interested in your opinion,' Tara said coolly, and strode across the kitchen to lift two mugs off the old pine dresser for herself and Mick.

'There's an oul' sayin' that comes to mind when I look at you,' Shay stated gravely, as though passing a death sentence, 'and when I listen to yer fancy accent, "Put a beggar on horseback and she'll ride him to hell!"' He shook his fist dramatically. 'Mark my words, Tara Flynn – for for *hell* is where yer big ideas are goin' to take you!'

Shay's cutting words pierced his daughter's heart as surely as an arrow would have done. Unwittingly, he had echoed the very words that Rosie Scully had used, when she had shown Tara the door, on her last visit to Ballygrace House.

Suddenly, a shadowy figure appeared at the bedroom door. All eyes turned to look at the frail old man, dressed in woollen vest and long johns – one arm supporting him on the frame of the door. He took a moment to get his breath back after the exertion of climbing out of his high bed and walking across the room.

'Shay,' Noel Flynn wheezed, 'for Jaysus' sake – will you go home? Haven't you done enough harm for one night?' He gave his son a long piercing look. 'You've said things you should never have said to that girl . . . you've excelled yerself, man.' Then Noel swayed on his feet and his breathing changed to short, rapid bursts.

A cold shiver washed over Tara, when she noticed the old man's lips starting to tinge with blue. She pressed the back of one hand against her own lips – to stop herself from crying out her hidden fears and worries about her granda.

There was silence for a few moments – save for the slow ticking of the clock on the mantelpiece – as all eyes were fixed on the swaying figure.

Eventually, his breathing eased and he mustered enough energy to continue. 'Go home, Shay,' he rasped. 'I'm not able for this carry-on any more.'

Shay Flynn wisely stepped out into the night, banging the door behind him.

The sound of light rain on her bedroom window woke Tara around seven o'clock the following morning. The morning of the party. In place of the excitement that had filled her mind for weeks, she was only aware of a dull headache and swollen eyes from all the crying she had done last night.

She forced herself to think of Gabriel – that was the only thing that could possibly make her feel better. He had been her last comforting thought before going to sleep last night after everything that had happened. She closed her eyes tightly – ignoring the throbbing behind the sockets – until until a picture of him came into her mind. A picture of him sitting opposite her in Bewley's that day in Dublin, and him smiling and chatting to her.

After a few minutes, she opened her eyes again, and let her gaze wander to her new rig-out, which hung outside her wardrobe door. Instead of the happy feeling she should have had, there was a nagging anxiety – the result of the horrible argument she'd had with her father.

Arguments with him were common enough, but the words that had passed between them on this occasion had gone straight to the very core of her. His parting words in particular, had done all but completely shatter her confidence.

After Shay had left, Tara had made a mug of tea for herself and Mick, and had taken one into her granda's bedroom. She needed to check that he was okay, and the tea was the only excuse she could think of for going in to him, without making her anxiety obvious.

Mercifully, he seemed none the worse for the upset. He was propped up in his bed, with his prayer book in his hands and his brown rosary beads spread out on the top of the worn grey blanket. His lips were back to their usual pale colour, and his breathing was more relaxed.

'Pay no heed to him, mavourneen,' Old Noel said soothingly, moving his legs to let Tara sit down on the bed beside him. 'When that fellow has drink taken, he would argue with the divil himself.' He looked up at the thatched ceiling and clucked his tongue in annoyance.

'Did you hear what he called me, Granda?' Tara said, hugging her mug of hot tea comfortingly to her chest. 'He called me a *beggar on horseback*. Isn't that a terrible name for a father to call his own daughter?'

'Pay no heed to him,' the old man said. 'It was the drink talkin' – not the man. He'll be sorry about it all in the cold daylight.'

'Granda?' Tara whispered. 'D'you think I'm making a fool of myself? D'you think I'd be better off staying at home instead of going to the party?' When the old man hesitated, she rushed on. 'I don't mind about my new costume and things – I can save them for Christmas. They won't go to waste. I was thinking . . . I could ask the fellow with the hackney cab in Daingean to drop Madeleine's present in, with a note saying I was taken sick.'

Noel took a sip of the milky tea Tara had pressed into his shaky hands, then he looked up into the sad face of his beloved granddaughter – the young woman who had brought so much light and love into the latter years of his life. For a few fleeting seconds, he saw the little girl in her face – the motherless child he had been unwilling to accept. The child he had grown to love in a fierce protective way.

It was strange the way things turned out, he thought. He had resigned himself to a life of hard work and no female company in the house after Hannah died. Little over a year later, everything had been turned on its head. Tara Flynn had indeed turned everything upside down. He had never had an empty moment after that, his eyes constantly on the burnished curly head as it bobbed from one thing to another, in and out of the house. He had taken her to school every morning until she was big enough to go by herself. Then he had waved her off at the door, watching until the red halo was only a speck in the distance.

Noel was acutely aware of the lack of a woman's hand about the house, to guide the little girl in the ways only another female could. To be there for her coming home from school – especially in the dark winter evenings – with newly baked bread and a bowl of hot soup.

But there was no woman. For whatever reason, God had seen fit to remove the two women in the child's life – her mother and her grandmother. There was only himself and Mick, and there was no danger of his bachelor son ever getting married. The only girl Mick had ever had a notion of, Kitty Dunne, had been wooed away from under his nose, while Mick was still making up his mind.

No – there had never been any womankind in Tara's life and there wasn't a damn thing that Noel could have done about it. When she had the chance of going to live with her father and Tessie in Tullamore, Tara had kicked up against it, and had refused to stay. Old Mrs Kelly had been a good help in guiding Tara, but she was only a neighbour, and an elderly woman after all.

As she grew older, Noel watched her pore over her homework books, night after night. And he had smiled at her determination, like the times she had sieved the black flour to make cakes during the Emergency – and then all the efforts to save money for her bicycle.

In the last few years, he had seen the biggest changes take place – from when she had taken up the piano and then started minding the bigger poultry at Christmas. Lately, her energies had gone into her work in Tullamore and her evening classes – while still keeping up with the work around the house, and managing a smile and a cheery word for the people who came to buy eggs.

At times, Noel felt the girl was driven, and he told her so. Tara would only shake her head and laugh. She pushed herself to the limits at everything. Her only indulgence was when she sat down with her books or magazines. Apart from then, she was constantly on the go.

It surprised him too, the company that Tara kept. After all her attempts to improve her speaking and clothes and everything else, she still had plenty of time for poor little Biddy Hart. Not so little now, Noel reminded himself. Only last Sunday she had walked back to the house after Mass, and had sat chatting to Tara over a drink of tea and a slice of Mick's fruit cake. Biddy had changed a lot in the last few years – not in the same way as Tara had – but enough to make her unrecognisable from the poor orphan of her earlier years.

Now – earning a few pounds cleaning the priest's house and working mornings in the bakery in Ballygrace – Biddy had filled out, and was as well dressed as any girl in the village. According to the rubbish that Shay talked after a few pints, she was as popular as any with the lads, too.

Too popular, Shay had said, hinting at more.

Noel wasn't interested in Shay's hints about Biddy or anyone else. Tara was too level-headed to be influenced by any of her friends' behaviour, and anyway she didn't go near the dances or places like that with Biddy. Their friendship was limited to the odd trip into the shops in Tullamore and a chat after Mass on a Sunday.

'Granda?' Tara suddenly said, rousing the old man out of his thoughts. 'Would I be better off missing the party? Am I only making a fool of myself?'

'No!' Noel's voice was stronger than Tara had heard for a while. 'You were invited, weren't you? Pay no heed to that *amadán* of a father of yours . . . and you go to the party as you planned. You're as good, if not better, than any of the others that'll be there. And hasn't the girl kept good faith with you over the years?' He reached out and patted Tara's hand. 'You go to the party – you'll learn nothing about life sitting home by the fire, and you do that too often these days. If there's nobody to yer likin' at the local dances or hereabouts, then you'll have to cast your net further. You have to do what pleases you, Tara, because nobody else is going to do it for you.'

Tara put her mug down on the chest of drawers by the bed. 'Oh,

Granda,' she said, putting her arms round the frail old man. 'What would I do without you?'

'You'll do fine, Tara Flynn,' he replied. 'Never doubt yerself – you'll do just fine.'

And with her granda's encouraging words rattling around in her head, Tara threw the bed clothes back and jumped out of bed to meet the day ahead.

Chapter Ten

'**M**other, stop fussing about – everything's fine.' Madeleine Fitzgerald gave her mother a big smile, and fluffed up the stiff taffeta skirt of her pale blue dress.

Elisha gritted her teeth and turned back to the exquisitely dressed tables laden with an array of food and drinks. *Keep calm, keep calm – you can't lose your temper tonight,* she told herself. *Just pray to God she doesn't start fiddling with the damned record player again.*

'You *promise* you won't keep coming in when everyone's dancing?' Madeleine checked for the umpteenth time. 'Any teenage parties I've been to never have parents in for dancing.'

'I've already told you that I won't interfere,' Elisha sighed, checking the pile of lace-edged napkins. 'Ella or Mrs Scully and I, will be here to greet your guests, and take their coats and things. Then, we'll disappear until it's time to serve the food – *exactly* as we agreed when we discussed things last week.'

Madeleine smiled again and looked at the time on the ornate clock on top of the white marble mantelpiece. 'They should be arriving any time in the next half an hour.' She hesitated for a moment. 'Do you think I look nice? Is my hair and my dress all right?'

No – damn you! Your hair and dress don't look all right, Elisha wanted to scream. Instead, she gripped the edge of the table tightly. After a moment, she slowly turned round to face her daughter. 'Your hair is lovely,' she lied. 'The hairdresser made an excellent job of straightening it all.'

'And the dress?' Madeleine looked down at herself and then fluffed out the stiff skirt again.

'Lovely,' Elisha said in a faint voice. 'Just the thing for a modern girl's party.'

Satisfied, Madeleine skipped across the room like a giddy six-year-old to her new record player. She started checking all her records again, carefully taking them out of the sleeve, and reading the names on each one aloud to herself.

'I'm just going upstairs for a moment,' Elisha said in a tight voice, 'to check on the spare bedroom for your friend.' And then, exerting considerable control not to rush from the room, never mind the whole house, she walked out at her usual dignified pace.

Back upstairs in the refuge of the spare bedroom, Elisha Fitzgerald sat down on the edge of the ornate brass bed. What – she thought to herself – was to be done with Madeleine? The party had been a focal point for months now, something to keep her mind distracted from all the nonsense which seemed to obsess her and make her do the first thing that came into her head. Her hair, for instance – her beautiful, white-blonde crowning glory – sheared off on a whim just the other night.

The Mother Superior of the boarding-school had been in a dreadful state when she phoned to say what had happened. Apparently, while the other girls were at supper, Madeleine had gone into the sick bay looking for an aspirin. Finding no one there, she had lifted the small scissors used for cutting bandages and had attacked her own hair. The strangest part of all, the Mother Superior said in a whisper, was that she had left the six inches of golden tresses that she had cut, spread out perfectly in a circle on the sick-bay floor. Just like the rays of the sun. The poor Matron had a terrible fright when she found Madeleine sitting cross-legged in the middle of the arrangement talking to herself.

The Mother Superior had suggested yet another little 'rest' from school might do Madeleine good. If that didn't work – perhaps the Fitzgeralds might consider removing their daughter *permanently* from the school at Christmas.

Her lengthy absences meant that she had little or no chance of passing her exams in any case, and perhaps the pressure of studying might not be the right thing for someone with such a delicate nature.

What was to be done with Madeleine if she left school? Elisha wondered. Gabriel was the only person who seemed to get through to her, who was able to distract her from her moods. But he was no longer available, as he spent most of his term-time in Dublin. There was always the possibility of a position in William's auctioneering business, if only Madeleine's temperament was stable enough.

Although she was desperate for something to occupy her daughter, Elisha knew that having Madeleine working in the public eye would not do William's business any good, if her behaviour was not dependable. Elisha looked across the room to where she could see her reflection in the mahogany wardrobe mirror. Her fair-coloured hair, now greying at the sides, was swept up in its usual neat chignon, and her pink twinset and pearls blended perfectly with her softly flared check skirt. Her gaze drifted upwards to her face, and there – in the hollow cheeks and the dark shadows under her eyes – she could see the strain of the life she had endured in recent years. First, her old life in Blackrock, shattered by William's foolish and spendthrift ways, and now – when he seemed to have things back on an even keel – this dreadful business with Madeleine. All the dreams Elisha had of going shopping in Dublin with her beautiful, blonde elegant daughter! Lunching out – sharing confidences about clothes and men – perhaps the odd weekend over in London – all in tatters. Just like Madeleine's hair.

The glorious white-blonde hair that was now cut above her ears in a severe bob, the best that the most expensive hairdresser in Dublin could do, with the ruined mess she had been presented with. The new style did nothing for Madeleine's bloated face and body. And these recent demands about getting her own way, not caring who was listening when she ranted and raved. And now this ridiculous obsession about the Ballygrace girl, Tara Flynn.

Where would it all end? And what of the future? What lay ahead for Madeleine? The doctors, whilst consoling, had guaranteed nothing. Take the medicine and hope for the best. If this was the best – what was to come?

Abruptly, Elisha got to her feet. She smoothed down her skirt, and then she smoothed down the green satin quilt on the brass bed. If only, she thought, she could smooth the other areas of her life so easily.

She glanced in the mirror, straightened her pearls, took a deep breath and went downstairs to face the evening ahead.

Tara set off on her bike for the party, after Mick had checked the front and back lights for the third time. Her granda had been insistent on it, although she had told him everything was all right and that it was only a mile to Ballygrace House. Even if the bike got a puncture, she assured him that it was a mild night, and would take her less than half an hour to walk there. The two men had seen her out to the cottage gate, Mick still in his floury work-clothes from the bakery, and her granda in a dark cardigan over his waistcoat to keep out the November chill.

'Why don't you get the Daingean hackney car?' Noel said, as though he were used to calling hackney cars every week of his life. They had, in fact, only used it once before, when he and Mick were late in finding out about a funeral. 'It would only take Mick a short while to go out to Daingean on the ass and cart . . . and I'll pay for it meself.'

'You'll do no such thing!' Tara said, giving him a hug. 'I've everything I need strapped on to the bike now. I'd be there *walking* it, before Mick even got to Daingean on the ass and cart. Now, go back inside, before you catch your death from pneumonia!'

Noel cleared his throat. 'Please yersel' . . . but the offer of the car is there.' Then, as she hitched her dress and coat up well away from the oily chain, and mounted the bike, he called: 'Enjoy yersel'! Ye can tell us all about it in the morning when ye come home – and remember, Tara Flynn – you're as good, if not better, than any that will be there.'

As she rode along the dark winding lane to Ballygrace House – lit only by the glow from her bicycle lamp – Tara went over everything she had packed for her night away. In the weekend case strapped on the carrier at the back of the bike, was a blue-striped wynceyette night-dress and matching dressing-gown, and some new underwear. She had bought those along with the case the previous week in Tullamore.

Her purchases had accounted for another few pounds of her precious savings disappearing, but it was money well spent. For travelling back in the morning she had chosen a heavy brown skirt with a beige-flecked cardigan, and a brown velvet bow to tie her hair back. She also had a flowered sponge bag with her toothbrush, toothpaste and a small bar of lavender soap.

Madeleine's present and card, and Tara's satin shoes were in the basket on the front of the bike. She would step out of the sensible leather loafers she had on for cycling, and slip on the satin shoes when she arrived at Ballygrace House.

When she turned in the gateway, Tara walked the bicycle quickly on up the drive, willing herself to feel confident as she drew nearer to the brightly lit house. *What can they do to you*? she asked herself. Hadn't she received an invitation to the party, the same as all the other guests? She wasn't a gate-crasher. She had been *invited* to the party and *invited* to stay overnight at the house. She was dressed suitably for the occasion, and she had a perfectly acceptable present. All in all, she was as good as any of the others, and, remembering her granda's words – looks-wise, she was probably better than most.

With those inspiring thoughts uppermost in her mind, Tara pressed on, allowing herself no time for second thoughts. As she had planned in advance, she pushed the bike round the near side of the house, where she could conceal it behind a thick bush. Then, very quickly and quietly, she changed into her satin party shoes and took off her camel coat. She took a small hairbrush from her coat pocket and drew it through her long curly hair several times.

Tara untied the case on the back carrier of her bicycle now and put her hand in a little pocket in the front for a sheet of folded brown paper. Deftly, she wrapped her leather loafers in the paper, and then slipped them into the side of the case. The paper would ensure that no gravel from the bottom of the shoes would mark her clothes.

Then, with her coat and the birthday present in one hand, and her overnight case in the other, Tara walked round to the front of the house and mounted the front steps of Ballygrace House.

As the doorbell sounded once again, Elisha Fitzgerald moved down the hallway towards it. 'If you show the other two girls into the sitting-room,' she called back to Madeleine, 'I'll attend to the next arrival.' She checked her watch just as she reached the door and wondered again, where on earth William and Gabriel had got to. They had arranged to take some people from England to look at land out in Kildare earlier in the afternoon. It was now quarter to eight, and there was still no sign of them. Elisha sighed to herself. She should have known better than to depend on William, especially where Madeleine was concerned. Like an ostrich, he preferred to bury his head in the sand.

Elisha had met most of the invited twenty-odd guests, and knew their parents from church or from charity events in the Midlands area. The majority were girls from Madeleine's boarding school, although the two who had just been dropped off in a hackney car from Tullamore were daughters of a business acquaintance of William's, whom no one knew very well.

He had invited them on an impulse – during a particularly satisfactory business lunch a number of weeks ago – and had received the sharp end of his wife's tongue for doing so. There was no room for impulsiveness with regard to Madeleine at the moment, she told him, and whilst the girls at school would make allowances for her unpredictable behaviour – strangers might not be so kind. Bearing that in mind, only ten boys had been invited to the party, and they were sons of family friends or schoolmates of Gabriel's.

Whatever picture Elisha had painted in her mind of Tara Flynn, the elegant young woman with the flowing Titian hair was most certainly not that. For a moment Elisha was caught off her guard, her brow in a deep frown, as she struggled to remember which of Madeleine's schoolfriends could possible fit this striking description.

Not one came to mind.

'Good evening, Mrs Fitzgerald,' Tara said confidently, deliberately relieving her hostess of her embarrassment. 'I'm Tara Flynn.'

'Of course . . .' Elisha said, momentarily flustered. She took the girl's outstretched hand. 'Do come in . . . you're very welcome.' And as Elisha Fitzgerald looked from Tara's well-cut, impeccable outfit up into the piercing green eyes, she instinctively thought to herself: *You were wrong, Elisha. Whatever else you have been right about in your life – you were wrong in your judgement about this girl.*

Tara lifted her case and followed Madeleine's mother into the hallway.

'I think,' Elisha said, 'that it might be best if we sort out your bags.' She turned and gave Tara a little smile. 'You're staying in the guest bedroom upstairs, so I'll show you up now, then you can come downstairs and meet the others.'

'Thank you,' Tara replied. 'That's very good of you.'

Then, loud music suddenly blared from the dining-room downstairs, drowning out further conversation. By the time they reached the bedroom at the top of the winding staircase, someone – presumably Madeleine – had turned it down low enough to allow Elisha to explain how to use the bedside lamp and where the bathroom was.

Tara returned her look, appearing more confident than she felt. 'I'm sure everything is fine,' she said, giving a smile. 'The room is really lovely . . . thank you for having me to stay.'

It would have been too hypocritical for Elisha Fitzgerald to say, 'not at all' or 'you're very welcome' – so instead she said: 'I'll leave you for a few moments to let you get sorted out. I'm sure you'll find your way back downstairs to the dining-room.' As she backed out of the bedroom, she added: 'I'm afraid it's simply a case of following the music.'

'Thank you,' Tara repeated. 'I'll be down in a few minutes.'

When the door closed behind Elisha Fitzgerald, Tara gave a huge sigh of relief and said 'Thank God' to herself. She put her case on the bed – pausing to stroke the satin embroidered quilt – and hung her coat on a hanger on the back of the door. Then slowly, her hands folded behind her back, she turned and viewed the room that she would sleep in that night.

A feeling of both nervousness and exhilaration ran through her, as she realised that she had indeed been accepted as a family guest. Madeleine's mother – although very proper and uppity – had been nice to her. *She had really been nice!* Mrs Fitzgerald had brought her upstairs, and spoken to her in the polite way she would speak to any visitor. Tara knew it was early in the evening, but it was a start – and a very good start.

She looked now, a relieved smile on her face, at the green velvet curtains with the matching, tasselled pelmet and the creamy-painted windowsills. She studied the dark, polished wooden floor and the floral rug with the long green fringe, which was exactly the same shade of green in the curtains and on the bed. Her gaze wandered to the satin bolster and pillows, and then she gratefully recalled an article in one of her ladies' magazines, which said to remove the top pillow at night, and sleep on the bottom plainer one. The top pillow – according to the article – was for 'decorative purposes only'.

Tara gave a wry little smile, as she remembered not so long ago, when she had slept on bleached flour bags for pillows and sheets before she had persuaded her granda and Mick to part with a few shillings every week, to a traveller from Dublin who came in his van selling proper sheets, blankets and quilts. They still had the old rough blankets though, and even her own bedroom – which was the best in the cottage – was still a million miles away from anything in this room.

Tara moved over to the walnut dressing table, sat down on the velvet chair with the carved legs and looked at herself in the mirror. Her eyes were gleaming – gleaming with delight and achievement – and a feeling which ran much deeper. A feeling which told her that she was quite comfortable in this magnificent house.

Then, hearing another car coming up the drive, Tara quickly checked her appearance again, making sure that her underskirt was not showing under the burgundy dress. She ran her fingers through her long hair, then took her satin clutch bag from the case, and pulled out a powder compact. Checking carefully in the little mirror in the lid, she patted powder on her cheeks and nose, and then she applied a light coat of lipstick. After giving one last glance at her whole reflection, Tara took a deep breath and opened the bedroom door.

She was halfway down the staircase, when she heard a car door banging and then voices coming towards the house. One voice in particular halted her in her tracks.

Tara stood, framed against the marble staircase, when Gabriel Fitzgerald opened the front door of Ballygrace House. There was a stunned silence, during which both pairs of eyes locked together. Whatever had attracted and impressed him about Tara that day in Dublin, he could feel even stronger now.

Then the front door opened behind Gabriel, and an older man dressed in a navy cashmere overcoat and pale blue silk scarf came rushing in. He – just as Gabriel had done – halted and stood transfixed as Tara continued her graceful descent of the stairs. Naked admiration, which came from long experience in assessing women, shone in William Fitzgerald's eyes. He caught his breath as the fine wool dress moved easily with her, outlining the curve of her thighs and her shapely long legs. The shining band of satin and the innocent little bow then drew his eyes upwards to her heavy voluptuous breasts.

Just in time, William Fitzgerald stopped himself from gasping aloud. Instead, he lifted a silk hanky to his mouth and gave a genteel little cough.

'Father,' Gabriel said in a croaky voice, 'this is Tara Flynn . . . Madeleine's friend.'

'My dear,' William Fitzgerald came gushingly forward, 'you're most welcome.' He reached a hand out to guide her down the last few steps. Her slim hand slipped perfectly into his larger smooth hand and the slight nervous tremor was not lost to him.

'Thank you,' Tara replied, hoping that she did not betray how uncomfortable she felt, with father and son still staring at her. As she descended the final step, Madeleine came down the hallway towards them.

'Tara! You came!' She hurtled down the hallway like an excited young colt and almost threw herself on her friend. 'Mother said she showed you to your bedroom – do you like it?'

'It's grand – it's really lovely,' Tara replied. For a moment she struggled for words – shocked at the drastic change in her friend's appearance. It had been some time since she had last seen her, but it seemed impossible that someone could change to the extent that Madeleine had. The most striking difference was the loss of her beautiful long blonde hair – and the substantial weight gain. The dress she was wearing made her arms look like two pink sausages, and her eyes seemed to have sunk into the doughy pale mound of flesh which covered her delicate nose and finely sculpted cheekbones.

'Come into the dining-room,' Madeleine said excitedly. 'Some of my friends have already arrived, and I want to introduce you to them.'

Tara's hand suddenly flew to her mouth. 'Your present,' she said. 'I've left it up in the bedroom!'

'That's not like you!' Madeleine laughed and turned to her father. 'This is the most intelligent and organised girl I have ever met. When I was at school in Ballygrace, she used to help me with my maths and English. She works in the accounts department in the distillery in Tullamore *and* she attends evening classes too – don't you, Tara?'

Tara's face and neck flushed. 'You make it sound much more grand than it is, Madeleine.' She turned back towards the stairs, glad of the chance to extricate herself from the tense atmosphere. 'I'll just go and get your present . . . I won't be a minute.'

When Tara returned, she was introduced to the two other guests, sisters called Sarah and Fiona from Tullamore, then she handed over the birthday gift.

Madeleine was thrilled with the cameo brooch and the lovely card which Tara had picked for her. 'Look, Mother,' she said, holding the little box out, 'it matches the earrings that Gabriel bought me – isn't that a coincidence?'

There was silence for a moment, while Elisha pondered the situation. 'Yes,' she finally said, 'that certainly is a coincidence.'

There was silence for a moment, while Elisha pondered the situation. 'Yes,' she finally said, 'that certainly is a coincidence.'

Gabriel decided to own up. 'It's not really . . . I actually bumped into Tara in Dublin. She'd just bought the brooch, and I thought it would be a good idea to buy you the matching earrings.' He laughed and ran his hand through his blond hair. 'You should have known I couldn't have picked something as nice as that on my own.'

'Thank you, Tara,' Madeleine said sweetly. 'If you hadn't met him, I would have probably ended up with a riding helmet or another pony book!' She held out her arm. 'Do you like my watch? Mother and Father bought it for me.'

Tara moved closer to admire the gold watch with the ruby and diamond face. 'It's beautiful, Madeleine,' she said, 'absolutely beautiful.'

The phone rang in the large hallway and Elisha rushed out towards it. She held the receiver to her ear for a few moments then said: 'Yes, I perfectly understand. Thank you for ringing.' She turned, then walked back down into the kitchen where William was pouring himself a glass of red wine.

'That's another guest offering their apologies,' she said tersely.

'That's nearly half the number of guests who were invited.' She looked at her own wristwatch. 'It's eight o'clock, and only three have arrived so far.'

William took a mouthful of his wine. 'It's early enough yet.' Elisha did not look convinced. 'Why were *you* so late? You promised you'd get back in plenty of time.'

'Business,' William replied, 'just business. Anyway, I'm here now, am I not?'

'You *are* here for the evening,' Elisha checked, 'aren't you? Even Mrs Scully is late. She was supposed to have worked right through until tonight, but apparently her daughter is due a baby at any time, and she had to go home for a few hours. She said she would be back as soon as possible.' She looked at her husband pleadingly. 'I need you here tonight – I couldn't cope on my own.'

William fingered his dark moustache. 'Is there a particular problem?'

'A *particular* problem? How can you ask such a stupid question?' she snapped. 'You only have to look at and listen to Madeleine, to know that there's a problem.' She pressed the back of her hand to her forehead. 'I'm absolutely dreading tonight.'

'If it doesn't turn out too well, we can always take her out for a meal in Dublin to make up for it,' William suggested.

Elisha looked at her husband with contempt. 'That's your answer to everything, isn't it? Just throw money at any problem and that will solve it.'

The doorbell sounded again and then, almost simultaneously, the back door in the kitchen opened and Mrs Scully came bustling through. 'She'll last another night, I'd say,' she said referring to her pregnant daughter, 'so I came back as quick as I could.'

William drained his glass then moved towards the hallway. 'You sit down and relax for a few minutes,' he said to his wife. 'I'll get the door.' Elisha turned to Mrs Scully. 'I'm glad you could make it back in time for the party starting. Ella has been here all afternoon and she'll be here as long as you need her tonight. She's in the dining-room just now, checking the napkins and cutlery.' Ella was Mrs Scully's help, a young girl who Rosie regularly described as 'neither use nor ornament'. The housekeeper kept the inoffensive maid's nose to the grindstone, with the more menial jobs such as emptying ashes from the fire and carrying in the turf.

By nine o'clock, only eight guests had arrived. Less than half the number expected. The three boys and five girls chatted in little groups and listened to the record player, while Madeleine went back and forth, checking on the phone calls of apology that had come consistently all night. According to the messages, a significant number of guests had gone down with a mysterious illness. To Elisha's relief, Madeleine seemed to accept all the excuses, and was now back in the party room, chatting animatedly to her guests.

The two girls from Tullamore who had arrived first, Sarah and Fiona, were very shy. They were only fifteen and sixteen, and were obviously younger and less sophisticated than the others. For the first half-an-hour Tara sat beside them, chatting about music and the latest fashions. Whilst doing so, she kept her eye out for Gabriel, who was – on his mother's instructions – moving around the room chatting to the guests in turn. Tara contented herself to wait, knowing that he would eventually reach her.

Sarah and Fiona admired Tara's outfit and had said how they wished they were allowed to choose their own clothes. They asked her all about the shop in Dublin that she had bought the costume from, and she described the big stores she had shopped in. The other three girls had been polite but reserved, standing in a corner whispering among themselves. The boys were little better – giving furtive glances at the girls and telling each other mildly suggestive jokes.

Madeleine floated between the guests, asking their preference in records and showing them the gifts she had received, seemingly unperturbed by the large number of guests who had not turned up. Tara wasn't too sure how many people were actually invited to the party, but judging by the tables of food and drink, she reckoned that Madeleine had been badly let down.

Madeleine's father had come in to chat for a while and then he had gone round handing glasses of wine to all the guests. The two younger girls Tara had been chatting to had refused, saying that their parents had warned them not to dare touch alcoholic drinks. William had smiled understandingly and brought them glasses of lemonade instead.

Tara accepted the beautiful crystal glass from him – and told herself off for having a vivid imagination when she thought that his fingers had stroked hers when he gave her the glass. She sipped the white wine slowly, acquainting herself with the cool dry taste. She had tasted beer and sherry at Christmas and when she had a cold, her granda had bought a small bottle of whiskey and made her a hot toddy – but wine was a new thing altogether. With every sip it seemed nicer, and holding the crystal glass by its long graceful stem, she felt quite at ease with herself and her surroundings. After accepting a second glass of wine from Gabriel and having a short chat with him, she hardly noticed when Mrs Scully and Elisha came through to serve the buffet.

The food – though beautifully presented and plentiful – was not as ostentatious as Tara's father had described. Tara positioned herself at the end of the table where Mrs Fitzgerald was serving, keeping her distance from her old adversary. She picked up a cream china plate edged with gold, and silver cutlery wrapped in a pink damask napkin, then waited while Sarah and Fiona picked what they fancied from the array of food.

Tara gave a casual glance to the bottom of the table, where the other guests were being served by Mrs Scully. She could hear the housekeeper patiently explaining about the sauce the chicken breasts were in, to one of the boys. Her manner was completely different to how Tara remembered and could only be described as grovelling. Tara presumed that the boys were from the 'better-class' families and therefore deemed worthy of civility.

When it came to Tara's turn to be served, Mrs Fitzgerald gave her a pleasant smile. 'Please help yourself to any of the dishes that you fancy, dear. If you're not sure about anything, just ask.'

Tara thanked her and looked along the length of the table at the plates of cold ham, chicken, pork, sausage rolls, vol-au-vents, sausages on sticks, potato salads and several other dishes she had never seen before. Very deliberately, she then set about choosing the dishes she had never tried plus a few familiar selections in case she had problems with the more unusual ones.

As Tara moved away from the table with her modest plate of food, she was acutely aware of Mrs Scully who was standing only feet away.

Her first instinct was to quickly turn away and walk to the far corner of the room but she steeled herself, and moved directly in front of the housekeeper.

'Can I get you anythin', Miss?' the old housekeeper said in a brusque tone as Tara passed.

At the sound of her voice, Tara froze like a moth trapped in candlelight, then, very slowly, she turned to face the old woman. For a moment their eyes locked, then Tara's gaze moved to scan the food in front of Mrs Scully. 'I think,' she said, looking down at the barely touched platters of food, 'that I have all I want, thank you.' Then, her eyes moved slowly and deliberately back up to look into the old woman's face.

'You're the . . .' Mrs Scully faltered, her face taking on the appearance of a lightly boiled beetroot, 'you're the young Flynn one, aren't you? Noel Flynn's grand-daughter?'

Tara held her gaze fast, instinctively knowing that she would cross the path of many Mrs Scullys – the sort who would hate her for daring to step out of her class.

'You're right – I'm indeed Tara Flynn,' she replied with a bright smile.

Mrs Scully's eyes narrowed. 'You're so well got up in yer fine clothes, that I'd have hardly known ye . . .'

Tara raised an indifferent eyebrow. Then, she leant across the table, and said in a low, icy voice: 'But you *don't* know me, Mrs Scully. You might know my name and my family connections – but you don't know anything about *me* at all.'

The housekeeper's eyes opened wide in shock and her heavy body started shaking with rage. What was it about this flame-haired, tall girl that got her goat up so much? Then, as the housekeeper opened her mouth to retaliate – to to say something which would expose this Flynn one for the lowly brat she undoubtedly was – Elisha Fitzgerald moved down the table beside them.

'Are you all right, Mrs Scully?' she asked, her brow furrowed in concern. She looked from the housekeeper to the young woman standing in front of her. 'Has Tara everything she wants from the buffet? We must make sure that Madeleine's friends have everything they want tonight.'

Tara smiled. 'I have everything I want, thank you, Mrs Fitzgerald.' She made to move away, then, on second thoughts, she turned back. 'Mrs Scully was just informing me that she knows my grandfather, weren't you, Mrs Scully?'

'Yes,' the old woman snapped, looking fit to burst a blood vessel. 'Indeed I do! And not only yer grandfather – but but every breed and bit of ye!' She took a deep breath, as though building herself up to scatter all the skeletons out of the Flynn family cupboard.

'Well,' Elisha said, 'that's very nice, isn't it? Now, Tara,' she said, guiding the young girl away from the table, 'let me get you a glass of wine to accompany your meal.'

'Thank you,' Tara replied, 'but I already have one which I've hardly touched. I'm not too used to wine and I don't want it going to my head.'

'Very sensible, but make sure you enjoy yourself. Madeleine is so pleased you have come.'

After checking on the other guests, who seemed to have little to say for themselves – and Madeleine, who was saying rather too much – Elisha made her retreat to the drawing-room. There, she found herself wishing that the house had been full of girls like Tara Flynn, instead of the handful which had actually come. How could she have been so naive as to think that word of Madeleine's 'problem' had not got round to all the families in the area? How could she have imagined that her behaviour at school and in church had not given the gossips plenty of tittle-tattle about the Fitzgeralds?

She sank into a leather armchair by the side of the fire, and lowered her head into her hands. How much more of this could she take? Surely all the years of anxiety and shame over William's gambling and womanising had been enough? The move to Offaly had been her decision and her decision alone. But it had still taken its toll. William may have been embarrassed about their move to 'The Boghole of Ireland' – one of his many derogatory descriptions of the Midlands. He resented his loss of authority and financial control – but what of her feelings? Elisha had had to leave a beautiful home behind in a refined area, with several staff at her beck and call. All a far cry from Mrs Scully and Ella.

She had to make lame excuses to friends and neighbours about having relatives near Tullamore who had offered William a wonderful business opportunity which they could not resist. Lies – all lies. And it was she who had had to come up with each and every lie, because William – like his business and gambling deals – had simply crumbled under the pressure.

And Elisha had carried everything through, until the lies had become the truth. Until William had redeemed himself and now had a more prosperous business than the one in Dublin. He had lately been offered the chance to open another auctioneer's office in Naas, making the prospect of a return to Dublin a possibility in the future.

Gabriel had succeeded well at school and was now coping with university and even Elisha's own health had improved. Her difficulty in sleeping and her general anxiety had improved greatly after the first couple of years in Ballygrace. She had now actually grown to love the peace and beauty of the countryside. So much so, the idea of moving back to Dublin held no great interest at present.

Since their move to Offaly, a huge mountain had indeed been climbed. Now – with the summit in clear view – was the immense effort going to be for nothing? Were they going to slide back down to the bottom again – on the back of Madeleine this time?

A knock came to the drawing-room door. Elisha quickly got to her feet and smoothed her hair and her skirt down.

After being bid to do so Mrs Scully came into the drawing-room. 'They're all fed and watered, as far as I can see,' she said to her employer in a flat tone. 'There's a terrible lot of stuff left – it's a crime when ye think of all them starvin' children in the world. Do you want me to start coverin' it or putting it away in the pantry?'

Elisha shrugged. 'I'd give it a while longer – they might eat more later. If not, you're welcome to take what you can carry home with you.'

Mrs Scully kept a solemn demeanour, even though she had just been offered what would feed her, and her extended family, for several days. She wasn't happy with being snubbed in front of the young Flynn one earlier on, and she was going to make Elisha pay for it one way or the other. The food was no compensation for being belittled. It was a perk of the job she was well used to. She had in fact earmarked a good-sized piece of bacon earlier in the evening to bring home with her. 'I'll see what's left,' she sniffed, 'and if it's the kind of thing they fancy, then I might take a few bits home with me.'

'Have something to eat yourself and take a glass of sherry or wine, or whatever you prefer,' Elisha said. 'And go and put your feet up in the kitchen. We can have a break for an hour or so before going back to the party.'

'Whatever ye like,' Mrs Scully said, refusing to be softened. She turned on her heel and stomped out of the room. '*Party – me arse!*' she said under her breath. '*I've had more feckin' laughs at a wake!*'

As she poured herself a large glass of sherry to ease her agitation, the housekeeper – in a rare flash of insight – suddenly realised why she hated Tara Flynn so much. She reminded her of her own sister, Cecelia. Her sister who was in America this thirty-five years. Cecelia had been a pretty nineteen-year-old, with an uppish attitude and big ideas, when Rosie, at twenty, was made junior housekeeper in one of the big houses in Tullamore.

Rosie had been delighted with herself, because she could rise at six o'clock, wash and dress, and be at the big house for half-past six. She was paid reasonably well, and it would let her save towards her wedding day to Jimmy Scully.

'How can you *bear* to be a servant to those people?' Rosie could still hear her sister say. 'And are you sure you want to be married to someone like Jimmy Scully? He's a nice enough lad, but you won't go very far with him. You should emigrate to England or America and make a decent life for yourself, instead of skivvying for other people! You're clever enough and should make more of yourself.'

Rosie had seethed, and hoped and prayed for her younger sister's downfall – but it seemed a long time in coming. Cecelia had got herself a job in one of the best draper's shops in town, where she didn't have to start until half-past nine in the morning. She got a discount on all the nice clothes, and stepped out for work every morning wearing her gloves and hat, as though she were going to a wedding. Her well-groomed hair was long and curling, while Rosie's thin mousy hair had to be kept short and neat for work.

It was worse when, a year later, their mother insisted that Cecelia was her bridesmaid at the small unglamorous wedding.

'You should have landed yourself a big farmer like me, Rosie,'

Cecelia had whispered, as they lay squashed together in the three-quarter size bed, the night before the wedding. Then she told Rosie all about the son of a big Protestant farmer from Carlow who was working in town, who had an eye for her. 'Of course I won't let him lay a hand on me unless he asks me to marry him. I want somebody to take me out of all this. I want a life where I don't have to lift a hand . . . I want somebody else to do all the dirty jobs.'

'And what about yer soul?' Rosie had snarled back. 'You'll be damned to hell if you marry a Protestant!'

'It'll be time enough to think about hell when I'm dead!' Cecelia said with a tinkling laugh. 'But if I marry a big farmer with plenty of money, then at least it won't be a hell on earth.'

Jimmy Scully would never have dreamt of laying a hand on Rosie before they were married. She would have marched him straight up to the priest if he had even suggested it. She was a decent, God-fearing Catholic girl, and she knew where allowing lads to put their hands on you led to. You only had to listen to the priest giving out from the pulpit on a Sunday, about the temptations of young people who danced too close together. In any case, sex was only something that women put up with – the side of marriage that you gritted your teeth and got on with.

Six months later, Rosie found out that Cecelia had no such scruples about the Carlow farmer 'laying his hands' on her. It was touch and go when she confronted him about the baby. His family put up all sorts of arguments and threatened all sorts of things. But in the end, he agreed to marry her in the registry office in Dublin, before they set off for a new life in America.

It didn't seem like thirty-five years ago when her parents had ranted and raved and cried. Thirty-five years ago since Cecelia had made a mockery of the family and still went her own selfish, uppity way. All that distance to America, and leaving everyone else behind to face the gossip and the jeering. And if Rosie met Cecelia tomorrow, she would hate her with the same venom she had felt all those years ago.

She would hate her, because Cecelia had been right.

After a short spell in New York City, they moved further up the state. They moved into the country, where they ended up owning a farm ten times the size of the one in Carlow. Cecelia had never dirtied her hands. She had maids like Rosie to do everything – even change the nappies of her two sons and two daughters. At one point, she had the cheek to write and say she would pay Rosie's fare, to come out and visit her in America. The letter – and the other letters which followed – had gone straight in the fire unanswered. As far as Rosie and the rest of the family under her influence were concerned Cecelia was dead and gone.

Rosie had gone to Mass every Sunday, and occasional weekdays, praying piously for Cecelia's soul. It was an absolute certainty that it was damned forever. And over the thirty-five years, as she worked hard cleaning her own house and other people's houses, Rosie wondered if Cecelia might have been right. Secretly, she often wondered how different her own life might have been, if she had set her sights just that *little* bit higher than Jimmy Scully.

It was all water under the bridge now, because Jimmy was dead – and Cecelia was as good as dead.

Rosie screwed up her eyes, and threw back the glass of sherry.

Gabriel knocked on the drawing-room door. 'Madeleine's fine,' he reassured his mother with a bright smile. 'She's the best I've seen for ages. There's dancing going on now, so it's not too bad . . . I'll get back in, because there's only four boys between six girls.'

'Thank you, Gabriel,' Elisha said quietly. 'I'm keeping out of the way. I know Madeleine doesn't want me checking up on things.' She hesitated. 'You will let me know if there's any problems . . . if she changes moods.'

Gabriel nodded. 'She's spent most of the time dancing with Tara . . . she's a nice girl and very good with Madeleine. She seems to know how to handle her better than the others.'

'I noticed that myself. She's a very beautiful-looking girl, too – isn't she?'

Gabriel raised his eyebrows. 'She is indeed.'

A few minutes later, William appeared in the drawing-room with two glasses of champagne and two smaller glasses of whiskey on a tray. He set the tray down on a side table, and then he handed one of the champagne glasses to his wife and lifted the other for himself. 'Here's to the future,' he said, lightly touching her glass with his own. 'I've a feeling things are going to get better.'

Elisha sipped her champagne and said nothing.

By half past ten, all still seemed well. Fortified by several stiff drinks Elisha found that she was fairly relaxed. Even if the guests decided to leave now, it was a reasonable time to end a party, she consoled herself. Given the situation, the evening had not turned out too badly. She and William had actually sat together listening to the radio, and apart from Mrs Scully coming in with more turf for the fire, and later bringing in a plate of party food for William, they had not been disturbed by any problems from the social gathering.

Elisha was so relieved that she told Mrs Scully that if she cleared and covered the remaining food, that she could cycle home now, rather than wait until all the guests had gone.

At the back door, she gave the housekeeper her extra wages for the evening's work, saying: 'You needn't rush back too early in the morning, as we'll have a later breakfast. We'll go to one of the later Masses in Tullamore, so if you're here for around half past nine, that would be fine.'

'I'll do me best, for I'll have to be up for first Mass meself in the mornin', if I've to cycle back here,' Mrs Scully said with a tight mouth. Then, after tying her headscarf tightly on her head she added: 'I'll bid you all a goodnight, ma'am . . . and I hope the young ones enjoy the rest of their party.'

As she cycled back into Tullamore on her loaded bicycle, Mrs Scully cursed a vengeance on Tara Flynn for showing her up in front of her employer that evening. The young cur – the cheeky, impudent whelp – the uppity little bitch! Her mind conjured up words too bad to even voice in her head. And the way the impudent little brat had wafted down the table, as thought she was used to fancy dinners all her life – instead of the bacon and cabbage and spuds she was reared on.

Mrs Scully's eyes took on a hard furious glint as she pedalled along, remembering how Tara had dared to look and speak to Mrs Fitzgerald, as though they were equals! Instead of keeping quiet about her poor, motherless background – the foxy-haired bitch had flaunted it.

Curse a hell on Tara Flynn! Rosie Scully hissed into the dark night sky – *and curse a hell on all belonging to her!* Then, the worst of her thoughts rattling through the midnight air, the old woman consoled herself that she had not only taken as much food as her bike could safely carry – but a bottle of sherry too! And if she got the chance in the morning, she would slip off with as much again.

Oh, it would take more than a few extra shillings, and a few bags of fancy food, to make up for the blow she had been dealt by Elisha Fitzgerald and that fecking little hoor! A few glasses of sherry would help to douse the worst of it tonight – but make no mistake – that young brat would pay for what she had done this night.

Be it long – or be it short – Tara Flynn would rue the day she crossed Rosie Scully!

Elisha looked into the glowing fire and thought to herself how strange it was that this particular cloud had a silver lining. How strange that on a night when she had been so tense and worried about Madeleine, that she should now feel relaxed sitting in front of the fire, listening to music with William. It had started off as merely a diversion, something to take her mind off what might happen in the room across the corridor, but had turned into something different.

William looked relaxed himself, sitting with his glass of whiskey in one hand, and the other hand thrown carelessly across the back of the sofa, tapping his fingers in time to the classical music. It was a very long time since Elisha had seen him look like that – looking as though he was enjoying being in her company. But more importantly, he had actually listened to all the worries she had poured out about Madeleine.

'If you like,' William suddenly said, sitting up in his chair, 'I could ring the specialist myself on Monday. I'll ask his opinion on whether Madeleine should continue at school, or come and work for me in the auctioneer's office instead.'

Elisha's heart soared. 'Would you?' she said in a whisper. 'I would be really grateful.'

William swallowed the last mouthful from his glass. 'Yes,' he said decisively, 'I feel that some sort of action is required here. Perhaps studying is placing too much of a strain on her mind . . . a change of environment might do her good.' He leaned across to Elisha's chair, and patted the back of her hand. 'It may do you some good, too –

seeing her every evening and weekends at home, as opposed to worrying about what she's getting up to at school.'

Elisha wondered how she would feel having Madeleine around more often. Especially if her behaviour was so unpredictable. Before she had time to ponder it, the sitting-room door flew open.

'Mother!' Madeleine said rushing in. 'D'you mind if we come in here to use the piano? Vincent has been learning to play jazz – and if we can persuade Tara – she's wonderful on the piano, too!' She gave a childish giggle and flounced up the skirt of her dress. 'She might play us some nice hymns – did you know she often plays the organ at Mass in Ballygrace?'

Elisha smiled. 'Very nice. I've no objection to anyone playing the piano – have you, William?'

'None whatsoever,' William said, getting to his feet to turn off the radio. 'Bring them in and let's hear all this wonderful talent.'

'Great!' Madeleine dashed off along the hallway and a few moments later returned with her guests in tow.

'Come in,' Elisha said brightly, lifting the piano lid up. 'We're looking forward to hearing all this musical genius that Madeleine has been telling us about.'

Vincent Byrne played first. He played a few American jazz tunes very competently and then he played some traditional Irish airs. Everyone sang along to 'Danny Boy', 'The Meeting of the Waters' and several other well-known songs. When Vincent finished playing, Madeleine and Gabriel played a funny little duet that they had learned years ago, and everybody laughed and joined in the chorus.

When they had finished, Elisha looked to the back of the group and said: 'What about you, Tara? Madeleine tells us that you're very accomplished on the piano.'

Tara blushed and looked slightly flustered. 'The music I play is not very entertaining – it's not really party stuff.'

'If you don't know any other pieces, you could play us a nice hymn – one we all know the words to.' Madeleine reached her hand out to take her friend's. 'Try something – *please?*'

Tara looked back at her and then slowly nodded her head. All eyes were on her as she squeezed through the group of teenagers and went to sit behind the beautiful grand piano.

As she had passed her by, Elisha noticed that Tara had taken her suit jacket off. She looked now at the girl's simple, short-sleeved burgundy dress which complemented her slim figure and her hair so perfectly. She noticed her smooth blemish-free arms, and her long artistic fingers as they roamed along the keyboard preparing to play.

William Fitzgerald had moved away from the group, to a side table which held a variety of bottles and decanters. He poured himself another generous whisky, to help him to withstand the next hour or so until the party broke up. Although he was a communicator of great skill when it came to business matters, he tended to take a back seat in social occasions, especially when it involved his own family. He returned to stand at the fire, his elbow leaning on the lower part of the fireplace, where he could observe Tara Flynn from a good vantage point.

The picture of this strikingly attractive girl descending the staircase had flitted in and out of his mind all evening. He watched her closely now, her slender hands poised above the keyboard and her green eyes closed against distractions.

Neither he nor Elisha had any expectations and were both caught off guard when they recognised the first few bars of Beethoven's 'Moonlight Sonata', being played by a very talented and practised hand. They looked at each other with surprised, raised eyebrows.

William listened and watched intently as Tara's whole body moved in time to the perfect music. Her eyes, when they occasionally opened, looked only at the keys, and when she tilted her head slightly he could see a faraway look in them. His gaze was drawn to her arched back, and thrust-out breasts, as she played the more passionate parts of the sonata.

As he listened, images floated in his mind of Tara Flynn sitting on the piano stool quite naked. Then he fantasised that she was sitting astride him – both naked now – as he made love to her.

When the piece came to an end, there was utter silence followed by a rowdy applause – jolting William back to reality.

Much later – after all the other guests had gone home, and Madeleine, Gabriel and Tara were asleep in their respective bedrooms – Elisha Fitzgerald turned over in bed and said to her husband: 'I wish we could find a reason to have Tara Flynn stay here more often. I really feel that she has a calming effect on Madeleine, and I'm sure the party would have been a complete disaster if it hadn't been for her.'

William shifted onto his side, his back to his wife. 'If you feel the girl is a help to her, then we must make sure Madeleine spends more time in her company.' He gave a little cough. 'Did I hear someone say that she was good with figures – accounts and suchlike?'

'Yes,' Elisha replied, 'Gabriel mentioned it to me. Apparently she attends night classes, and has passed a number of exams already. Have you noticed how well-spoken she is? And her taste in clothes is impeccable. It's extraordinary to think she's from local people – she's such a striking girl.'

'I didn't really notice her until she played the piano,' William lied, 'but yes – I suppose she is rather striking.'

'Gabriel seems quite taken with her,' Elisha commented. She thought for a moment. 'I don't think he has his eye on her or anything . . . do you? It would cause more trouble than it's worth, if we were to encourage any interest in that direction.'

'No,' William replied, 'I don't think we need worry there. Gabriel spends most of his time in Dublin.' He paused for a moment. 'Perhaps if I were to offer Tara a position in the auctioneering office in Tullamore, she could work alongside Madeleine, showing her the ropes, and being a sort of companion at the same time. What do you think?'

'Oh, William!' Elisha raised herself up on her elbow and turned towards her husband in the darkness. She reached a hand out to touch his shoulder – and waited for a few seconds. There was no response. He kept his back to her.

'I think that's a marvellous idea,' she said quietly, trying not to show just how delighted she was. She had prayed and prayed for weeks – since the hair episode – for a solution to this problem. And the solution had come, in the shape of Tara Flynn.

Then, as she eased her head back down on to her pillow, William unexpectedly turned towards her. Without a word, he took her in his arms. Then – since they were in the same bed for the first time in ages – he made love to her.

And, for the first time in a long time, Elisha did not resist him.

She did not resist him for two reasons. One – because he had been unusually attentive to her earlier in the evening, and two – because he had now handed her the solution to a major problem.

William rolled back to his own side of the bed, feeling pleased with himself and guilty at the same time. When they had first got into bed, he had not considered that sexual intercourse might take place. Sexual relations had not existed between them for a very long time. Much longer than William cared to remember. He had hoped that when he had got his businesses on an even keel, that the physical side of their marriage – which had died when everything went wrong in Blackrock – might return. They had automatically gone into separate rooms when they moved to Ballygrace House. Even though things had certainly improved, Elisha had never once suggested that they share a bedroom again.

How tonight had happened was beyond him. He had presumed they would go into their own rooms when they came upstairs around half past one, with William carrying a tray with a final hot whiskey for both of them. Elisha had opened her bedroom door, and gestured to him to go on in with the tray, and then somehow, he had never got round to leaving the room.

In bed, his thoughts had returned to Tara Flynn, as had Elisha's thoughts – although on an entirely different vein. They had the redheaded girl to thank for their conjugal bliss tonight. It was the thoughts of her that had coursed the blood through William's body as he made love to his wife.

Elisha had never been interested in the physical side of marriage, and because of that, he had been left with no option but to seek physical comfort elsewhere. Of course, when the disaster had struck with his business finances and his foolishness over gambling, Elisha had suddenly hit him with knowledge of the various women he had kept company with.

She had crucified him with that.

And yet, when things had improved, she had made no move to rectify the situation, obviously expecting him to lead a celibate life, whilst confined to a loveless marriage.

For several years after the move to Offaly, he had lived the life of a monk. But it had made no difference and, up until tonight, he had firmly believed that any intimacy between them was gone forever.

Some time ago, he had taken up with Philippa – an attractive English Protestant widow who lived in Athlone. A childless, discreet woman in her thirties, who missed the physical side of marriage even more than he did, she was a salve to his bruised male ego. He did not see her very often – given the time and distance in travelling – but when he did see her, he made up for the absence of pleasure with his wife. He had to be very careful indeed, for tongues wagged harder in the country than they did in Dublin. A word in the wrong place could jeopardise all that he had worked for.

Lately, Philippa had been making noises about moving back to England as she wished to marry again before it was too late. She had asked William outright about his intentions towards her and he admitted that their relationship could never be anything other than casual. Since his marriage had been solemnised in the Catholic Church, it was a marriage for life. She had subsequently, but sadly, told him that their days were numbered, as she wished to marry again and have children before it was too late.

He had not given much thought to the future or how he would cope without the female company he had enjoyed with Philippa. It had been sheer luck which had brought her into his life – through selling a few acres of land for her – and he was unlikely to come across another like her in the area. Another woman who would accommodate him in her own luxurious home, who had no inhibitions sexually – and who had asked nothing in return.

Perhaps, William thought to himself, Tara Flynn might be open to some sort of arrangement which might benefit them both. From the little he had seen and heard of her, perhaps she might be willing to trade her company for a step up the social ladder – via a career in his business.

He turned over in the unfamiliar bed. Tomorrow was another day. And after the pleasant surprises that he had encountered today, who knew what it might bring?

Chapter Eleven

Tara had been awake for over an hour when Madeleine came tapping on her bedroom door. 'Are you awake?' she called in a high-pitched excited tone. 'I've got something to show you.'

'Just a moment,' Tara called back. She reached to the bottom of her bed for her striped dressing-gown.

Madeleine came in, still in her night attire. 'That's lovely,' she said, pointing to Tara's gown. 'Considering your unfortunate background you have wonderful taste in clothes. Even Gabriel has commented and boys don't usually notice things like that.'

Tara pulled the dressing-gown on, trying desperately to hold back the sharp retort which had sprung to her lips. 'I may not have had the privileged upbringing you have enjoyed, Madeleine,' she said, failing miserably, 'but I would certainly not describe my upbringing as "*unfortunate*". For one thing – I was brought up to have the good manners not to insult people.'

'I'm sorry . . . I'm sorry . . . I'm sorry!' Madeleine said in a small, watery voice.

Tara paused, her feelings wrestling between hurt for herself and compassion for her confused friend. 'It's all right, Madeleine,' she said, putting her arms around her. 'I'm sorry too, for being so snappy with you.' Tara guided her over to the bed and they both sat down on it.

'I really didn't mean it,' Madeleine sniffed. 'I was only trying to tell the truth – I didn't mean to insult you.'

'It's okay. It's okay. We'll just forget it – let on it never happened.'

Madeleine sniffed again. 'It's just that I've promised someone to always tell the truth – and please don't ask me who it is, because I can't tell you.'

Tara felt a funny shiver run down her spine. 'It doesn't matter, Madeleine. I've already told you that.' She paused, searching for the right words. 'You can still tell the truth though and not hurt other people's feelings.'

'How?' Madeleine looked genuinely interested.

'Well,' Tara said 'you don't have to say everything that comes into your head . . . for example, you could have just said that my dressing-gown was nice, without saying all the rest.'

'But all the other thoughts in your mind are the truth,' Madeleine protested, 'and if you don't say them, you're committing a sin – the sin of omission. I really know what I'm talking about, Tara. I've been instructed by a very important person.'

'No,' Tara said, shaking her head. 'You've got it wrong. The sin of omission is when you deliberately omit doing something or saying something that could help someone else. What you said to me earlier on was *not* helpful in any shape or form – it was hurtful.'

Madeleine put her hands over her ears. 'Oh – I'm so mixed up now. I don't know what is the truth – and what is false. My brain gets so mixed up at times.'

Tara put her arms around her again. 'You shouldn't think about things so much, Madeleine. Just try to be nice to people and everything will be all right. If certain people are not nice to you, then just try to avoid them – that's what I do anyway.'

Madeleine started to rock back and forward on the bed. 'Oh, my God,' she began chanting out loud, 'I am very sorry that I have sinned against thee, because thou art so good, and I will not sin again.'

'Madeleine, stop it!' A feeling of dread was washing over Tara. 'You haven't done anything wrong – so why are you saying the Act of Contrition?' She gripped her friend firmly by the shoulders and turned her round so they were facing each other. 'You'd think you'd murdered somebody to hear you going on.'

Madeleine suddenly relaxed and a big smile spread over her face. 'I feel much better now. I know that – if by mistake – I committed a sin, that God has forgiven me.' She delved her hand into her dressing-gown pocket. 'I said I had something to show you, didn't I?'

Tara nodded, trying not to show her bewilderment.

Madeleine took a folded paper from her pocket and handed it to

Tara. 'I've been having some problems recently, trying to decide about my future – about whether I should stay on at school or not, that sort of thing.' She joined her hands now, as though in prayer. 'Anyway, I decided to pray for guidance, for a sign – that sort of thing. And I received it. What do you think?' She waited expectantly.

Tara unfolded the paper. When she saw what it was, she folded it back up. 'It's about the Missions in Africa, Madeleine. Everybody got one when the Mission was on during the summer.'

'Oh sure, I know what it is.' She gave a big smile. 'But I'd thrown mine in the fire when I came back from church and I never gave it another thought. And then, when I was worrying about what to do with my future, I said a prayer . . . and it appeared in the kitchen on the dresser. When you think about it, it's nothing short of a miracle! At the least, it's the answer to my prayer. God wants me to help in the Missions.' Madeleine suddenly grabbed Tara's arm. 'I think he wants me to be a nun, Tara! And you're the first person I've told.'

Tara looked back down at the folded paper and then she looked back up at her friend. 'Do you really want to be a nun, Madeleine? Is it something you've been thinking about for a long time?'

Madeleine wrinkled her brow in thought. 'No, not really . . . I just know that I want to help people less fortunate than myself, and when I saw the paper about the Missions, I suddenly thought that maybe I should be a nun.' She turned towards the window, a faraway look in her eyes. 'The world's a terrible place, Tara. We need to do everything we can to save it. If people don't stand up for what is good – then the evil forces will take over. I've been trying to explain that to people in school and when I went to the cemetery last week, but people just don't understand.' She turned back to Tara, her eyes bright and shining. 'The word of God doesn't only come through priests. God works in very strange ways, you know. Sometimes he chooses someone very ordinary like myself to be his messenger. Sometimes you have to do things which other people think are strange, to bring his message to the world.' She looked down at the folded Mission sheet. 'I'm waiting for another sign . . . from the person who gives me my instructions. Soon, I'll know what I have to do next.'

The hairs stood on the back of Tara's neck. 'Have you told your mother and father about this? Do they know about the person who's giving you instructions?'

'No . . . I haven't told them anything at all. It's too early for them to understand that their daughter has been chosen for something so special. You're the only one I've told.' Madeleine's face suddenly creased with anxiety. 'You won't say anything, will you?'

'No,' Tara said slowly, 'but I think you should tell them soon.'

Madeleine stood up now. 'I feel much better now I've told you. I knew *you'd* understand, because you're so clever. I'm actually surprised that they've chosen me to be the messenger and not somebody clever like you. It's strange, because I'm sure people would listen to you quicker than they'd listen to me.' She walked towards the door and then she said in a surprisingly normal voice, as though the previous conversation had not taken place, 'I'll leave you to get dressed, then we'll go down for breakfast. I'm sure I can smell father's kippers frying.' She gave a childish giggle. 'They make an awful smell, don't they?'

The nerves that Tara felt at having to sit down to breakfast with the Fitzgeralds were multiplied by all the weird things that Madeleine had said to her upstairs. Thankfully, both Madeleine's parents seemed in great form this morning and there was a pleasant chat going on at the table when she and Madeleine came down.

Everyone smiled and said 'Good morning', and Tara's mother asked if she had slept all right, and if she had found the bed warm and comfortable enough. She also complimented Tara on her skirt and cardigan and said how fetching the checked ribbon looked in her hair.

There had been no awkward moments with the food this morning, as she was familiar with the hot buffet which had been laid out on the sideboard. Tara followed Madeleine as she lifted a warm plate and helped herself to sausage, bacon, black and white pudding and a fried egg.

Madeleine poured out two small glasses of fresh orange juice and handed one to Tara. Then, they both sat down at the huge mahogany table with their plates. A radio was on in the background, and any silences were filled with the hum of low music or the chatty voice of the radio presenter.

Tara was grateful to see young Ella bustling around this morning and not Mrs Scully. The girl had said: 'Excuse me, Miss,' to Tara as she stretched past her with a rack of freshly made toast, and had smiled pleasantly when she removed her breakfast plate. Tara smiled back at the girl, suddenly feeling a bit uncomfortable about being served by her. Ella reminded her of Biddy and some of the girls she had gone to school with, and she would hate to be served by any of them. She turned back to the conversation at the table, and pushed the thoughts aside.

Tara was pleased when Gabriel, after pouring coffee for himself, had turned to her and said: 'You prefer coffee if I remember, don't you, Tara?' And she was so delighted he had remembered that she said, '*yes*' – even though she had planned on having tea, to see if it tasted the same as they had at home.

'Tell me about the work you're doing in the distillery, Tara,' Madeleine's father suddenly said, giving her a warm smile.

Tara felt her cheeks and neck going red, as the whole family gave her rapt attention. After a stuttering start, she began to relax a little when she realised that she was successfully answering every question William Fitzgerald asked her.

'What about reception work?' he quizzed now. 'Do you have much experience dealing with the public?'

'Oh, yes,' Tara replied. 'I work the telephone switchboard and I cover at the reception desk when the usual girl is on her lunch-break. I covered for her full-time when she was off work sick a few weeks ago.'

'Do you think there's much opportunity for promotion?'

'Well,' Tara ventured, 'Mr O'Hara, my boss, has said that I should be eligible for promotion *and* a pay rise, if I pass my exams at night classes after Christmas.'

'That's what I like to hear,' William commented. 'You're obviously a career-minded young woman. But tell me now,' he said thought-fully, 'if you had the chance of promotion with another company, how would you feel?'

Tara looked blank. 'I can't imagine that happening. I'm still very young and I have a lot to learn yet.' She took a sip of her coffee. 'I'm only too delighted with the position I have, and besides, there's not too many offices in Tullamore that I could move to.'

The conversation was suddenly interrupted as the front doorbell rang.

Elisha looked at her watch. 'That's strange,' she said. 'We don't usually have callers at this time on a Sunday morning.'

The heavy foot of Mrs Scully – slower than usual from her late night and a drop too much sherry – passed by the dining-room, on her way to answer the door.

The scruffily dressed man on the doorstep caught her unawares for a moment. 'Yes?' she said sharply, knowing she recognised him, but not sure from where. She was just about to tell him that he had no right coming to the front door when she suddenly recognised him. Her face lit up and a glint came into her tired eyes.

The man removed his greasy working cap, and stood clutching it to his breast with both hands. 'Beggin' yer pardon, ma'am,' he said respectfully, 'but could you tell me if a Miss Tara Flynn is in the house at the minute? To the best of me knowledge, she was supposed to have stayed the night here.'

'Tara Flynn?' Mrs Scully repeated, taking in his unshaven face and the working clothes that looked as if he had slept the night in them. 'And if she is here,' she said in a brusque manner, 'who should I say is looking for her?'

'Shay Flynn, ma'am,' he said, wringing the cap between his hands now. 'I'm her father. I wouldn't be botherin' youse all now . . . but I've got to bring her home because—'

'If you would just step inside,' Mrs Scully said, her voice suddenly sweet. 'I'll go and check whether yer daughter is here.'

Like a condemned man who was ordered to move forward to the firing line, Shay Flynn reluctantly stepped inside the front door of Ballygrace House.

Rosie Scully almost danced with delight along the hallway to the dining-room, all tiredness miraculously gone. So gleeful was she, she had to stop at the door for a moment to compose herself before going in to deliver the message.

God had indeed answered her prayer from last night – the quickest answer to a prayer she had ever received in her life.

She gave a little cough, and knocked on the dining-room door before walking in. 'Excuse me for interruptin' you all now,' she announced, 'but there's a man at the front door, and he's lookin' to have a word with Miss Madeleine's guest.'

Elisha turned to Tara. 'Had you arranged for someone to collect you?'

Tara's stomach suddenly tightened. 'No,' she replied quickly, gripping the handle of her newly filled coffee cup, 'I have my bicycle . . . I wasn't expecting anyone.'

Mrs Scully puffed up her chest. 'Well,' she said in a loud voice, 'there's a man at the door, claimin' to be yer father.'

'My father?' Tara repeated in a high stupefied voice.

We're not so smart now, Mrs Scully thought triumphantly to herself. *But just hang on, there's more to come, ye uppity little brat.* She turned to her employer. 'Shall I show him in?' she said, giving a big smile.

'Yes – yes. Of course,' Elisha said, 'show him in,'

'No!' Tara protested, getting to her feet. As she fumbled to put the cup back into the saucer, dark splashes of coffee spilled onto the snowy lace tablecloth. Tara's hand flew to her mouth in horror. 'I'm so sorry!' she gasped.

'Don't worry, Tara,' Elisha said quickly, 'Ella will get that out with bleach.'

'I'm sorry . . .' she repeated, pushing her chair back, 'I'll just go and speak to my father at the door.'

But it was too late, for Rosie Scully was tapping her way down the hallway, hellbent on bringing Tara Flynn's father into the dining-room. Nothing would give her greater pleasure than to see the Fitzgeralds' faces when they beheld the sight she would present before them. A sight which would tell them once and for all that Tara Flynn was not the sort they should be welcoming into their home.

'If it's all the same wi' you, ma'am,' Shay said, backing off, 'I'd sooner have a word with her outside – in private.' He knew before he came up the rhododendron-lined driveway that he was trespassing on the territory of the Quality – but he wasn't going to make a complete eedjit of himself by walking in on their breakfast.

'Come in!' Mrs Scully hissed. 'The Missus sent me to bring you in.'

She wasn't going to have this curly-headed *amadán* ruin her finest moment.

'What is it?' Tara came rushing down the hallway. Having made a fool of herself by spilling the coffee, she couldn't bear to have anything further happen.

'I'm sorry for comin', Tara. I knew ye wouldn't want me to – but I was made to come for you.'

Tara stopped in her tracks when she saw Shay's ashen face and trembling hands. She had a horrible feeling that something even worse than spilling the coffee, or having her father appear at the Fitzgeralds' house looking like a tinker, was about to happen.

'What's wrong?' she asked, oblivious to the smug Mrs Scully standing at her elbow, and the figures coming out of the dining-room behind her. She took a few steps nearer her father. 'What's wrong?' she asked again.

Shay wrung his cap unmercifully, acutely aware that all eyes were on him. 'It's . . . it's yer granda.'

There was a silence.

'He's had another bad turn?' Tara asked in a calm voice – too calm to be normal. 'We need to get him into hospital this time. I'll get my things –'

'No – no!' Shay blurted out. He grabbed clumsily at his daughter's hand. 'Yer granda,' he said in a deep, sorrowful voice, 'died at seven o'clock this morning.'

Somewhere, at the back of Tara's mind, her father's words registered, and she knew she should say something – do something. But her body would not react. It was paralysed, rooted to the spot.

She felt someone put an arm through hers. 'Come on, Tara,' Madeleine said in a gentle voice. 'I'll help you to get your things.'

Shay turned towards the door. 'I'll wait for you outside,' he said quietly, and before anyone could argue he had opened the door and made his way down the stairs.

When Tara lifted her spinning head, Mrs Scully looked her straight in the eye, with a look of pure triumph on her face.

Then the housekeeper – satisfied that the little Ballygrace brat had been seen in her true colours – said in a cheery voice: 'I'll make a fresh pot of tea, and ye can have it once the visitors have gone.'

William Fitzgerald gave the old woman a withering look. 'I don't think anyone requires tea, Mrs Scully. You can go ahead now, and clear up the dining-room.'

Nothing, not even a sharp reprimand from the Master, could dampen Rosie Scully's jubilation. 'Whatever you like, sir,' she said, and scuttled off down the hallway, glad to be on her own – so that she could smile as broadly as she wanted.

Fifteen minutes later, Tara found herself seated in the back seat of the Fitzgeralds' car. William had sent Shay on ahead, saying he would bring Tara in the car, as she wasn't in a fit state to cycle.

Shay was perplexed. Weren't things bad enough with him having to go up to Ballygrace House, without them having to drive Tara home in the fancy car? And – even worse – maybe they would be looking for the price of the petrol when they arrived at the house. 'Sure, I could put her up on the bar of me own bike,' he said to William Fitzgerald,. 'She'd be as right as rain by the time we get back.'

'No,' William said in a firm voice. 'You go on ahead – we'll follow you shortly.' He closed the door, which told Shay the conversation was over.

Shay threw his leg over the bike and muttered to himself: 'Mick can answer the door when they arrive, for I haven't the price of a feckin' drink this mornin' – never mind a gallon of petrol.'

Madeleine had packed Tara's things, while Elisha instructed Mrs Scully to bring Tara a hot brandy. After she had drunk as much as she could politely bear of the strong sweet drink, they set off in the car. William and Gabriel in the front, and the two girls in the back.

For once in her life, Tara had taken a step socially upwards without being aware of it. She had never sat in a private car before. She got in and out of the car, without giving it the slightest thought.

Her thoughts today – and for some time to come – were very firmly focused: on how she would cope without her beloved granda.

Chapter Twelve

The funeral the following Tuesday was big by local standards. The whole village of Ballygrace turned out, along with mourners who had travelled from farther afield, and three priests – not counting their own. Tara spoke to Madeleine and Elisha Fitzgerald, when they came to the front pew to offer their sympathies to her and the rest of the family. When Tara looked up at them, she noticed that Madeleine's eyes looked heavy and when she spoke she was like someone who was half asleep.

Elisha had kept a tight grip on Madeleine's arm and, having offered a few words of sympathy to Tara and her family, she guided her daughter to a corner at the back of the church. Life had been absolute hell with Madeleine since all the drama on Sunday morning. After dropping Tara out at the cottage, she had ranted and raved about how the old God was a vengeful God – always punishing people. She announced that a new, kind God was coming down to earth, to recruit people in the fight against evil, and that she was only waiting for a signal to join them.

An emergency appointment was arranged with the doctor. He prescribed medication to 'calm Madeleine down' until she saw the specialist in Dublin the following week. The medication certainly had calmed her, and had given them all a good night's sleep, but Elisha was on edge all the time, not knowing what to expect next.

Having to attend a funeral mass was the last thing they needed – given Madeleine's obsession with religion at the moment – but it was something that could not be avoided.

Biddy was in the church, too. She was sitting with Lizzie Lawless in the little side aisle, to the right of the coffin. Tara noticed that Biddy looked very thin and white, and had dark rings round her eyes. Both her friends looked terrible. In the midst of her grief, Tara wondered what on earth could be wrong, for them *both* to look so unwell.

Unlike her own family, nothing terrible had just happened to them.

Tara hadn't realised that her granda was so well known out of the village. It made her feel very sad when people came up to her and said that they'd known him years ago, and what a fine man he was. It made her realise that there were parts of her granda's life she knew nothing about – that she would never know about now. Worse still were the ones who came up to her and told her how they'd not only known her granda – but they'd also known Tara's mother when she was a young girl. The tears she tried to control had got the better of her when she met those people. Concentrating on everyone else at the funeral had not worked.

Her father had smartened himself up for the occasion and, with a tidy haircut and a dark suit, he showed signs of the handsome young man he once had been. Under the gimlet eye of Tessie, Shay had behaved with proper decorum and had not besmirched his father's memory by drinking too much at the funeral.

Tara could hardly bear to look at him.

The woeful row he had caused the night before her granda died was still too fresh in her mind. Mick had tried to explain that her granda had a bad heart condition and that, given his age and everything, it was bound to have happened at some time. There was no good in blaming Shay. Sure, hadn't they argued nearly every week of their lives? Even the local doctor had spoken to her at the wake, echoing Mick's words.

But Tara had her own thoughts – and she still blamed her father.

Joe had come down from the seminary in Dublin and attended the funeral with his weeping old grand-aunties, who linked arms with him on either side. Their moods swung constantly throughout the ceremony – alternatively delighted with the attention they got because of their holy nephew and distraught at having lost their only living brother.

In a moment of distraction during the funeral Mass, Tara found herself staring along the pew at Joe and wondering what he was thinking. At times, his face was like a statue, showing no emotion whatsoever. At other times, he had a serene little smile pinned on his face. The sort of understanding smile, Tara reckoned, that priests must find useful when listening to the woes and wants of their parishioners. Nodding and smiling, without actually saying anything, could serve many a situation. It could be interpreted any way the person liked. Tara wondered if they were taught how to smile like that in the seminary, because the priest who had driven Joe down for the funeral had the same little smile on his face.

As they walked out of the church behind the coffin, it suddenly struck Tara that she had no idea what Joe was thinking of during the funeral, because she didn't know her brother at all. She had seen him every Christmas, Easter and summer holiday, and they had talked about things like music and reading, but Joe had never once volunteered any information about his life in the seminary. Any questions that Tara had asked had been given the briefest of answers – accompanied by the little smile.

Even today at the funeral he had offered his hand in sympathy to her as though he was practising for all the funeral masses he would say in the future. And she had responded with the same reverence she had given the parish priest. Not the way a sister would respond to a brother. He had shown no emotion about his grandfather's death – just a sorrowful nod of the head and the same little smile. When Tara thought of it, Joe never really knew her granda either.

When Tara went back to work the following week everyone she knew came up to offer their sympathies again, even though a number had attended the funeral or the wake the night before. On several occasions throughout the first day she found herself dissolving into tears, but after a while she made herself concentrate on other things and not think of her granda all the time. It was impossible not to think of him at home. Even though Mick had got rid of his pipe and clothes, there were reminders of him everywhere.

Two or three weeks after he died, Tara was given a rise at work. Absolutely delighted with herself, she pedalled home from work as quick as her legs could go. She put the bike in the turf shed, then ran in the back door as usual to tell her granda all about it. Except that her granda wasn't there. Scalding tears ran in rivers down her cheeks.

Her granda would *never* be there again.

*

On the day Noel Flynn was buried, Biddy Hart discovered that she was pregnant. Unfortunately, the discovery took place in the presence of Lizzie Lawless, who had dragged her straight to the doctor's surgery after the funeral. Nothing terrible had happened to her in the doctor's, for Doctor Devine was a pleasant, understanding man who had told her she was not the first girl it had happened to – and she would not be the last. 'Wouldn't you agree?' he had said to Lizzie and Lizzie had said 'Indeed,' through clenched teeth.

Biddy was relieved that Lizzie had taken the shocking news so calmly – but her relief was short-lived. It was an entirely different matter when they got back home. Biddy found herself being thumped about the four walls of the kitchen by Lizzie's fists, and as a finale was beaten on the arms and legs with a stick which Lizzie used for herding the cow.

'That's all the thanks I get for giving you a decent Catholic home!' she raged. 'I wish I'd never set eyes on the pair of ye. You and that Nora Quinn. *You* especially – like mother like daughter! And weren't you given to me by the nuns, so's that you'd have a chance in life, and not end up goin' down the same road as yer mother?'

What road? Biddy wanted to ask, as she cowered in the corner beside the sacks of potatoes and flour. Her body was sore from the beating and her mind reeling from the things Lizzie had said about her mother. She was eighteen years old and had been living with Lizzie since she was four. In all those years, Biddy had never been able to get a word out of her about her background. All she knew was that her mother was dead and that nobody knew anything about her father.

'Who else would have been good enough to take in the daughter of a whore, who committed suicide? Only a saint!' She held the stick above Biddy's head. 'Who's the father? Who's the one that interfered with you?'

'I don't know,' wailed Biddy. 'It was a dark night . . . and there was a few of them. I couldn't see their faces. They pulled me into the bushes.' Biddy had practised this answer when they were sitting in the doctor's surgery.

'What?' Lizzie said, her mouth hanging open in shock. 'You don't mean to tell me there was more than one?'

'I was frightened to tell you,' Biddy sniffed, hardly able to believe that her story seemed plausible to Lizzie. 'Because I didn't know what they were doin'. . . I didn't know if it could make me have a baby.'

Lizzie gave her another clout. 'Don't tell me you're such an innocent that you didn't understand . . . you're trying the same tack as that Nora Quinn! She made out she didn't know she was expectin' until she was six months gone – and that she didn't know how she got that way. But she knew all right. I've since heard that she landed in a home for unmarried mothers in Dublin. She knows all right now, when she's down on her hands and knees scrubbin' floors in the convent every day, instead of the comfortable job she had lookin' after the priest.' Lizzie slowly straightened up, as though all the anger and fight had seeped out of her. She threw the stick on top of the sacks. 'You're sure you don't know who the boys were?'

Biddy shook her head – so relieved that the beating was over, she was unable to speak.

'We'll have to tell Father Daly . . . to see what he can arrange. He was the one that sorted out the place for that Nora.' Lizzie's face was pinched and tight, and her voice weary. 'He was good to her, even though the little bitch wouldn't tell about the father. It's a nice how-d'ye-do, having to tell him I've another one in the same position. The only savin' grace about it is that we can say *you* were tampered with against yer will. He might look upon it in a kinder light. There's women in this place would kill for a job cleanin' for the priest. The pair of ye were privileged – and look how ye've repaid him!'

Biddy struggled to her feet. 'D'you want me to tell him?' she ventured.

'No, I feckin' well don't!' Lizzie responded. 'You impudent brat! Won't that look nice – you walkin' into the priest's house – as brazen as brass – tellin' him all yer dirty business!'

Biddy hung her head, causing locks of hair to fall down over her eyes as a shield against her foster-mother's searing gaze.

Lizzie stomped over to coat-pegs at the side of the range. 'I'll go and see him this very minute, before that "know-all" Mrs McCarthy appears to make his supper. I'll be needin' to say a prayer to the Holy Spirit, on my way up to the priest's house.' Lizzie shoved her arms into her coat sleeves. 'I'll be prayin' for guidance as to how to explain *this* situation.' She pulled a crumpled headscarf out of the coat pocket and tied it tightly under her wrinkled chin. 'I hope I get my reward for all this in heaven – because I'm certainly not gettin' anythin' for it on earth!'

Lizzie made for the door then, her hand on the latch, she turned back to the craven Biddy. 'Not a word to that Dinny when he comes in – or anybody else. If you open yer mouth,' she warned, 'I'll feckin' well murder you.' She banged the door behind her, almost taking it off the hinges.

The minute Lizzie was gone out of the cottage, Biddy shifted from her hidey-hole corner to put the kettle on the fire. She examined the sore bits on her arms and legs where the stick had landed and reckoned she'd have a good few bruises in the morning. She'd feel better after a strong cup of tea and a couple of aspirins.

When the kettle had boiled, she sat up on Lizzie's settle bed with her tea and a slice of soda bread and jam and smiled to herself. She thought about how she would tell Dinny the news about the baby. She wondered what he would say. She bit into the bread. He might suggest that they should run away together and get married.

She pulled her knees up and hugged them to her chest – a position she liked when she was thinking of something nice. If they got married quick, she could wear the light-coloured suit that Tara had given her, before it got too small, and she was sure that Tara would let her borrow a hat.

Dinny couldn't use the excuse that she was too young now. If she was old enough to have a baby – then she was old enough to get married. A baby! she thought, hugging her knees tighter and rocking from side to side on Lizzie's bed. Biddy had wanted a baby for as long as she could remember. Something of her own. Somebody who was a blood relation – for she didn't have a blood relation in the whole wide world.

Biddy looked up at the clock. Dinny would be in from work shortly. She hoped he came in before Lizzie came back from seeing the priest. She smiled, wondering if he would bring her any presents this evening. She combed her hair and washed her face, then peeled some potatoes – to sweeten Lizzie's temper – and put the kettle on the fire. She would make a pot of tea for Dinny the minute he came in, and they would sit chatting over a cup each. Then, she got out the sweeping brush and gave the kitchen floor a good going over, and straightened up the chairs around the table.

The scrunch of gravel outside heralded Dinny Martin's arrival. Biddy quickly put the steaming kettle back over the fire to bring it back to the boil, and ran out to meet him.

'Jaysus!' Dinny exclaimed irritably. 'You nearly feckin' well knocked me and the bike over.' He stood the bike up against the side of the cottage and, ignoring the slighted Biddy, walked into the cottage, with her trailing behind. 'Well?' he grunted. 'What was all the commotion about – and where's Herself?'

Biddy tucked her hair behind her ears, to show off a pair of earrings Dinny had bought her a few weeks before. 'She's up in the priest's house.' Then, before he got any of his funny ideas, she quickly added: 'She could be back any minute.' She poured the water in the teapot on top of the leaves.

Dinny hung his jacket and cap on the hook behind the door and then came over to the fire. After coughing to clear his throat, he spat in the flames, narrowly missing the kettle. 'What's up?' he demanded. 'I know by the head on you, that there's somethin' going on.'

'I have some news that concerns you,' she said. 'I was at Doctor Devine's this afternoon.'

'What news would that be?' he asked warily.

Biddy stirred the tea leaves round in the pot with a long spoon, then left it to brew for a few minutes.

'What news?' Dinny repeated, taking a half-smoked cigarette from his pocket. He struck a match on the stone fireplace.

'I'm havin' a baby,' she said in a low voice. 'It's due in May.'

There was a long silence, while Dinny took a deep drag on his cigarette. 'And have you,' he said, 'informed the lucky father yet?' He casually removed a stray piece of tobacco from his tongue.

Biddy looked up at him. 'Amn't I informin' him now?' she demanded, hands on hips.

Dinny gave her a sidelong grin – a sneering grin which froze her heart. 'From what I hear,' he said, going over to the table for the sugar and a teaspoon, 'there's been a more than me pokin' the fire – a *lot* more.'

'That's a load of feckin' lies!' Biddy protested. 'You know fine well you're the only man I've been with.'

'Oh?' he said, pouring his own tea out into the mug. 'And what about the fine young fella I saw you with in Tullamore, not too long ago? A young fella by the name of PJ Murphy.'

Biddy's face coloured. How did Dinny know about PJ? It was months ago and she'd forgotten all about it. Dinny never chatted with any of the young ones in Ballygrace, and she'd made sure she only met PJ in Daingean or Tullamore. The last time she was to meet him, he hadn't turned up. 'Sure, he only took me to the pictures twice . . . he's only a young lad . . . he wouldn't know what to do.'

Dinny roared out laughing. 'He knew what he was doin' all right, when he had you up against the church wall. And you knew what you were doin', when I saw you leadin' him by the hand, round the back of the church.'

Biddy swallowed hard. 'It was harmless,' she insisted. 'I've never let anyone touch me but you.'

'So *you* say.' He gulped at his tea.

'Dinny?' Biddy looked up at him, with big tears in her eyes. 'I promise you – there was nobody else. I only went out with that lad because some of the girls were teasin' me about you. They were blackguardin' you . . . jeering at me livin' in the same house and everything. I got mad wi' them. They were sayin' that maybe we got up to things when Lizzie was out. I thought if I went out with PJ that they would stop goin' on about me and you.' She lowered her voice. 'I've always been careful never to let anybody know about us . . . but it'll be hard to keep this quiet for long. I'm over three months gone, and it'll be startin' to show soon.'

He looked directly at her now, his eyes narrowed with suspicion. 'It's not mine! We always did it standin' up – and I always pulled out in time.'

'Not always!' she retorted – panic starting to set in. Dinny was her only hope now. 'Remember the night you were drunk . . . and we went into the hayshed?'

The lodger's face was stony. He reached a hand out and grabbed Biddy on the fleshy part of her thigh. 'Don't try to hang this one on me . . . nobody will believe you. I have it out all over Ballygrace and

Daingean about you, since I saw you wi' the young lad. You're known far and wide as an easy little hoor. Nobody will believe a word out of yer mouth.' He tightened his grip. 'If you point the finger at me – you'll be sorry.'

'But Dinny . . .' her voice faltered. 'I thought we would get married . . . you always said when I was old enough.'

'Married?' he said sneeringly. 'You must be feckin' well jokin'!' He drained his mug, and threw the end of his cigarette in the fire. 'There's a widow-woman out near Tyrellspass, who's been offerin' me a room these last few years. Her house is cleaner than this oul' kip – *and* she makes a decent bite to ate.' He sniffed in a derisory manner. 'I'll be takin' her up on it, so.'

He said nothing about the fact that the widow-woman also had two young daughters, aged thirteen and fifteen. A fact of more interest to Dinny, than the clean house and good food their mother would provide. The daughters would hold his attention for a few years before they grew too old and too clever for him – just as Biddy Hart had done.

Lizzie appeared back a short time later. 'Get yerself up to the priest's house this minute,' she said to Biddy, when Dinny was out of earshot. 'He says he'll hear yer confession before Mrs McCarthy comes to make his supper.'

'I don't want to go to Father Daly,' Biddy dared to say. 'I don't want to go back to work in the chapel house either.'

Lizzie's face was a picture. She pointed to the door. 'Get yourself out this minute, you ungrateful little brat! You should be on yer knees thankin' God for the goodness of Father Daly. You should be grateful that he's willin' to even recognise you, after what's happened.' She lowered her voice. 'If word about you expectin' a bastard gets around Ballygrace, then you're on yer own! The only chance we have is if the priest can get it adopted.'

'This is indeed a sorry situation,' Father Daly said, letting Biddy in through the back door. The heavy-jowled, balding priest locked it behind her, so that they would not be interrupted. 'You poor child,' he said, patting her shoulder. 'It's always the innocent ones who are caught out . . .'

At that very moment, Dinny Martin was cycling to Tyrellspass, his meagre belongings tied on the back of his bike, and ten shillings poorer after paying Lizzie what he owed in rent. 'You're a big-hearted woman,' he had said to Lizzie as he went out of the door. 'But I don't think I could stay on under the circumstances. That Biddy isn't right in the head. Askin' me to marry her – an' me ould enough to be her father!'

Dinny had made sure he got in first with the story, so's that no one would be likely to believe Biddy. 'She's so desperate to give a name to her bastard, that she'd point the finger at any man. You wouldn't have to throw a stone very far to find several fathers for her child – but I'm not takin' the rap for that!' Dinny shook his head. 'It wouldn't be safe for me to be livin' under the same roof as the likes of her . . . she could accuse me of anything. I'm goin' while I still have me good name.'

'The little scut!' Lizzie had snivelled. 'I don't blame you one bit, Dinny Martin, and I'll not allow anybody else to blame you either. You've been a good lodger to me, you always kept yerself to yerself – and now I've lost you on account of that lying little wretch!'

An' even worse, she said to herself – *I've lost the good money you were payin' me*!

Chapter Thirteen

❧

December, 1950

The week before Christmas, Olive the receptionist came through to the accounts department looking for Tara. 'There's a man asking for you at reception,' she said. 'He's very well spoken and smartly dressed – so we'd better not keep him waiting.'

Tara felt a wave of relief that it wasn't her father again. However, as she followed Olive through to reception, she felt vaguely anxious as to who else it could be. If it was one of the bosses from Dublin, at least she was well dressed too, in her dark green tartan suit and green velvet hairband.

Whoever it was, *nothing* could be worse than when her father arrived last Monday morning, still drunk from the night before. He was morbid – weeping about his dead father – and looking for money. Thankfully, Olive had discreetly called Tara out, without anyone else noticing. After Tara had propelled him out of the building and round the corner, Shay was full of apologies. He tearfully explained how he had been short-paid the previous week, and they had little or no food in the house.

'I'll call round to the house at one o'clock and sort out the situation with Tessie,' Tara said. Then – wagging a finger in her father's face – she had warned him: 'But don't you *ever* come into my work again.'

After a quick discussion with her stepmother at lunchtime, Tara left ten shillings on the kitchen table. 'I'll help you and the children any time, Tessie,' she said sympathetically, 'as long as it's not going on drink.'

'I'm nearly out of me mind,' Tessie confided. 'He hasn't put in a

157

full week's work since his father died. He keeps blamin' it on himself. That row they had just before he died – and of course he's drinking all the more to try to forget. He'll be lucky if he has a job to go back to tomorrow.'

William Fitzgerald was the last person Tara expected to see in reception. He stood up when he saw her and held a hand out. 'I'm so sorry to disturb you, Tara,' he said, although the smile on his face looked more delighted than apologetic.

'Is it Madeleine?' she whispered.

'No – no,' he said, still smiling. 'It's not about Madeleine. It's more of a personal nature. I wondered . . .' He reached inside his navy cashmere coat for his fob watch. 'I wondered if you were due to have lunch soon?'

Tara looked at her wristwatch. It was ten minutes to one. 'My lunchbreak is at one o'clock.'

Just then, Mrs Reilly, the office manageress, came into reception carrying a sheaf of papers. 'Oh, Mr Fitzgerald!' she said in high excited voice, coming over to them. 'How are you?'

William stretched a hand out. 'I'm very well indeed,' he said, smiling at her in such a way that her face went quite pink. 'I hope you don't mind me disturbing your staff – but I had a message to deliver to Miss Flynn.'

'Tara?' Mrs Reilly shifted her spectacles further up her nose, and then looked at Tara.

'Yes,' William said, still smiling, 'she's a close friend of my daughter, Madeleine.'

Tara's brow deepened in a puzzled frown. Only seconds before he had told her that his visit had nothing to do with Madeleine.

'Oh . . .' Mrs Reilly said, shuffling her papers. She hadn't realised that Tara Flynn had friends in such high places.

'I believe,' William said, 'that she's due to go for lunch in a few minutes. I wondered if I might wait here for her?'

'Wait? Oh, no – she can go now. Sure, It's nearly one o'clock anyway.' She looked at Tara. 'Go on, Tara – don't keep Mr Fitzgerald waiting. He's a very busy man.'

Tara rushed through to the cloakroom, for her coat and clutch bag. She paused for a moment to glance at her reflection in the mirror, then she quickly patted a little face powder on, and a light coat of lipstick.

'There's a small restaurant not too far out of town,' William Fitzgerald told her in the car. 'I thought you might like it. I often bring Madeleine there for lunch.'

Tara thought of the sandwiches wrapped in brown paper that she had left behind in the office. 'I don't usually go out at lunchtime,' she announced, suddenly feeling bowled over by the suddenness of the situation.

'Of course not,' he said, as they drove along Patrick Street and swung up into Tullamore High Street. 'It will be a nice treat for you today.' He glanced casually at her. 'I'm sure a lovely young lady like you enjoys a treat now and again.'

There was a pause, and then Tara heard herself saying: 'If you don't want to discuss Madeleine . . . then why have you come to see me?'

'I want to put a proposition to you,' he said simply. 'I want you to come and work for me. I'll explain it over lunch.'

They drove the rest of the way in silence.

'Is this all right for you?' William asked, as he directed her towards a corner table in the dimly lit restaurant. He smiled when Tara said it was lovely. When they reached the table, he said 'May I?' and helped her out of her coat. In doing so, his fingers touched the nape of her neck. 'You have the most luxurious Titian hair,' he said in a low voice. 'Has any man ever told you that before?'

Tara gasped in shock at both his touch on her bare skin and the compliment he had paid her. Before she could reply that, yes, – his son Gabriel had used the exact same word to describe her hair – a waitress rushed over. She relieved William of Tara's coat and then waited until he had removed his own.

'We'll have a bottle of Beaujolais,' he told the waitress, and then he held out Tara's chair.

Tara was relieved that the menu was fairly basic. She ordered steak in a cream sauce with roast potatoes and a selection of vegetables.

'A good choice,' William commented, then said to the waitress, 'I'll have the same myself.'

He poured them both a glass of wine, then he clinked his glass against hers. 'Here's to our working future together.'

Tara glanced up quickly. 'I don't mean to be rude . . . but isn't it a bit early for that yet? We haven't even discussed it, and you might not find me suitable.'

William Fitzgerald laughed out loud, then he leaned across the table, and looked straight into her green eyes. 'Oh, I think I'm going to find you suitable, Miss Flynn. *Very* suitable indeed.'

The following Sunday, the whole family attended the early eight o'clock Mass for Noel Flynn's month's anniversary. Shay and Tessie came over in their ass and cart with all the children, and joined Mick and Tara in the front two pews. The solemn-faced Joe appeared with Molly and Maggie in a car driven by the priest from Tullamore. Various other cousins and relations joined them at the front of the church, too, as was the custom for anniversary masses.

In between thinking about her granda and how much she missed him, Tara reflected on the huge changes which had come about in her life since he died. She was due to start working for 'W Fitzgerald, Auctioneer' after the Christmas holidays, with more responsibility and with a higher salary than she had received in the distillery. She would work for a month, learning the business from the pregnant secretary who was leaving and who would not be returning after the birth.

After her own training period, Tara would then teach and supervise Madeleine in the more basic tasks of the office, such as handling the telephone and sorting out leaflets advertising land or property for sale. This was on the presumption that Madeleine would be well enough to start work. At present, she was in a private hospital in Dublin, receiving treatment for her psychiatric condition.

As Tara had expected, things had also changed at home. But she had not expected things to change to the extent they had. Her uncle Mick had taken to going out in the middle of the week, which was unusual for him. Occasionally, when she had come home after her evening classes, the fire was completely dead and the house empty and freezing. Tara didn't complain because Mick never interfered in her life – but deep down, she felt sad that another comforting part of her life had now disappeared.

After the anniversary Mass, her father and his family came back to the house, along with a few of the neighbours. Tara tied her hair back and put on a pinny, then she and Mick set about cooking rashers and sausages, black and white pudding, mushrooms and fried eggs. The previous evening, Mick had backed several loaves of soda bread and a large fruit cake.

A local woman named Kitty Dunne – a small, neatly dressed woman with bright eyes – was introduced to Tara as an old friend of the family. She had very generously brought some bacon and sausages with her, and two large apple tarts. She was particularly nice to Tara, and had even offered to give a hand with the frying. When her offer was declined, she sat chatting away to Mrs Kelly and Tessie over a cup of tea.

After the meal, the guests went home in dribs and drabs, and suddenly, Tara realised that there was only herself, her uncle Mick and Kitty Dunne left.

Kitty was busy telling Mick all about her own husband's funeral last year, and how the poor man had been sick for years. 'I had to sell the farm for a finish,' she said. 'I couldn't manage it on my own. It wasn't big enough to pay a man to work in it, but it was too much work without Sean.'

Mick nodded understandingly. 'A farm is a twenty four hour job, ma'am. Even the few cows we have here now would take up most of the evening. When I come in from the bakery, I'm out in the yard and the garden for the rest of the evening.'

'Oh, I can see the work you've put in,' Kitty said admiringly. 'The yard is spotless sure, you could eat your dinner of it, it's so clean – and all the lovely flowers at the front.' She smiled at Mick, and asked: 'Who minds the poultry?'

'Oh, that's Tara's end of things,' Mick said proudly. 'She feeds and looks after them all year, and I kill them for her. This weekend is our busiest time, for all the geese and turkeys have to go for Christmas.' Mick's face became sad. 'Me father used to help her with them . . . when she was small and he was fit.'

Kitty sighed. 'Things change. Isn't it a blessing that we can't see into the future? Sure, you can only plan a day at a time – isn't that all you can do?'

'Indeed,' Mick said. 'Indeed, that's all you can do.'

Tara offered Kitty another cup of tea.

'You're a good girl, and I'm grateful, but I must go home,' Kitty said. 'I've bed linen to iron, and bread to bake, and hopefully I can catch the fire before it goes out on me altogether.' She gave Tara a warm smile. 'That was a lovely breakfast. Mick's a lucky man to have such a handy girl around the house, although he's not as useless as some men I've met.'

Mick got to his feet now, and followed her to the door. 'Thanks for coming now, ma'am . . . it was good of you,' Tara heard him say, as they walked out. Then, she heard Kitty giving a little laugh: 'Will you go away out of that, and don't be "ma'aming" me, Mick Flynn! It's *Kitty* to you, and always has been. Haven't we known each other since we were in Mrs Donlon's class in school?'

Mick must have said something funny in return, because they both burst out laughing. Then, Mick walked alongside Kitty, while she wheeled her bike to the end of the lane. Tara had a funny feeling as she watched them from the window. She hadn't realised that it was *Mick* that Kitty knew. She had presumed it was her Granda. She'd never known Mick to chat so easily to anyone before, never mind a woman. It was yet another change in the life she had been so certain of.

Tara turned away from the window, feeling a sudden chill go through her.

Chapter Fourteen

The Christmas week came and went in a flurry of goose down and snow. It was the quietest Christmas that Tara had known, and she missed her granda so much, she felt a physical pain when she thought of him. Even the news that he had left her three hundred pounds in his will had given her little comfort. She had felt shocked at first that her granda had left that kind of money at all. Mick told her that one of her granda's bachelor brothers in America had left him most of the money a few years ago, and Noel had carefully added his life savings to the amount.

'Me father wanted you to have it,' Mick said. 'He said he was only sorry he didn't have it when you were younger . . . when your mother died, to have made life a bit easier for you then.'

Tara had stared at Mick for a few seconds, then she rushed into her bedroom and cried for two full hours.

When she went to pay the cheque into her account, Tara felt guilty that she should have the rewards of her granda's hard work, and that he hadn't used at least some of the money to make life easier for himself. He had left a certain amount to Mick and Shay and Joe, but had left Tara the greatest part of the money. According to what Mick told her, her granda reckoned that it would make up for losing her mother at so young an age, and for having such a feckless father as Shay. Only a token amount was left to Joe, because Molly and Maggie had intoned that they planned to leave the future priest and his church all their worldly goods.

On Christmas Eve, Tara went to Midnight Mass on her own, because Mick preferred the early Mass in the morning. Normally she would have stood at the church wall after Mass chatting to people as they came out, but it was a blustery night. It had started off with a light shower of snow, but had ended up with heavy rain.

Tara saw Biddy across the church, sitting beside the stony-faced Lizzie Lawless. She had caught Biddy's eye at the communion rails, but she and Lizzie had disappeared when mass was over. Tara didn't feel like going back to the house on her own, but she had no option, because she wouldn't be welcomed in Lizzie's. Anything which sounded like enjoyment or frivolity – even at Christmas – would not be welcome at Lizzie's.

She thought about calling in on Mrs Kelly, but apart from the Christmas candle in the window, there was no sign of life when she passed her cottage.

As she opened the cottage door, then fumbled in the dark to light the lamp, it suddenly struck Tara how lonely her life was at times. All the other girls in the village would have walked down to church, linking arms and talking about boys. Afterwards, they would have run home in giggling groups, two and three under the one umbrella, trying to keep out of the rain.

Apart from rare outings with the girls at work, and the occasional night at the pictures with Biddy, Tara never went out. She had no time, with her night classes and piano lessons, and all the work she had to do at home. She wondered now if all the hard work would be worth it, in the long run. She knew she was aiming for more out of life than the other girls from Ballygrace. They would be content with a job in one of the factories or shops. Passing the time and earning money, until they got married to a lad they would probably meet at one of the local dances. Tara knew of three girls in her class at school who were already married, and one of them even had a baby.

But on nights like this, Tara wondered what drove her to walk such a different path from the others. Tonight she would have given anything to sit by the fire chatting with another girl. Someone to chat to about ordinary things, like her granda and the Christmases they'd had when she was little. Someone to sit and have a glass of sherry with, and a slice of the Christmas cake that Kitty Dunne had handed in.

But there *was* no one to sit and talk to. And there was no point in brooding about it. Resignedly, Tara banked up the fire, lit a fresh candle – and went to bed.

Christmas Day wasn't as bad as Tara expected, because they had asked Mrs Kelly to come over for lunch at one o'clock. Mick had got a large goose cooked in the bakery, and Mrs Kelly did a nice stuffing and roast potatoes to go along with it. She told Tara that she had enjoyed cooking for them, because recently she had lost all interest in it. It wasn't worth the effort just for herself.

The two aunties in Tullamore had asked Mick and Tara to join them and Joe on Christmas Day. Mick had declined on behalf of both of them, saying that he'd rather be at home, since it was the first Christmas without his father. As it turned out, Joe was laid up over the holidays with flu, and it was just as well since he could have passed it on to the others.

Later on in the evening, after Nelly Kelly had gone home, Mick announced that he was going out for an hour. Tara knew that it couldn't be for a drink, because the pubs were closed on Christmas Day, but she felt she had no right to question him. Once again, Tara was left with her own company. She listened to the radio for a while, and then went off to bed early with a book.

Biddy appeared at the cottage the next morning – St Stephen's Day – with two tickets for a New Year's Eve dance in Tullamore. Tara couldn't refuse because Biddy said her ticket was a Christmas present, in return for the lovely perfume and soap which Tara had bought her. Biddy did not divulge the real motive for going to the dance. She had heard that PJ Murphy would be going, and she desperately needed an excuse to see him.

'Will Lizzie let you into Tullamore for a dance?' Tara asked doubtfully. 'You said she was being very awkward at the minute.'

'She's awkward *all* the time,' Biddy stated. 'But I'm going whether she likes it or not. I'm eighteen years of age, and I'm fed up being treated like a child. Anyway, it might be the last chance I'll get to go to a dance until . . .'

'Until when?' Tara asked, cutting two slices off the Christmas cake.

Biddy gulped. She nearly said '*until after the baby's born*' because she couldn't think about anything else at the moment. 'Until . . . St Patrick's night.' She fiddled with her newly washed hair. 'You know what Lizzie's like . . . it could be St Patrick's night before she'd let me out again.'

Tara checked the tickets. 'It would be terrible if Lizzie stops you at the last minute, and she's contrary enough to do it.'

'I'm positive. I'm definitely goin'.' Biddy's eyes glinted with excitement. 'I've decided what I'm wearin' already. It's a real fancy affair – and I've seen a dress in Tullamore that I'm goin' to buy for it. It's bright pink, and it has a real low neck.'

'Not *too* low, I hope?'

'Just low enough!' Biddy laughed. Low enough to let PJ Murphy know what he was missing, and to bring him scurrying back to her. 'I'm goin' in to Tullamore to buy it as soon as all the shops are open again.'

'Is it expensive?' Tara asked.

Biddy shrugged. 'I can't remember the price, but I know I have enough put by. The priest gave me some extra money in me hand, instead of givin' it all to Lizzie. An' I've been promised a bonus at the bakery too, because I'll be puttin' in extra hours over Christmas. I chat up all the oul' fellas in the bakery and the delivery men, and they've all been promisin' me a tip for Christmas. God, the older men are easy fooled!' she said with a raucous laugh. 'Except yer Uncle Mick of course. He's a confirmed bachelor, and I've too much respect to be trick-actin' wi' him.'

'He'd tell you where to go quick enough – the same Mick,' Tara warned her. 'You should be more careful, you know, Biddy. Your messing about could land you in trouble one of these days.'

'Ah, sure they know I'm only codding them,' Biddy said, like a woman of the world. 'They're all harmless enough. Anyway, I've been workin' hard these past few months, so I deserve a new dress for once.' She felt bad for telling Tara a pack of lies about getting tips and everything, but she couldn't explain that she'd saved up twenty pounds out of the money that Dinny gave her for being 'nice' to him. If she couldn't have him, at least she could buy a fancy dress and have a night out dancing with other boys, to spite him.

Tara poured out two mugs of tea. 'I'll have to think about what to wear myself.'

'Sure you have a wardrobe full of clothes – you've plenty of choice.

I'm all excited about this dance,' Biddy said dreamily. 'It's the first New Year's dance I've ever been to in Tullamore.'

As she walked back to Lizzie's, Biddy thought that it wouldn't be long until the baby started to show, and how everything would then change. She was already starting to feel a bit sick in the mornings and she was more tired than usual. Deep inside she was delighted at the prospect of having a baby of her own – someone that would be a real blood relation – but she was terrified about the reaction she would get from other people.

Tara was a big worry. Biddy didn't know how she would react at all. Maybe she would never speak to her again. Tara was very holy. Apart from mass on a Sunday she also went during the week if she could and to Confession every Saturday night.

It was funny, Biddy mused, how she and Tara never talked much about boys or anything personal like that. She reckoned it was because they liked different sorts of boys.

The boys Biddy liked were *not* the sort of boys that Tara would bother with, so there was no point in getting into rows over it. Tara only approved of boys like Gabriel Fitzgerald – but Biddy thought there was no fun or *craic* with ones like *him*. The sorts of things that Gabriel would likely talk about would be boring oul' books and studying, or even worse – religion and politics. Biddy shuddered at the thought.

God knows what would have happened if Tara knew about her and Dinny. Dinny had buggered off to Tyrellspass, and she hadn't heard a word from him since. She'd tried numerous times to tell Lizzie what Dinny had been up to for years, but Lizzie had walloped her with the broom for daring to say such a terrible thing about the poor lodger.

She would probably have *murdered* Biddy if she knew the truth about Dinny and the others. Biddy wondered if PJ Murphy would be at the dance and, if he was, what she would say. It was a bit awkward because she hadn't seen him since that last night in Tullamore. They were supposed to have met to go to the pictures in Daingean the following Sunday, but he hadn't turned up.

She wondered what the chances were of him being the baby's father. She didn't really know how a baby was conceived, but from the little she did, she reckoned that there was no real chance of the baby's father being Dinny or PJ. Out of the *three* men that had 'tampered' with Biddy, the one she truly wished was the baby's father – was PJ.

The real father would remain a dark secret. A secret that Biddy would take to her grave.

In the meantime, she would stick to the story about the three boys dragging her into the bushes. At least the bit about there being three of them was the truth – but only one of them was a boy. Whenever the time came to tell Tara her secret, she would stick to the safe story.

If the truth came out, Biddy knew she wouldn't have a friend in the whole wide world.

Madeleine was allowed out of hospital in time for Christmas. She came home the same day that Gabriel broke up at university, which took some pressure off Elisha. On Christmas morning the family drove into Tullamore for twelve o'clock Mass. Elisha decided that it was best not to rush Madeleine too early. The new drugs the hospital had prescribed – although effectively controlling the more worrying aspects of her behaviour – made her sluggish for the first few hours of the day. She looked more like her old self. Her hair had grown a bit, and she had lost some weight. There was no mention about God talking to her or any of the other voices she had been hearing.

Elisha decided that this year Christmas celebrations would be kept to a minimum because of Madeleine's condition and because Elisha was now wary of inviting people, after the fiasco of her daughter's birthday party.

'I really feel people are not as concerned about Madeleine as you think,' William said on Christmas afternoon, as he, Elisha and Gabriel were relaxing with a drink. 'I'm sure there would be no problems if we were to invite a few friends over to celebrate St Stephen's night.'

Elisha went to the sitting-room door to check that Madeleine was upstairs, and out of earshot. She came back a few moments later, biting her lower lip. 'I wouldn't feel confident enough . . . not yet.'

'For heaven's sake, isn't she back to her old self?' William sighed. 'She's very quiet and is hardly likely to offend anyone. We can't live our lives in perpetual fear of what Madeleine *might* do or say.'

'It's too early,' Elisha insisted. She walked over to the large bay window, a deep frown forming between her brows. 'I couldn't relax . . . I would be watching her all the time . . . worrying what was going through her mind.'

'Look, Mother,' Gabriel intervened, 'if you would like to invite friends for drinks, then ask them. I'll be quite happy to sit upstairs with Madeleine . . . listening to music or playing games. Father's right – we can't live our lives worrying about Madeleine all the time.'

Elisha stared out of the window at the bare, wintry garden. 'I'm not sure – it wouldn't be fair on you.'

William came over to stand beside her. 'How would it be,' he said, putting his arm around her, 'if we invite her young friend from Ballygrace? It would keep Madeleine company, and leave Gabriel free to mix with the other guests. It would also give . . .' He paused. 'I can't think of the girl's name . . .'

'Tara,' Elisha said helpfully. 'Tara Flynn. You'll have to remember that if she's going to start working for you soon.'

'Yes, indeed,' he said, guiding her back to the fireside. 'It would also give *Tara* a distraction from her situation at home . . . her grandfather's death and all that sorry business.' He seated Elisha, then poured them both a small sherry. 'I think having a friend here to occupy Madeleine would serve the purpose. I could also talk to Tara about her position in the office, and the particular jobs I would like her to pass on to Madeleine, when she's ready.'

Elisha looked thoughtful. It would indeed be a relief to have Madeleine out of the house, and have someone else taking responsibility for her. 'I see your point about inviting a friend over,' she said slowly, 'but I have reservations about Tara Flynn.'

'Oh?' William raised a surprised eyebrow.

'Her class,' Elisha said bluntly. 'However the girl may present herself, she's still of the peasant variety.' She took a dainty sip of the sherry. 'I know it's wrong to judge people on what they have . . . and normally I'd be the last to do it. But we have never had this close contact with her sort before. Working for the family is one thing, mixing socially is another. I'm just not sure if it's the right thing to do. I'm not sure if it's the right thing for Madeleine. It's as if we are saying she's not worthy to have the same class of friends that the rest of the family has.'

'Mother,' Gabriel said gently, 'Madeleine has *no* other friends. It's over a month since her birthday party, and not one of her school friends has contacted her. Any Christmas cards she received from them had little messages saying how busy they would be over the holidays. They were quite plainly stating that they would not be available to visit her, or have her visit them.'

William gave a little sigh of relief, and settled back in his armchair. It was very gratifying to have Gabriel argue his case for him. It was a delicate one, because he did not wish to appear to have any personal interest in Tara Flynn. He had always conducted his previous liaison in Athlone with great delicacy. Now that the affair was over and done with, there was a gap in his life. A gap that he felt might be filled with the daily contact of a beautiful young woman with striking red hair.

'Tara Flynn is not an *ordinary* girl,' Gabriel continued, still fighting Tara's corner. 'She's not to be compared with the others from Ballygrace. She's highly intelligent, well read, and is currently educating herself at evening classes to a higher standard than many of the so-called gentry. To look at her – her clothes and the way she carries herself – she could easily be mistaken for one of the girls from Madeleine's boarding school. In fact, she's better spoken and has more interesting conversation than *any* of those girls.'

'But her *father* . . .' Elisha persisted in a high voice. ' *"Peasant"* is the only word to describe the man. According to Mrs Scully he's also a *drunk*, and an incompetent husband and father . . .'

Gabriel shrugged. 'She's never lived with him. She was brought up by her grandfather, who was a respectable man.'

Elisha turned to William. 'What do *you* think?'

'Mmm?' William looked at her in a deliberately distracted manner, designed to convey disinterest in the situation. 'I can't see that it would do any harm. I'm quite prepared to stick my neck out for Madeleine's sake, and have the girl work in the office.' He leaned across and patted his wife's knee. 'The home is your domain, and you must decide as to whether you want the girl as a friend for Madeleine, or not.' He smiled warmly. 'As always, I have complete faith in your judgement.'

Tara came to spend St Stephen's night with the Fitzgeralds. William had driven Madeleine over to the cottage to ask her around lunchtime, and they picked her up at seven o'clock that night. Tara said that she would be more than happy to cycle over, rather than have William going to the trouble of driving out to the cottage again.

'It's my pleasure, dear,' William said, looking deep into her eyes. 'And in any case, the weather report is none too good for the next few days.'

As Tara closed the door after they had gone, she thought how William Fitzgerald had the exact same blue eyes as his son, although one was fair and the other dark. She smiled and wondered if Gabriel would look as young and handsome as his father when he reached middle age.

Tara's visit on St Stephen's night went so well that she was invited to join the family again for lunch on New Year's day. She had actually been asked to stay overnight on New Year's Eve, but she had apologised, explaining that a friend had bought her a ticket for a dance in Tullamore.

'Are the tickets for the dance all gone?' Madeleine asked eagerly.

Gabriel stood behind his sister, frantically shaking his head.

'Yes, I'm afraid they are,' Tara replied. 'Biddy said she got the last two tickets.' She consoled her by saying, 'I think it might be full of old farmers – not the kind of place you'd like, Madeleine. I'm only going because I don't want to let Biddy down, since she paid for the tickets. If it's a good night, I'll go with you another time. I'm led to believe they have a dance every month in that hall.'

Later on, Gabriel quietly thanked Tara for putting Madeleine off the dance. 'She's just not well enough for public places at the moment,' he explained. 'Maybe in a month or so.'

All the Fitzgerald family were grateful to Tara. Not only had she conducted herself well within the family circle, but she had also given a very good account of herself with their guests, two businessmen and their wives, who had travelled over from the Birr area.

They were quite unaware of Tara's background, and had assumed she was a friend of Madeleine's from boarding school. No one asked directly about her family; they seemed much more interested in the accounting work she had been doing in the distillery, and the fact she was going to work for Fitzgerald's auctioneering business in the new year.

After supper, when the women had gone through to the sitting-room to have coffee, and Madeleine and Tara had departed upstairs, the three men and Gabriel sat in the dining-room with cigars and brandy.

'An exquisite-looking young woman,' David Coombes, a balding, wealthy businessman commented to William, 'and such striking red hair.' He leaned forward. 'And a fine pair of breasts too! Oh, a man could be sent mad with the likes of those breasts . . . and the thought of that soft hair tumbling down over them – all naked and bare!' He laughed softly and dug William in the ribs. 'Some hope we'd have of that – I say – some hope we'd have of that at our age!' He pointed his half-smoked cigar in Gabriel's direction. 'It's a young buck the likes of Gabriel she'd be looking out for, wouldn't you say? A young buck?'

William took a mouthful of his brandy. 'Indeed,' he said aloud, 'indeed she might.' And there again, he thought to himself, indeed she might not.

'I can't believe the difference in Madeleine when Tara is here. She really knows how to handle her,' Elisha said in amazement to William, after the guests had departed. 'For the first time in weeks, I felt I could relax in my own home without having to check on her every five minutes. Tara talks to her about ordinary things, and if Madeleine wavers off and starts talking about religion or other inappropriate subjects, she just guides her back to the main topic again. She's more in tune with her condition than some of the doctors we've been paying good money for. Gabriel was right – we shouldn't judge people by their backgrounds. The girl is a godsend – no less than a godsend!'

Biddy called for Tara on New Year's Eve as planned. She cycled over, an hour earlier than planned, in a high state of excitement, wearing her new pink dress and a nice belted coat which Tara had grown out of.

'You look lovely!' Tara said, smiling in admiration, when she opened the door. 'What have you done to yourself?'

Biddy did a pirouette round the floor and then proceeded to regale Tara with all the details of her new hairdo and the new makeup she had bought. 'Mary McGinn – from up the backroad – she's learnin' to be a hairdresser. She's really brilliant; she copied the style from a magazine.' She took off her chiffon headscarf, and patted the piled-up hair, held together by hairclips and hairspray. 'D'you like my nail varnish? It's called "French Chiffon". I got it from the chemist's in Tullamore, and the girl picked me out a pink lipstick to match.' She pursed her lips together in a kissing motion for full effect.

'You look great, Biddy – just great,' Tara said, although she wasn't quite sure about the make-up. For her own taste, it looked a bit on the heavy side. Still, looking at the attractive girl in front of her now, Biddy was a million miles off the poor, starved little orphan Tara had known when they first started school together. Although still on the thin and small side, she had developed into a very good-looking young woman. The poor, straggly hair was now a rich healthy brown and the dirty clothes were a thing of the past since she was allowed to do her own washing when she was doing the priest's.

'Did you have trouble from Lizzie about going out?' Tara called from her bedroom as she changed into her own outfit. Earlier in the evening, when Mick had gone out on one of his recent jaunts, she had filled the tin bath and soaked in front of the blazing fire.

'Lizzie gave me no trouble at all,' Biddy replied, 'because she's in bed again with the runs. She was up the whole night with the diarrhoea.'

'Again? She's had a lot of trouble with that recently, hasn't she?'

'She has,' Biddy said lightly. 'And it's me that knows all about it – runnin' about emptyin' buckets and everythin'. It would turn yer stomach.'

Tara pulled an agonised face. 'Has she been to the doctor?'

'She says she'll call him out tomorrow if there's no improvement. She'll likely be fine by then.' She looked into the mirror above the fireplace and admired her new hairdo again. 'It does her no harm to have to take to her bed now and again. It makes her a bit more pleasant when she knows she's dependin' on you,' Biddy said unsympathetically. 'How many people would be willing to clean up all the mess, and have to cut up newspaper and everythin' for a cantankerous ould' witch like her?' She gave a little laugh. 'It's a pity she doesn't have the diarrhoea more often – she might be more civil to people then. The only thing she has any regard for is money.'

'As long as it's not too serious,' Tara said with a frown. 'It's very bad for you to have anything like that for long. It's weakening to the system.'

'Oh, there's no fear of anythin' serious happening to Lizzie,' Biddy said. 'She'll be up and about in the mornin', moanin' and groanin' as usual.' She lifted the kettle from the hearth and put it on the hook over the fire. 'Will I make us a cup of tea while you're gettin' ready, Tara?'

'Grand,' Tara called back, 'and you can cut some cakebread and cheese, and a slice each of Christmas cake. We'll have to keep our strength up, if we're going to be dancing all night and cycling there and back!'

After queuing in the cold for twenty minutes to get in, it was a relief for everyone when the dance hall doors were opened and the crowd surged in. The hall – its cold walls normally bare and bereft of any adornment – was festive and welcoming with garlands of holly and ivy, and brightly coloured paper decorations. There was even a Christmas tree with shiny ornaments and coloured lights to the side of the stage.

'Isn't it beautiful?' Biddy breathed, excited before the evening had even begun. She couldn't wait to get into the ladies' cloakroom to divest herself of the coat and show off her new dress. 'Won't it be great when we get the electricity in Ballygrace? We'll all be able to have Christmas trees with coloured lights then.' She giggled and nudged Tara. 'Can't you just imagine Lizzie's face if I asked her to buy a Christmas tree and fairy-lights?'

Once all the checking of hair and the re-applying of powder and lipstick had been completed in front of the mottled old mirror, the girls hung up their coats and scarves in the cloakroom, and went back into the main hall.

'Your suit's lovely, Tara – that dark wine colour looks well with your hair. Where did you get it?' Biddy asked as they looked for a place to sit.

'Dublin. It's the rig-out I bought for Madeleine's party. I thought it would be warmer since it has a jacket.' She gave a laugh. 'And if I get the feet danced off me and I get too hot, I can always take the jacket off.'

The three-piece band started up with a quickstep, and within seconds, several female couples were out on the floor getting into the swing of things. Groups of males of all ages lined along one wall of the hall, while the girls sat primly on the wooden forms on the opposite side, waiting until the band struck up in earnest.

Biddy and Tara walked halfway down the hall, Biddy greeting anyone she knew with a loud 'how-ya' as they passed. They found a space on one of the forms and sat down.

'Won't you be cold?' Tara commented as Biddy took her cardigan off, to reveal the low-cut, sleeveless dress. 'It's freezing in this place.'

Biddy rubbed her goose-pimpled arms. 'I'd sooner be cold than look like an oul' granny in a knitted cardigan.' She gave Tara a sidelong grin. 'Hopefully, I'll soon have a nice pair of arms to keep me warm. Did you see who's just walked in? And don't make it too obvious that you're lookin' at him.'

Tara kept her head straight, and swivelled her eyes to the door. 'That PJ Murphy?' She pulled a distinctly unimpressed face. 'Don't tell me you still have a notion of him – and him after standing you up?'

'He might not have been let out that night,' Biddy said defensively. 'His mother and father are fierce strict.'

'He made no effort to let you know,' Tara pointed out, 'leaving you waiting in the cold. I'd have nothing to do with him, if I were you.'

But you're not desperate for a father for yer baby, Biddy thought. 'I'll see what he has to say for himself if he dances me later . . . but I won't go runnin' after him.'

As soon as the band struck up the first proper dance, both girls were met with a rush of partners, and no sooner had they sat down when the same thing happened for the next, and the next dance again. Tara realised her lie to Madeleine about the dance being full of farmers was nearer the truth than she thought. As soon as they asked her where she came from, she found herself engaged in conversation about all the great grazing there was out in Ballygrace.

After putting up with several heavy-footed farmers tramping on her toes, Tara made her way back to the ladies' cloakroom in search of Biddy, who had disappeared ten minutes earlier. The last Tara had seen of her, she was in a deep conversation with PJ Murphy at the side of the dance floor. She presumed they had gone outside for a breath of fresh air. At least she hoped that was what they had gone outside for.

At times, Biddy's behaviour when she was around lads worried Tara. She seemed to play up to anyone who would give her a bit of attention – even if she'd only been introduced to them. In the last year or so, Tara had heard rumours about Biddy too – terrible rumours about her going with men – which she had ignored.

She had ignored the stories because it was usually someone like her father who spread them, or some of the women gossiping in the doctor's surgery or queuing in a shop. Her innate sense of privacy about her own life made her unwilling to listen to gossip about anyone else. Especially when that gossip was about Biddy – her only real friend in the village. Whatever was said about Biddy – whether it was the truth or lies – Tara would defend her to the last.

When she emerged back in the hall, trying to look casually round the place for her friend without looking desperate, Tara felt a hand on her arm.

'May I have the pleasure, Miss Flynn?' a familiar voice said. Tara's legs suddenly felt weak. It was Gabriel Fitzgerald – looking like a film star in a navy corduroy jacket.

'I'll just put my bag down on the form,' she said, attempting a casual manner.

In seconds she was back beside him and they stepped out on to the dance floor. 'I didn't know you were coming to the dance,' Tara said as they moved around the floor, in time to a slow waltz. 'You never mentioned it when I said I was coming with Biddy.'

'That's because I didn't know I was coming,' he replied. 'I didn't know anything about the dance until you mentioned it the other night. The following day, a fellow from university – from Birr – rang me and asked if I knew of anything going on for New Year's Eve.' He looked down at Tara and gave a little laugh. 'And then I remembered the farmers' dance.'

Tara looked at him with a mischievous glint in her eye. 'I was telling the truth when I told Madeleine it would be full of farmers. I've danced with four of them tonight and I've got the bruises to prove it. All they could talk about was their grand cows and sheep, and how much land their families owned.'

'They must have been trying to impress you, Tara,' Gabriel said, laughing again. 'Farmers never divulge how much land they have unless they have something to gain! I'd watch yourself there – they must think you'd make a grand farmer's wife.'

'Go away with you!' Tara retorted. 'Me with a farmer? Can you imagine it?'

He slowed down for a moment, then held her at arm's length as though studying her carefully. 'No,' he said in mock seriousness, 'I don't somehow see you as a farmer's wife. It's the legs. I couldn't really see you in wellington boots somehow.'

Tara pushed him playfully and he caught her round the waist. His hands reached under her jacket, so that there was only the fabric of her dress between them, and pulled her closer to him. So close, she could feel his warm breath on her neck. Then she was suddenly conscious of the touch of his fingers. For a fleeting moment, it felt as though he was actually touching her bare skin and a strange, warm feeling spread throughout her body. So warm, she was afraid that Gabriel could feel it too.

As they danced round the floor, chatting and joking lightly with each other, Tara wondered if Gabriel had planned to meet up with her tonight, or whether this was just a casual thing to him. She had no way of knowing. She would just have to be patient and wait.

After what seemed like ages, the dance number finished, and almost as quickly another one struck up. They started dancing again – closer this time. Without a word being spoken, Tara knew that she was going to spend the rest of the evening with Gabriel Fitzgerald.

When it came to the break for tea and biscuits, Gabriel joined the queue for the refreshments and Tara went round the hall looking for Biddy. She found her in a corner, leaning up against a window-sill and still talking very earnestly to PJ Murphy.

'Are you okay, Biddy?' Tara asked, throwing a disapproving eye at her companion. 'I looked for you earlier, but I couldn't find you.'

'I'm sorry Tara. I got chattin' to PJ. I saw you on the floor with

Gabriel Fitzgerald, so I knew you were all right.' She looked across the hall where the queue was lined up outside the kitchen. 'Have they started serving the tea yet?' she said, changing the subject. 'I could do with a cup . . . I'm feelin' a bit light-headed.'

PJ got to his feet rather unsteadily, showing signs of having indulged in a festive drink before coming into the hall. 'I'll fetch it for you,' he said thickly. 'I'll be back in a minute.'

Tara folded her arms and put her head to the side in an inquisitory manner. 'Well,' she said, 'what excuse did he give you for standing you up?'

'His feckin' ould mammy!' Biddy said bitterly. 'She says that PJ should be doing a line with somebody more suitable – one of the girls from the local farms.' Tears welled up in her eyes and she dropped her head and looked down at the floor. 'She says I'm not good enough for him.'

Tara leaned against the window frame beside her friend, and put her arm round her. 'Come on, Biddy – he's not worth it. There's plenty of boys like him around. Don't go making a fool of yourself over him. You could do a lot better than him – there's plenty of boys out there on the dance floor who would be interested in you.'

'But I haven't got the time to waste on looking for another lad, and anyway, he likes me . . . he told me only a few minutes ago,' Biddy snivelled. 'It's only his ould mother that's coming between us.'

'What's the big rush?' Tara said lightly. 'We're only eighteen years old – sure we've got our whole lives ahead of us.'

'You might have plenty of time –' Biddy said, then she bit her tongue, realising that she was divulging more than she intended to.

Tara caught sight of Gabriel's blond head weaving its way through the crowds. She signalled to him and he came over to the two girls. 'Hello, Biddy,' he said warmly, 'I haven't seen you for a while.' He handed Tara a cup of tea and the one intended for himself he handed to Biddy. The small gesture wasn't lost on Tara and she gave him a grateful smile.

'There's more – there's more!' he said in a jokey fashion, digging out several custard creams from his jacket pocket and handing them to the two girls. 'You're looking very well,' he said turning to Biddy. 'That's a lovely dress you're wearing.'

'D'you think so?' Biddy managed a watery smile, always receptive to a compliment. 'How's Madeleine? I heard she's not been too well in herself . . . I'm sorry to hear it.'

Gabriel dug his hands deep into his jacket pocket. 'She's grand at the minute, Biddy,' he said quietly. 'I'll tell her you were asking for her.'

PJ came back a few minutes later, with a half-cup of tea, having spilt the rest in the saucer on the way back. Seeing Biddy already with a cup, he proceeded to drink it himself.

A strained atmosphere which had not been there before descended on the group, and it became patently obvious that PJ was not at ease in either Tara or Gabriel's company.

He didn't seem anxious to be with Biddy either, Tara thought, from the way he kept watching the other girls in the dance hall. Tara quickly finished off her tea, and when the band struck up again for the second half of the night, Gabriel guided her back on to the floor.

'Biddy's looking great these days,' he commented. 'You'd hardly know her. I don't mean any harm, but she was a sad-looking sight at school. I always felt rather sorry for her. It's nice to see her looking so well.'

Tara nodded. 'Yes, she does look well.' Privately, she thought that Biddy wasn't quite herself tonight – it was probably all that business about PJ. 'What about your friend from Birr?' she said, changing the subject. 'Is he still around?'

'Oh, he's fine,' Gabriel replied. 'He came with a few others, so he won't be at a loss. They have a car with them, so they can head off any time they like.'

'What about you?' Tara dared to ask, leaning back slightly so that she could see the expression on his face. She had watched Biddy making a fool of herself with a man tonight, and she wasn't about to make the same mistake.

'I'm in no rush home tonight,' he told her. Then, he pulled her closer to him once again, and kissed her full on the mouth.

Oh, Gabriel! Tara thought, as his lips pressed harder, and her heart started racing. *This is what I've been waiting for all my life. This is why I've never let another boy near me. This is what I've worked every minute of the day for – to belong to you and your world!*

A long moment later, after he had stopped to let her catch her breath, he whispered in her ear: 'Do you know that you're the most beautiful girl in this hall, Tara Flynn?' And when she laughed in embarrassed disbelief, he added: 'You *are* beautiful – beautiful and elegant – and I only came here tonight because of you.'

The rest of the dance passed in a wonderful haze for Tara, and she stood in the packed hall clinging to Gabriel, hardly noticing when the bells were rung to herald in the New Year. Later, she caught sight of Biddy in the crowd, and pushed her way over to put her arms round her and wish her 'Happy New Year'.

'I don't feel as if it's going to be a happy new year,' Biddy said, looking very woebegone. 'I think it might be for you – but definitely not for me. I think it's going to be the worst year I've ever had.'

'Don't be so morbid,' Tara told her, the ecstatic happiness she felt shining in her own green eyes. 'We're young – we've got our whole lives in front of us.' She paused for a moment. 'Look – I've had some awful things happen to me this past year. Losing my granda was the worst thing I could imagine . . . but I know he'd want me to be happy.' She touched her friend's arm. 'I know Lizzie gets you down at times, but she's letting you out more – things will get better soon.' She looked over Biddy's shoulder at the sullen-faced PJ. 'If he's messing you about, then just forget him. There's plenty more fish in the sea.'

Biddy dropped her eyes. 'I know he's not the best . . . but he'd do. If he would just have me – he would suit me fine.' The band struck up another waltz. Tara suddenly felt the urge to have Gabriel's arms around her waist again, so she patted Biddy's arm soothingly and told her she'd see her later.

The rest of the night flew by and suddenly Tara was standing hand in hand with Gabriel Fitzgerald while the band played the 'Soldiers' Song' – heralding the end of the dance and the start of another year. They had another long kiss and, although the floor was now crowded with other courting couples, it was as if she and Gabriel were the only other people in the whole place.

Shortly afterwards, Tara went back into the cloakroom for her coat and scarf, keeping an eye out for Biddy as she went. But there was no sign of her or the skulking PJ. Arm in arm, she and Gabriel filed out of the smoky hall behind all the other dancers, then they went round the side of the hall to collect their bikes.

'Biddy's bike has gone,' Tara told Gabriel in a surprised tone, as they wheeled their bikes out on to the road. 'She must have gone on ahead.'

'Don't worry,' Gabriel replied. 'We'll probably catch her up on the road somewhere.'

Biddy had gone on ahead with PJ, and they were walking out the Cappincur road – she pushing the bike and her escort on foot. She was glad when the dance had finished, because, on their own, she could demand his full attention. She also wanted to dodge Tara, because she knew PJ would take the chance to head off, if her 'posh' friends joined them again. Biddy also knew that she had to take this chance to sort things out about the baby. She couldn't take the chance of anyone spoiling it again.

'Are you sure?' PJ repeated stupidly for the fourth time.

'I'm sure.' Biddy was getting fed up with his questioning. 'I've been to the doctor's and I'm due the end of May.'

'But we did it standin' up against the wall,' he protested, giving her Dinny's old argument. 'It's not supposed to happen if you do it that way.' He paused to light a cigarette to calm his nerves. 'And anyway . . . surely you can't be expectin' after doin' it for the first time? You said it was the first time – didn't you?'

'What d'you feckin' well take me for?' Biddy challenged. 'A dirty little whore or somethin'? Of course it was the first time. You were a bit quick, that was all – but we definitely did it.' Her mind worked quickly. 'I read about it all in a book, so I know for a fact.'

PJ drew deeply on his cigarette. 'I never read books,' he said lamely.

'You should,' Biddy said, more kindly. 'You learn a lot of things from books. Anyway, what are we goin' to do?'

He shrugged, then turned his head away. 'Me mammy will kill me stone dead,' he said in a low voice. 'You don't know what she's capable of. She's worse than any man when she starts.'

'What about me?' Biddy said. 'What am I supposed to do? I've no family to help me out or anythin'. The priest says if there's no lad to stand by me, then I'll have to go into a convent for fallen women in Dublin.'

PJ hunched his thin shoulders and took another drag on his cigarette.

'You wouldn't let that happen to me, would ye?' Biddy beseeched. 'You'll ask yer mother about us gettin' married . . . won't you?'

'*Married?*' he repeated in a horrified tone, picturing his mother if he told her. 'Sure, I'm only seventeen years old. I'm too young to be married.'

Biddy threw her bike in the ditch. 'You weren't too feckin' young when you had me up against the church wall,' she roared into his face. 'Were you?'

'I can't get married!' he roared back on the verge of hysteria. 'We weren't even courtin' – sure, I hardly feckin' knew you . . . and we were only at it the once.'

'It was long enough,' she said. 'Just the once was enough to have me expectin'.'

PJ threw the half-smoked cigarette away and then he stared up into the sky, as though seeking divine inspiration.

Biddy reached out and tentatively touched his hair. When he didn't move, she put her arms tightly round him. 'It'll be all right,' she said soothingly. 'It's just the shock – I was the same. I know we're fierce young to be gettin' married and everythin' – but wouldn't it be grand to have the baby, and still be young ourselves?'

PJ said nothing. He just stared over Biddy's shoulder into the blackness of the night.

When Tara and Gabriel rounded the corner on their bikes a short while later, they came upon the other pair standing like statues, with Biddy's arms still wrapped possessively round the boy she hoped would be her husband.

'C'mon, Biddy,' Tara called as she came upon her friend. 'It's after three o'clock and we've a good bit to cycle yet.'

PJ took the chance to extricate himself from Biddy's grip. 'I'll have to go home,' he said, heading back in the direction of Tullamore. 'I'll see you.'

'*When?*' Biddy called back loudly, picking her bicycle up from the wet grass. 'When will I see you?'

'Soon enough,' he replied, and then – without a backward glance – he disappeared into the darkness.

Gabriel cycled with the girls as far as the finger-post showing '*Ballygrace – 1 mile*'. Then, after whispering something in Tara's ear and kissing her lightly on the lips, he turned off for Ballygrace House. Tara stared after him until his shape disappeared in the early morning mist.

'That was a good night, wasn't it?' Tara said as she and Biddy got ready to start on the last leg of their journey. She buttoned her coat up to the neck and tied her headscarf tightly under her chin, aware of the biting cold for the first time since they left Tullamore. 'The dance was great,' she said in a faraway voice, thinking back to the slow waltzes she and Gabriel had earlier in the evening. 'It was a great idea of yours to go to the dance – thanks for buying me the ticket.'

'I'm glad you enjoyed it,' Biddy said over her shoulder as they mounted the bikes again.

'It's hard to imagine that another year has started already,' Tara commented as they cycled along. 'I wonder if there will be many changes ahead for us?'

'I wonder,' Biddy repeated.

Then, the two friends cycled along in silence, each deep in her own thoughts.

Chapter Fifteen

❧

1950

If Rosie Scully still bore a grudge against Tara Flynn, she kept it well concealed on New Year's Day as she served lunch. She and young Ella dished up roast beef and Yorkshire pudding – which Tara had never eaten before – thick slices of honey-coated ham and a selection of vegetable dishes. This was followed by sherry trifle and left-over Christmas cake. Although she liked to provide good, well presented food at all times, Elisha Fitzgerald did not like waste.

Mrs Scully kept a tight smile pinned to her face – even though she had earmarked the remaining quarter of the Christmas cake for herself – and offered the dishes to Tara in the same polite manner as she did to the members of the family. The sweetcake, she had planned, would accompany her nightly glass of sherry, which she had also purloined from the Fitzgerald household. No matter – she would make up for it with the tin of luxury chocolate biscuits she had hidden in the depths of a kitchen press, to be retrieved on her way out tonight.

Tara murmured a polite 'thank you' to the housekeeper as the meal was served to her, but avoided any eye contact with the older woman. Lying in bed that morning Tara had made several New Year's resolutions, and one of them was to treat Rosie Scully with no more than the polite indifference she would accord a waitress in a tearoom. She would no longer care what other people thought of her – especially begrudging people like Mrs Scully.

As she sat across the table from Madeleine and her handsome brother, Tara thought over all the promises she had made to herself earlier on that day. Her main resolution for the coming year was to continue to improve herself as far as she could in all areas. She reckoned she could do this without spending a lot of money – apart from one major indulgence which she knew would shock both her family and neighbours. This year, Tara was determined to buy herself a good, second-hand piano. She urgently needed it to increase practising her music to gain the grades necessary to teach the piano to younger pupils. She hoped another year of intensive practice would get her to the required standard. This would yield her yet another source of income and ensure that her own musical skills continued to flourish.

To compensate for the outlay of this major luxury, Tara reckoned that she could manage quite well on the good-quality clothes she had accumulated over the last few years, without buying any more for a while. She would work hard in her new job in the auctioneering business, and she would study so that she would pass her exams in the summer, which would allow her to dispense with her evening classes. She would also continue with her little poultry business and the weekend bookkeeping in the shops in Ballygrace.

Although those little jobs didn't earn a lot of money, Tara saved everything she got from them. She also intended to save even more this year from her new auctioneering position because her promotion meant that she would be earning a bit more, and her outgoings would be less.

Her Uncle Mick had been adamant in his refusal to take any money off Tara for her keep, saying that she wasn't a lodger in the cottage. He also said that the time could come when Tara might be thinking of moving to Dublin – or even emigrating to England. Big jobs – the sort he knew that Tara was studying and working hard for – were not easy to come by in places like Tullamore. If she wanted to move, then she would need plenty of money behind her.

Mick Flynn's words had greatly disconcerted his niece, causing her to ponder over why he had thought she might want to move away from Ballygrace. She was sure that she had never given anyone that impression, far less Mick, who had never interfered or shown the remotest interest in her future before. Her granda had been the one to whom she had confided all her hopes and dreams for the future.

Maybe, she told herself, Mick was only trying to fill her granda's shoes in his own ham-fisted way. Whatever good intentions her bachelor uncle had in mind, Tara had *no* intentions of moving to Dublin or England – or anywhere else for that matter. Ballygrace was the only place that held her interest – because Ballygrace was where Gabriel Fitzgerald lived, and the only place where she was likely to see him.

Tara enjoyed New Year's Day lunch and the light conversation which took place during and after it. Unlike St Stephen's Day – when several other people had joined the Fitzgeralds – Tara was their only guest. She was most careful to give each member of the family her undivided attention, as she was determined not to give Gabriel the impression that she had come solely to see him.

Back at the cottage that evening, Tara wondered if she had given Gabriel less attention than the others – but knew it was no bad thing. Instinctively she knew that if a man was worth having, then he was the one who would have to do all the running in the courtship. As she had witnessed with Biddy and PJ Murphy – if a girl made herself too available, he often lost interest.

The day had been a great success in many areas. Tara had automatically reached for the correct cutlery and glasses without having to plan every move in advance, and had also managed her way around the extensive cheeseboard at the end of the meal, without choosing anything which was truly awful.

She used the opportunity to ask William Fitzgerald lots of questions about the office work, and was confident enough to laugh when Gabriel lightly mocked her for taking notes down about her allotted tasks.

'I wouldn't encourage him by working during your own time,' Gabriel said, passing Tara a glass of red wine. 'He'll have you staying behind working overtime every evening, if you show too much willingness. My father can be a ruthless taskmaster.'

William had thrown his head back and laughed aloud along with his wife and the young people. He had every intention of keeping the delectable flame-haired Tara Flynn behind in his office every night if he got the chance – and her scribbled list would certainly not include the activities he had in mind for her.

After the first day working in Fitzgerald's auctioneering business,

Tara knew she was going to love her new job. She found Patricia McManus, the older secretary, to be pleasant and helpful. Bridie, the pregnant girl she was replacing, was equally pleasant, and full of chat about her forthcoming baby. After the first morning, Tara had very quickly picked up how to operate the telephone system. It was actually easier than the complicated system used in the distillery, and she had also acquainted herself with both the filing and the bookkeeping systems.

The area Tara found more interesting was the property side of the business. She found herself captivated by the sheaves of paper giving descriptions of property for sale in Kildare and the surrounding districts. The Offaly end of the business seemed to deal mainly in land sales. Tara had never concerned herself with house prices before, and found it fascinating to compare the prices of houses and businesses. She found herself staring open-mouthed as she examined a particularly fancy brochure which gave details and photographs of a large Georgian building, similar in size to Ballygrace House. The price took her breath away. She closely scrutinised the details about each room and then she got a sheet of headed notepaper and copied down all the financial details, so that she could work out the full cost of buying such a grand house when she got home later. It struck her immediately that the inheritance from her granda would have to be multiplied many times to afford such a place.

With the long dark January evenings, and her time taken up with studying and music, Tara saw very little of Biddy. On one particular occasion when they met outside the church after Mass, Biddy was muffled up in a heavy coat and scarf, and didn't look herself at all. She gave Tara a little wooden jewellery box for her eighteenth birthday, which had been two days before. Tara was delighted and thanked her friend for both the gift and for remembering her birthday.

'Did you get any other presents?' Biddy enquired.

Tara shook her head. 'My father would never think of anything like that – he's not like Madeleine's father. And Mick's run off his feet with the bakery and the outside work.' She sighed and looked down at the jewellery box. 'It was always my granda who remembered my birthday.'

'I haven't been well,' Biddy told her in a sorrowful voice, 'and Lizzie won't let me outside the door. That's why I never got up with yer present before. She even had the priest goin' on at me.'

'Well, at least she's looking after you,' Tara consoled. 'Did you ever see that Murphy fellow again . . . the one at the New Year's Dance?'

Biddy kicked at an icy puddle with one of her thick scuffed boots. 'He was supposed to meet me last week, but he never turned up. I sent a message on Friday, to a girl who works in the factory with his brother, to meet me yesterday evenin' – but he didn't turn up again. An' when I got home, Lizzie half-killed me for bein' out. She laid about me wi' the brush.'

'But you know what she's like about you going out – surely you knew what you were letting yourself in for?'

Biddy sighed. 'She'd been up wi' the diarrhoea all night again – so I thought she'd be asleep and not miss me. Anyway, it would have been worth the beating if PJ had bothered to turn up.'

'But he didn't – and you had to pay the price for it. When will you learn that he's just not worth it?' Tara shook her head and tutted, angry at Biddy for making so little of herself. 'It's for the best. You'll meet somebody better than him.' She put her arm round her forlorn friend. 'The way the boys run after you, you'll have no trouble meeting someone else.'

Biddy gave her a long, strange look, then she asked: 'What about Gabriel Fitzgerald? Are you still doing a line with him?'

Tara cringed inwardly at the idea of describing her friendship with Gabriel as 'doing a line' – the local description for courting. 'He's gone back to university in Dublin,' she said casually, as though she didn't mind. 'I probably won't see him again until Easter.'

'You should get yourself up to Dublin some weekend and see him,' Biddy advised, a livelier look now in her eyes. She always seemed to brighten up when the subject came round to boys and courting. 'What if he meets someone else at the university? There's plenty of girls in Dublin, you know.'

Tara shrugged and clapped her gloved hands together to warm them up. 'If he does, he does. I've no intentions of running up to Dublin after him.' *Why, oh why*, she asked herself, *was Biddy bombarding her with all these questions*? Questions that she had not allowed herself to dwell on. Each word felt like a stick being poked into an open wound.

'Maybe you working for his father now would put him in an awkward situation,' Biddy went on. 'It can be fierce awkward when you're workin' for people you fancy.'

'Maybe,' Tara mused. Then, attempting to get Biddy off the subject said: 'Madeleine is helping out in the office now.'

'Madeleine?' Biddy said with wide eyes. 'Sure, I thought she was still sick in the head. I heard tell just the other day that she was in and out of an asylum in Dublin.'

'If that's what the people in Ballygrace are saying,' Tara snapped, 'then the people in Ballygrace should mind their own business. They don't know anything about Madeleine Fitzgerald, because if they did, then they would know that she's fit and well at the minute.'

'Oh . . . that's grand,' Biddy replied, momentarily lost for words. She knew full well that Tara was directing some of her anger in her own direction. 'I'm glad poor Madeleine's feelin' better – I always liked her. They're nothing but a pack of feckin' sneers in Ballygrace.' Then, seeing Tara's disapproving look she blushed and said: 'Excusin' the language – but they've even told some terrible lies about me in this place. The people of Ballygrace haven't a good word for anybody. Sure, they've even found fault with yourself – *you*, who's never done anythin' worth talking about.'

Tara did not rise to her friend's bait. She had always kept herself to herself in the village and listening to gossip only infuriated her. It brought up such a rage it almost frightened her and made her feel like challenging the person who had instigated the talk. But that only led to rows. And rows in public – as her granda always said – made women no better than fishwives. Tara Flynn had never met a fishwife but, from the way her granda had spat out the word, she never wanted to be described as one.

Back at the cottage after Mass, as she revived the dying turf fire, Tara could not stop herself going over the conversation she had with Biddy. It had certainly touched a raw nerve. By throwing herself into work in the auctioneering office these last few weeks, she had attempted to block all thoughts of Gabriel Fitzgerald out of her mind. He had explained his situation quite plainly to her, the day before he went back to Dublin. He had come into the office in Tullamore – when he knew his father was elsewhere – and hung around until it was Tara's lunch break. They had then gone to a tearoom together and had chatted seriously about their friendship for the first time.

'I really enjoy being with you, Tara,' he had said looking deep into her eyes. 'Much more than I enjoy being with any other girl. But –' he paused, and swallowed hard as though there was a huge lump in his throat, 'I'm . . . I'm afraid I'm not in a position to promise anything. My parents have spoken to me recently – impressed upon me how I have to concentrate at university, because my grades in the exams at Christmas were very poor. They think it was because of Madeleine . . . all the recent upset. But really, I know it's because I've been thinking too much about you.' He lowered his eyes. 'I've several years studying ahead of me . . . After that – who knows what will happen?'

This was not what Tara had expected to hear. Foolishly, she had let her imagination run riot when Gabriel had asked to see her at lunchtime. It had run so far, that she had found herself imagining that he would confess to being in love with her. He would then ask her if she would be patient until he had finished his studies. And of course – she would be patient. She would gladly have waited. Only now, there was no guarantee that there would something worth waiting for. He was more or less telling her that she should *not* wait.

Another girl in her position might have been devastated – but Tara Flynn was not just another girl. Any feelings she had, would be buried deep inside. She would carry on as though nothing had happened. She would not let him know how hurt she was. She was not like Biddy Hart. She did not, *and would not*, wear her heart on her sleeve.

'I have plans too,' Tara replied in an even tone. 'And I wouldn't be in a position to promise anything either.' She had then looked him straight in the eye and even managed a smile which looked entirely sincere. 'I hope I didn't give you the impression that I was expecting anything from you, Gabriel, because that was not my intention. You surely must consider me a foolish, inexperienced girl altogether, to think that a few kisses at a New Year's dance could turn my head.'

Gabriel flushed deeply. 'I consider you no such thing . . . I obviously haven't explained myself very well.'

'I think you've explained yourself perfectly well.' Tara looked at her watch, and then bent down to retrieve her handbag from the side of her chair. 'I must get back. Patricia and Madeleine are due their lunch-break in ten minutes.'

Gabriel leaned across the table, and covered her hand with his. 'We can still see each other – can't we? When I'm on holiday, that kind of thing. I don't want the feelings between us to change . . . it's just that it's the wrong time.'

Tara drank the last mouthful of her coffee, then – as though she was hardly aware of it – slid her hand away from Gabriel's. She tucked her hair under her hat, then lifted her coat and scarf. 'We'll see what happens,' she said agreeably, and then swept out of the tearoom. She would not let him see how crushed his words had left her. And never again would she let her imagination run away with her feelings where a man was concerned.

Since then, Tara had kept herself busy in mind and body. She had put Gabriel to the back of her mind, and not allowed herself to dwell on the situation. She didn't have the time to spend brooding over it. Perhaps it was for the best, for all her other responsibilities seemed to fade into the background when Gabriel Fitzgerald was around. If she was not disciplined with herself, thoughts of him disrupted her studies, her piano playing and her work at both the office and home. It was in her own interests now to forget him.

She moved to put the pot of potatoes she had peeled before Mass, on the blazing fire, then she put the smaller pot containing chopped carrots, turnip and parsnips on beside it. The piece of beef for her and Mick had already been cooked the previous night and only needed warming up, when the vegetables were almost cooked.

By the time the meal was ready, Tara wondered where Mick had got to, for he had not come in from eleven o'clock Mass yet and it was quarter to one. Since her granda had died, they were fairly easy-going about Sunday lunchtimes, but today was different. She had wanted to get the meal over fairly early, because she had business in Tullamore.

She ate her own, and left Mick's meal in a covered dish, over a pan of boiling water to keep it hot.

A short while later, he came bustling through the door, red-faced and apologetic. 'I'm sorry now, me girl, keepin' you back from yer bite,' he said, taking off his best coat and cap, 'but I got chattin' after Mass.'

'It's okay,' she told him, getting a cloth to remove the steaming pot from the fire. 'I've had mine.' She set the hot plate with Mick's meal out on the scrubbed pine kitchen table.

Mick washed his hands then poured himself a tumbler of milk from the pitcher on the deep window-sill. Then in his slow, methodical way rolled his shirt-sleeves up to his elbow before sitting to eat.

'I'm going into Tullamore on the bike,' Tara said, pulling on her heavy tweed coat. 'I'm going in to look at a piano—'

'A piano?' Mick said, an alarmed look on his face.

'A second-hand one – remember? I mentioned it to you the other week.'

'And where were you thinkin' of putting it?' He said, gesturing round the kitchen. 'Sure, there's hardly room to swing a cat in here.'

Tara pinned a large brooch to her thick scarf, and then pushed her hair up under her beret. 'We'll just have to move things round a bit,' she said, pulling on her gloves. She gave her uncle a beaming smile. 'I promise I won't play it too loud – and I'll learn a few tunes that you can sing along to.'

Mick's mouth opened and shut like a fish – with not a word coming out. He was at best a man of few words, and whatever he wanted to say on this occasion would not take shape on his tongue. Eventually, as Tara lifted the latch on the door, he managed to shutter out: 'Don't be too hasty – take your time in case they diddle you out of yer money.'

'Don't worry,' Tara reassured him. 'I've been pricing pianos for weeks and I know exactly how much I'm going to pay for one.'

Tara was hardly out the door five minutes when Mick Flynn had his coat and cap on and was cycling in the opposite direction. He had been waiting for the right time to give Tara the news and it had never come. Tonight he would tell her and she would have to make up her mind what to do after it.

*

After viewing the piano and tentatively agreeing on a price, Tara called in on her grand-aunts before cycling back out to Ballygrace. The welcome she received from Molly at the door, was more than she expected.

'Come in, Tara,' the bent-over little woman said, ushering her into the dark hallway.' And it's welcome you are, my girl – welcome!'

Tara felt a little pang of sympathy as she followed the elderly woman down the hall and into the kitchen. It seemed only like yesterday when the two aunties were walking in their sprightly way with straight spines and steady feet. All of a sudden, they both seemed to have aged and grown doddery on their feet. She supposed it wasn't that surprising, since they were both in their seventies.

'And look at the grand surprise we have here,' Molly announced excitedly as she ushered Tara into the warm kitchen. 'We were just saying that a bit of young company would do you good, Joe. God must have been listening to our prayers.'

It turned out that after returning to the seminary in Dublin after the Christmas holidays, Joe had been struck down with a severe throat infection, and had been allowed home to recuperate. Molly and Maggie fussed about now, making tea and cutting bread and cake, and insisting that Joe and Tara go into the sitting-room with its nice warm fire, where they could talk 'young people's talk' on their own.

'Don't put yourself to any trouble. I had my lunch before coming out,' Tara said, as her coat and scarf were swept away to warm by the kitchen range. She wondered what she would say to her brother, because she was ignorant as to the life he led in the seminary – and because they had never spent much time alone before.

Joe saved her the immediate problem of thinking up a topic of conversation, as he went to dig out some records to play on the gramophone. 'You like classical music, Tara – don't you?' he asked in a croaky voice.

'I do . . . I like all kinds of music, classical and modern.'

'Maybe you'd give us a few tunes later,' Maggie suggested brightly. 'Joe hasn't heard you play for ages.' When Joe turned his attention to the gramophone, Molly bent towards Tara and whispered: 'The doctor took some tests on Friday . . . they think he might have glandular fever! At the very least, it's that bad flu, which they say has claimed a good many over in England. Don't you think he looks desperate?'

Tara nodded in agreement and then Molly scuttled off to make the tea. When Joe came to sit on the chair opposite her, Tara examined him at closer quarters and reckoned her brother did indeed look desperate. He had lost weight from his already slim frame, and his face had a dampish pink pallor, which was most unusual for him. His thick black hair – normally well controlled by a hair preparation – looked wild and unruly, and for the first time Tara was struck by the strong resemblance he bore to their father.

'Have you seen my father or Tessie lately?' Tara asked, since Shay had come into her mind.

'He called in yesterday evening,' Joe said, 'but he got a cool reception, so he didn't stay long.'

'Was he drunk?' Tara queried.

'He wasn't bad – but I could tell he had drink taken. And unfortunately, so could Molly and Maggie.'

Tara sighed disapprovingly. 'Did he have anything to say for himself?'

'Very little, but then –' Joe gave a sudden, uncustomary smile, 'if he had anything to say, I shouldn't think he would say it to me. He treats me as if I've just come down from another planet.'

Tara gave him a quizzical look. He had never spoken of, far less criticised, his father before. 'That makes two of us then, because he has very little to say to me either. We always end up in a row, especially when he has drink taken.'

Joe gave another smile – a gentle smile. 'I don't think he'll ever change. It's sad really to think about it, to have lost his wife and then lost his son and daughter too.'

'He has another wife and another family, Joe,' Tara reminded him. 'He got a second crack at the whip, and he doesn't seem one bit the better for it. He treats Tessie very shabbily, spending money she needs for food and clothes for the children.' She stopped, unaccustomed to talking in such a personal way. But, having suddenly opened the floodgates, the flow of words refused to be dammed. 'He's never stopped to think of *us*, has he? We got no second chances. We lost a mother when we were young, and then we were split up because he couldn't look after us on his own. We've had no mother or father in our lives and he never stops to think of us. He's too busy drinking every penny he has, feeling sorry for himself – and making a damned fool of himself.'

There was a silence for a moment. 'I didn't know you felt like that, too,' Joe said quietly. 'I'm always praying for forgiveness, for the hard thoughts I have about him at times.'

'He used to cause terrible trouble out at the cottage when my granda was alive,' Tara went on, 'but thankfully, with the weather being so bad at the minute, he hasn't called out so much.'

'Doesn't Mick miss the company? I thought they went out together at the weekends.'

'I think Mick meets him in Tullamore for the odd drink, so that we don't have the trouble getting him home late at night.' She looked at her brother now, who had become more like a real person, and less like a priest. 'Mick's changed since my granda died . . . in fact everything's changed.'

'In what way?'

'Oh, nothing terrible . . . he goes out more often and—'

'Tea!' Molly suddenly chirruped, bringing the intimate conversation to an abrupt end. Tara sat and ate the sandwiches and cake, and drank tea with her brother and her aunties. Afterwards, they insisted on her playing some of her pieces on the piano for Joe. She could not refuse, since she always left her sheet music at their house between lessons and practising. Joe was profuse in his praise of Tara's playing – urging her to go straight on from one piece to the next. 'You have a wonderful talent,' he told her, his eyes shining as she played her favourite 'Moonlight Sonata'. 'I didn't realise I had such a clever sister! You definitely outclass me as a pianist.'

Tara felt a lovely warm glow run through her. It was wonderful to feel that somebody actually cared about anything she did. Apart from her granda, nobody else in the family had ever shown a *real* interest in her. Of course, she knew that her father and Tessie and her Uncle Mick had no real knowledge about her music and studies, and so she avoided the subject, not wishing to talk over their heads. She also knew, deep down, that they didn't really know what to make of her at times – everything about Tara always seemed different.

It was nice to feel comfortable with someone who understood her, and didn't make her feel quite so odd. Someone who now seemed more like a real brother and less like a stranger.

Joe played a few pieces on the piano next – proving himself to be every bit as competent as his sister – and then he and Tara played several duets to the delight of Molly and Maggie.

Tara told Joe and the aunties about her plans to buy the piano. 'It's beautiful,' she said with shining eyes. 'It's walnut wood, and has lovely flowers carved in it, and two candlestick holders. It has a nice matching stool with a tapestry seat which lifts up to hold the books.'

'And aren't you the clever girl to have saved up money to buy such a thing?' Maggie said. 'Your mother would be proud of you!' She looked over at Joe and gave him an encouraging smile. 'She'd be proud of *both* of you. A clever girl with a good job and such a talent for the piano, and then the crowning glory of having a priest for a son.' She turned her smile, now beaming, to her sister. 'Amn't I right, Molly? Having a priest in the family is the greatest honour to be bestowed on any family?'

Molly clasped her hands together as though in prayer. 'Indeed it is!' she said passionately. 'It's the greatest honour for any family. No matter what sacrifices have to be made.'

'Oh, no sacrifice is too great,' Maggie echoed, 'when we know that at the end of it, Joe will reap the rewards of a life serving God.'

There was a silence during which all eyes turned towards Joe.

'Please God,' Maggie said in an emotional voice, 'that you'll be returned to the full of your health, and soon be able to go back to your college in Dublin.' She looked at Tara with clouded eyes. 'He hasn't even been fit enough to attend Mass these last two Sundays. Him who liked to attend daily Mass during his holidays. Father Higgins was good enough to bring him the Holy Eucharist during the week, when he was doing his parish sick visits.' She turned her gaze back to Joe. 'Please God, you'll be on your feet again soon and back to your holy studies.'

Joe, against all the aunties' arguments about catching pneumonia, saw Tara out into street. 'I enjoyed our chat by the fire,' he said quietly, 'and I enjoyed hearing you play the piano. Maybe you would call in again?' He paused, then added hurriedly, 'Only if you have the time . . . I know you have a busy life with work and everything. It's just –' his eyes dropped to the frosty ground, 'I very rarely have any company apart from Molly and Maggie . . . and the priests and nuns. To be honest with you, I find the days very long and depressing at home.'

'I would imagine you're missing the seminary and all your priest friends,' Tara said sympathetically. 'Tullamore must seem very dull to you after Dublin.'

Joe looked back at her, the white of his eyes standing out against his flushed hot skin. 'I have no great friends in the seminary,' he said in a croaky, desperate whisper, 'and the days were even longer and more depressing there. I'm sure that's what has me so ill . . .'

Tara felt a cold chill run through her. 'Have you said anything about this to Molly and Maggie?' she ventured. 'Have you said how you feel about the seminary . . . how it's affecting your health?'

Joe ran his hands through his curls – the dampness from his constant fever making the locks stand on end. 'It would kill them,' he said in a flat voice. 'They've only lived for my ordination these last ten years. They've scrimped and scraped, and gone without them-selves – to have the honour of a priest in the family.'

'Maybe,' Tara suggested, 'if you take a good long break from the seminary . . . you might feel different. When you feel depressed, everything looks dark and pointless.'

He nodded slowly and frowned as though in deep thought. 'Maybe . . . maybe, indeed.'

Tara cycled back, taking care with the patches of frost which were settling on the road. Her mind flitted from delight over the prospect of owning an elegant walnut piano with candlesticks – to dread over her brother's illness and his uneasy mind. What a predicament he was in, she thought. If he was to decide that the priesthood was no longer his vocation in life, then he would have to live with the consequences. However much it affected him – it would destroy his two old aunties.

Darkness had just fallen on Ballygrace as Tara approached the cottage. The place looked better lit than usual, with an oil-lamp shining from both the front bedroom and the kitchen. She dismounted from the bike and put it in the shed at the side of the cottage. After paying a quick visit to the grim wooden lavatory at the bottom of the garden, she entered the house the back way. As she opened the heavy door, Tara was instantly aware that there was more than Mick in the cottage.

'Come in – come in and warm yourself by the fire, my girleen,' Mick called with a heartiness bordering on falsity. 'Isn't that the cold night coming on us? Kitty was just saying that there's snow in that wind. Snow, begod! Isn't that all we need?'

'I don't know about snow,' Tara answered with a smile, 'but there's a frost settling on the ground. You'd want to be careful out on a bike later on.' She came to stand by the fire to warm her freezing hands. 'How are you, Mrs Dunne?' she asked pleasantly.

'Oh, I'm fine, Tara,' Kitty replied, giving an anxious smile, 'and thank you for asking.' She suddenly rose out of the comfortable rocking chair that Noel Flynn had sat in for most of his life. 'Begging your pardon,' she said anxiously, 'but maybe 'tis your own chair I'm sitting in?'

'Not at all,' Tara reassured her. 'I'm going to have a cup of hot tea and then I'll set a little fire in my room to study for the evening.'

'I have the kettle boiled an' all here for you, girl,' Mick said, rushing to put it back on the fire for a few minutes. 'And then we'll all have a cup of tea, for Kitty's only here these last few minutes herself, and hasn't had a drop yet.' He went back over to the table, and busied himself with the teapot and cups. 'And how did you get on with your piano?' he called in the hearty manner again.

An uneasiness settled on Tara, for everything about this situation told her there was something afoot. Something that concerned Kitty Dunne, and something that was going to have a big effect on Tara herself.

Eventually, after much humming and hawing, and beating around the bush, the news finally emerged. Mick was to be married to Kitty Dunne – and in the very near future. Apparently, Tara discovered, they had been sweethearts may years ago – but then Mick had gone to work in England for a couple of years. In the meantime, thinking he was gone forever, Kitty had married someone else. It was only at her granda's funeral, that he and the recently widowed Kitty had become friendly again.

'It will make no difference to you, Tara,' Mick said in a blustering manner. '*That* I can assure you. I promised me father that there would always be a home for you here. I have a will made out to that effect, so that when I pass over meself, the cottage will be yours.'

Tara nodded slowly, trying to take in the implications that this news would have for her. Then, her serious expression melted into a warm smile. 'I'm delighted for you, Mick . . . for you both. I wish you the best of luck,' she said sincerely. She then moved and gave them both a hug and a kiss to verify her words.

'Well now!' Mick said, flustered by the unusual show of affection. 'Kitty brought a bottle of sherry with her, so maybe we could crown the occasion with a little drink?'

Over the sherry, it transpired that, with Tara's agreement, Kitty would move into the cottage after their marriage.

'Sure, the old farmhouse down by the canal is far too big for her,' Mick explained. 'It's fierce cold in winter, and the windows are shivering and shaking with the icy wind. It's too far out from Ballygrace for any kind of comfort, with regard to the shops and the church.'

'It was fine when I was younger; the few miles cycle didn't bother me. But as I'm getting that bit older, I feel nothing about it suits me at all – so I'm going to sell it,' Kitty explained, 'and let out the few acres of land to a neighbouring farmer.'

'And then we'll build on next year,' Mick added, his face red from all the unaccustomed talking and explaining. 'We'll build on a bit at the back of the house, to give us all a bit more room – a bit more comfort.'

'I'll be able to pay for that,' Kitty said hurriedly, 'when I get the proceeds from the farmhouse.'

'And then,' Mick said, finally reaching the pivotal point for breaking the news this evening, 'we'll have more room for yer piano.'

'I have a few bits of furniture to bring with me,' Kitty said weakly. 'I couldn't leave them behind.' She gestured to the kitchen and living area which made up only a modest-sized room. 'This room would only hold a few more items, so I'll have to squeeze the rest into the bedroom.' She then blushed at the mention of the room she and Mick would be sharing. 'Next year, when we've added on to the house—'

'Now about the piano—' Mick blusteringly started to explain again.

'Forget the piano,' Tara interrupted. 'It was only a notion I had . . . it's not important.'

'Indeed we will *not* forget it,' her uncle said in a high voice. 'Just as soon as we have the room, you'll have your piano. In fact,' he said, nodding for confirmation in his intended bride's direction, 'you can have a whole band in here, my girleen – if it's to your liking.'

'Indeed,' Kitty agreed, 'if that's what she wants. This house will be yours, Tara, and every stick that belongs in it – as your Uncle Mick said. And it will be yours when I've added the bit on too, because you've been kind enough to welcome me into the house and to allow me to live with ye, when we get married.'

Tara took a deep breath, and – for the sake of her kindly uncle who had lived as a bachelor for the last fifty years – she gave a big smile and said: 'Have you picked a date yet, for the wedding?'

That dark January evening had not finished with its surprises for Tara Flynn. As she saw Mick and Kitty Dunne off, the worst news of the day was making its way through Ballygrace village in the distressed shape of her long-time friend, Biddy Hart.

Tara was sitting staring into the fire, still stunned by Mick's news, and trying to work out exactly what effect Mick getting married was going to have on her. It was easy enough to cancel the piano. That was no problem. She could continue to practise at the old aunties. But there were other issues to take into account – issues that were much more serious. Her continuing to live in the cottage meant that they would have to 'build on', and building on to the little thatched house would change it forever. It would not be the same place she grew up in. And eventually, she would leave – maybe to get married. But even if she didn't get married, she would have to consider leaving Ballygrace and moving somewhere that would afford her more opportunities.

Mick's words about her maybe moving to Dublin or even England suddenly came back to her mind, causing a heavy feeling to settle over her. She had secretly hoped that if she kept improving herself and saving, that one day Gabriel Fitzgerald might ask her to marry him. After their last meeting that did not seem so likely.

If marriage to Gabriel Fitzgerald was not an option, then perhaps she might meet someone of his type. But she knew of no others like him in the area and did not have the connections or the transport to be introduced to those further afield. It suddenly struck her, that in order to meet the right sort of husband, or have the right sort of career, she might have to move *herself*. She had some very hard decisions to make. Not right away, but soon enough to start thinking about it.

Tara was woken out of her reverie by a sudden, violent banging on the front door. Surely, it could not be Mick back so soon? In any case, he always came by the back door. With a thumping heart, she rushed to open it.

'I'm sorry!' Biddy said, bursting through the cottage door. 'I know it's dark and late – but I had to come tonight. Lizzie and the priest are takin' me to some place tomorrow, and God knows when I'll ever see you again!' Biddy's eyes were almost jumping out of her head. 'I could end up like Nora Quinn – and never be heard tell of again.'

'What are you talking about, Biddy?' Tara asked, almost dizzy with confusion. She ushered her friend into the warm room. Biddy's coat and hair were cold and damp. Tara started to help her out of the coat, and was even more confused when her friend struggled to keep it wrapped round her. 'I'll dry it out by the fire,' Tara told her. 'You'll catch pneumonia if you go back out in that damp coat.'

'Maybe that would be the best thing for me,' Biddy stated. 'Maybe if I died it would solve everythin'.' She sat down in the rocking-chair and huddled over the fire, still hugging the coat tightly to her.

Tara went over to the kitchen table where the celebratory bottle of sherry was standing. She filled a glass to the brim and handed one to her friend. 'Drink that up,' she ordered. 'It will do you good.'

Biddy sat sipping the drink and staring into the fire, while Tara got the kettle boiling again and waited until her friend was ready to talk.

'If I tell you something,' Biddy started, a sob already in her voice, 'will you promise me two things?'

Tara nodded solemnly.

'Will you promise to still be my friend – and will you promise to tell no one?'

'I promise,' Tara said sincerely.

Biddy took a deep breath. 'I'm expectin' a baby in the summer,' she said in a leaden voice, '. . . and they're takin' me up to Dublin tomorrow. To a place for fallen women.'

Tara's hands flew to cover her shocked face. 'A baby? I don't believe it! You can't have . . . you haven't *been with* anyone . . . have you?' Surely her friend wasn't the sort of girl to have let a boy touch her before she was married? Surely the rumours about Biddy were only *rumours* . . . and that deep down she was like herself, saving her virginity for the special person that would become her husband?

Biddy's lowered eyes told the truth.

After a few moments, Tara found her voice again and whispered. 'Maybe it's all a mistake?'

Biddy shook her head, a stricken expression on her face. 'I found out before Christmas . . . the day yer granda was buried. I didn't want to tell you about it when ye had yer own troubles.'

A tiny sword pricked Tara's heart at the mention of her beloved granda and caused a pain under her ribs. Oh, how she wished he were back here, to protect and advise her against all these terrible things that were happening to her.

'Who,' Tara said hesitantly, 'is the father?'

Biddy looked up at her with red-rimmed eyes, and then started on the story she had rehearsed as she walked down to Flynn's. 'It's that boy from Tullamore . . . that PJ Murphy.'

'Him?' There was silence for a moment. 'Does he know? Is he going to take responsibility for you?'

The tears came gushing out of Biddy now, and she rocked herself back and forward in the chair for pathetic comfort. 'He's gone!' she wailed, accepting a clean hanky of Mick's which Tara had taken from the clothes pulley. 'And his oul' mammy came out to see Lizzie, and then the priest was brought in. She said that she would strangle PJ before she'd let him be tied in marriage to the likes of me. And . . . ' she paused to dab her eyes, then blow her nose loudly on Mick's hanky, 'and both Lizzie and the priest said that Mrs Murphy was right, that a boy from a decent family couldn't be saddled with me. Then Lizzie said that I had been tellin' all different stories about the father. That I'd been accusin' innocent people. She said to PJ's mother that you could fling a stone and it could land at any one of a dozen boys I'd been with.'

Tara gasped in horror at the insinuation. 'What happened then?' she asked, dreading the answer.

'Mrs Murphy said that she was sendin' PJ away to Galway or Cork . . . or some far-flung place, to help his uncle out on the farm. She said she hoped I was happy now that I had deprived a good God-fearing mother of her favourite son . . . and that she would never forgive me to her dyin' day.' She stopped to dab her eyes again. 'She was terrible to me . . . and Lizzie agreed with every word, and then the priest said that he was going to solve the problem for everybody. He said that he was goin' to take me to this place in Dublin in the mornin' – where I would be a torment to nobody. He said that after a while, when PJ had learned his lesson about interferin' with bad girls like me, that his mother would forgive him and let him come home.'

There was a silence, then Tara asked the question that had been on her lips since Biddy came in. '*Why*, Biddy –' she asked, '*why* did you let PJ Murphy touch you? Didn't you know it was wrong? Did you not know this might happen?'

Biddy dropped her gaze to the floor. How could she tell Tara that she found it very easy to let the young, attractive PJ touch her, after all the things she'd done with Dinny and . . . other things she couldn't bear thinking about.

'I never gave a thought to havin' a child,' she explained, 'then, when I found out . . . I thought it would be grand to get married and have a baby. I've never had anybody belongin' to me before . . .' She broke off, and dissolved into a greater flood of tears than before. 'I'm ruined . . . ruined!' she wailed. 'Me whole life's ruined!' Biddy suddenly lunged forward and grabbed Tara's hand. 'An' I haven't a friend in the world apart from you, Tara. Nobody will bother with me when word of this gets out. Promise me, *please promise me*, that you'll still be my best friend?'

Tara felt her throat closing over, for she suddenly realised that she was now losing *her* best friend, too. She would have no one to talk properly to any more. Even if her granda was still alive, she didn't even know if she could have told him something so awful as this anyway. She couldn't tell *anyone* about this . . . not just yet.

Why, she asked herself angrily, could she not have a mother like every other young person? A mother was the only one who could have advised her on how to help the sad, fallen girl who stood weeping in front of her. A silly young girl who had given her precious virginity away to an even sillier young boy.

Suddenly, Tara knew what she should do. She would follow the instructions she heard often at Mass – she would listen to her own conscience. She took a deep breath, and then putting her arms around Biddy, said: 'Whatever happens now or in the future, Biddy, I'll always be your friend.'

Chapter Sixteen

Spring came early in Ballygrace. On St Patrick's Day, when she was in the back garden feeding the poultry, Tara noticed some daffodils peeping through the grass at the bottom of the apple tree in the garden. A feeling of hope came into her heart as she looked at the tight yellow buds.

She turned back towards the cottage, checking items on the washing line as she passed. She stopped to take down the lighter things, underwear and blouses which were still slightly damp, but perfect for ironing. The heavier things, the dresses and sweaters would need another hour or two in the breeze. They would be pressed and packed in her case, by the time William Fitzgerald came to pick her up at seven o'clock that evening.

Madeleine had been up and down since Christmas, coming into work when she was well enough, and staying at home with her mother when she was not. By the end of February, Madeleine was on the best medication that had been tried so far, and making great progress – and Elisha was at the end of her tether. A bad bout of flu, which had swept Tullamore and the surrounding area, had left her weak and nervous.

'You need a break,' William had said at breakfast the previous Monday morning, as he sat opposite his pale and edgy wife. 'You need to get away.'

'How can I possibly get away?' Elisha asked in a tone as dull as her grey complexion. 'Who would look after Madeleine?'

'I would – with some help, obviously. She's much better now and she's occupied from Monday until Friday in the office.'

'What about the rest of the time? There are the evenings and the weekends, which are the most difficult times for her. How would you cope?'

He reached across the table and stroked her hand. 'Leave that to me,' he said reassuringly. 'I think a break over in London in your delightful sister's company would do you the world of good.' He smiled fondly at her. 'I've already spoken to Frances, and she would love to have you – in fact, she insists that you come.'

Elisha's expression softened at the mention of her younger sister's name. Frances was indeed elegant, delightful company, and she lived close to the city centre – and all the big department stores in Oxford Street and Bond Street where Elisha loved to shop. 'I must admit that the thought of seeing Frances appeals to me,' she said in a brighter voice, 'and the shops will have their spring stock in. I need a new outfit for Hillary Duffy's wedding in May. If I buy it in London, it's unlikely that anyone will be wearing the same outfit.'

'That's the situation settled then,' William said, dabbing his mouth with a napkin and rising from the table. 'I'll call in at the travel agent's at some point this morning, and book your flight.'

'Are you sure?' Elisha asked again, all sorts of problems running through her mind.

'I'm certain.' He gave a broad smile. 'We can't have you attending Hillary Duffy's wedding in an ordinary old outfit from Dublin, can we?'

The following Saturday, after Elisha's departure, William asked Madeleine if she would like a friend to stay while her mother was in London. 'I'm just concerned about you being on your own too much,' he had pointed out. 'I often have commitments in the evening and at the weekend. I would hate you to get depressed again – and I thought perhaps that if you had company, you might feel better.'

Madeleine shrugged. 'I feel fine at the moment,' she said, 'but it would be nice to have Tara over now and again. She always cheers me up. She might be glad of a change herself, because her uncle got married last week, and I think she feels in the way with his new bride.' She gave a peculiar little giggle. 'I can't imagine a couple in their fifties getting married.' Then, just as quickly, she became serious again and said: 'It would also give us a chance to go over the accounts system at the office, because I'm still struggling with that.'

'That's it settled,' William said with delight. 'We'll drive over to Ballygrace tonight, and you can put the idea to her.'

The plan to bring Tara Flynn closer to him had worked perfectly. He had taken his time, in order not to arouse suspicion from his wife or his daughter. Hopefully, his patience would soon be rewarded.

The guest bedroom in Ballygrace House was exactly as Tara remembered. And, it was an answer to a prayer. She had not hesitated – even for a second – when Madeleine came bounding through the cottage door, and had pleaded with her to come to Ballygrace House '*even for a little while*'.

It had been very embarrassing for Tara on the night of Mick and Kitty's wedding, when all three of them had come back to the cottage. Tara thought they might have had a night away in a hotel in Dublin, or even a bed and breakfast in Tullamore, but they had laughed and said they were a bit old for a honeymoon. The walls were good and thick, but Tara had gone to sleep with the blankets over her head, just in case any alarming noises penetrated through to her own bedroom. She had gone to sleep every night since in a similar manner, and although she had not actually heard anything, her imagination had worked overtime, preventing her sleeping properly – and leaving her exhausted in the mornings. A break away was exactly what she needed. It was probably what Mick and Kitty needed too, because she knew they were both embarrassed facing her in the mornings.

Tara hung her freshly ironed clothes up in the wardrobe in the guest room in Ballygrace House. She had never used it before, because she had only ever stayed overnight, and had no need of it. She examined the wardrobe interior, fascinated by all the different compartments behind the three mirrored doors. The middle part was the same as a normal wardrobe with a rail, but the other two parts with shelves and drawers were more interesting. She took her time putting her hats in the top part, and then carefully hung her scarves on the special narrow rail with clips to stop them sliding off. Her sweaters went on the open shelves, and her shoes on the bottom shelves. Her underwear, stockings and night-dresses she put in the matching dressingtable drawers, and her dressing-gown on the fancy brass hook on the back of the bedroom door.

As she breathed in the fragrance of the dried lavender mingled with the smell of furniture polish, Tara felt such a surge of relief to be in this room. This beautiful, elegant room. She went over and stood in front of the glowing fire in the white marble fireplace, then she stretched on tip-toes to look at herself in the mirror above. It was over four months since the first time she had come to Ballygrace House – and four months since her granda had died. Such a lot had happened in that time.

It was amazing, she mused, as she threw herself down on top of the green satin quilt, how comfortable she now felt in this house. How the things which had intimidated her so much, no longer bothered her. Before, she would have worried about creasing the bed coverings, or have been hesitant about putting toiletries out on the dressingtable – as though someone would scold her for making herself at home in a place she had no right to be. Someone like Mrs Scully. But those days were gone – and gone for *ever* as far as Tara was concerned.

Although she had only been working for William Fitzgerald for a few months, she knew she had already earned his respect as a good employee. He was delighted that Tara had picked up every skill that Patricia McManus had shown her, and had even introduced several new ideas, which the older secretary had praised her for.

Tara had become more acquainted with land evaluation, and had accompanied her boss in his car to places like Mullingar, Athlone, Portlaoise and Birr. On a few occasions they had stopped off for lunch and chatted over the morning's business.

Each time she went out with William Fitzgerald, Tara found that she was more comfortable and confident in his company. Apart from using the opportunity to learn more about the business, Tara discovered that he was an easy person to talk to. He confided to her all his worries about Madeleine, and about the effect it had had on his wife. He talked about his plans for the business, and told her how he had started from scratch in Tullamore fourteen years ago, and was now one of the biggest businessmen in the Midlands.

'Hard work and persistence is the key to prosperity. Keep at it, and never give up,' he told her, time and time again. 'Anyone can do well, if they stick to that philosophy.'

Tara listened, and took in everything that he told her. William

Fitzgerald was an interesting and attractive older man. Although sometimes – she had to admit to herself – she wished she were riding in the car and dining in the fancy restaurants with his son. But that was highly unlikely because Gabriel was living in Dublin, and was not due home again until Easter. By that time, Elisha Fitzgerald would be home, and Tara would be back in the cottage with Mick and Kitty – and seriously pondering her future.

Mrs Scully had met her at the door on that first Sunday evening, and had taken her coat and hat and scarf from her – in a most civil manner. It was just as well, because Tara had decided to tackle the situation once and for all, if she had not been accorded the same respect as any other guest. Whether it would mean confronting Mrs Scully herself, or complaining to Madeleine's father, was immaterial. She would deal with the situation as it arose.

As if she had sensed Tara's attitude, the housekeeper had told William Fitzgerald that the fire was now blazing in Tara's bedroom, just as he had instructed. 'And if there's anything you need, Miss,' she had said in a courteous, albeit unsmiling manner, 'you only have to ask meself or young Ella.'

The situation at the cottage with Mick and Kitty couldn't continue. They were bending over backwards to be kind and accommodating to her – but she didn't belong there any more. It was as though a door had closed on her life, and there was another door waiting to be opened. It was up to her to pick the time and the place.

She supposed that Tullamore was the obvious choice to move to – for the time being at least. It would mean that she could walk to work every day, and she would be close to town for her evening classes and her music lessons. She would wait until Madeleine's mother came home from London, because she could always use Ballygrace House as a bolthole to escape from her real – very unpredictable – life.

The first two weeks at Ballygrace House passed by quickly. Every morning Madeleine's father drove her and Tara into the office in Tullamore. He normally waited long enough to check the post and make a few phone calls, and then he would go off to check any interesting land or property which was due to come on the market.

Twice in the third week, he had asked Tara to accompany him for the purpose of taking notes and, he explained, to monitor how Madeleine coped in the office without Tara's guidance.

Apparently the first day, a Tuesday, that Madeleine was left on her own with Patricia, she had coped very well. She had worked through the list of instructions which Tara had left on filing and on re-doing the window display. The second day, the following Friday, things had not gone quite so well.

William had taken Tara off to a stud farm in Kildare. 'We're meeting people from Dublin at the farm,' he explained as they drove along the winding roads in the late morning sunshine. 'I'm hoping they'll put in a good bid for it.'

'What would you like me to do?' Tara asked.

William gave her a broad smile, the white tips of his teeth showing beneath his meticulously groomed moustache. 'I'd like you to enjoy the run out to this lovely place.' He reached across and patted Tara's hand. 'Then, I'd like you to use your dazzling looks to good effect with the clients.'

Tara turned towards him, a look of alarm on her face. 'What do you mean?'

He laughed loudly. 'Relax! I'm paying you a compliment – you're a very beautiful young lady.' There was silence for a few moments as he negotiated a bad bend in the road. 'I want you to enjoy a nice day out of the office, to have the chance to look at a charming, very desirable property.' He paused again. 'The sort of property an elegant young lady like yourself might think of buying in the future.'

'*Me?*' Tara looked at him quizzically. 'You're codding me, aren't you?'

'Not at all,' he said coolly. 'Who knows what circumstances you might find yourself in.'

Tara turned away towards the window, so that he could only see her lovely red hair rippling down over her shoulders. 'It would be way out of my reach,' she said in a deliberately offhand manner, 'and any other *ordinary* person.'

'But that's the whole point, Tara. You could hardly be described as an ordinary person.'

Tara's face coloured up. 'I know exactly what I am, Mr Fitzgerald,' she said quietly, 'and I'm not ashamed of my background. My family might be ordinary, working-class people – but they are good and decent people. My grandfather brought me up with proper manners and instilled in me the necessity of a good education. He brought me up as well as an old man in his circumstances possibly could . . .' Then to her embarrassment, a lump in her throat stopped her saying any more and tears started pouring down her face.

As soon as they rounded the next bend, William Fitzgerald stopped the car with a screech of brakes. 'Tara . . . Tara,' he said in a strange voice. 'I never meant to upset or insult you.' He delved in his coat pocket for a handkerchief, then, putting one hand under her chin, her turned her face towards him and carefully dabbed her eyes.

'I'm so sorry for upsetting you,' he said kindly. 'I really did mean it as a compliment.'

Tara took the handkerchief into her own hand, and rubbed her eyes hard with it. 'No . . . no,' she protested, 'it's me who should be sorry . . . sorry for being so stupid, crying like this.' She paused and swallowed hard. 'It's just that . . . things are difficult at home just now – and I suddenly remembered how nice it used to be with my granda.' Then, to her horror, the tears suddenly came again – this time overwhelming her in sobs. She was so upset that she hardly noticed when William Fitzgerald's arms came round to comfort her.

Eventually, when the tears and sobs had subsided, William reluctantly released his hold on her. 'Are you all right, Tara?' he enquired gently.

Tara nodded. She took a few moments wiping her tears away, and then she took out her compact and checked her face in the mirror. 'Oh, God!' she whispered, dropping her head so that her hair fell down in two rippling curtains. 'Look at the state of me – and we're meeting those people shortly.'

'Take your time,' he said reassuringly. 'We're not meeting them until half past eleven. We'll be there long before them.'

Very quickly and with trembling hands, Tara applied a layer of powder on her face, which she hoped would conceal the huge blotches which had spread all over it. She didn't know which had unnerved her most, the fact that she had broken down and cried in front of her boss, or the fact that he had put his arms around her.

When she felt composed enough, they continued on their journey, arriving a good ten minutes before the prospective buyers. The stud farm was every bit as impressive as William Fitzgerald had described, and the house was outstanding – even bigger and grander than Ballygrace House.

'Have a look round before they arrive,' William suggested, as he sorted through the documents he had brought with him. 'The rooms upstairs are fascinating.'

Tara went upstairs in search of a dressingtable, grateful for the chance to check her face again before the people arrived. She found a large gilt mirror at the end of the wide hallway, and was relieved to see that she didn't look as bad as she thought. A light application of lipstick and a quick brush of her hair made an immediate improvement. Thank goodness she had worn one of her better suits today – a heather-coloured skirt and jacket, with a roll-necked cream blouse. Hopefully, it would take the attention away from her blotchy face.

As she wandered from one elegantly decorated room to another, she pondered over the situation in the car with her boss. He had been very kind with her when she got upset – and had been most apologetic when she had accused him of mocking her. A wave of embarrassment washed over her when she thought of how she had spoken to him.

Then Tara heard William Fitzgerald call her name, and say that the people who were coming to view the property had just pulled up outside. Giving one last glance at her reflection in the hall mirror, she turned and walked smartly along the hall and down the stairs to where her employer was waiting. Waiting, with a little smile on his lips – which Tara noticed. And stark admiration in his eyes – which she did not.

The business was over and done with in under an hour, and William was pleased – confident that the people would put in a good bid at the auction later in the week. 'I think,' he said as they drove through Kildare town, 'that we'll celebrate with a nice lunch. I know a hotel outside the town that has a good wine list.'

This was a place William frequented on a regular basis when he came over to the races. It was also a place his wife knew nothing about, because as far as she was concerned, his gambling days were long gone. It was very convenient for him to have property in outlying districts, as they gave him the perfect excuse to disappear to the odd race, when the excitement in the property business was not enough to quicken his pulse.

'What about Patricia and Madeleine?' she asked, feeling uneasy again. 'What about their lunch break?'

'I'll ring from the hotel but I'm sure it won't be a problem. You obviously forget, Miss Flynn,' he said raising his eyebrows in a humorous manner, 'that I am the boss.'

As soon as they were settled at a table in the restaurant, William went off in search of a telephone. He returned five minutes later with a satisfied smile. 'They'll have separate breaks for today,' he informed her. 'I explained that the business was taking a little longer than expected – so you'll have to back me up on that when we get back to the office.'

'I feel very guilty,' Tara told him, 'sitting in this lovely place, while the other two are stuck in the office.'

He learned across the table and patted her hand. 'You will have to get rid of those sorts of feelings, if you're going to be a successful businesswoman. There will be many occasions when you'll have to tell a white lie. In fact, it's a beneficial, nay – an *essential* talent to be able to lie properly in business.'

He laughed, and Tara suddenly noticed how the corners of his eyes crinkled in a very attractive way. Not as attractive as Gabriel – but attractive, nevertheless, for an older man. Then, ashamed of her silly thoughts, she bent her head and concentrated on the menu.

They chatted lightly through the meal and wine, and around two o'clock set off back to Tullamore.

'I'm sorry about the conversation we had coming in this morning,' William said, as they left Kildare town, and drove through the quiet country roads. 'I'm afraid I came across as rather insensitive, when really—'

'No,' Tara hastily interrupted, feeling more confident after two glasses of Beaujolais. 'It was childish of me to get so upset.'

'What I was trying to say,' he went on, 'is that I really admire you – the way you've educated yourself out of your class. It may surprise you to know that my own background is not dissimilar to yours.' He paused for a moment. 'My own family were good, God-fearing people, but they had no ambition. They knew their place, and were happy to stay put in it. But I wasn't. I suppose I've always wanted more.'

Tara looked at him, amazed at what he'd told her about his ordinary background – and even more amazed as to why he should tell her all this personal information.

'The thing is,' he continued, 'there's a price to be paid for ambition . . . and there's a price to be paid for all the things that ambition brings. I've paid dearly for all the things I've had in my life.' He came to a halt as a flock of sheep crossed the road from one field to another, checked by a black and white collie and a farmer wielding a large stick. 'My wife's family were much wealthier, of course,' he said, putting the car into gear again when the last sheep was safely across. 'They were highly suspicious of me at first.' He gave a little laugh. 'Some of them have never stopped being suspicious of my business dealings throughout the years, but I've managed to outwit them all. They thought we were finished when we moved to Offaly, that I'd be happy playing the country gentleman – but they were wrong. My businesses are nearly as profitable as they were in Dublin. Despite what many people think – I reckon that in the future, people will prefer to live in the country as opposed to the city.' He turned to Tara. 'What do you think?'

She considered his words carefully. 'I'm not sure,' she replied. 'It's not something I've ever thought about.'

'Take my advice – think ahead! In this sort of business, you have to look at what *might* happen in the future, as opposed to what is happening right now. England is a good example to follow in the property and building field.'

When they returned to the office, Patricia was in a fluster.

'Everything all right?' William asked in a light manner, hopeful of avoiding any sort of fuss.

'Everything in the office is fine . . . it's *Madeleine* I'm worried about. She went out for a walk round the shops at one o'clock,' Patricia explained, a panicky note in her voice. 'She said she would only be gone half an hour and then she would come back to relieve me. Of course, I had no intention of going out and leaving her on her own, but I knew you would prefer her to be back in the office.' She looked down at her watch. 'It's nearly three o'clock. She's been gone two hours.'

'How did she seem?' William asked, his brow furrowing.

Patricia bit her lip. 'She seemed a bit agitated all morning . . . and I . . . I heard her talking to herself . . . as though there was someone with her.'

'Shall I go and look for her?' Tara said quickly. 'I know the shops we usually look around when we're together.'

William looked grateful: 'If you wouldn't mind . . .'

Tara found her friend outside a shop that sold holy statues and pictures. Madeleine was holding a picture of the Sacred Heart high above her head and talking out loud. People were staring at her from a distance, while others were crossing to the opposite side of the street.

'Jesus spoke to me, Tara!' Madeleine gasped. 'He showed me the wounds in his hands and in his side. He told me that he wants me to be his special messenger . . . He's got lots of plans for me. And so have all the other saints. They don't want me to be a nun in the Missions straight away, they say that there's work to be done in Ireland – and I'm the person to do it. Do you know what I replied, Tara?'

'What?' Tara managed to make her tongue say.

'I said: "*Thy will be done!*"' She looked anxiously at Tara now. 'Do you think I was right to say that? Do you think it was all right to quote the scriptures? Do you think it was a good answer to give?'

Tara took the picture from her, hoping Madeleine did not notice her trembling hands. 'Yes, I think that was a very good answer.' She tucked the picture under her arm, and caught Madeleine's hand in hers. 'We'd better get back to the office now . . . Patricia's waiting to have her lunch.'

'I can't believe that I've been chosen . . . like Bernadette in Lourdes and the children in Fatima!' Madeleine whispered as they walked down the street together hand-in-hand. 'I never thought I was so special. I never felt that something like this was going to happen to me.'

William Fitzgerald was waiting outside the office door. His jaw sagged when he saw the glassy look in his daughter's eyes. 'The car's outside,' he said quietly. 'I think it might be best if we went straight home.'

Shortly after they arrived home, a doctor came out to Ballygrace House to see Madeleine. He spoke to her for a while, and after giving her an injection and some tablets, he said to William Fitzgerald: 'That lot should quieten her down. I should imagine she'll sleep for the rest of the day. If by any chance, she reacts against the medication – or if you notice any deterioration in her behaviour – phone me straight away.'

William nodded and handed the doctor some notes. 'Thank you for coming out so quickly.'

The doctor stuffed the notes in his pocket. 'It's an unfortunate business for any family to have to handle – but they're making great strides in the medical field with regards to psychiatry. Who knows what the future holds? There are new drugs being developed every day.'

William closed the door after the doctor with a heavy feeling in his chest. Thank God Elisha was not at home for this latest episode, otherwise he would have had a bigger problem on his hands. One female with nervous problems was quite enough at a time.

'Is she going to be all right?' Tara asked when William came back into the sitting-room.

'I hope so, but we'll have to wait and see.' A thought suddenly struck him. 'Do you mind staying here tonight? While Madeleine is not . . . not quite herself. I should think she'll sleep for the rest of the evening and night. Will you be bored?'

'Not at all,' Tara said agreeably. The circumstances at Ballygrace House with Madeleine might be bad, but they were still better than going back to the cottage to play gooseberry with Mick and Kitty. 'I'm happy here. There's plenty to keep me busy.'

'What will you do?' he asked curiously, coming over to sit on the armchair opposite her.

She shrugged. 'The piano – or I might do some studying or reading.'

'There's the gramophone or radio,' he suggested lamely. 'I'm afraid I have a meeting with a solicitor in Tullamore in an hour, and I've got to go to the office to pick up some documents first. I'll have to leave you here alone.'

'That's okay,' Tara reassured him. 'I'll be fine, and I'll keep checking on Madeleine every so often.'

He looked at his watch. 'It's half-past four. Mrs Scully or Ella should be in shortly to make the evening meal. I don't think Madeleine will be up to eating, but you can ask them to leave out something cold for her and me.'

'I'll do that.'

William got to his feet and made for the door. Then suddenly, he swung back round, and came to stand in front of her chair. 'Tara . . .' he said in a funny hoarse voice, 'I'm very grateful for everything you've done. Both in the office and especially for all the help you've given Madeleine.'

'She's my friend,' Tara replied, feeling slightly unnerved by his closeness. 'She's been my friend for a long time.'

He reached out and took her hand in his. 'You're a beautiful young woman and very kind.' He closed his eyes for a moment. 'I've enjoyed having you around the house. It's been very difficult for me lately with Madeleine's illness and her mother's condition.'

'Mrs Fitzgerald?' Tara was confused, and more than a touch disconcerted by the fact he was still holding her hand.

'Yes,' he said solemnly, nodding his perfectly Brylcreemed hair. 'She suffers from a nervous condition, too. Different from Madeleine . . . but there's definitely a weakness there. It comes on every now and again, and I could see the signs recently. That's why I insisted she had a break away for a while. She's not really a strong person.' He gave a little smile, and squeezed her hand tighter. 'Not like you. I know you're still young – but you're mature in many ways. An old head on young shoulders. I couldn't imagine anything ruffling you. You seem so single-minded and determined about your life.'

'I'm not too sure about that.' At that moment, Tara realised she felt more sorry for her boss than intimidated by him. 'I was very shaken when my granda died. And now I'm very confused about whether I should move to Tullamore.'

'I think,' he said, lightly kissing her hand, 'that would be a very wise move.'

Before Tara had a chance to pull her hand away, a deliberate cough at the sitting-room door suddenly alerted her and William Fitzgerald to the fact that they were not alone. He moved quickly to his feet.

'I knocked,' Mrs Scully stated, her beady eyes dancing, 'but ye were so busy that ye didn't hear me.' She looked from Tara's burning face to William Fitzgerald who was bristling with suppressed anger. 'I'm very sorry if I burst in on ye both,' she added, not sounding in the least sorry at all.

'You burst in on *nothing*,' William retorted in a loud voice. 'But if you knocked, you certainly didn't knock loud enough.' He lowered his voice. 'We've had a very difficult afternoon with Madeleine, and Tara's feeling rather upset after it all. If you would be so kind as to prepare her a meal, I think it might help matters.'

'Whatever you say,' Mrs Scully said, turning on her heel. She had seen and heard all she wanted, and was not going to stand around while William Fitzgerald thought up some ridiculous lie to cover up what was going on. She must have been blind not to notice it before! Why else would the likes of the Fitzgeralds bother with Tara Flynn? And to think they were using that poor lunatic upstairs as an excuse for their shenanigans. She only hoped she could get away early enough this evening to cycle into her second cousin in Ballygrace, to make sure that this juicy bit of scandal was spread around before the morning.

'I'm sorry,' William said when the housekeeper had closed the sitting-room door behind her. 'I was only trying to show you my thanks for all you've done for Madeleine . . . I would pay no attention whatsoever to Mrs Scully. She saw nothing which could be misconstrued. If I hear she has been gossiping – she'll be dismissed immediately.'

Tara closed her eyes and nodded. There was no point in attempting to explain the ways of village tittle-tattlers like Rosie Scully to someone so removed from it all like William Fitzgerald. How could he understand women whose lives were so empty of excitement that they filled their days feeding off the misfortunes of others, like pitiless vultures.

A small sigh escaped from Tara's lips. She knew from the look in the old woman's eyes, that something nasty would be made of the innocent scene she had walked in on.

Tara passed the next few hours practising on the grand piano and sorting through notes for her forthcoming accounting and shorthand exams. She was thankful when it was young Ella who knocked on the sitting-room door, to inform her that her meal was ready in the dining-room.

The salmon, boiled potatoes and glazed carrots were as tasty and beautifully presented as all the other meals in Ballygrace House, but Tara had no appetite. Whether it was due to the large lunch she had had earlier in the day, or the upsetting events which had followed – she could not stomach the meal.

When Mrs Scully appeared in the dining-room with a dish of trifle, her hawk-like eye fell on the barely touched meal. She clapped the trifle down some distance away from Tara, then reached across the table to remove the plate with the salmon. 'I suppose you're not used to being fed such grand meals at home,' she said scathingly. 'I suppose bacon and cabbage would be more in yer line?'

Tara gripped the edge of the table, rage coursing so fast through her veins that she felt dizzy. 'I beg your pardon?' she said in a steely voice. 'You are very mistaken if you think for one moment that I value *your* opinion.' She paused, making sure that her words had sunk in. 'I have no interest, whatsoever, in anything that you think – so I'd be grateful if you would keep your personal comments to yourself.'

The china plate that Rosie Scully was holding tumbled out of her shocked hands and fell back on the table, splattering the salmon and vegetables all over the lace cloth. 'You little whore!' she hissed between clenched teeth. 'Don't you have a quare nerve – comin' in here, as if butter wouldn't melt in yer mouth! First you have yer eye set on young Master Gabriel, and when he's not around, you make yerself available to a married man. A man ould enough to be yer father!'

'How dare you!' Tara was up on her feet now, flaming with anger.

But Rosie Scully thought herself well entitled to be giving an opinion and was only gearing herself up to battle. 'I know *all* about you, Tara Flynn,' she spat disdainfully. 'An' I know all about yer little whore of a friend – Biddy Hart! They've got her well out of the way at the minute – an' the little bastard in her belly.' She snorted loudly. 'An' you won't be long in followin' in her footsteps, by the cut of you!'

'You're nothing but a bad-minded old woman!' Tara pushed the chair back against the wall. 'I'll speak to Mr Fitzgerald when he comes back tonight – and I'll tell him everything that you've said.' She walked towards the door, struggling to control the wave of anger which was still rising inside her in a frightening way.

'And, I,' Mrs Scully said in a sneering voice, her eyes narrowed in hate, 'will be letting Mrs Fitzgerald and everybody in Ballygrace know about *your* sinful shenanigans with a married man! And you – with a brother that's in for the priesthood.'

Tara turned slowly and looked the housekeeper straight in the eye. 'Some terrible things must have happened in your life, to have made you such a bitter and twisted old woman.'

Rosie Scully's mouth dropped open in shock.

'*Nothing* you can do or say will have any effect on me or the way I choose to live my life.' And with that, Tara held her head defiantly high, and walked out of the room.

Never had an evening passed in such a painfully slow manner. Tara found reading and studying impossible, and she had no heart for playing the piano. The radio playing quietly in the corner was the only distraction from her thoughts. That, and the periodical checks on her sleeping friend.

She had already planned what she was going to tell William Fitzgerald about Mrs Scully. She would tell him how she found the situation intolerable and that she was leaving Ballygrace House first thing in the morning. Asking him to choose between herself and the housekeeper was unfair, and she had no wish to put him in that position. However, pleasant and convenient it was for her to stay in the house, she could not trust herself to control her temper again, should she be goaded by the old woman.

The telephone in the hall rang twice, and Tara heard footsteps on the tiles outside as someone answered it, but she could not tell whether it was Ella or Mrs Scully. Then later the younger maid came into the sitting-room to put more turf in the basket. She was as pleasant as usual, and gave no indication as to whether or not the gossipy older woman had said anything about the argument.

Around ten o'clock, Tara heard William Fitzgerald's car sounding on the gravel outside. She was on her feet at the fireplace when he came into the room.

'Sorry I was so long,' he said, going over to the drink decanters on the sideboard. He poured himself a large whiskey. 'But it was a good evening's work. Everything seems to be in order with the stud farm.' He held up a crystal decanter. 'Would you like a sherry, Tara? Or a glass of wine?'

Tara shook her head. 'No, thank you . . . I think I'll go off to bed now.'

'Are you all right?' he said, looking closely at her. 'Has anything else happened with Madeleine since I left?'

'No, she's been sleeping all the time.' She hesitated for a moment, then decided to take the bull by the horns. 'It's actually Mrs Scully. I don't know if you're aware . . . but she has a strong dislike for me.'

He sighed and raised his eyes to the ceiling. 'Has she said or done something to upset you this evening?'

Tara turned away from him, and stared into the fire. 'I don't want to cause any trouble, especially with Madeleine being ill and Mrs Fitzgerald being away. It might be best if I left. In fact . . . I think I should go in the morning. Madeleine will be fine if she has one of the maids here to look after her.'

'No –' he said angrily, 'you will *not* go. You have to tell me what she said.'

Tara took a deep breath. 'She said something about you and me . . . about walking in on us earlier on. Then she was particularly nasty about my friend, Biddy.'

'That's it!' William said. 'I won't have that meddling old woman causing trouble in this house. I'll sort her out once and for all.' He banged his whiskey glass down on a small table and stalked out of the room. Tara listened and could hear his footsteps as they went all the way down the hallway towards the kitchen.

But William Fitzgerald was too late, because Rosie Scully was already on her way, pedalling with all her might to her second cousin's in Ballygrace. Determined to do her worst.

The following Saturday morning, when Tara cycled back to Ballygrace to do the bakery accounts, she knew immediately that the housekeeper had spread her poisonous lies.

'And how's that young Fitzgerald one getting on?' the bakery owner's wife said, poking her head into the small office. 'I wouldn't normally go sticking me nose in – but I hear that you're lodging out at Ballygrace House.'

'She's fine,' Tara replied, not lifting her eyes from the accounts sheet.

Mrs O'Neill lingered in the doorway, reluctant to leave the conversation without having gained even a snippet of news, to add to all that she'd got from the butcher's wife. 'And how,' she said, in an uncommonly friendly manner, 'd'you find livin' up in Ballygrace Castle?' She used the childish, old name for the house. 'It surely must be a big change for you, and your family only cottagers.'

Tara still did not lift her head. 'The house is fine, and Madeleine's fine,' she said in a flat, disinterested voice.

'And how,' Mrs O'Neill looked back into the shop to check there were no customers, 'is Mr Fitzgerald himself? I hear the Missus has gone abroad for a while and he's left there on his own.'

Tara turned to face her. 'Apart from seeing him in the auctioneer's office, I wouldn't know how he is,' she said evenly. 'It's none of my concern. I rarely see him in the house, as he works most evenings.'

'Is that a fact?' The baker's wife was delighted to have got some information out of her. 'Surely he comes home for a bite to eat now and again?' She paused. 'Doesn't Rosie Scully from Tullamore keep house for them there?'

Tara sucked her breath in at the mention of the name.

'I'd say,' Mrs O'Neill went on, 'that *she'd* put a goodly dinner down to him in the evenings. I hear from her cousin that she's a fine cook.'

Tara stood up and closed the account books. She had it in her mind to tell this woman exactly what she thought of Rosie Scully, but to do so, would only put her on the same level as the scandalmongers. 'As I said before,' Tara's voice was icy, 'it's none of my concern. Now, if you'll excuse me, is Mr O'Neill there? I need a word with him about the accounts.'

The baker's wife folded her arms across her chest. 'I'll get him for you now.' Then, taking one last stab, she added: 'That's a grand job you have in that office. I saw you the other day in Tullamore with Mr Fitzgerald, all got up in the front of his car. You looked to be fine and friendly with him.' Then, delighted that she had broached the scandalous subject, she turned on her heel and went in search of her husband.

Tara was met with a similar reception in the village shop when she went to sort out the books for them a short while later. A group of gossiping women went deadly silent when she came into the shop. 'And how's yerself, young Miss Flynn?' one of the women called as she passed by them by on her way upstairs to the office.

'I'm fine, thank you,' she said in a clipped tone, hurrying on with her business.

The woman winked at her two companions. 'I say you'll be missing your friend, Biddy Hart, these days.'

Tara ignored the comment, and started to mount the steps.

'I suppose you've enough company out there in Ballygrace House with Mr Fitzgerald?' one of the other women called after her in a jeering voice. 'You wouldn't have much time to be thinkin' about the likes of Biddy Hart now . . . or yer Uncle Mick.'

When Tara reached the door of the office, she closed it firmly and then turned and pressed her back flat against it. At long last, by her association with the Fitzgeralds, she had given the local gossips the ammunition they thrived on. And even better, it had come hot on the heels of the news about Biddy and the baby.

Tara's shoulders slumped against the old cracked door, and tears came into her eyes. This was the reason she had always kept herself to herself – deep down she knew she was vulnerable to attacks like this, for daring to be so different from the other girls. Whether there was any truth in the gossip was of no odds. They would pass from one to another, adding a bit here and there, delighted to have something on 'that uppity Tara Flynn' at last.

Later that afternoon when Tara called back in at the cottage, she was relieved to find that the gossip had not reached Mick or Kitty's ears as yet. She gave them a brief outline of the animosity between herself and the housekeeper, and told them to ignore any rumours about her, because it was malicious lies spread by Mrs Scully.

Kitty had been kind and understanding. She bustled about sorting Tara cold ham and tomatoes and freshly baked cake bread, while Mick had sat grim-faced and saying little. As he passed her on his way out to the yard, he had patted her shoulder with a comforting hand. 'Pay no heed to her or her kind,' he said quietly. 'She's only an oul' begrudger – jealous because you're makin' something of yourself.'

Their attitude had lifted Tara's spirits a little but she felt guilty for not telling them everything. But how could she? How could she explain that the housekeeper had walked in on William Fitzgerald kissing her hand? She knew that it looked strange to an ordinary person, never mind one with a bad mind like Rosie Scully. But it had meant nothing. Nothing at all.

William Fitzgerald had apologised to Tara for putting her in such a compromising situation, or – what had been construed as a compromising situation – by the housekeeper. He had brushed it off as an insignificant incident, which should be forgotten by both herself and the housekeeper. He said that he would confront Mrs Scully about her general attitude to Tara. Depending on how contrite she was, he might give her a severe warning and another chance. The thought of sacking her and having to find a replacement in his wife's absence, he explained, did not sit easy with him. He had enough to contend with, without having domestic problems. He smiled and said he was fairly sure that the housekeeper would not wish to lose her job over such a minor matter.

Tara had not felt reassured by his view on the matter, and was sure that Rosie Scully would never admit to being in the wrong. She felt even less reassured now, having suffered the backlash of it all from the local gossipmongers – and she wondered how wise she had been to agree to return to Ballygrace House that evening. She had given no promises about staying for the rest of the month that Mrs Fitzgerald was away but, for her friend's sake, she would spend a few more days until William made other arrangements.

Madeleine was up and about when Tara returned to the house. She had shrugged off the heavy sedation of the previous night, and her eyes were bright and alert. 'I'm so glad you're here,' she said, when young Ella showed Tara into the sitting-room. 'I've been bored all afternoon. Daddy's been gone since lunchtime, and there's only been Ella and me in the house all day.'

'I'm glad you're feeling better,' Tara said gently. 'Now that you're up and about, is there anything you'd like to do?'

'I was just thinking,' Madeleine said with a faraway smile, 'that I'd like to do a jigsaw. Gabriel and I used to make jigsaws a lot when we were younger . . . I really miss him for things like that.' She paused for a moment. 'I've some new jigsaws upstairs that I haven't even opened.'

For the rest of the evening, Tara and Madeleine fitted pieces of a fragmented portrait of the Virgin and Child which Madeleine had bought in a religious shop in Dublin. Thankfully, there had been no sign of Mrs Scully around, and when William Fitzgerald returned around half-past nine, Tara went off to bed, pleading a headache. After the awful day, she just wanted to fall asleep and blot everything out.

Madeleine was up and about from six o'clock on Sunday morning. Although she did not actually come into Tara's bedroom to wake her up, her movements in the hallway outside, and her footsteps tripping up and down the stairs made certain that Tara would not go back to sleep.

It made no difference, Tara thought as she dressed. She had slept very badly in any case. Her mind had kept going over and over the situation about William Fitzgerald and Mrs Scully. She had a horrible feeling about it all but there was nothing she could do. She had never done the housekeeper any harm and yet the woman seemed to hate the very sight of her. And she had now to contend with her reputation being torn to shreds in Ballygrace.

Over breakfast, William told Tara that Mrs Scully had sent a message in with her grandson that she was ill and would not be back at work for some time. 'Doesn't want to face the music,' he commented, 'but she'll eventually have to face it. She won't receive a penny from me, until I have a full explanation for her behaviour.'

Tara listened to him and politely nodded her head. She was heartsick of the subject.

Madeleine made a fuss when her father suggested that she should perhaps not go to Mass for once. 'No!' she protested. 'I can't miss Mass – it's a mortal sin.'

'I think,' William said, 'that we might have a drive out today. We'll go to Mass in Birr for a change. It's a fine day, and we'll all benefit from the fresh air.'

All three set off in the car, Tara feeling both relieved at not having to face the gossips at Ballygrace Church, and apprehensive about how Madeleine would behave in church after her performance on Friday.

When they arrived at the church, William motioned that they should sit in one of the back pews, nearer the door. He stood back to allow the girls in before him, and Tara went first, ensuring that Madeleine was in the middle. As soon as Mass started, Tara noticed that Madeleine was becoming agitated. She watched the priest and listened to his words intently, her eyes narrowed in concentration. Every so often, she rocked backwards and forwards as though she were in a trance. And every so often, William reached forward and put out a discreet hand to halt the rocking. But within minutes, Madeleine started again.

'Are you all right?' Tara asked her several times but Madeleine didn't react. She just continued looking with intense concentration at the altar, or rocking back and forth. Tara noticed people further along the row nudging each other and whispering.

When Communion time came round, Tara was greatly relieved when William indicated that they should quietly leave by the back door. In the coming and going of the Communion queues, they were hardly noticed. Madeleine, thankfully, made no protest at being ushered out, and for the second time in as many days, she was quickly bundled into the car and driven back to Ballygrace House.

As soon as they arrived back at the house, William did as the doctor had instructed and gave Madeleine more of the medication. By the time lunch was ready at two o'clock, she was once again upstairs heavily sedated, and Tara found herself dining with William alone. Given the tense circumstances, he was charming company as usual.

After lunch, Tara excused herself, saying that she had a backlog of studying and piano practice to catch up on, and she spent the rest of the afternoon and early evening in the sitting-room, working on her own.

Around six o'clock, Tara decided to have a walk out in the fresh air before supper. There was no sign of William or his car, and Tara presumed that he had gone off somewhere when she was playing the piano, his car engine drowned by the music.

As she walked through the grounds and down the driveway, she wondered how Kitty was coping with the poultry. Mick's new wife had bent over backwards to be helpful to Tara, and kept apologising, saying that she hoped Tara wasn't staying at Ballygrace House on account of her having moved into the cottage. Tara told her several times that it wasn't the case, but the fretful look on Kitty's face had said she was not convinced.

As she paused to examine a bush full of tight purple buds, Tara's mind suddenly flitted to Biddy and the baby. It should be due in the next few months and she wondered how her friend was coping with it all. She had received two letters from the convent in Dublin that Biddy was staying in, saying she was being treated all right, and had made friends with some of the other girls. The letters surprised Tara, for they were written in a tidy script, and the spelling and grammar was much better than she would have expected.

'*They say the baby is to be adopted,*' Biddy had written on tear-stained paper, '*and will be given to a good family who have the money to look after it. Father Daly has been up to see me a few times. I don't really like him coming up but he's the only visitor I have. He says that he won't help me anymore if I argue with them about taking the baby away. I suppose it's the best way. What could I give a child and me only an orphan myself? If you ever get the chance to come up to Dublin, Tara, please, please come and see me. You can get a bus to the convent from O'Connell Street, it only takes about twenty minutes.*

If you don't manage to get up to Dublin, I will see you after the baby's born. I'll phone Father Daly and let him know when it comes. Some of the nuns are nice to me here, and some of them are horrible – giving out all the time, and making us do all the cleaning and the laundry. One of the younger nuns, Sister Agnes, has been very kind to me, and she has helped me with my writing and spelling. I've got much better than when I was at school, and going into classes saves me from doing all the housework. Sister Agnes says I'm quite clever, and she's much nicer than the teachers were to me at school.'

Tara realised with a sudden pang that she missed Biddy very much. Maybe next weekend she might take the train up to Dublin to see her. They might be very different in their ways, and in their taste in boys, but Biddy was a true friend – and she knew how to keep a secret.

Never once had she mocked Tara for her 'fancy ways' or for the serious manner she took her studies and music – and for her interest in Gabriel Fitzgerald. And she knew Biddy would understand how awful things were over this business with Rosie Scully.

Tara sighed deeply, wishing that she could cycle out to Ballygrace to sit and chat with her friend for a half-an-hour. She wondered if Biddy would come back to live in the village again after the baby was born and adopted. She didn't know how she would advise her, because if people could be so awful over a lie started by a jealous housekeeper, what would Biddy have to face on her return? The priest might be on her side, and he could remind his parishioners about the way Jesus treated Mary Magdalene – but that wouldn't help Biddy when she encountered the acid tongues of the women on her own. In any case, Lizzie Lawless was unlikely to take her back in, given all the terrible things she had spread in Ballygrace about her.

When Biddy had initially left for the convent in Dublin, Tara had a small idea in the back of her head, to ask Mick if she could move in with her when she came back. That plan seemed to have been made a long time ago, long before Mick changed from a confirmed bachelor into a married man with a cottage bursting at the seams with Kitty's beautifully polished furniture. There was no room in the cottage for Biddy now, just as there was no room in it for Tara's piano – and however Mick and Kitty would have liked otherwise, there was less room in it every day for Tara.

She came to the conclusion that really she was no better off than Biddy at the minute. She couldn't go back to her homeplace for much longer either. She had no family who could offer her a better situation, for Shay was never a bit better off at the beginning of one week, than he was at the end of the previous one. She knew if she were really desperate, that there was always Joe's little room going spare, during term-time at Molly and Maggie's. Tara shuddered at the thought of the dark little house full of holy pictures and statues, and she remembered the last time she'd seen the hunched-up, sick Joe, being fussed about by the two old aunties. No – she shook her head, her long red curls swinging violently from side to side – the aunties' house was not a viable option either. Just the thought of it made her feel shivery and claustrophobic.

Tara turned when she reached the bottom of the drive and then slowly started to walk back to the house again, her forehead creased in thought. She still had a few hours' studying to do, and she knew she must put all these morbid thoughts out of her head, and get on with it.

Around eight o'clock, the headlamps of the car shone as they came up the driveway. Tara was greatly relieved, because just minutes before, Madeleine had come floating down the stairs in her dressing-grown, her blonde hair bobbing gently about her shoulders. From the minute Tara caught the glassy look on her friend's face, she knew all was not well. When she heard the peculiar ramblings which came out of her mouth, and then the all the crying and sobbing, she was positively worried.

Tara had sat her in a chair by the fire with a blanket, and after calming her down, tried to tease out of her what was the matter. It was difficult to make any sense of the things Madeleine was saying, but Tara found the gist of it to be religious. 'We have to put the radio on,' she told Tara in a near-hysterical voice. 'I'm waiting for a message . . . a sign.'

'Why the radio?' Tara asked, completely confused.

'Sometime the messages come through the radio . . . it's the only way they can communicate from Africa.'

'Africa?'

'The nuns . . . the ones who give the signs.'

Ella knocked on the sitting-room door to say that she would be putting supper out in the dining-room in ten minutes. Tara thanked her and said they would be along shortly, when Madeleine suddenly cut in. 'You've been tampering with the radio . . . haven't you?'

'What radio?' Ella's face was a picture of confusion. 'I never touched any radio.'

Madeleine stood up, a pinkish tone suffusing her neck and face. 'Don't lie to me!' she said hysterically. 'You're the one who's been interfering with things . . . touching the papers and the books! Contaminating everything . . . spreading the work of the devil!'

'Sorry, Miss Madeleine,' Ella stuttered, backing out of the door, 'but I don't know what you're going on about. As God's me judge, I never touched any radio! I never touched anythin'.'

At that point, William appeared at the sitting-room door. 'What's all the commotion?' he asked, looking from Ella to Madeleine. 'Has something happened?'

'It's Miss Madeleine,' Ella said, her voice high and breathless. 'She thinks I've been touchin' things . . . her radio and books an' that!'

Madeleine's eyes were heavy and brooding and she twisted a strand of blonde hair between her fingers. 'She's contaminated the holy scriptures . . . she's interfered with the radio reception, so that I won't receive my messages.'

Ella's hand flew to her mouth, and she shook her head from side to side in stifled denial.

'Messages?' William was deliberately calm as he took off his hat and scarf. 'And exactly what messages would you be referring to, Madeleine?'

'The messages from my Guardian in Africa,' she said wearily, as though everyone should have known. Her voice now sounded dull and flat, as though all the energy was seeping out of her.

William stared at her for a few seconds, and then he wheeled round to the young maid and said in a low but kind voice: 'Go about your work, Ella – and forget about all this business.'

'The supper –' Ella struggled out, 'it'll be ready in a few minutes.' She then took to her heels and fled along the hall to the safety and normality of the kitchen.

'I think,' William said, guiding his daughter by the arm into the sitting-room, 'that we need to check on your medication.'

'I've already taken my medication,' Madeleine replied, struggling out of his grip. 'It makes me feel funny . . . all sleepy. I'm sure I'm missing signs because of it.'

He rolled his eyes to the ceiling. 'I'll ring Dr McNally later and we'll see what he advises. In the meantime, we'll have something to eat in a sane, civilised manner.'

Madeleine froze. 'I'm not having anything to eat if that girl has prepared it!'

'Ella's a very good cook,' Tara said quietly, 'and she's a very nice girl, too.'

Madeleine put both her hands tight on her throat. 'I won't eat it! I won't eat anything she touches.' She turned to her father and flung her arms around him – feverishly clutching at him like a distressed child. 'Ella . . .' Her voice was high and hysterical. 'Ella is controlled by the devil! He has told her to kill me . . . and she's been poisoning my food!'

'Don't be ridiculous,' William gasped, struggling to extricate himself from his daughter's arms without upsetting her further. He straightened up his collar and tie, trying to regain his composure. 'This is utter nonsense, Madeleine! Ella's a completely harmless girl.'

Madeleine gave a loud whine like a wounded animal and cowered against the wall, her arms covering her head. '*You* understand, Tara, don't you?' she sobbed. 'Please say you understand. Everyone else is against me!'

Tara went over and very gently put her arms round her friend. 'You're all right, Madeleine,' she said in a soothing voice. 'Of course I understand you.' She held her for a few moments until she felt Madeleine relax against her. 'Come on, we'll go into the sitting-room, and I'll play your favourite tunes for you.'

'Will you? Will you play me some Christmas carols?' she asked pleadingly. 'They're my favourite. I like to think of Jesus when he was a baby – all nice and innocent. Before all the terrible things started happening to him.'

Tara motioned her to go into the sitting-room. 'If you find the music in the bookcase for me,' she bargained, 'then I'll play anything you want.'

As soon as she was in the room and out of earshot, Tara turned to William Fitzgerald. 'I think,' she said quietly, 'that Madeleine's medication might not be helping her. I've never seen or heard her like this before.'

William ran his fingers through his hair. 'If you can keep her occupied . . . then I think I should phone Dr McNally now.'

The doctor was out on an urgent call with a sickly young baby, and it was some time before he could be contacted, and then make his way out to Ballygrace House.

Madeleine, having tired of the musical session, said she was going upstairs to read. Tara continued to practise some of her own more difficult pieces on the piano, to pass the time until the doctor's arrival.

'I'll get it,' William Fitzgerald told the nervous young housemaid when the doorbell sounded. 'You can get off home early tonight, Ella –

it will make up for the upset with Madeleine earlier on.' The gesture hid the fact that he did not wish the young girl to be around, should there be any problems later in the night with his daughter.

When he and Doctor McNally mounted the stairs, the problems which lay ahead were all too apparent. In the half-hour or so since she had been alone, she had very quietly accumulated every holy picture, statue and cross in the house, and spread them out from the top of the stairs all the way along to her bedroom door.

Pinned on the bedroom door was a large notice – scrawled in charcoal on white paper: '*I am The Way, The Truth and The Life.*' And underneath it: '*Satan – Get thee behind me.*'

'I think,' Doctor McNally said slowly, 'we are looking at hospital treatment. Given the serious nature of things and the travel factor – Maryborough would be advisable.'

There was a silence, while William contemplated the doctor's verdict. 'Hospital, yes – but not Maryborough. It's too close . . . word of her condition would have spread round the Midlands by tomorrow morning. When she recovers, she would never be allowed to forget it.' He shook his head. 'Elisha's not bearing up too well at the moment. She's gone to London for a break. If I have to tell her that Madeleine's in Maryborough Asylum then . . .'

Dr McNally nodded his head vigorously. 'Yes, yes – of course.' His brow creased in deep thought. 'If it's Dublin, I'm afraid I'll have to sedate her. Otherwise, you may have trouble . . . with the journey being that much longer.'

The evening was more difficult than anyone envisaged, with Madeleine refusing to open her bedroom door – and then cowering in hysterics when her father finally burst the lock. After a long time patiently explaining to her about the doctor and the hospital, eventually Madeleine had to be restrained by William and Tara, while Doctor McNally gave her a sedating injection.

It was not far off midnight when William pulled in at the hospital in Dublin. Together, he and Tara managed to get Madeleine out of the car and into the building. Another hour passed sorting out administrative details, and then more time settling Madeleine into a private room. Some time later, weary and tired, they set off on the return journey to Offaly.

*

Tara found it strange coming into Ballygrace House in darkness. Most of the lamps were burnt out and it was unusually chilly in the house, since the fires had died down.

'I think the kitchen would be the warmest place,' William decided after inspecting the fires in the reception rooms. He re-lit the main lamps, and then led the way down the hall to the kitchen. An inviting, comforting warmth greeted them on entering Mrs Scully's domain. 'I'll make us both a hot brandy, then I'll boil some water for a stone jar for your bed. Ella will have stoked up the fires in here, so the stove is fairly hot.'

Tara followed behind, her thoughts lingering back in the events of the awful evening. She sat down in the big armchair by the fire which was slowly coming back to life and hugged her coat around her, as her employer rattled about in the unfamiliar territory of the kitchen cupboards.

After a few moments opening and closing doors, William gave a sigh of relief. 'Here we are!' he said brightly, producing two large brandy glasses. 'They're especially thick – to withstand the heat.' He then poured two large measures into the glasses, and two spoonfuls of sugar in each.

It occurred to Tara that she should say she had never tasted hot brandy and might not like it – but she kept quiet. After everything that had happened tonight, trying out a new drink was hardly a trial. In any case, William Fitzgerald had told her that hot brandy was the best thing to revive anyone after a shock, or if they were feeling chilled. Since they had experienced both those very situations, it was the most appropriate drink.

William actually looked more in need of something to revive himself, Tara thought. His face was an unusual greyish colour, and the bones high in his cheeks seemed more pronounced than normal. Tara supposed it would be strange if he had not shown signs of strain, at having his only daughter committed to a mental hospital – and she shuddered at the thought of poor Madeleine lying sedated in a hospital room tonight.

'Here we are,' William said coming across the stone floor. He handed her the brandy glass, wrapped in a thick napkin. 'That will take the worst of the chill out of you. Drink it up quickly while it's hot.' He then sat down in the armchair opposite the fire to her.

As she took a tentative sip of the scalding drink, it dawned on Tara that she was probably sitting in Mrs Scully's armchair. She wondered what the gossipy old woman would make of the situation, if she were to walk in and find herself and William Fitzgerald seated together once again.

After a few minutes silence, William leaned forward. 'I don't know how I can ever repay you for all you've done, Tara.' He looked down into his steaming brandy glass. 'It's been the worst night of my life,' he said in a choked voice. 'I feel like a monster, committing my own daughter into a locked ward in a mental hospital.'

'It was the only thing you could do,' Tara said weakly. Then another little silence fell between them. Tara felt she should say something more to comfort him – but *what* could she say? Her mind was almost numb from going over the situation, wondering if *she* could have done more than she had to prevent Madeleine being sedated and taken into that place. It was the most awful thing she had ever witnessed. She had often heard stories in the village about lunatic asylums, and the terrifying things that went on in them – but never once had she ever imagined herself being inside one. And never, when she was growing up in awe of her wealthy friend, could she have ever imagined taking Madeleine Fitzgerald into an asylum.

Since she could think of nothing of any comfort to say to her boss, she swallowed another sip of the hot golden liquid, holding the glass tightly in cupped hands. It tasted nice in a bitter-sweet way, and it was certainly warming her. She closed her eyes, imagining the golden heat travelling through her body.

'You must be very tired,' William said with concern.

'No . . . no.' Tara sat up straight in the armchair. 'I was just thinking about Madeleine – wondering how she is.'

'I should imagine she's sleeping by now. At least – I hope the poor child is sleeping.' He looked deep into the fire. 'What kind of torment must her mind be in . . . to come out with all those things?'

Tara could not summon up a helpful answer, so she took another mouthful of the brandy. It tasted even nicer this time.

William put his glass on the tall mantelpiece and then took his coat off, before sitting back down again. 'I know her mother has suffered with nervous trouble . . . but nothing of this nature. She certainly never had any of this religious mania.'

Tara, now warmed by the flaming fire, slipped her arms out her coat, too. The skirt she was wearing was a bit creased, but for once, she was not troubled by her appearance. She sat back in the armchair, her feet tucked under her, sipping her drink and listening while William Fitzgerald talked about all the worries he had about his wife and daughter.

He talked and talked – in an intimate way he had never talked to a woman before. After a while, he got up and poured them both another hot drink – and then he resumed talking again.

The third time he got up to replenish their drinks, Tara held on to her almost empty glass, refusing any more. 'My head's spinning a little,' she confessed. 'I'm afraid I'm not used to strong drink.'

'I'll take your glass anyway,' William said, in a voice mellowed by the alcohol. 'I'll just add a drop of boiling water and sugar to what's left, to heat it up for you. After that, you must go on up to bed – and a nice warm bed. I have the kettle boiling for your stone jar, and I'm going to fill it, and put it into your bed right now.' He paused and smiled, the corner of his eyes crinkling up.

As she watched him, Tara was struck by the resemblance between William Fitzgerald and his son. Thinking of Gabriel now, she felt a stabbing sensation in her breast. Oh, how she wished he was here in Ballygrace House now, with his beautiful blond hair and blue eyes. How she wished he was here, stroking her hair and telling her that everything about Madeleine, and everything at home, would be all right.

'The one good thing out of all this,' William suddenly announced, 'is that neither of us has to go into the office in the morning.' He gave a wry smile and bowed. 'I formally give us both the day off.'

'But what about . . .'

William bent down and pressed a finger to her lips. 'Shhhh . . . what happens in the office tomorrow is not your department. Your department is to sleep in bed all morning . . . like a good little girl.' He held his finger to her lips for a few moments longer.

Tara turned her head, feeling vaguely disconcerted with the

physical contact. She focused her glazed eyes on the glowing fire, while he fixed the hot stone jar and took it upstairs.

A minute or two later, he was back downstairs whistling an old Irish tune as he made the drinks. William Fitzgerald – who had never lifted a hand in any kitchen before – discovered something about himself at five o'clock on that dark spring morning. He discovered that he was deriving the utmost pleasure from the simple rituals of making drinks and filling a stone jar for Tara Flynn. He imagined how it would feel to make a light breakfast for her, and then carry it upstairs to her bedroom – and then sit on the end of her bed while she ate it. This – from a man who had previously believed that satisfaction was derived purely from what women *gave* to him – was a revelation indeed.

As she watched the flames flickering and dancing, Tara wished again with all her heart that she was alone in this cosy, warm kitchen with Gabriel Fitzgerald – and not his father. Her thoughts – hazy from the brandy – drifted back to the New Year's Ball and all the hours they had spent wrapped in each other's arms. She slipped her shoes off now, ignoring the soft clatter as they hit the stone floor, and then she drew her knees up higher, hugging them close to her body.

An unexpected, cosy feeling stole over her – blanking out the horrors of the night – and making her feel relaxed and mellow. She was still in this pleasant daze when William Fitzgerald returned with two steaming drinks. She happily accepted hers with the reassurance that he had added only hot water and sugar, to the small amount of brandy she had left in the bottom of her glass.

As he took a gulp of his own strong drink, William felt no guilt at deceiving the breathtakingly beautiful girl opposite him. He had in fact added another good measure of brandy to her glass. He knew that she was already showing the signs of having drunk too much but, if she had another drink in her hand, she would be more relaxed – and she would stay with him longer. He found himself enchanted by the easy, unselfconscious way she was talking and listening to him. It was so deliciously different to the formal manner she adhered to in the office. He loved sitting so close to her, even when she was staring into the fire, wrapped in her own private thoughts. It was like sitting looking at a beautiful, flawless painting. Except this painting was living and breathing – and had the most voluptuous breasts he had ever seen.

He took another sip of his drink, grateful to the alcohol for putting distance between himself and all the horrendous happenings of the previous night. He had thought when Elisha went over to London that an emotional burden had been lifted from his shoulders. A few weeks away from each other would surely help ease the tension which had been growing again between them.

He had been certain that Madeleine was on the road to recovery and would soon transform back into the blonde, well-groomed girl she had been. He had been considered her eventually taking over and running one of his offices in the not too distant future. Certainly not the undertaking office. He shuddered at the thought. He could hardly bear to go into the place himself, and given Madeleine's nature, it definitely would not suit her. The auctioneering office in Tullamore would be worth considering. It would give her a status as a businesswoman in the immediate locality and it would keep everything in the family.

And then of course there was Tara to consider – the beautiful, elegant Tara – who, in the last few weeks, had become as real in his affections as any of his family. He stole a glance at her now – the sort of glance that a smitten young boy would steal. Her glorious red head was bent in deep thought. The sight sent a rush of pure lust ripping through his body, so fierce he was afraid she would see his discomfort.

He gripped the stem of his brandy glass to stop himself reaching a hand out to her. The hand of a drowning man. A man cast adrift in a loveless marriage – a marriage which had long grown cold.

He took a gulp of his drink – to force back all the thoughts which were threatening to erupt in a volcano of words declaring his longing and desire. He lowered his head and only allowed himself the small pleasure of staring at her shapely ankles and her stockinged feet.

He had plans for Tara Flynn – big plans. He was going to move back into the property business in Dublin. All his misdemeanors from the past were now forgotten and he had redeemed his reputation. Recently he had been approached by old Dublin associates, interested in property around Kildare and Naas. Stud farms and riding schools were becoming big business in those areas, and there were many people interested in cashing in on it.

An auctioneer's office in Dublin would save a lot of travelling and with the dazzling Tara Flynn running it, he would be guaranteed plenty of business. He would rent an apartment for her in the city centre. An elegent place for an elegant lady – tastefully furnished – that would serve as a retreat for him when he was visiting the city.

'My two best friends . . .' Tara ventured in a wavery voice, 'both of them . . . have gone away.' She lifted her head up to look across at him and was surprised at how difficult the small gesture was. 'Both of them – Madeleine and Biddy – are in Dublin . . . and I'm left down here in Ballygrace . . . all on my own.'

William could see quite plainly that the brandy had done its job. 'Biddy?' he asked.

'Yes,' Tara said thickly. 'Biddy . . . Biddy's having a baby.'

William's eyes narrowed in interest. He vaguely remembered Tara mentioning this girl's name before. He wondered if this was the girl Mrs Scully had been gossiping about. 'And this, Biddy – is she a married lady?'

Tara swung her head rather violently from side to side. 'No . . . no. Some boy . . . he took advantage of her. They sent her to a convent . . . to a place for fallen girls.'

He nodded, surprised that the fairly religious, highly principled Tara would have a friend in such a position. The pregnancy was one thing – but the home for fallen women was another thing entirely. 'Dreadful business for a young girl,' he said diplomatically.

'She's a very *good* girl,' Tara said with emphasis. 'She's had a terrible life . . . she's an orphan.' She halted for a moment, then added in a tearful voice: 'And poor Madeleine . . . I hate to think of her in that place, too.'

William's heart sank. 'It's too damned awful,' he agreed in a broken tone. 'And I can't bear the thought of explaining it to her mother and Gabriel. Elisha's very delicate at the moment – and Gabriel's due to sit exams shortly – pretty tough exams. He didn't do as well as he'd hoped at Christmas so he has to put a big effort into his work this term, if he doesn't want to get thrown out.' He sighed and ran a hand through his hair. 'His mother is finding things difficult enough, coping with Madeleine. If Gabriel comes home without any prospects, I think it will break her completely.'

Tara lifted the glass and took another drink of the sweet lukewarm brandy. She wanted to ask William if failing his exams was the reason Gabriel hadn't been home for some time. Perhaps he felt he had nothing to offer a girl at present – not until his studies showed more success. Perhaps he had only cooled towards her until his future was more secure. A little glimmer of hope came into Tara's heart.

'Of course,' William went on, 'a man looks at these things differently. If one path in life doesn't work out, you simply change to another one. Gabriel could always come into the property business with me. It would just be a case of toughening him up a bit. He's inclined to be a bit on the dreamy side.'

Tara moved in her chair to reach the small table and put her glass down very carefully. 'I think,' she said, unravelling her long legs from under her, 'that I should . . . go to bed.' She got to her feet rather unsteadily.

'Must you?' William's voice was anxious. Having opened up to her about all his family life, he wasn't ready to let her go just yet. He had enjoyed their conversation immensely, and there were many other things he wanted to tell her.

'Yes,' Tara replied thickly, 'I must go.' She searched a foot around the chair until she found one shoe, then she did the same with the other, staggering slightly as she did so. She stood up straight, throwing her mane of red hair back from her face. 'I'm sure . . .' she said, 'that Madeleine will soon be better . . . that everything will soon be better.'

William drained his glass and stood up, too. 'Thank you, Tara – you've been such a comfort to me tonight.'

'I'm glad I could help.' She turned and started to negotiate her unsteady way towards the kitchen door. Then, she swung back, suddenly remembering her handbag, and collided into him. 'Oops! Sorry . . . I'm so sorry!' she said, reaching a hand to the door handle to steady herself.

Both his arms came round her waist immediately. 'Okay, now?' he asked, his hands tightly holding her young firm flesh. The nearness of her made William feel almost faint, and the light scent from her hair made his hands shake ever so slightly.

'Yes,' she replied, straightening herself up. 'Sorry . . . but the brandy seems to have gone to my head a bit.' As she excused herself, a niggling little voice in her head suddenly alerted Tara to the fact that she was all alone in Ballygrace House with William Fitzgerald. A hot, nervous feeling swept over her and she was acutely aware of the pressure of his fingers and the nearness of his dark, male body. Trying not to show her panic, she eased herself out of his arms and started for the door again. 'I'm really not . . . not used to strong drink.'

William Fitzgerald stood watching her as she swayed her way out of the room – and used every ounce of willpower to control the passion which was coursing through all the veins in his body.

Chapter Seventeen

As she undressed in her cold bedroom, Tara murmured to herself how kind William Fitzgerald was, for he had not only slipped the hot stone jar into her bed, but he had also taken the trouble to light the oil lamps for her. Several times, as she removed her stockings and undergarments, she had to grip the bedside table to steady herself – and she told herself off for being such a silly girl as to drink all that hot brandy. She hadn't felt too badly, she remembered, until she had drunk the third glass – the one with only hot water and sugar. She shook her head. Never, she decided, would she drink hot brandy again.

She fiddled about for a while with the tiny pearl buttons on the front of her long lace-trimmed cream night-dress. Having succeeded in fastening it, she padded across the bedroom floor in her bare feet and quenched both lamps. Then, she slid in between the smooth flannelette sheets and laid her fuzzy head on the green satin top-pillow which for once she had forgotten to remove.

She stretched out her-long legs, luxuriating in the warmth of the stone bed-warmer, and thought of Gabriel Fitzgerald. It had heartened her to hear how hard Gabriel was concentrating on his studies. It suddenly all made sense to her, that *of course* he would have to put a greater effort, if he were planning on a solid career for the future. And if she, Tara, played her cards right, perhaps there was a chance that *she* could be part of that future with him. By the time he finished university, she would have passed all her exams at night school and would be well on with her piano exams. Certainly, well enough qualified to teach the subject at an elementary level, and earn some more money to add to her precious savings. She closed her eyes now and, still thinking of Gabriel Fitzgerald, she drifted off to sleep.

Some time later Tara was suddenly woken. It was still dark in the room, and somewhere in her befuddled brain, she was vaguely aware of a presence in the room.

Perhaps, she thought, perhaps it's Gabriel – sneaking in to give me a goodnight kiss! She almost giggled, the effects of the brandy still working. Then, she chided herself. How could she even imagine Gabriel getting into the same bed as her? She was obviously dreaming again. She turned over on her side, facing the wall. She had had lot of dreams about the handsome blond Gabriel over the years. When she remembered some of them the next morning, she often blushed, wondering where the sinful thoughts came from.

She was still hazily unconcerned when she felt the heavy weight lie down on the opposite side of the bed beside her. And then, she felt a warm breath on the back of her neck and a gentle hand reaching out to caress her shoulders. Then the hand moved to gently touch her hair.

Gabriel! She wasn't dreaming – he was here in the room and in the bed beside her. She gave a little moan of pleasure and then she turned in the darkness of the room to face him – to say his name – and warn him that someone might come in and catch them together. But before she could get her tongue around the words, he pulled her in his arms and crushed his mouth on top of her parted lips. Then he kissed her with an urgency she had never experienced before, and suddenly she was aware of strange, warm feelings in her body she did not know existed. Her body trembled and she clung tighter to him as he moved his mouth to kiss her eyes, her neck, and started down towards her breasts.

Then, as his hands moved to the tiny pearl buttons – the buttons she had struggled to fasten earlier on – Tara suddenly was wide awake. Her hands flew to the neck of her nightdress to prevent him opening it, but then his weight moved on top of her. Before she could do anything, she was pinned beneath this warm, heavy weight. Pinned beneath a naked, muscular male body – which was not Gabriel's – and when she realised who it was, she was paralysed with fear and horror!

'Tara . . . Tara, my love!' William Fitzgerald's voice moaned, his hands reaching down her body now, pushing up her nightgown –

searching for the lithe limbs beneath. The limbs that had so captivated his thoughts these last few months.

'No!' Tara gasped, trying to push the heavy weight off her. 'No . . .
please! No!'

'Shh . . .' he told her drunkenly, 'we both deserve a little comfort . . . no one need know . . . we're not doing anyone any harm.'
Then he turned towards her and smothered her mouth with kisses
while he pressed the hardness of his body against hers.

'No!' Tara screamed. 'Don't . . . please, don't!' But as the sound
echoed round the bedroom, she knew that there was no one within
miles who would hear her cries. Realising that she had only herself to
depend upon, she summoned up every ounce of energy she possessed,
and then – with all her might – she pushed him away.

But it was useless. In a split second he was back on top of her again,
one hand moving over her breast, and the other forcing her thighs
apart. And all the time moaning – saying her name over and over
again – telling her how much he adored and worshipped her and had
wanted her all these months. How she had brought sunshine into his
life and made him forget all the burdens he had to endure. Tara heard
nothing of his words or excuses, as she struggled in vain against his
fingers pressing hard into her flesh, and his mouth crushing once
again upon hers.

Gradually, Tara became still. A cold, stark fear which had stolen
over her body, told her that that the inevitable would now happen
and to struggle would only make it worse.

There was only one point later when Tara struggled again. When
William Fitzgerald thrust himself inside her, she gave a scream which
came from the depths of her soul.

After that, she was silent. She was silent as she mourned the loss of
her virginity.

The virginity she had been saving for William Fitzgerald's son.

PART TWO

Man cannot discover new oceans,
until he has the courage
to lose sight of the shore.

ANON.

Chapter Eighteen

❧❧❧

June, 1950

The crowd surged forward. 'Thanks be to Jaysus!' a sandy-haired man said loudly in a thick Dublin accent. 'That was the worst boat journey I've ever had. Every feckin' pint I supped came back up quicker than it went down!' He gave a raucous laugh, then looked around the other passengers to see who was laughing along with him. To his satisfaction, several others joined in, making disparaging remarks about the boat company and the rough journey across.

Tara looked over her shoulder at the pale-faced Biddy and raised her eyebrows in disapproval. 'If I ever come on a boat again,' she whispered indignantly, 'I don't care how much it costs – I'm coming first class!' The loud-mouthed Dubliner had nearly driven them mad on the journey from Dublin to Holyhead and try as they might to escape him, they always seemed to run into him again. They moved along the ramp, stopping and starting to let travellers change cases from one hand to another, or for parents to pick up tired children in their arms.

'Are you all right?' Tara said, glancing back at Biddy. 'Are you sure you can manage that case?'

'I'm fine,' Biddy replied. 'But I'll be a lot better when we get off this boat.'

Tara looked at her watch. 'I hope the train has waited for us,' she said anxiously. 'It would be terrible to miss it and be stuck in a strange place for hours.'

'We've still to go through the Customs.' Biddy took the opportunity

247

to move into a space in the crowd alongside her friend. 'D'ye think they'll say anything to us? D'ye think they might take us into one of the rooms?'

'Not at all,' Tara said in a crisp voice, although in truth she wasn't one bit sure of what might happen.

The passengers walked in single file now as they came to Customs clearance. Tara glanced back anxiously every now and again, to check how Biddy was doing. It was just over two weeks since she'd given birth to a small, premature baby boy, and she was still bleeding heavily. The stern-faced Customs officers looked closely at each person as they passed by. They had already selected three people from the crowd to open their cases or bags but when Tara and Biddy came up to the desk they just nodded and told them to pass through.

'It must have been our good clothes and hats,' Biddy said in a voice breathless with relief. 'I'm glad you made me dress up for travellin'.'

Tara slipped her free arm through Biddy's and gave her a comforting squeeze. 'We had nothing to hide, so it wouldn't have mattered even if they had stopped us.' She heaved a sigh of relief when they were told that the train to Manchester had waited for the boat passengers. 'We'll be fine now,' she assured Biddy, as they boarded the train. 'It's only half-past two. It'll still be daylight when we arrive in Stockport.'

'Don't we have to go to Manchester first?' Biddy enquired anxiously. 'I'm sure that's what Father Daly wrote down on the bit of paper.'

'We take this train to Manchester, then we'll have plenty of time to catch a connection from Manchester out to Stockport,' Tara told her.

After looking in a number of carriages, they were lucky to find two vacant seats – side by side – in the very last one. There had been an almost empty carriage further along but when Tara slid the door open, she realised why. The drunken Dubliner was stretched out, taking up a full row of seats for himself and there were three other men seated opposite him, with open bottles of beer in their hands. Tara had quickly banged the door shut and motioned to Biddy to keep moving on.

'It must be busy because it's a Friday,' Biddy said. 'I heard the trains from Dublin are fierce busy on a Friday, too.'

A pleasant, elderly man from Galway very kindly lifted their cases up on the rack above their heads, then, when they sat down, proceeded to ask them both which part of Ireland they came from. Tara hesitated for a few seconds, then she said: 'A small place near Tullamore.'

Thankfully, the man didn't know Tullamore as such, although he had neighbours who had connections in Mullingar, which wasn't too far. He went on to regale them with details about the funeral he was travelling to in Ardwick, a district of Manchester. Normally, in a situation like that, Biddy would have been the one to do all the chatting, but since she wasn't at all herself, Tara ended up listening and asking all the right questions.

The train journey was quite pleasant and while Biddy and the man from Galway dozed, Tara looked out of the rain-dotted window at the scenery as they passed through the lovely countryside of Wales and then out into the more industrialised areas as they approached England.

At least, she thought to herself, she was in a better situation than when she arrived in Dublin, last Tuesday afternoon. She had company with her in the shape of Biddy, and she had an address to go to. She sighed and looked out at the station they had just pulled into. It was a place called Chester, a place she had never heard of. Just like she had never heard of Stockport.

The jolt of the train stopping woke Biddy. She looked round the carriage with bleary eyes, not sure for a moment where she was. 'Are we in England yet?' she checked with Tara.

'We are,' Tara said, patting her arm. 'We've another bit to go yet before we reach Manchester, then we've to change trains for Stockport.'

'I would never have managed this journey on my own,' Biddy whispered. 'I keep thanking God for sending you up to Dublin when he did. When you walked in the door of the convent, I couldn't believe it – it was like a miracle.'

Tara smiled back. 'It was an answer to my prayers too, Biddy,' she replied in a low voice. 'And whatever happens, we'll make it work.'

'When Father Daly first gave me the name and address of Mrs Carey in Stockport, I told him I couldn't go to England – then I thought about it. Where else would I go? I couldn't go back to Ballygrace – not that Lizzie Lawless would have had me back anyway. I'd even thought of asking you if I could come and live with you and Mick, but then you wrote to me and told me about him getting married. That was some shock! I would never have imagined Mick getting married in a million years.'

Tara nodded. 'I'm glad for Mick. Kitty's a nice woman, and he deserves it. But I have to admit, it was a big shock for me too.' And one of a number of shocks, Tara thought to herself. And if Biddy knew what had happened at Ballygrace House – the real reason she had left Ireland – she would have had the biggest shock of all.

As if she had read Tara's thoughts, Biddy suddenly said: 'I can't believe what's happened to Madeleine.' She shook her head sorrowfully. 'Her family must be in a terrible state – her being in a mental hospital. You wouldn't think anything bad like that would happen to the Fitzgeralds. The Quality don't usually get things like that happenin' to them.'

Tara looked out of the window at the little splashes of rain that had just appeared on the glass. Oh Biddy, she thought to herself, if only you knew the things that happen to the Quality, you would never look up to them again. 'I think Madeleine will have to spend a long time in hospital,' she said, 'but I'm sure she'll eventually get better.'

Some time later the train pulled in at a drizzly Manchester, and a porter told them to hurry up as a train was leaving for Stockport in five minutes. The next train-ride was a short one, taking them out through the city overlooking the offices and houses as they went along. Thankfully, the rain had stopped by the time they arrived in Stockport. The girls alighted from the train with their cases, and then stood looking at each other, unsure as to what to do next.

'If you wait here with the luggage,' Tara told her friend, 'then I'll go and ask at the ticket desk if they know whereabouts in Stockport Shaw Heath is.'

The ticket clerk told them that they should get a taxi to Shaw Heath, because, although it wasn't very far, it was all uphill, and would be heavy going if they were carrying luggage. He pointed to a taxi rank right outside the station and said they would be at the address in less than five minutes.

The black Hackney cab turned up on to a busy road and both girls craned their necks as they drove along, trying to get a better view of Stockport town, the place that was now their new home.

'Have you been to Stockport before, girls?' the small, stocky cab-driver asked in a strong North-West accent.

'No,' Biddy replied, 'we've just moved here.'

'Very nice,' he said, 'very nice.' He then proceeded to give them a guided tour of the area as they passed through. 'We're out of the main shopping area up here, and we're heading out of the town. This building to the left of you is the library, and that building straight in front of you on the same side is the Town Hall.' He laughed. 'It's called the "Wedding Cake" because the shape at the top looks like one.'

'It does!' Biddy said excitedly, pointing at the huge structure. 'Look at it, Tara. And it's a lot bigger and fancier than any of the buildings in Ballygrace or Tullamore.'

'Where's that?' the cab driver enquired, turning the taxi into a street on the right. 'Somewhere in Wales?'

'It's in *Ireland*,' Tara said in a clear, clipped tone.

'You'll be at home here then,' the man laughed. 'There's plenty of Paddies around these parts.' He turned down another road. 'We're going into Shaw Heath now. What street did you say it was?'

'Maple Terrace,' Biddy said, her voice sounding breathless.

Tara took her purse out of her handbag, and started to sort out the correct change for the taxi. It was difficult getting used to the different pennies and ha'pennies and shillings, sixpences and threepenny bits. Biddy hadn't a clue and couldn't tell one coin from another, so she had left it all up to Tara to sort out fares, money for tea and anything else.

The taxi came to a stop outside a row of red brick terraced houses on a cobbled street. 'Here we are, girls – this is Maple Terrace,' the driver said, getting out to help them with their cases. 'What number did you say, love?' he asked Biddy.

'Number twenty,' Biddy said, trying not to giggle at being called 'love'.

The driver strode on, checking the numbers on the houses. He turned in one of the gateways, deposited the cases on the doorstep, and then rang the bell.

The girls followed behind. Tara gave him the money, with a few coppers extra for a tip. 'Thanks, love,' he said warmly, 'and if you need a cab, you'll find me most evenings down by the station.' He gave them an appraising glance. 'I'm sure two fine-looking girls like yourselves will be out on the town in the evenings. I often go to the dance halls round Stockport and Manchester when I have the night off – so I might run into you at a dance some evening.'

When the cab pulled away, the girls looked at each other. 'The nuns in the convent kept warning me about the dance halls in England,' Biddy said to Tara. 'They said they were nothing but dens of iniquity.'

Before Biddy could elaborate any further, an elderly woman with coiled grey hair and a cross-over pinny opened the door.

'Yes?' the woman said, her eyes flitting from one to the other and then settling on the suitcases. 'Can I help you?'

'Mrs Carey?' Tara asked, and when the woman confirmed with a nod, she continued. 'I'm Tara Flynn, and this is Bid – Bridget Hart. Father Daly over in Ireland said you might have rooms here.'

'*One* room,' Mrs Carey corrected in an accent which betrayed Irish origins, tempered with a heavier Manchester accent. 'He only wrote about *one* girl. I haven't the room for two.'

Tara's heart sank. She knew everything had gone too smoothly to be true.

'We could share . . .' Biddy said, looking at Tara for support.

Mrs Carey shook her head. 'It's the smallest room in the house, not enough room to swing a cat in it.' She pursed her lips together, and shook her head. 'I've only the room for one. You'll have to decide between you, which one has it. Father Daly had no right sending two of you, when he sent word to me that there was only *one* coming.'

'We want to stay together. Would you know of anywhere else that might take two of us?' Tara asked, trying to keep calm. 'Are there any other lodgings about?'

Mrs Carey crossed her arms high on her chest and put her head to the side. 'Oh, there's lodgings about all right but whether they're *decent* lodgings is another matter—' She stopped abruptly, and turned her gaze on a tall elderly man who was walking up the street towards them. 'You'd better lift those cases and come inside,' she said irritably, 'before someone falls over them and blames me.'

They followed her up two little steps, which were painted a blood-red colour to match the door and then down a dim hallway, lit only by a small red bulb situated under a picture of the Sacred Heart.

'Drop your cases at the door, until I write a couple of addresses down for you,' she said sharply.

The girls followed her until they found themselves in a steamy kitchen which smelled of stale cabbage, and had a large round table set for eight people. They stood silently, Biddy with her fingers crossed behind her back. She was desperately hoping that Tara wouldn't blame her for the predicament they were in, because she had assured her that there would be room in this house for two lodgers.

Mrs Carey took a pen and paper down from a shelf and wrote down the addresses. 'If neither of you want the room,' she said, handing Tara the piece of paper, 'Then I'll let you get on your way. It's Friday and I have fish and chips to cook for the men coming in from work shortly.'

Biddy's mouth watered at the mention of the fish and chips. She hoped that they would soon be sitting down eating a meal themselves, for they'd only had a bar of chocolate in the train station in Manchester, since their sandwiches on the boat.

'How far would these places be?' Tara asked anxiously, dreading the thought of traipsing around the strange cobbled streets in the dark.

'Just a couple of streets away,' the landlady said. 'You'll be there in a few minutes. I'll see you to the door, and I'll point out the direction. You should be all right in one of those places. It's not too busy a time of the year yet. It gets worse in the summer, when the younger ones leave school and are looking for a job and digs.'

Out in the strange cobbled streets once again, Biddy said to Tara: 'I'm glad we're not stayin' in that house. It had a funny smell – and I didn't like her one bit.'

'I didn't care for her either, but at least it would have been a roof over our heads.' Tara consulted the piece of paper. 'Right,' she said in a determined voice, 'we have to cross this road now and turn left. It should lead us into Willow Terrace and we're looking for number thirteen. And say a prayer,' she instructed Biddy, 'that the rain doesn't come back on. All we need is to get drowned as we're walking along, and we'll be nice-looking sights turning up at anybody's door.'

'They say number thirteen is fierce unlucky,' Biddy said glumly, picking up her case. 'I hope this one is better than Mrs Carey's.' Then, she suddenly smiled. 'Did you notice that she had the electric lighting, Tara? There wasn't a candle or an oul' oil lamp anywhere. Won't it be great to live in a house with the electric lighting?'

'Don't mind about the lighting, Biddy,' Tara said, as they walked along. 'It's finding a bed for the night that's more important.'

The next two houses they called at had no vacancies. A man who answered the door in the second house had scrutinised them closely and said: 'Are you Irish?'

'We are,' Tara replied, thinking he might have relatives over in Ireland. 'We're from the Midlands—'

'In that case,' he said, stepping back inside, 'you can *keep on looking*. I've had to get rid of two drunken Micks in the last month, and I vowed never to take in any of them in again! In my opinion, they're nothing but ignorant, ill-educated, drunken louts! So I'll say good day to you.' And with that, the door was banged firmly in their faces.

'Well!' Tara said indignantly. 'I don't believe what I've just heard.'

Biddy touched her arm. 'Father Daly warned me this might happen. He said that some of the English can't stand the Irish. He said we were to keep our heads down, and be careful of which Irish crowds we associated with.' She sucked in her breath, and said in a wavering voice: 'I'm glad we didn't get a room in that house – I told you number thirteen was unlucky.'

Tara lifted her case up again, her heart as heavy as the luggage. '*Where*,' she sighed, 'do we go now?'

They trudged back along the damp unfamiliar streets, being careful to pick their steps over the rough cobbles lest they should twist an ankle and add to their misfortunes.

'How are you feeling?' Tara asked Biddy as they turned a corner and came upon a row of shops. 'Do you feel you need to sit down yet?'

'I'm all right for a bit longer. If we don't get something soon, maybe we could go somewhere for a cup of tea.'

'If you mind the cases for a few minutes,' Tara suggested as they came upon a newsagent's shop, 'I'll run in here and buy a newspaper. You never know, they might have lodgings advertised in them. I'll ask if they know where we can get a cup of tea while I'm in.'

Tara seemed to be gone an awful long time. Biddy kept moving the cases in closer to the shop wall, afraid someone might trip over them. People seemed to be in a hurry, she thought, rushing in and out of the little row of shops. Several times she had to stop herself from saying '*Hello*' to people, if they caught her eye. Tara had warned her not to make free with anyone, as the English liked to keep themselves to themselves. It would be no problem to Tara, Biddy thought, for she kept herself to herself all the time.

'Good news,' Tara said, coming rushing out of the shop with yet another bit of paper. 'The people in the shop are from Mayo and they've given me the address of a nice English woman who takes in lodgers.'

Biddy joined her hands. 'Thanks be to God!'

'I didn't notice going into the shop,' Tara said, pointing to the newsagent's window, 'but there are advertisements for lodgings stuck up here. And apparently the English woman came in yesterday and put a notice in saying she had two vacant rooms. They said she has a huge house, just along the street here. Seemingly she takes in a lot of Irish lads and the newsagent said she might be glad of the company of girls for a change.'

Both girls left the cases for a moment and walked to the end of the row of shops, to look down the street.

Biddy looked up at the top of the building where the street names were positioned. 'We're back in Maple Terrace,' she said incredulously. 'All these streets look the very same.'

'It's not Maple Terrace that we're looking for,' Tara told her. 'It's actually Maple *Grove*, and it's somewhere down the bottom of the street. Apparently there's a little road that goes in on the right-hand side and the house is just off there.'

They went back and picked up the cases. 'Please God,' Biddy said aloud, 'that we'll be lucky this time. I'm not fit to be walking about for much longer.'

'Here,' Tara said, taking her case from her, 'I'll carry this for you and you carry my handbag. We won't be long getting there.'

They walked along the street in silence, Tara breathless from carrying the two heavy cases and Biddy deep in thought. She didn't want to worry Tara but she was still bleeding heavily, and she needed to get to a toilet where she could change her sanitary pad and underwear. The tops of her legs were also chafed and sore, where the large hospital pad had been rubbing against her skin.

At last, they reached Maple Grove and the big house that the newsagent had described to Tara. 'Cream front with pillars and stained-glass window over the door,' Tara read from the paper, 'and we have to ask for a Mrs Sweeney.' She dropped the cases once again and strode in the gate, up the high white-painted steps, and rung the bell.

Within seconds, a petite attractive woman in her late thirties, with bright blonde hair, a red dress and bright red lipstick came to the door.

'Yes, love?' the woman said in a strong Manchester accent. 'What can I do for you?' She gave Tara a big smile.

'The newsagent at the corner gave me your address. She said you had some vacant rooms.'

'Already?' the woman said, her eyes wide with surprise. 'I only put that notice in yesterday.'

'Do you still have the rooms?' Tara asked anxiously.

The woman looked over her head at Biddy who was standing at the gate. 'How many rooms were you looking for, ducks?'

'Two,' Tara said, her voice slightly breathless – dreading the same response as the other places. 'It's for my friend and me . . . but if you don't have two rooms, we would be very happy to share.'

'Come in. Come in, love,' the woman said warmly, opening the door wider, 'and call your friend to come in, too. We can't stand outside doin' business, can we?'

Tara's heart leapt with relief – things were going to be all right after all. 'I'll just go down and help her with the cases,' she said.

'It's brighter than that other house we were in, thanks be to God!' Biddy whispered as they followed the woman down the white-painted hall, 'and it smells a lot better, too.'

'We'll go into the front room,' Mrs Sweeney said, opening a door off the hallway, 'because we won't get a chance to chat with that rowdy lot in the kitchen. They're always the same on a Friday when they've just been paid.'

They put their cases down on the floor and then Biddy suddenly blurted out: 'I'm beggin' yer pardon, ma'am, but have you a lavatory I could use, please?'

'There's one at the top of the stairs, love,' the landlady said, then went out into the hallway to direct her. 'Your friend looks a bit peaky,' she said when she came back into the room. 'Has she been feeling poorly?'

'I think,' Tara explained, 'that she's a little tired. We've been walking about with the cases for a while.' She hesitated for a moment. 'She also has problems every month . . . you know, women's problems.'

'Say no more!' Mrs Sweeney rolled her eyes to the ceiling. 'I used to have the same trouble myself when I was her age.' She leaned forward. 'Tell me about yourselves now, ducks, and what's brought you to Stockport.'

Tara took off her black felt hat. 'My name's Tara Flynn, and my friend is Biddy – Bridget Hart. We're from County Offaly in Ireland, and we went to school together.'

'That's lovely,' the woman said, putting her hand out for Tara to shake. 'I'm Ruby Sweeney – pleased to meet you, I'm sure. A lot of the lads I get here are Irish, and I always find them a nice bunch – at least they think of their mothers when they're away from home.' She took the top off her pen. 'Now, I think we had better get down to business. I have two rooms vacant, on account of a building contract that has just finished. Some lads from Scotland who were working on a hotel out by the airport.' She sat back in her chair and studied her prospective boarder. 'They were quite happy sharin' a room – and sharin' the cost. I don't know how you would feel about sharin' a room.'

Tara's mind worked quickly, taking in the financial and personal implications. 'Is there a big difference in price?'

'It's one pound and fifteen shillings each a week if you're sharing,' Ruby stated, 'and two pounds five shillings each if you want separate rooms. They are both fairly big rooms with double beds in each.'

'I think we might be best to start off sharing, and when we find work we can perhaps think of separate rooms.'

'You haven't got jobs then?' the landlady said, her voice high with alarm. 'D'you mean to say you've come all the way over from Ireland without jobs?'

'It's not a problem,' Tara reassured her quickly. 'We can pay a month's rent in advance.' When the landlady still looked doubtful, Tara reached into her handbag, and drew two five-pound notes and several one-pound notes out of the back compartment of the new leather purse she had bought in Dublin. She had learned already – in the week she spent in Dublin – that money talked. 'In fact,' she said, placing the notes on the table, 'I'd be happy to pay *two* months' rent in advance, although I'm sure there will be no problem about us finding work.'

'What sort of work would that be?' Ruby said smiling, looking at the money.

'I'm looking for some sort of clerical or bookkeeping position.' Tara noticed that the landlady looked impressed. 'And Biddy has experience in a variety of domestic work. She was a priest's house-keeper and she kept a bakehouse in order.' Tara was glad that Biddy wasn't around to hear herself being elevated from a maid in the priest's house to housekeeper, for she was more inclined to play her positions down.

'I thought you both looked like teachers when you turned up at the door,' Ruby confessed, 'and with you being so well-spoken and everything.' She put a finger under her chin, a thoughtful look on her face. 'I don't know anybody in the clerical line who could help you out finding work – you might have to go to an employment agency for that. But I'm sure I could put a word in somewhere for Bridget.'

'That's very good of you to offer.' Tara turned now as a pale-faced Biddy came in the door. 'I'm just explaining that we both hope to find work as quickly as possible – isn't that right, Bridget?'

Whether it was the thought of work in her weakened condition or whether it would have happened in any case – Biddy swayed for a few seconds in front of Tara and the landlady, and then promptly fainted at their feet.

Chapter Nineteen

Tara huddled in an armchair by the big bedroom window until one in the morning, staring out into the brightly lit street. She found the street lighting strange after a lifetime of dark country nights. Twice she had got into the double bed beside Biddy, closed her eyes and tried to sleep. But her mind refused to stop going over the terrible things that had happened – and imagining even worse things that might lie ahead in this strange place. All the relief she had felt at finding a place to stay had now evaporated, and was replaced with an awful, cold fear in the pit of her stomach. A cold fear which reminded her that she was hundreds of miles and a dark sea away from her home and family in Ballygrace. The home she could never return to after the dreadful thing that William Fitzgerald had done to her. The thing she could never bring herself to tell anyone – not even Biddy.

When Biddy had come round from her faint last night, Ruby Sweeney had bustled about making her a cup of hot, sweet tea. After the tea, the landlady had shown them the double room on the second floor which was to be their new home for the next couple of months at least. There were three bedrooms and a large bathroom, which Ruby said would be used by all the occupants of the rooms on that floor.

The girls' bedroom was of a reasonable size and clean, with a double bed decked with a faded pink candlewick bedspread, and a fringed rug on top of a brown linoleum floor. There was a large double wardrobe which had seen better days, a matching dressing table with a circular mirror and three deep drawers, and a small cabinet at either side of the bed. The walls were adorned with large cabbage-rose wallpaper, and the bright pink of the roses had been picked out to paint the skirting-boards and door.

'It's lovely,' Biddy gasped, sitting down on the bed to feel the soft bedspread. Compared to Lizzie Lawless's run-down cottage and the sparse cell she had occupied in the convent, it was unadulterated luxury.

'It'll do grand, thank you, Mrs Sweeney,' Tara added, as she pushed pictures out of her mind of green satin quilts and bolsters, and the fine furniture she had come to love in Ballygrace House.

Two older men – builders from Wexford – were called upon by the landlady to lift the girls' cases upstairs. The men were obviously planning a night out, for one of the men had shaving foam round his ears, and the other was in the middle of polishing his 'low shoes', usually only worn by Irish men when they were going out at the weekend.

'I feel terrible disturbing them,' Tara said. 'We could have managed to lift them up ourselves.'

'Why have a dog and bark yourself?' Ruby had said, as the two men brought the cases in. 'I have them paintin' and decoratin' for me in the summer and I get them to do any odd jobs about the place. They love doin' it – it makes them feel at home.' She introduced the girls to the two men and then left them chatting for a few moments, discussing the different parts of Ireland where they and the other lads living in the house came from.

A short while later – after donning a frilly flowery apron over her red dress – Ruby had brought both girls into the kitchen and sat them down at the big pine table for the traditional Friday night tea of cod and chips. 'Is it any wonder you're poorly, love?' she said to Biddy, heaping a pile of mushy peas on her overflowing plate. 'Traipsing round the streets in the rain and not having a bite inside you for hours – and then havin' your monthlies on top of all that! I'd like to see how any man would manage with all that we women have to put up with.' She set the pot with the peas back on the gas cooker and then lifted a plate of bread and butter from the work-top and placed it on the table between the two girls. 'My advice to you young girls is to have a quiet night in tonight and a long lie in the mornin'. Monday is time enough to be looking for work.'

Obviously, the offer of two months' rent in advance had quashed any fears Ruby might have of her two lodgers being unable to pay their way. She turned to Biddy now, wagging a warning finger. 'If you run into any of the younger lads in here later on, don't let any of them try to talk you into goin' out tonight. They're nice enough lads, but, naturally enough, they're after anythin' in a skirt. Have a quiet night in, and then you should take a walk into Stockport tomorrow afternoon and have a look at the shops.' She touched Tara's shoulder in a conspiratorial manner. 'I must admit I spend more than I should on clothes and the hairdresser's myself – it costs me a bloody fortune havin' me roots done every few weeks and a shampoo and set every Friday for the weekend.' She fluffed up the back of her peroxide-blonde hair in a preening, model-type gesture. 'I only had it done this morning. I'm afraid my attitude is – if you work hard for your money, then you're entitled to spend it on yourself. And anyway, the men who lodge in this house always appreciate a woman who looks after herself – not like my husband, Bert Sweeney.' She rolled her eyes to the ceiling. 'He was a right miserable old sod – wouldn't let me spend a penny on meself! He would have had me goin' around lookin' like a bleedin' rag-woman if he'd had his way.'

There was a shocked silence and then Biddy started to choke on a pea which had gone down the wrong way.

'Are you all right, love?' Ruby asked, pouring her a glass of water from the jug on the table, and when Biddy confirmed with a nod that she was, the landlady continued: 'As it happened, Bert Sweeney was killed crossing a road in Manchester – a bus it was. He was drunk of course, entirely his own fault. Anyway, if he hadn't been killed then I would have had to divorce him, so it saved me the trouble. I got this house from the insurance money – so at least I didn't suffer five years of marriage to him for nothing.' She waved her hands about, taking in the expanse of the kitchen. 'Take it from me, girls, the satisfaction of owning your own house beats the satisfaction a man can give you – any day of the week.'

There was an embarrassed pause, then, feeling she should say something, Tara ventured: 'How long is it since he died?'

'Seven years ago last December, love,' she said. 'It was the best Christmas present that I ever had.'

'D'you think,' Biddy asked, wide-eyed and fascinated, 'that you'll ever get married again?'

Ruby threw her head back and roared with laughter. 'Not bloody likely! Once bitten, twice shy. I'd sooner live over the brush with a man, any day, than get married. At least you can walk away from them without worryin' about divorce. Anyway, I've worked too hard to get this house in shape to share it with a man. Not that I don't like them, mind – they have their uses.' Then, noticing the shocked look on the girls' faces, the bubbly blonde woman suddenly became serious. 'Oh hell, I forgot about you being Irish! I'll bet you two are Catholics, are you?'

Both girls nodded.

Ruby looked flustered. 'And there's me rattlin' on about divorce and everything. Sorry, ducks. You don't have divorce in Ireland, do you? But then,' her face broke into the irrepressible smile again, 'you probably don't have rotten men like Bert Sweeney in Ireland either.'

'It doesn't matter,' Biddy said, anxious to hear more of Ruby's life story. It made her feel much better about her own problems. 'We'll have to get used to different ways – we're not living in Ireland now.'

Tara shot Biddy a disapproving glance which Biddy either didn't see or decided to ignore.

'That's very true, love,' Ruby agreed. 'It's easier if you do in Rome what the Romans do.' She looked up at the kitchen clock. 'I'll have to run and get changed,' she said, untying her apron strings. 'I'm off to the bingo. I'm meetin' some of me mates down the town at half-past seven. Friday night's bingo night,' she explained, 'and then a drink down the George pub after. Put your dishes in the sink and I'll sort them out when I come back in tonight. If you want to make a cup of tea later, help yourself. There's a packet of Rich Tea biscuits at the side of the caddy.'

'What d'you make of her?' Biddy whispered when they were alone. 'She's very glamorous altogether for an older woman, with her blonde hair and everythin'.'

Tara shrugged and looked down at the remainder of her fish and chips which for some reason now, she could not eat another bite of. 'She seems nice enough . . . in her own way.'

'She's gas!' Biddy went on. 'I think it'll be great living in this house.

Did you hear what she said about the lads going to the dancing and everything? It sounds as if there's as much goin' on in Stockport as there is in Dublin.'

Tara lifted her head abruptly. 'Why did we come to England, Biddy?'

There was an awkward silence. 'You know why, Tara. Because of . . . to get away from . . .'

'We came to get away from all the gossiping people in Ireland,' Tara reminded her, 'and to get a fresh start in a place where no one knew us.' She took a deep breath. 'I think the last thing we need is to get involved with lads.'

Large tears loomed in Biddy's eyes. 'I didn't mean any harm . . . I was only sayin'.'

Tara took a deep breath, anxious not to upset Biddy, but concerned at the same time. 'We've a lot more important things to sort out before we can be thinking of dance halls and the like. We have work to find, and as soon as we can afford it, we must find a better place than this.'

Biddy gestured with her hands around the kitchen. 'But it's grand here, Tara. It's nice and clean and warm and everythin'. I think it's a lovely house.'

'That may be, but a lovely house full of working men is no place for two girls.' Tara pursed her lips together. 'And there's the religious side to take into account. Father Daly even gave a sermon on it one Sunday – about the behaviour that goes on in the dance-halls in England, about the living in sin and the drinking and everything.' A picture suddenly crept into Tara's mind, bringing her out in a cold sweat. A picture of William Fitzgerald handing her a glass of brandy. She shuddered at the memory.

Enough had already happened back in Ireland – Tara would make sure that she and Biddy made no more terrible mistakes.

Oblivious to her friend's fears, Biddy kept her head down, in case Tara realised that all the things she was saying about England were the very reasons Biddy had been happy to come. When Father Daly had presented her with the boat ticket to come over to Stockport – whilst at the same time warning her about all the evils in England – she had thought how exciting and glamorous it sounded.

'We must get work as quickly as possible,' Tara decided, 'and then we can afford to get out of Mrs Sweeney's and into a *decent* boarding-house.'

Biddy looked down at her empty plate, and then – for want of something better to do – she reached for another piece of bread and butter, and ate it without tasting a bite. She always felt at a loss with Tara when she started going on like this about ordinary people. Mrs Sweeney seemed a good sort to Biddy, far better than Lizzie Lawless and some of the other religious types that came to mind. Ruby Sweeney was the sort of person you could talk to, the sort of person who would understand how some things just happened. Well, as far as Biddy was concerned, from what she had seen of Ruby Sweeney's house, she was quite content to stay here indefinitely. If Tara was insistent on moving out, then she would cross that bridge when she came to it.

The landlady had looked in on the girls again on her way out to the bingo. 'There's two hot-water bottles hanging on the back of the pantry door. You can fill them before you go to bed.' Then, looking at Biddy sympathetically, she said: 'It might help to ease the cramps in yer stomach, love – it usually helps me. There's a few magazines and a radio in the sitting-room, so you can make yourselves at home for the evening. I'll chat to you in the morning about the extra for the electric fire in your room and about the hot water for baths.' She smiled at Biddy again. 'I hope you're feelin' better in the morning, ducks. You don't look quite so peaky now.'

Biddy nodded, her face glowing with this unaccustomed motherly attention.

Then, as a parting gesture Ruby added: 'Ignore any noise later on. It'll only be the lads comin' back from the dancing with a few pints in them. They have their own front-door key, so they shouldn't disturb you too much. Ta-ra now – see you in the morning.'

After they had cleared their dishes, the girls went upstairs to unpack and sort their clothes into the wardrobe and dressingtable drawers. Later on, they came back down to the sitting-room and sat listening to the radio. Tara sat by the coal fire reading a book she had bought in Dublin, while Biddy flicked through fashion magazines and fiddled about with the radio, tuning it into all the strange British stations until she found a music one she liked.

Around ten o'clock, Biddy offered to make them tea, and a while later she brought two mugs of tea and the packet of tea biscuits back into the sitting-room. They listened to another radio show of popular music and then after that, they filled the rubbery hot-water bottles, and went upstairs.

'I'll have to find a chemist first thing in the morning,' Biddy said, bitting her lip nervously, when she came out of the bathroom. 'I've nearly run out of sanitary towels. I'm using twice the usual amount because I'm bleeding so heavily.'

'We might have to find a doctor if you're no better during the week,' Tara said looking concerned. 'I'm sure you should have some kind of check-up after a few weeks.'

Biddy shook her head, her eyes large with fear. 'No . . . I don't want anybody findin' out about the baby. I'm sure I'll be grand after a few more days.'

Biddy fell asleep in minutes, lulled by the comfort of the flannelette sheets and the heavy blankets, while Tara's racing mind would not let her find the peace she needed to drop into sleep.

She looked out of the bedroom window now, seeing nothing beyond the pane of glass a few feet away. She shivered and pulled the colourful crocheted shawl which had earlier adorned an armchair round her shoulders. What if Biddy was *really* ill? What if Ruby found out that she had fainted not because of her monthly periods but because she had just given birth to an illegitimate baby? And even if Biddy was okay, and they weren't thrown out of their lodgings, what if they didn't find work?

What if . . . ?

Tara's mind ran on and on – refusing to be still. After a few more minutes, she eventually dragged her stiff, cold limbs out of the armchair and across the floor to the tallboy in the corner of the room. She reached for her handbag and unzipped the small pocket inside it. She took out a pair of white glass rosary beads that Nelly Kelly, her old neighbour, had given her on the day she left Ballygrace. She kept these for everyday use in her handbag, while another pair were safely buried in a drawer in the dressing-table. Those were special ones which she would not risk using. They were the old brown wooden beads which had been held in her granda's hands – every single day of his life.

Clutching the glass beads tightly, she crept back into her side of the unfamiliar bed and curled up in the same way she used to do as child. She lay rigid, making sure that not one inch of her body touched her friend's. Apart from the nightmare night with William Fitzgerald, Tara had never shared a bed with anyone since she was a child.

She felt for the cross on the end of the string of beads, and pressed it to her lips, then she started. 'The Joyful Mysteries,' she mouthed soundlessly, lest she should waken Biddy. 'The first Joyful Mystery – the Annunciation. Please God and Our Blessed Lady – don't let me be pregnant after what William Fitzgerald did to me! Our Father who art in heaven . . .'

By the time she reached the Glorious Mysteries, Tara had dropped into a deep sleep, clutching the beads tightly to her chest.

Biddy was much better the following morning. 'It was me own fault,' she said to Tara. 'I should have known not to go so long without eating. I feel much better after the fish and chips and a good night's sleep. It's the best sleep I've had for months.'

'Good,' Tara said, giving her a relieved smile. 'We'll have our breakfast, and then we'll go out and find a chemist for you. Thank God it's not raining like yesterday.'

Biddy sniffed the air. 'There's a grand smell of cooking coming from downstairs. What time is it?'

Tara checked her watch. 'Ten o'clock! We've slept it out.'

Biddy threw back the bedclothes. 'I'll run to the bathroom first, and I'll be dressed in ten minutes.'

'There's hot water in the bathroom,' Tara informed her, 'so take your time and have a good wash.' Biddy's hygiene had improved over the years but she was still inclined to only wash when she felt she really needed it. Tara felt she had to keep a close eye on Biddy's ablutions, given their close sleeping arrangements. 'I'm going to enquire about having a bath tonight. Won't it be grand to just run the hot water into the bath from a tap? No more carting pans of water into a tin bath!'

'D'you know, Tara?' Biddy said, gathering the dressing-gown that the nuns had given her round her shoulders. 'Now that we're livin' in this lovely place, with the electric lights and everythin' – I feel as if I've died and gone to heaven!'

Tara lay on her own side of the bed for a few more minutes, thinking about what Biddy had said. In many ways she was right. The place was lovely and Ruby Sweeney seemed a nice woman. But there was something about the place that bothered Tara. Perhaps it was all the trouble with William Fitzgerald which made her very wary of people who seemed too nice too soon. Or perhaps it was the thought of all the other lodgers in the house being men – and the way Biddy was reacting to it all. She seemed too excited and only too willing to be drawn into a new life they both knew nothing about.

Listening to Ruby Sweeney talking about divorce and 'living over the brush' with men had appeared to whet Biddy's appetite. And Tara was sure that it was only a matter of time until she spilled all the business about the baby to the landlady, or someone else who would offer a sympathetic ear.

Maybe, Tara thought, *she* should have been more sympathetic herself to Biddy about all she had gone through having the baby early, and then having it wrenched away for adoption. She felt a bit guilty about that, but every time the subject of how Biddy became pregnant in the first place was approached, Biddy clammed up and the conversation fizzled out.

Tara was at a loss how to help or console her friend over losing her baby but the one thing she was definite about was that Biddy must not get herself into that situation again. But it was not going to be an easy task, for Tara noticed that even the mere *mention* of boys and dance halls brought a glint into Biddy's eye. God knows what she would be like when she eventually got the chance to go into the dance halls around Stockport and Manchester. Last night it was the only topic of conversation that she was interested in when she was chatting with Ruby and the lads.

Tara sighed and sat up in bed. Coming over to England had given both her and Biddy a clean slate, and it was imperative that they did not blot this one. There was no one here who knew anything about William Fitzgerald and the gossip that had swept Ballygrace about her relationship with him – thanks to Mrs Scully.

But there was no Rosie Scully in Stockport, and – Tara vowed – there would never be a man like William Fitzgerald in her life again.

*

Ruby had breakfast ready and waiting for them in the warm kitchen. 'Bacon, sausage and eggs, and black pudding all right for you, ducks?' she asked, heaping the food on their plates. 'All the Irish lads love their fry-ups at the weekends. I've just washed up after four of them – so I thought you two would be the same. It'll keep you going for a while, and then you can get something to eat in Stockport when you're out at lunchtime. I only do meals in the evenings – and the Sunday dinner at three o'clock. The lads usually get something at the pub on a Saturday, or some of them go to a football match or whatever takes their fancy.'

After breakfast, the two girls sat at the table drinking tea, and listening to more of Ruby's outrageous stories about her husband. Two young men in their late teens appeared at the kitchen door – a tall one with dark hair and a smaller one with bright red hair.

'Sorry we're a bit late for breakfast, Ruby,' the tall one said in a thick Dublin accent, 'but we missed the late bus back from Manchester last night and we'd to walk a few miles before we picked up a taxi.'

'Oh, you poor lambs!' Ruby exclaimed. 'Your feet must be killin' you.' She put the huge frying pan back on a ring on the gas cooker. 'Sit yourselves down, and have a cup of tea with the girls – they're Irish too – so you'll have plenty to talk about. I won't be two ticks gettin' your sausages and bacon going. We can't have two growin' lads going out on an empty stomach.' She put six large sausages, two black pudding slices, tomatoes, and four rashers of bacon in the sizzling fat. She then went to the larder and got four eggs to fry with bread.

The lads in Sweeney's boarding house paid her well every Friday night, and Ruby reckoned that as long as she kept them well fed she would never be short of lodgers.

'Whereabouts are yez from then, girls?' the taller of the two boys asked, his eyes darting from one to the other with great interest.

Tara sighed inwardly as Biddy introduced them both and then started to regale the boys with all the details about Ballygrace and Tullamore. The boys took turns in asking questions, but were quick to focus their attention on Biddy when they realised that Tara was not so forthcoming. A tape recording, Tara thought cynically, with all their personal details might save them going over and over the same story, to every Irish person they came across.

'And where are ye from yerselves, boys?' Biddy asked, her eyes shining, and her Irish accent thicker to keep up with the boys' heavy Dublin accents.

'I'm Sonny – I'm from the Liberties, and Danny's from Kildare.'

'Kildare?' she said, putting her head to the side in a dreamy fashion, 'that's where the Curragh Racecourse is, isn't it?'

Tara's throat tightened at the mention of Kildare, remembering the day she had spent there with her old boss. 'Come on, Bridget,' she said, standing up. 'We've got business to do in Stockport, and it looks as if it might rain later.'

'I'm just having another half-cup of tea,' Biddy replied casually, reaching for the teapot. 'I'll catch you upstairs in a few minutes.'

'Your friend Tara,' Ruby commented to Biddy when Tara went out, 'likes to keep herself to herself. You're very different to be friends. She's a bit of a lady, isn't she? More on the posh side?'

Biddy thought for a moment, not realising the slight which had just been paid – inadvertently – to herself. 'Yes,' she said with a nod, 'I suppose she is a bit posh – but she's the best friend I've ever had.'

'I knew we shouldn't have worn these hats today,' Biddy complained, hanging on to the brim of a brown feather-trimmed one that Tara had lent her. 'It's far too windy and not one other girl we've passed has been wearing one. I don't think hats can be fashionable in Stockport this year.'

'It's worth it, for appearances' sake,' Tara sighed, 'in case we see any work advertised. We can just walk in, knowing that we're well-dressed.'

'I don't know many cleaners or people who work in bakeries who wear hats,' Biddy grumbled, ''cos they're the only jobs I'm qualified for.'

'Stop moaning, Biddy,' Tara said sharply. 'We've more to be worrying about than whether hats are fashionable in Stockport.'

'It's okay for you, going for fancy jobs in offices,' Biddy retorted, 'but I feel like an oul' granny in this hat.'

Then, a gust of wind suddenly whipped the green felt hat from

Tara's head and sent it spinning into the middle of the road. 'Jesus! I'll have to catch it,' she shouted, running out after it. 'It's my best hat and the only one that matches this coat!'

A double-decker bus coming down the road towards them sounded its horn loudly, and then screeched to a halt. 'It's lucky you're good-looking, or I might have run over it!' the bus driver called. Then, he and the passengers at the front of the bus, looked on with amusement while a thoroughly embarrassed Tara retrieved her hat from the middle of the road.

She gave a wave of thanks and came running back towards Biddy. 'I've never felt so shown-up in all my life!' she gasped, her face bright red. Then, when she saw Biddy's heaving shoulders and her face crumpled with suppressed laughter she started to titter in spite of herself.

Both girls broke out roaring and laughing, so hard that Biddy had to hang on to a high wall for support. 'Oh, Tara – you should have seen yer face when the wind lifted the hat clean off yer head – it was a picture!'

'What's that they say?' Tara giggled. 'Pride comes before a fall!' She gripped the hat firmly in her hand and then, in a suitably contrite manner said: 'I think we should just *carry* the hats today – until we get some decent hatpins. Unless, of course,' she added, 'we're actually going in somewhere that requires one.'

'Halle – bloody – luia!' Biddy yelled, taking the hat from her head and twirling it around on her finger.

It took the girls nearly half an hour to walk down into the town centre. They stopped along the way to look at the Town Hall again. Tara was delighted when she saw a poster advertising a piano recital on in the Town Hall that evening. The top of the bill was a young Scottish girl, whom Tara's old piano teacher had heard play in Dublin and had described as a 'magnificent classical pianist'.

'I'd love to go to that tonight,' Tara said, pointing up at the poster. 'If I pay for your ticket, Biddy, will you come with me? I'd hate to walk into a big place like that on my own.'

'Us – go out – tonight?' A smile spread on Biddy's face. Although she wasn't in the least bit interested in piano recitals, it was a chance to get out and about in this exciting town at night. You never knew who you might meet in a new place. 'Grand!' she said enthusiastically. 'I'd love to go, too.'

They passed an estate agent's on the way down to the shops but, being Saturday, they had closed for the half-day. Tara examined the board with pictures and details of the houses for sale, while Biddy walked a few shops further down to look in at a ladies' fashionwear shop. The first window in the estate agent's dealt mainly in the small 'two-up, two-down' terraced houses in the immediate vicinity, while the window displayed the bigger, detached, and more prestigious houses which were described as being in 'the desirable residential areas'. The prices for the bigger houses took Tara's breath away, for they were much higher than those in Ireland – those within her auctioneering experience in the Midlands. Dublin, no doubt, was a lot dearer than down in the country.

But the prices of the smaller houses were not too bad, and even the three-bedroom terraces were not unreasonably priced – given the fact they had the luxury of bathrooms and running hot water. There were some houses, depending on condition, which were advertised for four and five hundred pounds. Tara suddenly thought of the money she had locked in her suitcase back in the bedroom. There was over three hundred pounds – in fact it was nearer three hundred and fifty pounds. It was all the money she had withdrawn from her bank account in Tullamore – the money she had been left by her granda, plus the money she had saved herself. It dawned on her that if she worked hard and saved every penny for a few more years, then she could afford to buy a house for herself.

As she stared in a mesmerised fashion into estate agent's window, an incredulous idea came into Tara's mind. If she got a good job in an office, with a good salary, then she should be in a position to apply to the bank for a mortgage, which meant – she could afford to buy a house *now*!

She knew all about mortgages. William Fitzgerald had explained them in great detail to her, over their lunches together, saying that in order to accumulate money you had to be willing to take a risk. He also told her that property was the best investment that anybody with spare money could make. 'Take a tip from a gambler,' he had once said, looking into her green eyes. 'Good land and property are the horses to back – as long as you have the patience.'

The money to pay the mortgage would come not just from her salary, but the money from renting out spare bedrooms to girls like herself and Biddy. She would keep enough to buy a piano, and would then make more money from that giving piano lessons at the weekend and in the evenings. Tara pressed the back of her hand to her mouth, feeling almost giddy with the real possibility of this monumental idea. *Was she going mad?* she asked herself. Who would give a girl of eighteen a mortgage? It was highly unlikely. And yet, a little voice at the back of her mind told her to pursue the idea – for there was sure to be a way round it.

'Tara,' Biddy suddenly called, emerging out of a shop doorway, 'come and look at this dress – I think it would really suit you.'

Tara turned away from the estate agent's window and went to join Biddy, knowing full well that however nice the dress was, she would *not* buy it. From now on, every penny she made would go towards the purchase of her own house.

Her own house with her own piano in it.

Chapter Twenty

Elisha Fitzgerald stepped out of the car, and paused for William to escort her up the front steps of Ballygrace House. Mrs Scully was waiting for them, a welcoming smile on her face and the door held wide.

'Thanks be to God!' the housekeeper said, taking Elisha's vanity case and handbag from her. 'Welcome back to Ireland, Ma'am. It'll be nice to have things back to normal, now that ye're home.'

'Thank you, Mrs Scully.' Elisha's voice was weary though polite. 'It's nice to be back home.'

'I'll have the dinner on the table in half an hour,' Mrs Scully said ingratiatingly. 'An' I've done one of yer favourites: chicken and ham with a nice sauce, and roast potatoes and carrots and peas.'

'I think Mrs Fitzgerald would like to go straight upstairs now – she's rather tired after her flight,' William said curtly. 'I'll come down and let you know when we're ready to eat.'

'Whatever ye like now,' the housekeeper said agreeably. 'Whatever ye like.'

When they were in Elisha's bedroom on their own, William closed the door and then went and stood with his back to the glowing fire. 'I don't know who is the more shocked – you or I.'

Elisha opened one strap on her case and then the other. 'I did,' she said, keeping her eyes on the case, 'actually contemplate an abortion.'

William's eyes bulged. 'No?' he gasped. 'Surely not?'

She slowly nodded her head. 'I am forty-three years old.' She paused for a moment, then took a long, deep breath. 'I have a daughter in a mental asylum, a son who is twenty years old – and I am expecting another child. After all those years without any – any affection between us – and now *this*. If it wasn't so ludicrously sad, it would be laughable. I feel as though God has played some awful trick on me!'

William strode across the floor and put his arms around his wife. 'There are two of us involved in this situation – it could be a fresh start for us both. Perhaps – perhaps it is a blessing in disguise.'

Elisha pulled away from him, smoothing down her immaculate hair with trembling hands. 'I fail to see any blessing in it. Whilst I feel better in myself after the break away in London, I still have to face all this business with Madeleine, knowing that in a few months' time I am going to have another child wholly dependent on me for the next twenty years . . .' She halted now, obviously distressed. She drew a handkerchief from her coat pocket and dabbed her eyes. 'What if the child has the same condition as Madeleine?' she said in a whisper.

'The chances of that happening are very small,' William countered. 'It's not a hereditary condition – I had all that out with the psychiatrist in Dublin.'

'Thank God for that, at least,' Elisha sighed. She took her coat off and laid it on the bed for Mrs Scully to put away later. Then she changed her outdoor shoes for a more comfortable pair. 'And you say Dr McNally wanted to send her to Maryborough Asylum?'

William nodded. 'It was simply a matter of proximity, to get her attended to as quickly as possible – but I said we wouldn't hear of it. I insisted on having her admitted to a hospital in Dublin.'

'You did the right thing.' There was a conciliatory note in her voice. 'Although I felt angry at the airport when you told me about Madeleine having been in hospital since shortly after I left, on reflection it was probably the right thing to do.'

'You needed the rest.' William fingered his moustache. 'She's well looked after in Dublin. They say it would be best if she stays there for some time, to let them try out the different medications and then monitor the effects. Eventually, they hope to have her on a medication which will eradicate the religious delusions and the voices . . .' He hesitated for a few moments, then cleared his throat. 'And all the distressing symptoms she told the doctors about.'

Elisha's hands flew to her ears. 'Don't go on! I can't bear to hear any more about it.'

'I'm sorry . . .'

'Mental illness is the most awful scourge for a parent to bear! I feel so helpless. When I was over in London, I kept going over and over it in my mind – trying to work out why it should have happened to Madeleine.' She looked at her husband, her eyes clouded with worry. 'I keep wondering if it's something *we* did – if it's our fault – something about the way we brought her up.'

'No – no!' William held his hand up, halting her flow of recriminations.

Elisha shook her head and sat down in the wine velvet armchair by the fire, wringing her hands in agitation. 'I can't help but think we're being punished for something wrong we did.'

'We gave her a good home, a good education, ponies, ballet lessons – everything we could. I refuse to take responsibility for her illness – and I refuse to let you take it either. The psychiatrist was emphatic – this illness just strikes at random.' He knelt at the side of the armchair and put his arms around her, and was grateful this time that she did not flinch from his touch. 'We have nothing to fault ourselves over. We did our best.'

Rosie Scully bustled about downstairs, humming contentedly to herself whilst checking that everything was just as it should be for dinner. She had been happier these last few weeks than she could remember being for a very long time. Things were back in order in her life, now that she was reinstated back where she belonged, in Ballygrace House.

It had been a case of 'not missing the water until the well runs dry', as Rosie had found to her cost, the few weeks she had been out of a job. For a start, there was her wages – the loss of them had left a big hole. And then there were all the little perks like the leftover food, the odd bottle of sherry, the cast-off clothes that the Missus gave her for the family, the old curtains and bedding. The list of stuff that had come from Ballygrace House was endless, and even over that short period, it was sorely missed.

But funnily enough – the biggest loss had been the status that the job had given her. She hadn't realised just how much people had deferred to her because of her position. For example, the people in the butcher's shop in Tullamore – the shop which delivered the meat to Ballygrace House – had been distinctly cool to her when she had called in the other week for her own bits of things.

'Heard you've left the Big House, Mrs Scully,' the woman who served over the counter had commented, hardly a week after she'd been out of it. 'Have you found another place yet?'

'I'm not lookin',' Rosie had snapped defensively, then had gone on to lie: 'I've – I've only been out on account of my varicose veins – I'll have to wait an' see what the doctor says.' Then, covering all options lest the she should have been sacked in her absence, she added: 'He might say I'm not fit for work for a while, wi' the standin' and everything. I'll just have to wait and see.'

'Oh, I'd be careful if I was you. There'll be plenty of women looking for a position in Ballygrace House,' the shop assistant stated. 'I wouldn't go advertising the fact you're thinking of leaving, or there'll be a queue of them outside the house lookin' for your job, before you've even made up your mind.' She'd clapped Rosie's half-pound of sausages, her bacon rashers and black pudding on the counter. 'That'll be four and fivepence, please.'

Rosie had bit her lip as she passed over two half-crowns. She hadn't been given the usual coppers off the price, and every item had been weighed exactly to the half-pound.

'You'll be missing the good cuts of beef and the turkeys and hams, I would say,' the shop assistant had said as a parting remark. 'The Fitzgeralds only live off the best.'

Rosie had not meant to stay away from Ballygrace House for so long. She'd only meant to give William Fitzgerald a day or two to cool down about the way she'd attacked that brat, Tara Flynn. But things had got a bit out of hand.

Rosie had in fact cycled out to Ballygrace House the Monday morning after Madeleine had been taken to hospital – and the morning after William Fitzgerald had gone into Tara's room. She clutched in her hand a doctor's note excusing her absence. The note described her illness as 'high blood pressure', as opposed to the varicose veins she had told everyone else. It was then she had en-countered Tara Flynn once again.

Rosie lifted a pan of carrots off the stove, and drained the boiling water from them – a broad smile on her face at the memory. Oh, God worked in strange ways. If she hadn't come to Ballygrace House that morning, she would never have caught them rowing in the kitchen, with the Master apologising over and over again to her about something he'd done. Rosie had stayed outside – hidden among the rhododendrons – until the uppity little brat had gone. And for all her bad thoughts, she had found herself actually shocked at the thought of them in that big house all on their own – Tara Flynn and the Master.

And they had been in the house all night too, on their own. She had discovered from Doctor McNally when she'd been in to see him. He had let it drop when he said about Madeleine being taken into hospital late the night before. It didn't take much to put two and two together, to work it out what William Fitzgerald had been apologising about.

Oh, things were different now that Tara Flynn was gone forever from Ballygrace House. And Rosie Scully had heard it from her own lips that she wouldn't be back.

'I don't want a lift from you – now or ever!' Tara had dared to shout at William Fitzgerald. 'I came into this house for the first time on my bike – and I'll go out of it the same way.'

'Please, Tara . . .' he had cried, coming down the stairs after her.

'Just drop my case at the office,' she'd said coldly. 'I'll pick it up with the wages I'm owed tomorrow morning.'

'You're not leaving your job, too – not on account of this?' His voice was desperate. In all her years at Ballygrace House, Rosie had never heard him like that before. 'You've worked so hard, and have a brilliant future ahead of you – don't throw it all away over this . . .'

Tara had wheeled the bike out from the side of the house and then, without a backward glance, had cycled on down the drive.

And thank God and his Blessed Mother that she had, Rosie thought, for things had started to look up from that moment on. The housekeeper decided to creep away from Ballygrace House without making her presence known. Her business would keep. She could tell it was definitely not a good time to throw herself at her employer's mercy. She would manage another week or two without the money. And hopefully he would cool down in the meantime and forget any bad feelings against her.

And so, a couple of weeks later, Rosie Scully cycled back to Ballygrace House and knocked on the back door. When he answered, Rosie had put on a show like she'd never done in her life before. 'Oh, Mister Fitzgerald!' she'd said, almost falling in the door. 'I hope you'll give me another chance – I wasn't meself at all these last few weeks. I've been havin' trouble with me blood pressure – it was nearly through the roof, it was that high.' She handed him the note from the doctor and managed to squeeze out a few tears at the same time. 'All I want is to get back to normal – get back to me work.' When he hadn't protested, she started to take off her coat. 'I'll give the whole house a good goin' over – for I know it won't have got much more than a lick and a promise from young Ella, while I was away.'

William had stared through her, as though she wasn't really there. Then, finally he said: 'This can't happen again. You have been with us long enough to know your place. Servants cannot interfere with any family business, or any guests we choose to invite to this house.'

'Oh, it won't happen again,' Rosie assured him, dabbing at her watery eyes. 'It wouldn't have happened only for the blood pressure . . . and I'm on tablets for that now.' And she meant every word of her apology, because now there was no Tara Flynn to rise her she would be as meek as a mouse.

Nothing could rise her again, now that little uppity brat had gone from Ballygrace House, gone from her good job in Tullamore – gone from the Midlands entirely. It had been the talk of the place, Tara Flynn walking out of the auctioneer's office and disappearing to Dublin. Then – according to the housekeeper's cousin from Ballygrace – there had been more talk, saying she had gone to England. And not only had she gone to England, but she had been accompanied by that ungrateful little whore that Lizzie Lawless had fostered. The one who had dared to blame poor Dinny Martin for getting her in the 'family way'.

Through subtlety and innuendo, Rosie Scully had sown the seeds of scandal regarding Tara's departure. She had hinted at some sort of 'friendship' between William Fitzgerald and the foxy-haired madam from Ballygrace. She said nothing definite, which could be traced back to her, but the rumours had flown round the village and reached the ears of anyone who knew Tara Flynn. It had even been suggested that she had left after finding herself in the same predicament as her friend.

It had given Rosie the utmost delight when the rumours had come full circle and she was approached in Tullamore after Mass last Sunday, and asked if she had heard anything about Tara Flynn's hasty departure. 'What goes on in Ballygrace House,' she had said piously, 'is no business of mine – or anyone else's.'

Chapter Twenty-one

Tara had never heard music like it. She sat, transfixed, as the exotic woman's fingers roamed over the piano keys, making the most beautiful sounds. Several times, tears came into Tara's eyes as a particular piece transported her back to Ireland. 'Moonlight Sonata' took her back to Ballygrace House and Madeleine's birthday party. Images of Gabriel Fitzgerald and her dancing on New Year's Eve floated through her mind, of the afternoon they spent in Dublin . . . of the first time he had kissed her.

The beautiful music surrounded her, reminding her of all the silly, romantic dreams she once had – and rebuking her for the silly, romantic girl she had once been. It all seemed a lifetime ago, not just months.

When the Scottish pianist moved on to Chopin, Tara thought of her brother, Joe. She pictured them both that last afternoon taking turns on the piano – much to the delight of the two old aunties. She must write to him this week, she suddenly thought. She had promised to write as soon as she was settled in at her new address.

Tea and biscuits were served at the interval and there was also a bar.

'Shall we have a drink?' Biddy suggested, her eyes scanning the crowds for a glimpse of any young people among all the ancient music enthusiasts in their fur coats and evening dress. 'I could get us a sherry each if you like.'

'No,' Tara whispered sharply, 'tea will do us fine. We can't afford to throw money away, when neither of us has a job.'

Biddy sighed inwardly and took a sip of her pale, weak tea. She had never been so bored in all her life. Her legs were stiff and aching, and her backside was numb from sitting on the hard seats for so long. She hoped with all her heart that things would look up when she got a job. Spending an evening out at a place like this was worse than going to a funeral.

When Biddy went off in search of the 'ladies', Tara left her seat and wandered through the crowds looking at the beautiful architecture of the impressive Town Hall. She took in the ornate ceilings and stained-glass windows, and compared them to some she remembered back in the big houses she had seen in the Irish Midlands. How she would love a house with all these beautiful old details, she thought to herself. It was funny she should feel that way, because when she had admired a beautiful moulded centrepiece in Ruby Sweeney's sitting-room, the landlady had announced that she couldn't wait to get rid of it.

'As soon as I can afford to replace all these old-fashioned lead windows, then the ceilings are the next job,' Ruby had stated. 'I want them lowered with a false ceiling, to cover up all the ugly looking borders and light surrounds. They're dead old-fashioned now, they are.' She had shaken her head in amusement at Tara. 'You're a funny little bird at times. For a young girl, you have an old head on those shoulders.'

Tara had stopped to examine a plaque on the wall when she overheard a woman at her elbow saying: 'That young pianist has made her mark in the musical world already, and apparently a lot of her success is down to her husband.'

'Is he here tonight?' the woman's companion asked.

'He's the distinguished old fellow who changes the pages of her music – the one with the little grey beard and moustache.'

'You're joking!' The companion laughed. 'He's never her husband – he looks more like her father.'

'Well,' the first woman said in a low voice, 'according to what I've heard, he's nearly old enough to be her *grandfather*. He's in his late fifties, and she's only in her early twenties. He discovered her when she was playing in a small local concert in the highlands of Scotland. He's a wealthy Italian and apparently he owns a castle in the highlands. I've heard it said he's a millionaire. He happened to attend the concert to support the fund-raising, and discovered this young musical genius.'

'She's obviously no fool,' the companion said lightly. 'It's the quickest way for a young woman to climb the ladder in all walks of life – marrying an older, rich man. By the time he's dead, she still has her whole life in front of her.'

Tara went back to join Biddy at their seats and, when the curtain lifted on the beautiful Scottish pianist, she suddenly noticed the distinguished, handsome man who introduced her again to her audience, and then escorted her proudly to her seat at the piano. And then, as the enchanting music surrounded her, Tara wondered if perhaps there was something in the conversation she had heard.

She turned to Biddy, and said in a low voice: 'You know that older, handsome man who's on the stage with the pianist?'

Biddy sat up straight – a startled look on her face. She had just succumbed to the overwhelming urge to drop off to sleep, lulled by the funereal music. 'Who?' she whispered. 'The oul' fella with the grey hair?'

'He's her husband . . . and he's an Italian millionaire.'

'Go away with you!' Biddy replied, straining her neck to look up at the stage. 'He's *ancient* . . . he looks older than yer Uncle Mick.' And, Biddy thought to herself, he looks so old he makes Dinny Martin look like a young fella. 'I don't know how she can get into bed with him. I don't care if he is a millionaire – I'd sooner have a nice, ordinary young lad any day of the week.'

Biddy was the first to find work, and not just one job – but *two*. The following Monday morning while she and Tara were having breakfast, Ruby had told her of work that was going in one of the big hotels in the town. 'A fine big place it is too, and they've just built a big extension on to it,' Ruby said. 'Twenty bedrooms, so I believe, and they're looking for more chambermaids and waitresses, and kitchen staff and the like.'

'A hotel?' Biddy said nervously. 'D'you think they'd give me a job in a fancy hotel? With me bein' a stranger here – and no one to speak up for me?'

'Course they would, love!' Ruby said, patting her hand. 'I'll speak up for you – I'll tell them you can turn your hand to anything. I've never had a lodger like you before – in and out washing dishes for me, and yesterday you had the potatoes and vegetables peeled for the whole house in under an hour. You're a little gem – any hotel would be glad to have you.'

Biddy blushed. 'I enjoy helping and anyway I've been doin' it all me life. Sure, I was no better than a slave in Lizzie Lawless's house, and I never got so much as a word of thanks. A clout around the head was all you would get out of her.'

'She sounds a right evil old witch!' Ruby commented with narrowed eyes. She found all Biddy's stories about Ireland fascinating, in the same way that Biddy loved hearing hers. 'I don't know how you stuck it so long.'

Tara pushed her chair back from the table. 'I'm going upstairs to get my coat on,' she told Biddy. 'Then we'd better get down into Stockport, or we'll have wasted the whole morning.'

Ruby pulled a face behind Tara's back. 'You'd better go, ducks, or you'll be in trouble. I'll write down the address of that hotel for you, and you can call in. Oh, and if you don't mind me sayin', love,' she added, 'I would speak slowly if I were you – sometimes your accent's a bit hard to catch when you talk quick, like.'

'Thanks,' Biddy said, not in the least bit offended. 'I'll try and remember that.'

Once again – at Tara's insistence – the two girls donned their smartest coats and hats over light summer dresses.

'How are you feeling?' Tara asked as they walked along the main road.

'I'm grand now, thanks,' Biddy replied. 'The bleeding's eased off.'

'Do you ever . . .' Tara hesitated, 'do you ever think of the baby?'

'Now and again . . . but I find it hard to remember, as if it was all a dream. It's like it happened to someone else. I can't imagine myself as the mother of a baby boy.'

'You know you can always talk to me about it,' Tara offered. 'That's if you want to.'

'Thanks,' Biddy said quietly, then she pointed across the road at a big white building. 'I think that's the hotel Ruby told me about.' She read from the bit of paper. *The Grosvenor Hotel. Ask at the reception desk for Mr Timpson.*

The reception area was dark and forbidding, with wood panelling, old beams, and ornate paintings hanging on the walls. When Biddy nervously, and slowly, explained her business to the young lady behind the desk, the receptionist contacted Mr Timpson on the phone.

'Straight up the stairs,' she pointed to Biddy, 'and it's the second door on the left. Mr Timpson says he'll see you right now.'

Biddy gave Tara a rather anguished look as she ascended the staircase, as though she were making her way up to an executioner.

Tara sat on a sofa in the reception area while she waited for her friend, taking in all the architectural and decorative details around her. She stood up at one point, to examine a heavy old painting in a gilt frame, when a door swung open behind her and two smartly-dressed businessmen – and elderly white-haired man and a tall, good-looking, younger man came through it. She turned away, focusing her attention on the painting.

'It's perfect,' the elderly man stated, 'and it blends in so well with the main building that you would be hard-pressed to tell that there's a hundred and fifty years of a difference.'

'I'm glad you're satisfied with the work,' the younger man said in a rich, deep voice. 'They're a good bunch of lads – I've used them for a number of contracts recently.'

Tara's ears suddenly pricked up, for the second voice she heard had a definite Irish lilt to it. The accent was certainly smoothed at the edges – probably by many years spent in England – but it was Irish nevertheless.

She gave a quick glance over her shoulder, and was mortified to see the younger man staring straight at her. She turned away quickly, her cheeks flaming, and kept her back firmly to them until she heard them go out of the door.

A short while later, a more buoyant Biddy descended the stairs than the one who had gone up. 'I've got it!' she said, waving a sheet of paper in the air. 'I start tomorrow.'

Tara gave a big smile of relief. Thank God one of them had a job already. Even better that it was Biddy, for she had very little money with her. If she hadn't found work, Tara would have had to pay both their rents, when it next came round.

'It's in the kitchen,' she told Tara as they walked towards the town centre. 'I'll be working shifts – sometimes until the early hours of the morning, because they do meals and dinner-dances at the weekends. An' Mr Timpson says that he'll give me a trial behind the bar, because they could do with a pretty barmaid to bring the men in.' Biddy giggled with delight. 'Imagine anyone callin' *me* pretty!'

'But you *are* pretty,' Tara told her. 'When you do your hair nice, and have good clothes on, you look lovely.' Tara's words were sincere, for Biddy had indeed improved greatly over the years.

'D'you think so?' Biddy's voice was unsure. 'Lizzie always used to say I was an ugly little brat.'

Tara put her arm round Biddy's shoulder and pulled her playfully towards her. 'Do you honestly think I'd have a best friend who was ugly?'

Biddy looked up fondly at her – delighted to hear herself described as Tara's *best* friend – and then they both roared with laughter.

Tara had no luck at all with the four estate agents that she tried in Stockport. 'I'm sorry we've nothing here but we have a new office just opened in Bramhall,' one of the secretaries told her. 'It might be worth your while giving them a ring.'

They had an early lunch in a cafe of soup and bread, and then they had a look around the shops again before going home. Back in their lodgings, Ruby met them on the stairs carrying a load of blankets and sheets. Biddy quickly told her all about her job in the Grosvenor Hotel.

'Clever girl!' the landlady said. 'An' I've got good news, too. You hadn't left five minutes this morning, when I had two lads turn up at the door lookin' for lodgings.' She nodded to the pile of bedclothes in her arms. 'I'm just going to make up their beds – they're in the room opposite you two. A nice Geordie lad – from Newcastle, you know. The other one's a fine handsome black lad from somewhere out Bolton way. He says a lot of the landladies wouldn't let him put a foot over the door on account of him bein' black – in't it shockin'? I've had quite a few blackies lodgin' here, and I've found nowt wrong with any of 'em.' She winked at the two girls. 'He's a fit-lookin' lad and you know the reputation they have with women. I'd watch yourselves, if I were you two. He's just about your age. Just make sure he doesn't turn into the wrong room after he's had a few drinks, or you could be up all night.' She gave a great roar of raucous laughter.

Unable to help herself, Biddy gave a bit of a titter, then covered her mouth with her hand quickly when Tara gave her a stony look.

'How about you, ducks?' Ruby asked Tara. 'Any luck?'

Tara took her hat off and shook her head, sending her coppery curls flying. 'No . . . nothing,' she said with a shrug. 'I've been given a number to ring in a place called Bramhall. I thought I might try them later this afternoon.'

'Oooh, Bramhall!' Ruby said, tipping the point of her nose with her forefinger. 'It's *very* posh out there. That's where all the big nobs live.'

'Is it far from Stockport?'

'No, love, it's only a couple of miles away – about twenty minutes on the bus.'

Later on that afternoon, Tara went out to the nearest telephone box with a handful of coins. The number rang and rang but was not answered. She checked her watch – it was quarter to two. Maybe, she thought, they were on a lunch break, and decided to take a walk down to the newsagents to pick up a magazine. It was still too early in the day for the evening newspaper, which Ruby had said was the best paper for job adverts. She would walk out and buy that later on in the day.

When she tried the phone number again, this time it was quickly answered. Tara briefly explained her business, telling the girl on the other end that she had been advised to ring by the Stockport office.

'I'm afraid the manager is out at the moment . . . do you have a phone number he can contact you at?' And when Tara replied that she didn't have a phone number, the girl then asked her to call back in an hour or so.

Tara's heart sank as she put the phone back in the cradle. She knew it was silly getting so frustrated, since she had only been in England a matter of days. But now she had this great plan in her mind, she was desperate to get things started – and securing a job was the very first task on her list.

Biddy met her at the door when she returned, drying her hands on a kitchen towel, and her face red with excitement. 'You're never going to believe this,' she told Tara. 'Ruby's asked me if I'd like to help her out with the housework and cookin', and she says she'll pay me for it!'

'But I thought you were going to work at the hotel?'

'I'm going to do *both* jobs,' Biddy said proudly. 'I'll be working shifts in the hotel – mostly late ones, so I can help out here with the breakfasts and preparin' the evening meals. Up until a few weeks ago, Ruby had an older woman coming in every day, but she had a stroke, so Ruby's had to manage on her own since. She was looking for somebody and she says I'm the quickest worker she's ever seen in a kitchen!'

'That's grand,' Tara told her warmly. 'I'm delighted for you. You've done a lot better than me.' She took off her coat and hung it on the hall-stand. 'I've had no luck at all. I've to ring that place again in an hour – but I'm not holding my breath.'

'Oh, you'll be fine,' Biddy said. 'You'll get something shortly. With all your qualifications and everythin', sure, they'll be queuing up for you.' She turned towards the kitchen. 'I'm helpin' Ruby with the vegetables for the dinner and then I'm going to bake a few apple tarts for after it. You should see the price she's payin' in the baker's for them! I said I could make her three for the price of one.'

'Good for you.' Tara smiled at her friend. 'I'm going up to the bedroom to write a few letters, until it's time to make that phone call again.' She had promised to write to Joe and Mick and Kitty, and to her old neighbour Mrs Kelly, but up until now had put it off.

Biddy rushed off back into the kitchen, delighted with herself about securing two jobs in the one day, and secretly proud of the fact that for once she had succeeded where Tara had failed. She said as much in passing to Ruby, and the landlady had laughed and said: 'You know the old saying, ducks – every dog has its day!'

Tara was no more successful in contacting the manager of the estate agent's the second time round. Apparently, the secretary told Tara, Mr Pickford had only been in the office briefly, and had to rush out somewhere else. He did however, leave a message to say that if she would like to call out to the office at ten o'clock on Thursday morning, he would see her then.

She was so disappointed that she couldn't face going straight back to her digs and instead walked towards the shops on Shaw Heath. She posted her letters and then walked towards the Catholic Church. Both she and Biddy had gone to eleven o'clock Mass at Our Lady's on

Sunday morning and she had been entranced by the beautiful big church.

She quietly opened the main door, and went inside. The church was cool and surpringly bright, with the afternoon sunshine pouring in through the multi-coloured stained-glass windows. She walked up the aisle, genuflected at the main altar, and went to a small side altar which had a stand for candles in front of a statue of the Virgin Mary. She picked up a box of matches from the stand, then lit two of the little round candles. She took her purse out of her handbag and found a sixpence and pushed it in the coin slot in the tin box on the stand. Then, she knelt down in front of the candles, bent her head and started to pray – praying harder than she had ever done before.

Since Biddy was busy working, Tara spent the next few days getting to know the area on her own. She made her way down to the library in Stockport – bigger than any library she had ever seen – and filled a card in to become a member. Then, another afternoon, she decided to catch a bus out to Manchester, to see if there was any work there. Although she would have preferred the company, she was glad that Biddy was now fully occupied with work, because she would have no time on her hands in the evening, to think about going out and about.

Manchester was a fascinating city, although Tara thought it was definitely not as friendly as Dublin. She enjoyed walking round the big department stores and took her time looking at the fashions and trying out samples of the various perfumes. She was tempted once or twice to buy something, but she stopped herself. Every time she felt the urge to spend money, instead she pictured a huge house with a grand piano – and she felt strong enough to resist.

Again she had no luck with finding work in any of the estate agents', but she gathered leaflets and brochures of property for sale, to browse through at home later. As she looked through a display of houses for sale in the Didsbury area, it crossed her mind how much more organised the English estate agents were compared to the ones she knew in Ireland. Even the ones selling the smaller houses had printed sheets with a photograph of the house, while the bigger houses had fancy brochures giving more details. Presumably, she thought, the auctioneers in Dublin were more up-to-date with their businesses than the smaller ones like Fitzgerald's. If she could turn the clock back, she could have given William Fitzgerald some advice for a change – instead of all the advice he had constantly bombarded her with.

A hot flush came over her neck and face and her heart started its now-familiar pounding. This always happened when her mind wandered back to William Fitzgerald and then to that terrible night in Ballygrace House. Quickly, she turned on her heel, out of the office, and back into the fresh air where she could breathe deeply.

As the days went by, Tara got to know more of the other people who she was sharing lodgings with in Ruby Sweeney's house. Surprisingly, the men and even the younger lads were all very pleasant and mannerly. Any time she and Biddy walked in on them playing cards in the kitchen, or carrying on in the hallways upstairs, they always apologised for any coarse language the girls might have overheard.

After a few days, she noticed that they didn't apologise in the same way to Biddy, if they thought Tara was out of earshot. They were much more relaxed in Biddy's company, and teased her and told her corny jokes, and the other night had asked her to join in a game of cards.

Biddy had looked at Tara and then said: 'I haven't time now, lads . . . maybe later.'

Although the men had been obvious in their admiration of Tara when they first met her, they soon realised that she had no interest in them and her cool demeanour was her way of keeping them at arm's length.

On the Thursday morning, Tara lay in bed until she heard the last of the men leaving for work and then around half-past seven she got up, went into the bathroom and ran a hot bath.

Afterwards, back in the bedroom, she roughly dried her long hair with a towel, combed it out, and then quickly got dressed. She decided on the camel swagger coat and black hat over a light dress. She always felt confident in that outfit, and if it was too hot she could carry the coat and hat. This morning Tara needed every little boost she could muster up. If she didn't find suitable office work soon, then she would have to take any job she was offered.

Downstairs later, she and Biddy joked together as Biddy served up her breakfast. 'I didn't even hear you getting up this morning,' Tara said, taking a sip of the coffee that the landlady had bought in especially for her. She was the first lodger to ever ask for coffee, Ruby said. All the others were perfectly happy with tea.

'I was up at six o'clock,' Biddy said proudly. 'Six of the lads are working up in Carlisle and they had to be on the road early. I'll have a longer lie-in tomorrow – Ruby says she'll do breakfast, because she wants me to cook tea for the men coming in from work in the evening.' She leaned across the kitchen table and whispered to Tara: 'I think she has a new boyfriend, because she says she's going into Manchester shoppin' in the afternoon, and staying on to have a meal and then go to a show in the Palace Theatre.'

'Good for her,' Tara said, taking a bite of her toast and marmalade.

'Ruby has a very glamorous life,' Biddy said, giving a dreamy smile.

It was a nice spring morning, and although Tara was preoccupied with more serious thoughts, she enjoyed the run out to Bramhall on the bus. The further out from Stockport she went, the bigger and more expensive the houses looked. The black and white Tudor-style timber buildings particularly caught her eye and she felt slightly guilty thinking how grand they looked compared to the plainer Georgian houses back in Ireland.

Ruby had told her to look out for Bramall Hall when she came near to the village. She spotted the ornate gatehouse easily but had to crane her neck to catch the tiniest glimpse of the building itself. It crossed her mind for a moment that if she were on her usual mode of transport – her bicycle – she could have dismounted and had a few minutes looking round, before resuming her journey. As the bus moved on past the park, Tara promised herself she would come out and visit the hall and the surrounding park on a nice sunny day.

She alighted from the bus in the middle of the small shopping area and then, after carefully checking the directions, she walked down to a corner to cross the road. Suddenly, a shiny black car came speeding round the corner, and swerved on to the opposite side of the road, to avoid hitting her. Startled, Tara stepped back on to the kerb, her heart thumping with fright. When she composed herself, she turned to look at the offending car.

The driver leaned across and rolled down the passenger window. 'Sorry! I took the corner a bit quick – are you all right?' It was the handsome businessman who had stared at Tara in the Grosvenor Hotel, the day that Biddy was being interviewed. He looked at her now with bright, interested eyes.

'I'm fine, thank you,' she answered abruptly and started to walk on up the street. She heard the car engine start up again, and when she glanced behind, she found that he was following her slowly.

She kept her gaze straight ahead, grateful for the wide brim on the hat which shielded her face, and with her heart thudding she searched for an escape route. A few yards down the street she saw a narrow alleyway between two tall buildings and she took her chance and stepped into it. She walked along the alley, quickly and purposefully, dodging the puddles and broken glass which littered the pathway.

When she felt she was far enough away from the street she stood in a doorway and looked back, checking if the black car had gone. To her relief, there was no sign of it. She stood for a few moments longer until she was satisfied that he had indeed gone, then tiptoed her way back out into the street.

Thornley's Estate Agents office was on a corner at the end of the main street in Bramhall Village. Since she was a few minutes early, Tara looked at the displays on the three big windows outside. A quick glance told her that the houses in the area were much pricier and more 'upmarket' than the ones she had seen for sale in the Stockport branch.

She checked her watch again, then taking a deep breath, she opened the door of the office and walked in. When she introduced herself at the desk, one of the girls showed her to another smaller office. 'Mr Pickford will see you now,' the girl said in an accent similar to Ruby's.

Half an hour later, Tara walked back out through the office with the balding, bespectacled manager behind her. 'This, ladies,' Mr Pickford said in a officious tone, 'is Miss Tara Flynn. She will be starting work here next Monday morning.'

The interview had gone perfectly, Tara recounted to Ruby and

Biddy over a cup of tea back at her lodgings. Apparently, Suzie – one of the girls in the office – had been on a month's trial and had not lived up to expectations. This, the manager had said in a bristling manner, was due to her casual manner with customers and her abysmal spelling. She would be leaving the following day, Mr Pickford had said, and Tara would take up the vacant position on Monday.

'You will, of course, have to fulfill a probationary period,' he added, then asked Tara her reference from her previous employer in Ireland and any certificates she had with her.

A hot flush swept over Tara's face and neck as she handed him the envelope containing her excellent Leaving Cert results, the certificates she had gained from her night classes – and the reference which William Fitzgerald had left for her with the wages she was owed.

'These all seem in order,' Mr Pickford said, looking over his half-frame spectacles, 'but the proof of the pudding is in the eating, as we discovered in the case of Suzie. We shall have to see how things work out.'

Thornley's Estate Agents was a very different kettle of fish to Fitzgerald's Auctioneering business, as Tara quickly found out. Mr Pickford prided himself on 'running a tight ship', where the customer was always treated with the utmost respect and no effort from the staff was ever too great.

'We are in one of the most prestigious districts of Stockport,' he told Tara the following Monday morning in front her new colleague, Jean. 'We have competition in the way of another very well established business just along the road. We must do everything to ensure that Thornley's have the edge over them. Remember,' he said, throwing an eye at Jean, 'we're not in the business of selling tins of baked beans here. We are asking clients to spend hundreds – and sometimes thousands – of pounds.'

The first week in her new job flew by, and Tara found that keeping busy was the best cure for the dark thoughts that often plagued her. She was up in the morning at seven o'clock and out of the house by eight o'clock. During the day she had little time to ponder over her old life, and by the time she came back to her lodgings at six o'clock in the evening, she was tired out.

On the Friday evening, she came home from work to be met in the hallway by Biddy, who was sporting a new, shorter hairstyle. 'I've got the evenin' off from the hotel,' she said excitedly, 'and some of the Irish lads have asked us to go to the dancing, the Erin Ballroom, in Manchester.' Ignoring Tara's stony face, she went on quickly. 'The lads have only said that they'll take us to and from the dance hall – they're not tryin' to chat us up or anythin' . . .'

Ruby suddenly appeared out of the sitting-room, her arms folded defensively over her high bosom. 'Get yourselves off out for the evening,' she said, looking directly at Tara. 'It'll do you good to loosen up a bit – two nice-lookin' girls like yourselves. You've been here for a fortnight now, and apart from goin' to work, church and down to the library – you haven't stirred out of the house. It in't natural to be stuck indoors all the time.'

There was a silence for a moment. 'I'm not sure,' Tara said slowly. 'I don't know if I feel up to going out tonight.'

Biddy looked from Tara to Ruby – not quite sure which side to fall on. 'Maybe when you've had somethin' to eat . . . I've done you some lovely floury potatoes and parsley sauce to go with the fish tonight.'

'A proper loyal friend she is,' Ruby commented, patting Biddy on the back. 'The lads were all content with the usual fish and chips and mushy peas. She cooked the potatoes specially for you.'

'Thanks, Biddy,' Tara said, deliberately ignoring the landlady. 'Maybe I'll feel brighter when I've had something to eat. We can talk about it later on. I'll just drop my things off upstairs, and I'll be back in a minute.'

There was another silence as she mounted the stairs and Tara could feel both sets of eyes boring into her back. Just as she was turning in her bedroom door, Sonny – the Irish lad from Dublin – called to her from the bathroom door.

'Are you goin' to the Erin tonight with Biddy?' He stood smiling at the bathroom door, stripped to the waist with a razor in one hand, and a towel in the other. His face was lathered with shaving soap, and as he spoke, globules of the lathered soap dripped on to the floor.

'I'm not sure,' Tara said for the second time, opening her bedroom door. 'I'll see how I feel later.'

In the privacy of her bedroom, Tara dropped her coat and bag on a chair, then sank down on the side of the bed. The last thing she felt like tonight was going dancing. And, she thought, she had a number of very good reasons for feeling like this. For a start – she genuinely didn't feel too grand. Her head was fuzzy and aching and she felt generally out of sorts. It was probably the fact she had worked flat out all week and was up earlier than usual in the mornings.

Tara suddenly dropped her head in her hands. *Please God*, she thought, *please don't let it be anything else! Don't let me be in a worse predicament than Biddy was!*

She felt little better after the special meal her friend had cooked for her – and felt guilty every time she looked at Biddy's hopeful face.

'Come on, Tara,' Biddy coaxed, putting a dish of rice pudding in front of her. 'Ruby's right,' she said, using the landlady as a backup. 'It'll do you the world of good to get out and have a bit of a laugh.'

Tara looked up at her friend. 'Aren't you worried about going out, after what has happened to you?'

Biddy shrugged and stared at the floor. 'It's in the past – and I can't keep payin' for my mistakes forever.'

'But, Biddy,' Tara presisted, 'the lads that have asked us to go to the dance . . . they're no different from that PJ fellow from Tullamore. You could see no wrong in *him*, and just look where it landed you.'

Biddy shook her head and tears welled up in her eyes. 'It wasn't all *his* fault . . . his mother wouldn't let him marry me.' She gave a loud sniff. 'It's not fair that you keep remindin' me about what happened. I came over to England to start a new life. If I wanted to become a nun, I would have stayed in Ireland.'

'I'm only trying to help you,' Tara snapped, getting up from the table, 'but if you're determined to go your own way, there's nothing I can do about it.'

'What about yer rice puddin? Are you not goin' to eat it?' Biddy said in a choked voice, then tears started to run down her cheeks and her shoulders dropped dejectedly.

'Oh, Biddy . . . ' Tara's tone suddenly softened. She went over and put her arms round her friend. 'I'm sorry. I didn't mean to hurt you – I'm just so worried about what might happen you – about what might happen to us *both*. Everything is still very strange and new here.' She patted Biddy's back as though she were a child. 'And I was worried about you being sick – the way you were when we first came over.'

'Sure, I'm fine now, Tara. Everything's back to normal. You've nothing to worry about. Nothing is going to happen to either of us.' Biddy wiped her tears away with a hanky and gave a faint smile. 'Nothing could ever happen to *you* – and I promise I won't do anything to let you down. I know I'm not the cleverest person in the world, but honest to God – I've really learned me lesson.'

Tara sat back down at the table, struggling with the temptation to pour out her own awful story to Biddy – to let her know that something terrible had indeed already happened. But then, she thought, *What good would it do?* It was bad enough for Biddy having to deal with the loss of her little baby, without giving her more worry. And what would she think of Madeleine and Gabriel if she knew what their father had done?

It would be time enough if the worst thing happened. Then, every single plan she had made would crumble to dust. And all because of her naiveté and too much brandy.

She spooned a small amount of strawberry jam on her rice pudding, which she didn't in the least feel like eating now. 'Let me see how I am after a bath.'

'If you don't feel up to going out, we can go the next time I'm off,' Biddy said, but there was a note of hope in her voice. 'I was going to get me hair done anyway – it was in bad condition and I needed a few inches off it.'

Tara felt slightly better after her bath and, after thinking about it all again, she decided that perhaps it would do no great harm to go to the dance. She was in her dressing-gown and combing her long hair out when Biddy tapped at the bedroom door.

'How d'you feel now?' Biddy stuck her head round the door, her fingers crossed behind her back.

'I suppose a couple of hours out won't kill me,' Tara replied, 'but if the dance hall's rough, or if any of those boys start bothering us, then I'm coming straight home.'

'Oh, *they* won't bother us,' Biddy said in a rushed, excited tone. Unknown to her friend, she would go round all the lads who were still in the house – this very minute – and warn them to behave when they were anywhere near Tara. 'Ruby said that the Erin's the best-run dance hall about. She said they're very strict about who they let in.' She made to close the door again, terrified that Tara might change her mind.

'Biddy . . . have you decided what you're wearing?' Tara asked.

'I'll have to wear me blue dress. It's the only one that zips up,' Biddy said quietly. She'd tried the other two on before Tara came in and was shocked at how terrible she looked in them. 'I've put on a bit of weight on me stomach since . . .'

'The blue dress always looks nice on you,' Tara reassured her. 'I'll only be another ten minutes, then you can get in to get ready.'

'We've plenty of time. I'll just finish clearing up the kitchen.' Biddy closed the bedroom door and then made straight to warn Sonny and Danny to be on their best behaviour. She didn't want anything spoiling their first night out, in case Tara refused to go dancing with her again. Several of the lads in the house had asked Biddy if she would partner them to the dance tonight but she had refused, saying that she would rather go with her friend.

'You're not goin' to the dance wi' Tara Flynn?' Sonny had jeered over breakfast this morning. 'Sure, she wouldn't be able to dance. She walks with her nose in the air and her back's so straight you'd think she had a brush stuck up her arse!'

'That's not a bit funny,' Biddy admonished him. 'You shouldn't be jeerin' her just because she's more educated than us.' She gave him a poke in the arm. 'All the lads we knew back home thought she was very good-looking.'

'Oh, she's good-looking all right,' he had said grudgingly, 'but sure, she'd hardly give you the time of day. She could be a bit friendlier, her being Irish and all, and livin' in the same house as us.'

'She doesn't mean any harm. She's just different,' Biddy said defensively. 'And anyway, she's been more than good enough to me.'

Sonny slid an arm around Biddy's waist. 'Sure, wouldn't I be good to you, if you would only give me the chance.'

Biddy giggled and pushed him away.

Ruby stood at the front door as the group of six lads – four Irish, the Geordie lad and his black friend, Lloyd – and Biddy and Tara all trooped out in their finery. She made a joke of carefully inspecting each one as they passed by with perfectly coiffed hair, and picked odd bits of fluff from jackets before letting them out the door. 'Yer mothers would be proud of your shiny shoes and your smart suits. I dare anyone to say that Ruby Sweeney's lodgers aren't well turned out!' she said with vigour. 'The nerve of some of them stuck-up landladies, who have the bloody cheek to turn their noses up at the Irish lads – calling them dirty Irish Paddies!'

Tara cringed inwardly at hearing the Irish described in such a way but hid it with a smile when Ruby patted her arm, and said: 'You look lovely in that green dress and the matching hairband really shows off your red hair. Have a good time, ducks – I'm sure you'll enjoy yourself when you get there.'

The boys all went upstairs on the double-decker bus, because it allowed smoking, while the two girls went inside. When the conductor came downstairs to collect the fares, he told Biddy and Tara that their fares had already been paid by their friends.

'That was good of them,' Biddy said hastily, 'but I'll make sure that we don't get landed with them for the night, just because they've paid our bus fares.'

It would have been the same story at the dance hall, but Tara and Biddy insisted on getting into the queue before the boys, and determinedly handed over the money for their own tickets. When they got inside the hall, there was a good crowd already gathered, waiting for the band to strike up.

Tara was heartened that the Erin Ballroom was nicer than any she had been to in Ireland. There were proper seats and tables all round the hall, and there was a balcony above – altogether a very glamorous place. They handed their coats in at the cloakroom and then Biddy suggested that they should get a mineral from the bar.

'I don't fancy fighting my way through that noisy crowd,' Tara said hesitantly.

'I'm well used to crowds with working in the Grosvenor,' Biddy laughed. 'You go and find a table and I'll get us a drink at the bar. What d'you want to drink? D'you fancy trying something like a sherry or a Babycham?'

'No – no!' Tara shook her head vigorously. Alcohol was the last thing she intended to have – the memory of the last time she drank was still too raw. 'I'll have a mineral . . . a lemonade or something.' She found a table to the side of the dance floor, which would let them move on and off the floor easily, without pushing through lots of other tables. Then, when she was seated comfortably, she allowed her gaze to wander round the dance hall – being careful not to catch the eye of any men who were staring at her.

On the whole, she was pleased to note how well-dressed both the males and females were. Considering the disparaging remarks that had been levelled over the years at the Irish, for their lack of hygiene and sophistication – there was little evidence to prove these remarks in the dance hall tonight.

Most of the people in the hall were definitely Irish, from the chatter at the tables around her, Tara mused. They must be in good jobs, which would allow them to dress so well and to pay for lodgings, and to probably send something back home to help their families out.

According to Ruby, some of the lads in the boarding house were earning very big money labouring on building sites, having been taken on by Irish building contractors. They needed no education for this work, which was just as well, for many of them had left school at twelve and thirteen. As long as they were prepared to put in the work when they first came over to England, then they could learn a trade as they went along. It was true that they had to work long hours for this. Some of the lads were out of the house for twelve and fourteen hours at a time – and they grabbed the chance of work on Saturdays when they were paid at time and a half.

When they were standing at the bus stop, Tara had heard Sonny say they'd better not drink too much beer tonight, on account of having to get up for work again at six o'clock in the morning. Saturday night, they would be back in the dance hall again, or perhaps at the cinema or a pub somewhere. From what Tara could see of the Irish in England so far, it was definitely a case of working hard and playing hard.

For herself, she would quite happily forego the playing part, and tomorrow night when Biddy was working in the hotel, she would be content to sit in her bedroom reading and making plans for her future.

Within seconds of the band striking up, the dance floor was filling with couples. Tara had just leaned forward to comment on the fact when she felt a hand tapping her on the shoulder.

'Will we have a dance?' Lloyd, the young black fellow from the boarding house asked, while his friend Jimmy took to the floor with Biddy.

They were excellent dancers, and Tara found herself and Lloyd circling the floor with great ease. After a few rounds of the floor in silence he asked: 'Is this your first time here?' and when Tara confirmed it was, he said: 'Mine, too. They seem friendly enough and the band's good. D'you go to many dances?'

Tara smiled back at him. 'No, not really. This is the first dance hall I've been to since I've come to England, and it's a nice place.' They chatted easily for the rest of the dance and another one, and then Lloyd escorted Tara back to her seat where they changed partners, and she danced with Jimmy while Lloyd danced with Biddy.

Until the band took a break, the girls were never off the floor and while Tara was flattered by the attention, Biddy was positively giddy with excitement. 'This has been the best night of me life so far,' she said, her eyes darting round the groups of boys. 'They're all real gentlemen, aren't they?'

'Most of them seem very nice,' Tara agreed, 'and they're all good dancers.' Although she had come to the dance under duress, it had not been as bad as she had expected. All the boys she had danced with had been pleasant and polite, although some had been slightly the worse for drink – and they were always the ones Biddy seemed to have the best laugh with.

Sometimes Tara wished she could throw herself into mixing more – enjoying things the way Biddy did – but her serious nature prevented it. And anyway, she reasoned, they liked different things. She had got as much enjoyment from the piano recital the other week as Biddy got from the smoky atmosphere of the dance hall.

As she glanced round the hall, Tara suddenly realised that not one of the boys she saw – in their shiny shoes and smart suits – held any attraction for her. All these boys who had Biddy in a state of elation if they so much as spoke to her, seemed so young and gauche to her. If she was brutally honest with herself, she found them boring.

Whilst being pleasant enough, their conversation was all the same.

The well-settled ones usually started off asking where *she* came from, then chatted about where *they* came from, the great jobs and digs they had, and the great money they were making in England. Alternatively, some of them would ask her what she thought of England and before she got a chance to reply, they would say how homesick they were for Ireland, and would be out of this feckin' hole of a country as soon as they'd made enough money to set themselves up properly at home.

Once again – as she did when she was in Ballygrace – Tara found herself pondering over the fact that she was so different from Biddy and all the other girls in the dance hall. Why she wasn't satisfied with the things they wanted out of life?

She had felt happy when she was younger with her granda, and then later in Ballygrace House with Madeleine and Gabriel. It all seemed such a long time ago. And after the awful catastrophe that she had been stupid enough to let happen, those happy times were gone forever.

'I think I'll come here every weekend I'm free, from now on,' Biddy said, picking at a handful of peanuts. 'Some of the girls from the hotel come here, and we could all meet up when we have the same nights off.' She looked round the hall again. 'I think it's a very glamorous place altogether. Better than any of the dumps in Ireland.'

'Ah, Biddy,' Tara said, giving her a knowing smile, 'you were pleased enough with the dance halls over home, this time six months ago. You're not going to go all English on us, after only a few weeks in the place, are you? You're not going to be one of those Irish who haven't a good word for the place they came from?'

Biddy grinned back. 'Sure, I'm only enjoying meself and tryin' to fit in, Tara. Isn't that what we're supposed to be doin'?'

'It is indeed,' Tara laughed. 'Sure, I'm only codding you.' Then, she glanced at her watch, wishing it was the end of the dance, and not just the break.

A few minutes before the band was due back on, the girls fought their way through the crowds – ignoring wolf-whistles and offers to buy them a drink – and made for the ladies' toilets. Tara looked around her at all the girls laughing and chatting, and titivating themselves in front of the mirror, and she thought back to the New Year's Eve dance in Tullamore.

A terrible ache spread through her body as she remembered how she had danced with Gabriel Fitzgerald, and the many times he had kissed her on the way home. The ache turned into a short but sharp pain, low down in the pit of her stomach, and she was grateful when one of the toilet cubicles became vacant, and she could lock herself away from view of the other girls.

A few minutes passed, and then she came back out of the cubicle – a different Tara Flynn. This girl was light-headed with relief and glowing with delight. The dull ache had manifested into a small, but recognisable stain on her white knickers. A small bloodstain that put an end to all the weeks of worry, terrified that her dreadful coupling with William Fitzgerald would result in a pregnancy.

With shaking hands, she had applied the sanitary towel and belt she had carried every day in her bag since she had come over to England. Her period, which she usually dreaded, was the best thing that had happened to her in a long time.

'Are you all right?' Biddy asked, as she waited while Tara washed her hands.

'I'm more than all right,' she told an astonished Biddy. 'I'm so all right, that I feel I could dance all the way from here to Timbuktu!'

Tomorrow morning, straight after breakfast, she would walk down to the church and light a candle in gratitude for her prayers being answered.

Around twelve o'clock, the girls left the dance hall with a large group heading for the late-night bus back to Stockport. Biddy had been true to her word, and though she had got into a huddle in a corner a few times chatting to lads or girls, she had stuck close to Tara for most of the evening. As they turned on to the main road, a large black car slowed down to take the corner and Tara was startled when she recognised the driver.

It was the same man who had followed her along the street in Bramhall a few weeks ago. The man from the Grosvenor Hotel. The car went on for a short distance and then drew up outside the Erin Ballroom. Tara gripped Biddy by the coat sleeve, pulling her to a halt, while the rest of the crowd moved on.

'What's wrong?' Biddy asked.

'Hang on,' Tara said quietly, guiding them into the shadow of a doorway. 'I just want to watch that car for a minute.'

'Who is it?'

'I'm not sure who he is but I've seen him a few times recently. I'm just wondering what he's doing at the dance hall at this hour of the night, when the place is closing up.'

They both watched as the tall handsome man in a dark overcoat stepped out of the car. Sidestepping the groups who were still coming out of the building, he went up the front steps and walked purposefully into the hall.

'He's very good-looking, whoever he is,' Biddy commented. 'How d'you know him . . . have you spoken to him?'

'Not really,' Tara said evasively, moving back into the street again. 'I was just curious when I recognised the car again—' She grabbed Biddy's arm again. 'We'd better hurry or we'll miss the bus home.'

Chapter Twenty-two

'What exactly has happened in this house, since I was last home?' Gabriel Fitzgerald demanded of his father and mother. The tray with the tea and scones which Mrs Scully had prepared for his arrival lay untouched on a side table. 'The last time I phoned – when Mother was in England – I was told that Madeleine was improving, and that she was being cared for at home and work by Tara Flynn.'

'That *was* the case –' William Fitzgerald started to reply.

'And now,' Gabriel went on, extremely agitated, 'I find that Madeleine's in a mental institution and Tara has disappeared off to England.' He looked from one parent to the other. 'It doesn't add up. Tara has always been a good friend to her . . . she understood her condition. I just can't imagine her walking away from her family and good job – without leaving an address or anything.'

'Gabriel,' Elisha sighed, holding the back of her hand to her forehead, 'I'm afraid you'll just have to accept that we don't have the answers to your questions. In fact,' her voice grew weaker, 'I asked your father the same questions myself, when I returned from London.'

William drew himself up to his full height. 'I don't understand the fuss that's being made about this very ordinary young girl.' He cleared his throat. 'We have far more important matters to deal with at present. The fact of the matter is, Tara Flynn was publicly embarrassed by Madeleine's behaviour on a number of occasions, and no young girl likes to be put in such a compromising position. Secondly, everyone knows that she and Mrs Scully had some sort of ridiculous feud running between them. After one of their disagreements, Miss Flynn more or less asked me to choose between them – which I found highly presumptuous of her! Needless to say, Mrs Scully is still with us.' William regarded Gabriel closely, hoping that the explanations he was offering would settle the Tara Flynn situation once and for all. 'Thirdly,' he continued in a determined tone, 'I hear she was offered a job in England, which proved too exciting an opportunity for her to miss. I believe she travelled with a young lady who had just given birth to an illegitimate baby which was subsequently taken off her for adoption.'

Elisha nodded her head. 'I always thought she was a girl with extraordinary ambitions, given her rather basic beginnings. I would imagine that Ballygrace and Tullamore were not big enough for her.'

Gabriel walked across the room to the window and stood with his hands folded behind his back, trying to make sense of his father's explanations.

'Your mother is correct.' William smiled gratefully at his wife. 'The girl was neither fish nor fowl. She didn't fit in with her own kind, and she was struggling hard to fit into the class above her station. And as everyone knows – it isn't easily done.'

'I disagree!' Gabriel wheeled round angrily on his father. 'This class thing is nonsense. *You* above all people should know that – you moved up the social ladder yourself.'

There was a stunned silence in the room, for this was the first time Gabriel had ever challenged his father on anything of this nature.

William's face drained of all colour. 'Exactly what,' he said in an icy tone, 'are you implying?'

'I am *implying* nothing.' Gabriel's voice was equally cool and not in the least repentant. 'I am *stating* that if it is all right for one person to step out of their class, then it should be all right for others to do the same. Tara Flynn is an intelligent, decent girl, and no one with an eye in their head could ever describe her as *lowly*!'

Elisha rushed across the room and put her arm through her son's. He had taken the news of her pregnancy surprisingly well – which she had dreaded telling him. But the great relief she felt was now being threatened by this current issue. 'Gabriel – Gabriel – I really don't know why we are arguing about the girl. We really have enough worries with poor Madeleine and with . . .' She lowered her head, unable to find the delicate words to describe her pregnancy.

Gabriel moved his free hand to cover his mother's. 'The fact is,' he said, looking from one to the other, 'I came home from Dublin this weekend with the intention of asking Tara Flynn to become engaged to me – and to marry me when I've finished my studies.' Before they could utter a word, he added determinedly: 'No matter what happens, I fully intend to find her!'

Rosie Scully's ear was glued to the keyhole of the sitting-room door. She had come to ask if they wanted more tea, and to check what time they wanted dinner served tonight. Instead, she had heard raised, angry voices, and constant referrals to that conniving little bitch – Tara Flynn. Now her head was reeling from the last thing she had heard Gabriel shout at his parents – that he was going to find Tara Flynn, and then he was *going to marry her!*

'Over my dead body,' Rosie whispered, 'will Master Gabriel bring that foxy-haired little whore back to Ireland!'

Chapter Twenty-three

The following Monday morning Tara stopped to check through the pile of post at the front door on her way out to work. Her face brightened when she saw there were two letters bearing her name, and one addressed to Bridget Hart. All three had Irish postmarks. She lifted her own and Biddy's, and left the rest on the table at the door. She ran back into the kitchen where Biddy was clearing up after breakfast.

'A letter for you, Biddy,' she said, sliding it across the big table, 'and believe it or not – *two* for me! The first I've had since coming to England.' She examined the postmarks on the envelopes. 'The one with the Dublin postmark must be from Joe . . . and the other one,' she pondered, 'I think – is from Kitty and Mick.' She put both letters in her handbag. 'I'll keep them to read on the bus.' Then, catching the sombre look on Biddy's face, she asked: 'What's the matter?'

'It's nothing,' Biddy said, stuffing the letter into her apron pocket. 'I think it's just another letter from Father Daly.' She carried on clearing the table.

'Have you written back to tell him you've settled down in Stockport?' Tara said, biting into a triangle of toast that had been left in the toast rack. 'Have you told him that you've got yourself *two* jobs?'

Biddy shook her head, and carried a stack of breakfast plates over to the sink.

'You *should* write to him,' Tara advised. 'I think it's very good of him keeping in touch . . . there aren't many priests who would have been so helpful to you, Biddy. I know the lodgings he suggested didn't work out, but if it wasn't for him, we wouldn't be over here in good jobs.' She looked at her watch. 'Oh, God – I'll have to run or I'll miss my bus!'

Joe had no great news in his letter. It was all about the exams he was sitting, and how he was more or less recovered from his glandular fever. He'd had a relapse since she had last seen him in Dublin, but it was not as bad as before. He said he was still worrying about studying and that he found it hard concentrating at times. He was delighted to hear that Tara was settling in over in England, and had done very well landing a good job so quickly. He finished off by asking *her* to pray for *him* – for a special intention.

Tara folded his letter and put it back in the envelope. She looked out of the bus window, thinking it was strange that a student priest should ask her to pray for him. It really should, she thought, be the other way round.

The other letter was signed from her Uncle Mick and Kitty, although it had actually been written by Kitty. It said more or less the same thing as Joe, about being pleased she had found a job and was settling in. Kitty quickly went on to say that Mick had been to a solicitor to make a will – and that the cottage would be Tara's when he died. In the event of Mick dying first, it would be hers immediately, as Kitty would vacate the cottage to go and live with a widowed sister in Tullamore. The letter closed saying they both missed her and hoped she might come back for a holiday in the summer.

Tara signed deeply. Poor Mick and Kitty. They still felt guilty about her leaving first the cottage, and then leaving Ballygrace. How could she explain to them that, while she had felt in the way, the final decision to leave had been forced on her by circumstances they could never imagine?

Mr Pickford was already in the office and bustling around when Tara arrived at twenty to nine. 'Nice and sharp, as usual, Tara,' he commented, as he passed her by with an armful of files. 'We have a busy, busy day ahead of us. I'll let you get settled, and then I'll go over a few things with you.'

Tara hung up her hat and coat and then went into the small kitchen. The kettle was already boiling on the electric stove, so she put a spoonful of coffee in a mug and mixed it with a drop of milk. She then made a pot of tea with the remainder of the boiling water, and left it on the top of the stove. Jean was always a little behind the others in the morning, and was often too late to start the process of making tea before the office opened. So, without making an issue of it, Tara made sure she had a pot of tea ready for her colleague coming in.

She also discovered that their starchy boss appreciated the gesture too, and had recently taken to having the kettle boiled for her arrival. All in all, Tara felt it was worth the trouble, as it seemed to start everyone off in a more pleasant mood – giving a homely start to a formal day.

'Thank you, Tara,' Mr Pickford said politely, when she put the mug on his desk. He motioned to her to sit down on the chair opposite him. 'I have a meeting in Manchester later this morning, which means I won't be here when a very important client calls in. I'd like you to deal with him, as opposed to Jean.' He took a delicate sip of his tea, and then surveyed Tara over his little spectacles. 'This client – Mr Frank Kennedy.' Mr Pickford gave a rare smile. 'He's a fellow countryman of yours, I'm led to believe. He started off buying old properties and renovating them – then selling them off as flats. But recently, he has moved into the building business, estates of thirty and forty modern houses. Apparently he can't build them quick enough, and some are selling before the foundations are laid.' He pushed his spectacles higher on his nose.' We've sold a number of his properties through the Stockport and Manchester offices, and now he's given *our* branch his new estate to handle, since it's nearer to Bramhall than the other offices.'

'What would you like me to do?' Tara asked.

Mr Pickford took a large file from a drawer in his desk. 'He's calling in to check some sample brochures that we've had designed.' He opened the file, and laid a selection of the brochures in front of Tara. 'I'd like you to go over these with him, and have him choose the most appropriate one.'

The rest of the morning – which the girls presumed would be more relaxed due to Mr Pickford's absence – was one of their busiest. The phones rang incessantly, and customers seemed to appear one after the other.

'Will you be all right on your own?' Jean asked Tara at twelve o'clock. 'I wouldn't have planned to meet my friend for lunch, if I'd known that Mr Pickford was going to be out.' She picked her umbrella out of the stand. 'I have my lunch in the office most days and the one day I decide to go out, it's pouring down.' She hesitated at the door. 'I feel bad leaving you on your own.'

'I'll be fine,' Tara reassured her. 'Things seem to be slowing down a bit now.'

After Jean had gone, Tara sorted out some filing, and then started on a pile of letters which were waiting by the typewriter on a small desk at the back of the office. Since starting work in Thornley's Estate Agents, Tara had picked up many new skills which were necessary for a modern expanding business. The telephone system was much more up-to-date than the one she had used in Tullamore, and everything from the filing cabinets to the typewriter was new to her. But the biggest differences were the sort of clients who were selling property and the customers who were buying. Back in Ireland, Fitzgerald's Auctioneers had mainly dealt with farmers and people who could afford the larger properties. Few ordinary people like her own family had ever frequented business premises. Here, in Bramhall, she was meeting all kinds of people, from working-class newly married couples who were buying their first house, to wealthy landlords who were looking for large properties to split up and rent out as flats.

Apart from her genuine interest in the business, according to Mr Pickford, Tara's courteous, yet confident manner with the customers was her greatest strength. Whether people were buying small two-up, two-down houses, or seeking an extensive property with tennis courts and swimming pool, Tara gave them all the same respectful attention.

She lifted her head now from the typewriter, as the office door opened with the resulting tinkling bell. She stood up and quickly moved towards the front desk, a welcoming smile on her face.

'I'm Frank Kennedy,' the tall, dark-haired man said, 'Mr Pickford told me that the brochures would be ready today.'

Tara was suddenly rooted to the spot. It was the handsome Irishman who had nearly run her down – the one from the Grosvenor Hotel and the dance hall. She quickly composed herself. 'I'll – I'll get them for you now,' she said briskly, turning towards Mr Pickford's office.

'Hang on there a minute,' he said as the back of her curly red head disappeared from view. 'That's surely an Irish accent, is it not?'

'It is,' Tara called back. She lifted the file containing the brochures from her boss's desk, and then stood for a few moments taking several deep breaths, before returning to the main office.

'Here you are,' she said, deliberately looking at his dark rain-splashed overcoat, as opposed to his face. She slid the file across the counter to him.

He caught her wrist lightly and, instinctively, Tara looked up into his face. She knew he was handsome, even from a distance, but she was surprised to find that close up he was even more attractive. The thick black hair, barely tamed by some preparation, set off startlingly blue eyes and even white teeth.

'I didn't know you worked in here. How come I've never seen you when I've been in before?'

She pulled her hand away, trying to remind herself that he was a very important customer – in fact *the* most important customer on the office books. 'I haven't been here long – just a few weeks.'

'I saw you in the Grosvenor Hotel recently, and along the main street here in Bramhall. If I remember, you almost stepped out in front of me.' He viewed her with narrowed eyes. 'I wondered who you were – but it never crossed my mind you might be an Irish girl.'

'Well, now you know,' she said curtly. 'And if I recall correctly, it was *you* who came flying round the corner in your car.'

He threw his head back, and laughed out loud. Then, he suddenly stopped, and stared unashamedly into her eyes.

Tara felt herself shrinking from his gaze. There was something about this smooth, polished man that reminded her of William Fitzgerald, although he was much younger. She turned back towards her desk, willing Jean to come back early. 'I'll leave you to concentrate on the brochures.'

'Time enough for that,' he said, casually leaning on the counter, his folded arms on the unopened file. 'What's your name, and which part of Ireland are you from?'

Tara put a fresh sheet of paper in the typewriter, and again reminded herself that this was a very influential client. To be obviously rude to him – and perhaps be reported to Mr Pickford – would not help her career at all.

'My name's Tara Flynn,' she replied, 'and I'm from County Offaly.'

'Indeed,' he said in an amused tone. 'The King's County itself!'

Tara bent over her machine and started to type.

'I'm a Clare man, myself,' he volunteered, his eyes watching her every move. 'I've been over in England for these past twelve years.' He paused. 'How long did you say you've been over here?'

'I didn't say. I've been here just a month,' she replied. 'Now, if you would be good enough to excuse me, I have some work to do.'

'You won't have had much time to look around,' he mused. 'There are some nice places to see, art galleries, museums and theatres and the like. Then there's Bramall Hall, Lyme Park – and there are some lovely restaurants. Sure, it would be a whole new world for you, coming from the bogs of Offaly. Maybe I could show you round?'

Tara looked up at him now. He really was the most insufferable man, so easy and sure of himself. 'There's more to Offaly than the bogs,' she informed him in a curt manner. 'And I'm perfectly capable of finding my way around Stockport or any other place.'

A broad, amused smile spread on his face. 'I'm sure you are – you seem perfectly capable all round.'

The door bell tinkled again, and a couple who had been in earlier that morning came in. Tara fought back a huge sigh of relief and jumped up from her desk to attend to them.

'We'd like to make an appointment to view two of the three-bedroom houses we discussed this morning,' the woman said, sliding across the printed details she had been given earlier on.

'Forgive me for interrupting,' Frank Kennedy said in a most charming way, 'but there are some modern, three-bedroom houses coming on the market in the next week.' He passed a brochure across the counter to the woman. 'They have the most up-to-date kitchens and bathrooms in them.'

'Oh!' the woman said, holding the brochure out to her husband. 'They look really lovely – maybe we could view them as well.'

After they had left, Frank Kennedy winked at Tara and said: 'A good businessman never misses an opportunity.'

In spite of herself, Tara smiled at his cheek.

Capitalising on the slight thaw in her manner, he asked: 'Would you like to come to dinner with me tomorrow night?'

'No,' Tara replied, without even considering his offer. 'I'm very busy in the evenings.'

'How about an afternoon out then?'

'I'm sorry,' she said, looking him directly in the eye, 'but I'm much too busy at the moment.'

The main door opened again, and Tara was delighted when she saw both Mr Pickford and Jean shaking the rain off their umbrellas.

'Ah! Mr Kennedy!' Mr Pickford looked delighted. He put his wet umbrella back in the stand. 'Has Tara been looking after you?'

Frank Kennedy threw a glance in Tara's direction. 'She has indeed – I have all the brochures here.'

'Excellent.' Mr Pickford motioned his worthy client towards his office door. 'If you would be so kind, Tara,' he said over his shoulder, 'perhaps you might bring us in two cups of tea and some biscuits.'

'Isn't he just gorgeous?' Jean whispered dreamily, when the door closed behind the two men. 'I've heard people saying he's nearly a millionaire! Kennedy's have all the main building contracts in Manchester and Stockport. It was his builders who did the big extension to the Grosvenor Hotel.'

Ah, Tara thought, *so that's why he was in the hotel, the morning that Biddy had her interview.*

'He's just bought up another row of houses in Wilmslow,' Jean said knowledgeably. 'He does them up, then either sells them or rents them out.' She tucked her bobbed blonde hair behind her ears. 'Everything he touches turns to money. And,' she said, rolling her eyes meaningfully, 'he's *single*. Funnily enough, I heard he only lives in a little flat himself, somewhere out in Stockport. He's just broken up with a girl here in Bramhall. Her family have a huge house with stables and a tennis court and everything. From what I hear, he's very generous, but he never stays with the same girl for long.'

'I'm afraid he's not my type at all,' Tara called from the little kitchen. She poured the steaming water from the kettle into the teapot. 'He's just a bit too obvious. If you threw a penny, you would hit ten of his kind.'

'I wouldn't mind meeting even *one* of his kind,' Jean laughed. 'He's definitely the most handsome man that's ever walked in this office door.'

Biddy sat pondering over her letter, during her afternoon break in the empty bar of the Grosvenor Hotel. Father Daly intended to come over to Stockport some time in May. There was a convent in Buxton – about an hour's drive away – and he would be staying there. He said he would definitely meet up with her, and would do his best to find out any news about the baby. Biddy screwed the letter up into a ball, and threw it into the rubbish bin. She wanted to forget all about Ballygrace, and she wanted to forget all about the baby. It was hard to imagine it had ever happened, and yet it was only a month ago.

But Biddy had learned from it. She would never let that happen to her again – not until she got married. She had learned that there were ways to prevent having a baby. Ways nobody had ever talked about in Ireland. And she would never let an older man near her again either. Just the thought of it all now made her feel sick with shame.

'A drink, Biddy?' Fred, the burly part-time barman said, putting a glass of lager down on the table in front of her. 'When the cat's away,' he said, going back to the bar to pull himself a pint, 'the staff will play.' Fred only worked part-time in the bar, as he was a semi-professional wrestler during his hours off.

Biddy glanced anxiously at the door, terrified she might be caught drinking during her working hours. 'Did Mr Timpson say when he would be back?'

'This evening sometime,' Fred said, tilting the glass to get a good head on his beer. 'If he comes in early, just grab your glass and make for the sink. I'll tell him you were helping me to clear up.' He filled his glass, and then came to sit down at the table beside Biddy. 'Are you all right, love?' he asked her in a concerned tone. 'You've been very quiet all day.' Then, his face turned bright red, as it often did when he talked to a girl.

'I'm grand,' she replied, giving him a weak smile. 'I'm just a bit tired.'

'No bloody wonder.' He took a long drink from his glass. 'You've been working here since seven this morning, and when you finish here at four o'clock, you're back working in the boarding house.' He shook a warning finger at her. 'You want to take it a bit easier – you're too hard on yourself.'

Biddy took a sip of her lager, and leaned closer to Fred until their bare arms were touching. 'It's nice to know that somebody cares about me.'

'I bloody well *do* care about you,' he told her, his colour deepening at the confession. 'You're only a slip of a girl, and you need lookin' after. I only wish I could look after you a bit more . . . but with me wrestlin' and everythin', I'm not around as much as I would like.'

Biddy drew a finger along the dark hairs on his forearm. 'It's nice havin' a big strong man lookin' after me.'

Fred put his glass down on the table, and wiped his mouth with the back of his hand. 'If you like, we could go to the pictures on Thursday night. It's the only night I'm off at the minute, what with me trainin' and everything.' Then, he reached over and kissed Biddy full on the mouth.

A lovely warm feeling came over her as she kissed him back. Maybe Fred would be the right sort of man for her. He was only a little bit older than her, in his late twenties. And although his brown hair was thinning a bit, he was the strong, manly sort who would look after her well. Fred would make sure that nobody took advantage of her.

The only problem was the boys in the boarding house, because Biddy liked a few of them there, too.

If she agreed to start going steady with Fred, it would mean she couldn't go dancing with them any more. She pulled away from him now, and took a drink of her lager. She could always keep things with her and Fred secret. He needn't know about her going dancing with Sonny and the others, when he was travelling away with his wrestling. And, Biddy thought, since the Grosvenor was too posh for the lads at Ruby's, they weren't likely to meet up with him in there. She would play it safe, not settle for anyone too soon. She looked up into Fred's face and gave him a big smile. 'The pictures on Thursday night would be grand.'

Chapter Twenty-four

'Please, William,' Elisha Fitzgerald said, 'go and see Gabriel first. Even if it's only for an hour . . . look in at the university and see how he is. It's not far from the hospital, and you can drive down and pick up Madeleine after you've seen him. Perhaps he might come home *next* weekend, if he knows that Madeleine is being allowed home visits again. I know he sees her regularly in the hospital, but it would be so much nicer to have them both in the house again.'

It was ironic to be bringing an unplanned third child into the world, when she had just lost the other two children she so desperately wanted to keep. She winced and rubbed her hand along her lower back, to ease the deep ache which was there day and night. This pregnancy had been far more troublesome than her previous two. But what else could she expect? She was now a woman in her forties, as opposed to one in the bloom of her youth. She hardly dared look in a mirror these days. She dreaded the dark circles she would see under her eyes from lack of sleep, which only emphasised the lines around them.

William sighed. 'I'll call in . . . if that's what you want. But there's no guarantee that he'll see me. He's refused all telephone calls since he last came home.' William had felt the onslaught of age in recent months, mainly due to disturbed sleep. But his insomnia was not a result of physical discomfort – rather a discomfiture of the mind. He only seemed to fall into sleep, to awake in a cold sweat – with a picture of a stricken Tara Flynn etched in his brain.

When he looked back over the last six months, it was as though he were looking down a long black tunnel, viewing the actions of another man. A ridiculous, middle-aged, lust-filled man. How could he have been so stupid and blind as to imagine that a girl like Tara Flynn would have any interest in him? How could he have been so stupid?

A horrendous claustrophobia washed over him. 'I'll just have a walk out in the garden for a few minutes, to clear my head,' he said abruptly, making for the door.

'Shall I ask Mrs Scully to bring you some aspirin?' Elisha called after him, but whether he heard her or not, he did not reply.

William walked down the path at the side of the house, and then out into the garden. He stopped dead once he was out of sight. He stood for a few minutes and breathed deeply of the rhododendrons and the azaleas – but he gained no pleasure from the sight of them, nor from their faint damp scent. Nothing gave him pleasure any more.

He walked further down the garden, and then out towards the paddock where the ponies had grazed. On her last weekend home from the hospital, Madeleine had refused to go anywhere near the family pets, saying the ponies were beasts of the devil. When he and Elisha had tried to talk to her, she had rushed upstairs and locked herself in the bedroom.

Hours later, when William had burst the bedroom door in, they found her lying on the bed, semi-conscious, after repeatedly slashing at her wrists and arms with a tiny blade she used for sharpening her pencils.

The following day, after Madeleine had returned to the hospital, the faithful ponies that had carried her and Gabriel round the fields of Ballygrace House, were sold to a riding school.

William kicked out aimlessly at a stone as he walked around the field, the wind whipping his jacket from the back and lifting wisps of his well-groomed hair. However hard he tried to divert his thoughts from the terrible thing he had done to Tara Flynn, it always came back to haunt him. And lies had now become so ingrained in the pattern of his everyday life that he was starting to believe them himself.

Gabriel had been like a dog after a bone, refusing to let the matter of the girl rest. He had ferreted around, firing one question after another – trying to work out why she had suddenly left without a word of explanation. Finally, after interrogating Mrs Scully to the point of tears, he had headed back to Dublin, saying that he would not rest until he found Tara Flynn.

What might happen if Gabriel succeeded was William Fitzgerald's darkest nightmare. Should it become known what actually happened in Ballygrace House, he would face complete ruin. He suddenly felt dizzy, faint at the thought. He could face prison! His family would disown him – and he would lose his reputation forever. Pinpricks of sweat broke out on his forehead. Already, due to the pressures of Elisha's pregnancy, they were back in separate bedrooms. Even worse, Elisha had moved into the bedroom that Tara had occupied during her stay in the house. Until now, he had managed not to put one step over the threshold of that bedroom. It was as though the spectre of Tara Flynn was inside the room – waiting to exact her revenge.

He turned back towards the house now, the strong breeze a balm on his perspiring face.

Another thought had occurred to him during his meanderings this morning – a thought that brought a sliver of hope to his tortured mind. Perhaps, if he were to find Tara Flynn and go down on his knees – humble himself in front of her – perhaps she might absolve him, as the priest had done in confession. And then, if Tara Flynn was as generous as he hoped and prayed for, he would plead for her absolute silence.

Mrs Scully was waiting in the hallway with a glass of water and two aspirins, when he came back into the house. 'They're givin' bad weather around Dublin and the Midlands for the afternoon,' she announced gravely, having just heard it on the radio. 'High winds, seemingly. Dreadful for the time of year.'

Her employer raised an indifferent eyebrow. 'Indeed?' he said, in a lifeless monotone. He swallowed the two aspirins, then handed her back the empty glass. With leaden arms he lifted his hat and coat from the hall-stand, and then took his car keys from the hook on the wall.

Elisha came to the sitting-room door. 'You won't forget about Gabriel? I would come with you but . . .' She looked down at her bulging stomach. Then, suddenly self-conscious, she straightened up, and attempted her usual regal posture.

'No, no,' William said hastily. 'The journey would be too uncomfortable for you. The road beyond Edenderry is particularly bad – pot-holes everywhere.'

She nodded her head. 'Have a safe journey.' When the door closed behind him, she went into the dining-room, and stood watching with huge empty eyes as the car roared down the drive.

William called at the university office, and asked if Gabriel might be excused a class to have an early lunch with him. He was not surprised by the cool reception, and was perturbed to notice that his son seemed to have lost some weight in the few weeks since he had last seen him.

'Have you found Tara's address in England yet?' was the first thing Gabriel asked, after they exchanged a terse greeting.

William shook his head, then gave the reply he had rehearsed. 'Her family – the uncle in Ballygrace and his wife – say they haven't heard from her. Whether that's the truth or not, I have no way of telling.' He paused for a moment. 'I promised your mother I would call to see you . . . she's very concerned about you.'

Gabriel dropped his eyes to the ground. 'How is she?'

'Bearing up – considering her condition, and all the worry with Madeleine.'

'I saw Madeleine a few days ago,' Gabriel said now. 'She seemed calmer – more at ease with herself. She said she was looking forward to going down to Ballygrace for the weekend.'

'Your mother asked me to mention that Madeleine is coming home *next* weekend also.' He took his hat off, and moved it round in a circle between both hands. 'She wondered if you might do the same. She thought it would be nice to have the whole family together again.'

They walked along towards Grafton Street, their silence covered by the usual city noises, and their bodies angled against the bracing wind, which Mrs Scully had correctly forecast. William gripped his hat tightly in one hand, after barely rescuing it from the wheels of a butcher's van.

'Where would you like to eat?' he now asked his son.

Gabriel shrugged. 'Anywhere but Bewley's.' Sitting in the same restaurant that he had sat in with Tara would have just been too painful.

*

William heaved a sigh of relief when he started the car up again, and set out towards Madeleine's hospital. Having lunch with Gabriel had not been quite the ordeal he had feared, but it had not, by any manner of means, been easy. It was as though Tara Flynn, with her flowing red hair and brilliant smile, had been sitting between father and son in the restaurant. Not in body, but definitely in spirit.

Gabriel had offered a curt apology for his outburst on his last visit home. In retrospect, he realised he should have spoken out to the family about his intentions towards Tara at Christmas. More importantly, he realised that he should have made his intentions known to Tara herself.

'I just presumed,' he told his father, utter wretchedness written all over his young handsome face, 'that she would *always* be there. I know she had feelings for me that were understood without being spoken.'

William had felt an arrow of guilt pierce his heart. He had been so, *so* blind – to everything but his uncontrollable lust – that he had not recognised the obvious attraction between his own son and Tara Flynn.

Gabriel swallowed hard, unused to speaking so honestly to his father. 'I presumed I had all the time in the world – that I could concentrate on my studies, and then return to Tara when it was all over. Maybe,' he confessed, hanging his head shamefully, 'in my snobbish stupidity, I thought I might meet someone at university who was of my own class. I thought that I might meet someone who made me feel the same way that she did. Someone who had shared my privileged upbringing. But I was *so* wrong! Class and money have nothing to do with it. A beautiful, intelligent girl like Tara Flynn does not to come round twice in a man's life. I was an immature fool, I should have spoken out when I had the chance – and then I might not have lost her.'

Oh, how I wish you had spoken out at Christmas, William thought sadly, sipping his coffee. But then, would things have turned out any differently? Even if he had not become foolishly obsessed by the girl, he rationalised, Elisha would not have gone along with Gabriel's wishes. Tara was fine as a friend for Madeleine – but only when all the other friends had deserted her. The stark reality was that Tara Flynn would not have been entertained at Ballygrace House had it not been for Madeleine's misfortune.

When he had paid for the meal, William impulsively reached across the restaurant table, and clasped Gabriel's hand. 'Some things happen in life – dreadful, unimaginable thing – that are out of our control.' He paused, desperately searching for the right words. 'Then there are other things, which we must take control of. Learning from our mistakes is the greatest lesson of all. And undoing any harm that can be undone.' He stood up from the table. 'I wish I had been a better example to you . . . perhaps it's not too late for me to learn yet.'

Madeleine was waiting in the day room for her father. She was, as Gabriel had said, much calmer than recently. William also thought she looked bright and cheerful, and pretty. The way she used to look, before her illness and all the pills had taken their toll.

'I'm looking forward to coming home this weekend,' Madeleine said, planting an unaccustomed kiss on his cheek.

'I wish the weather was milder for us travelling back,' William said, smiling warmly at her. 'It's bad enough struggling against the wind, but now we have hailstones and rain to contend with, too.'

'I don't care what the weather's like.' Madeleine slipped her arm through her father's – another rare gesture of affection – as they braved the gusts of wind to run out to the car. 'I feel so much better,' she explained as they turned out the drive. 'I haven't had those silly voices in my head for a while. I think my new medication is definitely working. I feel so well that I think I could do anything now.'

William said nothing. Madeleine's moods were like a pendulum, and good moods like today were not to be depended upon.

They drove through Dublin, and then out along the country road towards Offaly. Madeleine chattered on, while William concentrated on negotiating his way through poor visibility. As they neared Edenderry, the rain eased off and a weak ray of sunshine peeped through the clouds.

'Look, Daddy!' Madeleine suddenly shrieked, her eyes dancing with delight. She tapped at her window, pointing up towards the sky. 'A rainbow!'

William lowered his head and turned to look out of the passenger window, feigning interest to please his daughter. Until the situation was rectified with Tara Flynn, until he had made some sort of amends, nothing in life could hold any interest for him again.

He looked up into the sky, and there, in all its glory, was the brightest and most perfectly formed rainbow he had ever seen. The sight of it brought unexpected tears to his eyes.

'A rainbow means good luck – you can make a wish on it,' Madeleine babbled excitedly. 'Maybe things are going to get better for everyone. Mother will have a lovely new baby soon – and that's a fresh beginning for the family. And maybe I'll hear from Tara soon.' She turned back to the window, and stared straight up at the rainbow. 'I think I'll make *that* my wish. That very soon I'll hear some news of Tara.'

William blanched at the mention of her name. He closed his eyes – just for a moment – as the dreadful guilt engulfed him once again. But it was a moment too long – that gave him no time to react – when a monstrous beech tree suddenly tumbled from the side of the road, down on top of his car.

A huge, unrooted monster – freed from the earth by the raging winds – which crashed down upon the car, crushing the life from the father and daughter within.

Chapter Twenty-five

The same Friday morning, Tara arrived at work more than half an hour early. 'Mr Pickford?' She looked apprehensively into her boss's office. 'I wonder if I could ask your advice?' She put a cup of tea on the little drink mat on his desk.

Mr Pickford looked alarmed. 'Advice?' His voice reached a higher pitch than normal. 'Advice pertaining to what, exactly?' He lifted the cup and took a mouthful of the steaming tea.

Tara felt all her confidence starting to drain away. 'How would a young woman . . . like myself . . . go about obtaining a mortgage?'

Mr Pickford's eyes bulged behind his thick glasses. He set the cup back down on his desk. 'A mortgage, indeed . . .' He came round to sit on the corner of his desk. He folded his arms and pushed his glasses higher on his nose. 'Are you planning to be married?'

'No . . . no. Not at all!' Tara replied. 'I have some savings,' she explained, 'and I feel it might be wiser to invest it in property. Just a small house . . . nothing grand. I thought it might be better to buy something, rather than paying out rent.'

'Yes, indeed,' Mr Pickford said. 'I can see your point entirely.'

'Another thing,' Tara went on hurriedly. 'I want to buy a piano. I couldn't have one while I'm still in lodgings, and I really need it to keep up my practice. I've found a music teacher near where I live, and I'm going back to lessons soon, to finish off the examinations I started in Ireland.' She bit her lower lip. 'If I had my own house, there would be no problem about the piano. I also thought I might take on some pupils myself in the evenings . . . young children just starting out.'

Mr Pickford raised his eyebrows in surprise. He had no idea that

Tara had such an interest in music, but then, he rarely had personal conversations with his staff. 'Of course you would need a piano, under the circumstances. Now regarding the mortgage business – your age, unfortunately, may well go against you. You're somewhat younger than the average house buyer. But – there are exceptions to every rule. It would all depend on your circumstances. Your work record, previous bank accounts, references and so forth. And of course,' he emphasised, 'you would have to have saved with a building society for some length of time. Prove yourself, as it were . . . before they would consider giving you a loan.'

Tara nodded. 'Which building society would you recommend?'

'Oh, any of the large ones. There are several with branches in Stockport. I would suggest you open an account straight away and put any savings you have into it. What they want to see, is a regular amount going in every week or month, which would indicate that you could afford the payments if they gave you a loan.'

'Yes, I understand. I'll call into one of the building societies in the next week or so.'

'You could take a longer lunch hour this afternoon,' Mr Pickford suggested, 'and go into Stockport then. I think we could spare you this once, since you more than make up your hours at other times.'

Tara clasped her hands together. 'Oh, that would be grand . . . are you sure you wouldn't mind?'

'I think we can make an exception, on *this* particular occasion,' Mr Pickford replied carefully.

That afternoon, Tara came back to her office in Bramhall, with a building society account book in her handbag. The sense of exhilaration which ran through her, every time she looked at the book, was something she had never experienced before.

'This,' she whispered to herself, as the bus turned towards Bramhall village, 'is just the start. This is the first rung on the ladder.'

When she returned from work that evening, she had an unexpected visitor. Exactly how Frank Kennedy found where Tara lived she wasn't sure. It didn't seem like the sort of information that Mr Pickford would give to a client. Perhaps, she thought, it was Jean who told him. When she confronted him in Ruby Sweeney's sitting-room, she discovered she was wrong on both counts.

'I confess to having followed you home from work,' Frank Kennedy told her with a gleam in his eye, which said he was not sorry at all. 'It was the only way I could get to know where you lived. Mr Pickford wouldn't be the sort to divulge that kind of information – and it would have put me at a disadvantage in our business arrangements if I had asked him.'

'You have a real nerve coming here,' Tara told him angrily, as she paced up and down the sitting-room floor. 'If I'd answered the door instead of Mrs Sweeney, I would never have let you over the doorstep.' She stopped and looked him in the eye. 'I've refused you *three* times in the last fortnight. What makes you think I'm going to change my mind, just because you've had the cheek to ask me again?'

'I've got something very special to celebrate,' he said, smiling up into her lovely face. 'And I would like *somebody* very special to celebrate it with me.'

'What's the big celebration?' she asked, her green eyes narrowed sceptically.

'I've just closed an important deal today,' Frank Kennedy said in a low voice. 'I bought the Erin Ballroom.'

Tara's mouth opened in an 'o' of surprise. He had obviously been checking things out at the dance hall, the night she and Biddy saw him.

'Come out with me tonight,' he pleaded. 'I've got to go to Dublin tomorrow for a few days, so tonight's the only free night I have. We could go out for a meal, somewhere nice in Manchester – or whatever *you* want to do. It would mean an awful lot to me.'

The instinctive refusal of his attentions suddenly froze on Tara's lips, at the thought of him owning such an important business. *Perhaps*, she thought, *I could learn something from this Frank Kennedy. He's come over from Ireland, just as I've done, and he's obviously prospered in a big way. He's done exactly what I want to do. Who better a person to learn from?* 'If I do agree to come out with you,' she said, 'then I want my friend to come, too.' Tara knew for a fact that Biddy had the evening off, and she never refused the offer of a night out.

'A chaperone?' he asked, with an amused look on his handsome face. 'Bring whoever you like – as long as *you're* joining me, I'll be delighted.' He stood up now. 'I'll pick you up at half-past seven – if that's all right with you?'

'Actually,' Tara said, walking to the door, 'eight o'clock would suit me better. I have some things to do.' She may have agreed to go out with him but she wasn't going to make it easy.

'Eight o'clock it is.'

Biddy was thrilled to bits about being asked to accompany Tara on her date. 'What are you wearin'?' she asked excitedly as she rushed around the kitchen, determined to have all her chores finished early. 'We'll have to really dress up if we're going into Manchester – it's bound to be fierce posh. What d'you think I should wear?'

'Whatever you feel happy in,' Tara replied.

'I didn't know you knew Frank Kennedy,' Ruby said, rushing into the kitchen.

'Why?' Tara asked. 'Do *you* know him?'

'Not *personally*,' Ruby admitted, with a toss of her blonde, candy-floss hair. 'I only know him by sight. Some of the lads I've had boarding here have worked for him. He's a demon worker himself by all accounts, on the job at the crack of dawn. Even though he wears a white collar now, he can still wield a shovel with the best of them.' She gave Tara a sidelong grin. 'You're a dark horse, aren't you?'

'What d'you mean?' In spite of herself, Tara's face broke out in a smile, too.

'I thought you weren't a bit interested in lads . . . the way you've given the bum's rush to all the young fellas in here. Now I know why! You're more interested in the *bigger* fish.' She gave Biddy a knowing wink. 'She's certainly landed herself a big fish there – plenty of money, and good-lookin' too!'

'To be honest,' Tara said, sitting down at the table, 'he's been driving me mad for weeks, calling in at the office every other day. The thing is, he's one of our most important customers, and I don't want to offend him to the point that he takes his business to another estate agents.' She sighed deeply. 'He found out where I lived, because he followed me back from work. I've only agreed to go out with him so that I can explain in a nice, reasonable way that I don't want to get involved with him.'

'But, why?' Ruby was astounded. 'What's wrong with him?'

Both the landlady and Biddy started at Tara, waiting for her answer. How could she tell them that she was frightened of him? That for all her outward sophistication and confidence, she was frightened of getting close to any man.

'I'm sure there's nothing wrong with him,' Tara replied. 'It's me . . . I don't really want to get involved with anybody at the moment.'

'Get away with you!' Ruby said, ushering her out of the kitchen. 'Get yourself upstairs and get all dolled up. You're nowt but a young girl, and you should be enjoyin' yourself. You take things far too seriously. You should take a leaf out of Biddy's book.'

Biddy shot Ruby a warning look. She didn't want Tara to know all about Fred and the other things she confided in the landlady. Tara wouldn't understand, and would only harp on at her about not trusting fellas, and how they were only interested in one thing. What did Tara know about lads? Apart from a childish interest in Gabriel Fitzgerald, sure she knew nothing about them at all!

Tara sat at the small dressingtable, combing out her long red hair. Then, she applied a light coat of foundation make-up, mascara and lipstick. She had taken her time choosing what to wear tonight, as she had never dined out in Manchester before. Eventually, she settled for an olive green straight skirt, with a matching button-up jacket with a darker green trim. After trying several different pairs, she settled on black suede court shoes with a matching bag. A pearl necklace and earrings finished the outfit off. Elegant, but not showy.

Biddy wore one of her newest dresses, a turquoise one with white polka dots with a new white clutch bag. Hardly a week went past that she didn't buy something from her wages. Practically every penny went on clothes, make-up and jewellery. Cheap and cheerful, and always the height of fashion. As far as Biddy was concerned, the days of Lizzie Lawless and the dirty, hungry orphan were long gone.

Frank Kennedy appeared at Sweeney's door on the dot of eight. He presented Tara with a bunch of colourful flowers, and then made a great fuss complimenting them both on their attractive outfits. Biddy was highly delighted at being driven into Manchester in his fancy black car, while Tara sat in the front trying to maintain a composed, unruffled manner. She didn't know whether to be pleased or dismayed at how well Biddy and Frank hit it off immediately.

'Six months ago, back in Ireland,' Biddy rattled on, as is she'd known him all his life, 'if anyone had told me that I would be driving into Manchester to a posh restaurant in such a posh car – I would have said they were mad!'

'Ah,' Frank replied, 'but you're not in Ireland now, Biddy. Over here in England, everything is possible. I had very little myself, when I came over here first.'

'And which part did you say you're from?' Biddy asked, immediately feeling more comfortable with him.

The restaurant was lovely – flowing pink tablecloths with fresh flowers and candles. As they walked in, Biddy suddenly clammed up, overwhelmed by the grandeur. When the head waiter motioned them forward, she clutched her bag tightly in both hands, and meekly followed Frank Kennedy and Tara to their table.

Tara, knowing her so well, was aware of Biddy's discomfort. She leaned across the table to her. 'You're well used to restaurants now, with working at the Grosvenor.'

'This is a good bit posher,' Biddy said, sinking lower down in her chair as the waiter approached their table.

'That doesn't matter,' Tara assured her. 'The people working here are the same as the ones working in the Grosvenor. They're doing the exact same work as you and the other staff do.' She smiled encouragingly. 'Tonight's different for you. It gives you a chance to see things from the customer's point of view. It'll help you in your own work.'

'I never thought of it like that,' Biddy said, brightening up a morsel.

The waiter passed round wine lists, and then Frank asked of there was any particular wine the girls preferred. Seeing the look of panic on Biddy's face, Tara leaned across to Frank: 'You choose. I drink very little in any case.'

The meal was ordered, with Tara subtly guiding Biddy through the menu, and then all three sat sipping the German wine which Frank had chosen, whilst waiting to be served. After quickly gulping down her first glass of wine, Biddy became more relaxed, and was chatting animatedly when the waiter came with the first course. Frank had picked a fish starter, while the two girls settled for mushroom soup. All three had steak in a red wine sauce to follow, served with a variety of vegetables. Even though she had eaten a full meal back at Ruby's, Biddy tucked into her meal with great relish, a second glass of wine having removed any lingering inhibitions.

Tara was still sipping her first glass, ever mindful of drinking too much, when she realised that she was actually enjoying herself. Frank Kennedy was very entertaining company, good at relating funny tales about when he first arrived in England, and about the different men he worked with on the building sites. For someone who was so well-spoken, and reportedly so wealthy, he had no airs and graces about himself.

After finishing her chocolate and cream dessert, Tara excused herself and went to the ladies room. When she came back, Biddy and Frank were in such a deep conversation that they were unaware of her approaching the table.

'The only lad Tara's ever shown any interest in,' Biddy was saying, 'is Gabriel Fitzgerald. The Fitzgeralds are a fierce wealthy crowd from Ballygrace – *real* Quality. Ballygrace is where me and Tara went to school. Tara was best friends with Madeleine, Gabriel's sister. Of course,' she quickly added, 'she was always best friends with *me*, too.'

'I thought my ears were burning when I was in the ladies',' Tara said lightly, sliding into her seat. 'I hope I haven't missed anything interesting.'

Biddy took another gulp of her wine. 'I was only tellin' Frank about us at school – about you, me and Madeleine.'

'I was hoping Biddy might divulge a few secrets from your past,' Frank said, laughing, 'something that would convince me you're not *completely* perfect, but alas, it seems there are no skeletons lurking about.'

Before Tara could think of a reply, the waiter appeared at her elbow with a cup of tea for Biddy and two cups of coffee.

The combination of wine and relief at having survived an evening in such a posh restaurant made Biddy even more animated in the car on the way back home. With little persuasion from Frank – and none from Tara – she launched into singing a medley of old Irish songs and kept them entertained for the whole journey.

When they reached Sweeney's, Biddy then insisted that Frank come in for a cup of tea. 'We have a nice sitting-room,' she babbled on, 'probably not as posh as yer own house, but it's a hell of a lot nicer than the one I left behind in Ballygrace.'

'Frank's been in the sitting-room, *twice* this evening already,' Tara said patiently, 'and he has to be up early to go to Dublin in the morning.'

'My flight's not until tomorrow evening,' Frank corrected her, getting out of the car. 'So I'll be happy to take you up on the tea, Biddy.' Tara glared at him, but he just grinned back. 'You can't get rid of me that easily, Miss Flynn!'

As they were mounting the steps, the front door suddenly flew open. 'Thank God, you're here!' Ruby exclaimed, ushering them all inside. 'The priest is here – and he has some news for you. I'd just got in from the bingo. He's ever so nice – I made him a cup of tea while we were waiting.'

The colour blanched from Biddy's face. '*Father Daly from Ireland? He's not due over yet.*'

'No, love,' Ruby said, shaking her blonde head. 'It's one of the priests from the local church in Shaw Heath,' Ruby stated. 'He says he got a phone call from a priest in Ireland, to give you the news.'

Tara's heart lurched, as she followed the petite landlady into the sitting-room where the priest was waiting.

'Ah, yes,' the priest said, standing up, 'I recognise you girls now. I often see you at eleven o'clock Mass on a Sunday – particularly the taller one here. I'd recognise that red hair anywhere.'

Biddy bit her lip. Since coming to England, her attendance at Mass had lapsed. Often, she had to work at the Grosvenor on a Sunday morning, and the times she wasn't working she was in bed recovering from a late Saturday night at the Erin ballroom. Anytime Tara asked her had she got to Mass, she simply said she went to another church near the hotel.

He gestured to everyone in the room to sit down. 'Girls,' he said, sitting back down himself, 'I got a call from your parish church in Ireland earlier this evening, asking if I would pass on some news to you both.' He took a little black notebook from his pocket, and checked one of the pages. 'A Mr . . . Michael Flynn . . .'

Tara's hand flew to her mouth. *Oh no, not something wrong with her Uncle Mick!*

'A message was sent *on the behalf* of a Mr Michael Flynn,' the priest went on.

Tara blessed herself, relieved that there was nothing wrong with Mick.

The priest paused for a moment. 'I'm afraid there's been a terrible tragedy in the village – and in the same family. A family that's known to you both.'

Tara and Biddy darted anxious glances at each other.

'Apparently,' the priest said, 'a William Fitzgerald and his daughter Madeleine were killed this afternoon coming from Dublin in a car.'

Madeleine and her father! Tara suddenly felt very strange. Her head spun the way it had the night she drunk the brandy. It was as though everything around her was not real – as if it was all made of cotton-wool or candyfloss. Her head sunk into her hands and she closed her eyes and the rest of the conversation seemed to be taking place miles away.

'What happened?' Biddy asked fearfully from under lowered brows.

'A massive tree crashed down on the car – they didn't have a chance. They were both dead when a farmer came upon them a short time later. Apparently they had galeforce winds all over that part and there's been a number of accidents.'

Tara felt strong arms come round her.

'Are you all right?' Frank Kennedy said in a low, concerned voice.

She opened her eyes, but immediately the dizzy feeling returned. Trying to fight it, she struggled to get to her feet – but the strong arms forced her back down into the chair again.

'I've got some brandy in the kitchen,' she heard Ruby saying. 'That'll help bring her round.'

Brandy . . . not brandy, Tara thought *Madeleine's dead . . . and William Fitzgerald is dead. And it's all my fault! He said he was sorry – he even cried – but I wouldn't forgive him. I was stupid. I should never have been there on my own with him that night. I should have gone back to the cottage to Mick and Kitty. And poor Madeleine . . . I never got round to writing to her. I couldn't let myself think about her, because she reminded me of what happened . . . All me, me, me! Selfish, selfish, selfish.* Tara groaned aloud, and then the tears started to all.

'You're all right, Tara,' Biddy said soothingly, stroking her friend's hair. 'It's one of them terrible things that just happen. Nobody can help it.' Biddy looked at the priest and then at Frank Kennedy. 'Madeleine was Tara's *other* best friend,' she explained, 'and Mr Fitzgerald was her boss. She worked at his auctioneer's office.' Then, carried away by the undivided attention of both men, Biddy embellished further. 'Tara often stayed with them out in Ballygrace House . . . she was like one of the family.'

Ruby's high heels could now be heard tapping their way along the tiled hallway and back into the sitting-room. 'Here you are, ducks,' she said, thrusting a hot glass wrapped in a napkin into Tara's hand. 'Drink that up, and you'll feel much better. I've put plenty of sugar in it.'

Tara gazed down into the glass, then, as the distinctive smell of brandy reached her nostrils, the floor came up towards her. She slumped forward in a dead faint.

'I feel so embarrassed,' Tara said, leaning against Frank Kennedy's car. She felt much better now after a walk in the fresh air. 'The brandy nearly scalded poor Ruby and it went all over her good carpet.'

Frank took her hand in his and was delighted when she didn't pull it away. 'You had a terrible shock tonight,' he said soothingly, 'and everyone understands that. I'm just glad I came into the house with you, otherwise you wouldn't have made it over for the funeral in time.'

Tara shivered at the mention of the word 'funeral'. 'Are you sure you can organise me a plane ticket for tomorrow?' she asked quietly.

'No problem.' His manner was reassuringly confident. 'I only booked mine the other day and there were plenty of seats available on the flight. Anyway I know one of the girls in the booking office.' He reached a hand out and touched her hair gently. 'I'll ring the airport first thing in the morning, and if you ring me around ten o'clock, I'll be able to tell you the arrangements.' He dug into in the breast pocket of his jacket, and took out a business card with his address and phone number on it.

'It's really good of you,' Tara said, taking the card. 'I don't know what I would have done without you . . . I still feel as though I'm asleep, and that I'm going to wake up in the morning and find out it was all a bad dream.'

'If there was any way that I could make that happen,' Frank said, 'believe me – I would.'

Tara had dreaded going to sleep, afraid of the nightmares that would come when she closed her eyes. She eventually fell asleep around two o'clock and when the bright sunshine woke her at eight o'clock she was surprised that she had slept so soundly and had not dreamt at all. Biddy had obviously crept out of bed earlier and gone down to start the breakfasts for the lads who were working the Saturday morning shift.

Tara sat upright in bed. Just before she had gone to sleep last night, she had decided that she would go into Stockport for a black outfit for the funeral. The black winter coat she had worn to her grandfather's funeral was back in the cottage in Ballygrace, and anyway, it was much too heavy for this time of the year. She would have to get a lightweight jacket or suit. She had bought very little since arriving in England, she reasoned, and the suit would be useful for work. She wondered vaguely about whether she should wear a black hat, and then, with a pang of sadness, she remembered the black lace veil she had worn to her Granda's funeral. It was still hanging in her little wardrobe, back at the cottage.

In a short time she was bathed and dressed, then she headed downstairs to the kitchen.

'How are you now?' Biddy asked sympathetically. 'D'you feel better?'

Tara nodded, although her pale face and the dark circles around her eyes were a contradiction.

Biddy poured Tara a cup of coffee. 'Could you manage a fry?' she asked. 'I've got some bacon and sausages under the grill.'

'No . . . no,' Tara said, shaking her head. 'Just toast will be fine, thanks.' She looked at her watch. 'I've got to run into the shops in Stockport now for a few things.'

'What about Frank?' Biddy asked, putting two slices of toast under the grill. 'Haven't you to phone him this morning?'

'I'll do it from Stockport.'

'Tara?' Biddy said hesitantly. 'You're not thick with me . . . about not going to the funeral?'

'No . . . no. I can understand your reasons for not going.'

Biddy hung her head. 'I couldn't face going back to Ballygrace . . . seeing Lizzie Lawless, and knowin' that everybody's talkin' about me havin' the baby.' She turned back to the grill to check the toast. 'I don't think I could ever face goin' back to Ireland again. I want to forget that Ballygrace and Ireland ever existed.'

Frank Kennedy was true to his word. When Tara rang him, he told her that he had organised her plane ticket and said he would pick it up that afternoon on his way to the airport. 'I'm afraid I have some business in Manchester later this morning,' he told her apologetically, 'so I'll have to meet you in the airport at four o'clock to check in. The flight goes out at five.'

'I'll go back to the house and get packed now.'

'The funeral is on Monday, isn't it?' Frank asked.

'Oh, yes—' Tara suddenly looked flustered. 'What about coming back?'

'I've booked a flight back on Monday evening. That *is* what you said?' There was a small pause. 'I can always change it.'

'No . . . Monday's fine. I don't want to stay any longer. And anyway, I have to get back for work. Mr Pickford was very good about letting me have time off for the funeral, and I don't want to take advantage of him.'

When she arrived in the check-in department of Manchester Airport, Tara found a seat and looked around to see if Frank Kennedy had arrived yet. It was her first time in an airport, and as she watched the other passengers coming and going, she wished that this first flight over to Ireland had been for a happy occassion. She wished it had been a proper holiday – after a decent length in England. A holiday that would have allowed her to enjoy the hustle and bustle of the airport.

She had opened her handbag, looking for a hanky to wipe a stray tear, when she saw Frank Kennedy's tall frame coming through the crowds. She lifted a hand to wave at him, and was shocked at the overwhelming relief she felt when he waved back and came rushing towards her.

'Have you been waiting long?' he asked anxiously, sitting down beside her. His piercing blue eyes took in every inch of her beautiful, but pale face. He felt such a strong, physical stirring just looking at her. No woman – and there had been plenty – had had such an effect on him. She touched every erotic feeling he had in his body, and every fantasy he had in his mind. He swallowed hard. God knows how he would feel when he was finally allowed to touch her.

'No,' she whispered, 'I just arrived a few minutes ago.'

'Would you like something to eat?'

'No, thanks. I'm not very hungry.'

'You said that this was your first time flying – are you nervous?'

Tara shrugged and gave him a weak smile. 'I haven't really had time to think about it, but I'm sure I'll be fine.'

He took the plane tickets out of his inside pocket. 'If we check in now, we'll have time for a coffee or a drink before we board.'

Later, when Frank was at the bar, Tara thought how lucky she was to have met him now. How would she have managed all of this without him? It was amazing how he had walked into her life at the right time. When she thought about the times she had turned him down, been almost rude to him – and yet he had still come back. He was definitely a persistent man, one who did not give up easily.

She looked across the airport lounge at him now. She found herself examining the way his pinstripe suit jacket hung perfectly on his square shoulders. As he turned towards her, carefully balancing a tray, an unexpected warmth ran through her body, and she suddenly realised that in spite of her earlier misgivings, she was actually attracted to him. In fact she was extremely attracted to him. This was indeed a revelation to her, because Gabriel Fitzgerald was the only male who had ever had that effect on her.

'I've just been thinking,' he said, putting the laden tray on the table. 'Wouldn't it make more sense if you stayed in Dublin tonight?' Frank lifted a small bottle of red wine and a glass and placed them in front of Tara, then did the same for himself. Then he put a plate with sausage rolls and sandwiches between them on the table. 'I don't think you'll have much luck getting a train down to Tullamore by the time we arrive in Dublin,' he explained. 'I would be happy to run you down. I'm picking up a car at the airport – but unfortunately I have a business dinner this evening and it could be very late by the time it's over.'

'I hadn't given a thought about getting down the country,' Tara confessed, her face flushing at the oversight. 'Everything has happened so quickly.'

'I'm booked in at one of the hotels in the centre of Dublin,' he told her, 'and it will only take a phone call from the airport to book another room. I'm free tomorrow and I can run you down to Offaly then.'

'No . . . that would only inconvenience you,' she protested. 'I can catch a train down easily.'

'Have you told your family when you're arriving in Offaly?'

'No. The priest in Stockport said he would phone back to Ballygrace, and let them know that I would be down for the funeral at some point over the weekend.'

'So they're not expecting you tonight?'

Tara shook her head. 'They're the sort who'll just take me when I arrive.'

'Frank Kennedy!' a distinctly Irish accent suddenly boomed from across the airport lounge. A short, portly man was making his way across the room towards them. 'Bejaysus, it's yourself indeed! Is this you off home for the weekend?'

Frank quickly got to his feet. 'I won't be a minute,' he told Tara, his brow suddenly furrowed. He went across to meet the man but, instead of bringing him to join them at the table, he guided the older man towards the bar.

The Shelbourne Hotel was beautiful. Not wishing to let Frank know that she had never stayed overnight in a hotel before, Tara stood quietly while he organised a single room for her. She again wondered about him. About the great ease with which he did everything. As though he were born into such a gracious lifestyle.

So far, Tara had purposely kept things impersonal but had overheard some of the things he had told Biddy about himself. According to what he had said, he was reared in County Clare, in an ordinary family. And yet, from the casual manner he displayed towards the manager, and the confident way he was signing the hotel register – he looked as though he had been brought up in a family like the Fitzgeralds.

At the thought of poor Madeleine and her father, the dreaded feeling of sadness and guilt washed all over her again, making her feel quite weak.

'Are you all right?' Frank Kennedy held out a key with her room number attached to it.

'Yes,' Tara lied, 'I'm grand.' How could she explain to him the guilt she felt about neglecting her sick friend, and the fact Madeleine had died not even knowing where Tara was?

Tara's bedroom was beautifully furnished and decorated, and spacious for a single room. Frank's room was right next door. The fact that he was so close did not bother her, and she had not flinched when he told her. Not so long ago it would have bothered her a great deal, but she knew – without a doubt – that Frank Kennedy expected nothing from her at present.

From the first time he had spoken to her, he had confessed to finding her beautiful, sophisticated and intelligent. But she had known all that, even before the words had formed on his lips. William Fitzgerald had opened her eyes as to how men act when they lust over a woman. She had not been mature or experienced enough to recognise it at the time – but she had grown up very quickly, these past few months.

Frank apologised profusely about having to leave her alone in the hotel while he attended his meeting, but Tara told him she would be perfectly fine on her own.

'I'm not very good company at the moment,' she said. 'I might have a walk around the city later on, and then I'll have something to eat.'

'You're sure?' he checked, knowing that she would cope perfectly well on her own. He found Tara Flynn's independence quite refreshing. Most of the women he knew – much older, and much more worldly – would not feel comfortable in a hotel or even a cafe by themselves. But then, Tara Flynn was not like any of those other women. And that was the very thing that held his attention. That, and her obvious physical attractions, which put her in a league of her own.

Chapter Twenty-six

Kitty burst into tears when she opened the door and found Tara on the doorstep on Sunday afternoon. When she walked into the cottage, Mick's face turned a deeper shade of red than usual and when he stood to give her a hug, he almost squeezed the life out of her.

Moments later, the older couple suddenly became very formal, when they noticed Frank Kennedy standing by his black shiny car. In the midst of even the most terrible crisis, they always remembered their place in life. Just by the look of his car and his clothes, they knew that Tara's companion was a cut above them.

Around four o'clock, after a cup of tea and a slice of Kitty's home-made apple tart, Frank excused himself, saying that he would drive into Tullamore and find himself a hotel or lodgings for the night. 'I'll call back for you about half-past six,' he told Tara when she came out to see him off.

'Look, you don't have to come to the church with me,' she said quietly. 'You don't even know the family and apart from me you won't know a soul.'

'What else would I be doing?' he replied. 'I'd like to come with you . . . if it's not pushing in.'

Tara hesitated for a moment. 'That's fine. I'll see you at half-past six then.' As she waved him off, she pushed away thoughts of how incredible it was that Frank Kennedy should be in Ballygrace at all. Less than a week ago, she wouldn't have given him the time of day, and yet now she felt she had known and depended on him all her life. Not since her granda had another person looked after her the way he was doing now.

When Frank arrived back, Tara asked him to leave the car at the cottage, for she knew that there were so few cars round the village it would only command great attention. Attention she was desperate to avoid.

'I know it's probably the wrong time and place to say it,' Frank whispered as they walked along behind Mick and Kitty, 'but you look beautiful in black – the mantilla really brings out the red in your hair.'

'Thank you,' Tara said quietly. She stared straight ahead, thinking that it was indeed the wrong time to say such a thing. But telling him so would not make the situation any better.

They walked along in silence, then after a few minutes Frank whispered: 'Are you all right?'

'It's very difficult,' Tara said quietly. 'It's just about the most difficult thing I've ever had to do.'

'The girl – was she a very close friend?'

'Yes,' Tara sighed. 'I've known Madeleine since I started school, and we've been friends since then. I worked in her father's auctioneering office, before moving to England. Madeleine had been very ill. She was in hospital in Dublin . . . with some sort of mental illness. I had been staying at Ballygrace House just before that, looking after her.' Tara said nothing about Gabriel Fitzgerald. What was there to say in any case?

'I'm very sorry.' Frank sounded awkward for the first time since they had met.

Then they came in sight of the church and the crowds that were lining the streets waiting for the hearses to come from the mortuary in Tullamore. The Fitzgeralds were the most important family in Ballygrace and people from far and wide had travelled for the funeral.

Tara's heart sank at the thought of having to join all these people – people who had gossiped about her and sniped behind her back. Of course, no one would say a word to her face. That was not the way they worked. She had checked with Mick and Kitty earlier in the afternoon as to whether people had said anything after she had left Ballygrace for England.

'No – not a word – in all honesty,' Kitty had blustered. 'The odd one might have asked how you were keeping and how young Biddy was – but nobody said anything *direct*.'

Tara had not questioned them any further, knowing that if anything *had* been said, her uncle and his wife would say nothing, to save her feelings.

Hot tears welled up in Tara's eyes now, making the crowds of people ahead disappear in a watery blur.

'Here – here you are.' Frank handed her a white starched handkerchief, which had been well laundered by the fussy woman who looked after the domestic side of his life in Stockport. 'You can keep it.'

Tara dabbed at her eyes and nose. 'I still can't take it in. I can't believe they're dead . . . that I won't ever see Madeleine again.' Her voice disappeared into a whisper. 'I should have gone to see her before I moved to England, or at least written to her. I feel so guilty!'

Frank put a comforting arm around her shoulders. 'Now why should you feel guilty? You had nothing to do with the accident – nobody had. It was an act of God. Only he knows why it happened.'

After a few moments, Tara eased away from his arm. Then she pulled the black veil down so that it covered her eyes. Apart from her own appearance at the funeral, she knew that Frank Kennedy's polished appearance, his expensive pinstripe suit and his confident demeanour, would attract the curious eyes. To be seen with a wealthy-looking stranger's arm around her, would definitely cause a stir among the mourners.

She had noticed the curious looks on Mick and Kitty's faces when she brought him into the cottage, and as soon as he left, she explained who he was. Tara had elaborated on the fact that he was an important client of Thornley's Estate Agents, and had then lied, saying that her boss had arranged the lift with Frank Kennedy from Dublin. She said nothing about having arrived in Ireland the previous evening, or about staying in the Shelbourne hotel.

They walked along the road, Tara looking straight ahead, until they heard Mick call to them from the crowd. They joined him and Kitty, and then they waited until the two hearses could be seen coming along in the distance.

As they were unloading the coffins from the big black hearses, the mourners quietly filed into the church. Kitty ushered Tara and the two men in with the first crowd, to make sure they got a seat. There were so many people there, that a large number would spill out into the churchyard.

Tara slipped into a seat at the back of the church, pulling the lace mantilla further down over her eyes. She then knelt down, closed her eyes, and tried hard to concentrate on saying a prayer for Madeleine and her father's souls. Her efforts proved futile. Every time Tara got halfway through a prayer for the dead, a dreadful picture of a drunken William Fitzgerald formed behind her closed lids.

Later, when the church was full, the congregation stood up and then the organ started to play a slow, mournful hymn. The two coffins were carried in one after the other.

The sight of the coffins and the sad music brought scalding tears to Tara's eyes. Then, she felt a terrible crushing feeling in her chest, when she caught sight of the familiar blond hair. Gabriel Fitzgerald, tall and dignified, walked behind the polished mahogany procession, supporting his mother on his arm. When they passed her by, Tara's eyes were wide and stunned when she realised that Elisha Fitzgerald was very obviously pregnant.

Tara's heart began to beat rapidly and her throat ran dry. Surely Kitty must have known about Madeleine's mother? *Why hadn't she written and told her?*

My God . . . Tara thought. *What if . . . what if that dreadful night had resulted in me being made pregnant by William Fitzgerald? What would it have done to this poor, tired-looking woman? A woman who looked too old and too weary to become a mother again. What would it have done to Elisha Fitzgerald's mind, to have known that her husband had raped a young virginal girl?*

Apart from the issue of a possible pregnancy, Tara knew that if Elisha ever found out about the rape, it could quite easily push her over the edge. It could make her mentally ill, especially after losing her husband and daughter. And then, what would have happened to the poor innocent baby Elisha was carrying? There was only Gabriel left in the family to shoulder all that pain, should the truth behind Tara's disapperance ever become known.

Tara lifted her eyes up now to the altar, in front of which the two coffins were now being placed on metal stands. They would stay there overnight – side by side – in the empty, dark church. She stared at the gleaming, expensive coffins, and thought of the father and daughter encased within.

She thought of Madeleine riding her pony, Madeleine at her eighteenth party, Madeleine ranting and raving about going to the Missions. She thought of the crushed and broken Madeleine in the coffin, ready for her final journey. Then, she thought of William Fitzgerald and how he had cried the night he took her virginity – and how he had cried like a wounded animal the following morning.

Tara looked up above the altar now, to the broken figure nailed to the cross. As she stared at the sorrowful, familiar effigy, Tara vowed that Elisha Fitzgerald would never know anything about that terrible night.

Chapter Twenty-seven

Biddy stared across the kitchen table at the slim, blonde girl. She felt like throttling her, as the girl sipped daintily from a cup of tea and then took a long, dramatic drag on her cigarette. Sally Taylor had only been in her aunt's lodging house for one night, and yet she was acting as if she owned the place already.

'I'll have another cup of tea, Biddy, if you've any left in the pot,' Sally said in a strong Liverpool accent. Then, without even looking at Biddy, she slid her cup across the table.

'I'm not too sure about all this business,' Ruby said to her niece. 'I don't want your mother coming over here, blamin' me for you leavin' home.'

'She won't,' Sally said, narrowing her eyes against the cigarette smoke. 'They're glad to get rid of me. Now she's gorra new boyfriend, she'll want the house to herself.'

'The thing is,' Ruby said, examining her newly painted red nails, 'I'm not sure if this house is the best place for you. Apart from Biddy here and her friend Tara – there's only workin' lads in the house.'

'*You* said you liked it here, didn't you?' Sally said accusingly to Biddy. 'You said last night that it was a good laugh here with all the lads.'

Biddy's face coloured up. Sally Taylor had been introduced to her the previous night, when Biddy had finished a late Saturday shift at the Grosvenor. She had stayed on until around twelve, having a few drinks in the bar with Fred, and then she had walked home. The Babychams she had drunk had made her relaxed and chatty, and she had sat up for another hour, drinking tea and telling Sally how much she loved Stockport and living in Ruby's house.

Sally had sat quietly, taking in everything that Biddy had to say, and then she announced that she was thinking of moving into her aunt's lodging house permanently. 'She wouldn't charge me anythin' until I found a job, and then she wouldn't look for much – bein' that me mam's her sister, like.' She had puffed on her cigarette. 'Yeah, old Ruby would let me have the run of the place. I could come and go as I like here.'

From that minute, Biddy started to feel uneasy. She and Ruby got on very well, and Biddy had taken to telling the others in the hotel that the landlady was like the mother she never knew. In fact, living in Sweeney's boarding house, Biddy was happier than she had ever been in her life. She had her best friend with her, and although Tara nagged a bit she was easy got round, and when Tara was out, she could have a good laugh with all the lads.

The appearance of the blonde, over-confident Sally had thrown a spanner in the works. If she didn't rapidly improve her attitude, something would have to be done. Biddy passed the fresh cup of tea back to Sally now and bit her tongue as the girl lifted the biscuit tin with the chocolate ones in it, and helped her self to two. They were *special* biscuits, reserved for Biddy and Ruby when they were in the house on their own in the afternoons. Occasionally, Tara might have one, but she would never touch the tin, unless she was offered. And now – here was that little blonde brat helping herself to them, without so much as a 'please' or a 'thank-you'.

Biddy went over to the sink. She washed the cups and saucers, and then started peeling the vegetables for the Sunday lunch, leaving the niece and aunt to their family chat. As the long curls of potato peel started to fill the basin, Biddy wondered how Tara was getting on back in Ballygrace. Just the thought of the place sent a shiver through her body. Nothing – not even the death of a friend – could entice her back to Ireland now. She rubbed the back of her damp hand over her forehead. It wouldn't surprise her if she *never* went to Ireland again. She had no interest in the place any more.

Then, a cold shiver crept over her, as she thought of Father Daly's impending visit.

'What are the fashions like in Ireland, then?' Sally asked, stubbing her Woodbine out.

'What d'you mean?' Biddy said defensively. She had already been the butt of Sally's 'Irish jokes', and wasn't going to walk into any more.

'I'm only askin' – what are the fashions in Ireland like? Are they as up-to-date as around here?'

'There's plenty of big shops in Dublin,' Biddy replied, 'and you can buy any type of clothes you like, as long as you have the money. The clothes are every bit as good as any in Stockport.'

Sally sighed. 'That doesn't say much about Dublin! The fashion in Stockport and Manchester's bleedin' dowdy. You want to get yerself over to Liverpool some time – the shoppin' there's brilliant.'

Ruby leaned across the table, and tapped a blood-red fingernail in front of her niece. 'If Liverpool's that bloody good, then you want to get yerself off back home.' 'She looked at her watch. 'I'm sure there's a train to Liverpool later on this evenin.'

'I didn't mean it *that* way,' Sally protested. 'I love Stockport, and anyway, me mam's havin' a bad time with her nerves. She's driving me up the bleedin' wall.'

'Knowing you, lady,' Ruby retorted, 'it's the other way round. It's likely *you* that's drivin' *her* up the wall. You're a right rum 'un, you are!'

'Oh, Aunty Ruby!' Sally giggled, coming round the table to give the landlady a placating hug. 'I don't mean any harm. You know what I'm like – us bein' family and everythin'.'

The vegetable knife dropped into the murky depths of the basin. 'I'll be back in a minute,' Biddy said, and suddenly rushed out of the kitchen door.

She took both flights of stairs two at a time, then made for her bedroom door. When she got inside, she flung herself on the bed and buried her face deep in the pillow. Why, oh why, she wondered, did things never go right? Why does everything *always* get spoiled? Scalding tears spilled onto her pillow. Since she had come to Stockport, her life had changed in the most wonderful way. All the bad things about Lizzie Lawless . . . and Dinny and the baby and . . . *everything* had been left behind. She had become a new person, a girl who had money and could afford nice fashionable clothes. A girl who could have a bath as often as she liked. She had become an *ordinary* girl. The kind of girl she had always wanted to be.

Tara would die if she knew it – but Biddy had even told Ruby about the baby. One night, when she had come in from the late shift in the hotel, Ruby had been sitting alone by the fire in the sitting-room. She was holding a glass of whisky and dry ginger, and she was crying. Two coal-black streams of mascara poured down her rouged cheeks unchecked. More shocking still was the way Ruby had carelessly rubbed the sleeve of her pristine white cardigan over her tear-stained face.

'Have a drink with me, ducks,' Ruby had begged, in a voice thick with alcohol. 'I hate drinkin' on me own – it only makes me feel worse. I was hopin' you'd be in soon, all the others have gone to bed.' She tottered over to the glass display cabinet and took out another tumbler. She put it on the coffee table beside the bottles, and poured a generous measure of whisky topped with the dry ginger.

'Thanks,' Biddy said, perching on the end of the sofa. She'd already had three lagers with Fred after work, and didn't really feel like another drink, but she would never hurt Ruby's feelings.

'This is a terrible day for me!' Ruby said, leaning her elbows on her knee, and letting her blonde head sink into her hands. 'This is the anniversary of the day me baby should have been born. Twenty-one years ago it was. It would have been twenty-one today!'

'Your *baby?*' Biddy stupidly repeated. 'But sure, you never had any children . . . did you?'

'No, ducks,' Ruby snivelled. 'But I *should* have done . . . I should 'ave had a baby . . . if I'd never had it aborted. If I'd never have killed the poor little thing.' She wiped her streaming eyes with her other sleeve. 'Me mam *made* me. I were only seventeen . . . nowt but a bloody kid meself.'

'An abortion!' Biddy whispered. 'Was it terrible?' She had heard dark stories about abortions.

Ruby took a big gulp of her whisky and then grimaced, as though she were being forced to drink arsenic. 'It were bloody awful! The bastards almost butchered me to death. It were a husband and wife together – and she was worse than him. Supposed to be a doctor an' a nurse.' She sniffed loudly. 'I were sick for weeks, and they left me in such a state that I couldn't have any more kids. Maybe me an' Bert would have had a happier marriage if I'd been able to have kids.' She held her glass up to Biddy, as though she were proposing a toast. 'Make sure *you* have kids – it's a lonely life for a woman who's not been blessed with them.' She took another swig of her whisky.

'I've already had a baby,' Biddy said in a whisper.

'Have you, love?' Ruby didn't sound a bit surprised.

'Just before I came over here . . . I gave it up for adoption.'

'Life's bleedin' unfair,' Ruby said.' 'I would 'ave loved a baby.'

'I couldn't have kept it,' Biddy explained, her eyes fixed on the rug in the centre of the floor. 'In Ireland they're fierce strict about things like that, an' I had no mother or no family to help me out. Tara's the only one who knows over in England . . . apart from you now.' A panicky feeling suddenly came over her, at the fact she had exposed her carefully guarded secret. 'You won't tell anyone, will you?' There was silence for a moment. Then, Biddy lifted her eyes and looked anxiously at the landlady. But Ruby was fast asleep.

The following morning when Biddy was frying sausages and rashers of bacon, Ruby had patted her shoulder and said: 'Thanks for listenin' to me last night. Don't mind me, I'm a silly bugger when I'm pissed. I've got a right sore head this mornin'. How are you?'

'I'm grand,' Biddy said, giving a relieved smile. She had hardly slept all night, worrying about the terrible thing she had divulged to the landlady.

'Don't worry,' Ruby said, as though she had read Biddy's thoughts. 'Anythin' that was said last night is between you, me and the gatepost.'

From that morning on, Biddy had felt a special bond with the landlady. They both shared a secret – and Ruby's secret was darker than hers. She felt as though a great weight had been lifted off her mind. Ruby thought no less of her, even though she knew about the baby. Everything had been grand, even the bad news about Madeleine and her father hadn't spoiled things. Oh, it was a terrible business, and she pitied the poor family. But she had never really been that close to Madeleine. They had nothing in common, with Madeleine being Quality, and if the truth be told, Biddy was jealous of Tara's friendship with her.

Now, there was nothing to worry about. With Madeleine gone, Biddy would be Tara's best friend.

Everything had been working out fine and grand, Biddy thought, as she lay on the bed. Until that Sally Taylor had appeared on the scene. In twenty-four hours, everything had been turned upside down. Ruby had a loyalty to the girl – being her aunt – but at the moment she was definitely seeing the spiteful Sally through rose-tinted glasses.

Biddy sat up now and wiped her eyes. She would do nothing for the time being. She would go back downstairs and do her work, and she would be as pleasant as she could to Sally. Maybe things would settle down in their own time. She went into the bathroom and washed her face. She glanced in the mirror and was relieved to see she looked more or less back to normal. Then, she took a deep breath and descended the staircase.

As she walked along the hallway towards the kitchen, Biddy's body suddenly went tense when she heard Sally's high-pitched laughter. She hovered about at the kitchen door, waiting until the conversation between aunt and niece had died down to enter.

'You'll have to find some sort of work if you're staying,' she heard Ruby say.

'I could help you out here,' Sally suggested.

'That's Biddy's job and she's a damn good little worker. I don't need any other help.'

Biddy's heart soared at the landlady's praise. She stood listening, hoping for more.

'But it's not fair. She's already got a full-time job in the hotel,' Sally pointed out. 'And she's not here all the time, you said so yourself. I could cook and do the cleanin' up the mornings she's not here. I wouldn't ask for anything, my board and lodgings would be enough.'

'You, m'lady,' Ruby laughed, 'could sell ice to an Eskimo.' She paused. 'It's early days yet. Just let me think it over.'

Biddy put her hand on the doorknob.

'I don't mean no harm to her like,' Sally ventured, 'but it's not really fair that an *Irish* girl should come over here and take *two* jobs off us English. Surely one job's enough for her? She's landed on her feet here with you, Aunty Ruby. Most places would have run her the minute she opened her mouth. Those Irish can be awful ignorant – imagine havin' a name like Biddy! It's like something out of the ark.'

'Enough of the jeering,' Ruby said sharply. 'Biddy's a nice girl and I wouldn't let Tara Flynn hear you calling the Irish ignorant! She'd have your guts for bloody garters! She's a lot more refined than you or even me. You should see the fella she's gone over to Ireland with this weekend, he's practically a millionaire, and good-lookin' too. Be very careful what you say about the Irish – for they're what's keepin' this house going.'

'Oh, well,' Sally said petulantly, 'that's me put in me place.'

Biddy opened the door. 'Sorry about that,' she said walking over to the sink. 'I was a bit short-took, it must have been somethin' that I ate at the hotel last night.'

'What's the name of your hotel?' Sally asked, twisting a strand of blonde hair round her middle finger.

'The Grosvenor,' Biddy replied.

'Well, if that's what the food does to you,' Sally scoffed, 'remind me never to eat in there. It sounds a right dump.'

'*You'll* never need to worry about eating in the Grosvenor,' Ruby laughed. 'You could never bleedin' well afford to!'

Sally raised her eyebrows. 'An' who says I'd be paying for it?' She drew her fingers through her peroxide hair, feigning a model-like mannerism. 'Isn't that what men are for? Just give me time to find me feet here, an' I'll soon have all the lads in the house fightin' over who's paying for me!'

Biddy smiled to herself, and went back to peeling the potatoes.

Around three o'clock, all the lads gathered in the kitchen for their Sunday dinner.

'What's to do with the fancy table?' Jimmy, the lad with the Geordie accent, asked. 'It's not Christmas or Easter or anythin' is it?'

'There's no special occasion,' Biddy told them, 'not as far as I know.'

'Sit down, lads,' Sally commanded, as familiar with the lodgers as if she'd known them for years. She stood one hand on a hip and gave a little pout to show off her new orangey-pink lipstick. 'Youse lads have been working hard all week, and youse deserve to sit down at a nice table now and again. An' anyway,' She added, giving a giggle, 'I wanted to prove that I'm more than just a pretty face. As me mam says, you don't have to be plain to be practical.'

'We're spoiled for choice here,' Lofton laughed, 'between the blonde and the brunette beauties! And both of them able to cook and clean. What more could a man want for?'

The other lodgers gave a whoop of appreciation, and while Biddy was pleased with being called 'the brunette' she was more than annoyed with Sally. Much to her gall, Ruby's niece had insisted on helping to prepare the meal, and had then set the table in a fancier manner than normal. She had raked around the kitchen, looking in cupboards and pulling out drawers until she found a matching plastic salt and pepper set, to replace the huge tin of salt with the rusty edge and the small box of pepper. The plastic salt and pepper set was adorned with a picture of the seaside on one side, and '*A Present from Blackpool*' written on the other. Sally had also dug out some green paper serviettes which were left over from Christmas. The fact that some had a spring of holly in the corner, and others were decorated with small poinsettia flowers, failed to diminish Sally's enthusiasm about bringing an elegance to Sweeney's Sunday dinner table.

'What are we supposed to do with these?' Jimmy asked, holding up a serviette.

'Keep your nose clean,' Ruby said, walking into the kitchen. She threw a warning eye at Sally. 'And that goes for everyone.'

As Biddy had anticipated, all the lads were eager to have Sally join them at the Erin Ballroom for the Sunday night dance. After they had finished their sherry trifle and tea, they all took turns at trying to persuade her.

Sally made a good show of looking doubtful. 'I'm not sure,' she said, batting her sooty-black eyelashes. 'I should really wait until I've found a job, before I start goin' out.'

'One night won't do any harm,' Biddy said, then she added generously, 'an' if you're short of money, I'll pay you in. I got me wages on Friday.'

'Would you?' Sally squealed with delight. 'That would be great! What time do we need to leave?'

'We usually catch a bus around eight o'clock, so's we have time to call in at one of the pubs in Levenshulme, for a drink before the dance.'

Sally pushed her empty trifle plate away and stood up. 'I'd better go and have me bath now,' she announced. 'It takes bleedin' ages gettin' me hair set and dry.' And then, without a backward glance at the dirty plates and pans, Sally took her leave.

After she had cleared up, Biddy brewed a pot of tea and then carried two cups and two chocolate biscuits upstairs to Sally's bedroom.

Sally, wearing a bright yellow dressing-gown, was busy putting curlers in her hair. 'Ta, Biddy,' she said, taking a sip of the tea and a bite of her biscuit. 'D'you know somethin'? I think you and me's going to be good mates.'

'It's grand to have another girl around the house,' Biddy said with a smile. She casually leaned against the dressingtable drinking her own cup of tea. 'What are you wearin' to the dance?'

Sally held up a shimmery blue top. 'You don't think it's a bit too brassy for an Irish dance hall, do you?' she asked. 'I've heard that priests sometimes come into Irish clubs, to check how the girls are dressed.'

'It's fine,' Biddy assured her. 'I've never seen a priest in the Erin Ballroom. It's a very glamorous place.'

Sally sipped at her tea in between putting in rollers and smoking a cigarette. 'You haven't any nice nail varnish and some remover, have you? Me nails are chipped, and I forgot to bring my own stuff. I'd borrow me Aunty Ruby's – but have you seen the bright red stuff she wears?' She gave a sneering laugh. 'I wouldn't be seen dead in it!'

'I've got a nice pink nail varnish that'd match your lipstick,' Biddy told her. 'I'll get it for you when I've washed up the cups.'

Sally drained the remains of her tea, and pulled a face. 'You want to tell my Aunty Ruby to buy some decent tea. I'll bet she buys the biggest and cheapest box in the shop.' Sally rolled her eyes mockingly. 'She can be a right cheapskate at times . . . me mam reckons she's makin' a mint out of runnin' this place.'

Biddy took the cup off her. 'I'll be back with that nail varnish shortly.'

Back in her and Tara's room later on, Biddy chose a pink dress to wear to the dance. She was confident she looked nice in it, because the last time she'd worn it, loads of the lads had complimented her on it. She laid it out on the bed along with her stockings and clean underwear, then she gathered her washing things together and headed for the bathroom.

'I think Sally's in the bathroom,' One of the lads called, as Biddy passed his open bedroom door. 'She's in and out of it, like a fiddler's elbow,' he laughed.

Biddy knocked gently on the bathroom door. 'Will you be long, Sally?' she called. 'I've still to get my bath.'

'Eah . . . d'you think you could you use the one downstairs?' Sally called back. 'I might be a bit longer.'

'Okay,' Biddy said agreeably. 'Call into my room when you're ready for goin' out.'

Biddy was pleased with the way her *brunette* hair had curled tonight. She twisted this way and that way on the little stool, looking in the mirror at her hair. She liked the way the lads had described her as a *brunette*.

After the bad start with Sally, she had now decided that tonight was going to be a good night. She could feel it in her bones. As she applied her lipstick, she thought how well things were working out for her in Stockport. She loved her work in the Grosvenor, and she loved working with Fred the barman. It was grand to have him to go to the pictures with, or to go out for a quiet drink now and again, without feeling that she was stuck with him. Biddy knew she wasn't ready to get stuck with anyone just yet. Not after the business with the baby.

Because of Fred's wrestling commitments, he wasn't around much at the weekends. The weekends were when he made his big money travelling to places like Liverpool and Newcastle. He said some weekend he'd take Biddy with him to watch him fight, but she didn't really fancy the thought of watching two big men knocking the hell out of each other. And Fred was a nice lad – she wouldn't want to watch anyone hurting him.

Anyway, with Fred not being about too much, it left Biddy free to do what she wanted when she wasn't working. And to see whoever she liked. She gave her hair a good squirt of lacquer and woundered if she should take up smoking full-time. She had tried it once or twice with the other girls in the hotel but only recently had got the hang of inhaling the smoke. Earlier on in the kitchen this evening, she thought that Sally looked quite sophisticated when she was smoking, and she woundered if she might look more attractive if she were to take the habit up, too.

Biddy looked in the mirror now and held her lipstick between her two fingers as though it were a cigarette. She threw her head back the way Sally did, to avoid getting smoke in her eyes. She moved around on the stool, pretending she was chatting to people, and waving the cigarette about so that people would notice her painted nails.

Biddy put the lipstick back into her make-up purse. She would try a cigarette at the club tonight, and see if she could copy the way Sally smoked. If she felt comfortable, then she just might take it up full-time.

There was a tap on her bedroom door. 'Are you ready?' Sally called. 'The lads are waitin' downstairs.'

'Arc you all right?' Biddy asked her, as they walked along the street. 'You seem a bit quiet.'

'I'm fine,' Sally said, chewing furiously on a piece of gum. 'What are the lavvies like in this place?'

'The lavatories? Oh, they're grand – well, they're grand at the beginnin' of the evenin', but they get terrible messed up by the end of the night.' She gave Sally a side long glance. 'And sometimes you have to wait in a fierce queue to get anywhere near them.'

A frown crossed Sally's face and she chewed her gum all the harder.

As soon as they arrived in 'The Wheatsheaf' pub for a drink, Sally disappeared off looking for the ladies'.

'Is the young blondie one all right?' Sonny, the Dubliner asked. 'She's not joinin' in the *craic* like she did earlier on.'

'I don't know what's wrong with her,' Biddy said with a shrug, 'Ruby said she's inclined to be on the moody side at times.'

'Not like our little darlin' Biddy!' he said, leaning over to put a friendly arm around her. 'You're always the one way, whatever the weather.'

Biddy said: 'Go away with you!' but she was secretly delighted, and deliberately leaned against him so his arm stayed around her.

After a few drinks, everyone started to move out of the pub in the direction of the Erin Ballroom. Biddy suddenly felt a hand clutching her coat sleeve as she walked out into the street.

'Wait on us, will you?' Sally asked, her eyes wide with anxiety. 'I need to go to the bleedin' lavvie again . . . I've got terrible cramps in me stomach.'

'I think she must have the runs! She's been in and out of the bog all night,' Danny called loudly as Sally rushed back into the ladies', her cheeks flaming red.

Biddy told the lads to go on ahead, and she stood waiting in the pub doorway until Sally eventually appeared. 'Are you all right?' she asked again. 'You're lookin' fierce pale.'

'Am I?' Sally asked, in a voice that was not so sneeringly confident as usual. 'Should I put a bit of rouge on, d'you think?'

'You can wait until we get to the Erin,' Biddy said, pulling her arm. 'The lads went on ages ago, and they said they'd try to keep us a seat. If we don't get a move on, we mightn't get in at all.'

They had to stand nearly a quarter of an hour in a queue to get into the dance hall, and as soon as they got inside the door, Sally disappeared in the direction of the ladies' room. Any sympathy Biddy might have had for her, was lost because Sally hadn't said 'thank you' to Biddy for paying her bus fare and the entrance charge to get into the ballroom. She'd also accepted drinks from the lads without so much as a thank-you, as if she was doing them a favour. This, Biddy knew, would be the pattern if Sally was to stay on permanently in Stockport and she dreaded the thought.

The band was brilliant, and as soon as it started playing Biddy asked Sally if she wanted to get up on the floor.

'Maybe later,' Sally replied in an off-hand manner. 'We'll give them a chance to warm up first.'

'I thought you were always the one first up on the dance floor,' one of the lads called across the table to her. 'You were braggin' about that this afternoon. We're all dyin' to see how you shape up.'

'I have to be in the mood for dancin',' Sally said in an irritated voice. 'An' I don't like all this Irish music – I prefer the more up-to-date stuff that you get in the dances in Liverpool.'

'If Liverpool's that great,' Sonny said with his Dublin candour, 'you should go back there.'

'Oh, I didn't mean it like *that*,' Sally said quickly. 'It's just I'm not used to it – it'll probably grow on me.'

'Come on then,' he said standing up, 'let's see how good you are at jiving.'

She glanced over anxiously at Biddy, who was just making her way to the dance floor with one of the other lads.

Biddy looked over at Sally several times, wondering how she was feeling. She didn't look as if she was enjoying herself at all. All the other couples on the floor were laughing and chatting and singing along with the band, and really throwing themselves into the serious business of jiving. Sally was holding herself very stiffly and not looking at all like the great dancer she had boasted to be earlier on. Then suddenly, mid-dance – and without a word of explanation to her dancing partner – she took flight in the direction of the lavatory.

'Jaysus!' Sonny, said as he passed Biddy on his way back to the table. 'How did we get landed with *her*? She's as odd as two bloody left shoes.'

Ten minutes later, a red-faced Sally appeared back at the table.

All eyes were on her.

'I'm feelin' a bit poorly,' she said moodily to no one in particular. She had turned her seat away from Sonny, blocking him out from her view and ignoring the fact she had left him standing on the dance floor like a complete idiot. Apologies were not something that came naturally to Sally Taylor. If they had, she would never have left Liverpool in the first place. For all her stories, it was obvious that she found running away easier than saying she was sorry.

When the dance was over, Biddy stood waiting for Sally at the door of the dance hall, just as she had waited for her in the pub earlier in the evening. She said nothing when a pale and sweaty-faced Sally eventually came out. They walked together to the bus stop in silence.

'Why didn't you go off with that fella from Manchester that you were dancin' with half the night?' Sally suddenly said, as they boarded the late-night bus. 'Didn't you fancy him?'

'He was all right,' Biddy replied, 'but I didn't like the thought of leavin' you to go home on yer own.'

Sally bristled at Biddy's pity for her. 'I would have been fine,' she countered. 'I could have gone back with the lads from the house.'

'They might not have been very nice to you,' Biddy said quietly. 'They've been laughin' and jeerin' at you goin' to the lavatory all night.'

Sally coloured up. 'D'you think they noticed I had the runs?' she whispered. 'I'd die if they knew that.'

Biddy nodded gravely. 'I think they did.'

Back at Sweeney's lodging house, there were the usual cups of tea and banter after the night out.

'So you weren't impressed with the Erin Ballroom?' Sonny asked Sally.

'It was okay,' Sally said, drinking a cup of water. She was frightened to drink anything else, and reckoned that the few drinks at the Erin had made her condition worse. She'd had to rush upstairs to the lavvie the minute she'd come into the house. 'It was just the mood I was in . . . I'd probably give it another go again next week.'

'Well, I reckon that you wasted your money tonight,' Sonny commented lightly.

Biddy bit her tongue, and didn't say: 'Well, actually, it was *my* money, not hers.'

'What d'you mean?' Sally put the cup down and folded her arm defensively. She often liked a good row with a lad that fancied her – she found that it made them run after her all the harder. Unfortunately, her stomach was not in the mood for a row tonight.

'Well,' he said, looking at the other lads in a sniggering manner, 'I reckon that you would have had a better evenin' for the price of a penny.'

'What the bleedin' hell are you gettin' at?' Sally snapped.

Sonny was not in the least bit fazed. He had already decided that her pretty face and blonde hair were all she had going for her. He liked a girl who didn't mind enjoying herself and having a laugh. In his book, Sally was too full of herself – and he was still annoyed at being left standing on the dance floor without a word of apology. 'I'm just sayin' that you might have had a better time if you'd put a penny in the slot of a public shithouse. You could have saved yer money and saved yer legs runnin' backwards and forwards, because you were in it the whole bloody night!'

Sally opened her mouth to answer him, but her words were drowned in jeering laughter from the other boys.

'Just ignore them,' Biddy said, getting up from the table to put her arms round the blonde girl. She walked her out into the hall. 'You go on up to bed, and I'll bring you a cup of boiled milk in a minute. They say that's the best cure for diarrhoea.' Her voice softened. 'I'm sure you'll feel fine in the morning . . . d'you want me to give you a call around seven to help with the lads' breakfasts?'

Sally paused for a moment. There was no way she was going to face that jeering pack again. Not in the morning – not ever. 'No . . . if I feel fine in the morning, the only thing I'll be doing is headin' back home.'

'But I thought you were stayin'?' Biddy asked in a shocked tone. 'I thought you an' me were goin' to be great pals?'

A sudden cramp came low down in Sally's stomach. 'Sorry, Biddy – but I think I was a bit hot-headed when I left me mam's. I only did it to spite her.' She turned towards the stairs. 'Maybe you could come and visit me in Liverpool. I could really show you how to have a good time there – the dance halls are tons better than that crappy place tonight.'

'Thanks, Sally – I'd like that,' Biddy said in a cheerful voice, and went back into the kitchen to boil the poor girl's milk.

Chapter Twenty-eight

Tara was up early on Monday morning. She had slept surprisingly well, but when she awoke with daylight glinting through the curtains in her old bedroom, she sat up with a heavy feeling in her heart. This was her last day in Ballygrace, and it was going to be one of the worst days of her life.

'A good breakfast will set you up for the day,' Kitty said, as she bustled about organising the table. 'I've baked some brown and white cakebread, because I know you like it. No doubt yer friend will have a fry in the hotel in Tullamore, so he'll be well set up too. He seems a grand fellow – have you and him been courting for long?'

'We're not courting . . . we're just friends.' Tara chose her words carefully. 'I've only known him for a short while. He's one of the customers in our office and my boss knew he was coming over to Ireland this weekend.'

'He's been very good to you,' Kitty said. 'He seems to think a lot of you.'

'Yes,' Tara agreed, 'he has been very good.' She knew she was deliberately being evasive with her aunt, but what was there to say?

'When do you think you'll come home again?' Kitty started spreading thick, creamy butter on the home-made bread.

'I don't know . . . it depends on work and everything.' How could she say she was saving every penny towards buying her own house in England, and that a holiday would take a big chunk of her money? And that wasn't the only reason. There was Gabriel Fitzgerald – and he was only one of a number of other reasons.

'I'm just thinking about your father,' Kitty said quietly. She turned towards the new range they recently had installed. 'He's been asking about you a lot. In his own way, I think he misses you.'

'How is he?' Tara asked, feeling a stab of guilt. 'I would have gone to see him and Tessie – but there just isn't the time.'

'We'll give him your excuses, tell him you were only here over-night.' She put a plate full of rashers, sausages, black and white pudding, and an egg in front of Tara. 'He got the sack out of the factory.'

Tara sighed. 'What happened this time?'

'The same as usual – drink and missing time off work.'

'They'll be struggling, Tessie and the family.' Tara lifted her knife and fork. 'Thank God he left me with me granda – I don't know what would have happened to me if I'd been brought up with him. We've never seen eye to eye.'

'And yet he has a fondness for you,' Kitty said. 'You can tell by the way he talks about you. He was fierce worried when you went off to England like that. He was back and forward here for weeks, checkin' if we'd heard anything from you.'

'Was he?' Tara said with some surprise.

'And he heard that Mrs Scully was gabbin' about you bein' sacked by the Fitzgeralds, and he tackled her about it. He told her in no uncertain terms that you'd left of yer own choice – which was the truth.' Kitty smiled. 'I believe she's buttoned her lip a bit more since then.'

Tara's heart sank at the mention of her old adversary. She had caught a glimpse of the housekeeper being helped into the church the previous evening, shrouded in two huge black mourning shawls. A long one around her ample body, and a heavy black veil over her head and shoulders. Two other women had linked her in, while she sniffled and cried into her hanky. In spite of her feelings towards the nasty old woman, Tara had felt a twinge of sympathy. Life would never be the same for Rosie Scully ever again. Instead of looking after a family, she would only have Mrs Fitzgerald and the new baby. They would all rattle about in that big empty house.

Mick joined them at the table and the conversation changed to the more mundane business of the poultry. As they ate their breakfast, the thought struck Tara that Elisha Fitzgerald might not stay in

Ballygrace House on her own. With Gabriel in Dublin, she would have no family close by. She would probably sell up and move back to Dublin.

Tara's fork halted halfway to her mouth. If her intuition was correct – *today* might be the last chance she would have to see Gabriel Fitzgerald.

Frank turned up in plenty of time for the funeral Mass, dressed immaculately in a sober black suit and tie, and a sparkling white shirt. Kitty fussed about getting him a cup of tea and some of her bread, which he politely ate, even though he had eaten a huge breakfast already.

In the midst of her confused thoughts about the funeral and Gabriel, Tara noticed how relaxed Frank seemed in the modest little cottage, chatting to Kitty and Mick. He was sitting now discussing the turf-cutting up the bog with her uncle, in the same easy manner he had discussed the different wines in the fancy restaurant in Manchester.

Frank Kennedy was a man for all seasons. A man who would fit in well with the lower classes or the Quality, and be accepted by both.

He was so different from Gabriel Fitzgerald Tara thought. Frank was a grown, independent man with his life already in order and his future well mapped out. And Tara knew instinctively that if she wanted it there would be a place for her in Frank Kennedy's glittering exciting future. Something told her they were a pair of a kind.

As she sat opposite him, at the scrubbed kitchen table that had been part of her childhood, she felt a surge of warmth towards him. The sort of feeling that she had only ever felt towards Gabriel. As yet, Frank did not engender the feverish excitement that came instinctively at the sight of her first, young love. But the possibilities were there.

Kitty pointed out several times that was a slight drizzle as it neared the time for the eleven o'clock funeral mass.

'That's no problem,' Frank said cheerfully. 'We'll all go up the church in the car, so.'

Tara saw Kitty's eyes light up at the prospect of a ride in the fancy motor, and she bit back her automatic refusal. 'That would be grand,

Frank,' she replied instead. What difference would it make now? Everyone had seen her in the church last night, and there would be no novelty in her appearing today. With the weather being so miserable, people would be rushing, heads down against the rain, and probably wouldn't even notice who had arrived in the fancy black car. She could slip in and out of the church unnoticed, without having to face the gauntlet of the other parishioners, heading to church on foot.

Tara gritted her teeth when they arrived at the church to find a huge crowd waiting on the funeral cars arriving. The weak sunshine had seen off the recent drops of rain. The situation was made even worse when several of the men moved to the gates, presuming that Frank Kennedy's car was one of the official mourning cars, or at least a VIP from Dublin who had come to mourn William Fitzgerald.

Her face burned red under the black mantilla, while Frank came to open her door, and then the passenger doors at the back for Mick and Kitty. As they gathered themselves together to make for the church, two shiny funeral cars rounded the corner and slowly loomed towards them.

'We'd better stand a minute,' Kitty whispered urgently to the others. 'It would look bad if we walk into church before the family now.'

All four stood silently as the cars came to a halt at the church gates only yards away from them. Tara turned back towards Frank's car, giving the impression of having left something inside it.

'Is there anything wrong?' he said, coming towards her. 'Have you forgotten something?' He made to open the car door.

'No . . .' she replied in a low voice, her body still turned towards the vehicle. 'I just didn't want to stand gawking when the Fitzgeralds are walking into church.'

There was a small silence, then Frank said: 'I think your friend has just seen you – the tall fellow with the blond hair.'

Tara lifted her head abruptly, and there, striding across the road was Gabriel Fitzgerald, looking unfamiliar in a dark hat which covered most of his hair. She gasped aloud, wishing desperately that she could run away.

He was closer now, taking off his hat. 'Tara?' he said. 'It is you, isn't it?'

Tara raised the front of the black veil, so that he could see her face. 'Hello, Gabriel,' she said in a measured tone, her heart thumping. In the months since she had last seen him, he was taller and looked older – like a grown man. He was an older, sadder version of the boy she had known. 'I'm so sorry about everything . . . about Madeleine and your father. It's terrible . . . the worst news I've ever had.'

'Did you come back home for the funerals?'

Tara inclined her head. 'Yes, of course. Wherever I was, I would have come back for Madeleine.' Her eyes filled with tears.

Gabriel nodded. 'We wondered where you'd gone . . .' He looked back in the direction of the funeral party. 'I'm afraid I have to go.' He took a step backwards, now looking straight into Tara's eyes. Gazing at her . . . as if he had never seen her before. 'Could I see you later on this evening – or maybe tomorrow? There are some things that Madeleine would have liked you to have . . . and I'd like to talk to you myself.'

For a timeless moment – a moment stolen from New Year's Eve – Tara looked back into his eyes. Even in the midst of his misery and grief, she could not fail to recognise the message that was there for her. It was the same stark look of physical attraction that she saw in Frank Kennedy's eyes daily. Gabriel Fitzgerald wanted to see her because he wanted to resume their prematurely ended relationship.

Tara's heart surged with all the old feelings for him – and she almost found herself saying '*yes*' that she would meet him tonight or tomorrow morning. '*Yes*', she would meet him any time he wanted.

Then, the reality of the present, awful situation came flooding back. The reality of Madeleine and her father's deaths. The reality of William Fitzgerald having raped her.

'I'm sorry, Gabriel,' she whispered in a croaky voice, 'but I . . . we . . . have to catch a plane early this evening . . . back to England.'

Gabriel shifted his gaze to Frank.

'This – this is a friend of mine from England,' Tara said. 'Frank Kennedy.'

Frank immediately stretched a hand out and shook Gabriel's. 'I'm very sorry for your troubles.'

There was a long pause.

'Thank you,' Gabriel finally replied in a clipped tone, his eyes narrowed as though he had a severe headache. 'I must go now.' He put his hat back on.

'Maybe . . .' Tara ventured, 'you could leave the things at the cottage . . . with my uncle. If it wouldn't be any trouble.'

Gabriel gave a vague smile and nodded. 'Yes . . . yes, of course. I'm glad things are working out well for you in England, Tara.' He reached for her hand, and held it for a moment.

Then, as quickly as he had appeared, he abruptly turned and vanished in the mist of tears that now filled Tara's eyes. She closed her eyes tightly and took a deep breath. When she opened them a few moments later, there was a determined figure marching purposefully towards her.

'A fine thing when a father has to come lookin' for his daughter!' Shay Flynn cried, loudly enough for anyone within yards of them to hear. He was all got up in his best black funeral suit, with a clean white shirt and a black tie, his curly black hair sleeked down in a tamer manner than usual. 'A fine thing I say, because – by all accounts – she has no intentions of coming looking for me!' He threw a scathing glance in Frank Kennedy's direction, letting him know that he had heard all about *him* too, and wasn't in the least bit daunted or impressed.

'Daddy—' Tara started to explain.

'And you all got up like the Quality for the Fitzgeralds' funeral!' Shay continued his diatribe, hands on hips. 'And ye wouldn't even give your own father the time of day! Disappearin' off to England with hardly a word, and then you sneak back without lettin' yer closest connections know! Yer poor mother – and yer granda,' he added as an afterthought, 'would turn in their graves if they were alive today.' He blessed himself. 'God rest their souls.'

'But I only came down overnight,' Tara explained breathlessly, feeling she would collapse if another unexpected person crept up on her.

'Oh, you were seen! You were found out!' Shay said, waving away her excuses. 'You were seen at the church last night, and it was reported back to me in a pub later. Bad news travels fast in Ireland!'

Tara's eyes narrowed at the mention of the word 'pub'. 'I'm only over for the funeral and I'm leaving straight after it for the airport. I'm back at work first thing in the morning.'

'Oh, *flying* is it now?' Shay said, his eyes looking her up and down. '*Aeroplanes*, begod! And you couldn't look in on yer poor oul father in Tullamore? You couldn't get yer boyfriend to bring you in to see me in his fancy car?'

Tara sighed in exasperation, aware that they were giving great entertainment to all the mourners going into the church. 'Frank's just a friend. We've had no time – it wasn't deliberate.' Her voice softened a little. 'Surely you wouldn't have expected me to miss Madeleine's funeral?'

'No! Indeed I wouldn't,' Shay spluttered, his face red with indignation, 'but I wonder if you'd be so quick to come back, if it was *my* funeral? Yer own poor father's funeral?'

'Come on now, Shay,' Mick intervened, pulling at his brother's arm. 'There's no need for that kind of talk outside of the church.'

Shay shrugged him off. 'She's no daughter of yours remember – only a niece,' he said churlishly.' And you're not the one that's been made little of. Parading herself around Ballygrace as if she was one of the Quality herself. She wouldn't spare a thought for her poor oul' father. Oh, no – no fear of that! An' him havin' a hard time of it, with no job an' hardly a penny comin' in to the house.'

Tara drew herself up tall. 'I'm going into the church right now,' she said determinedly. 'If you come back to Mick's after the funeral, we can have a chat then . . . and I'll see what I can do.' She had every intention of leaving an envelope with money for him in the cottage in any case. She only hoped Tessie was about, and that she could put the money in her safekeeping rather than her father's. She knew only too well that it would burn a hole in his pocket until he reached the nearest pub.

Shay's attitude suddenly changed and his high colouring began to fade. 'I'm not lookin' for anythin' off ye – no begod,' he countered, as though she had wounded his pride. 'Well . . . nothin' that I won't pay ye back . . . when I'm on the pig's back again.'

The pig's back? Tara thought as they walked across to the church. For an insane moment she had to stop herself from laughing out loud. She daren't even glance at Frank Kennedy, for she knew he would have seen the ludicrous side to the situation too. When was her father ever on the pig's back? Things never went well for Shay, because he never allowed them to.

Any pig's back he had ever sat on gave him a very short ride indeed!

Due to the delay, the group had to split up inside the church and squeeze into any vacant spaces in the pews. Tara and Frank found seats halfway up the church, while the others went nearer the back. Where Shay went, Tara had no idea, but she was glad he had melted somewhere into the congregation away from her.

'I'm really sorry about my father,' Tara whispered to Frank when they were settled in the church. 'I should have warned you about him . . .'

Frank shrugged and smiled. 'I've met his type before,' he whispered back. 'Sure, I have a few like that in my own family. Are you all right? Did he bother you?'

Tara rolled her eyes. 'I'm well used to him.'

Where normally one priest would have served the funeral Mass, there were six in attendance at this particular one, showing the high esteem the Fitzgeralds were held in. Tara's thoughts flitted backwards and forwards during the ceremony, dredging up early memories of her and Madeleine starting school together, embarrassing memories of the first day she walked to Ballygrace House, happy memories of Madeleine's birthday party . . . and then the awful memories of Madeleine's decline into mental illness.

However she looked at it, Tara could not understand what had gone wrong with her beautiful friend who seemed to have everything. All the advantages that Tara had lacked and sometimes envied. She came to the conclusion that money did not necessarily guarantee happiness. Look at all the money William and Elisha Fitzgerald had, and yet he had obviously not been happy in his marriage. If he had been happy, he would never have done the terrible thing that had made Tara move to England. The congregation rose to their feet, and without even knowing she was doing it, Tara followed suit automatically.

At Communion time, she saw the blond head of Gabriel as he went to kneel at the altar rails. Her heart leapt once again at the sight of him.

It was just as well that she didn't have time to meet up with him. Whatever he had to say, nothing could ever come of their relationship now.

In many ways the Fitzgeralds' funeral was one of the most formal, dry-eyed affairs that Ballygrace had ever seen. None of the locals – apart from Tara Flynn and the servants – had ever got to know the family well. It was in fact surprising that the funeral was held in Ballygrace at all. Tullamore with its much bigger and more imposing church would have seemed the most obvious choice – but Elisha Fitzgerald had deliberately chosen the small local church, hoping that it would draw less attention to the sad funeral service. Her plan had not succeeded. Mourners had travelled from far and wide and the crowd now spilled out into the courtyard of the church. They stood in silence, although they could neither hear nor see any of the service.

When the ceremony was over and the church doors opened, brilliant sunshine greeted the congregation. The coffins were carried out first and then the family and other mourners followed. The hearses were followed to the end of the village and then a large number of the people departed for home while the serious mourners carried on to the cemetery for the burial service.

Tara had thought long and hard about going to the cemetery, and decided that she would not. It would involve all the business of cars coming back, and in order to be sure of a lift she would have to take Frank. Also, there was the question of whether she would be asked to join the funeral party back at Ballygrace House or wherever they were having the customary refreshments. Between all that and the awkwardness of seeing Gabriel again – Tara decided that it was best to finish her public mourning in the church.

The Flynn contingency drove back to the cottage in Frank Kennedy's car, Shay unusually complain at the thought of the forthcoming boost to his finances.

'Did you see that oul' Scully one?' he said in an amused tone as they drove along. 'She collapsed coming down the aisle, and had to be helped to her feet by the two hefty daughters. She was worse than Our Lord under the cross!' He clucked his tongue in disapproval. 'I'd say she was more worried about the thoughts of lossing her job an' the money, than seeing off oul' Fitzgerald an' his daughter.'

Tara pursed her lips tightly but said nothing. She had no wish to be a hypocrite defending Rosie Scully. She had indeed seen the house-keeper's performance in the church.

When the Fitzgeralds, their relations, and people of renowned respectability had gone down the aisle behind the coffins, the main group among the local women mourners had been the Scully family, headed by the housekeeper herself. Rosie's gimlet eyes had peered through the gap in the black veil, scrutinising each and every pew, to see who had come to pay their condolences. And more importantly – to see who was missing.

Her eyes had lit on the elegant Frank Kennedy – he being a black stranger – then darted to the sophisticated woman by his side. An overwhelming rage had risen inside her when she realised that the woman in the sombre finery, was none other than that brazen brat, Tara Flynn!

Her watery eyes bulged with hate as they met the unflinching, brilliant green eyes. The green eyes that looked back defiantly, re-fusing to be intimidated by Rosie Scully – or anyone else like her – ever again. The housekeeper read the message in those eyes, saw the grand clothes and the distinguished man by her side. At that instant she realised that the battle between herself and Tara Flynn was over.

They would never again meet on common territory.

It was only a matter of time now, Rosie had forecast that morning. Only a matter of time until she was put out to pasture. Like a worn-out oul' heifer. There were no doubts about it. Elisha Fitzgerald would move to Dublin or London until after her child was born, and Ballygrace House would be closed up and maybe even auctioned off. There would be no more big houses to look after. Not by Rosie Scully. Her housekeeping days were over.

Even before the deaths of William Fitzgerald and his daughter, Rosie had known her days were numbered. The last weekend that Gabriel had come home, he had caught her with her ear glued to the sitting-room door. She had been eavesdropping on a row between him and his parents, having been drawn like a magnet when she heard. Tara Flynn's name being bandied about in angry tones.

Her fatal mistake had been getting down on one arthritic knee to see through the keyhole. When she heard Gabriel yelling that he intended asking the Flynn one to marry him, she had frozen on the spot. She was still rooted, unable to move, when the hot-headed young man had yanked the door open, and came flying out of the room. Rosie's pretence at polishing the brass on the door – without the necessary polish and cloth – had cut no ice with Gabriel.

'You,' he had yelled, 'are a traitor in this house! Over the years you have been rude to guests and have spread malicious rumours about them. My mother should have got rid of you long ago!'

Rosie had staggered to her feet. 'Indeed an' I haven't done any such things!' she spluttered. 'I've always thought the world of the family – every one of ye – and defended ye to everyone outside that would run ye down.'

But Gabriel did not have the patience or the interest to listen to her excuses. He turned away and then ran up the stairs, taking them two at a time.

'Is there a problem?' William Fitzgerald called from inside the room.

'No . . . no, sir,' she had called back in a shaky voice. 'It was just a small accident . . . me and Mr Gabriel bumped into each other in the hall.' She put a hand on the jamb of the door to steady herself. 'No harm done – I say. No harm done.'

But harm had indeed been done, and Rosie Scully was both perpetrator and victim at the same time. She had caused the problem by her own devious nature, and she knew that the time was coming when she would have to suffer the consequences.

The housekeeper made sure that she had kept to her own corner of the house until Gabriel had gone back to university. Things seemed to have settled down and she had almost put the incident to the back of her mind when she overheard her own name being discussed by William and Elisha. There had been no eavesdropping on this occasion, and it was quite by accident that she heard the conversation on the upstairs landing, as she was slowly mounting the stairs.

'I was informed by one of the girls in the office that Mrs Scully has been gossiping in Ballygrace about Gabriel and Tara Flynn,' William told his wife.

'What sort of gossip?'

'Apparently she's been spreading it around that Tara had thrown herself at him, and had hoped to eventually trap him into marriage. The implication was that she planned to lure him into a relationship, which would result in a pregnancy and a shotgun wedding.'

'Surely not?' Elisha gasped, groping her way to sit down upon one of the deep window-ledges on the landing. 'Mrs Scully wouldn't do such a thing – I've always found her to be loyal.'

'Then you are very fortunate, my dear,' William replied, both hands gripping his jacket lapels. 'I'm afraid I have caught her out gossiping on numerous occasions recently.' He took a deep breath. 'She even made suggestions about the poor girl throwing herself at *me* when you were in London.'

Elisha's head sunk into her hands.

'It would be laughable,' William said, stroking her hair, 'if it weren't so serious. Can you honestly imagine a young beautiful girl like Tara Flynn being the slightest bit interested in an old man like me?'

'She'll have to go,' Elisha said in a low voice. 'We can't allow this sordid nonsense to go on. She can't be trusted any more . . . God only knows what she might say next. Our private lives are becoming common knowledge – fodder for the locals.'

'Don't upset yourself,' William soothed. 'I'm sure no-one takes any notice of the old crone. It's only people as low as herself who would pay any attention to her ludicrous gossip.'

'Nevertheless – she'll have to go,' Elisha repeated. 'We'll leave things as they are until after the baby's born and then we'll talk to her.'

'I'm sure a few pounds' pay-off will take the sting out of it for her, although it won't replace all the perks she has helped herself to from the larder and the sherry stock.'

'We've been too soft with her for too long,' Elisha said, getting up on her feet again. Sitting on a hard surface had started nagging cramps in her back.

Very slowly, and very carefully, Rosie Scully had retreated back down the stairs and into the kitchen – her head a complete whirl after what she had just heard. They were going to get rid of her after the baby came! That was only a matter of a couple of months – weeks even. And she only trying her best to uphold the family name. Not once had she said anything wrong about Mr and Mrs Fitzgerald – in fact she loved bragging about them and all the nice things in Ballygrace House. Sweet Jesus! It was the only thing she'd ever had to brag about in her life. Oh, she might have said the odd thing about Gabriel and Madeleine, how they were spoiled with their ponies and everything, but criticising them was only another way of bragging. Of highlighting the difference between the Quality and the ordinary folks.

She had looked around the warm, cosy kitchen. The home from home, that would be no more. The same went for the thick slices of the best pork and beef, the butter and the eggs, and the comforting glass of sherry that gave her miserable life a small glow. Everything would be gone but not forgotten. With that final thought, Mrs Rosie Scully had lain her head down on her heavy, work-scarred arms and wept.

Later, when the Fitzgeralds had come back down the stairs and acted as if everything was normal, the housekeeper had felt a little ray of hope. Maybe – just maybe – if she kept things ticking over nice and quietly, they might change their minds. They might forget all about the ups and downs. Oh, and she would keep her mouth shut – good and tight. As if she had a zip sewn over it. There was no need for any more talk. Tara Flynn would be put out of her mind forever. With the new baby due soon – and Rosie Scully an old hand at making up bottles and changing nappies – happier times could be round the corner.

It was the sound of all those lost dreams ringing in her ears, coupled with the sight of Tara Flynn, that had brought Rosie Scully to her knees in Ballygrace church. Down she went like a sack of spuds, the black veil slithering over her face and chest, as she sprawled out on the cold church floor.

There was a commotion for a few moments, as arms flew from all quarters to heave her back to her feet. She was guided into the nearest pew, her heavy coat loosened, and told to lean back and take deep breaths. By the time she had straightened up again, and was once again wearing her shawl in a dignified manner, Tara Flynn and her distinguished escort had already filed out of the church.

Tara felt guilty as she watched her father and Frank chatting back at the house. She had run Shay down to the lowest, and yet here he was, being as charming and personable as anyone could expect. To give Frank his due, *he* had made a great effort with *everyone* he had been introduced to. Again and again, Tara had to remind herself that she had only got to know this man recently. This handsome, wealthy, intelligent man who she had utterly depended on through this terrible weekend.

'So ye reckon there's always work across the water?' Tara heard her father say now. 'An' would ye say that even an oul' fella like meself would find it easy to get work . . . well-paid work?'

'The kind of work that's available would be very hard work,' Frank said seriously, 'heavy labouring. It wouldn't suit an idle man.'

'Begod no,' Shay agreed, his curly black head bobbing up and down. 'And what manner of foreman would want to take on an idle man? Only an eedjit!'

'Exactly,' said Frank, turning to accept a cup of tea from Kitty.

Shay took a cup from her as well, unusually profuse in his thanks.

'How are Tessie and the children?' Tara asked the question in all sincerity, but also as a diversion from the disconcerting conversation she had just overheard. The thought of her father ever coming over to England brought a strangling feeling to her throat.

'Oh, they're grand,' Shay said affably, 'not a bother on them. Tessie will be sorry she missed you.' He looked Tara in the eye. 'She thinks very highly of you, you know.'

There was an accusation in his voice which Tara did not miss. 'And I think very highly of Tessie too,' she replied curtly. You could only think highly of a person who put up with her father, day in, day out. 'Tell her I'm sorry I missed her this time. I'll see her and the children next time I'm over.' She leaned closer to her father, so no one else would hear. 'Make sure she treats herself and the children out of the money – make her buy a nice dress or something for the summer.'

'Begod, I will,' Shay beamed, patting the breast pocket of his jacket, where the money was safely tucked. The thought of it suddenly struck a chord. He waited until Tara was distracted then he looked over at Mick, trying to catch his attention. When he did, he made the gesture of drinking a pint to him, an indication that they might slip off to the pub. It was the done thing among the locals to give the deceased a liquid send off, and particularly necessary on such an auspicious occasion. It wasn't every day that Ballygrace saw a double funeral – never mind the fact that the departed were Quality. Mick lowered his brow, shook his head, and mouthed 'later' back at him.

Shay swallowed his disappointment along with one of Kitty's sultana scones, and pondered on his discussion with Frank.

Tara found it very strange parting with Frank Kennedy. He got a taxi from Manchester Airport to drop her off at Sweeney's, and then said he must head back to his own place to sort out some paperwork.

'Won't you come in for a cup of tea?' She asked him through the taxi window, She was surprised at how easy it was to say that to him now. Only last week she had been thinking of every way to avoid him.

'Thanks, but – no,' he replied. 'I'll be in touch with you in the next day or two, when I've had time to talk over your situation with the building society.'

'That's good of you,' she said quietly. 'And Frank . . . thanks again for everything this weekend. I would have found it very difficult without you.'

He stretched his hand out of the window and pulled her closer to him. 'It was my pleasure.'

His dark brown eyes looked deep into hers, and she could feel his warm breath on her face. Before she could stop herself, Tara leaned forward and kissed him on the mouth. In a moment, his arm came tightly round her neck, holding her very close to him. She had really meant it as a quick gesture of thanks, but somehow, it had turned into something else.

As Frank's lips pressed hard against hers, Tara felt a shiver of pleasure run through her body. How long it would have lasted, she didn't know, but the taxi driver brought it to a quick end when he coughed loudly.

'I'd better let you go,' Tara said, moving reluctantly away from the taxi window.

'I hope,' Frank replied in a low voice, 'that you won't let me go. I'll be in touch soon.'

She lifted her bags from the kerb, and then stepped back as the taxi pulled away. She could still see Frank's arm waving from the end of the road. And she was still quivering from his kiss.

Biddy was on a late shift at the hotel, and since Tara was too exhausted from travelling to wait up for her, it was the Tuesday evening after work before they had a chance to catch up on each other's news.

'I went to Mass this morning down at Our Lady's Church,' Biddy told Tara. 'I know it wasn't the same as being at the funeral, but I felt as though I was taking a little part in it.' She lowered her head. 'I lit a candle for Madeleine and her father – and I lit one for you as well. To make sure you didn't have a crash in the plane.'

'That was nice of you, Biddy. The plane was absolutely fine.' Her face softened. 'I said a prayer for you in Ballygrace Church, too.'

'Did you?' Biddy looked delighted. 'How was everybody? Yer Uncle Mick and his wife?'

'They were fine,' Tara told her. 'But it was very sad looking at the two coffins . . . it was the worst thing I've ever seen.'

'Did you see Gabriel?'

'Yes, he spoke to me just before the funeral.' A silence fell between them, then Tara said: 'How was the weekend here?'

Biddy brightened up a bit – but not too much, in case she might appear disrespectful to the dead. 'There was this girl here . . . Ruby's niece. She was planning on moving in, but she changed her mind and left this morning.' And she then proceeded to relate the saga of Sally and Sunday night at the Erin Ballroom.

Chapter Twenty-nine

'You can start house-hunting now,' Frank Kennedy told Tara as they came out of the building society the following week. 'And considering you're a single young woman – I reckon they've been very fair with you.'

Tara was grinning from ear to ear. 'I'm delighted! But I'm sure they wouldn't have agreed to a mortgage without you vouching for me.'

'The fact you got an excellent reference from the estate agents, and had a good bit saved up really clinched it,' he told her. 'Hard cash always talks, and the more money you have, the more you can borrow.'

For a moment Tara was reminded of William Fitzgerald and the advice he was always giving her. She quickly brushed the thoughts aside. 'I'm going to start looking at houses straight away,' she told him enthusiastically.

'I'm glad you didn't put all your money down as a deposit,' Frank said. 'It means that if you run into any difficulties with people paying rent you'll always have something to bail you out.'

'I have plans to make sure I *never* run out of money,' she told him earnestly. 'I'm going to look for an evening or weekend job – anything at all. I would prefer if I could get work bookkeeping, but I'm quite happy to try my hand at something different, so long as it pays.'

'If you're working evenings and weekends,' Frank said with a frown on his handsome face, '*when* will I get to see you?'

'We'll see each other – don't worry,' she reassured him. 'We'll cross that bridge when we come to it.'

*

Three weeks later, Tara had laid the foundations for her new life. With Frank's help, she found a large Edwardian semi about a mile from Ruby Sweeney's. It was closer to her office in Bramhall and only five minutes walk away from the Park Hotel where she would work as receptionist two evenings a week and Saturday and Sunday mornings. Frank had also helped her to find the job.

The house was situated on the corner of a tree-lined avenue, with lawns to the front, side and the rear. It was a beautiful redbrick semi-detached house with three bedrooms, and on the first viewing, Tara fell in love with it. There were details like the mosaic-tiled hallway with the sweeping staircase, the marble fireplaces, the intricately patterned, stained-glass windows, and the servants' bells in the kitchen, which made her think of Ballygrace House. Although different in many ways, the English house had a similar feeling of grandeur – and it made Tara worry about how she could even think of affording such a place. Although the building itself was solid enough, it needed quite a bit of work done both inside and out in the garden, which was completely overgrown.

'I wouldn't have advised you to look at it if I felt you couldn't afford it,' Frank stated, as they were being shown round the house for the second time that week. 'I know it needs a bit of work, but I can get that done for you at cost price. I know electricians and plumbers who are quick and cheap,' Frank smiled now. 'Well, quick*ish* and cheap*ish*, for workmen!'

They both laughed. This was just another of the things which made Tara warm to Frank Kennedy. His down-to-earth manner and good sense of humour made her feel happy to be around him – more and more of the time.

They paused on the staircase to study the beamed hallway and the beautifully carved, dark wood panelling on the walls. Frank ran his hand over the grained wood. 'All the original features are still in the house. Nowadays,' he pointed out, 'a lot of people think that's old-fashioned and are busy ripping them out. If you leave them as they are, I'm sure they will be a selling point for the house in the future.'

Tara looked doubtful. 'I'm still not sure I can afford it. I'd really only thought of buying a little two-up, two-down. Using one bedroom myself and renting out the other.'

When they reached the top of the stairs, Frank threw open a bedroom door, revealing a large, airy room with an ornately decorated ceiling and more of the beautiful stained-glass windows. 'You could fit three single beds into this room. That's three weeks' rent.' They moved on to an equally large bedroom next door. 'That's another two weeks' rent,' he commented. 'You'll find that the rent easily covers your mortgage, without having to put any of your wages into it at all.'

'What about furniture?' Tara suddenly thought.

'Second-hand,' Frank replied. 'There's loads of places around Stockport selling second-hand stuff. And the more you buy from the one place, the cheaper you'll get it. You only need basic stuff for boarders. Think about Ruby Sweeney's. It's clean and tidy, but the furniture is basic and cheap.'

They went into the bedroom which faced out to the front. Tara walked over to the large bay window and looked down into the garden. Frank pointed out a school across the road, saying that it would be quiet in the evenings and weekends, and during the summer holidays. The boundary fence of the school had flowering cherry trees, and large beech trees lined the pathway outside. She looked, imagining how the garden with the sad-looking apple tree and the overgrown flower borders would look after a good week's work.

Suddenly, all her fears melted away and Tara decided that this was the house she really wanted. Frank was right. There was no point in buying a smaller house outright, which would involve no great effort or sacrifice. Money not committed would just disappear, he had warned her. 'I've made all my money from chancing my arm,' Frank admitted. 'You have to think big – that's the way all good business-men work.' He grinned at her. 'When you find how easy it is to make money from renting, I guarantee you'll be looking for a second house in the not too distant future.'

Tara was shocked and disappointed when Biddy said she did not want to move into the house with her. 'But I thought we had always planned on that,' she said in a hurt voice.

'That was in the beginning,' Biddy said apologetically. 'That was before I had started work in the hotel and at Ruby's. Livin' here suits me fine. I like Ruby and it's handy for work and everythin' else.'

'But we've only been over in England a short time,' Tara argued. 'I thought we'd stick together for the first few years.' She lowered her head. 'Is it because of *me*, Biddy? Is it because you think I'm too serious . . . that I'm not as easy-going as Ruby and the lads?'

Biddy shook her head. 'No – no, of course it's not! It's not anything that . . . I just don't want to move. It's the first place I've ever felt happy in me whole life, and I don't want to leave it. I like helpin' Ruby, and I know it's stupid . . . but I have a funny feelin' in me bones that if I move from here, things will start to go all wrong again.' She put her hand on Tara's shoulder. 'Don't be bad friends with me over it, Tara – please!'

'We won't fall out over it,' Tara conceded, although she had no understanding of Biddy's fears. 'We're adults now, and I've got to make decisions that suit me, and you've got to make decisions that suit you.'

Biddy wasn't being awkward when she told Tara she was afraid to move. She felt safer with Ruby than she'd ever felt in her whole life, and she wasn't ready to give that up just yet. Lately, there seemed to be reminders about her old life around every corner. A little foxy-faced Irishman man had come into the hotel bar the other day, and after chatting for a few minutes, had asked Biddy where she came from. When she told him, he laughed aloud, saying he was from Edenderry in Offaly. He said he had been a postman for two years in Ballygrace, before moving over to Stockport.

'It's a fierce small world,' he told her, 'and none of us would want to be hiding secrets from anybody, for you never know who you might meet. Oh, we'd all be quickly found out.' Biddy had failed to halt his searching questions. Within minutes, he had pinned down that she was one of Lizzie Lawless's orphans. There was no way of hiding it. He had asked straight out who her connections were, and exactly what house she had been brought up in.

He said that he was back and forward to his elderly parents in Edenderry fairly often and that he could look in on Lizzie, if Biddy liked, and give the old woman her best wishes. Thankfully, Fred had appeared with the man's drink just at the right time and it had given her the chance to escape to the kitchen. She had stayed in there helping to wash up until the man had gone.

Biddy knew, without a shadow of a doubt, that the next time he was in Offaly he would run about with more legs than a hen to make enquiries about her. And the people he met would not be slow to relate the story about her bastard baby, and about poor Dinny Martin who got the blame of being the father.

Just the thought of it made Biddy shudder and feel sick.

What if the foxy-faced man came back into the hotel, and told the story to Fred? All the work she had put into her fresh start in Stockport would have been for nothing.

It didn't bear thinking about.

The visit from Father Daly tomorrow didn't bear thinking about either – the visit he had cancelled a few weeks ago, and then suddenly wrote the other day to say he had managed at long last to organise. *Nothing*, he had written, would prevent his visit this time.

The visit that Biddy was dreading.

It was just another tentacle stretching out from the dark waters of Biddy's past in Ballygrace. And the only safe raft in the middle of all this was Ruby Sweeney's house. The house that Biddy could be another person in. A ordinary girl, living in an ordinary house. The house that *nothing* would make her leave, for the time being. Not even her long-standing friendship with Tara Flynn.

Father Daly arrived at six o'clock the next evening. He had sailed over the previous night from Dublin on the boat, and then driven from Holyhead to the convent near Buxton. After a couple of hours' sleep in the afternoon, he had eaten something light and then had made his way out to Stockport to see Biddy.

'Well, well, well,' he said, when Biddy opened the front door to him. He took off his black hat, revealing sparse grey hair, and looked her up and down. 'If I met you out in the street, I wouldn't have known you . . . not a bit of it.' He stepped inside the lodging house. 'That certainly makes up my mind,' he said. 'We must eat out at a nice restaurant tonight. Only the best for such a sophisticated young lady.' Food and drink was a very important factor in the parish priest's life, as was borne out by his purplish nose, heavy jowls and good-sized paunch.

Biddy tried to smile, but her mouth froze in a tight line. 'If you come through to the kitchen, I'll introduce to you to my landlady – Mrs Sweeney. Tara's upstairs, I'll give her a shout in a few minutes.'

'So, the situation with the address I gave you didn't work out?'

Biddy shook her head. 'She would only take one of us, and we didn't want to separate.'

'You're happy and content here?' the priest checked.

'I am.' There was no mistaking the determination in Biddy's voice. 'I have no intention of moving for the foreseeable future.'

Father Daly pursed his lips and bobbed his head up and down.

Several of the Irish lads were still eating their evening meal in the kitchen. Seeing the clerical collar, they downed knives and forks and stood up respectfully. There was also an element of guilt, wondering if the priest could tell that they had abandoned their Sunday Mass and Catholic duties since coming to live in England.

'Finish your meal, lads,' the priest said in an over-jovial jovial tone, squeezing Sonny on the shoulder for good measure. He stretched a hand out to Ruby Sweeney. 'So this is the lady who has been looking after my young parishioners?' He shook Ruby's hand. 'A fine place you have here.'

He was sitting down at the table, drinking a cup of tea and eating a slice of apple tart, when Tara came in. 'Tara Flynn,' the priest said, getting to his feet. 'Terrible business about your young friend and her father. Ballygrace hasn't got over it yet.' He held her hand tightly between both of his. 'I never got a chance to talk to you at the funeral. I believe you came and went very quickly. I called down to your uncle Mick the day after, but you'd already gone.'

'Work, Father,' Tara said quietly, easing her hand out of his grip. 'I could only get a day off work, so I had to travel straight back.' Already, Tara was feeling uncomfortable with this man of the cloth.

'Ah, yes,' he sighed, sitting back down. 'Unfortunately, the English don't make the same ceremony out of funerals as we do.' He gave a little smile in Ruby's direction. 'Who's to say which is the right way and which is the wrong? I'm afraid in Ireland, we still stick to the traditional ways of doing things. The mourning can take up to a week.'

'You have the day off tomorrow?' The priest waited in the hallway, as Biddy was making upstairs to get her new summer coat. When Biddy nodded, he said: 'Good. In that case, bring a few personal items in a bag, just in case we stay overnight in the . . . convent. You'd better warn the landlady, too.'

Biddy stared at him with wide eyes. 'I'd rather come back,' she said quietly.

The priest's eyes narrowed. 'We have a number of things to talk about, Bridget, and it may take longer than a few hours.' He jingled his car keys. 'Run upstairs and get what you need,' he said firmly. 'Somthing nice and feminine. I'll wait for you in the car.'

As they drove out through Stockport and into the rolling hills of Derbyshire, Father Daly did most of the talking. 'Have you a boyfriend?' he asked, holding the steering wheel in one hand, and unbuttoning his white collar with his other.

'Not really,' Biddy replied, looking out of the car window at the hills and ploughed fields.

'I mean,' Father Daly said, 'have you a boyfriend like PJ Murphy or . . . Dinny Martin? A boyfriend who you let kiss and feel you?'

Biddy kept starting out of the window. 'No, they're just friends.'

'So, there's no chance of any more babies for the time being?' he said in a low voice.

'No . . . and I have no intentions of having any more. Not until I'm married.'

'Very sensible,' the priest commented. 'It's a pity you didn't think of all that before.'

'I was young . . . I didn't know any better.' She turned towards the priest. 'When I came to you at Confessions for the first time – when I told you about Dinny – I was only fourteen years of age. What did I know?'

'Our Lady was only a young girl when she gave birth to Our Lord,' he replied, throwing the clerical collar over his shoulder into the back seat. 'The age business has nothing got to do with religion – it's a culture thing.' He waved his hand in the air. 'They're all man-made rules and laws. Look at the business with Jesus and Mary Magdalene.'

Biddy bit her thumbnail and stared out of the window.

'Jesus,' the priest went on, 'didn't care for the rules and conventions of the Jewish faith at the time. He consorted with her, when no one else would bid her the time of day.' He put his hand on Biddy's knee. 'Just like me with you, Bridget. When everyone else in Ballygrace cast you aside, because you brought an illegitimate child into the world – who stood by you? Well?'

Biddy looked out of the window again, and tried to move her leg out of his grip.

'*I* stood by you, did I not?' he said, sliding his hand up between her thighs. 'I sorted you out with the convent in Dublin, and then with all the adoption business.' His hand moved up to the fleshy part at the top of her legs. 'I've always looked after you . . . my own little Mary Magdalene . . . and you must always look after me.'

Biddy squeezed her legs together tightly, until he moved his hand. A short while later, they veered off the road which went to Buxton, further into the Derbyshire country.

'I thought you said we were goin' to Buxton?' Biddy said sharply.

'Did I?' he said in an amused tone. 'Well, we might call in there after breakfast in the morning. The nuns said, if I could make it, they'd like me to say a late morning mass.'

'Where are we goin' now?' Biddy asked quietly.

'To a nice hotel,' he replied. 'Somewhere that we won't be known. We'll have dinner there tonight, and then we can go out for a walk or a drink later.'

Biddy slunk down in her seat and stared straight ahead. The ghosts of Ballygrace had caught up with her once again.

Chapter Thirty

The legal and financial business of buying the house was completed by the end of October. Two of the lads from Ruby's who were painters and decorators gave all the rooms a coat of paint, which made a huge difference. Tara then advertised in the local hospitals for any nurses who needed lodgings, and placed an advertisement in the local papers for 'professional business-women'.

Whilst the paperwork was being done on the house, Tara had accumulated the necessary furniture and had stored it in a warehouse belonging to a friend of Frank's. She had originally planned on second-hand stuff for the bedrooms she would rent out and new furniture for her own bedroom. But, when she looked at the new stores in Stockport, she changed her mind. There was no comparison between the quality and beauty of the old carved furniture and the characterless modern stuff.

Another thing which swayed her, was the similarity of a marble-topped mahogany bedroom suite to one she had seen in Ballygrace House. In the end, she bought pine furniture for the spare bed-rooms, a three-piece suite for the sitting-room, and a dining-room table and chairs, from an Italian dealer in Stockport. She also bought the mahogany bedroom suite for herself, plus a number of large rugs.

'I was told you would take something off the price for cash,' Tara said confidently.

'You're a good businesswoman, and know how to drive a hard bargain,' the Italian had laughed, but he knocked a good bit off the price, and threw in a dark wood coffee table and a hall stand as well.

There were other necessary items which Tara could not buy second-hand. She took her time comparing prices of curtains, towels, bedding, pots and pans, a kettle and a teapot and other odds and ends. When she was satisfied she had the best deals, she bought those, too. Luxury items such as pictures and ornaments she decided could wait.

The piano, sadly, would have to wait even longer. Tara had visited a huge musical shop in Manchester, and had priced the sort of piano she wanted. Even the most basic model was out of her reach at the moment. She could have signed up to buy one on a hire-purchase agreement, but every instinct told her not to do so. If anything should go wrong at all with the rent – then she might not be able to meet the payments on the piano.

However disappointed she felt, Tara would not let it spoil the excitement of moving into her new home. She knew without a shadow of a doubt that she would eventually get her piano – and exactly the type she wanted. It would be worth the wait.

As Frank promised, all the work that needed doing in the house was completed within a week, and the following Saturday he helped her to move in.

'Didn't I tell you it would be all right?' he said with a grin, as he helped carry in the last piece of furniture. 'It's all ready for your lodgers to move in tomorrow.'

So far, Tara had interviewed and accepted three young nurses who would share the big room. A schoolteacher in her thirties, who had come to Stockport, would move into the room with two beds. Miss Woods said she would prefer to pay extra for a room on her own, rather than share with a stranger. When she got to know the other teachers in the area, she said, she would perhaps be willing to share.

'Fine,' Tara had agreed. The woman looked so harmless and repectable, that Tara felt she would be a steadying influence on the younger, giddier nurses. She understood the teacher's feelings because she was delighted to have a room to herself, after sharing for so long with Biddy. She told Miss Woods that if she could find someone to share the room within a month, she wouldn't charge her the extra for having the room to herself in the meantime. This, Tara reasoned, would save her having to advertise and interview people, and then take a chance on them. She was quite sure that Miss Mary Woods would find her a perfectly acceptable lodger who could afford to pay the rent on time.

Tara gave the furniture remover five shillings for his help, then she whispered to Frank: 'You haven't forgotten tonight, have you?'

'Not at all!' He smiled and ran a hand through his dark hair. 'I'm really looking forward to it. It's not often that a beautiful young lady insists on taking me out for a meal.'

'It's the first time I've done such a thing myself,' she smiled, 'but it's the least I can do, to thank you for all your help.'

Frank bent his head and lightly brushed his lips on hers. A hot feeling of passion rose up in her immediately, and her body instinctively started to move to meet his. Then she drew back, conscious of the fellow watching from the van.

'I'll pick you up at seven,' Frank told her, as he climbed in the removal van, 'and then you can decide where we're going.'

When she closed the front door, a wave of excitement – different from the one Frank had just evoked – ran over her. She pressed her spine against the heavy wooden door, and looked around the imposing reception hall and the swirling carved staircase. *You, Tara Flynn,* she said aloud, *own this beautiful house. You own every single bit of it . . . and it's just a start. Sometime in the future, you're going to own somewhere every bit as grand as Ballygrace House!*

Biddy called to her friend's new house to see how things were going around six o'clock. Tara was in a dressing-gown with her hair wrapped up in a towel.

'I can't believe me eyes!' Biddy said, as she opened one door after another. 'I've never seen anythin' so grand-lookin' – it would put you in mind of Ballygrace Castle. You'd think you'd been livin' here for years.'

'You don't think I'm mad for having bought it?' Tara said quietly, when they were sitting at the small table in the kitchen later, sipping tea.

Biddy reached out and took Tara's hand. 'This is the sort of place you belong . . . where you've always belonged.'

'Thanks, Biddy,' Tara whispered. 'It's just that when I was younger I could never have imagined myself owning a house like this.'

'When we were younger,' Biddy replied, 'there was a lot of things I could never have imagined happenin' to me . . . terrible things I wish had never happened. It's only when you get older that you realise how bad they were.'

'Are you thinking about the baby?' Tara asked cautiously.

Biddy sighed and looked down into her cup of tea. 'That's the worst thing. Lately, I keep wondering what it would have looked like . . . whether it would look like me or . . .'

Tara reached over and put her arms round Biddy's shoulders. 'We all have things we regret happening.'

Biddy looked up at her friend, large tears in her eyes. 'You never did anything wrong in yer life, and apart from Gabriel Fitzgerald, you never even looked at any of the local lads. And even then, I'm sure you only kissed him . . . isn't that all?'

Tara nodded. How could she tell Biddy that Gabriel hadn't done anything wrong? How could she say: *It wasn't Gabriel – it was his father!* Looking back, she wished now she had lost her virginity to Gabriel Fitzgerald, for although it would have been a sin, it would have at least been *normal*.

'What about Frank?' Biddy asked. She loved girlish gossip, and it wasn't often Tara was in the mood to talk like this. 'He's a bit older than you . . . he doesn't look the type that would wait forever for . . .' She wiped away her tears with the back of her sleeve. 'He's so handsome he could have any girl he wants.'

Tara took a deep breath. 'To be honest, I'm worrying about it. So far, he's been quite content with kissing and cuddling . . . but I don't know how long that will last.'

Biddy drained her tea. 'Just make sure you don't make the same mistake I did,' she warned. 'There are things a man can buy to make sure that nothin' happens. Things that stop you havin' a baby.'

Tara coloured up. Trust Biddy to assume the worst. 'I don't think I need to worry about anything like that.' She looked at the clock. It was twenty to seven. 'I'll have to get ready now,' she said getting to her feet. 'Frank will be here any minute.'

'Oh, I nearly forgot,' Biddy said, lifting up her handbag. She took out a small, tissue-wrapped parcel and handed it to Tara. 'It's only a little thing . . . I'll get you a decent present when I get me wages.'

Tara opened it carefully. It was a holy-water font, with a picture of Mary and Joseph and the baby Jesus on it. 'Thanks, Biddy – it's lovely,' she said gratefully, 'I'll put it by the front door.'

Later that night, after a lovely meal in Manchester, Tara had cause to remember Biddy's words. Since she had always invited Frank in for a cup of tea or coffee at Ruby's, he had automatically got out of the car and followed her into the new house. As soon as the front door was closed behind them, he pulled her back and wrapped his arms around her.

'You are the most beautiful girl in the world,' he whispered, whirling her round and burying his face in her hair. 'And it's nice to have you to myself at last. We never have any time on our own at Ruby's; there's always an audience around. Sometimes I feel that we're like two teenagers, with everybody checking up on us.' He gave a laugh and then started to kiss her neck and throat in a small pecking manner. 'It's ridiculous – and me the age I am.' He suddenly stopped and looked deep into her eyes. Then slowly, he guided her backwards, until her back was pressed up against the wood panelling which she had polished lovingly earlier in the day.

Then, he bent his head and kissed her full on the lips – light at first, then much harder. Harder and deeper than he had ever kissed her before. His arms tightened round her, and then Tara felt his full weight pressing against her, pinning her against the wall, as his mouth crushed down on hers. His body moved even closer to her, until she could feel the unmistakable male hardness pressing into her groin.

Suddenly, William Fitzgerald's face swam before her eyes. It was *him* all over again . . . *his* hands, *his* mouth, the hard part of *his* body pressing into her. A feeling of revulsion and nausea overwhelmed her, and she violently moved her head sidewards to prevent Frank kissing her, then went limp in his arms until he released his hold.

'Is there something wrong?' he asked, his voice slightly hoarse.

Tara avoided his gaze. 'I'll put the kettle on,' she said quietly. She slipped past him and opened the kitchen door.

Frank followed her into the kitchen, a deep frown on his handsome face. 'Have I done something wrong?' he asked again.

'No,' Tara replied, keeping her back to him as she filled the kettle. 'Would you mind checking the fire in the sitting-room? I banked it up before we went out, but it might be a bit low.'

A short while later she came into the sitting-room with a tray of tea and fruit cake. The fire had come to life again, and Frank was sitting on the sofa. Tara placed the tray on the coffee-table, and after pouring out the tea she sat down in one of the armchairs.

'What's wrong, Tara?' Frank said again, this time sounding really worried. 'Have I suddenly got the plague or something? Even with all the crowd in Ruby's you managed to sit closer to me than this.'

Tara swallowed hard. 'It's just that we're not usually on our own . . . and I feel a bit overwhelmed.'

There was silence for a few moments, then Frank got to his feet and came over and crouched down by her chair. 'It's okay, Tara,' he said in a comforting tone. 'Everything's okay. If you feel I'm rushing you, then I'll back off.'

A wave of relief washed over her. 'I'm sorry,' she replied in a tiny voice. 'I'm just not ready for anything – for anything – physical. It's something I never planned on before . . .' How could she say '*before marriage*' to this older, sophisticated man? 'I've never been in a relationship like this before.'

'That's okay,' Frank said soothingly, his finger tracing a pattern on the back of her hand. 'We've all the time in the world.' He leaned forward and kissed her gently on the mouth. 'You're very special to me – and I can wait as long as you want me to. You're worth waiting for, Tara Flynn.'

The lodgers moved in the following day as planned. Tara felt a wave of pride when she heard the admiring comments about the newly painted bedrooms, the furniture and the nice bedspreads. This is only the start, she said to herself. The first rung on the ladder to becoming a fully independent woman. Just as long as the rents come in regularly, and the mortgage and bills are paid – everything will work out fine.

Getting into a routine the first week was much harder than Tara had anticipated. It meant rising at six-thirty to get herself sorted out for work, calling her boarders, and then rushing downstairs to the kitchen to start cooking breakfast for everyone. She ruefully thought how easy she had had it in Ruby Sweeney's boarding house, with Biddy serving breakfast most mornings, and having a hot meal put down to her by Ruby or Biddy every evening.

Coming in after a hard day's work in the office was worse still, knowing that there were potatoes and vegetables to be peeled, and meat to be cooked for the hungry boarders. And then there was the shopping in between which Tara had quickly worked out, would have to be done during her lunch-hours. If she waited until after work to do it, it just slowed the whole evening up.

By Friday evening of the first week, Tara realised that turning dreams into reality came with a price – hard work and exhaustion early in the evening. It did not however, deter her in any way. When the boarders came in from work and handed her their rent money, she felt a glow of satisfaction, which made everything worthwhile.

That first Friday evening – after the evening meal was over and everything cleared up – Tara sat at the kitchen table and wrote out a new timetable, shopping list and menus for the following week. She could now see that there were ways that she could save time, like setting the breakfast table the night before, and asking the girls to sign a weekly sheet for cooked breakfasts or toast or cereal. Also, a neighbour she bumped into, had offered to do the weekly washing of towels and bed linen for a very fair price.

'You're surely not changin' all the beds every single week?' Biddy had gasped when she heard. 'Ruby does it every fortnight.'

'But she deals mainly with working lads,' Tara reminded her, 'and most of them would happily go *months* without clean sheets. I have nurses and teachers, and they expect different standards. Don't forget we changed our own bed at Ruby's every week, and even Ruby did her own.'

Biddy shrugged. 'I'm just thinkin' of the extra work for you. It can't be easy for you on your own, and havin' to do a full-time job yersel.'

'I'm managing,' Tara said confidently, 'and it will be worth it in the end.' She comforted herself with the thought that if everything went to plan until Christmas, then she could think of taking on someone like Biddy to share the cooking and cleaning chores. But for the time being, she was more than willing to keep things running on her own.

Tara was also happy with the way things were turning out with Frank. The more she saw of him, the more relaxed and confident she felt in his company. She had warned him that she wouldn't have much time on her hands for socialising for the first few weeks, and he had understood completely.

'You're preaching to the converted,' he had told her when he popped into the office on Friday afternoon. 'I had to do the same thing myself when I came over to England first. It was a case of working and sleeping for the first two years, and it wasn't easy. The other lads were out drinking and dancing from Friday evening until Sunday night, while I was still slogging it out. But that dedication,' he pointed out, 'is what makes the difference.'

'You don't mind not going out this weekend?' she had said. 'I feel exhausted, and I still have a lot of things to sort out.'

Frank shook his head. 'It's not a problem. In fact, since I have the time on my hands, I think I might head over to Ireland for a few days, or even the week.'

Tara raised her eyebrows in surprise. 'Again?'

'I could do with visiting my mother and father. I didn't get down to Clare when I was over with you, and they write every week asking when I'm coming home.' He shrugged. 'I mightn't make it back for Christmas, so I'll go now while things are quiet. All the contract work seems to be going well. The teams I have at the moment can be trusted to work away on their own.' He stroked her hand discreetly, lest Mr Pickford should be watching. 'And since you're not available, I'll only be at a loose end. I'll call in at the travel agents shortly, and I'll take the first flight I can get.'

Tara felt a pang of disappointment. Not going out with him was one thing, but knowing he was across the sea from her was another. 'You'll let me know as soon as you get back?' she said anxiously. 'I should be more organised by next weekend, and I'll be ready for a night out then . . . besides, I'll miss you.'

'Good girl,' he said giving her a wink. 'I'll ring you at the office as soon as I get back.'

'You've made a good contact there,' Mr Pickford commented as the door closed. 'Frank Kennedy has an excellent business head on his shoulders. I'm sure his speaking to the building society on your behalf was instrumental on the mortgage going through so easily.'

'I think it certainly helped,' Tara agreed.

'Having said that,' Mr Pickford peered over the top of his spectacles, 'I'm sure he can see the same ambitious qualities in yourself. Like attracts like. I'm sure you'll do very well in your boarding business.'

Tara gave her boss a warm smile and turned back to her typewriter.

The second week of running her small boarding house went more smoothly. All the little changes had made a big improvement to her routine. When Friday came round again in the office, she found herself reaching for the phone in the hope it was Frank back in Stockport. By five o'clock, she had resigned herself to the fact that he was still in Ireland.

It was Tuesday of the following week when he eventually called from Country Clare. 'I'm really sorry,' he said at the other end of a crackly line, 'but there's a few problems I need to sort out – and a bit of business. I hope to be back at the end of the week.'

The end of the second week came and went, without another word from Frank. By that time, Tara was feeling tired and edgy, and unable to concentrate on anything.

Perhaps, she found herself thinking, he has decided to move his business over to Ireland. He obviously had contacts in Dublin and further down the country. Surely, she reasoned, he would have told her of any such plans. Or would he? Had he reacted badly to her rebuff the last night they were together in the house? Was it possible that he had decided she wasn't worth waiting for any longer? He had pointed out that he was a mature grown man, and although they had never discussed it, Tara knew that he must have had physical relations with some of the women he had courted before meeting her.

It was definitely a case of not missing the water until the well ran dry. Until he had gone, Tara never realised just how big a part in her life that Frank Kennedy played: all the business with buying the house, organising the jobs that needed doing, and a million and one things that she needed just to talk over with him.

And of course, it didn't end just there. Tara found she actually missed his hugs and kisses, and his soothing words of encouragement. Over the two weeks she had spent on her own, she had gone over the situation between them, and had come to the conclusion that there was no comparison between her relationship with Frank, and what had happened with William Fitzgerald. She realised that Frank was not capable of hurting her in that way – he was too genuine for that.

'I'm off this evening,' Biddy said when she called round on Sunday afternoon. 'Some of the lads are going to try a new dance hall in Stockport – why don't you come with us?'

Tara put down her sewing needle. She was busy hemming a pair of curtains for the bathroom. 'I can't,' she sighed. 'I don't know whether I'm coming backwards or forwards, I have so many things to do.' Today already, she had left the cooked breakfast in the oven for the boarders, worked the ten until two shift in the hotel reception, cooked lunch, and still had evening Mass to attend.

'You haven't been out with us for ages,' Biddy said in a wounded tone. 'Surely you can manage *one* night when Frank's not here?'

Tara paused. She had been so caught up in the new house, that she had not had much time for Biddy lately. However different paths their lives might take, Biddy was very important to her. She had to make the time. 'Okay,' she said, forcing a bright smile on her tired face, 'maybe a night out would do me good.'

It might take my mind off Frank too, she thought.

Even before they stepped inside the dance hall, Tara had her doubts about this new place. The queue outside had taken ages to move, and there had been a lot of pushing and shoving from some fellows who were obviously the worse from drink.

When Lloyd was shunted into Biddy by one of the drunks, he turned on them saying: 'Where's your manners? That's a young girl you nearly sent flying into the wall!'

'Listen to the darkie!' one of the drunks jeered. 'Talking as if he owned the place. I'll bet he's just swung out of a tree in the jungle.'

'Mind your mouth!' Sonny warned him.

'Dirty bleedin' Irish . . . they're as bad as the fuckin' blacks!' another lout called from the queue. 'You should all get back to yer own countries, and leave us in peace.'

At that point the doors opened, the crowd surged forward, and the argument was swallowed up. Tara heaved a sigh of relief when they were safely inside and she saw the trouble-makers heading off to a lounge in another part of the building.

'The music's grand, isn't it?' Biddy said excitedly. when they took to the dance floor. 'It's a change from that oul' Irish music in the Erin, isn't it?'

As usual, they were not short of partners, as the fellows from Ruby's boarding house danced with them one after the other. Although they were not exactly her type, over the months Tara had got to know them better. She found that they were all decent young fellows, and they were also very good dancers. She was pleased when the tall, graceful Lloyd danced her, as it gave her a chance to say she felt awful about the abuse he had taken from the drunks earlier on.

'It don't matter,' he said, smiling at her in his shy way. 'I'm used to all that shit . . . I get it on the building sites regularly.' He clapped a hand over his mouth. 'Sorry about the language . . . I shouldn't have said that to a lady like you.'

Tara laughed. 'I've heard a lot worse in Ireland, but I'm grateful for the compliment.' She relaxed in his arms, chatting and enjoying herself as he guided her round the beautifully polished floor. When the music finished, they stood chatting for a few moments then the band struck up a Glenn Miller number. Lloyd asked if she wanted to stay up for another dance.

Before Tara had a chance to reply, two rough hands grabbed her by the shoulder and swung her round. 'You dancin'?' one of the drunken louts from the queue asked, his gaze disorientated and his mouth slack from the effects of the alcohol.

Tara froze. Her immediate reaction was to walk off the dance floor, but something held her back. She looked at Biddy. Sonny – having been elbowed out of the way – had left the floor, and Biddy was now dancing with the fellow's equally drunk companion. It was the rule in most of the dance halls that you did not refuse to dance with a man, and although she felt repulsed by her partner, she realised she had little option. She gave a shrug of apology to Lloyd, knowing that he would be the target of the drunk's anger if she refused him.

Reluctantly, she moved into his outstreched arms. As soon as they moved together, Tara felt as though she were tangling with an octopus with no sense of direction as he roughly propelled her round the floor.

'What's a nice girl like you,' he slurred in a Manchester accent, 'doin' with a dirty black nigger?'

Tara stiffened up. 'He's a very nice lad, and he's neither dirty nor a nigger,' she replied frostily. 'For your information he happens to be West Indian, and *I'll* dance with whoever I like.'

He grinned, impressed by her spirit. 'You're another Paddy, then? You don't look nowt like a Paddy.' He leered drunkenly at her. 'You're the best-lookin' Paddy I've ever seen!'

Tara turned her face away from him, feeling revulsion at his beery breath and the smell of sweat emanating from his armpits. *The cheek of him!* Criticising Lloyd – a boy who was meticulous in his hygiene and dress. He was the most fashion-conscious of all Ruby's male boarders, often accompanying Biddy on her shopping trips to buy the latest style of shoes, shirts or ties.

They circled precariously round the floor, Tara deliberately looking over his shoulder at the other dancers, the bar or the floor. Looking anywhere except at her partner. When the dance eventually ended, Tara pulled away from him.

'We'll stay up for another one.' he told her, gripping her by the arm.

'No thanks,' Tara said firmly, pulling away. 'I'm sitting the next one out.'

He put his other hand round her waist, ignoring her refusal. 'You've been up with the fuckin' darkie for more than one dance,' he snapped, 'an' if a darkie's good enough to dance with, then I'm not goin' to be refused.'

'Let me go!' she hissed, pushing him so hard that he staggered backwards into the other dancers. Someone pushed him away and he staggered again – as though doing some elaborate sidestep dance – and eventually landed on his backside in the middle of the floor.

'Fuckin' Irish bitch!' he yelled, his voice echoing loudly round the dance hall.

In seconds, two burly men with white shirts and red dicky-bows appeared on the scene. Taking an arm each. they yanked the drunk off the floor and propelled him towards the main door, as he kicked and cursed in protest. They were followed by his three loud-mouthed friends, one of whom stopped to call back to Tara: 'All the Irish and darkies in this place are dead!'

The manager of the dance hall, outraged that such an incident should happen on their opening night, insisted on calling two taxi cabs to ensure that Tara and the others got home safely.

'That's the first and last time in that place,' Biddy moaned as she got out of the taxi at Ruby's. 'We'll stick to the Erin Ballroom, or the other Irish places in future. At least we're mixin' with our own kind there.'

Tara bade them all goodnight, and then the taxi took her off to the peace and safety of her own house – and to her thoughts of Frank Kennedy.

On Tuesday evening after the office had closed, Tara was walking along to her bus stop when a familiar black car pulled up. 'Frank!' she called delightedly, running round to the passenger side of the car. She opened the door and jumped in. 'What happened? I thought you would have come back sooner.'

'Did you miss me?' he asked, hugging her tightly.

'Indeed I did!' she replied without hesitation. 'You wouldn't believe how much I missed you.'

'Well now,' he said, leaning back in his seat to look at her, 'I'm delighted I went away, if that's the effect it had on you.' His brown eyes twinkled. 'Maybe I should go away more often?'

'Don't you dare!' Tara said. 'I had a terrible weekend without you.'

Frank started up the car. 'What was so terrible about it?' They pulled off in the direction of Tara's house.'

'I went with Biddy and the others to a new dance hall in Stockport,' she told him,' and there was nearly a fight. This drunken fellow was really annoying me up on the dance floor.'

Frank looked alarmed. 'Did he hurt you?'

'Not at all,' Tara reassured him. 'The staff made short work of him. But we had to come home in taxis, in case they were waiting for us outside.' She hesitated. 'They were really horrible to us because we were Irish, and they were worse to poor Lloyd.'

'Lloyd?'

'The nice black fellow in Ruby's.'

'His colour no doubt,' Frank said, shaking his head.' 'It's the first thing eedjits like that go for. No one got hurt though?'

'No . . . no.' Tara hesitated for a moment. 'Was there a problem in Ireland? With you being so long.'

Frank negotiated the bend past Bramhall Hall, then started up the hill towards Davenport. 'There was a bit of a to-do in the family, and my mother and father took it badly. I couldn't leave them until things were looking a bit better.'

'What happened?' Tara asked curiously. Then, colouring up with embarrassment, she said: 'Unless it's personal, of course.'

Frank kept his eyes on the road. 'It's my younger sister – she's got herself into a bit of trouble with a local lad.'

'Oh . . . I'm sorry to hear that,' she said quietly.

Frank shrugged. 'She's not the first and she won't be the last. The problem is, she's only seventeen, and the lad's not up to much.'

'Will they get married?'

'That's not on the agenda.' he said almost snappily. 'I had to drive her up to an aunty's house in Donegal. She's going to stay there until after the baby's born. She's going to have it adopted, and then she can come home with no one the wiser.'

'I'm sorry.' Tara said again.

'Anyway.' he said suddenly sounding cheerier. 'Will we go out tonight? We can go for a meal or we could find out if there's anything good on at the pictures.'

Tara linked his arm and learned her head on his shoulder. 'I'm really pleased you're back.'

He took his left hand from the steering-wheel, and tousled her curly red hair. 'Not half as pleased as I am.'

Later, Tara lay in bed going over the evening in her head. Tonight Frank had behaved like a perfect gentleman – just as he had promised. He had made no physical advances towards her apart from a few tender kisses. But she realised that this could not go on forever.

After the awful night at the new dance hall, Tara knew she didn't want to go back to that kind of social life again. Although she liked being with Biddy and the lads, she knew that *their* idea of a good night out was not hers. The fiasco on Sunday night had merely confirmed it. While she was still perturbed by the incident, when she called at Ruby's the night following the incident, the others – including Biddy – had been joking and making light of it. As far as they were concerned, it was par for the course of being Irish people in England.

The fact that they were willing to accept such bad treatment appalled Tara, and she knew that not all Irish people were the same. Even though Frank owned the Erin Ballroom, it was only a money-making business to him. It was not part of his social life, and he never went into it as a customer. His dealings with the place and the other ballrooms were strictly business. For pleasure, he went to places that were quiet and discreet, and where people judged him on his achievements, and not his nationality or accent.

Through her relationship with Frank Kennedy, and her previous friendship with the Fitzgeralds, Tara now leaned that way too. She was held in high esteem in her office, and with the banks and building societies. It was a natural progression of the way she had lived her life in Ballygrace. She had never been one of the main-stream crowd, and even if she wanted to, she would find it very hard to start now.

Having always been an individual, she found it easy to continue along that familiar path. Besides, she was no longer lonely. Frank had changed all that. With him by her side, she would not have to worry about being abused by drunks on a dance floor, or dreading who she would have to sit beside on the late bus back home. But Tara knew that in order to keep a handsome, successful man like Frank Kennedy at her side, a price would have to be paid.

The price would include forgetting that Gabriel Fitzgerald ever existed – and also forgetting that his dead father had raped and robbed her of her virginity. It would mean learning to show her feelings in a normal, healthy manner – instead of cringing every time Frank laid a hand on her.

To continue onwards and upwards with her new ambitious life, she – like Biddy – must leave the ghosts of Ballygrace behind.

Chapter Thirty-one

'Are you sure you shouldn't try to phone Tara first?' Tessie Flynn said anxiously, handing her husband a pile of freshly ironed clothes. 'She mightn't take kindly to you landin' on her without any warnin'.'

'Phone – me arse! What would the likes of me be wantin' wi' a phone? Isn't she me daughter – me own flesh and blood?' Shay stuffed the carefully ironed shirts and underclothes into a battered holdall. 'It'll be time enough for her to know that I'm comin' when I arrive tomorrow. Sure, you know what Tara's like. If she was in bad humour, she could find a million excuses to stop me goin' over – and the very next day she could be moanin' and givin' out that I never took the trouble to go an' see her.' He lifted the brown paper bag containing his working boots and squeezed them into the holdall. 'And in any case,' Shay went on, 'wasn't it Frank Kennedy that encouraged me to go over? Wasn't it *him* that told me there was a job waitin' for me any time I wanted? Since when did I ever need Tara's permission to go anywhere?'

'That was months ago.' Tessie wearily reminded him. 'It's nearly December now, and there mightn't be the same work going.'

'Well, there's one thing for sure,' Shay stated. 'There's more work goin' on over in England, than there is in this feckin' kip of a place!' He yanked a bit of string through holes he had made in the top of the holdall to replace the broken buckles.

'Can you not wait until after Christmas?' Tessie pleaded. 'Jimmy Doyle said he could get you work in the creamery over the Christmas holidays.'

'Feck the creamery,' Shay said, 'and feck Jimmy Doyle! I'm not goin' back into that place to be treated like a young school lad. Now, Tessie,' he warned, 'I have no more time for arguments. I've to be outside church in ten minutes to catch a lift from the priest. If I miss him, I've no other means of gettin' to Dublin.'

He walked over to the door, where his good black winter coat was hanging on a nail. It was a cast-off of Joe's which the trainee priest had grown out of. Shay wore it for Mass on Sundays and special occasions like funerals. He put it on now, as it was easier to wear the heavy coat travelling, than have it all creased by carrying it in a bag.

'But think of the childer over Christmas,' Tessie implored. 'They'll be askin' where you are . . . and if Santy's bringin' them anythin'.'

'There's a better chance of Santy comin' to them if I get a few weeks' work behind me in England.' Shay's eyes lit up at the thought. 'Sure, it could be the makin's of us. If I can get a decent job wi' big money, then we could all be movin' to England! This time next year, we could all be on the pig's back.'

Tessie looked back at him with dark-ringed eyes. Shay was always full of big plans that came to nothing. Since being fired from the factory earlier in the year, he had been in and out of various jobs – none of which lasted very long due to his drinking.

He had been harping on about going to England since Tara's visit, saying all he needed was the fare over and he'd be gone like a shot. Tessie had taken no notice of him – but last night he had fairly taken the wind out of her sails. He had come back from visiting Mick and Kitty in Ballygrace – surprisingly sober – and brandishing the price of a single ticket from Dublin to Holyhead. He made no mention of the extra few pounds. Mick had given him, which was concealed in his inside pocket.

'It'll be the grandest Christmas we'll all have this year,' he prophesied. 'There will be no shortage of anythin' once I get settled in across the water. Oh, you know me once I get started. I'll be workin' every minute there's daylight – from dawn until dusk.' He rubbed his hands together gleefully. 'There'll be no holdin' us this Christmas – Santy will be humpy-backed carryin' turkeys and toys into the Flynns' house!'

'You'll definitely come home for Christmas?' Tessie asked anxiously.

Shay made the sign of the cross on his chest. 'As God's me judge.' Then, he gave his wife a kiss, and the children a salute of farewell. He lifted the battered holdall, and made his way out of the house and into the cold winter air.

A feeling of exhilaration raced through Shay's wiry body as he walked jauntily towards the church. He felt so good, he could have tap-danced his way along the icy street. For years he had dreamt of having this wonderful freedom, far away from all the responsibilities and feelings of inadequacies that pervaded his life. And now – at long last – his dream was coming true.

Shay had no intentions of returning to Tullamore for Christmas. None whatsoever. Like a dog let off the leash, he would not return to captivity for as long as he could help. And he hadn't really lied to his wife. He said he would return for Christmas, but he had not specified which one. Christmas of the following year would be soon enough for him.

Oh, he would certainly do his bit by Tessie and the kids. He would send home the guts of his first week's wages the very minute it was put in his hand. And he would send home the *second* week's as well. If the money was as big as he heard tell, they should have the finest Christmas they'd ever had. That should please Tessie and ease his conscience at the same time.

He would only need a few shillings for himself. He wasn't a selfish man. Enough for a couple of pints after a hard day's work. Sure, didn't any man deserve that? He wouldn't need to concern himself with lodgings or the likes. Hadn't his eldest daughter bought a fine house for herself, and was taking black strangers in off the street? What objections could she possibly have to putting her own father up?

Shay smiled to himself. For once, he was definitely on the pig's back.

Tara was looking forward to the first Christmas in her own house. It would be lovely and peaceful, and she was planning a well-earned rest. She had over a week off work, from Christmas Eve until after New Year. And the best bit about it was the lodgers. All of them were heading to their respective homes for the holidays. Tara would take things easy, with only the few hours' work in the hotel reception over the weekend. They were busy and she couldn't let them down. Still, there would be no rushing cooking breakfasts and in the evenings she could suit herself. She was always welcome for an evening meal at Ruby's, and she and Frank would probably eat out on other nights.

Things were quiet in the office at the moment. Mr Pickford was using the time to sort out a new filing system and although Tara and Jean were kept busy, it was in an easier manner than normal. She had written earlier on to Kitty and Mick, explaining that she had now bought the house and apologising for not making it back for Christmas. She planned to send them something nice for Christmas like a fancy bedspread, or maybe some sheets and pillowcases – something special that Kitty wouldn't find locally. She would send money to her father and Tessie as usual, and clothes and books for the children. Tara felt books were very important, and doubted whether Shay would encourage the children to read, the way her granda had always encouraged her.

She was planning to write to Joe again before Christmas, too. He would be back in Tullamore as usual in a few weeks. She had written over a month ago to give him her new address, but so far had heard nothing from him. Life as a trainee priest, Tara supposed, was probably very busy. In the next few weeks, she would shop for all her Christmas presents and then get them posted nice and early. Then, she would begin to wind down, and look forward to the rest over the holidays.

Biddy was more rushed off her feet than ever. The Grosvenor Hotel had started its Christmas functions in mid-November, and the restaurant and bars were heaving with office 'do's' nearly every night of the week. Biddy didn't mind a bit. Whether she was cleaning the guest rooms upstairs, serving behind the bar, or cleaning up in the kitchen – people appreciated her willing and cheery manner. Her bulging purse at the end of every night was evidence of the appreciation, as she received more tips than any of the other staff.

At Sweeney's boarding house, Biddy and Ruby had got back to their usual way of running things, after the Sally episode. Biddy still giggled to herself when the thought of Sally rushing to the bathroom every ten minutes came into her head.

She and Ruby were the only females in the house now, and that was exactly how Biddy liked it. Having said that, Tara had never been any competition where the lads were concerned and there were odd times when Biddy missed sharing a room with her.

Although Tara was only a ten-minute walk away, Biddy had little time on her hands for visiting just now. Things had really moved forward with herself and Fred the hotel barman, and they were going out a lot more. In order to see more of Biddy, Fred had dropped some of his weekend wrestling bouts, and had asked the assistant-manager if they could be rostered to have the same nights off together.

Up until recently, Biddy had kept her social life with Fred and her nights out with the lads in Ruby's very separate. It had been a case of hedging her bets. Whilst Fred was very attentive and good to her, he wasn't exactly the kind of fellow Biddy had imagined settling down with. Although he had a pleasant nature, no one could have described the muscular, red-faced Fred as handsome.

The lads in Ruby's were a different matter . . . especially Danny and Sonny. Biddy had always had an eye for them, but no matter how many nights she went to the local dance halls with them in a group none of them ever asked her on a proper date. Biddy couldn't work out what she was doing wrong, because she knew they often took other girls out to the pictures.

It was a funny situation, because, on a couple of occasions late at night, she had found herself kissing and cuddling on the settee with one of the lads. If the truth be told, she had been in that position with nearly all of them – even Lloyd, the black lad, and one of the older men who'd been nice to her as well.

A few times she had even let Sonny or Danny into her bedroom when Ruby wasn't around. They reminded her of her old love from Ballygrace – PJ Murphy. And like PJ, they didn't stop at the kissing and cuddling for long. Their hands were quick to unbutton her blouse, loosen the hooks on her brassiere, then roughly fondle her small breasts. And recently, she had even allowed them to slip their hands up along her legs, and fiddle around with her stockings and suspender belt.

It was funny that after all the years of letting Dinny do whatever he liked to her, that Biddy now found herself unable to go any further than kissing and petting. She always stopped when it started to get really serious. The picture of the little baby she had left with the nuns always came into her mind. Another little orphan baby – just like the abandoned baby she once was. No matter how much she was enjoying the kissing and cuddling, she couldn't ever let that happen again.

'It's all right,' Danny had coaxed on one occasion, his hands roaming urgently over her body. 'I've got one of them rubber things.' He started to unbutton his trousers. 'I'll put it on and we won't need to worry about anythin'.'

Biddy had pushed him away, muttering it was the wrong time of the month. Reluctantly, he had buttoned himself back up, then, cursing under his breath, had left the room. The next morning when she was going to the bathroom, she had overheard him and Sonny talking as she passed their bedroom door.

'Did you have much luck with little Biddy last night?' Sonny asked.

'Nearly,' Danny bragged, 'I'd say it won't be long now. I'm gettin' closer every time. I'd say she'd have let me ride her last night, if it hadn't been for her woman's trouble.'

Sonny roared with laughter – much to Biddy's shame. 'She's the only girl I know who has woman's trouble every week instead of every month! She's used the same oul' line wi' me as well, on several occasions.'

'I'll bet you a pound, that I ride her before you,' Danny stated.

'You're coddin' yersel', man. Biddy's only up for a kiss and a bit of an oul' feel. She's savin' the rest for her weddin' night – like a good Catholic girl.' Sonny gave a mocking laugh. 'We may look elsewhere. I think we'd have more chance wi' Ruby.'

Biddy heard a hand being slapped on the bedside cabinet. 'There's the pound,' Danny challenged. 'I bet you I'll ride her before Christmas is over. An' I'll do it for the price of a couple of "Babychams" at the dance hall. Wait and see.'

'You'll get no peace from her if you start that business,' Sonny warned. 'She'll be lookin' for a weddin' ring off you before you know it.'

'You must be jokin'!' Danny sneered. 'She might put up a decent breakfast – but she's not the type you'd want to look at every mornin' for the rest of yer life.'

'If that's yer attitude,' Sonny laughed, 'then you'd better keep yer mickey tucked in yer trousers. That one's desperate for a man to marry her. You can see it leapin' out of her.'

Biddy had turned and tiptoed back to her own bedroom. Once inside, she had crawled into her double bed, pulled the covers over her head – and quietly bawled her eyes out.

The next morning at work she agreed to start 'going steady' with Fred. And that very night – she brought him round to Ruby's and introduced him to all the lads. Biddy could see they were impressed that she had such a big, strong-looking boyfriend. When they found out Fred was a wrestler, they were even more impressed.

Strangely enough, a few weeks after they found out about Fred, Danny asked Biddy if she'd like to go to the pictures with him. He obviously saw her as more attractive, now she had another lad after her. Even though her initial reaction was one of delight, Biddy quickly remembered the conversation she had overheard about herself.

'Thanks for asking me, Danny,' she said, giving a bright smile, 'but I'm not interested in goin' out with anybody except for Fred.'

The surprised look on Danny's handsome face said it all. *Never*, Biddy vowed, would she give any man the chance to use her again.

Chapter Thirty-two

Shay pressed the doorbell, and kicked the snow off his good low shoes again. He knew he'd have been better off wearing his old working boots, but Tessie had warned him that Tara wouldn't be impressed if he turned up looking like a tramp. He put his holdall on the step, cupped his hands together and blew into them. If he thought it was fierce cold leaving Ballygrace, the cold in Stockport was fiercer still.

A dainty, blonde woman in a tight-fitting dress opened the door. She looked at him expectantly.

Shay stood tall inside his priestly son's cast-off coat. 'Sorry to be botherin' you, ma'am,' he said, vaguely tugging his forelock. 'But would you, by any chance, have a Miss Biddy Hart here?' Shay kept his eyes glued on the prettily made-up face, not daring to let them roam in the direction of her ample breasts.

Ruby Sweeney gave him a beaming smile. 'You've come to the right place, but I'm afraid she's not in at the minute. She's gone shoppin' down town with her boyfriend.'

Shay's shoulders drooped in disappointment. This was the second blow he had been dealt in the last half an hour – and maybe he was about to have the second door shut in his face. He suddenly felt very weary from the long journey and the effects of all the beer he had drunk on the boat last night.

'Come in, love,' Ruby said warmly. 'We can't have you standin' on the doorstep in all this snow. And anyway, Biddy won't be that long. Not on an afternoon like this.' She held the door open wide, to allow Shay and his shabby holdall to pass through.

'That's very kind of you, ma'am,' he said, taking off his cap to reveal his boyish, curly hair. 'You see, it's really me daughter I'm after. She would be a friend of Biddy . . . a Miss Tara Flynn be name.'

'*Tara?*' Ruby's voice was high with surprise. 'You're *Tara's* father?'

'I am,' he smiled, 'for me sins. I've just travelled over on the boat from Ireland.'

'Fancy that! I bet it was bloody parky on a boat in this weather?'

'Indeed, it was, ma'am.'

'Tara boarded with me until she got her own place,' Ruby informed him now. 'Hasn't she done well, since comin' over to England? She's a very clever young lady, but I have to say – she doesn't take her lovely red hair after *you* anyway!' Ruby gave a tinkly little laugh. 'Mind you,' she said admiringly, 'you've got a fine head of dark hair yourself . . . Mr Flynn.'

Shay beamed, delighted with the unexpected compliment, and suddenly not feeling quite as tired after all. 'Shay's the name,' he said, holding his hand out.

'An' mine's Ruby.' The landlady smiled warmly as they shook hands. 'Ruby Sweeney.'

Ruby guided him into the kitchen. 'Sit down, love,' she said, pulling out a chair. 'You look chilled to the bone. I'll get you a nice cup of tea to warm you up.' Ruby turned to put the kettle on the gas ring. 'I just took it off the boil when you rang the bell. I was about to make meself a brew.'

'A cup of tea would be grand, ma'am,' Shay said gratefully, taking in Ruby's neat little bottom and her fine legs. 'I'm sorry to be puttin' you to any bother, but I've been traipsin' up and down the town lookin' for where Tara lived. Then – when I eventually found the right house – I was told she was at work.'

'Work?' Ruby was confused for a moment, since it was Saturday afternoon. 'Oh, the hotel! She works Saturday afternoons in the reception.' She paused, hand on hip. 'I suppose it was one of them snooty teachers or nurses that answered the door. Didn't they even ask you in?'

'Well, you see . . . the way it happened,' Shay explained, 'when they said Tara wasn't there, I asked for a Biddy Hart – so they sent me here.'

Ruby poured the boiling water into the teapot, tutting all the while.

'What a welcome for you! All the way from Ireland, an' then being kept on a bleedin' doorstep in the snow. You always imagine that them educated types would have more manners – but you would be surprised at some of them. Especially them dried-up, old spinstery teachers.' She turned back to him now, allowing the tea to brew. 'Have you been in Stockport before?'

'It's me first time in *England*,' Shay confessed, 'never mind Stockport.'

'Aw . . .' Ruby said sympathetically, 'you must be absolutely knackered, if you've been travellin' all night.'

Shay looked up into the landlady's eyes. It was a very long time since he'd had anybody fussing over him – especially anyone like this vivacious, blonde, busty woman. 'I'm tired from traipsin' around, all right,' he admitted, 'but a cup of tea, and havin' a lovely girleen like you to chat to, will soon knock the sleep out of me.'

'I'll be happy to chat to you,' Ruby simpered, 'As long as you're happy to keep callin' me a *girleen!*'

They both roared with laughter.

Tara was rooted to the spot in the hallway. 'Did he give his name?'

'To be frank with you,' Mary Woods said, 'I could hardly make out a word the man said. He's *Irish* – that much I do know – although his accent is nothing like yours or Mr Kennedy's. After that, I'm afraid he lost me.'

'But you said he asked for *me* by name?'

'I could just make out your name, and when I said you were out, he then asked for your friend, Biddy Hart.' Miss Woods looked most annoyed at this unwarranted interrogation. 'I'm sorry I can't give you more information,' she said haughtily, 'but I could barely understand a word the man said.'

Tara's heart sank. 'What *exactly* did he look like?' she asked quietly, dreading the reply.

The teacher sighed in exasperation. 'I'm really not very good on descriptions . . . I think he had darkish hair . . .' She paused for a few seconds, then called in to her colleague, who was busy marking schoolbooks in the dining room. 'Vera? Did you manage get a good look at that Irish fellow who came to the door?'

'A dark-haired man with a cap,' Vera called back. 'Average height . . . a working man I would say, by the look of him. Wearing a smart-looking top-coat, although it was a bit on the big side for him.'

Mary Woods shrugged and nodded. 'That just about sums him up.'

'And you say you gave him the address of Sweeney's lodging house?'

'Not exactly. He showed me a letter addressed to Miss Bridget Hart, of Maple Terrace in Shaw Heath. It was written in the finest handwriting, so it was easy to make out,' Miss Woods explained – as though she were talking to one of her slower pupils. 'So I pointed him in the right direction.'

'I see,' Tara said, feeling rather faint at the thought of who her visitor might be. Her only hope was the top-coat. Shay had never possessed a decent winter coat. 'I think perhaps I'll take a walk down to Sweeney's and find out who the person is.'

'I should imagine it's some fellow looking for a bit of work in the garden or some such thing. Even though he was Irish, he didn't strike me as the sort of man you or Mr Kennedy would be acquainted with.'

Tara turned towards the door. 'Would you explain to the others that the evening meal might be a bit late? I'll do my best to be back as quickly as possible.'

'Of course,' Miss Woods said, suddenly noticing that Tara had gone quite pale. Feeling guilty about her earlier, abrupt manner, she said: 'Vera and I could peel the potatoes and vegetables for you, if it would be of any help.' She didn't want any discord between them, because Tara Flynn was an excellent landlady, and the standard of her house was better than anywhere else in the area.

'Thank you.' Tara forced a smile. 'That would be a great help.' She equally wanted no problems with her lodgers. They were a rare breed: quiet, teetotal, early-bedders who paid their rent on time.

She hurried off down the icy road as quickly and as safely as she could. Please God, she prayed as she went along – please don't let the Irishman in the top-coat be my father!

*

Biddy recognised the voice and the unmistakable hearty laugh the minute she stepped in the door. 'It's Tara's father!' she told Fred in an astonished voice. 'What's he doing here?'

She was even more astonished when she opened the kitchen door, and found Shay and Ruby cosied over glasses of hot whiskey, chatting and laughing as if they'd known each other for years.

'Biddy!' Shay exclaimed, sweeping her into her arms. 'Biddy, me oul' pal!'

Biddy was so shocked that for a few seconds she was speechless. Never, had Tara's father spoken to her in such a familiar manner – far less grabbed her into his arms!

'Fred . . .' she finally stuttered out, 'this is Mr Flynn – Tara's father.'

'Shay's the name,' he said, grinning ferociously at Fred, and pumping the wrestler's arm up and down. 'All me friends, for their sins, call me Shay!'

'Pleased to meet you, Shay,' Fred said, his face turning its usual beetroot red.

Shay sat back down in the chair, and took another mouthful of his hot whiskey. It was the second glass since his tea and sausage rolls. He beamed round at the other three. If this was life in England – Shay Flynn couldn't get enough of it! Drinking hot whiskies in the company of an attractive woman, and not having to put a foot outside the door for the use of a lavatory was luxury indeed.

If this was what his first afternoon over the water brought – he could only wait and wonder at the other delights which were sure to follow.

'Frank Kennedy guaranteed no such a thing! He did not *guarantee* you a job in England!' Tara told her father in an outraged voice. Although they were in the privacy of Ruby's front room, she was finding it very hard to keep her tone low enough not to be heard. 'You had no right,' she stated, pacing up and down in front of the fireplace, '*no right whatsoever* – to just turn up here without a word.'

'Sure, I had no time, Tara,' her father argued, 'and anyway – I was desperate. There's Christmas comin' up in a few weeks, and we haven't so much as a ha' penny for Santy to come to the childer.

And don't forget, there's a whole crowd of them at all ages to be fed and clothed – never mind Santy.' He shook his head sadly. 'Those poor childer are not as lucky as you an' Joe were. Sure, you were spoiled wi' yer granda an' yer Uncle Mick . . . and wasn't that Joe treated like a prince wi' the two oul' aunties?'

Tara took a deep breath. There were a million truths she'd like to scream at her father – but she knew she could talk to doomsday, and he would not understand one word.

'Surely,' she said in a more patient tone, 'you could have got work back in Tullamore? There's always work going in the hotels and in the creamery over Christmas.'

Shay shook his head. 'It's changed days since you left,' he said mournfully, as though Tara had been gone for years. 'They expect you to work for nothin' over there. And anyway – it was Tessie who had the whole idea of England in her mind. It was *her* who made me come over.'

Tara folded her arms and raised her eyebrows in disbelief. She waited – scepticism written all over her face – to hear how her downtrodden stepmother had suddenly become a dictatorial tyrant.

'It was *her*,' Shay went on, dropping his gaze to the floor. 'Sure, she's never let up about England since the Fitzgeralds' funeral. Since I happened to mention about Mr Kennedy offerin' me a job, she's been on about it, mornin', noon and night.' He gave a quick, sideward glance to see how Tara was taking the story. 'I never would have landed on you like this, if it hadn't been for her. Sure, she only *begged* yer Uncle Mick to lend me the price of me ticket.'

'I don't believe one word of it!' Tara suddenly rounded on him. 'Tessie would never let you off to England on your own. She knows fine well you can't be trusted to hand over money you've earned in Tullamore – far less depending on you to send money across the Irish Sea!'

'Tara, Tara . . .' Shay's voice was low and genuinely hurt. 'What did I ever do that makes you talk to yer poor father in such a desperate way?' He shook his head. 'Didn't I always do me best by you? An' me – left a young widower when yer poor mammy died. Sure, I was beside meself wi' grief.' He paused. 'It was the greatest sacrifice of me life, havin' to give you an' Joe up, but I *had* to do it. I had no choice, girl . . . I had to do it for yer own sakes.' He looked her straight in the eye, convinced of the truth in his own words. 'When me an' Tessie got married, sure we were desperate to have you to live with us, but you wouldn't come. You made yersel' sick every night until we brought you back to yer granda . . . God's me judge, if I'm not tellin' you the truth. Even then – at five years old – you were determined to get yer own way!'

Tara sank into an armchair, momentarily overwhelmed by the onslaught.

Quick to realise he had gained an advantage, Shay ploughed on mercilessly. 'I thought you'd be pleased to see me . . . the way I was lookin' forward to seein' you. I was delighted at the thoughts of me an' you – me eldest and me most *favourite* daughter – spendin' a bit of time on our own . . .' His voice trailed off in a theatrical manner. 'I thought we could make up for the time we missed when you were small – but bein' the soft eedjit that I am, I never realised that you'd be *that* ashamed of yer poor oul' father.' He shook his head sadly, then stuck the knife right in. 'I wonder what yer poor dead mother, and yer poor oul' granda would make of it all?'

To Tara's immense relief, a knock suddenly sounded on the sitting-room door. The situation between herself and her father was too volatile for her to make any instant decisions.

'It's only me,' Ruby said, sticking her peroxide head round the door. 'I hope youse won't mind me pokin' my nose in . . . only I was goin' to make a suggestion that might help youse out.'

'Not at all,' Shay said magnanimously. 'Wouldn't we be only too delighted to have yer opinion – a intelligent lady like yersel'.' He patted the settee for Ruby to sit down, as though he were in his own house. In the short time he had spent with the landlady, he knew that they were kindred spirits, and that any suggestions she might make could very well be to his own advantage.

'I was just thinkin',' she said, eyeing Tara warily, 'that maybe your father would be interested in lodgin' *here* for the time being. No offence or anythin' . . . but I don't think those spinster teachers you have up there would be his cup of tea. I couldn't imagine him feelin' comfortable in a house with the likes of *them*.'

Shay shrugged his shoulders. 'To be honest, they weren't exactly to me tastes,' he said in all seriousness – then added hastily: 'Although I'm not a person that likes to pass remarks on others.'

'Neither am I, love,' Ruby agreed, 'but sometimes the truth has to be told. They're not suitable people.'

Tara suddenly felt the most outrageous urge to roar out laughing. It was like finding something absurdly funny in the middle of a funeral wake. If only Miss Mary Woods and Miss Vera Marshall were present to hear themselves discussed, as being unworthy of sharing a house with *that Irish fellow*, as they had described him.

'But what about work?' Tara said instead of laughing. 'I have no idea how Frank's business is going at the minute . . . and whether he needs any more labourers. He might not remember even talking to you about work.'

'Well, we can soon find out,' Ruby replied officiously, 'but if he thinks anything of *you*, I'm sure he won't have forgotten about your father.' She turned to Shay. 'And that's another good thing about being in Maple Terrace – you would be livin' here with workin' men like yourself. If Frank Kennedy has nothing for you, I'm sure some of the other lads will know where there's work goin'.'

Tara felt both relief and dread at the same time. The immediate sense of relief at not having Shay under her roof – and an even greater relief, of not having the hullabaloo she envisaged if she had dared to refuse him.

The dreading part came when she thought of him making himself so at home in Maple Terrace, just ten minutes' walk away from her. The responsibility of it all, and the ramifications of a close friendship between himself and Ruby – was too desperate to even think about.

'He can't be all *that* bad,' Frank consoled her, as they drove out to Buxton for a piano recital that night. 'I'll give him a start on the building site out in Bolton, on Monday morning. The early rise and the long drive there and back will soon sort him out. The money's good, but he'll only be fit for bed when he comes home every evening. If he's genuine about doing it for the family, then he'll keep his head down and be too busy working to bother you.' He smiled reassuringly at her. 'On the other hand, if he's only come over here for a bit of a dodge over Christmas, I'd say he'll be gone by the end of the week.'

Tara shook her head. 'I'm still in a state of shock . . . my heart dropped like a stone when Mary Woods launched into the story about this strange Irishman in the fancy top-coat.'

Frank took his eyes off the road for a moment and they were twinkling mischievously. 'You have to admit that there's a funny side to it, Tara – when you think of the two teachers not knowing the dreadful Irishman they were talking about just happens to be your father!'

'Don't!' Tara warned. 'Just don't!'

Biddy lay on her bed, staring up at the ceiling. The letter which Shay had given her had been torn into a hundred tiny pieces and flushed down the lavatory. It was from Father Daly. The priest explained that he had tried to get a few days off over Christmas, to come over to the convent in Derbyshire again. Unfortunately, things had not worked out with a replacement priest and he would have to spend Christmas in Ballygrace. He did, however, plan to come over in February. That was definite. He reminded her of the nice time they had spent together on his last visit, and how very much he was looking forward to repeating it all. And perhaps – in the meantime – they could both be thinking of ways to make the visit even more interesting this time.

Father Daly also added that he hoped that she was behaving herself like a good Catholic girl. He reminded her about the evils of the pubs and the clubs in England, and said not to forget to attend Mass and confession. *Going to confession* he underlined in his letter, was particularly important. Even priests were tempted by sin.

Confessing regularly, he wrote, gave *everyone* a clean page on a regular basis.

Biddy turned over on the bed and buried her face in the pillow. Tonight at work, she was going to tell Fred she had made up her mind about her Christmas present. This afternoon when they were in Stockport, he had stood outside a jeweller's shop, pointing out diamond engagement rings. When he was met with complete silence from Biddy, he suddenly changed tack and started suggesting real gold watches or fancy charm bracelets instead.

Most girls started off with a bracelet with one or two charms, and then added the others as they could afford them – or received the little trinkets as gifts. Frank told Biddy that he would buy her a bracelet so heavy with charms that she wouldn't be able to lift her wrist up. He could easily afford it he bragged. All the money he had made from wrestling – the money he never had the time to spend – was gathering interest in a local building society. The money was waiting patiently, until he found the right girl, to put down as a deposit on a nice little two-up, two-down.

He had then gone on to say that maybe she would like to go out to Preston with him over the Christmas holidays, to meet some of his family. Fred was the youngest of a family of five, and his parents were getting on a bit.

Biddy had told him that although they were courting, she didn't want him to think that she was really *serious* about him at the moment. She said it might be best if they left visiting his family for a bit longer, and if they bought each other something small for Christmas, and not too personal. After all – Biddy pointed out – she wasn't even twenty yet.

Fred had muttered. 'I was only thinking . . .,' and then blushed to the roots of his thinning hair.

Now – after receiving Father Daly's letter – Biddy knew the answer she should have given Fred Roberts. She realised now that she needed this big, kind bear of a man to act as a barrier between herself and the awful – sometimes, unspeakable – things in life. She had already seen the effect Fred's presence had on the lads in Ruby's. They now looked at her with respect, and where they had often laughed and jeered at her, they now took her opinions more seriously. They treated her more like Tara now – more like the decent girl she always wanted to be.

With Fred by her side, Father Daly would have to take Biddy more seriously too. He would soon realise that when she said '*no*' she meant it. If he persisted in his ungodly attentions, then he would have to face the consequences.

When she arrived in the Grosvenor for her eight o'clock shift tonight, she would tell Fred that she would be delighted to choose an engagement ring for her Christmas present. She would also tell him that she would be proud to marry him, as soon as he liked.

Then, tomorrow morning, she would sit down and write a letter to Father Daly, telling him all about her wonderful news.

Chapter Thirty-three

Having barely recovered from the shock of her father's arrival, Tara received two more surprises the week before Christmas. One was unbelievably wonderful, and the other rather disturbing.

A huge lorry had appeared outside Tara's house around nine o'clock on the Saturday morning. She was in the process of drying her hair when one of her nursing lodgers came tearing upstairs calling that Tara had to come to the door to sign for a delivery.

'Tell them it's a mistake,' Tara called back from her bedroom. 'I haven't ordered any furniture.'

The man at the door was insistent. The item most definitely had to be delivered to a Miss Tara Flynn. He had winked at the nurse, saying that it was a surprise Christmas present.

Eventually, a harassed Tara came flying down the stairs in her dressing-gown. 'I did *not* order anything,' she said breathlessly. 'It must be a mistake.'

But it was no mistake. The black-polished baby grand piano, decorated with a huge pink ribbon and a bundle of mistletoe, was addressed to Tara Flynn.

'There you go, love,' the delivery man said, handing her a fancy envelope. 'That'll solve the mystery for you.' He raised his eyebrows. 'And when we've brought in the piano, you can sign the documents and we'll be on our way. I've a boss who times every bloomin' delivery.' He motioned to the other men in the lorry to get started. Moving a grand piano – albeit a baby grand – was a delicate and intricate manoeuvre.

Tara opened the envelope with shaking hands. It was an old-fashioned Christmas card, with a picture of a Victorian family gathered round a piano singing Christmas carols, with the words 'To a very special person' inside.

The handwritten part said: '*Looking forward to many pleasurable hours, listening to your sweet music . . . Love, Frank.*'

He called round later that evening to check that the piano had been delivered in perfect condition and that it was to Tara's liking. She ushered him into the dining-room, where the baby-grand piano stood in the huge bay window – as though it had been lovingly crafted with that particular spot in mind.

'Not being very cultured in the music department,' Frank explained, with that confident smile of his, 'I simply asked them to send the best piano they had in the shop.'

'Oh, Frank!' Tara said, running her hand over the creamy ivory keys – the keys of a brand new piano she had never expected to own for years. 'It's far too expensive . . . I really feel—'

'Do you like it?' Frank said, his eyes dark and serious.

Tara looked up at him, her own green eyes shining more brightly than ever before. 'Good God! Of course . . .'

'Then in that case,' he said simply, 'you must have it.'

And then later, after all the talk about the piano had been exhausted, Frank sat Tara down on the matching black-polished stool, and told her the bad news.

'I have to go home for Christmas,' he said, looking down at the pattern on the large fringed rug. 'I'm booked on a flight on the twenty-third.'

Tara's heart sank like a stone. 'But that's only a few days away . . .' She looked at his troubled face. 'Why? What's happened?'

'My mother,' he said quietly, 'she's very bad. She's had a couple of small strokes in the last week or two. It's probably all the business with my sister that's brought it on.'

Tara sat in stunned silence. All the weeks she had looked forward to this special Christmas. The first Christmas they would have spent together. She had imagined sparkling winter afternoons where they would go for walks in Bramall Park or maybe they would drive out to the Lake District. Frank had suggested that the other night. Then she had pictured them dining in dimly lit restaurants with real Christmas trees twinkling in the corner. And then the other evenings – when she had imagined them curled up together in front of a log fire in her sitting-room, and then later perhaps . . . curling up together in the same bed.

This Christmas, Tara had decided to give herself to Frank. To give herself in the loving, physical way a grown woman gives herself to a grown man. Because she knew now – long before the baby-grand piano had arrived – that, without a shadow of a doubt, she loved Frank Kennedy. It was not been the besotted, girlish love that she had felt for Gabriel Fitzgerald. And, although Frank was certainly hand-some and charming, it had not been love at first sight. It had been a slow-burning, gradual kind of love . . . the kind that just crept up quietly on you.

Frank lifted his head and met her tearful gaze. 'I'm sorry,' he said in a low voice.

'It's all right,' Tara told him. 'I understand.'

Tara's first Christmas in England, was the strangest Christmas she had ever spent. She rose early and walked down to first Mass. Afterwards, she came back to her empty house, and opened three small presents she had been given by Frank, a parcel which her brother Joe had sent, and a card with money from Mick and Kitty.

'*Pick yourself something nice*', Kitty had written. '*You have much better taste than me*'.

She had also written on the card that poor Mrs Kelly, Tara's old neighbour, had been taken into hospital. If and when she got better, she was expected to move to her daughter's in Dublin, as she wasn't fit to be left on her own. Kitty finished by saying the old cottage was all closed up, and looked very lonely.

Tara fought back tears as she thought of how kind Mrs Kelly had been to her when she was a child, but she pulled herself together, reminding herself that it was Christmas Day.

Frank's presents were next. She gasped at the silver and jade green necklace, which reclined in a satin-lined box with matching earrings. '*To match your unforgettable eyes*' he had written on a small card attached to the box. She then unwrapped a bottle of expensive French perfume, and a box of handmade chocolates. Whatever about his humble Clare origins, Frank Kennedy knew all there was to know about sophistication and style.

Joe had sent two books by Irish authors. '*In case you forget your Irish connections!*' was written on his card. Tara was delighted, and planned to start both books later on in the day. There was a letter inside, saying how well Joe had done in his autumn exams, and how he was spending Christmas as usual back in Tullamore. He sounded brighter and better than he had in some of his previous letters, which made Tara feel relieved.

She smiled as she turned the books over in her hands. Coincidentally, she had sent Joe books as well, but they were music scores that she had come across while in a shop in Manchester.

She mused to herself a while, thinking how different were the lives she and Joe led. Her thoughts wandered on to consider the *vastly* different lives that Shay and Tessie's family led – the mixture of half-brothers and sisters, and step-brothers and sisters. While Tara and Joe had been brought up without their parents, they had been taught and encouraged to read from an early age. Both of them seemed to have been born with a love of books and music, and her granda and his two maiden sisters, had provided the environment for that cultured side to grow.

There were no signs of any of the young Flynns leaning towards the more artistic side of life, as the elder two did. Tessie – a decent and hard-working mother – could just about manage to put a letter together, and that was the sum of her literary achievements. Shay had long left behind the interest in reading instilled in both him and Mick by their father. In the earlier days of his second marriage, any books he borrowed from his father or the library invariably ended up torn to bits or scribbled on by the kids. Shay gave reading books up as a bad job, settling for the odd edition of the *Irish Independent* when he was flush and the local weekly paper.

Tara was seated at Ruby's kitchen table with Biddy and Fred, three of the working lads who had not gone home – and her father.

'Isn't this grand?' Shay said, grinning at everyone, a paper hat balanced on his black curls, and a well-scraped plate in front of him. He held high his glass of beer. 'A toast to the fine cooks!' he pronounced loudly. 'That was the best Christmas dinner I've ate in me life – and cooked and served by the two loveliest girls in the country!'

Tara cringed, but smiled and held up her glass along with the others. She knew she should be more grateful to Ruby for asking her, but she would have preferred to spend the day on her own. Unfortunately, Biddy had told the landlady about Frank's untimely departure to Ireland and she had been railroaded into coming down to Sweeney's for her Christmas dinner.

It was very kind of Ruby, but Tara could not help feeling out of place. Biddy and Fred – who had announced their surprise engagement on Christmas Eve – were sitting making sheep's eyes at one another.

'You'll be the next one,' Biddy prophesied, her eyes gleaming with pride at the diamond ring on her left finger and the two bottles of Babycham she had just drunk.

Tara nearly said, '*I'm too young for engagements yet,*' but thought better of it, in case Biddy was offended. Instead, she smiled, and let Biddy think she was one up on her, having captured the burly Fred.

'By the way,' Shay suddenly said, 'did I tell you what happened about yer fine friends the Fitzgeralds?'

Tara's stomach did a somersault. 'No,' she said quietly, 'you haven't mentioned them.'

'Begod!' Shay said, raising his eyebrows in surprise. 'Well, I meant to tell you, as soon as I arrived.'

Tara waited patiently, like someone waiting to have a tooth pulled.

'Well now,' Shay started, 'it would seem that the house is to be sold.'

'Ballygrace House!'

'Ballygrace House indeed,' he confirmed. 'The mother had the other child lately – a boy by all accounts. I think it was not long after the funerals, for she went up to Dublin shortly after it. The young lad – Gabriel – wasn't that it?'

Tara's cheeks flamed. She nodded, willing Shay to hurry up.

'Well, seemingly,' Shay said, dragging the story out forever, 'he was going backwards and forwards from Dublin regularly over the summer. In fact,' Shay pointed his finger accusingly at Tara, 'he called out to Mick and Kitty, shortly after the funerals, lookin' – by all accounts – for your address in England. He said he had something belonging to his poor dead sister – the young mad one – that he wanted to give to you.'

'I never heard from him,' Tara said. 'He never got in touch.'

Shay shrugged. 'Maybe he left somethin' for you out at the cottage with Kitty – you'd never know. I wouldn't imagine it would be much. The Quality are renowned for bein' mean outside of themselves.'

'You were telling me about Ballygrace House,' Tara urged through gritted teeth. 'When did it go up for sale?'

'Oh, I don't think there's anythin' official like, but that's the talk around the place.'

'What about the auctioneering offices?'

'I know nothing about the others – but one in Tullamore is still carryin' on. I believe they have some young scut down from Dublin runnin' the place.' He looked over at Ruby. 'You know the type, have hardly finished havin' their arses wiped all, and they think they know it all.'

'The type that would try to teach their granny how to suck eggs!' the landlady added for good measure.

Tara struggled on for a few minutes more, trying to get more information out of Shay. But it was like getting blood out of a stone. He had told her all he could remember, and had then launched into a tirade of abuse against the gentry in general. It was a well known fact, he stated, that the gentry had been the downfall of the poor hard-working man in Ireland. Tara bit her tongue once again, amazed that her father had such an inflated opinion of his working capabilities.

The three lodgers had been in the pub since lunchtime and were struggling to speak in coherent sentences of any great length. The Geordie lad seemed to be having some difficulty getting the festive food from plate to fork, and then in the direction of his mouth.

This all went unnoticed by Shay and Ruby, who had downed a few drinks earlier on in the sitting-room, while Biddy had basted the turkey and roast potatoes under the proud gaze of Fred.

Shay had never looked so well. He had spent some of his hard-earned money on a new suit and a shirt and tie, and he had also got a decent haircut. He was well settled in Ruby's now, and had determinedly stuck with the labouring job out in Preston. 'You see, Tara,' he had explained a few days ago, 'it wouldn't be worth me while goin' over to Tullamore for Christmas. Sure, the money I'd spend on me ticket would cover the few bits and pieces from Santy.' He managed to look downcast for a moment. 'Needless to say, I'll be lonely without Tessie and the childer over the Christmas – but sure, isn't it solely for their benefit I came over?'

There were no signs of loneliness about Shay from what Tara could see. He looked more at home in Ruby's than he'd ever looked in his own house in Tullamore. Thankfully, he hadn't been the nuisance about her own place, as she had first feared. The frosty-mannered teachers had kept him at bay, and – as Frank had forecast – he was too tired from work in the evenings to be bothering her. Shay assured Tara that he was content enough with a few harmless pints of beer at the weekend with the older lads, or to join Ruby for the odd game of bingo.

'As long as everything is all right with Tessie,' Tara had ventured.

'Oh, indeed!' Shay confirmed. 'There's no need to be worryin' about Tessie. She's the finest. I phoned her at the hotel last week and she sounded in great oul' form – great oul' form altogether!'

The letter in the Christmas card Tara had received from her stepmother seemed to confirm Shay's words. Tessie had thanked Tara for the money and gifts for the children, and said between that and the money Shay had sent she'd never been so well off for a Christmas in years. Reading between the lines, it sounded as if Tessie was enjoying the benefits of Shay working in England – both from the money angle and the rest she was having with him not being around the house.

All seemed well indeed according to both Shay and his spouse. Tara would have liked to have felt reassured by that, but was somehow prevented by the lingering looks that passed between her father and Ruby Sweeney.

Tara pushed aside her suspicions, pinned a festive smile on her face, and reached for the other end of a cracker that Fred had just thrust in her direction.

Although let down by Frank's absence, Tara found she actually enjoyed the peace and quiet on her own. The days slipped away in a melody of beautiful music played on her wonderful piano at any time of the day which took her whim. The feelings which ran through her as she played her favourite pieces gave her great comfort. The piano became her substitute lover, bringing a surge of delight every time she walked into the room and beheld its beauty framed in the large bay window. Nothing – not even the day she realised she owned the house – compared with the pleasure Tara derived from owning such a superior, beautiful instrument.

At times she was reminded of the evenings in Ballygrace House, when she had played the piano with Madeleine and Gabriel listening, and then a terrible sadness enveloped her. She would weep and ask questions out loud in the room. *How could Madeleine be dead? How could such a young girl, who had hardly lived – who had never even had a proper boyfriend – be gone forever? How could God let such a thing happen?*

At those times, she played the louder, more violent pieces of music – her fingers flying up and down the ivory keys with amazing speed. She would play on and on, until she was physically and mentally exhausted. Then, the worst of the feelings evaporated, she would move on to the softer, more romantic pieces, until a more tranquil frame of mind returned.

Her mind then would return to Frank Kennedy, and she would wonder what the future held for them. She was quite resolute they would remain as a couple, but she was not at all ready for the step which Biddy had just taken with Fred. Tara had given them both her warmest congratulations, and promised Biddy that she would take her into the shops in Stockport to pick a nice engagement present as soon as the Christmas holidays were over.

But she did not envy Biddy one single little bit. What was right for Biddy, wasn't right for her. The life she and Frank were leading as a courting couple suited her perfectly. She enjoyed her evenings out with him, whether they dined at some nice restaurant, went to a musical evening, or went to the cinema. She loved his warm, entertaining company, and was happy for that to continue for the foreseeable future. She felt no need for engagement rings or talk of marriage.

Apart from Frank, Tara's work, her lodging house, her music – and her plans for the future – were more than enough to satisfy her for now.

The physical side of their relationship would sort itself out one way or another, Tara decided. Since Frank had been away, she was surprised to realise that she didn't feel quite so horrified by the thought of having a sexual relationship. Tara wasn't sure this was due to living in a big town where people weren't watching you all the time, or whether it was because her religious convictions didn't seem so important as they did in Ireland.

Or maybe it was because Tara wasn't so sure of God any more, after what had happened to Madeleine.

New Year came and went, and then suddenly, her old rigorous regime was back with a vengeance, as the lodgers started to return. Frank rang her at work the moment the plane touched down in Manchester Airport.

'That's my last visit to Ireland for a while, please God,' he told her. 'I've missed you more than you'll ever know.'

That evening he came round to the house, and they shut themselves in the dining-room, where Tara played one beautiful tune after another on the black polished piano.

'You're really not mad at me for going away over Christmas?' Frank asked quietly.

Tara shook her long red curls. 'I told you I understood . . . and anyway, I kept myself busy with the piano.' She looked up into his eyes. 'But I'm very glad you're back.'

Chapter Thirty-four

In her own eyes, Tara lost her virginity to Frank Kennedy during a weekend holiday in January. Her dreadful encounter with William Fitzgerald, she decided firmly, did not count. As a birthday present – and to make up for being away over Christmas – Frank had booked them into the Pine Lodge Hotel in the Lake District.

He phoned the hotel in advance, checking that there would be a choice of rooms available. Then, when he announced the surprise during her lunchtime on the Friday, he checked whether they were to have single rooms or a double.

Tara only hesitated for a moment. 'I think a double would be fine,' she said quietly.

'Are you sure?' Frank asked, his brow furrowed. 'I don't want you to feel . . .'

'You haven't made me feel pressurised. It's entirely my own decision.' Although she was nervous at the prospect, she managed a little laugh. 'I'm twenty years old – it's time I knew about the birds and the bees.'

'In that case,' he laughed, 'I'll make sure we have the suite which has the four-poster bed!'

The stately, elegant hotel was set on the banks of Lake Derwentwater and, as they drove towards it, Frank explained why he had chosen that particular place. 'The travel agent informed me that the scenery was the inspiration for William Wordsworth's poetry and Beatrix Potter's writing,' he told Tara. 'Since you're such a keen reader, I presumed you would appreciate that.' He smiled. 'I thought you might enjoy the chance to educate me on the literary side now, since you've been so patient teaching me all about the charms of classical music.'

Tara cuddled into his arm as they drove along. 'I am so excited!' she said with childlike delight. 'I can't believe how well you've organised all this. I would never have been able to get away if you hadn't sorted it out.'

'It's called cheek!' Frank laughed. 'Bloody cheek!'

Not only had Frank organised Biddy to look after Tara's lodgers, but he had also sorted things, so that she had the weekend off from reception in the Park Hotel. More and more, Tara realised the influence Frank Kennedy had with business people in Stockport. His name only had to be mentioned and she could see their eyes light up in interest.

And yet, around her, Frank had no false airs and graces. They talked about everything with honesty and ease. With people like Mr Pickford and her lodgers, Tara was friendly and polite – but extremely private. She did not discuss her relationship with Frank, nor did she feel compelled to explain or excuse anything about her father. The two teachers quickly realised they had made a blunder where Shay was concerned, when she brought him up to the house a few nights after his arrival in Stockport.

After insisting that he put his cap in his coat pocket, she had brought him into the house, looked the two straight-laced ladies in the eye and said: 'Miss Woods and Miss Marshall, I'd like to introduce you to my father – Mr Shay Flynn.'

The two ladies had blushed and shook Shay's outstretched hand. They were – as Tara had anticipated – much too polite to mention their previous encounter with 'that dreadful Irishman'. After that, they bent over backwards to be polite to their landlady's father on any occasions that they met.

There was nothing to hide with Frank. Knowing that his own background was so similar to hers, and that they shared the same outlook and ambitions in life, Tara could totally relax and be herself in his company. Even when they had got into the ornate bed for the first time, he seemed able to read her mind.

'Tara,' he said softly, as she slipped into the four-poster bed in her new satin nightdress, 'I know you're more religious than I am . . .

and I don't want you doing this, if you're worrying that you're committing a sin or anything like that.'

'I'm not worrying, Frank,' she replied. 'I'm grown-up, and I answer to my own conscience. And sure, if I do start to feel guilty – isn't that what Confession is for?' She laughed gently, having unwittingly echoed Father Daly's words to Biddy in his Christmas letter.

The physical bit was fine . . . much better than fine, Tara thought. She had not, thank God, seen William Fitzgerald's face when she closed her eyes, and she had not imagined that it was his skin next to hers, instead of Frank's.

The first time especially, Frank had been so gentle and caring with her – checking every few minutes that she was all right. While wordlessly reassuring him, Tara was relieved that she felt far more relaxed and confident than she had dared hope. If Frank had noticed that there were no bloodstains when they had finished loving the first time, he made no mention of it. Instead, he had kissed and stroked her, telling her she was the most beautiful, desirable woman in the whole world – and how he had dreamt of making love to her since the first time he had seen her in the Grosvenor.

Over the weekend they made love many times, often – to her own surprise – with Tara as the instigator. As soon as Frank's skin touched her smooth skin, all reticence melted away. But there was one particular moment when Tara was reminded of her past. Frank held her in his arms after the waves of passion had subsided, and whispered to her proudly: 'You're now a full woman, instead of my little virgin girl.'

For a brief second, Tara thought about telling him about what had happened with William Fitzgerald, but Frank had reached out for her again – and the moment passed. Some time, she knew she would tell him, because he was honest and open about himself, and because she knew he would understand.

Biddy was overwhelmed with relief when February came and went, without any word from Father Daly. Being engaged to Fred had given her a new purpose in life. Encouraged by Ruby – and by the silence from Father Daly – she had decided to wait a while before getting married, so that she could build up a stock of items for her 'bottom drawer'.

'Start as you mean to go on, love,' Ruby advised, as they sat in the kitchen chatting over a cup of tea. 'Make that Fred go shoppin' with you every week, and get him to buy you any nice clothes or things for the house that you fancy. Get everythin' off him while the goings good, for they all change when they get married.' Ruby pursed her red lips, remembering life with the late, mean Mr Sweeney. 'It suddenly becomes: "You can't have this; you can't have that! We've got the mortgage and the gas bill." Take my advice, Biddy girl. You want to get everythin' out of him now, while you have him in the palm of your hand.' She suddenly let out a dirty guffaw of laughter. 'Did you hear what I just said? Never a truer word was said by accident! It's when they're in yer hand, you can get anythin' you want!'

Biddy looked vague, then it suddenly clicked. 'Oh Ruby, you're terrible!' She laughed loudly along with the landlady. 'You're obviously taking a leaf out of yer own book,' she said. 'I noticed you got another big bunch of flowers yesterday.'

'Tulips and daffodils,' Ruby said casually, admiring her newly polished nails. 'A spring bouquet.'

'Do I need to ask who from?'

'You know fine well they're from Mr Flynn.'

There was a silence.

Ruby's eyes narrowed defensively. 'What about it? We're doin' nobody any harm. We're two middle-aged people just enjoyin' each other's company . . . a few drinks, the odd game of bingo, an' a bit of a laugh. Where's the harm in that? I'm not takin' the bread out of anybody's mouths. I make sure he sends the money home to his wife and kids every week. From what Shay's told me, there wasn't much goin' on between him and the wife in any case. You told me that yourself when he first arrived.'

Biddy nodded in agreement, not wishing to get on the wrong side of her good friend. She had told Ruby about Shay's wife always nagging him about work and being too fond of a drink. But she had no idea when she was gossiping with Ruby, that it would give the impression that his marriage was of no importance. 'It's Tara I feel sorry for . . . I think she might have an idea about—'

'Tara can have all the ideas she bleedin' well likes,' Ruby snapped.

'She's got nowt to do with me and Shay. An' anyway, people who live in glass houses shouldn't throw stones.'

'What d' you mean?' Biddy looked mystified.

'Just what I say. Look at the way she went on at you for havin' a bit of a laugh with the lads here, and yet she would dare anybody to say a word to her about her dirty weekends away with Frank Kennedy.' Ruby lowered her voice, and leaned closer. 'An' he's not all he's cracked up to be. I've heard rumours about that Frank Kennedy . . .'

'D'you mean about the backhanders in his business deals and everythin'?' Biddy asked. She'd heard murmurs about how Frank had given a backhander to the manager in the Grosvenor for giving him the contract for the extension. 'Sure, that goes on all the time in the building trade.'

'Well I know it goes on,' Ruby agreed, 'but it's not just his business wheelin' and dealin' I'm goin' on about.'

'What then?'

'It's his private life.' Ruby's voice dropped. 'Shay came across someone from Country Clare the other week, and when he asked this lad if he knew Frank Kennedy, the lad not only knew him, but everybody belongin' to him. Then, suddenly, he stopped dead, and asked Shay how he knew Frank', an' when Shay said that Frank was courtin' his daughter – almost engaged like – the lad clammed up. He said it wasn't for him to be tellin' tales about Frank Kennedy, and that it wasn't for one man to judge how another man conducted his private life. The lad said that you never knew when you might need Frank to put a bit of work your way, so it was best to keep your trap shut.' Ruby raised a pencilled eyebrow. 'It's not the first time I've heard stories about Frank Kennedy, an' you know the sayin' – where there's smoke, there's fire.'

'What have you heard?' Biddy's brow was furrowed.

Ruby drained the last mouthful of her tea, leaving pink lipstick round the rim of the cup. 'I'm sayin' nothin'. If there's any truth in the rumours, then Tara'll hear it soon enough.' Ruby shrugged. 'Maybe she knows about it already and is quite content. That grand piano must have cost him a bleedin' fortune.' She lifted Biddy's hand, and studied her engagement ring. 'Tara could have half a dozen of those for the price Frank Kennedy paid for that piano. Maybe she'd rather have a big house an' a fancy piano than a wedding ring. Maybe it suits her to turn a blind eye.' Ruby suddenly grinned. 'Maybe she's not as daft as the rest of us!'

Shay went back to Ireland for a visit in July. There were a few slack weeks at work, due to bad weather, and he suddenly decided to head home. He got a great welcome from everyone, and immediately decided that going to England was the best thing he had ever done. Instead of dodging people all the time, embarrassed over his unemployed state – he discovered that 'working away' made him a figure of great importance. Everywhere he went, he was greeted with: 'Howya, Shay! How's the work goin' over the water? You're lookin' well on it anyway.'

Shay swelled with pride, discovering that it was a much better feeling than the elusive state he had always pursued with alcohol. He also discovered that the more fashionable clothes that Ruby had insisted on him purchasing, made a great impression on everyone, especially his wife.

'We might go out for a walk this evening,' Tessie commented shyly on his second day at home. 'It's not often we get a fine evening and there's no good in havin' all those nice clothes, if nobody gets to see them.'

Shay had generously insisted on treating his wife to a new hairdo and a new dress – the first dress he had ever bought her – and then they both paraded round Tullamore that night in their finery.

'Shall we call in for a drink?' Shay suggested as they passed one of his favourite watering-holes.

Tessie looked hesitant, having good reason, going on Shay's past record.

'Sure, there's no need to be worryin',' he said, taking her by the elbow. 'I'll only have the two glasses of beer, and then it'll be straight home.'

And straight home it was. The younger children were put to bed, and the older children were out and about with the fine weather. For the first time in many years, Shay and Tessie were actually on their own.

Surprisingly, Tessie needed very little persuasion from Shay for them to creep into the bedroom, careful not to waken the children in the next room. The freshly washed hair, the new shirt, and the fact he was sober made Tessie suddenly feel she had a new and better man.

And indeed she had. For there were improvements in Shay she could never have dreamed of. Instead of the impatient, rough couplings she had been used to with her husband, here was a man who was taking his time to kiss her – not only her lips – but other parts of her body he had never kissed before!

Tessie gasped and blushed with embarrassment, but did not ask him to stop. If this was what living away from home caused – she wanted more of it! A sober, loving husband was something she thought only existed in romantic novels and women's magazines. Shay was obviously missing her so much that it had made him a more loving and considerate man.

Even if he only came home for two or three fortnights a year, it was worth it all. An added bonus was the less Shay was home the less chance of any more pregnancies.

There was nothing now, Tessie suddenly realised, that Shay's presence depended upon.

The children were better fed and dressed with the weekly money their father had been sending, and when he was at home he was interested in everyone and everything. All in all, peace and contentment reigned at long last in Flynn's house.

Whatever had caused the dramatic change in Shay, Tessie neither knew nor cared. As long as the money kept coming in, and Shay remained clean and sober – she was happy. If there was a woman, as she suspected, Tessie Flynn reckoned she had a lot to thank her for.

The two men recognised each other in the same instant. Frank Kennedy was on his way out of the airport to pick up a friend's car when he encountered Gabriel Fitzgerald who was on his way into the airport.

Gabriel was the first one to speak. 'Tara's friend, isn't it?' he said, stretching out his free hand. The other held a heavy leather suitcase. 'Gabriel Fitzgerald . . . from Ballygrace. You were at the family funerals.'

Frank nodded and gave him a very firm handshake. 'Frank

Kennedy. Nice to meet you under more ordinary circumstances. Are you travelling far?' he enquired.

'London – to visit my mother. She's convalescing at my aunt's with the baby.' He paused for a moment. 'Have you seen Tara recently?'

'Oh, indeed I have,' Frank laughed. 'Not two hours ago. She saw me off at Manchester Airport.'

'Really?' Gabriel sounded surprised. 'How is she?'

'She's grand. Tara's well settled over in England now. She's going to make a great businesswoman. She's well-versed in the estate agency business in Manchester and she also has her own boarding house. It's running so well that I'll be advising her to expand soon – take on another property, and hire someone to run it for her.'

'Really?' Gabriel said again, and immediately felt immature and stupid for repeating himself, under the gaze of this confident, older man.

'You sound surprised,' Frank said lightly. 'You obviously don't know Tara too well.'

Gabriel flushed red. 'I shouldn't be in the slightest surprised at anything Tara Flynn does. She's always been a very capable girl.'

'That's for sure,' Frank agreed.

'I wonder,' Gabriel ventured, setting his case down on the ground. He reached inside his pocket for a pen. 'I wonder if you could give Tara a message for me?'

'Certainly,' Frank said agreeably. He now set down his expensive briefcase.

Gabriel wrote down several phone numbers. 'If she's over in Ireland, she'll catch me at one of these numbers. We have Ballygrace House closed at the moment, but hopefully it will be open again soon – when my mother's back to full health.' He handed Frank the piece of paper. 'I have some things belonging to my sister, Madeleine . . . I know she would have liked Tara to have them. They were very close friends.'

'So I believe,' Frank said, tucking the paper into the top pocket of his jacket. 'Tara has told me *everything* about her life in Ballygrace before we met. Unfortunately, she doesn't have much time to spare on nostalgic trips home. Her business and *our* social life take up all her time.'

There was silence for a moment.

'Tara and I are due to be engaged soon,' Frank suddenly announced.

'Oh . . .' Gabriel flushed again. 'I didn't realise . . . Congratulations.'

'Thanks,' Frank lifted his case, and turned towards the exit door. 'I have a car to pick up now.' Then – without a word of farewell – he was gone.

Gabriel stared after him for several minutes, his forehead creased in thought. Then, he lifted his case and turned towards the departures board. Bumping into Frank Kennedy had clarified a few things which had been clouding his mind for some time. Although he had not witnessed the crumpled paper with the phone numbers blowing around the car park area, instinctively he knew that he would not hear from Tara.

It was suddenly crystal clear what had to be done. He was going over to London to see his mother – and to meet up with Olivia Freeman again. She was an old family friend, and they had known each other as children. Elisha and Olivia's family thought they were an ideal couple. Anyone who knew them thought they were an ideal couple.

Gabriel didn't really know how he felt about Olivia. He didn't know how he felt about any other woman – apart from Tara Flynn. He had been so slow to realise it. He had nearly been swayed by his parents and their view that she was not a suitable match for him. It had taken their parting for just a university term for him to realise how much Tara meant to him. He had thought them young, and with all their lives in front them. He thought he had all the time in the world to get his degree – and all the time in the world to decide about Tara Flynn.

And then fate had stepped in. With the untimely, shocking deaths of his father and Madeleine, he suddenly realised that life was precious and fleeting. He had learned a hard lesson and – cruellest of all – he had learned it too late.

The piercing ache he had felt in his heart when Frank Kennedy told him that he and Tara were to be married was almost worse than the pain he had felt at the double funeral. When he had spoken to her that day outside Ballygrace Church, he knew, beyond all doubt, that he loved Tara Flynn. He loved her with an intensity he had not realised he was capable of.

But now, he had to face the fact that his love was too late. He had been beaten to it by the successful, mature Frank Kennedy. Worse still, he thought miserably, was the knowledge that he had probably been beaten by a better man.

He forced his brain to digest the flight information his eyes had been staring at for five full minutes. Then he turned towards the Aer Lingus check-in desk. In a few hours he would be in London with his sick mother and baby brother.

Later tonight he would see Olivia.

Chapter Thirty-five

❧

Summer – 1952

Biddy had decided on an autumn wedding in late September. She had taken Ruby's advice and not rushed into marriage too quickly. A year and half since the engagement, and Biddy now had a bulging bottom drawer. It was filled with towels and dishcloths, tablecloths and bedlinen, cutlery and a dinner service, a variety of cushion covers and ornaments. Deposits had been paid on a three-piece suite, a bedroom suite and a double bed at the Co-op in Stockport. Biddy had a credit book, and she and Fred would make weekly payments on the furniture.

They had also been looking round at houses in the Shaw Heath and Edgeley area. Biddy stated quite firmly that she did not want to move far from Ruby's, as she intended to keep on both her jobs after they were married. They were in no rush about the house, as Ruby said Fred was welcome to move into Biddy's room after the wedding if they hadn't found anything they really fancied.

'It's a big step, buyin' a house,' Ruby had warned one morning, when all the men had gone to work. 'You don't want to rush into anythin' until you're a hundred per cent sure. That double room upstairs is there for you, as long as you need it.'

Biddy glowed with gratitude. As far as she was concerned, she was happy to stay forever in Maple Terrace under the caring eye of Ruby, but she knew it would be unfair on Fred. She knew that a married couple should have a place of their own. And yet, the prospect of being away from the dainty Ruby filled her with dread. Two years of the landlady's nurturing attention had only scratched the surface of

Biddy's deep need for a maternal figure in her life. Like a baby chick, enjoying the comfort and warmth of a mother hen, Biddy was reluctant to let go.

Ruby suddenly looked serious. 'Have you told Fred yet?'

Biddy lowered her head. 'I haven't had the chance.'

Ruby tutted. 'You're worryin' yerself over nothing. Fred Roberts worships the bloody ground you walk on! He's not goin' to dump you, because of somethin' that happened a few years ago. He'll understand that you were only a young girl, an' you didn't know any better.' Ruby bit her lip. 'He's a good man, and he won't want to lose you over that.'

Biddy nodded, tears welling up in her eyes. 'I know . . . but I just can't seem to find the right time.' She looked at Ruby, one tear sliding down her cheek. 'I think Fred thinks I'm a virgin. Because I wouldn't let him go the whole way, he thought I was afraid of him hurtin' me. He said not to worry, that I wouldn't feel so nervous when we were married.'

Ruby patted Biddy's shoulder. 'You'll be fine whether you tell him or not. He probably wouldn't know the bloody difference.'

When she finished clearing up the breakfast things, Biddy made to go upstairs, to get her things ready for her afternoon shift in the hotel. She paused at the kitchen door. 'Did you go to the doctor's yet?' she asked Ruby.

'Not yet,' the landlady replied casually, 'I've been so bloody busy recently.'

'Has it got any better?'

Ruby frowned, and pressed a small, manicured hand on one of her breasts. 'It's hard to tell . . . though I think the lump feels a bit smaller than the last time I checked.'

'What about yer . . .' Biddy blushed, 'what about yer nipple?'

Ruby took a deep breath. 'It's still leakin'. I think there might be a bit of an infection in it.' She smiled reassuringly at Biddy. 'If it doesn't clear up soon, I'll get myself off to the doctor's.'

'I think you should,' Biddy said, her forehead wrinkled with worry. 'It sounds as though you might need an antibiotic.'

Chapter Thirty-six

It had been almost two years since Tara had been back in Ballygrace and she found things very different. There was Mrs Kelly's cottage for a start. It was the sorriest-looking sight that Tara had ever seen. The old thatched roof had collapsed in the centre, leaving a gaping hole where the rain had poured through, destroying the bits of furniture that were left in it.

'Not one of her family bothered with it after she died,' Mick explained, as they stood outside the derelict cottage. 'Seemin'ly, there was a disagreement over whether they would keep it as a holiday home, or whether they would sell it, and divide up the money. Ye know the way families are. In the wind-up, they did nothin'. Then, last winter, durin' the bad storms, the roof fell in.' Mick gave a deep sigh. 'We contacted the lawyers in Tullamore to let them know – but nobody came near. It's been like that ever since.'

Tara turned back towards Mick and Kitty's cottage, her eyes blinded by tears. 'She was so good to me when I was little . . . and I never even made it home to her funeral.'

'Sure, none of us did, Tara,' Mick said sadly. 'Her family were all queer hawks. They buried her up in Dublin, straight out of the hospital. They didn't have the decency to put it in the paper. Nobody in Ballygrace knew for a week.'

But whatever Mick and Kitty said, Tara *did* feel very bad about it. Mrs Kelly's house was the only one she would have visited in Ballygrace, and it would have been nice to go across and spend an hour with her old neighbour, chatting about her granda, and all the things Tara had got up to when she was small. It felt very strange, to suddenly be confined to Mick and Kitty's cottage, most days and nights.

Mick took her out for a few jaunts in the new pony and trap. 'It could be a car, the next time you're home,' Mick said. 'There's a good few folk in Tullamore has them now. People you'd never have imagined would be interested in them. Mind you, there's no one has a car as fine as Frank's.'

Frank was over in Ireland for a week, and on this occasion had brought his own car over on the boat. Tara had decided on the spur of the moment to accompany him as far as Offaly.

'I'm sorry I can't invite you down to Clare,' Frank had said apologetically, 'but there's only the one spare room, and my mother's funny about having visitors.' He gave a deep sigh. 'She's been funny ever since my sister had the baby . . . I think it's some sort of depression.'

'It's all right,' Tara told him. 'There's plenty of time for visiting –' She had been going to add: 'when we get married', but had stopped herself just in time.

In all fairness, she had no one to blame but herself for the situation. When Frank heard that Biddy had got engaged, he had asked Tara then if she would have preferred an engagement ring to the piano.

'Definitely not!' Tara had laughingly replied. 'The piano's a million times better than any ring'

'That's fine,' Frank said in a relieved voice. 'I'm glad we're of the same mind. We know where we're up to without bothering about engagements and weddings for a while.' He had patted her on the head. 'It keeps things more interesting, if we have our own separate businesses and our own separate lives. I've seen too many marriages turn sour, when the novelty wears off.' Then, taking her in his arms, he said: 'We're not like Biddy and Fred . . . the novelty will never wear off for us.'

After a few days in Ballygrace, Tara wished she had suggested to Frank that they meet in Galway for a day or even overnight. But it was too late, because she hadn't thought of asking him for a phone number where he could be contacted. Instead, she contented herself with small forgotten pleasures like feeding the ducks and chickens, gathering gooseberries and strawberries, for Kitty to make into delicious pies and flans, and long walks along the country lanes she had known as a child.

She preferred this to walking along the streets of Ballygrace, where she felt so exposed and self-conscious. Where she was under scrutiny from the top of her curly auburn head, to the tip of her expensive, Italian shoes. In each and every shop a silence fell when Tara and her aunt entered. Then, the shop assistant would either become all officious, or else they would be over-friendly, determined to glean every ounce of information that they could pass on later. Tara, after several years of privacy in England, found it very difficult.

'Pay no heed,' Kitty advised, aware of her niece's discomfort. 'They do that to everyone who comes home on holiday. They mean no harm. By this time next week, they'll be talking about somebody else. They have little to entertain themselves here.'

When they called in at the bakery where Mick worked – and where Tara had helped at the weekends with the accounts – she suddenly remembered the other side of the people from Ballygrace. The owner of the bakery, who had been grateful for Tara's help in sorting out his unruly accounts books, came round the side of the counter full of smiles and hugs.

'Aren't you the sight for sore eyes?' the elderly man said warmly. 'Look at you, Tara Flynn! An' the fine lady you've turned out to be. Yer poor oul' granda would have been proud of you! What's all this I'm hearin' about you buyin' a grand big house over in England? An' how's little Biddy doin'?'

After that warm welcome, Tara suddenly relaxed, realising that many of the locals were delighted to see her home, and interested in how she had fared 'across the water'. Sometimes, she scolded herself, she was inclined to look at things in a black and white way. People were only people, in Ireland or in England, after all.

Quite a few asked after Biddy, and when Tara ascertained that the interest was genuine, she was happy to pass on the fact that Biddy was well and planning to get married. Only two women gossiping outside the Post Office had dared make any reference to Biddy's baby. One, goaded by the other, had asked if Tara could settle an argument. Was it true that Biddy Hart had taken the child over to England with her – or had she in fact, had it adopted? On that particular occasion, Tara had delivered the coldest, most withering look she could muster, and without a word had turned on her heel.

Father Daly dropped down to the house one evening, hearing that Tara was back home. Instinctively, she felt there was an ulterior motive to his visit. He started off jovial and interested in all her news, expressing his approval about the fact she was now, what he described as 'a woman of means'. Then, he went on to ask for Biddy. 'I believe she got herself engaged last year,' he said gravely.

'She's getting married in September,' Tara told him. 'Didn't she tell you?'

'No,' Father Daly replied, 'she did not. Is he a suitable match for her? Is he a practising Catholic?'

Tara said, yes, that in her opinion, Fred was an ideal match for Biddy. He was a kindly big man, who worshipped the ground Biddy walked on. As for him being a practising Catholic, Tara said as far as she knew, he was. She then went on to say how highly the management in the Grosvenor thought of Biddy, and how they were giving her a room free for the wedding reception, and a half-price wedding meal.

The priest had listened, brow wrinkled and balding head to the side, and then asked Tara if there was some writing paper and an envelope in the house. He quickly scribbled a note, and then asked Tara if she would *hand*-deliver a letter to Biddy. Apparently, he had written to her several times in the past year without a reply. She must have got at least one of the letters. The post to England, *presumably*, couldn't be that bad. The priest also told Tara that Lizzie Lawless hadn't been too great lately and it would be nice if Biddy spared a minute to drop a 'Get Well' card to her old foster-mother.

Tara took the letter from him, and bit her tongue about commenting on Lizzie Lawless.

'So, the wedding is the first weekend in September,' the priest mused. 'I must write that in my diary.'

As she saw the priest out to the door, Tara suddenly realised that he had only come for news of Biddy. Well, if Biddy wasn't interested in replying to Father Daly's letters over a year, she couldn't fathom out why he would keep on writing to her.

As though sensing her thoughts, he suddenly changed the conversation to Tara again. 'There's few would have expected you to have come up so far in the world,' he said condescendingly, 'given your disadvantaged background.'

Tara was incensed. 'Whatever you might think about my family being poor,' she snapped, 'I take exception to you describing my upbringing as "disadvantaged"!'

'Tara . . .' the priest said in shock, 'there was no harm intended . . .'

'My grandfather taught me to read before I went to school,' she said, ignoring his protestations, 'and I had more books given to me, and more time spent on me, than any child in Ballygrace. I would hardly call that disadvantaged, would you?'

The priest lifted his hat from the hook on the door. 'You're obviously in need of your holiday,' he said. 'Running a business in England must be very stressful indeed.'

Mick dropped Tara over to Tullamore on the Friday, and she visited Tessie and the two old aunties. Tara was delighted to see her stepmother looking better than she had for years, in a fashionable skirt and jumper, and her hair newly set. Tessie told Tara how going to England had been the making of Shay. Oh, he was a different man altogether, and as far as Tessie was concerned, she hoped the situation would continue until she had all the children off her hands. The two eldest were both in good factory jobs, and please God, Assumpta would follow them next year.

Tara said, in all truthfulness, that both Shay and herself were so busy working, that their paths only crossed on rare occasions. She agreed with her stepmother that he had certainly improved himself, and was glad he had kept his word about looking after his family financially.

'I'm sure you've been the making of him stayin' on the straight an' narrow,' Tessie whispered, as she saw Tara off on the doorstep. 'He's so proud of you, that he doesn't want to let you down.'

'I don't think it's anything to do with me at all,' Tara said hastily. 'I think he can take the credit alone for that.' Then, she hurried off just in case Tessie happened to ask any probing questions regarding Shay's accommodation, or worse still – how his landlady was treating him.

Molly and Maggie had failed a lot since Tara had last seen them, both now very wrinkled and bent over. The little musty house was still a shrine of holy pictures and statues, and their main topic of conversation was still Joe and the seminary. It wouldn't be long now, with the help of God and his Blessed Mother – the stooped old ladies told Tara – until Joe's ordination. They said, with shining eyes, that they both hoped and prayed that she would make it over for her brother's glorious occasion.

'Nothing,' Tara assured them, 'will make me miss Joe's ordination.'

After tea with Molly and Mary, Tara played a few of their favourite tunes on the old piano, and then she walked up to the shops in Tullamore for a breath of fresh air. She bought a tin of chocolate biscuits for the aunties and another one for Kitty. Then, she bought a nice Galway Lace tablecloth and napkins to take back to Ruby, and a lovely bedspread for Biddy's bottom drawer.

On her way back to the aunties' house, on impulse, Tara turned down Church Street. She paused for a few moments on the opposite side of the street from Fitzgerald's Auctioneers. Surprisingly, the office looked exactly the same as the last day she worked in it. Although perhaps, she thought, it might have had a fresh coat of paint.

She crossed the street, and then gave a cautious glance through the window, wondering if Patricia McManus was still there. Then, as she caught sight of a heavy, darkhaired woman, she suddenly remembered that Patricia had planned to retire the autumn that Tara had left. Disappointed, she turned away. She had only gone a few steps, when she heard the office door open, and then a woman's voice call out to her.

'Can I help you?' It was the dark-haired woman Tara had seen through the window.

'No . . . thank you,' Tara stammered, her face flushing. 'I was just passing . . .'

'You're welcome to come in and have a look around,' the woman said. 'We've some new brochures that have just arrived.'

Tara decided it was easier to explain. 'I used to work in the office,' she said, 'and I wondered if Patricia . . . Patricia McManus was still there . . . and then I remembered she was probably retired.'

The woman smiled and nodded. 'Yes, I took over her position. I see her at Mass most Sundays. I could tell her you were asking for her. What name should I say?'

'Tara – Tara Flynn.'

The woman raised her eyebrows slightly and nodded. 'Tara Flynn,' she repeated. 'I'll make sure I remember that.'

Tara couldn't tell if the name meant anything to the woman or not. 'So Mrs Fitzgerald kept the business on after her husband died?'

'Yes, she kept on all the businesses, although her son is in charge now. He has managers running all the offices.'

'Really?' Tara was shocked to feel her pulse quickening at the mention of Gabriel. 'I was very good friends with his sister, Madeleine. In fact, we worked together in this office for a time.' She paused. 'Is – is Gabriel in Tullamore often?'

'Occasionally,' the woman told her. 'He was down a fortnight ago. He comes to check how business is going and to air the big house. It's a pity to see such a lovely place all closed up, but of course he has no need of it.' She shrugged. 'You'd think Gabriel would sell it, because he spends most of his time in Dublin or London these days.'

'London?' Tara was taken aback.

'Oh, yes,' the secretary confirmed. 'He's engaged to an English girl. I hear he's to be married in the spring.'

Tara turned away. He hadn't even left a memento of Madeleine's for her.

'You're very quiet, Tara,' Frank said, as they drove out towards Dun Laoghaire on Monday afternoon. 'Did everything go all right?'

Tara pushed her sunglasses up into her hair. 'Sorry . . . I was just thinking. Yes – everything went fine.'

'Did you do anything exciting?'

'Not really. I visited relatives and went for long walks.' She smiled. 'And I ate too much of Kitty's lovely cooking.'

'Did you give any more thought to buying the other semi?'

'I've decided to have a word with Mr Benson in the building society this week,' she replied. 'So far, his advice has been good.'

'You should just go for it,' Frank told her. 'You couldn't get anything better than the house next door. It will let you keep an eye on everything. Whoever you decide on running it will be right under your nose, so there's less likelihood of you being ripped off. And,' he pointed out, 'you won't have any neighbours causing you problems.' He gave an impatient little sigh. 'You're mad if you don't move quickly, Tara. You'll lose any advantage you have, because it'll be snapped up fast.' Through a builder friend, Frank had found out that the other half of Tara's red-brick semi was due to go on the market next week.

The sun came out from behind a cloud and Tara put her sunglasses back over her eyes. She still wasn't sure about this latest idea of Frank's, and she wanted more time to think. 'I'll see what Mr Benson has to say.'

'You can easily afford it,' Frank persisted. 'You won't have any trouble finding boarders and the rent will easily pay the increased mortagage. You were worried sick when you took out the first mortgage and you've had no problems there. In fact,' he pointed a finger, emphasising his words, 'you'll be able to pack up the weekend job, and teaching the piano.'

'But I enjoy my teaching,' Tara said, 'and the money from that and the hotel lets me save, instead of having every penny swallowed by the mortgage.'

'Let's change the subject,' Frank suggested. 'See what Mr Benson has to say, if it makes you feel better.'

They chatted lightly for a while, Frank about his parents who seemed to get frailer every time he went home, and Tara elaborating further on how she had passed her time. They both carefully avoided any more discussion about buying the house. She told him every-thing, apart from her visit to the office and her walk out to Ballygrace House on the Sunday afternoon. What was there to say? That there was something about the big old house which drew her back there, seemed to beckon her, as though a small part of herself still belonged there.

Frank knew little about her involvement with the Fitzgeralds and there was no point digging over old ground now. Besides, even *thinking* about the sad-looking house, with its overgrown garden and shuttered windows brought a pain to the middle of her forehead. Talking about it would only make it worse.

They arrived in plenty of time to check in, only to find that the boat was delayed. There was a queue of cars in front of them waiting to board.

'I'll have to stay with the car,' Frank said, craning his neck to calculate how many cars were in front of them, 'but you can take the chance, if you want to stretch your legs.'

Quite a few passengers had the same idea. Tara strolled by the sea wall, away from the noisy lorries and cars. She walked until Frank's car was a black dot and the loudest noise she could hear came from the seagulls. After a short while, Tara found a newsagent's shop, and she went in and bought newspapers, a magazine, two bottles of lemonade and some chocolate. Afraid she would have trouble finding the car if the queue started to move, she walked back at a quicker pace to the rows of vehicles.

'Good girl,' Frank said, opening the newspaper she had bought for him. He gave her a flirtatious wink. 'What would I do without you?'

Tara laughed. 'Exactly what you did *before* you met me.'

The wait to get on the ferry seemed interminable. Officials in dark uniforms and stiff hats with clipboards walked up and down the queue, apparently checking lists. When any of the passengers challenged them about the delay, there always seemed to be someone else further along who could furnish them with all the reasons.

Tara had another short walk along the seafront, as her legs were starting to cramp from the constant sitting. Her mind flitted from memories of the week in Ballygrace to the semi-detached house she might buy in Stockport. Secretly, she had made up her mind to buy it, but, for a reason she wasn't quite sure of – she wasn't going to tell Frank just yet. It just seemed important to her that she made the decision entirely on her own. Although she was grateful to him for all his help, occasionally Tara found herself irritated at the way he took the credit for the success of her boarding house. He had said it so often that at times Tara almost forgot she had thought the idea up all by herself, long before she met Frank Kennedy.

She turned back towards the queue again, her long red hair streaming out in the breeze behind her, and a hand holding down the billowing skirt of her cream linen dress. From a distance she could see Frank leaning up against the side of the car. He waved when he caught sight of her, a big grin breaking out over his handsome face.

Tara waved back, suddenly feeling a surge of warmth towards him. She wondered now, as she got nearer to the car, how she could have been so awkward to him about the house business earlier on. There was not a woman in Stockport who would not be glad to step into her shoes, and walk out arm in arm with such a prosperous, attractive man. Maybe, she thought, I'd better meet him halfway, or he might start looking elsewhere.

Then, just as she was only half a dozen cars away from him, a man suddenly came flying past, knocking Tara into the oily bumper of one of the cars.

'Frank! Frank!' the man called. 'Thank God you're still here!'

Tara had barely straightened herself up, and was about to check the damage to her cream dress, when a young boy around ten years old and a slightly older girl came running after the man.

'Daddy!' the girl screamed hysterically. 'Daddy! We've been looking everywhere for you!'

Tara turned her head, and saw the two children hurling themselves against Frank. She walked forward to join them – but the chalk-white appearance of Frank's face stopped her dead in her tracks. She stood two cars away from the group and watched.

'It's Lucy,' she heard the man explain breathlessly. 'She had a bad fit after you left . . . the worst one she's ever had. I brought her and Carmel up to the hospital. There was no point taking her to Galway – they'd only have sent her by ambulance up to Dublin.'

'Daddy! Daddy!' the boy screamed now, climbing up Frank's legs. 'You'll have to come to the hospital. Lucy and Mammy need you! You can't go to England now.'

Tara observed the scene in front of her as though she were watching a film. And just like a film – this was not real. The boy and girl – with Frank's dark hair and eyes – couldn't be his children. The man – shorter and stockier than Frank, but with similar features – must be his brother. That's it, Tara thought. It's Frank's brother, and they must be Frank's nephew and niece.

But why, she asked her dazed mind, was the boy up in his arms, and crying '*Daddy*', over and over into his neck? And why was the girl hanging on to his hand, and pleading with him not to go to England?

Very slowly, Frank's head turned towards her. In the instant that

447

their eyes met – she knew. She knew from the pit of her sinking stomach, that these children were Frank Kennedy's and that the Carmel the man had referred to – was Frank Kennedy's wife.

Chapter Thirty-seven

Tara stood in a remote corner of the ship's deck, oblivious to the strong breeze that lifted and tossed her Titian hair. Her green eyes, concealed behind the sunglasses, stared out over the Irish Sea. She took a deep shuddering breath. Nothing could wipe out the memory of what had happened back in Dun Laoghaire – when she discovered that their whole relationship was built on lies and deceit. When the man she had grown to love was revealed as a complete stranger in front of her very eyes.

She kept replaying fragments of their short, terse conversation, over and over again. In the end, there had really been nothing to say. The family scenario which had unfolded before her told her everything she needed to know. If that had not been obvious enough for her, the shocked look on Frank's brother's face when he realised they were travelling together, removed any doubt.

Tara had retrieved her things from Frank Kennedy's car quietly and with no fuss. A scene was not appropriate, nor was it her style. From the stammered explanations he had attempted, Tara understood that Frank had a very sick daughter – some kind of brain tumour. The deterioration in the child was the only reason he kept returning to Ireland, he had quickly and tearfully explained. The marriage had been over years ago.

Tara had smiled at the two children, and said she hoped their sister was better soon – and that she would say a prayer for her. She said she knew their daddy from work, and that he had kindly offered her a lift back home to Manchester. She lifted her heavy case and said she would go to the booking office and get a foot-passenger's ticket to Holyhead.

'Are you sure you'll be all right?' Frank had stammered, his voice no longer sounding like his own.

'Perfectly sure,' Tara replied, avoiding his gaze. 'I think *you* have a lot more to worry about than me.' She paused, shifting the case from one hand to another. 'If I were you, I should plan to spend a lot more time with them in Ireland.'

'Tara . . . I'll explain when I get back,' he had said in a low, pleading voice, as she turned away.

'There's no need,' Tara replied in an icy tone. 'I have all the explanations I need. You would only be wasting your time.'

She stared out over the greenish-grey water now, grateful for every watery mile the ship put between herself and Dun Laoghaire. Between herself and Frank Kennedy. She knew now that when Frank did eventually return to Stockport there would be a wider chasm between them than all the miles these waters filled. It would be a chasm so wide nothing would ever breach it.

Tara suddenly spotted the first landmark of Holyhead. Today, she thought, removing her sunglasses, would be like the first day she and Biddy had arrived in England. It would once again be a new start. This time, she had a house behind her, she had several jobs which all brought in money – and she had her wonderful, grand piano. The only good thing left from their relationship.

Tara knew she was capable of starting all over again. Her life would go on – without Frank Kennedy.

Her life would go on without any man.

'The rotten bastard!' Ruby exclaimed. 'A wife an' a handicapped kid! I always knew there was more to him than meets the eye – didn't I, Biddy? I always said he was too sweet to be wholesome.'

Tara had got the taxi from Stockport train station to drop her off at Ruby's. She wanted to get the business of Frank Kennedy over and done with, and telling Ruby and Biddy was the first step. Talking about it made it seem more real. It made her face up to what had to be done.

'Oh, Tara, I'm really sorry for you,' Biddy said, her eyes filling up with tears. 'I was expectin' you to say you'd got engaged or some-thin' . . . but I never expected you to tell me that Frank was a married man.' She paused. 'I can't believe it – he doesn't even look married.'

'That's men for you, love,' Ruby said, putting a cup of tea in front of Tara. 'They never look like they're supposed to. I've had that happen to me more than once.'

There was silence for a moment – while everyone thought of Shay – but nobody actually said anything.

'You'll manage, love,' Ruby told her. 'You're like me – a a survivor. You'll manage without Frank Kennedy. The bastard! You'll go on to bigger and better things.' She took a sip of her tea. 'At least you're not walkin' away empty-handed. Thank God you got the piano out of him first!'

Ruby was due to go into hospital two weeks before Biddy's wedding. A biopsy on both breasts had showed up what the doctor described as 'something sinister'. An operation was now necessary to show up the full extent of the problem.

'I knew I should never have gone near the bloody doctor!' Ruby told Biddy the morning she was due in. She plunged the breakfast plates into the hot soapy water in the sink. 'Once they get their hands on you – you've had it.' Her voice rose an octave higher, as she viciously attacked a scrambled-egg pot with a scouring pad. 'Once they cut you open – you're a goner! I should never have let them bloody near me.'

Biddy's face was deathly white. 'You'll be fine,' she said comfortingly, although inside she felt more hysterical than Ruby. She twisted a strand of her black hair nervously between her fingers. 'Once you've had yer operation you'll be fine.'

'I'll not be bloody fine!' Ruby snapped. 'How will I be fine when I'm in hospital an' you're gettin' married?'

'You'll be out in plenty of time,' Biddy reassured her. 'The wedding's not for two weeks.'

'What about this place?' Ruby said, waving her hands around. 'You shouldn't be doin' all this. You shouldn't be usin' up holidays from the hotel to run this place, while I'm in the bleedin' hospital.'

'I don't mind,' Biddy said. 'I like cookin' for the lads.'

Ruby dried her hands on a tea-towel, then came to sit at the table. 'What about Shay?' she said, her voice suddenly quiet. 'How's he goin' to take all this?' Her shoulders slumped.

'Never mind Shay – it's yerself that's more important.'

'How's he goin' to feel about me if they chop off me breasts?'

'They won't,' Biddy stated, feeling sweat breaking out on her brow at the thought. 'They won't do anything like that.'

'An' you've that priest comin' next week, that Father Daly,' Ruby rattled on. 'You said he wanted you to go to that convent in Derbyshire again, for the—'

'The retreat,' Biddy finished for her. 'A retreat for women who are gettin' married.' A nauseous feeling came up into Biddy's throat.

'How will you manage? How can you plan yer weddin' and go to Derbyshire if you're runnin' this bloody place?'

'I don't want to go with him . . . it'll be a good excuse.'

'I don't know what's goin' to happen next,' Ruby whispered. 'I feel as though everythin's fallin' apart.'

Chapter Thirty-eight

Two days later, a car drew up outside Tara's house. She knew it was Frank before she opened the door. He followed her into the dark hallway and, without a word being spoken, followed her into the dining-room. Tara walked over to the bay window, and stood beside the piano with her back to him. Her red hair was drawn back from her face in an elegant knot, and her posture was straight and unyielding.

'Tara,' he started, 'will you listen to me while I explain?'

'Please do,' she replied, her tone icy and clipped. 'I'm sure I shall find it all very interesting.'

And she did listen. For nearly a whole hour she listened as he poured out his heart and his life. She standing like a statue with her back to him, and Frank sitting on one of the dark wood chairs he had pulled out from under the dining-table.

Tara listened to a story of an unhappy marriage to a local girl, which was forced upon them, when they were only seventeen. How even before the first child Lucy was born, he knew deep down that things would never work out. But he kept trying. Frank was hard-working and ambitious. Carmel, though outwardly a vivacious red-head, was at heart a homebody. A girl whose only ambition was to have a nice house in the same village as her brothers and sisters, so all her classmates could see how well she and Frank had done. Within five years they had the nice house, and another daughter, Sarah, on the way. By this time, Frank had started working in England. The big jobs and the big money were all to be had in England.

The plan was that Carmel would join Frank in England, after Sarah was born. He had now gone into the contracting side of the building trade, and as his reputation grew, work came in fast and furious. He found them a lovely, four-bedroomed, detached house in Edgeley in Stockport, and then waited until Carmel was ready to join him.

He was still waiting.

He travelled backwards and forwards on the boat and then when he could afford it, he travelled by plane. Carmel came for a couple of holidays, and hated it. She was overwhelmed by the crowds, by the traffic – and by Stockport in general. It didn't matter that the house was bigger and better than any house in the village in County Clare. Who was going to see it if it was over in England? By the time Declan was born, they both knew she would never move to England.

Tara knew the rest of the story about the growth of Kennedy's contracting business, so he didn't elaborate any further on that. He explained how he and Carmel had spoken about their situation at length, and how they had agreed to live separate lives for ninety per cent of the year. For the sake of both their children, both their families – and the Catholic Church – they would act as a normal married couple when he came home. Given the difficulties about obtaining a divorce and the fact that neither of them were planning to re-marry, it was the easiest option.

He then went on to painfully explain about his daughter's Lucy's illness. The tumour had been discovered shortly after he had met Tara. That was the reason for his unexpected return to Ireland last Christmas and the subsequent frequent visits. An operation had removed the tumour, but Lucy now suffered from severe epileptic seizures. The hospital expected her to gradually get better – but it was a long, painful process, and both wife and daughter needed all his support.

Frank thrust his fingers through his dark hair, then looked up at Tara for the first time since he had started the story. She still had her ramrod straight back to him.

'I want you to know,' he said now, 'that you're the only woman. I've ever truly loved in my life.'

Very slowly she turned to face him. She was crying. She faced him quietly and with great dignity, but she was crying all the same.

There was a huge, empty silence.

Frank ran a nervous finger round the collar of his white shirt. Every inch of him ached to cross the room and pull her into his arms. But he knew he dare not. He squared his shoulders – awaiting what was to come.

'It's over, Frank,' she finally said. 'It's finished.'

He stood up. 'I'll get a divorce – I promise you.'

Tara shook her head. 'No . . . it could never work. You have a wife and children.' She thought of adding '*You obviously have a penchant for red-haired women*', but decided that the petty comment was beneath her and belittled the situation.

Frank's throat suddenly felt dry. He swallowed hard. 'I should have told you when we first met . . . but I was afraid to . . . I was afraid I'd lose you.'

'It wouldn't have made any difference *when* you told me. A married man is out of bounds.' She ran her hand over the cool ebony top of the piano. 'We've had some good times, and I'm grateful for them – but you deceived me.' Tara's green eyes narrowed until they were hard emerald slits. 'You've deceived me in the most awful, despicable way . . . and I could never, ever, trust you again.'

Then, her head held high, and arms folded across her chest, she marched past him to the door. 'There's nothing more to say, Frank.' She held it wide open for him to pass through. 'Please go.'

Chapter Thirty-nine

Ruby's cancer was advanced in both breasts and had moved into her lymph nodes. As she lay in intensive care after undergoing a double radical mastectomy, her GP, Doctor Phillips shook his head in dismay. How could an intelligent, attractive woman ignore such obvious signs for months?

When she had come to his surgery the first time a couple of weeks ago, one glance at her breasts and nipples – particularly the right one – had made his blood run cold. Ruby Sweeney had been apologising for wasting his time, saying she knew it was only a silly little infection, and if he would give her an antibiotic, she would be on her way. He had to insist on having a look at her. She had held on for dear life to first her blouse, and then her bra. But the look in her eyes, when he eventually examined her, told him that Ruby had known there was something seriously wrong for months.

In the initial stages, fear – not the cancer – had been her biggest enemy.

Doctor Phillips hoped that they had caught the cancer early enough. Ruby was still under fifty and had always been in good health. With treatment, and the right attitude, she might well make a good recovery.

'Are you sure I look okay?' Biddy said, twirling round in the three-quarter length white wedding dress, the Wednesday before her big day. She tugged on the satin material at the hips. 'You don't think it's a bit loose on me or anythin'? We've three more days until the wedding – I still have time to get it taken in.'

'You look perfect,' Tara told her for the third time in as many minutes. 'You look absolutely beautiful. Are you happy with this?' She motioned to the satin bridesmaid's dress she was wearing. It had three-quarter fitted sleeves, a sweetheart neckline, and the dark green colouring contrasted very well with her hair.

'I'm delighted with it,' Biddy said, 'an' I'm glad we got a bridesmaid dress we both like.' Biddy took her headdress out of the box. It was a half-moon, sparkly, ornate affair. 'I'm havin' my hair set in curls first thing on Saturday mornin',' she explained. 'The lady in the bridal shop said the head-dress should just sit on top. It has a comb attached, but I can always stick a few hair clips in for safety.'

'I'll help you,' Tara offered. 'We'll make sure everything goes like clockwork.' She smiled and stifled a sigh of weariness. She had never felt so tired. It was only nine o'clock in the evening, but she had recently started going to bed very early, due to the busy schedule she had each day.

Since she and Frank had parted, Tara had filled the void he left with teaching extra piano lessons in the evenings and Saturday mornings. It brought in more money, and it had given her the financial confidence to go to the building society and ask for a bigger mortgage to buy the house next door. She hoped to know in the next few weeks whether or not they would loan her the extra money.

In the meantime, teaching and playing the piano took up every minute she wasn't cooking, cleaning, working in the office, or working weekends in the Park Hotel. It was ironic that Frank had bought her the beautiful instrument, and now it had replaced him in her heart. The piano gave her peace, pleasure and escapism – and the piano would never hurt and betray her.

Biddy sniffed, then went over to her dressingtable in search of a hanky. 'I wish,' she said sadly, 'that Ruby was here. It's taken all the good out of the weddin', her not being here. I wish she was out of hospital an' everythin' was back to normal.'

'It will be . . . soon.' Then, in an effort to distract Biddy's mind from her depressing thoughts, Tara lifted her bridesmaid's headdress and said: 'How would you like me to wear my hair? Up or down?' She sat the green headdress on top of her flowing hair.

'Either way,' Biddy replied. 'You're lucky. Your hair always looks lovely, however you wear it.'

Things could not have gone worse for Biddy in the week leading up to her wedding. Poor Ruby was going to be in hospital for at least another fortnight. The operation had been very serious, and she had reacted badly to the anaesthetic. Now, when she was just beginning to come round, she had developed a bad chest infection. On no account, the hospital said, was she well enough to go home, far less attend a wedding. The only consolation was the suggestion that Biddy and Fred come to the hospital and have pictures taken with Ruby. The nurse said that with a lacy nightdress, a bit of lipstick and some powder, Ruby would look like her old self.

Deep down, Biddy knew that her beloved friend and landlady would never be the same again.

Although Biddy had written to Father Daly saying that she didn't want him to come to Stockport to perform her wedding ceremony, he had ignored her. Instead, he had phoned the parish priest at Our Lady's Church in Shaw Heath, and arranged the whole thing behind her back. It was only when she went down to the church to sort out the flowers and the organist, that the parish priest said how nice it was for her to have her own priest from home to conduct the wedding.

Biddy had however, put Father Daly off the idea of coming over to Stockport last week, saying she had a very sick woman to visit each day, a boarding house to look after, and a wedding to arrange. He had written a nice letter back, saying he would wait until the week of the wedding, and call out with Biddy and Fred's wedding present to Maple Terrace on the Thursday night. Perhaps, he thought, they might take a last run out to the convent in Derbyshire, before Biddy was a married woman. Her stomach had turned over at the thought, for she knew that the word *convent* actually implied *hotel*.

Biddy had slept very little over the past few weeks. It had all started with worry over Ruby, and then it had gone on to anxiety over the wedding, and wondering if she was doing the right thing by marrying Fred. She still hadn't told him anything about the baby or Dinny . . . or any of the other things. Biddy was sure Fred loved her, but what man would be prepared to overlook all that? Everything was going wrong, and her growing dread about Father Daly's visit was now putting the tin hat on it.

After another night tossing and turning, Biddy woke up early on

Thursday morning. The black cloud of depression, which had been her constant companion lately, descended the minute she opened her eyes. And then she remembered. Last night she had made a decision which would settle things one way or the other with Father Daly. But first, she was going to cook breakfast for the lads, and then this afternoon she was going to visit Ruby.

Biddy was standing outside the women's surgical ward at five to three. Being a weekday, it was fairly quiet. Most visitors came for the evening visit between seven and eight. At dead on three o'clock, the ward doors were opened by a po-faced nurse in a white starched uniform, allowing the strong antiseptic hospital smell to waft out.

Walking down the long ward, towards Ruby's bed, Biddy felt her heartbeat quicken. She could see Ruby lying down in the bed. She quietly pulled out the wooden visitor's chair, and then sat nervously by the side of the bed, casting anxious glances at the pale sleeping form, dwarfed by the metal-framed bed. Ruby had always been a petite slim woman, but the last few weeks had taken its toll. She was now so thin her tiny bones barely caused a ripple in the bed.

Biddy's gaze travelled round the ward, taking in the regimented beds and metal lockers, the tops of which were adorned with 'Get well' cards, and vases of assorted flowers. Faded, sickly green curtains, were drawn back tightly on rails at the head of each bed.

Patients with visitors carried out conversations in low voices, conscious of disturbing their sleeping neighbours or being overheard. Every so often, a loud rasping breathing sounded across the ward, from a curtained-off bed. Apparently, another visitor had whispered to Biddy it was a young woman who had just recently been wheeled back from theatre.

After a quarter of an hour of the depressing ward, Biddy heaved a sigh of relief as Ruby's blue eyes flickered open.

The landlady gave her friend a big smile. 'Biddy . . . what're you doin' here?' she said, struggling to sit up. 'Haven't you got enough to do without runnin' up to visit me in the middle of the day?'

'How're you feelin'?' Biddy asked, her eyes roaming over the landlady's face for any small signs of improvement.

'Oh, I'm gettin' there . . . I'm gettin' there,' Ruby replied. 'I'm like an old workhorse. I think they'll have to shoot me first.'

Biddy laughed nervously, and – ignoring her friend's protests about wasting money – put a bunch of grapes and a bottle of Lucozade on top of her rusting locker. 'Ruby . . . can I ask yer advice on somethin'?'

'Course you can, love.' Her brow deepened into a worried 'v'. 'What's wrong? You're not havin' second thoughts about the wedding or owt?'

Biddy shook her head. 'No . . . it's Father Daly.'

'That nice Irish priest? Did he come over for the wedding then?'

'He's not nice, Ruby . . .' Biddy's voice suddenly sounded choked. 'He's not nice at all. He's a terrible man . . . an' he should never have been a priest.' All of a sudden, the sickly perfume from Ruby's white and yellow chrysanthemums, and the antiseptic hospital smell mingled together to make her feel dizzy and nauseous.

Ruby sat straight up in bed, smoothed down the cream cover, and clasped her hands on her lap. It was still an effort to remember not to cross her arms over the painful area which used to be her bust. 'I'm waitin',' she said softly, understanding and compassion written all over her face.

Biddy moved her chair so that it was angled away from the flowers, and took a deep breath. 'The baby,' she started, her eyes downcast, 'it wasn't PJ Murphy's . . .'

Ruby clasped her hands together so tightly that the knuckles went white – but she stayed silent.

'From the age of eleven,' Biddy went on, her breath coming in short, panting bursts, 'this man . . . Dinny Martin, a lodger in the house I grew up in . . . he used to touch me.'

Ruby reached as far behind her as pain would allow, and drew the curtain partway across to give them some privacy.

A tear slid down Biddy's burning cheek. 'I liked Dinny . . . I was as much to blame as he was. He used to give me sweets and little presents every time we . . .'

There was a silence.

'Did he – did he have proper sex with you?' Ruby asked quietly.

Biddy nodded, and searched for a hanky in her coat pocket. 'Not at first . . . it was when I was older,' she sniffed.

'An' this Dinny fella . . . is he the father of your baby?'

Biddy's eyes opened wide, and she suddenly looked like a cornered rabbit. 'No,' she whispered, shaking her head vigorously. '*Dinny's* not the father.'

'Then,' Ruby asked, her mind a whirl of confusion, 'if he's not the father, an' PJ what's-his-name's not the father . . . who is?' Then, as it suddenly dawned on her, Ruby's hands flew to cover her mouth. 'Don't tell me . . .' she whispered.

Biddy closed her eyes and swallowed hard. 'If it had been Dinny or PJ I would never have had the child adopted. Sure, I was an orphan meself . . . I wouldn't have done it to another human being . . . another poor little baby . . . if it hadn't been for what happened . . .'

'Look at me, Biddy,' Ruby said urgently. 'Look at me . . . and get all this off yer chest. You'll never know any peace until you tell somebody.'

Biddy lifted her sad, tortured eyes and looked up into the face of the only mother she had ever known. 'It's Father Daly,' she whispered. 'That terrible, evil man – is the child's father.'

For the next half-an-hour, Biddy talked while the sick Ruby held her hand and listened. Not once did the older woman reveal any sign of shock or disgust at the emotional outpourings that she heard. Occasionally, she muttered 'the bastard!' and gripped Biddy's hand tighter, and at one point she stopped her, and hissed: 'For Christ's sake, stop blaming yourself – you were only a bit of a kid. They were two grown men – an' they should bleedin' hang for what they done to you!'

By the time Biddy had told the whole story, it was coming to the end of visiting time. She dabbed her eyes and made to move.

'You just stay where you are, love,' Ruby told her when the bell sounded. 'It's another ten minutes before they throw you out.' She patted Biddy's hand firmly. 'You've talked for the last half-an-hour, and now it's my turn.' She gave Biddy a wink. 'We're going to sort that old pervert priest good an' proper. We'll sort him out that well, that he'll never want to show his face outside Ireland again. An' I guarantee you – he'll be heading back on the first boat from Holyhead in the morning.'

461

'How?' Biddy asked, her eyes wide. 'What can we do? No one will believe my word against a priest's.'

Ruby pulled her in closer to the bed. 'Listen to me carefully,' she said, her blue eyes narrow with determination, 'an' you must promise me to do *exactly* what I tell you.'

Chapter Forty

Father Daly arrived at seven o'clock on the dot on the Thursday evening. His purplish face, bloated from years of red wine and brandy, beamed with pleasure when Biddy opened the front door. He carried a box wrapped in wedding paper, which he said was a little piece of Ireland to remind Biddy of her heritage, and the fine workmanship of her fellow countrymen. It was a heavy vase made of Waterford Crystal. Biddy thanked him quietly, left him chatting to some of the lads in the kitchen, and then went upstairs to get her coat.

When she appeared downstairs a few minutes later, dressed in a belted blue woollen dress with a high collar and long sleeves, he apologised to the lads for having to rush off. 'A poor old nun from County Offaly,' he said piously, blessing himself. 'She's unlikely to last the week out, and it would ease her passage out of this world if she saw some faces from her home parish.'

His pious tune changed when he and Biddy were alone. 'Where,' he asked, as they went towards the front door,' 'is your overnight bag?'

'I have everything I need,' Biddy told him firmly.

'Surely,' he whispered, fingering the sleeve of her light wool dress, 'you have a more fetching outfit than that. Something that does justice to your trim figure?'

'My dress is fine,' Biddy snapped.

The unholy priest sighed, but decided not to pursue the subject any further.

Father Daly did all the talking as they drove out of Stockport. 'I believe there's a nice little hotel in Macclesfield,' he said casually, taking off his dog-collar. 'I thought we might have a meal, and then we can relax afterwards with a drink.'

'I think I could do with a drink *before* the meal,' Biddy said, checking the time on her watch. 'I could do with somethin' to relax me.'

A smile appeared on the priest's bloated face. He slid a hand over to her knee, then his fingers pressed firmly on her flesh. 'You can have as many drinks as you like, Bridget,' he told her in a throaty voice. 'As many drinks as you like to loosen you up. We don't want anything to spoil this special last night together.'

'We'll have a bottle of Beaujolais,' Father Daly beamed to the waiter, 'and a well-done steak each, with all the trimmings.'

He had changed his shirt in the double bedroom he had booked for them, and was wearing an ordinary striped tie. To all intents and purposes, he and Biddy looked like father and daughter. The priest was aware of this, and the idea that people might assume they were related made their rendezvous in the hotel all the more exciting to him. He looked round the restaurant, a smile of appreciation on his lips.

The waiter appeared back at the table and poured two glasses of wine. The priest took a mouthful from one and then nodded his approval.

'These are the important things in life, Bridget,' he said in a low, contemplative voice. 'Pleasant surroundings, candlelight, good food and wine, music and – most important of all – *stimulating* company.' He gave a little laugh. 'And you, my dear Bridget, are the most stimulating company I have ever enjoyed.'

Biddy took several gulps of her wine, checked her watch again, and then she said she needed to go to the ladies'. Once outside the restaurant, she asked a porter where the payphone was. He pointed her down a long narrow corridor.

Before she lifted the receiver, Biddy took a piece of paper from her handbag, and checked the telephone number and the hotel bedroom number that she had written on it. She knew she must not make any mistakes. Ruby had told her exactly what had to be done, and so far, Biddy had followed her instructions to the letter. And so far – everything had worked out exactly as Ruby said it would.

Biddy crossed the fingers of one hand and dialled the number with the other.

'It is the thoughts of your company,' Father Daly said, when Biddy returned, 'that has kept me going. Those thoughts have kept my spirits up during the lonely months in that cold, damp house in Ballygrace.' He leaned forward, beads of sweat standing out on his fleshy brow. 'I often think back to our first little encounters in my kitchen pantry. Do you remember?'

Biddy lifted her folded napkin, and smoothed it out on the table in front of her.

'*You*,' the priest continued, in the same sickly tone, 'who I thought to be a sweet innocent teenage girl. Then I discovered you were not such an innocent.' He held his wine glass by the stem, and moved it round in a circular motion. 'Not such an innocent at all . . . my dear Bridget. Oh, how you loved to talk about it . . .' He shifted about in his chair now, and then moved a hand down to adjust the front of his trousers.

Biddy's eyes flashed with anger. 'I was upset . . . after what had happened with Dinny. You're a priest – I thought I was telling you my Confession.'

'Confessions,' he said with a smile, 'are for the Confessional Box. You and I were in the kitchen pantry when you willingly demonstrated what you and Dinny Martin had been getting up to.'

'You *asked* me to show you,' she hissed. 'I thought you were going to speak to Dinny . . . tell him to leave me alone. I thought you would tell him that what he was doin' to me all those years was a sin. I was only a child when he started . . . I never knew what it was he was doin' to me.'

Father Daly glanced up and saw the waiter coming towards their table. 'Let us forget all about the past and enjoy our evening together, Bridget. Our time is running out.'

No, Father Daly, Biddy thought, it's not *our* time that's running out – it's *your* time.

Biddy dragged the meal out as long as she possibly could. She chewed every bite of her steak very slowly and deliberately. She then took her time equally slowly, choosing and eating a dessert.

'It's nice to see a young girl with a healthy appetite,' Father Daly said, signalling for another bottle of wine. His eyes darted from Biddy's face to her modest bust. 'And I'm delighted to see how well you've filled out since coming to England. You're obviously looking after yourself well.' He paused for a moment. 'This Fred fellow you're marrying, does he treat you well?'

'Yes,' Biddy replied honestly, 'he treats me better than anybody has in me whole life.'

'I hope,' the priest said, frowning deeply, 'that he won't cause us any problems in the future.' He reached a podgy hand across the table, and tilted Biddy's chin to make her look at him. 'You know I still intend to visit you? I'll be back to England once or twice a year, and I'll always come to see you. Let us never forget that we have a common bond, Bridget. God gave us the gift of a child. It wasn't something we asked for . . . nor was it something we wanted. But God in his wisdom gave us that child, so it must have been for a reason.'

He halted as the waiter returned with the wine and then continued when they were alone again. 'I keep regular checks on our son,' he informed Biddy. 'Being a priest I'm entitled to do that. He's being brought up with a professional couple in Dublin – the father is one of the top solicitors in the city who often acts on behalf of the church.'

Biddy's eyes widened in shock. 'Do they know anything about me?'

Father Daly took a sip of his wine. 'They know you're a poor orphan girl who got herself into trouble with a married man.' He leered at Biddy now, his eyes beginning to show the effects of the wine. 'It's true – technically, I *am* married to the church.' He leaned across the table. 'I may be a priest of God,' he whispered thickly, 'but I was created a man first – and I have a man's needs.'

Biddy shrunk back in her seat and checked her watch again.

After dessert, they both ordered a cup of coffee. 'Have whatever you like,' Father Daly said. 'The church is paying the bill.'

Biddy sipped at her coffee, while her free hand fiddled with her clip-on pearl earring. The earring suddenly clattered on to the table, and then bounced down on to the floor.

Biddy put her cup into the saucer, then tried to look under the table. 'Oh, father,' she said apologetically, 'I think me earring's rolled under yer chair. Could you reach it for me?'

'A pleasure for a fine young lady, Bridget.' Father Daly pushed his chair out from the table and bent down.

Quick as a flash, Biddy took two small tablets from her dress pocket, and dropped them into the priest's coffee. She lifted a teaspoon, and stirred the hot liquid, to help the tablets dissolve rapidly. Then, as the priest triumphantly exclaimed 'Got it!', Biddy sat back in the chair and tried hard not to smile.

Whatever happened later on in the evening, she would have the pleasure of knowing that Father Daly would not have a comfortable night. Judging by the excellent past performance of the laxative tablets on Lizzie Lawless and Sally Taylor, she could expect a reaction fairly soon.

Oh, the hours of secret laughter Biddy had enjoyed when she thought of Lizzie Lawless being confined to bed for days on end, due to a mysterious 'weakness of the bowels'. Biddy had laughed even louder when she thought of the brassy blonde Sally, who had threatened her own position with the lads in the lodging house. The memory of Sally scuttling cross-legged and red-faced to the bathroom every five minutes, and then her hasty exit from Stockport, had been a tonic in itself.

Now, it was Father Daly's turn to suffer the physical indignity of the cramps and sweats, and the mad dashes to make it to the lavatory before an embarrassing accident occurred. At times of trouble – when she had no verbal or physical recourse – Biddy had found the laxatives to be a basic but utterly effective line of defence.

After coffee and a few more drinks in the bar, Biddy said she would like to go up to the bedroom.

Father Daly's eyes lit with delight. 'Of course,' he said with a smile, 'we can order more drinks with room service, if we require it.' He finished his brandy off with a flourish.

As soon as they arrived at the bedroom door, Biddy excused herself and made for the bathroom a few doors down the corridor, leaving the priest to go into the bedroom on his own. She perched on the side of the clawfooted, enamel bath and waited. She hugged herself, rocking back and forth. Every few moments, she stopped and checked the time, wondering and worrying whether Ruby's plan would work.

Then suddenly, Biddy's heart leapt into her mouth as she heard the thud of several sets of footsteps coming up the wooden stairs. She hoped and prayed they were the footsteps she had been waiting for all night. Quietly and cautiously, she opened the bathroom door just a fraction. Just wide enough for her to check as to whom the footsteps belonged.

Then – like a bird that had just been released from captivity – Biddy's heart soared. She flew out of the bathroom door along the corridor to where Tara, Shay and Fred were standing, outside Father Daly's bedroom door. Fred came forward to greet her with outstretched arms.

'Thank God!' Biddy cried, running forward and burying her face in Fred's great chest.

Hearing the noise, Father Daly opened the door, his tie discarded and his shirt open halfway down his well-fed stomach. He stood bewildered and speechless, his eyes and mind working hard against the combination of wine and brandy, trying to make sense of the scene before him.

Tara moved first. 'I think,' she said, in a cold, uncompromising tone, 'that you might prefer us to speak in the privacy of the room.' Then, without waiting for an invitation, she brushed in past the priest, closely followed by her father, Biddy and Fred.

Father Daly – realising something was seriously afoot – automatically slid straight into his superior clerical role. 'Well, now,' he said, striding purposely across the bedroom. He stood, hands behind his back, against the window. 'To what do I owe the honour of this unwarranted convoy?' His voice dripped sarcasm and disdain.

Tara cut right across him. 'What exactly is your business with Biddy?' she said, advancing towards the window.

The priest cleared his throat and straightened his back. 'I am not in the habit of being spoken to in such a manner, young lady, and I most certainly will not be interrogated by the likes of you.'

'Perhaps you'd like to be interrogated by the *Gardaí* back in Ireland?' Tara said now, her face a picture of disgust at the thought of all the things he had done to poor Biddy. 'Or maybe the Bishop would like to hear all about a priest who has interfered with a young girl?'

'I deny everything that you've accused me of,' the priest said in a superior, bumptious manner. 'Where are all the witnesses to these dreadful accusations?'

Shay stepped forward. 'Maybe,' he said, eyeing the priest dangerously, 'it's not words that are needed here. It's not as if we're in holy Ireland now. Maybe, begod,' he turned to look at Fred, 'we need to take a firmer hand.'

The burly Fred suddenly moved across the room to face Father Daly. His big hand shot out, and pinned the rotund priest against the wooden cross of the window. 'I don't like what I've been hearing about you – about the things you're been doing to Biddy.'

Father Daly's blood pressure escalated. 'This is preposterous!' he said, attempting to struggle to struggle out of Fred's grip. 'Take your hands off me – I'm a man of the cloth!'

'A man of the cloth, me arse!' Shay spat. 'You have no white collar on now, and in my opinion, you should never have been let wear one! You're a disgrace to the church and all it stands for! Tamperin' with a poor young girl like Biddy, when she came askin' for yer guidance an' help.'

Fred suddenly snapped. His free arm moulded itself into a battering ram with a huge fist. It moved with lightning speed to connect with Father Daly's jaw, while the other giant hand held him fast – as a cat's paw would hold a mouse.

Realising there was no point in even attempting retaliation or escape, the priest opted for submission. His shoulders slumped and his head lolled to the side, blood dribbling from his fleshy mouth. 'You'll have to answer for this,' he warned through red-coloured spittle. 'I deny any accusations laid against me, and I'm prepared to do that in a court of law.'

Tara pushed between Fred and the priest. 'You,' she said, thrusting an accusing finger in the priest's bloody face, 'will most certainly answer for this. You will answer in the highest court – when you go to meet your Maker!' She paused. 'Your guilt and sins are written all over your face. Even as a child I knew you were not what a priest should be. And if I sensed that awfulness about you, there must be others who felt the same.' Tara's voice quivered, and her shoulders heaved with revulsion. 'You are a reptile of the lowest order. Make no mistake, one way or another, you'll pay for this. Tomorrow, I intend to write to the Bishop in Carlow and the parish priest in Tullamore, informing them of the terrible things you've done. Whether they choose to believe it or not, it will make them keep a watchful eye on you.'

Father Daly's face turned pale. To add to all this horrendous business, he now had an unusual nagging pain, low down in his stomach. 'They won't believe a word from the likes of you. You, who were the talk of Ballygrace and Tullamore, cavorting around the place in a car with a married man – namely William Fitzgerald.'

Biddy's hands flew to cover her face. She couldn't believe that the priest would say such a thing to her friend.

Tara flinched inwardly, but showed no signs of it. 'Unlike you,' she said, her head held high, 'I have a clear conscience. I did nothing wrong with William Fitzgerald or any man while I was in Ireland.'

The priest calmly took out a white handkerchief, and used it to blot up the blood pouring from his cut mouth. 'Everyone knows that's why you ran off to England. It's *you* who should be seeking absolution for your sins – not me.'

'Stop it!' Biddy suddenly screamed, tears streaming down her face. She pointed a finger at the priest. 'You know exactly why I came to England . . . and you know that Tara only came to keep me company. *She* has never done anything wrong.' Her voice was broken, tortured now. 'You are the most evil person I've ever known . . . and you've tried to ruin my life, and God knows how many other young girls' lives.'

The priest continued dabbing at his mouth, as though she had never spoken.

'It's all right, Biddy,' Tara said quietly, going over to put her arm around Biddy. 'He'll get what he deserves. When the Bishop receives the letter, he won't be practising as a priest for much longer. I'm sure we'll hear he's retired quite shortly – although it's swinging from the end of a rope he should be.'

A violent tension hung in the air around the room. Tiny beads of perspiration appeared on the Father Daly's forehead, due to the effort of clenching his buttocks together, to prevent the most humiliating accident that could ever befall a priest.

'Biddy?' Fred motioned his fiancée to come to his side. 'It's up to you now. Just say the word and I'll do him good and proper! I'd like to break his bloody neck. I don't care if they lock me up and throw away the key. I'll make sure he'll never lay another hand on you – or any innocent young girl again!'

Biddy's heart pounded with feelings of relief mixed with guilt. If only she was the innocent girl Fred thought her to be . . . if only he knew all the business with Dinny and PJ. But Ruby had warned her to say nothing more to Fred than was absolutely necessary. The less he knew, the better for Biddy. Men were only men. And after all, Ruby said, they still had their feelings.

Biddy came over to stand by the big, muscle-bound Fred. Fred her protector. Fred the man she was due to marry in two days' time. She looked up into the wrestler's face, her eyes full of gratitude and love. 'Leave him,' she said quietly. 'Let's get out of here. He's not worth dirtying your hands over.'

Under the circumstances, Biddy's wedding went off very well. The Grosvenor provided a sherry and whisky reception in the wood-panelled foyer, and a photographer took pictures in front of the ornate marble fireplace. Afterwards, everyone moved into a small function room where they dined on vegetable soup, roast beef and Yorkshire puddings, and sherry trifle.

Biddy wore her white, fitted, three-quarter length dress of satin overlaid with lace on the arms and bodice. Her sparkly headdress sat perfectly on her shoulder-length hair, specially curled for the day by a hairdresser. Tara had come up to Maple Terrace when Biddy had returned from having her hair done, and had helped with her make-up, and the pinning of her head attire.

The nice parish priest in the local church performed the wedding mass, saying how sorry he was that the priest from Ireland couldn't make it. No one mentioned the business with Father Daly. This was Biddy's special day, and it was an unspoken agreement that it should not be tainted by any reference to the priest.

Shay and the other lads from Ruby's lodging house, all looked very smart, albeit slightly awkward, in their best suits with red carnations in the buttonholes. Fred and his brother looked smarter still, in brand-new suits, and Tara Flynn caught the eye of every man in the church with her dark green dress, and her flowing russet locks.

The rest of the guests were made up of Fred's family and friends from Preston, some of his wrestling mates, and some of the hotel staff. The wedding celebration was also a 'leaving do' for Biddy, because she had now given up her job in the Grosvenor to run Ruby's lodging house single-handedly. Ruby had argued against it, saying that she could always ask Sally, her niece to come over from Liverpool. That had definitely made up Biddy's mind, and the following day she had handed in her notice. The hotel manager was very good, and said that there would always be a job there for her when Ruby was back in the whole of her health.

After the meal, the guests danced to a three-piece band which played regularly in the Grosvenor. Fred paid for the first round of drinks, and after that, everyone paid for their own. All in all, it was as nice a wedding party as Biddy could ever have dreamed of back in Ballygrace. She and Fred had received lovely wedding presents from his family and both their friends. Then Fred had given Biddy the best present of all as they posed for a photograph.

'This is the start of a new life for us,' he had whispered, 'and it's what happens from today that counts. The past is in the past.' Biddy's heart had *almost* soared into happiness.

But the wedding day, could not – and would not – be complete without Ruby.

There was a lump in Biddy's throat as she sat by Ruby's bed, resplendent in her wedding attire. Fred was in a chair next to her, and Shay, tearfully morbid after a few drinks, sat opposite, holding Ruby's limp hand. The wedding photographer – a wresting fan of Fred's – stood outside the ward smoking a cigarette, waiting for a signal that the patient had wakened up. As she studied the shrunken figure in the bed, for the first time ever Biddy noticed the landlady's dark brown roots showing through her peroxide blonde hair.

That inch of virgin brown hair, made Biddy feel paralysed by an inarticulate fear. Ruby Sweeney was meticulous in all aspects of her appearance – none more so than the upkeep of her bleached blonde hair. For Ruby to be unable to do anything about those dark roots – or worse still – to be unaware of them, filled Biddy with a terrible dread.

All three sat mute by the stricken landlady's bedside, waiting for her to take her place in Biddy's wedding album.

After the celebrations were over, Tara lay wide awake until the early hours of the morning. In the last few months, she had lost two more important people in her life. Biddy was only a mile or so away – but she was now a married woman. Fred, who was moving into Biddy's room, and Ruby were now her main priorities. Running the lodging house in Maple Terrace and visiting the hospital would take up all Biddy's time.

Frank Kennedy had disappeared from Tara's life, permanently. She had heard that he had gone back to Ireland for six months, and presumed it was to spend more time with his wife and family. Strangely, she didn't miss Frank as much as she thought she would. And stranger still, his absence did not cause the great pain it might. The greatest hurt had been to her pride. The fact that he had deceived her for all that time. But, she consoled herself, the most important thing was that she *had* got over it.

The whole business of Frank, and the awful revelations about Biddy and Father Daly and Dinny Martin had left Tara drained. It was all too awful. She now felt old and weary.

She stretched a hand out and checked the time on the clock again. It was nearly half-past two. Tomorrow was Sunday, and that meant early Mass, cooking breakfast for all the lodgers and then in the afternoon, working in the reception of the Park Hotel.

Monday would start her weekday routine off again with work at Thornley's Estate Agents, cooking dinner when she came in, and then teaching the piano in the evening. The winter and the start of another year in England was only months away. Months of the gruelling but satisfying routine that would fill a void in Tara Flynn's life.

A void which Gabriel Fitzgerald had completely filled for a short but glorious time. A void which Frank Kennedy had almost filled – but not quite. A void which Tara now knew might never be filled again, for she had lately come to realise that there were few men who she was actually attracted to. After Frank, she realised that she would rather be on her own, than make such a mistake again.

Hard work – and the security and independence it gave – would now be the mainstay of Tara's life.

Chapter Forty-one

✦

September, 1956

'I think,' Tara said, looking in the changing-room mirror, 'that this is perfect.' She had nearly said that the rich brown velvet coat and dress was 'perfect for an autumn ordination', but decided against it. This was London, where there were people of every creed and colour, and it was better not to bring religion into conversation with a stranger.

'It is, madam,' the sales assistant agreed, 'the colour is perfect for your striking hair.' She paused, pressing her finger on her lips. 'I'm sure there's a hat which would match it perfectly. If you don't mind waiting – I won't be a moment.'

Tara looked at herself in the mirror again. Harrods was the most expensive shop she had ever patronised, and this outfit was the most expensive she had ever worn. It worked out at a month's wages in Thornley's, and the hat, no doubt, would add another week's wages on top of that. Then there would be the shoes and the handbag. But it would be worth it.

Tara smiled to herself as she turned round in front of the mirror, her feet sinking into the plush carpet. The dress was short-sleeved and fitted her slim figure like a glove under the matching, slightly shorter 'swagger-coat'. It reminded her of the first decent coat she had worn as a teenager – only the other one had been fashioned in wool, in a camel colour. She shivered, remembering how she had nearly worn the camel coat on a shopping trip up to Dublin – on the day she had met Gabriel Fitzgerald.

The assistant reappeared at the curtain of the fitting-room. 'I think the hat is slightly darker, madam,' she said, holding it out.

Tara pulled the velvet hat low down on her brow, being careful not to crush the delicate bunch of cream and rust flowers that decorated one side of the brim. A glance at her reflection told her that she would pay the price, whatever it cost.

After lunch in Harrod's restaurant, Tara planned to shop for her handbag and shoes, and for a special present for her godson, Michael. Biddy and Fred's baby was due to have his first birthday the following week. It gave Tara the excuse to really splash out on him, as she adored buying the little boy presents. Biddy was always grateful for the gifts, since she had no family to buy him things, and felt awkward that it was Fred's family who bought all the presents. There was only really Tara left, who Biddy could consider close enough to be anything like a relative. Ruby – her mother and friend rolled into one – and who would have spoiled little Michael, was now dead and gone.

Ruby had lived long enough to hear of Biddy's pregnancy, but had succumbed to her illness just three months before the baby was born. The first year of treatment and physiotherapy seemed to have worked, and then gradually, Ruby discovered one malignant growth after another. All in new places. Eventually, the hospital sent her home to spend her last months among her friends and lodgers.

Shay had not left her side after the first summer of her illness, and when Ruby was no longer able to go out to the bingo or the pub, he lost interest in going out, too. In the latter stages, he and Ruby sat on either side of the fire, listening to the radio, and chatting over hot, weak brandies.

Shay had never been able to talk to anyone the way he talked to Ruby. They talked about everything together – and more importantly – they had laughed together. Shay had laughed more in the last few years with his landlady, than he had ever laughed in his life before. And he did not know how he was going to face a future without the little blonde lady who had brought so much love and laughter into his life.

Ruby Sweeney was no fool. She knew all this, because she felt exactly the same about Shay. Of all the men who had come and gone in her life – and all the lodgers who had come and gone through her door – Shay was the one she had found love and companionship with. When she first met him, she felt deep down that he was a decent man who had no confidence or pride in himself.

It had given Ruby the greatest pleasure to watch him go from strength to strength due to having a decent job, and more importantly – a decent wage. Ruby reckoned that the few years she had had with Tara's father had been the best they both had in their lives. But it could never have lasted. At some point, they both knew that Shay would have to return to his family in Ireland. Ruby had only borrowed him. The decision about when he would go back had now been taken out of their hands by fate. Shay would return when Ruby's time was up.

He had nothing left to stay for.

Biddy had nursed her surrogate-mother right up until the end, and was devastated when the inevitable happened. The fact that Ruby had left her the boarding-house in her will had not been any consolation to her. It was Ruby's dynamic presence, her cheery voice, and her motherly advice that Biddy wanted – not Ruby's house.

Around four o'clock, her shopping expedition completed, Tara caught a taxi back to her hotel in Victoria. She left a message in reception for her friend Kate – another redhead, but with a short and bobbed style – to call at her bedroom around six o'clock for dinner. Kate, who had replaced Jean in Thornley's, had arranged to meet her sister in London that afternoon, which left Tara free to shop for the special outfit on her own. This evening they planned to have an early dinner in the hotel, and afterwards head out to the opera in Covent Garden.

The girls had been planning this September weekend in London for ages, and for Tara it had been a complex task. She had to organise someone to cook the meals and clean up in her own house. The other part of the semi, which she had bought a few months after Biddy's wedding, was home to six nurses, and running well under the care of a local woman. The fact that Tara was literally through the wall from it, meant that the same standards were maintained in both houses. If Tara had anything to thank Frank Kennedy for, it was for encouraging her to take well-calculated risks.

The venture had gone so well that the Christmas after Tara had bought the second house, she was able to give up her weekend receptionist job in the Park Hotel. The spare hours on Saturday and Sunday afternoons now allowed her to take on more piano pupils, as she always had a waiting list of eager young pianists.

Technically, Tara did not need to work at all, as the rent from both houses, more than covered the mortgage, and left her with enough to live on comfortably. But however well things were going, it never occurred to her to think of giving up working for Thornleys, or her piano teaching. The money from both jobs she banked every week, as an insurance against the future. Tara Flynn, after only six years in England, was an independent young woman, and an owner of substantial property.

Although she took none of it for granted, Tara did not hesitate when it came to indulging her love of music and the theatre. She travelled into Manchester regularly to catch any new shows, opera or ballet. Lately, since she had become friends with Kate, she had taken to having the odd weekend away to places like Leeds or Newcastle. This trip to London was their latest foray into the shopping cities of England.

Tara and Kate travelled down on the train from Stockport, after work on the Friday night. They had been recommended the hotel by Kate's sister, who worked for a big travel agent in London. The hotel was minutes' walk from Victoria Station and Buckingham Palace, and overlooked the Palace Mews. On their first evening, particularly warm for the beginning of September, they took a walk all around the palace area, and then strolled through St James's Park, ignoring the admiring stares they drew from men. A strikingly attractive redhead was enough to catch any man's eye, but two beautiful girls with flaming red hair was enough to cause accidents.

When they grew tired of walking, the girls found a little Italian restaurant close by their hotel. As they chatted across the table lit with candles in wine bottles, Kate kept Tara amused with tales of ex-boyfriends, and scrapes she had got into in boarding school in Manchester. Tara, in turn, related stories of growing up in Ireland, shopping in Dublin, and how she had started up her little chicken and turkey business.

Although she was sorry when Jean left Thornley's Estate Agents to move to Newcastle, Tara was delighted with her replacement – the bubbly red-headed Kate. Kate Thornley was actually a granddaughter of *the* Mr Thornley, who had started the business up years ago, and her father was the major shareholder in the business. Kate, therefore, had a lot of clout with Mr Pickford when it came to odd days off, was mad about ballet and the opera and was never short of money. Her job in the estate agents was temporary – filling in until someone more qualified turned up to fill Jean's position – and her father's idea for keeping his flighty daughter occupied over the summer.

Kate had recently completed a college course in fashion and design, but had found no openings in that field around the North West. Eventually, she planned to head for Paris or Rome, to work for one of the big fashion houses, but for the time being she was content working with Tara in the estate agency office. Her hairstyle and clothes were always of the latest fashion, and lately she had set a trend in the area for the combination of tight sweaters, Capri pants and flat ballet pumps. The outfit looked stunning on Kate's petite, elfin figure. Tara – whose clothes veered more towards the more elegant and conservative – was also showing signs of Kate's influence, and had added the odd casual sweater and trousers to her own wardrobe. The fact that Kate was single, and available for nights out and weekends away, had made a huge difference to Tara's social life.

'Your outfit is wonderful,' Kate breathed, as she studied the velvet dress and coat which Tara had lain out on the bed for her inspection. She lifted the hat, and pulled it on her own head. It looked nice with her straight red bob, but did not have the same impact as it did crowning Tara's russet curls. 'It's much too sophisticated and expensive to be wasted on a boring church "do". We'll have to find you somewhere more exciting to wear it.' Kate was Church of England and only attended services at Christmas and Easter.

'*Heathen!*' Tara scolded. 'It might not seem very exciting to you, but my brother's ordination is a very important affair.'

Kate looked suitably chastised, then, tossing the hat on the bed, she spoiled it by asking: 'Will there be any handsome, eligible men at the ordination?'

'Handsome, eligible men? The place will be full of priests and nuns!' Tara shook her head in exasperation. 'I wonder, Kate Thornley, have you any decorum at all?'

The hotel menu was excellent. After some deliberation, Tara chose duck with port wine pâté and toast to start, followed by trout with almonds, while Kate opted for smoked salmon and steak in a pepper sauce. When they were offered the wine list, Kate waved it away. 'We'll have a bottle of Moët & Chandon, please.'

Tara's eyes opened wide with surprise. 'Champagne?'

Kate laughed. 'To toast your trip to Ireland – and your brother's ordination. And, to make up for being such a terrible heathen!'

The Opera House in Covent Garden was packed out for the Scottish Opera's rendition of Puccini's *Madame Butterfly*. Kate had booked the tickets weeks before, which saved them having to join the massive queue for seats. Once inside the foyer, both girls shrugged off the admiring glances cast in their direction by men of all ages. Their stylish outfits – Kate's navy and white Chanel suit, and Tara's wine, slim-fitting dress with a dropped waistline and flowing jacket – drew even more glances from the females.

'I'll just go and get a couple of programmes,' Tara said, pointing in the direction of the stall. 'I'll catch you back here in a minute.'

'And I,' Kate replied, with a twinkle in her hazel eyes, 'will look for the biggest box of chocolates I can find. I spotted the perfect box in a shop window on the way in.' She giggled, the effects of the champagne still evident. 'I'm in a chocolate mood tonight,' she warned, 'so you'd better watch out!'

Tara rolled her eyes in amusement, as the small, but distinctive form – her hair bobbing busily up and down – disappeared into the crowds. Wherever they went, Tara thought, Kate always livened things up.

Five minutes later, Tara was standing in the same spot, holding the programmes and craning her neck to look for her friend amongst the crowd. There was a great buzz of excitement in the air, as people rushed backwards and forwards, getting organised before it was time to take their seats for the performance. Suddenly, Tara felt a firm hand on her arm, and she turned towards Kate. Only it wasn't Kate

Thornley. Tara found herself looking up into the intense blue eyes of Gabriel Fitzgerald.

'Tara,' he said, his breathing sounding short. 'I can't believe it's you . . .' He leaned forward and pressed his lips lightly against her cheek. Then, he stepped back to look at her again, amazement and delight etched all over his face.

'Hello, Gabriel,' a calm voice replied. Considering her heart was hammering in her chest, Tara was amazed to discover it was actually her own voice. 'How are you?'

'I thought it was you – I thought I recognised your hair.'

Tara felt her hands clench and her throat tighten. 'I didn't know you liked opera,' she said – and immediately felt silly. Why shouldn't he like opera? And why should it be of any importance to her, whether he liked opera or not?

'I'm not very knowledgeable about it,' he confessed, with a grin. 'I thought I should take the chance to learn a bit more about it, since I'm living in London at the moment.'

So he was living in London, Tara thought. She wondered about Ballygrace House. Perhaps his English wife didn't fancy living in a remote village in the middle of Ireland? She looked up at him through lowered eyelids, and noticed how very blond his hair still was, although it was longer than she remembered. Little tendrils were growing down, curling at the back of his smooth neck. Gabriel had always been a very handsome boy – but now he was a devastatingly handsome man.

Her gaze caught his, and when she saw the look in his eyes, she felt the familiar tightening in her stomach. It was the same way he had looked at her on the night at the New Year's Eve ball in Tullamore, when they were teenagers. Tara turned her head away. She was obviously imagining it. Sure, wasn't he a married man by now? She clasped the programmes tightly to her chest, and started to look around the crowds. 'I'm waiting on my friend . . . I seem to have lost her.'

'You're not with . . .' he paused, the colour on his cheeks going deeper, 'you're not with the chap I met at the funeral?'

Tara's heart skipped a beat at the mention of both Frank and the funeral. 'Frank? No . . . no,' she said, her head shaking vigorously, and her voice slightly higher. She felt completely flustered now. 'I'm with my friend, Kate . . . we've just come down to London for the weekend.'

'Have you been back to Ballygrace recently?' Gabriel asked, his eyes taking in every inch of her face.

'No – not for a long time.'

'I left some things of Madeleine's for you,' he said 'at your uncle's cottage. I kept them . . . hoping I might see you.'

Tara swallowed hard to ease her dry throat. 'My aunt wrote and told me. Thanks, it was very thoughtful of you.' She looked down at the programmes. 'I've been really busy in Stockport,' she said, feeling guilty that she'd misjudged him about the mementos. 'I have a lodging business – plus my work – and everything. I'm going over soon, and I'll pick the things up then.'

'I believe you have some very nice property,' Gabriel said, and when he saw the surprised look on her face, he quickly added: 'I met your friend, Frank, in Dublin Airport some time ago.' He paused. 'It was around the time of your engagement.'

'Engagement?' Tara's brows shot up in amazement. She and Frank had never planned to get engaged . . . how could he? He had never mentioned meeting Gabriel Fitzgerald. What else, she wondered, had he not told her?

Kate suddenly appeared, grabbing Tara's sleeve in a flurry of excitement. 'Sorry,' she said, grinning from ear to ear. 'I met a guy from college who I haven't seen for ages. He was telling me all about this brilliant new designer who's opened a place in London. Apparently she's looking for staff –' Kate halted mid-sentence, suddenly realising that Gabriel was with Tara.

'Gabriel,' Tara said, 'this is my lost friend, Kate.'

He stretched his hand out.

'Gabriel's an old friend from home,' Tara explained. 'We're from the same village, and we went to school together. I was very close friends with his sister.'

Kate returned the warm handshake. 'Another Irishman abroad!' she joked, taking in every detail of his six-foot, blond good looks, and his expensive, well-cut clothes. 'Has Tara been boring you with all the details about her ordination over in Ireland? Or are you one of the lucky people who are going too?' Kate laughed. 'It's all she's talked about this weekend. We made a special trip down to London so's she could buy an really exclusive outfit for it – one that she wouldn't see duplicated in Dublin.' She touched Gabriel's arm and rolled her eyes. 'She's made it sound so exciting, I'm beginning to wish I had an invitation to it myself.'

'Kate!' Tara gasped, on the verge of wringing her neck. 'You really do exaggerate at times!'

'Who are you with?' Kate asked Gabriel, ignoring Tara's annoyance.

Tara blushed at her friend's forthright manner, although she had been dying to ask him the very same thing.

'I'm –' He coughed to clear his throat, 'I'm with a group.'

Tara's heart sank. He had not specified whether the group was family or friends. She was quite sure that his English wife must be part of it.

Kate smiled. 'I see you're one of these mysterious Celtic types. Tara can be a bit like that at times.' She turned to Tara, handing her a ticket. 'I'll catch you inside.' Then she had the cheek to add: 'Don't be late.'

Tara laughed and shook her head in exasperation

'She seems very nice – lively but nice,' Gabriel commented, obviously amused. Then, after a few moments' hesitation, he asked: 'This ordination, is it in Ireland?'

'It's my brother Joe – it's in Dublin.

'When?' he asked.

'Next weekend.'

'How long are you going over for?'

'Saturday until a week the following Tuesday. We have the ordination in Dublin on the Sunday, and then his first Mass in Tullamore the next Sunday.' It suddenly dawned on Tara why he was so interested. She gave an apologetic smile. 'I promise I'll pick up Madeleine's things when I'm in Ballygrace.'

'Did you know Ballygrace House is up for sale?' Gabriel said suddenly.

Tara's body stiffened. 'I heard rumours some time ago . . .'

He nodded. 'It's definite now. The board is up in the office window. Next year, it will probably be the auctioneering business.' He shrugged ran a hand through his fair hair. 'With my mother living in London – and I spend very little time over in Ireland, myself.'

A bell rang out now, signalling for people to take their seats. Gabriel looked down at his watch. 'I suppose I'd better make tracks.' He hesitated. 'I don't suppose we could meet tomorrow? Just for a short while.'

Tara's heart lifted – then, just as quick, she scolded herself. She had already been badly burned with one married man, the last thing she needed was getting involved with another. 'I'm sorry,' she said quietly, 'but we're travelling back home tomorrow.'

He nodded his head, as though he had expected a refusal.

'How is your mother?' she asked, as they moved along in the crowd towards the auditorium.

'Much better,' he replied, his arm guiding her. 'In fact, I think she might remarry soon.'

'Really?' Tara's voice was high with surprise.

'An Englishman. One of the leading barristers in London. He's very nice, and he's also very good with my young brother, William.'

Tara shivered. The boy was obviously called after his dead father. She looked up at Gabriel and smiled brightly. 'I'm delighted for her . . . please give her my regards.'

He stopped dead. Then, he reached out and took both her hands in his. 'My mother often talks about you,' he said quietly. 'It was only afterwards that she realised the extent of your support for Madeleine – even during the worst her illness. You were the only real friend she had.'

The mention of her youthful, golden-haired friend, suddenly brought a flood of tears to Tara's eyes. She eased a hand out of his grip, deeply embarrassed at showing herself so vulnerable, and dug into her jacket pocket for a hanky. 'I'm sorry . . .'

'It's me who should be sorry, Tara,' he said, manoeuvring her into a little corner, away from the crowds. 'So very, very sorry.' He reached for her, and pulled her into his arms.

Instinctively, Tara melted into his embrace, burying her head deep in his chest. Then, a little voice at the back of her head reminded her that Gabriel Fitzgerald was a married man. Gently, and without saying a word, she pulled away from him.

The second bell sounded, signalling three minutes until the start of the performance – and the end of her brief, but disturbing, encounter with Gabriel Fitzgerald.

Madame Butterfly went straight over Tara's head, as she sat through the performance. Watching, but seeing and hearing very little, her mind was completely taken up by the whole incident with Gabriel Fitzgerald and the effect he had had on her. How could she still have feelings for him after all this time? And after all that had happened with Frank? How could she be so immature and silly, to lust after another married man?

Occasionally, Kate dug her in the ribs to whisper a comment about the opera, or to push an immense box of chocolates under her nose. But even the sweet, cloying smell of the confectionery – which had Kate dipping into the box every five minutes – failed to tempt Tara away from her thoughts.

When the interval came, Tara said she didn't mind Kate rushing off to talk to her college friend again, and said she was happy to stay put in her seat.

'I thought you might want to see that handsome Irishman again,' Kate commented. 'I'm very surprised that you never mentioned *him* before. He is absolutely gorgeous.' Kate put her bobbed head to the side, and studied her friend carefully. 'I'm sure you're keeping something from me. I can tell these things, just by the way he looked at you.'

Tara shrugged. 'It doesn't matter how he looked at me – he's a married man.'

'Oh, well,' Kate said, rolling her eyes. She had heard the whole sorry tale about Frank Kennedy. 'Say no more.' She put the box of chocolates in Tara's lap. 'Help yourself while I'm gone. They might cheer you up.'

Tara's concentration was slightly better during the second half of the opera but she had lost the main thread of the story. She would have to ask Kate to explain it to her later.

When the performance finished, Tara asked Kate if they could move out of the Opera House as quickly as possible.

'I have no wish to see Gabriel Fitzgerald with his wife,' she explained. 'It was hard enough meeting him, after all this time.' She gripped the handle of her bag tightly. 'I just want to get out of here and forget that I ever laid eyes on him again.'

Chapter Forty-two

Tara looked along the pew at her father. When she caught his eye, she smiled reassuringly at him, and he winked back at her. He had changed so much since his return to Ireland. Some changes were for the better.

His hair was still the same curly black, but now he washed it more often. His suit and shoes were impeccable today. But then they would be. Today he was up in Dublin to watch his oldest son being ordained into the priesthood. This was a very special day – a day very few fathers ever got to see.

Shay stood tall beside his wife, his elderly aunts and his daughter. His brother Mick and his wife Kitty, were in the pew behind, with Tara's half-brothers and sisters. He was surrounded by his family on this special day, and he looked fit and well. Everything about Shay Flynn's appearance was for the better. Two years after her death, all those outward signs were still a testament to Ruby Sweeney's love and attention.

There were other noticeable changes about Shay. He no longer drank heavily – a couple of glasses of stout on a rare occasion. He could take it or leave it. Now sober, he never missed a day's work. When he came home from England, he had followed Ruby's instructions to the letter, and gone cap in hand to his old employers at the factory. He had explained how he was now off the beer and would be a model employee, an example to the others. Ruby was right. He was given a lowly job at first, sweeping the factory floor and cleaning the machines. Within a few months he was in a more respectable position, which he had maintained ever since.

But the biggest change in Shay was within himself. If the light had not gone out of his life, it had certainly dimmed. Never again would he know the love he had known with the blonde, busty landlady. He had been a lucky man to have known such a woman. He knew of no other man who had enjoyed such a glorious – albeit brief – liasion. His relationship with Ruby had filled every little gap he ever had in his life. Even the tiniest gap that a man is rarely aware of.

And he knew he would never be so fulfilled in his life again.

But Shay was resigned to it. He knew the path that was laid out in life for him, from now on. He would tread it firmly and with his head held high. Tessie had made plenty of sacrifices while he had been enjoying life to the full in Stockport, and now it was his turn to make the sacrifices for her.

His wife and his family were the main priority in his life, and he would stick to that into old age. He had made that promise to Ruby on her deathbed, and he knew – as sure as he had ever known anything in his life – that he would not break it.

Tara felt intensely proud of her brother. Since her arrival in Dublin yesterday, she had felt overawed by the magnificence of the occasion. There had been no point in travelling all the way down to Ballygrace, to travel back today, so she had booked into one of the city centre hotels. Not the hotel she had stayed in with Frank.

She had met up with Joe the previous night, and they had gone for a meal together. Although she had broached the seriousness of his vocation in her letters with him many times, she felt compelled to check one last time that he was truly doing the right thing. Like a bridegroom going into marriage.

'Yes,' Joe had assured her, with an affectionate pat on the hand. 'I have no doubts about what I'm doing with my life.'

'Don't be angry with me for asking,' Tara had said, her emerald eyes clouded with worry. 'It's just . . . a few years ago . . . you were having serious doubts.'

'It was glandular fever, and it left me very weak and depressed,' he explained, 'and my whole life seemed one big problem. Every little thing grew out of all proportion. But I took some time off, and, once I started to get back to full health, I could see what had caused it all.'

'You're sure?' Tara checked. 'You don't feel duty-bound to go through with the ordination or anything like that? One more or one less priest isn't going to make a whole lot of difference to God.'

Joe put his knife and fork down on the plate. 'Wherever do you get your ideas, Tara? You're talking like an agnostic.' He laughed out loud. Then, he suddenly looked serious. 'I'm sorry . . . your faith must have been really shaken by that priest from Ballygrace.'

Tara nodded her head. 'It has been *severely* shaken. He almost ruined Biddy's life.'

Joe took both her hands in his. 'I prayed for you and Biddy, when you wrote and told me.'

'I thought,' Tara whispered, 'that you might find it hard to believe. That you would think Biddy was lying. It's such a terrible thing for a priest to do.'

'It is a hard thing to believe,' Joe said gently, 'but human beings do terrible things . . . and priests are only human, after all. Don't forget, Lucifer, the devil himself, was an angel first. Hopefully, preists – like the one I intend to become – will make up for the sins of the odd bad one.' He paused. 'After a spell in a priests' retirement place in London, the Bishop sent Father Daly to work in a retreat house down in Cork, where he'll only be mixing with adults. He won't do any more harm to children in Ballygrace.'

'Thank God for that,' Tara had said quietly, 'and it's to be hoped, that he does no more harm *wherever* he goes.'

Watching the Bishop and the priests on the altar now, and Joe and his fellow seminarians – all in their celebratory robes – made Tara's heart swell with pride. It crossed her mind more than once as to how her long-dead mother would have felt on this special day – and how sad it was for Joe that she had not lived to see it. To most Irish, Catholic mothers, it would be a dream come true. Joe was nearing the age his mother had died. It was a strange, Tara thought, for a child to have lived into adulthood longer than a parent. More than once she had to wipe a tear away, while at either side of her, Maggie and Molly constantly sniffled into their hankies. And as the two wrinkled old ladies witnessed the Bishop laying his hands on Joe Flynn's head – their cup had finally overflowed. All the prayers and financial sacrifices offered up over the years had now borne the most wonderful, glorious fruit.

The buffet reception after the ceremony was held in the great hall of the seminary. Father Joe now an ordained priest, looked serene and calm as he moved around, chatting with members of his family, the Bishop and priests, and the young men with whom he had spent his years of training.

When they had finished eating, Tara, dressed in her new velvet suit and hat, watched as Joe guided his old aunties, to have a photograph taken with him and the Bishop. This last, unexpected gesture, was the icing on the cake.

'Well,' Shay announced, as they travelled back down on the evening train to Tullamore, 'at least we all passed oursel's. We mightn't be gentry, and we mightn't be a lot of things – but nobody can point a finger and say we let Joe Flynn down. As far as I'm concerned, we conducted oursel's wi' the greatest of eloquence.'

'*Father* Joe,' Molly corrected him, still snivelling into a hanky. '*Father Joseph Flynn*. From now on, we must remember to give him his proper title.'

The celebrations at the seminary in Dublin were only the start. Each day, visitors called both into the aunties' house in Tullamore and Mick and Kitty's cottage, offering their congratulations and handing in cards and small presents. Much the same sort of ritual as would be accorded for a wedding – except there was no bride. It went on right through until the following Saturday, with Mick proudly ferrying Tara and Kitty to and from Tullamore in his new Ford car.

'Not in the same league as yer friend, Frank's, car,' Mick had commented, 'but it's one of the first in Ballygrace. Not bad for the likes of us.'

'It's wonderful,' Tara said, smoothing the leather upholstery, but she said nothing about Frank. They had accepted her letter of explanation shortly after they parted. She had played things down, and kept it simple. Her aunt and uncle would only be horrified to know how he had deceived her. Like the business with William Fitzgerald – some things were better left unsaid.

At twelve o'clock on the Sunday – a glorious autumn day, fitting for the occasion – Joe said his first Mass in his home parish. This, as far as the family was concerned, was the *really* big occasion. This was when people of any importance in the town would be there to witness the Flynn's finest moment. Never again would they just be an ordinary family in the town. Father Joseph Flynn had lifted them onto a different plane.

Tears flowed from friends and family alike as this dark-haired young man, whom they had all watched grow up, now stood on the altar, a priest of God. Invitations had been issued to another buffet in the church hall, where the town celebrated their latest offering to the secular life. After this, the family all congregated back in the old aunties' for more tea, sandwiches and sweetcakes, and a modest sherry or whisky for those who indulged. Tara and Joe's piano-playing kept everyone in high spirits, as they played request after request of the old Irish favourites.

This special day was the aunties' 'swansong', as their entertaining days were nearing a close. Both of them were riddled with arthritis and suffered from failing eyesight. There were now cobwebs in corners of the fusty sitting-room, which would never have escaped them before, and cake crumbs and turf dust on the carpets – too small to be detected by their dim eyes.

Mick had driven Tessie and Tara out to Tullamore on Saturday afternoon, on the pretext of bringing extra delph and glasses, and they had given the whole house what the local women would call 'a good going over'. Carpets were brushed, cups were scoured clean of brown tea-stains, and smears polished off glasses. A few hours' work, and Molly and Maggie's house was like a new pin, as befitted the home-place of a newly ordained priest.

Later that night, the Flynn family, the parish priest and close friends were out in force again, dining in style in a hotel in Tullamore. Although the two old women had saved for years towards the celebratory receptions and meal, Tara and Shay had insisted on paying a third of the cost each. Shay still had little money to spare, but nowadays had a lot more pride. He had never done much for Joe over the years, and he was determined to do this one thing properly.

Although he mightn't be 'Quality', Shay had remarked more than once, Father Joseph Flynn had not been made little of.

Tara woke out of a disturbing dream around six o'clock on Monday morning. She looked dazedly around her old bedroom for a few moments, and then she remembered. She had been dreaming about Joe's ordination. It was hardly surprising, since the whole week in Ireland had been devoted to the religious ceremony. But in her dream all the celebrations had taken place in Ballygrace House.

She lay for a while, trying to go back to sleep. When that was impossible, she then tried to divert her thoughts on to other things, but however hard she tried, fragments of the dream kept floating back into her mind. Eventually, she decided to get up and make a cup of coffee. The kettle was just coming to the boil on the shiny, modern white cooker, when Kitty came tiptoeing out of her bedroom. 'I thought I heard you,' she whispered, going over to get the tea-caddy and another mug from the shelf. 'I've been wide awake for a while, too.'

They both sat down at the kitchen table, with their drinks and a slice of brown soda bread.

'Are you all right?' Kitty asked. 'You don't seem so bright this morning.'

'Actually,' Tara confessed, 'I had a silly dream . . . one of those dreams that you can't get out of your head.'

'What was it about?'

'Ballygrace House . . . and Madeleine.' Tara halted, unwilling to bring any more of the dream back to life.

Kitty pulled her dressing-gown tighter around her chest. 'I often get dreams like that,' she said thoughtfully, 'about the past.' Her face suddenly brightened up. 'You still haven't looked at the box that the Fitzgerald lad left for you. Will I get it now?'

Tara paused for a moment. 'I suppose I might as well get it over with.'

Kitty put her hand on the brown-paper-wrapped parcel in seconds. She had kept it in the bottom part of the dresser, so that it could be retrieved easily the next time Tara had come home. 'I wonder how long it will take for Ballygrace House to sell?' Kitty commented, as she put the small square parcel on the table. 'It's a fine big house, to be sure – but how many people would have the money to buy it around these parts?'

Tara opened the package carefully, aware that Gabriel Fitzgerald's hands had wrapped it and then tied the string into a small tight bow.

She caught her breath, even before she saw the contents of the beautiful jewellery box she had just uncovered. It made the little wooden box, that Biddy had once given Tara for her birthday, look plain and tawdry by comparison.

Madeleine's jewellery box was heavy silver, the top inlaid with a delicate mother-of-pearl design, based on the Book of Kells. The box alone was a treasured gift, and yet Tara could feel by the weight that it contained several items.

She unwrapped the tissue paper. For several moments she stared down at the cameo brooch she had given her friend for her eighteenth birthday. Then she pressed the back of her hand against her mouth to stifle the cry of sorrow. Sorrow for the beautiful, blonde girl, who was no more.

With her aunt's comforting hand on her shoulder, Tara gathered herself together, and opened three more tissue-wrapped packages.

'They're beautiful,' Kitty gasped, as Tara held up the cameo earrings, 'and a perfect match for the brooch.'

'Gabriel bought them for Madeleine,' Tara said quietly. Then, she opened the last two packages, as a mesmerised Kitty looked on. The long thin box contained a double string of pearls, flanked by tear-drop pearl earrings. The small square box held Madeleine's expensive gold watch, with the ruby and diamond face, that Elisha and William Fitzgerald had presented to their sad and disturbed daughter on her eighteenth birthday.

Tara stared down at the small display of jewellery on her granda's old pine kitchen table, almost bleached white with Kitty's hard scrubbing. Then slowly – very slowly – her folded arms leant on the table, and her glorious mane of russet hair came to rest on top. Then, with Kitty's arms around her, she wept and wept – for all the things that were gone.

'Are you sure you don't want Mick to bring you into Tullamore in the car?' Kitty asked anxiously later that morning, as Tara dusted down her old bicycle.

'Not at all. It's a lovely day, and it will do me good to get a bit of exercise.' She smiled warmly at her aunt. 'Sure, all I've done is eat and drink the whole week.'

Tara had forgotten how lovely it felt to have the breeze rustle on her face and neck as she cycled slowly along. It was only eleven o'clock in the morning and she was in no hurry on the last day of her holiday. Occasionally she dismounted from the bike, to stop and stare at cows and horses, or a familiar field or cottage which she remembered from long ago.

She waved to farmers passing on tractors, the odd car, and several asses and carts. Her cream lambswool twinset and Donegal tweed trousers set off the brown cameo brooch perfectly. A simple piece of cream lace held back her untameable curls, revealing the cameo earrings.

She had originally planned to pick up a few things from the shops for Biddy and Kate, but on arrival in Tullamore, she found herself leaning the bike on the wall outside Fitzgerald's Auctioneers. The main board mounted in the middle of the window showed an imposing view of Ballygrace House, Surrounded by several interior shots. Printed cards accompanied the photographs, giving the dimensions and descriptions of each room and drawing attention to particular outstanding points.

Later, Tara described it to herself as a sort of madness. She could find no other excuse for her sudden, impulsive behaviour. Without a moment's hesitation, she walked into William Fitzgerald's office where she had once worked, and asked the strange girl behind the desk for a brochure of Ballygrace House.

'Are you seriously interested in it?' the girl asked, handing her the details.

Tara looked at the asking price on the back page and took a deep breath. 'I might be.' Ballygrace House was worth more than the two houses she owned in Stockport put together. But not a huge amount more. She had forgotten the considerable price difference between Britain and Ireland. If really pushed – thanks to Frank Kennedy's tutoring – Tara knew she could find a way of affording the house.

Of course, she had no intentions of doing so.

'I could have someone there to show you round the house.' The girl looked at her diary. 'Three o'clock? Mr Costelloe is on his way out from Edenderry around then. I can ring him, and ask him to meet you out at the house.'

Tara's head started to reel at the thought.

Could she step over the threshold of that beautiful, but disturbing place again? Would the ghosts of Ballygrace House be there . . . waiting for her? The tragic Madeleine . . . William Fitzgerald . . . or the dreadful Rosie Scully?

It would be her last chance, ever, to find out. Her last chance to lay those ghosts, once and for all. Tara looked down at Madeleine's watch. She could have her shopping quickly done, and be back out in Kitty's for two o'clock. 'I'll be outside Ballygrace House,' she said firmly, 'at three o'clock.'

The girl opened the appointments diary. 'Your name, madam?'

'Flynn – Miss Tara Flynn.'

After a quick lunch, Tara asked Mick if he would take her for a short drive. He beamed and said he would be only too delighted to drive her anywhere she liked. He had planned on driving the three of them over to Tullamore that evening, for Tara say goodbye to her father and his family, and the old aunties. And tomorrow, he was due to drive to Dublin for the first time, to drop Tara off at the airport.

Slowly but surely, Mick was expanding his repertoire of routes around the country.

'It's not far,' Tara told him, 'but cycling would ruin my outfit.'

'Where exactly,' Mick enquired, 'would you be thinking of going?' He had a rag in his hand, to give the car another quick polish.

Tara turned towards her bedroom door. 'Ballygrace House,' she said in a firm voice. 'I'm going to have a last look at it, before it's sold.'

At her request, Mick left her off about a hundred yards from the driveway, around ten to three. 'Four o'clock should give me plenty of time,' she told him. 'If you don't mind coming back then.'

'Whatever you say, me girl,' he smiled warmly, 'whatever you say.'

It had been more madness that had made Tara change into her brown velvet Harrods outfit, her hair tucked under the low-brimmed hat. She saw the incredulous look on Kitty's face as she came out of the bedroom, wearing an ensemble that cost a fortune – and her only going to look at an old house.

But Tara was wearing the outfit as a soldier would wear a suit of armour. She would meet all those old ghosts as the equal she now was. *All* the clothes she had brought with her spoke of quality and money. Even the casual trousers she had changed out of would have been perfectly suitable for a meeting with an auctioneer. Years of experience in the estate agents' in England left her with no doubts as to how she presented to others. She came across *exactly* as she was – an educated, cultured young woman of considerable means.

Tara walked up the driveway of Ballygrace House, determined to see the place fresh, with her practised estate agent's eye. The grass verges were overgrown on both sides, and moss and weeds now covered the path. The ivy on the stone walls was struggling valiantly with the climbing.

As Tara rounded the bend and the front of the house came into view, it was apparent to her that no gardener's hands had touched the place for a long time. The rhododendrons were overgrown and now fought for space with indeterminable bushes. As she grew nearer, Tara was shocked to see the same neglect evident on the house itself. The grand, imposing building was now weather-beaten, its wooden door and window-ledges scorched and cracked. The painted steps which Mrs Scully had brushed and scrubbed daily were now down to the bare stone, and edged with moss.

All life and love had long departed from Ballygrace House.

The noise of an engine coming up the drive, heralded the prompt arrival of John Costelloe. Tara pulled the brim of her hat further down on her brow, in an effort to shield her eyes. Whatever her private feelings about the house, she would make sure that he only saw her as a prospective buyer.

John Costelloe struck her as handsome in an obvious way. Dark wavy hair and perfect white teeth. A similar type to Frank Kennedy. Instinctively, Tara was on her guard, but he was courteous and businesslike. After introducing himself, he opened the heavy front door of Ballygrace House – and started to show her around the house.

'If you have no objections,' she said, 'I would like a few minutes to look around on my own.'

For a moment he looked flustered, not used to dealing with such an assertive woman. It was normally men who dealt in property matters. 'No . . . that would be perfectly fine. I'll just wander around outside in the garden.' He paused. 'I'll be in and out, if you want to check any details.'

Immediately, Tara noticed that the bulk of the furniture was gone – presumably, shipped over to Elisha Fitzgerald's house in England. Some of it, perhaps, to Gabriel and his wife's home. The remaining furniture was covered in dustsheets, including the grand piano. Surely, she thought, Elisha or Gabriel would want the piano? Surely, they would not leave such a beautiful instrument?

Tara threw the white cover back and lifted the piano lid. She pressed a few keys. The tone was duller than she remembered. It obviously needed tuning, and was perhaps a bit damp. She pulled the stool out and sat down.

John Costelloe suddenly halted in his tracks, as he descended the front steps. For a moment he thought he was imagining things – then he realised that the beautiful music was coming from inside Ballygrace House. He moved down another step, then leaned across the wall to cautiously look in through the drawing-room window. There, seated at the piano, was the elegant woman in the brown velvet coat and hat. Her whole body swayed in time as she played a beautiful, haunting melody. When the piece ended, she paused for a brief moment, then she started on another. This one he recognised immediately – 'Moonlight Sonata.'

John stood mesmerised until she had finished. Then, she startled him further, when she slowly leaned forward on the stool, and pressed her hands and head onto the dark wood. She remained like that for a few moments, then she abruptly rose, closed the lid, and pulled the dustsheet down over the piano.

Later, as they walked through Rosie Scully's kitchen, Tara checked as to whether the brochure price was negotiable or not. That all depended, the auctioneer said, on Mr Gabriel Fitzgerald. Did she realise, he wondered, that Mr Fitzgerald was also the owner of the auctioneer's business, and John Costelloe's boss? He spent little time in Ireland these days, and even less in Tullamore. The best kind of boss to have, the young man joked.

Tara nodded and gave a faint smile, but said nothing. She walked across to the window, and looked out into the overgrown wilderness, that once had been a vegetable garden.

Eventually, after she had checked both upstairs and downstairs, the garden and the out houses, Tara steeled herself and started to ascend the staircase once again. There was one room upstairs that she had not been in. As she got nearer to the landing, her feet grew heavier – but she kept going.

This room was the main reason she had come to Ballygrace House today.

Tara hovered uncertainly outside the room for several minutes – unaware that John Costelloe was watching her every move from downstairs. Her palm was sweating, and her arm shook visibly as she reached for the door handle. Then she turned it, and stepped inside.

Tara held her breath for a few moments – then she gave the greatest sigh of relief. The bedroom was completely empty. Gone were the green curtains – daylight streamed in through the dusty window. And gone was the green satin bedding, the carpets, and all the furniture.

The dark place that Tara had held in her mind's eye for years – no longer existed.

The room William Fitzgerald had drunkenly crept into and then raped her had nothing to do with this empty, echoing room. She walked across to the window, the heels of her Italian shoes tapping on the bare floor. She looked down into the overgrown garden again – and felt nothing. Then she turned, and stared round the room one last time.

Then, Tara Flynn smiled. A little smile – but a real smile nonetheless.

She had put many months and many miles between herself and that unfortunate incident. She had grown up in between. A whole lifetime separated the girl from the woman.

The ghosts of Ballygrace House had been laid to rest.

Tara accepted John Costelloe's offer of a lift to the gates at the bottom of the drive. Mick was not due to pick her up for another quarter of an hour. She would enjoy a walk out in the fresh air, and meet him somewhere along the road.

John opened the passenger door for her.

'Thank you,' she said, 'you've been very helpful.' The car interior was hot and stuffy, so she removed her hat and let her russet locks tumble down freely.

'Your hair,' he suddenly blurted out, 'if you don't mind me saying – is beautiful.'

'Thank you,' Tara replied, with the distracted manner of a woman well used to receiving compliments.

The engine had just roared into life, when they heard another vehicle coming up the drive.

'Your lift, I presume,' John Costelloe said, letting the handbrake off.

'No . . .' Tara craned her neck. 'I don't think so.' Mick's car was not nearly as big, and anyway, he drove much more slowly than the car that was coming towards them.

'Jesus!' John Costelloe suddenly exclaimed, 'Look at the English registration – it must be the boss man himself.'

'Who?' Tara said, her heart starting to thud against her chest.

'Fitzgerald.' The young auctioneer's voice was suddenly low, and less confident. 'Mr Gabriel Fitzgerald.' He opened the car door.

Tara's heart was racing now, and her whole body shaking. What on earth was he doing here? And what possible reason could she give for *her* presence at Ballygrace House?

Gabriel brought the car to a halt with a screech. Then, he jumped out, and came striding towards the car.

There was nothing else for it. Tara opened the door and, as elegantly as she could, stepped from the car, gripping the hat tightly. She stood up, her legs like jelly. Then, her mind still working on an excuse, she squared her shoulders.

'Good afternoon, to you,' John Costelloe called to his boss, attempting to sound casual. 'I've been showing a client round the house.' He motioned towards the car. 'This is Miss Flynn. She's come to view the property. She's come all the way over from England.'

John Costelloe might as well have not been there, as the owner of Ballygrace House and the woman from England stared at each other.

'Tara,' Gabriel said. 'I was afraid I might have missed you . . .'

Tara's hand flew to the brooch on the collar of her coat. 'I have Madeleine's jewellery . . . thank you . . . but it was too much.'

Gabriel turned to his employee. 'It's all right, John – I'll see to things here. You can go now.'

They both stood watching until the car disappeared down the drive.

Then there was a silence.

Gabriel suddenly moved forward and put his hands on her forearms. 'Tara . . . I had to come and see you . . . to try to explain . . .'

Tara looked up at him. 'Explain what?' she asked quietly.

He gave a deep, weary sigh. 'Everything . . . all the things I should have explained to you years ago. The mistakes I should have apologised for.' His hands gripped her tighter. 'But I was young and I didn't have a clue about women or life.'

Tara felt a tightness in her chest and throat. 'What are you saying, Gabriel?'

'I'm saying that I should have had the guts to speak out against my parents. I should have had the guts to tell you about my feelings before it was all too late.'

Tara shook her head. 'Don't, Gabriel . . . please don't!'

'I may be making the biggest mistake of my life – but I don't care. Tara,' he said hoarsely, looking deep into her eyes, 'I love you – and I want you. I always have.'

Tara's heart lurched, her emotions doing somersaults at his touch. Then, reason took over, and tears sprung into her eyes. 'No, Gabriel – no!' she protested, pulling out of his grip. 'This is wrong . . . I won't have anything to do with a married man.'

Gabriel's brow deepened in confusion. '*Married?* But I'm *not* married.'

'I *know* you were married a few years ago,' she almost shouted. How could yet another man think she was such an innocent fool? 'The secretary in your office in Tullamore told me.'

He shook his head. 'No . . . no. I was *engaged* – but we never went through with it.' He paused, struggling to find the right words. 'She was only a family friend – a second best, after you.'

Tara looked up into his blue eyes, and the tears started to flow. 'No – you – your family, everybody thought I wasn't good enough. I can't go through this charade again.'

'Tara!' Gabriel gripped her arms again, and the velvet hat dropped unnoticed on to the gravel path. 'I love you! I love you with all my heart.' Tears filled his eyes now. 'God's my judge – my life has been worth nothing since you left Ireland. I knew I'd made the most dreadful mistake the minute I heard you'd gone.'

Tara started to struggle again. 'It's too late – it's much too late!'

'No!' he yelled, his voice echoing round the overgrown garden. 'Don't say that, Tara.' His voice suddenly broke. 'Is it Frank Kennedy? Is it still him?'

Tara looked away. 'It has nothing to do with him – or any man. Anything between me and Frank was over a long time ago.'

Gabriel held her at arm's length now, his confidence restored slightly. He reached a gentle finger to lift her chin. 'When I met you in London, I knew without a shadow of a doubt that I wanted to share the rest of my life with you.' He looked her straight in the eye. 'I came back to Ireland this morning, for one reason only. To confess my feelings for you – and to find out what you feel about me. Tell me honestly, and I'll go back to London in peace. I have to know, one way or another. Have you no feelings for me? No feelings at all?'

Tara's eyes clouded over. She moved her head away, so that he could not look into them and see her feelings. 'It's too late, Gabriel,' she said in a dull, flat voice. 'Too much has happened. We're older and we've changed. You live in London and I live in Stockport – we're miles apart. We're miles apart in every possible way. I have my work and my life . . . You have Ballygrace House and your work in London.'

'No, Tara! No!' he persisted. 'We can change it all. We're young. We could sell up everything – we could get married and come back to live here.' He waved his arm expansively, taking in the house and the grounds. 'You know the auctioneering business inside out – there's nothing we couldn't do together. We could make Ballygrace House a happy place again. We could get married and have children – children to fill this house with love and laughter.'

Tara's heart was racing so fast she thought she would choke. Everything she had ever dreamed of, dangled tantalisingly in front of her eyes. 'Are you mad?' she whispered.

Gabriel reached out and drew her into his arms. 'I love you – I love you so much, Tara Flynn – and I want you to be my wife.' His lips came down on her closed eyelids, and then on her mouth.

Tara felt her body go limp. She swayed against him, and their lips crushed in the most beautiful, passionate kiss. The sort of kiss she had only ever experienced with Gabriel Fitzgerald. The sort of kiss she would never find with any other man. Suddenly, the years in between fell away – and they were locked together.

'Tell me we have a future together,' he breathed into her flowing hair. 'I want you, and I need you. I don't care where it is – Ballygrace House or Timbuktu. As long as I have you – I don't care!'

'Oh, Gabriel!' she cried. 'I'm frightened . . . I want you . . . but I'm so very, very frightened.'

His lips brushed hers again. 'Hush, my darling . . . my darling, darling Tara – there's nothing to be afraid of, ever again.'

She looked up at him now, her eyes full of unconcealed love. 'How could it possibly work?'

'We'll make it work – don't doubt that for one moment,' he told her. 'We'll do whatever you want. I'll sell Ballygrace House and the auctioneering offices and come to Stockport . . . or we can both sell up, and move over here.' He lifted her hand and kissed it gently. 'Or, we can live like gypsies . . . and go from place to place.'

Tara turned her head and looked at the badly neglected, but still gracious building. A cloud moved, and the sun suddenly shone down on Ballygrace House. For a moment, the windows sparkled and the patchy paintwork gleamed.

Her heart lifted. 'Maybe,' she ventured, 'we could try. We could visit each other in London or Stockport at weekends – and see what happens.'

Gabriel kissed her hand again. 'There's no rush,' he told her. 'I can wait.' He looked across at the house now. 'I'll take it off the market, until you make up your mind.'

Then, as he pulled her into his arms once again, Tara Flynn knew that she had come home. As Gabriel had said, whether it was Ballygrace House or Timbuktu – as long as they were together – they would find a home.

THE END